Millennium's Eve

MILLENNIUM'S EVE

Ed Stewart

VICTOR BOOKS

A DIVISION OF SCRIPTURE PRESS PUBLICATIONS INC.
USA CANADA ENGLAND

More fiction by Ed Stewart

The Pancake Memos and Other Stories for Growing Christians
A Window to Eternity: Twelve Short Stories Based on the Sayings of Christ

Copyediting: Carole Streeter; Barbara Williams
Cover Design: Paul Higdon
Cover Illustration: Gary Meyer

Library of Congress Cataloging-in-Publication Data
Stewart, Ed.
 Millennium's eve / by Ed Stewart.
  p.   cm.
 ISBN 1-56476-133-9
 1. Journalists — United States — Fiction.   I. Title.
PS3569.T4599M55   1993
813'.54 — dc20   93-23790
                                                              CIP

---

1 2 3 4 5 6 7 8 9 10 Printing/Year 97 96 95 94 93

Millennium's Eve

To my wife, Carol.
Thanks for thirty years of love, friendship, and fun.
Here's to thirty more!

To our children, Kenneth and Kristine,
and our son-in-law, Jim.
I couldn't be more proud about being your dad.

And to our first grandchild, Olivia Rae.
You won the race with Gramps! You were born before the book!

The Lord bless you and keep you;
The Lord make His face shine upon you
and be gracious unto you;
The Lord lift up His countenance upon you
and give you peace.
Amen.

NOVEMBER 1999						
S	M	T	W	T	F	S
	1	2	3	4	5	6
7	8	9	10	11	12	13
14	15	16	17	18	19	20
21	22	23	24	25	26	27
28	29	30				

1999 DECEMBER 1999

S	M	T	W	T	F	S
			1	2	3	4
5	6	7	8	9	10	11
12	13	14	15	16	17	18
19	20	21	22	23	24	25
26	27	28	29	30	31	

JANUARY 2000						
S	M	T	W	T	F	S
						1
2	3	4	5	6	7	8
9	10	11	12	13	14	15
16	17	18	19	20	21	22
23	24	25	26	27	28	29
30	31					

(7) Days
Till
Millennium's
Eve

One

"I *hate* L.A!"

The words had been simmering inside Beth Scibelli long before she pulled out of the Galaxy Rent-a-Car lot at LAX. But after twenty minutes on the infamous San Diego Freeway—lurching forward and braking, lurching and braking a few feet at a time—her irritation boiled over and she spit the words out. Then she pounded the steering wheel once with her fist and growled the worst expletive she could think of. It still didn't quite capture her feelings, but her minor explosion helped take her mind off her disappointment and hurt, which, if she really thought about it, was at the root of her anger anyway.

The five-lane river of traffic engulfing Beth surged haltingly northward, every car, every shuttle van, every limo another insignificant swell in the confining current. All around her engines revved, turbos whistled, brakes squealed, horns blared. Occasionally the siren of a rescue vehicle or police car trilled from the surface streets. Jet shuttle copters swooshed across the dark, hazy sky following invisible air commuter traffic lanes a few hundred feet above the pavement.

"It's almost 1 o'clock in the morning," Beth snarled to the drivers around her, who were veiled behind chrome, steel, and darkened glass. "It's the start of Christmas Eve. Why aren't you idiots home putting up your Christmas trees or wrapping your kids' toys or whatever you do on Christmas Eve?"

Beth thought about using a stronger word than "idiots" but changed her mind, realizing she was guilty of whatever label she used, because she was helping to clog up the freeway too. Ever since she learned to drive on them fifteen years ago, L.A.'s freeways had been notorious for jamming up and slowing to the speed of a car wash at any time of the day or night—and the San Diego Freeway was right up there with the Santa Monica and the Ventura as the worst. Even the proliferation of the air shuttle network and the ambitious expansion of L.A.'s Metro rail system couldn't keep car-crazy Angelenos off the road.

Having been away from the freeways for eight years, Beth naively had hoped they would be better. She chided herself for her foolish optimism. "You're the real idiot for coming down here," she breathed bitterly.

Beth reached for the stereo controls in the center console between the two plush white leather bucket seats in her rented luxury Star Cruiser. She punched the FM band and turned up the volume, hoping to mask the muted traffic noises bleeding into the "soundproof" cabin.

"... Yuletide carols being sung by a choir, and folks dressed up like Eskimos ..." Beth wrinkled her nose at the song and pushed SEEK.

A tinny-voiced man was sing-songing through a monologue of some kind in a foreign tongue. "Silent Night" was being twanged on a weird-sounding instrument in the background. Beth groaned and pushed SEEK again.

"Decorations of red on a green Christmas tree, won't be the same if you're not here with me. . . . " Some cowboy was crooning the song. Beth made a gagging sound.

"Geez, it's not Christmas yet," she fumed aloud. "Isn't somebody playing something besides Christmas music? I *hate* Christmas in L.A!"

Keeping an eye on the bumper inching forward and stopping ahead of her, Beth fumbled in her large purse for a CD—*any* CD. She pulled out the first one she touched, shoved it into the console player, and activated a track at random. A stormy symphonic piece boomed from the speakers. French horns bellowed, strings moaned, cymbals crashed. Rimsky-Korsakov's *Scheherazade*, Beth recognized.

She turned the volume higher, wishing the rising decibels could somehow lift the Star Cruiser above the grimy city and rocket her back to the Northwest.

Beth's journey from Seattle to Los Angeles had begun positively enough. In September she had landed a lucrative contract to free-lance a supermarket paperback covering the big Unity 2000 rally at the Los Angeles Memorial Coliseum on Millennium's Eve. The project didn't promise to be as exciting as other free-lance writing assignments she'd accepted around the world in the last few years, but Beth couldn't ignore the substantial numbers on the bottom line.

The downside was going to L.A. Even worse, it would be L.A. on Millennium's Eve. *No wonder the money is so good,* Beth thought. *What journalist in her right mind wants to be in L.A. to welcome in the new millennium? Sydney would be beautiful this time of year. And São Paulo's ceremony ushering in the new millennium promises to be one of the most extravagant in the world.*

But the Bible-thumpers of America had chosen L.A. for Unity 2000, their spiritual launching pad into the next millennium. And a nice piece of work on the project would make several payments on Beth's lovely home overlooking Skagit Bay on serene Whidbey Island. *I can endure L.A. for a couple of days for that kind of money,* she encouraged herself.

Then there was the dreaded prospect of flying in early to spend Christmas with her parents. Beth had lived at home in the Los Angeles suburb of Woodland Hills until she entered USC and moved into a dorm. After graduation she migrated to Seattle to begin her career and peck away at a master's degree at the University of Washington. Since then she had purposely avoided spending Christmas in L.A.—

or any other time of the year, for that matter. L.A. had become too big, too dirty, too impersonal. Even the gleaming L.A. Lakers, Beth's idols in the '80s, had plummeted to lackluster mediocrity in the '90s. Beth had all but disowned L.A. as her hometown.

She wasn't exactly eager to visit her parents either. Jack and Dona Scibelli had become so religious since she entered college that Beth could hardly stand to visit them. She made a pilgrimage home only when free-lance assignments brought her to Southern California, which wasn't very often because she avoided those assignments like blind dates. Jack and Dona had made a few trips to Beth's island—when they weren't on some junket with their television pastor.

But when the Scibellis found out that Beth was covering Unity 2000, they were ecstatic. They would be attending the big gathering themselves, they had said. *Of course you will,* she thought wryly as they gushed to her about it over the phone. *Half the religious nuts in the country will be crammed into the Coliseum that night. You wouldn't miss a big hallelujah hoedown like that.*

Couldn't they all spend Christmas at home and welcome in the new millennium together, they had pleaded. The thought of spending Christmas in L.A. turned Beth cold. She loved Christmas in rural Oak Harbor, Washington, surrounded by stately evergreens and majestic Puget Sound dotted with white and green ferries and brilliantly lit pleasure craft. Her friends were in the Seattle area. There would be parties and gifts and perhaps a dusting of snow. And maybe even someone special to curl up with by the fire and listen for Santa and his sleigh.

But as much as she wanted to, Beth couldn't bring herself to refuse her parents' invitation. She didn't understand—and could hardly stomach—the fanatical religious practices that had dominated their lives since the early '90s. But they were still her parents, and their invitation had been so sincere. Besides, it would get her into L.A. a few days ahead of the hordes streaming into the southland for Unity 2000 and the many other new millennium celebrations, not to mention the Rose Bowl game the next day. And she could stay with Jack and Dona, which was rather critical since every hotel room from Santa Barbara to Carlsbad had been booked for months.

After finally agreeing to come, Beth found herself looking forward to Christmas at home. She hoped it would be the kind of Christmas she had enjoyed as a child, back in the days before Jack and Dona became immersed in the television congregation of evangelist Simon Holloway. Through November and early December, as she shopped for gifts for her parents, Beth envisioned the three of them at home decorating the tree, making fudge, and playing cribbage together—some of her warmest childhood memories. Foolishly she let her unbounded hopes create a fragile fantasy of Christmas in the family home in upscale Woodland Hills as it was twenty years ago.

But 120 miles out of LAX the romantic illusion she had fabricated quickly began to unravel. The Boeing 757 pilot announced that incoming flights were stacked up for landing. "We have to take a number, folks," he drawled. "We'll be pacing the coastline out here for about an hour"—which turned into two hours—"until the tower gives us a chance at a runway and a gate." *The least they could do is comp the cocktails,* Beth had thought impatiently, as she watched the lights of Malibu pass underneath her for the third time.

By the time the plane finally landed around midnight, Beth's warmly glowing vision of Christmas in L.A. with Dad and Mom was rapidly dematerializing. The airport was crowded with new millennium doomsayers thrusting literature in her face and rude travelers jostling her through the terminal and cutting in front of her at the baggage carousel. She had to fend off some kid who tried to separate her from her carry-on bag containing Jack and Dona's gifts.

Then, when she called her parents to let them know she was running late, the rest of her fantasy blew up in her face. "Your mother took advantage of a wonderful opportunity," Jack announced proudly, as if he'd just won the international lottery. "Rev. Holloway said on his program this morning that he had some last-minute cancellations at Jubilee Village for the Festival of the Nativity. So Mother called in and got a reservation on the spot. Isn't that great? She left today for Orlando. We both wanted to go, but you know how expensive airfare is at the last minute. She was so excited. She'll be at the Village until Sunday afternoon."

Beth shoved her compact personal phone into her purse with a sigh and a curse. She would have been angry at her mother for standing her up if she hadn't felt so sad and disappointed. *It serves me right,* she remonstrated herself as she wheeled her luggage to the curb to await the Galaxy shuttle. *I let myself believe it could be the same, but it's not the same. It will never be the same.*

To top it all off, the agent at the noisy Galaxy counter couldn't find her confirmation for the economy Star Chaser she had reserved two months earlier. "I'm very sorry." the girl said. "We're busy tonight, and your flight was delayed. All our Star Chasers are gone."

Beth was ready to blister the counter with a stream of well-chosen words, but the girl kept talking. "So we have a brand-new full-size GM Turbo Star Cruiser for you. Candy apple crimson. Hyperstereo sound and built-in phone and fax. No extra charge. Merry Christmas, ma'am."

It took a couple of seconds for Beth to realize her windfall. *Star Cruiser, top of the line, a $45,000 car with all the electronic doohickeys,* she thought. *Makes those dinky Star Chasers look like pedal cars.* A slight smile momentarily drained the tension from her face. She realized she hadn't smiled since lifting off from SeaTac. "Yes, Merry Christmas," she returned almost sincerely, as she scribbled her name on the contract and scooped up the keys.

The first bump to the rear of the sleek Star Cruiser snapped Beth back to the present with a start. The onboard computer's masculine movie-star voice temporarily cut into *Scheherazade* with a warning, "Caution to the rear. Caution to the rear."

Beth squinted into the rearview mirror at the blinding beams of a high-riding old Chevy Blazer directly behind her in the number four lane. A heavy, muffled Latin beat coming from the truck's stereo thundered above the loud strains of the symphony filling the Cruiser's cabin. A staccato of coarse male laughter from the Blazer pierced the music.

Beth glared in the rearview mirror. "Watch where you're going, you cretins," she growled at the silhouettes bobbing to the beat in the Blazer. She inched the Star Cruiser closer to a Cadillac limousine in front of her in the stop-and-go traffic.

The next bump was harder. The Cruiser lunged forward, but Beth stopped it just short of hitting the limo. "Caution to the rear. Check for possible damage," the computer insisted. Beth hissed angrily. The men in the Blazer laughed louder, then bumped her hard again.

Ever since Beth could walk, Jack Scibelli had taught his daughter never to back down from a challenge. His tutoring had stood Beth in good stead as a better-than-average high school and college basketball player and a successful journalist in the highly competitive global information market. But even Jack would have urged caution had he known what his daughter was about to do.

A carload of idiots intentionally bumping her on the crowded freeway in the middle of the night in the last place she wanted to be on Christmas Eve was the last straw. Beth lifted an unmistakable gesture of contempt for L.A., Christmas, and the creeps behind her into the glare of the Blazer's headlights and held it there, muttering a string of bitter curses into the mirror.

The response was immediate. The Blazer roared forward and bashed the candy apple Cruiser. *Crack!* If the Caddy hadn't moved ahead almost a car length, the impact would have launched the Cruiser into its trunk. Beth's head flew back and bounced off the white leather restraint, and she couldn't repress a loud gasp of fright. She heard the Blazer's high bumper scrape the Cruiser's rear deck.

The computer suddenly became adamant: "Collision to the rear. Damage confirmed. Assess damage before proceeding." A tiny dagger of fear slashed at Beth's seething anger.

Then a shadowy figure was at the passenger-side window reaching for the door handle. Gasping, Beth gunned the engine and jerked the wheel to the left. The Cruiser lunged toward a minivan in the next lane. Horns blared, tires screeched. Beth swerved back sharply and braked. Nowhere to go!

"Collision to the rear. Damage confirmed. Assess damage before proceeding," the computer demanded again.

"Shut up and help me," Beth growled at the voice.

The man was at the door again, a muscular Latino youth with a scraggly goatee, wearing a dark T-shirt and headband. Beth could feel the Blazer nudging the rear deck of the Cruiser again.

The locks, Beth! Mounting fear screamed at her. *Why didn't you activate the locks?*

Beth fumbled for the lock switch on the center console. But she was too late. The side door flew open, and the Latino thrust his head and shoulders inside and grabbed at her. Beth shrieked and cursed. She lashed out at him with her right hand, deflecting his arm and scratching him across the cheek. The computer interrupted itself: "Front passenger door open."

"Get out of here!" Beth screamed, adding a couple of vulgarisms she'd never used before. She kept slashing at him with her hand and nails. Horns from nearby cars blared objection to the youth's attack, but nobody stopped to help. Beth willed her anger to keep the intruder and her fear at bay.

"You got us in a wreck, chica" the youth growled, swiping at her arm. His breath instantly flooded the cabin with the stench of liquor, garlic, and hashish. "Pull your car to the side; we're gonna settle with you." A second kid jumped from the Blazer to stop traffic in the slow lane so Beth could be forced to the freeway's shoulder.

Beth knew the youths weren't interested in exchanging insurance information. She'd read about packs of hoods who could abduct an unsuspecting "accident victim"—usually female—on L.A.'s freeways, pick her car clean, and escape along the shoulder before onlooking motorists bothered to call 911 on their car phones.

Beth gunned the car forward half a car length, leaving her attacker spinning in the street and the door ajar. The traffic crept around her and blared at the kid holding back a lane of traffic now two car lengths behind the Cruiser. Beth grabbed the phone from her purse and punched 911. But the Latino dived headlong into the car, grabbed her arm, ripped the phone from her grasp, and threw it to the floor.

"Collision to the rear. Damage confirmed. Assess damage before proceeding. Front passenger door open."

Beth screamed and pummeled the man's face with her free hand. He seemed unfazed, as if numbed by drugs. The Cruiser pitched and nose-dived as Beth struggled to keep her foot on the brake while battling the intruder. The car's jerking motion swung the passenger door wildly open, then closed it hard on the Latino's foot, which dangled outside. He cursed bitterly in Spanish, grabbed her by the elbow with one hand, and reached for her throat with the other.

Then he was gone.

Beth heard a raspy yelp of pain outside the door, which gaped wide open again. Her assailant was sprawled face down on the pavement. A tall man wearing a maroon flight suit, black helmet and visor, boots, and gloves was perched on top of him. The man had the youth pinned to the ground with one knee, twisting one of the kid's arms behind him and jerking his head back by the hair. The big kid struggled wildly, and it was all the man in the helmet could do to keep him down.

"Don't just sit there, ma'am. Call the cops!" the man yelled at Beth, who sat stunned with mouth agape. *Scheherazade* continued to blare from the speakers, interrupted every five seconds by the computer's insistent admonitions about damage to the rear and the door being open.

Flushed and flustered, Beth shoved the gear shift to PARK and looked for her phone. It had disappeared in the melee. She fumbled at the console to kill the CD and activate the car phone. She turned on the radio by mistake. "Little Drummer Boy" was rum-pum-pumming. Beth cursed.

Suddenly the second Latino, younger, smaller, and more intoxicated than the first, pounced on Beth's rescuer from behind, knocking him off his captive. The two of them rolled on the pavement dangerously close to the tires of an airport shuttle van trying to ease around the fracas in the right lane.

All three men scrambled to a crouch at once. The man in the flight suit struggled to unzip a side pocket. Both youths charged him.

The gunshot made Beth jump and scream. She saw the larger kid fly backward, slam against the side of her Star Cruiser with a sickening crunch, and crumple out of view. The younger Latino backed off abruptly, turned on unsteady legs, and headed for the Blazer, which was revving for a getaway. A second shot caught the escaping hood midstride in the left buttock and sent him spinning and tumbling to the pavement, howling with pain.

"Call the cops now!" the man with the gun barked at Beth through the open door.

Beth frantically tapped the console selector, and the lighted display flashed back at her: FM, AM, CD, CB, FAX, PHONE. Before she could activate the key pad, an engine revved loudly behind her. She glanced in the rearview mirror to see the Blazer screech backward until it slammed into a truck behind it, then peel forward and jerk right, aiming for a space between cars in the number five lane.

The space was too narrow, but the panicked Latino driver went for it anyway. He floorboarded the Blazer toward his only escape route: the shoulder of the freeway. The Blazer barely missed the younger Latino but clipped the Cruiser's right rear quarter panel and the front bumper of an old beater Escort stopped in the number five lane. Beth gasped at the jolt and the bawling duet of high RPMS and rubber spinning on pavement. The computer almost seemed to lose control about the Cruiser being hit again.

The man in the maroon flight suit, who was standing in the gap between cars with his gun still smoking, dived and rolled in front of the Cruiser to evade the charging Blazer. By the time he scrambled to his feet, flipped up his visor, and took aim, the Blazer had fishtailed onto the shoulder and accelerated.

That's when Beth saw the motorcycle parked on the shoulder, which she realized belonged to the man who took on the hoods. The rear end of the Blazer slid into the bike and toppled it into a clump of oleander bushes alongside the shoulder. *This poor Good Samaritan is getting more than he bargained for out of his kind deed*, she thought painfully.

The man in the flight suit was suddenly on Beth's side of the car, pulling the door open. "Get out, please, ma'am," he commanded, reaching for her arm. "I have to follow that vehicle and apprehend the hit-and-run suspect."

Beth grabbed the wheel and braced herself to resist. "What do you mean, 'get out'?" Beth snapped defensively, fearing for an instant that the stranger might be just as intent on harming her as the Latino hoods were. "You . . . you can't take this car," she stammered, wracking her brain for a plausible reason. "It's a rental and it's damaged and I might have whiplash and I don't live in L.A. and—"

"I don't have time to argue, ma'am," the man interrupted, sliding his pistol into his flight suit and unsnapping his helmet strap. "I'm a police officer, and I have to follow that Blazer. Now please get out. I'll call for another officer to pick you up." He pulled off his helmet and tossed it into the back seat, then grabbed her elbow ready to pull her out.

She jerked it out of his hand. "You're not leaving me alone on the freeway in the middle of the night with two junkie lunatics and a million other people who don't give a rip. You take my car, you take me too." Beth surprised herself with her ultimatum. She wasn't really sure she wanted to go with the guy who had just saved her life, but she was positive she didn't want to stay behind.

"I don't really need the company, but I have to leave *now*. So if you're not getting out, move over." The man sat down and began forcing her across the console with his hips.

"Hey, wait a minute," she protested, not really resisting him but not ready to give up the driver's seat. "How do I know you're a cop? I've been away from L.A. for awhile, but I know a cop's uniform when I see it, and you're not wearing one." Her heart was still beating wildly.

"I'm off duty, ma'am," the man almost barked at her. "I don't have time to dig out my holocard, but I promise I'll show it to you later. Now get out of my seat."

The man didn't look like a policeman to Beth. His face was round and boyish, with the large, excited eyes of a twelve-year-old anticipating a game of Space Troopers and Aliens on a video monitor. But thinning sandy-colored hair and a day's growth of beard belied his youthful features. He was at least thirty, maybe even thirty-five, Beth assessed. And his bravery on the freeway and his authoritative tone seemed to back up his claim. Beth wasn't sure she was ready for it, but she took a deep breath, hiked up her long skirt as modestly as she could, and threw her slender, five-foot eleven-inch frame over the center console into the passenger's bucket.

The man had the Star Cruiser in gear and rolling before his door was closed. He punched the accelerator and swerved between cars and onto the shoulder. Beth watched the digital display race toward 70 MPH. She silently sucked a long breath and buckled in. Gravel peppered the wheel wells as the Cruiser flew along the paved shoulder past the freeway logjam. The computer chanted a new warning: "Exceeding legal speed limit." *Mandatory airbags are a wonderful thing in L.A.*, Beth whispered to herself.

The man in the driver's bucket flipped on the car's emergency flashers, then deftly switched the phone to hands-free mode, and punched 911.

"This is Sergeant Cole, LAPD, driving a civilian vehicle in pursuit of a hit-and-run suspect. I'm northbound on the 405 just south of National Boulevard. Patch me through to any law enforcement units in the vicinity." Sergeant Cole's even, commanding tone and firm, two-handed grip on the wheel nudged Beth's confidence in him a little higher. His excited, little-boy eyes were hawkish, scanning the pavement ahead illuminated by the Cruiser's high beams. Far ahead the Blazer was angling toward the off-ramp at National Boulevard.

In seconds two California Highway Patrol freeway cruisers and an LAPD helicopter checked in. "CHP 5110, I have two suspects disabled in the number four lane of northbound 405 approximately a quarter mile south of National," Cole reported in the crisp, emotionless dialect Beth often referred to as cop-speak. "Request that you secure the suspects and transport to LAPD."

They always say "suspects" over the radio instead of "bad guys" or "scum bags" or worse, she thought. She still wanted to see Cole's holocard, but she knew he had to be a cop. He had the lingo down.

"No problem, LAPD. We're en route. ETA one minute."

"By the way, CHP, the hashhead—correction—suspect I'm pursuing knocked my civilian Kawasaki into the bushes back there." Beth smiled at the slight crack in Cole's professional demeanor over his bike getting clipped. "Request that you secure it before one of the locals adds it to his collection."

"Affirmative, LAPD."

Cole leaned on the horn and kept flashing the headlights high-low-high-low. The Star Cruiser flew down the shoulder toward the off-ramp at National. The souped-up Blazer had already sped down the long off-ramp and turned right through a red light, sideswiping a pickup in the intersection before speeding east on National. The Cruiser was still a quarter mile behind him.

"Suspect has exited the freeway at National and is headed east. He's in an old, midnight-blue, hopped-up Chevy Blazer. Big, wide-track tires. California license five-Nora-Robert-Nora-zero-five-nine." Cole repeated the number clearly. "I'm in pursuit." Beth wondered how the sergeant had captured the license number during the fracas, something she never even thought to do.

"Roger, sergeant. This is Air 10. We'll be on scene in a couple of minutes. Over."

The light was green as the Cruiser approached National Boulevard at nearly 80 MPH. "Hang on, ma'am," Cole warned. *No way can we make this turn without flipping over,* Beth thought in mild panic. She grabbed the armrest in the door with her right hand and braced herself against the dash with her left. Cole braked hard at the last moment, flicked a glance left and right, then threw the cruiser adroitly around the corner in a controlled four-wheel slide before tromping the accelerator to the floor again.

She heard the clatter of a wheel cover hitting the pavement and turned to see the spinning chrome disc jump the far curb, skitter across the sidewalk, and crash into a doorway of a deserted building, sending a transient diving for cover.

Beth held her breath through the turn, exhaled, then sucked air again as the acceleration pressed her deep into the leather bucket seat. The digital display never dropped below 45 MPH around the corner and then climbed rapidly toward 90 as the Cruiser hurtled eastward on National Boulevard. The computer, which had given up its warnings about damage to the rear, went berserk. "Excessive speed. You are in danger of causing an accident. Excessive speed. You are in danger—" With barely a glance at the console, Cole tapped in an override command, and the computer went silent.

The Blazer was several blocks ahead of them, swerving sharply in and out of four lanes of light traffic on a street lined by mom-and-pop stores and two-story apartment buildings. The light at Military

Avenue was green when the Blazer crossed it, but it turned red before the Cruiser arrived fifteen seconds later. Cole slowed only slightly and laid on the horn. The side-street traffic hesitated at his warning, and he swept between the standing vehicles at 65 and accelerated again.

"Suspect still heading east on National between Military and Westwood. I'm in pursuit," Cole reported. Air 10 and four LAPD black-and-whites called back that they were converging on the location.

The journalistic side of Beth's brain was working overtime. She had a million questions she wanted to ask Sergeant Cole about police procedure for commandeering a civilian vehicle, strategy for a high-speed chase without red light and siren, and his qualifications and experience behind the wheel. She knew there was a dynamite first-person story here she could write about and sell—if she survived! She wanted to know the personal interest angles about Cole's family, how he got into police work, if he had ever been injured, how he felt about endangering the life of a citizen. But her sense of self-preservation kept short-circuiting her objective inquisitiveness. How could she concentrate on a story when she couldn't stop wondering how her own obituary would read in tomorrow's *Times*? She would do her best to help Cole keep them both alive *now*. The story—if there was to be one—would have to come later.

Up ahead the young hood driving the Blazer negotiated another tire-screaming turn in traffic onto Westwood Boulevard. "Suspect now heading north on Westwood," Cole reported matter-of-factly. Then he braked abruptly at the corner to snake the Star Cruiser around standing vehicles and gawking spectators.

Barely clear of the intersection Cole floored it again, rapidly gaining ground on the Blazer as they roared down tree-lined Westwood Boulevard at close to 80. Pico Boulevard, another major intersection surrounded by commercial buildings, was dead ahead. The Blazer jerked into a skidding right turn onto Pico. Beth could see the tires smoking and hear the squeal from three blocks away.

"There's another black-and-white coming at him on Pico, so he has to cut south again." Cole was talking to himself in a subdued but excited tone. "I could cut him off—" Suddenly Cole hit the brakes with such force that it threw Beth's full weight against the seat belts and snapped her head forward. Before she could catch her breath, he cut the wheel sharply to the right at 45 MPH, sending the car into a four-wheel slide around the corner and onto a side street parallel to Pico Boulevard. Beth tried to brace herself, but the momentum of the surprise turn threw her upper body sideways across the console into Cole's lap. Her flailing elbow caught him in the chest, and her long dark hair flew across his face.

As the sergeant straightened out with his left hand and accelerated into a residential neighborhood, he used his right forearm to shove Beth back to her side of the car. "I appreciate the interest, ma'am, but this isn't a good time for me," Cole said, keeping his eyes glued to the road.

"Say again, sergeant," Air 10 cut in. "I didn't receive your last transmission about a good time for you. Over."

This time it was Cole sucking air as he silently remonstrated himself for his flippant comment. "Disregard, Air 10."

Somewhere in her preoccupied, disconcerted brain, Beth subconsciously registered the data: *A little sense of humor; a little arrogance; a little vulnerability. I think there's a real man underneath that tough black-and-white exterior.*

"Suspect is eastbound on Pico approaching Overland," Cole called with increased excitement in his voice. "I'm cutting behind him in case he tries to escape south on Overland." The sound of a police chopper could be heard overhead, and the brilliant cone of light from its 30-million candlepower "midnight sun" swept the intersection of Pico and Overland.

As he approached Overland, Cole watched through the trees as the searchlight turned south. Then he almost shouted, "He's coming back! I've got you, you dirty—"

In the next instant Beth knew her life was over. Ignoring the stop sign, Cole cranked the wheel to the left and skidded the Cruiser into the wrong-way lanes of Overland Boulevard and into the high beams of the Blazer. They were within three seconds of a head-on collision, and Beth instinctively covered her face with her arms and screamed.

But the youthful Latino driver somehow sliced the Blazer between the approaching Cruiser and a parked car, scraping the sides of both, and roared on. Seconds later, as Beth fought to regain her breath, two wailing black-and-whites raced by, and Cole, cursing his failure to waylay the Blazer, spun the car around to rejoin the pursuit.

"Can't the other cops take it from here?" she cried, panting from her brush with death.

Cole didn't answer verbally, but his accelerator foot to the floor, his angry, straight-ahead glare, and the determined set of his jaw clearly announced his intention. The Cruiser flew over a set of railroad tracks and bottomed out with a deafening crunch, spraying sparks left and right like waves from a speeding boat. Beth and the sergeant bounced heavily and grazed their heads on the cabin's ceiling. Beth heard her luggage thumping against the lid and floor of the trunk. She winced, hoping her computer would survive the beating.

"Sergeant, we have you and the suspect in sight from the chopper," Air 10 alerted. "And the black-and-whites are on top of him.

Advise that you abort pursuit for your own safety. That Star Cruiser doesn't have the suspension to take many hits like the last one."

Cole exhaled his disappointment and punctuated it with a sharp, whispered curse. He could see the chopper's searchlight ahead and hear the trill of chase units all around them. But it was a few seconds before he eased off the accelerator. As he did Beth slowly released a lung full of air and relaxed her death grip on the safety belt.

"Affirmative, Air 10," Cole sighed. Beth thought he sounded like a little boy whose father just told him that he couldn't ride the roller coaster anymore tonight.

Two

Hours earlier the Arena had been rocking as 15,000 berserk Clippers' fans watched their team storm back from a 12-point halftime deficit to edge the Celtics by 3 in double overtime. It didn't matter that the rebuilding Celts were struggling to hold onto fourth place in the Eastern Conference's Atlantic Division. They were still the fabled Boston Celtics, the team of legends: Cousy, Russell, Havlicek, Bird. To the Clippers' faithful, beating the currently legendless Celts on their annual trip to the Los Angeles Memorial Sports Arena was as satisfying as beating one of the championship teams of the '70s or '80s in the NBA finals—which the Clippers had never come close to doing.

The Arena was silent now, dimly lit by a handful of security lamps in the ceiling and secondary light from the encircling ground- and arena-level concourses. Though swept clean of several hundred pounds of flattened cups and cardboard snack trays, the Arena still smelled of beer and popcorn. It was 2:30 A.M.

A slight, stoop-shouldered man wearing a concessionaire's uniform and cap entered the darkened Arena from the concourse at the lower level. He was pushing a dolly stacked with cartons and moved wearily across one end of the giant oval next to the playing floor.

The man paused just past the standard which suspended the basket precisely ten feet above the polished hardwood. His eyes, squinting behind thick, wire-rimmed glasses, swept the vast, darkened bowl, seemingly returning the gaze of thousands of invisible faces watching him roll his burden across the floor. Then, as if yielding to a ripple of applause from the crowd, the man left his dolly and stepped timidly onto the playing floor. The ripple cascaded to a roar. Embarrassed and yet warmed by the crowd's reception, the man lifted his hands to one large section of his invisible admirers and bowed slightly. He turned to face another section and bowed again, obviously reveling in the silent ovation, which was thunderous in his ears.

Having faced every section in the Arena and received the adulation graciously, the man walked to center court and began to speak, not audibly, but by mouthing words and gesturing grandly to his rapt audience.

"Hodge, are you in there?" The interrupting voice was that of a huge black man standing with hands on hips in the wide doorway on the next level up.

"Yes sir, Mr. Whatley. I'm here, sir." Hodge spoke in the slight brogue of a second-generation Irish commoner. He abruptly ended his command performance and hurried back to his dolly.

"C'mon, Hodge," Mr. Whatley called, more annoyed than angry. "I'm trying to finish up and get us out of here, and you're in there daydreaming again. Hey, man, everybody else is gone. Let's move it!"

Mr. Whatley wore the short-sleeved white shirt and tie of an assistant manager. But after an evening of supervising hot dog stands and several hours of cleaning and restocking them, his size 3X shirt was rumpled and smeared with mustard and catsup, and the wrinkled tails hung out. His stained, out-of-style tie was loose and askew at the collar and stuffed between the buttons of his shirt where the second and third rolls of flab converged.

"I'm sorry, Mr. Whatley," Hodge groveled. "I'll be right there, sir. This is my last load of buns, sir. I'm sorry, sir."

But in his haste to rock the dolly back onto its wheels, Hodge buckled the stack of cartons and they tumbled loudly to the cement floor. Several cello-wrapped packages of hot dog buns spilled out.

Whatley turned and waddled away, cursing about the lousy help he had to work with. Hodge scurried to pick up the buns and restack the cartons.

"I'm sorry, Mr. Whatley," he called after his boss. "I'll be right there, sir. I'm sorry, sir."

It took Hodge about twenty minutes to distribute three cartons of hot dog buns to the food stands around the concourse on the Arena level. He had already restocked the stands upstairs on the ground-level concourse. Meanwhile, Whatley paced impatiently near the staff exit at the back of the stockroom on the northwest curve of the Arena, complaining to the grizzled security guard sitting in a folding chair near the door reading a paperback novel.

"Why do I always get stuck with these brain-dead winos on my shift?" Whatley whined as he paced, his ponderous jowls jiggling with every heavy step. "Why should I have to stick around until this clumsy, slower-than-a-slug old coot finishes? Why can't I just leave him to work until dawn if he wants to, since you're here all night anyway? But no, the boss says I can't leave until everything's done. If help wasn't so hard to find, especially with all the Millennium's Eve stuff going on, I'd have Hodge's tired old butt back on the street where it came from."

The guard grunted sympathetically, but he hadn't heard a word.

Whatley stuck his head out the stockroom door and boomed into the concourse, "C'mon, Hodge, man. My woman's waiting. Let's go, Hodge."

Hodge's wimpy reply drifted back from a food stand somewhere on the lower level. "Almost finished, Mr. Whatley. I'll be right there, sir. I'm sorry, sir."

Hodge finally emerged from the employee locker room dressed in his street clothes and swinging a dirty, blue and white plastic picnic chest in one hand. Whatley studied the sorry-looking sight walking toward him in the stockroom. Hodge had stated on his application that he was fifty, but Whatley knew better than to believe what people said about themselves to get this minimum-wage job. Fifteen-year-old high school dropouts wrote down nineteen, and sixty-year-old bums wrote down forty. Whatley didn't care. If they showed up and did the work, what difference did it make? He had such a hard time keeping good help he could overlook just about anything on an application.

Still, Hodge wasn't much more than fifty, Whatley judged. His long, straggly hair sticking out from under his soiled Dodgers cap was the color of dirty straw with only a few wisps of gray. And although Hodge appeared on the skinny side—almost fragile—in the baggy jeans, sweatshirt, and frayed, oversized jean jacket he always wore to and from work, he was remarkably strong—slow and rather clumsy, but strong. Yet Hodge's frequent mental lapses convinced Whatley that the old man's hidden vices had aged him to within ten years of checking out—twenty years max.

And that face. Whatley had never seen a homelier face. His deeply lined skin was weathered to a reddish-brown, as if perpetually sunburned, with a bulbous, mottled nose supporting Coke-bottle lenses. He had the puffy red cheeks of a major league boozer. Hodge consistently showed up to work with two days worth of sparse, yellow-gray stubble. Whatley mused that Hodge probably shaved every day, but his razor couldn't get any closer to skin with the consistency of an old, worn catcher's mitt.

Hodge's lips were thick and usually cracked and scabbed. Whatley had never seen the old man smile, but he'd caught him yawning once, revealing a mouthful of yellowed, crooked teeth and the breath of a half-dead camel. Hodge's deep-set, jaundiced eyes, magnified by his thick lenses, peered blankly between thick, drooping lids and a set of bags that would have made the Samsonite people envious.

In a lot of ways Hodge was like any of the thousands of bedraggled, empty-eyed souls who wandered the streets of downtown L.A.—dopeheads, winos, and crazies claiming to be the reincarnation of Elvis or the emperor of a distant galaxy beamed to earth to recruit warriors. And Hodge's gaunt appearance had almost caused Whatley to reject him immediately when he applied at the Sports Arena-Coliseum complex six months earlier, suspecting him to be an AIDS victim approaching the advanced stages of the virus.

But Hodge's mandatory blood and urine tests for problematic drugs and all strains of the virus came back clean. Subsequent random drug tests were also negative. And though Hodge admitted to enjoying a bottle of muscatel on occasion, and often smelled like he used the stuff for cologne, he had never missed a day of work or showed up late or drunk. Whatley could only wonder how Hodge was masking the addictions and diseases that ruled the lives of countless others on the street who looked just like him.

Hodge's appearance was too great a liability for Whatley to put him behind the counter serving customers. So the assistant manager had confined him to cleanup and restock, which seemed to suit the wiry little bum just fine.

"Mr. Whatley, sir?" Hodge said to his hulking boss as the security guard fumbled through his ring looking for the door key.

Whatley backed off slightly and waved a blast of camel breath away without attempting to disguise his meaning. "Yeah, Hodge, what?"

"Sir, I wonder if you ain't heard from Mr. Teresina, sir, about next Friday night." His Irish accent had a sing-songy quality, but his blue-collar grammar made him sound out of tune.

Whatley blanked. Teresina. Friday night. He was clueless.

"Mr. Whatley, sir, you were gonna ask Mr. Teresina if I could trade with one of his workers at the Coliseum Friday night. Like I said, I'm a religious man, sir, and I would like to work at the Coliseum Friday night to see—"

"Oh, oh, yeah. Friday night, the big religious thing," Whatley cut in, his memory jogged. "Truth is, Hodge, I haven't had a chance to talk to Teresina yet. I'll do that tomorrow, Hodge, first thing, okay? Don't worry, I'll talk to him."

Whatley was lying, of course. No way was he going to trade Hodge for some unknown entity on the busiest night of the decade. Hodge wasn't much, but at least he was dependable. So what if the old coot wanted to see all those hallelujah hotshots in person lined up on the Coliseum platform like God's almighty all-stars. He could see them on the big screens in the Arena anyway. Hodge didn't have to be there in person.

The overflow from the Coliseum would probably push the Memorial Sports Arena to a new attendance record. Nope, Whatley wasn't letting Hodge out of his sight on Millennium's Eve. He just had to keep him on the string, convincing him that he would talk to Teresina at the

Coliseum about the swap.

The guard turned the key and swung the heavy metal door open. "Thank you, Mr. Whatley, sir," Hodge offered as he followed the big black man through the door into the cool December night. The lock clicked behind them. "Thank you again, sir. I appreciate it, sir." Hodge touched the bill of his dirty Dodgers cap respectfully.

Whatley didn't see it. He was already striding heavily toward the employee parking lot on the southwest side of the Arena. He was heading for a hot date with Shalonda Bankhead, a well-developed high school dropout who sold hot dogs on his shift and usually enticed a male customer to take her home after the game. Tonight was Whatley's lucky night.

"See you here Sunday night for the Knicks game, Hodge," he called over his shoulder. "Don't you be late, man, or I'll kick your butt."

"Yes sir, Mr. Whatley. I'll be here, sir. Good night, sir."

Whatley knew Hodge wouldn't be late, but the brusque warning was a habit.

Hodge stood in the glow of the floodlight illuminating the sidewalk just outside the stockroom door, watching Whatley lumber into the darkness. *Just one more week, you big slob,* Hodge mouthed after him silently, *and you'll wish to God you had been a little more respectful of me.* Then he regripped the picnic chest, jammed his free hand into the pocket of his ratty-looking jacket, and started home.

The first hours of Christmas Eve 1999 were clear and cold in L.A. Hodge puffed steam as he angled through Exposition Park on the north side of the Sports Arena. He had discovered several different routes from his place of employment to his cheap, rented bungalow. Tonight he decided to stay on the main drag: Figueroa.

The massive, ivy-covered walls of the Los Angeles Memorial Coliseum loomed dark and silent to his left at the west end of expansive Exposition Park. If it hadn't been so cold, Hodge would have walked around the giant bowl and thought about what was going to happen there Millennium's Eve.

Exposition Park was home not only to the Arena and the Coliseum but also to the Los Angeles County Museum of Natural History, the California Museum of Science and Industry, the Aerospace Museum, and the Afro-American museum. Hodge hoped to visit these attractions someday, but he had been too busy since arriving in L.A. almost seven months ago. As enjoyable as strolling leisurely through the museums might be, there were more important things to do than dally in the past. Hodge had already spent too many years in the past. There was really only one week of the past left, he reflected. At the stroke of midnight on Millennium's Eve, the future would commence. Hodge had been preparing for it for months, but he still had much to do.

He crossed Exposition Boulevard against the signal. Surface traffic was light for an early Friday morning in the city. But Hodge could hear the steady muffled hum of traffic on Interstate 110 running parallel to Figueroa two blocks east.

As Hodge veered northeast on Figueroa, he passed the sprawling campus of the University of Southern California on his left, its cement and brick buildings and tree-lined walkways well kept and imposing, and the University Hilton on his right. On other nights Hodge walked home on University Avenue through the heart of the historic private university.

Across Jefferson Boulevard from USC, Figueroa abruptly turned into a somewhat run-down, litter-strewn commercial district of dumpy little shops, all-night liquor stores and diners, pizza delivery joints, and bars. The sidewalks were nearly deserted. Most of Hodge's street brothers had found shelter for the night, except for a few hollow-eyed incognito "aliens" who were having difficulty locating their transporter pods for beaming back to their home galaxies. California Tokay, guzzled from a paper bag in a darkened doorway, really fouled up an alien's memory for coordinates. Hodge had learned early that if he walked briskly and purposefully in the early morning hours, any drunks, vagrants, or aliens on the street left him alone. So did the cops.

After several blocks, the northeasterly veering Figueroa finally overpassed noisy 110 as it shot straight north toward the Santa Monica Freeway. Hodge angled west at the overpass to Twenty-Third into a low-income quarter of older wood-frame homes and occasional two-story, '50s-style, stucco apartment buildings. The glare of the yellow-white industrial streetlights flooding Figueroa gave way to the much dimmer residential streetlights.

Hodge spotted the gang of four males several seconds before they stepped from the shadows between houses to block the sidewalk. He saw their cigarettes glowing in the darkness. Their faces were mostly shadows.

"Hey, old man, do you have something for us in there?" one of them exhaled toward him. The kid had a slight Southeast Asian accent.

Hodge gripped the handle of his picnic chest and walked around them without breaking stride or acknowledging their presence. He'd been hassled by gangs before on his walks home. Usually he ignored them and they left him alone—he looked too poor to have any money. But occasionally, like tonight, his picnic chest aroused more than a passing interest in kids who would snatch anything that could be traded for a hit of cocaine or an ammunition clip.

Another gang member, a white kid, and bigger, reached out and grabbed Hodge roughly by the arm as he attempted to pass, and spun him around. "Didn't you hear my friend?" he snarled. "What's in that thing with the handle?" Hodge thought the kid was overacting his toughness a little.

Hodge, who was an inch taller than the kid but about forty pounds lighter, leaned into his face. He gripped the chest tightly, while his free right hand remained stuffed in his jacket pocket. "Nothin' but a half a bologna sandwich and a few orange peels, punk," Hodge said forcefully just above a whisper, making sure his rancid breath pummeled the kid's nose. This was not the groveling persona Hodge often displayed for Whatley. This was the street-wise back-alley Hodge talking. He had learned during his first few days in L.A. that you can ignore trouble on Figueroa, but in the neighborhood you better be fast enough to outrun it, tough enough to overpower it, or smart enough to defuse it.

The gang member quickly let go of the old man's arm and stepped back, cursing and mumbling about Hodge's breath smelling like a toilet.

"I didn't think you'd be interested," Hodge said as he turned and continued walking down the sidewalk listening intently for footsteps. Sometimes kids came after him; sometimes they didn't. These kids did. Just as the big kid grabbed the handle of the picnic chest from behind, Hodge whirled, yanked it from his grasp, and flashed his knife in the dim light so the punks could plainly see it. It was a huge knife; the blade was a full six inches long.

"Take my word for it, punks," he said to the gang who had backed out of range. "A bologna sandwich, some orange peels, and a cooler ain't worth getting cut over. But if you insist, I'll sure accommodate you." Then he pushed the knife a little closer to them.

As Hodge figured, the four boys weren't up to hand-to-hand combat, and they continued backing away. Then they showered him with vile obscenities—promising to "get him" some night—before crossing the street and heading toward Figueroa.

Hodge watched until they were two blocks away, then, putting down the chest, carefully returned the knife to its sheath—sewn inside his baggy jean jacket.

At Estrella Avenue he turned right and walked into an even darker neighborhood. The DWP had long since given up replacing streetlights in this area, because they were almost always shot out the first night they appeared. Estrella was crowded with dilapidated, two-story frame houses from the 1930s that somehow had escaped both urban renewal and the riot torches of the '80s and '90s.

Hodge walked soundlessly down Estrella in the darkness, turned east at Twenty-First one block to Bonsallo, then north again. About halfway between Twenty-First and Washington he stopped at a driveway guarded by a rusty chainlink gate, lifted the latch, and stepped inside. He walked along the broken cement driveway beside a darkened one-story wood house to a tiny bungalow in the rear that once had been a garage. Even in the pitch darkness, Hodge walked straight to the front door of his bungalow and pulled a ring of keys from his pocket. He slipped one key in the deadbolt and unlocked it. Then he inserted a second key in the doorknob, opened the door, entered, and quickly locked himself in.

Hodge dropped the picnic chest inside the door, then moved through the ink-black darkness as if the room were fully lit. He stepped to each of the bungalow's three windows, which were installed years ago for light and ventilation when the garage was transformed into living quarters. But since Hodge moved in, the one-room bungalow hadn't seen the light of day. The windows were covered from the inside with tar paper and duct tape, soundproofed with scraps of cork sheeting, styrofoam, and cardboard, and securely boarded. Heavy dark curtains were draped across them. Hodge tugged at the curtains in the darkness, assuring that they were tightly closed. They always were.

Hodge walked to an old wooden desk in the corner nearest the door and turned on a small lamp. The room was cramped and cluttered. The desk was stacked with books and papers, as was the crude bookcase of cement blocks and unfinished boards standing beside it.

The low open-beam ceiling was stuffed with old insulation material and crisscrossed with frayed electrical wires. The walls were also well insulated. But the Sheetrock had been installed slapdash fashion and never taped or plastered. For all its unfinished appearance, the room was thoroughly weather- and soundproofed.

In one corner of the room was a sagging but neatly made single military-style cot. In the other back corner stood a toilet and tiny sink. A large, unframed mirror leaned against the wall atop the sink. A battered bureau stood next to the sink. A naked light bulb hung from a cord and socket above the mirror.

A rickety table stood in the remaining corner with a tiny, beat-up refrigerator buzzing and clicking underneath it. A corroded electric hot plate and cans and boxes of food cluttered the tabletop. A board supported by L-braces nailed to the wall in the "kitchen" was lined with a mismatched array of dented pans and chipped dishes.

In contrast to the somewhat disheveled perimeter, the center of the room looked like a carefully organized, low-budget work area. An eight-foot wooden table was spread with an array of simple tools. A large light bulb hung over the table.

Hodge stood beside his desk and touched a number of open books and papers strewn across it as if greeting cherished friends. His eyes darted from book to book, notepad to notepad, paragraph to paragraph, appraising words and phrases. Soon he was absorbed in the treasures before him. He absently removed his cap and jacket, sat down in an old wooden desk chair, and began poring over two large volumes, scribbling notes and sketching diagrams.

It was cool in the unheated bungalow, but Hodge didn't seem to notice. He moved from book to book feverishly, occasionally punctuating a discovery with a hum or grunt of delight.

Presently he rose and began pacing the small room. He circled the worktable repeatedly, reciting phrases he had written and gesturing emphatically. His eyes blazed with the fire of conviction, and he paced with a self-assured, almost arrogant strut. His voice rose with passion and conviction, as if his little bungalow was crowded with eager listeners. Small tears squirted from the corners of his eyes.

In the midst of his emotional presentation, he stopped and jerked stiffly upright, as if he had stepped on a live wire. The inner voice prompting the reaction buzzed like an alarm within him, arresting, compelling, more insistent than he had heard it in weeks: *Return to me! Hasten! Do not delay! Return at once!*

Hodge had dealt with this interruption for years, not without difficulty. Yet every rejection of the intruding authority had made the next rejection easier, though each recurrence rang with unnerving clarity: *Return to me! Hasten! Do not delay! Return at once!*

"You are not my master," Hodge spoke aloud to the gnawing interruption. "My master speaks with a gentle tongue, smooth as honey, like a friend. You speak with authority, like a father. I know my master's voice. I will not listen to yours."

Hodge had recited the lines countless times, just as the master had coached him. And as before, the alarming inner cry fell silent—for another season. Hodge returned to his pacing and impassioned preaching.

After several minutes the storm passed. Hodge returned to his desk and hovered over his notes, bracing himself with both hands, until his fervor ebbed to a few heavy sighs. It was nearly dawn, and he was utterly spent.

He moved slowly to the kitchen, reached behind a cast-iron pot on the shelf, and pulled out a nearly full bottle of brandy and a plastic cup. In contrast to the rest of his possessions, the bottle glistened. Hodge cradled it carefully. It was the only luxury he had allowed himself.

He poured half a cup and returned the bottle to the shelf. Shuffling to the mirror by the sink, he turned on the light bulb and studied his image in between small, reverent sips of the warming liquid. Then he set the cup on the ledge and began the process of preparing for bed.

Three

It was nearly 3 A.M. before Beth and Sergeant Cole had finished their video depositions at the scene of the Blazer driver's arrest. The drug-hyped seventeen-year-old Latino gang member had outrun the black-

and-whites for a couple of miles and gamely tried a few more high-speed evasive maneuvers. But his last trick, a too-fast, too-tight turn, flipped the Blazer on its side in a screeching, grinding, spark-spraying crash which startled awake a residential neighborhood just off Westwood Boulevard on Queensland. The kid sustained a shattered elbow, lacerated face, and abrasions.

The corner of Queensland and Selby looked like the site of an emergency vehicle convention. The mortally wounded Blazer was surrounded at odd angles by six black-and-whites, two red LAFD pump engines, an LAFD rescue truck, two private ambulances, and a tow truck. The emergency fleet sprayed the older, middle-class tract homes with brilliant red and amber lights. Residents huddled at the curb in bathrobes and blankets to gawk. A couple of TV vans were parked behind the emergency vehicles while their crews scrounged footage of destruction and injury for the early morning local news. The normally quiet neighborhood was overcome by the rattle of idling diesel engines and the crackle of amplified chatter from remote radios carried by the uniformed public servants swarming the scene.

CHP 5110 swung by the convention long enough to report that they had rescued Cole's bike and had ferried it to the CHP yard under the cloverleaf of the Santa Monica and Harbor Freeways. Except for a few scratches and a broken mirror, it looked okay, they said. The officers also said that the two wounded members of the Latin Barons had been taken to Daniel Freeman Hospital and treated for DAB wounds before being booked.

"DAB wounds? Treated then booked?" Beth quizzed a huddle of LAPD and CHP officers while Cole recited his version of the episode into the video cameras. She couldn't believe her assailants' gunshot wounds weren't more serious.

"Most of us carry these new DAB guns—DAB for 'drop and burn,' " explained a cop who was obviously schmoozing the tall, attractive, self-assured victim. He was little more than a rookie, but he did his best not to sound like one. He had dropped the customary cop-speak in favor of a pseudo-suave aren't-you-impressed-that-I'm-a-cop? approach.

"They're made entirely of plastic—polymers, really. See?" He put his DAB gun into Beth's hands. "It fires a gel capsule at high velocity that literally knocks the bad guy down, no matter how big or mean or zoned on drugs he is."

"Mm." Beth tried to sound impressed while examining the small black handgun. It had the weight and appearance of a loaded squirt gun.

"The capsule bursts on impact and splatters an acid that burns through the clothes and fries a few layers of skin. The burn isn't too serious, but it seriously distracts the bad guy until we can cuff him and scan him." The other officers grunted and nodded nonchalantly as if they DABed at least a dozen bad guys a day.

Beth shook her head in mock disbelief. "I was sure the big guy was dead or nearly dead. He slammed against my car like a side of beef. I'm glad he's locked up, but I'm also kind of relieved that he wasn't killed."

"That sleazebag got the hurt he deserved," interjected the short Hispanic CHP officer who had arrested the wounded hoods on the freeway. "He had some nasty burns on his neck and chest from being DABed at close range. But he also got a concussion and some deep bruises from bouncing off your Star Cruiser."

"And you should have seen the other kid," interjected his partner, a thin Asian officer with a neatly trimmed mustache. "There he was, crying in the middle of the San Diego Freeway with the backside of his jeans burned away and his little red butt sticking out."

The cops laughed louder than was necessary, Beth thought, like when something only moderately amusing breaks the stranglehold of tension in a difficult situation. She realized that the wild ride through West Los Angeles had been almost as terrifying for some of the cops standing around her as it had been for her. Beth couldn't help laughing with them, and she felt some of the tension drain from her as she did.

Inspecting the damage to her shiny red Galaxy Star Cruiser and its contents quickly sobered her up. The assault it endured from the Blazer resulted in a smashed taillight and a badly dented and scratched rear deck. The once-gleaming candy apple surface on the driver's side looked like it had been worked over by a gang of kids brandishing nails and screwdrivers. Beth wished she hadn't denied the additional coverage on the rental this time. She decided not to report the incident to Galaxy or her insurance company until she checked the car in on January 2.

They also checked the oil pan for her and reported no leaks were apparent. The Cruiser's trunk lid was jammed closed. So the young cop who had tried to impress her with his DAB gun pried the lid open with a crowbar and gave her a length of nylon cord for tying it down again.

Beth's luggage, the kind advertised to withstand the punishment of gorillas masquerading as airline baggage handlers, survived the ramming and the chase. But even a high-impact plastic case couldn't save her computer. The monitor screen was cracked, and the unit made an electronic spitting noise when she turned it on. She swore at the prospect of having to use a rental in L.A. until hers was repaired. And she hoped her auto insurance would cover both the Star Cruiser and her Nanotec 6000 computer. *Thanks to fiber optics, at least I can retrieve all my backup notes and research from home,* she thought with a measure of relief. She was also relieved to find her phone under the front seat, none the worse for the ordeal.

One by one the emergency vehicles left the scene in response to other calls. Beth offered to drive Cole to the CHP yard to pick up his bike. She felt obligated to thank him for saving her life on the freeway, even though she was far from thankful for the wild ride that further damaged her rental car, trashed her computer, and gave her an authentic near-death experience. Cole, who was animated and somewhat cocky while describing his part in the chase to the video cameras, didn't appear thrilled about her offer. But his departing colleagues had left him no alternatives.

"What branch of the police department are you in, sergeant?" Beth took a stab at small talk. Cole had fallen silent after giving her directions to the CHP yard several miles west of the accident just off the Santa Monica Freeway.

"I'm a patrolman, just like those officers back there," Cole said without emotion, staring straight ahead. The sullen silence that overcame him when he was called off the chase had returned. Beth thought she liked better the boyish enthusiasm and intense competitiveness he displayed during the chase.

"So you knew all those LAPD guys?"

"Fraternally, yes; personally, no. They're out of West L.A. Division. I work the Southwest Division, downtown L.A." Cole's eyes never left the Santa Monica Freeway stretched out ahead of them.

"I thought sergeants didn't have to work the streets. They get the computer jobs. Nine to five, coffee breaks, suede jackets, ties."

"Detectives and administrators maybe. But patrol sergeants patrol with their officers. We're kind of like point guards on a basketball team, coordinating the actions of the other officers."

Beth regarded Cole's barely civil demeanor as a challenge. At the mention of basketball, she tried another approach to crack him.

"You look like you could have played some basketball."

"Yeah, I played a little in college." Cole sounded only slightly more interested in the new topic. He still wouldn't look at her.

"What are you, about six-six?"

"Six-five."

"Where'd you play?"

"UCLA. Take the next freeway exit." Beth flicked on the turn signal and aimed toward the off-ramp.

"Mm, the mighty Bruins. Made it to the Sweet Sixteen a couple of times back in the early '90s. Were you on any of those teams?"

"Yeah, '92. Didn't play much. Played a little more in '93."

"I played for USC, '89 to '92," Beth said, almost a little embarrassed at her rather juvenile attempt to impress him. "We got a little NCAA tournament action ourselves in '92."

Cole mumbled an unintelligible response. Beth didn't think he could sound less impressed. He directed her into the driveway leading to the brightly lit CHP yard encircled by a ten-foot chainlink fence topped by rolls of razor wire.

"I appreciate what you did for me on the freeway," Beth said as she pulled up to the gate, trying to sound sincere without gushing. She had decided only to thank him for his help and forgo any comments about the chase.

"I'm a police officer, ma'am. It's my job to protect and serve," Cole said with a tinge of sarcasm as he reached into the back seat for his helmet. He avoided looking at Beth.

"But you were off duty, sergeant. You didn't have to stop."

"It's not exactly something you leave in your locker with your badge and uniform when you walk out at night. You see an out-of-towner getting jumped because she foolishly flips off a bunch of joyriding hashheads without the sense to lock her doors, you just react."

Beth's face flushed warm. *So that's the reason for the silent treatment,* she hissed to herself. *I'm just another dumb broad who was asking for trouble.* She had hoped that this rather good-looking, heroic officer was free of the macho, me-Tarzan attitude she found so offensive in many men her age. After all, he had rescued her from the Latin Barons and even called her "ma'am." But suddenly another hope exploded in her face, and she felt horrible for being so naive.

Beth's response was controlled but crisp with indignation. "Look, sergeant, I didn't challenge those creeps to a round of destruction derby on the freeway. But I wasn't about to let them get away with it either. I grew up in this rat hole of a city. Even though—thank God—I haven't lived here in a few years, I know if you back down to trash like that they'll run right over you. I did what I could, okay?"

"What you did was stupid." Cole's voice rumbled with emotion that had obviously been simmering beneath his cool exterior. "All you had to do was use that finger of yours to phone 911 as soon as the hoods threatened you, and an air unit would have been overhead in thirty seconds. They can laser-DAB a bad guy from 300 feet—they don't miss. But no, you have to take on the Latin Barons single-handedly. Geez, all this communication technology we've developed and you can't get a know-it-all broad to point her finger in the right direction."

"Maybe you forgot, sergeant, I'm the victim," Beth snapped, hurt and steaming.

"What do you know about being a victim, lady?" Cole almost shouted, finally facing her. Beth could see the veins in his neck bulging in the dim light. "You obviously have no clue what the Latin Barons or the Grave Warriors or some of our other fine citizens do to pretty girls driving alone at night. I've handled the bodies. I've seen the crime-scene pictures. You don't know how close you came to joining the gallery of pinup girls lining the walls of the county morgue." The truth of his words cut Beth deeply. She'd seen the pictures too. A classmate of hers at USC had been one of them.

"Yeah, but you saved me from the hoods only to nearly kill me off in that hell-on-wheels chase," she retorted spitefully. She was scrambling to defend herself, but she covered it by staying on the offensive. "I can't believe you played macho-cop chicken with a civilian in the car!"

"I asked you to get out of the car. In fact, I *ordered* you to get out. But, no, you had to play the tough chick with me just like you did with the Barons. That's two stupid decisions in a row."

"You . . . you have no right to talk to me like that," Beth sputtered. "I resent your, your—I resent you! I'm a citizen. You're a public servant. You're supposed to protect me, not harass me."

Cole gripped his helmet and jerked open the door. Flicking her a subtle sneer of triumph, he said, "I'm off duty, remember?" Then he stepped out, slammed the door, and strode brusquely through the gate and into the yard.

Beth was so upset she trembled. The disappointments and traumas of the last three hours suddenly began breaking over her like the killer surf that pounds the Southern California coastline in winter. Her high hopes for Christmas at home had blown up. The physical assault by the Latin Barons and the high-speed chase had terrified her. The brash judgmentalism of a chauvinistic cop had deeply wounded her, especially because what he said was true.

Beth struggled to fight back the pounding waves with her anger. *To blazes with L.A.! To blazes with my parents and Christmas! To blazes with the Latin Barons and DAB guns and Sergeant smart-mouth Cole! To blazes with Unity 2000 in the Coliseum! I want to go home!*

Beth felt the self-sufficient, hold-it-together-at-all-costs dam within her crumbling under the attack. Tears flooded her eyes and a sob swelled in her throat. She cursed her inability to control her emotions. She didn't dare put the car in gear and try to drive, but she wasn't about to give Cole the satisfaction of seeing her fall apart. She pretended to search her purse on the floor as a man in a maroon flight suit and black helmet riding a Kawasaki 1200 pulled out of the CHP yard and roared passed her toward the freeway entrance.

Suddenly the terror and bitter disappointment of the first three hours of Christmas Eve kicked Beth in the stomach. She clasped both hands to her mouth to stifle a moan, but failed. She quickly fumbled to lock the doors and shut off the engine; then the dam collapsed.

Four

It was shortly after 4 A.M., and Shelby Hornecker was suddenly and breathlessly awake. Her dream was the culprit again, the same vivid, suffocating dream that had interrupted her sleep sporadically for the last nine months. She lay still in her king-size bed with eyes closed, willing sleep to return and erase the familiar, pulse-quickening scene from her mind. Sometimes she did fall asleep again. But the dream never went away completely, because it was more than a dream. It was a living nightmare caged in her memory.

As much as Shelby wished that the dream was only a bizarre creation of her imagination, she knew it had really happened. The predawn phone call. The paralyzing message. The hysteria that swept like a range fire through the Horneckers' Spanish villa near Austin as Shelby numbly but dutifully woke and notified her staff. The live satellite coverage within minutes that allowed the world to view her private tragedy.

As usual, in the seconds following the dream's fresh assault, Shelby's senses groped the darkness of her surroundings for something comforting to hang on to. The familiar muted tick coming from the massive antique clock in the hall steadied her. The whisper of the climate vents assured her that the villa's computer-monitored environmental control system, including the security of the 600 acres of rolling hills surrounding the house, was fully operational. Silk sheets swathed her trim and shapely thirty-eight-year-old body. Her favorite fragrance, one of the most expensive in the world, wafted lightly through her expansive bedroom.

And, as usual, she grasped at the adornments only steps away from her bedroom suite, symbols of her worth in those frightening, lonely moments after the dream . . . an entire room stocked with finely tailored suits, dresses, and gowns. In her mind she fingered the wool, the silk, and the satin. In another room for coats, furs, shoes, and purses, the heady fragrance of imported leather and eelskin rivaled that of her perfume. There were ornate, heirloom boxes laden with custom jewelry. In her mind she affectionately fondled every ring, necklace, bracelet, and pin.

Calmed, she allowed her mind to stroll beyond her luxurious suite to inventory the trinkets and treasures embellishing the Hornecker villa. She swept through the halls and lolled in room after room. She itemized her possessions much like an insomniac counts sheep. Original watercolors, acrylics, and pastels. An antique porcelain doll collection. Mayan pottery and tapestries. And, outside, a herd of prize-winning Brahmans. . . .

Sleep returned, and so did the dream, beginning with the pulse-quickening beep of her bedside phone. Shelby saw herself flinch and gasp with fright. "Yes, what is it?" Her brain seemed stuffed with wool. Her voice was thick with sleep.

"Shelby, I don't know how to say this. Something terrible . . ." The man's voice broke. His attempt to stifle a wrenching sob failed.

The undisguised grief on the other end of the phone stung Shelby fully awake. She had never heard their good friend and self-assured partner so obviously distressed.

She glanced at the digital clock glowing on the nightstand. "Stan, it's 3 in the morning. Where are you? What's wrong?" Her mind was conjuring up answers by the dozen: *Eleanor or one of their children must be very ill. No, it's more serious. There's been an accident. A member of the office staff has been hurt or killed. . . .*

"I'm at home, here in Dallas," Stan's voice convulsed as he spoke. "I'm sorry to wake you, Shelby, but Eleanor said I should call you right away. Oh dear God, give us strength!"

"Stan, pull yourself together, man. What is it?"

Stan retched the words in bitter mouthfuls. "The team's plane . . . exploded this morning . . . over the Mediterranean. . . . Our film crew was killed . . . Kevin, Alyson, Dimbo, everyone on the shoot." Stan wailed uncontrollably. Shelby suddenly knew. "Adrian too, Shelby . . . down with the others . . . Adrian has gone home to be with Jesus . . . . I don't know what to say . . . . I'm so sorry."

The recurring dream always included several impersonally narrated clips from CNN's coverage: "Rev. Adrian Hornecker, age thirty-nine, the flamboyant Dallas televangelist, was killed this morning along with his award-winning film crew when his chartered jet exploded shortly after takeoff from Tel Aviv. Hornecker was returning to Dallas after filming the latest in a series of feature-length dramas based on the biblical account of the Second Coming of Jesus Christ. So far three Arab sects, all of which have publicly decried the pro-Israeli stance portrayed in Hornecker's internationally distributed films, are claiming responsibility for the bombing. Seventy-eight passengers, all employees or dependents of Victory Life Films, and a crew of six died in the explosion."

The narration accompanied footage of salvage boats crisscrossing fifty square miles of the eastern Mediterranean looking for bodies and debris, of which very little remained afloat.

The dream always ended with clips supplied to CNN several days later by Israeli television. It showed the youthful blond minister/filmmaker, briefcase in hand, smiling and waving to the crowd at the Tel Aviv airport as he boarded the charter. The voice-over of the network's touching human interest angle was ingrained in Shelby's memory: "Although Rev. Hornecker's remains went to the bottom of the Mediterranean with the others, remarkably, his locked briefcase, still tangled in the lines of a life preserver, was picked up by salvage boats. The case contained detailed plans for a prayer chapel to be built on the grounds of the couple's ranch near Austin, Texas. The chapel was to be a surprise for Shelby Hornecker, the late televangelist's wife and co-pastor of the Dallas-based Victory Life Ministries, in honor of their tenth wedding anniversary."

Shelby awoke again. The dream had terrorized her twice in one morning. *Why today of all days?* she wondered. *Christmas Eve. My first Christmas Eve service alone.* She chided herself for the negative thought. Adrian always scolded her for even the slightest hint of negativism.

The gentle chimes of the hall clock signalled 4:30 A.M. It was time to get up anyway. Shelby switched off the alarm before it sounded.

She swept her arm across the empty side of the bed. The sheets were cool, as they had been since February 2, the day Adrian left for Tel Aviv.

Actually, there were many nights in their nine years together when Shelby had slept alone, especially after the film ministry mushroomed. Ever the driven perfectionist, Adrian insisted on writing, producing, and directing every film himself — in conjunction with hired industry professionals who knew how to mold the televangelist's visions into reality on the screen.

Adrian's passion to produce Hollywood-quality "Last Days Evangelistic Thrillers," as he called them, caused him to spend weeks at a time on globe-circling location shoots and in Victory Life's Hollywood studios. Shelby was left in Dallas to coordinate the televised services from their lavish 4,000-seat auditorium near Arlington Stadium.

Every service featured a dynamic end-times video sermon by Adrian Hornecker. The live congregation watched the sermon on the huge sanctuary screen. But for the vast satellite congregation, the sermon was carefully edited into the live service to look like Adrian was there in the flesh. With the film ministry engulfing so much of Victory Life's funds, it was critical that Adrian remain highly visible and active to keep their television "partners" believing and giving. When Adrian was away, it was Shelby's job to keep up appearances.

Those were stressful days for Shelby, heading up the large ministry staff. And each of those days ended in Austin between cool sheets, with loneliness, anger, fear, suspicion, and longing her only bed partners.

Shelby touched her bedside intercom. "Good morning, Theresa."

It took a few seconds for Shelby's personal assistant and friend to respond. "Good morning, Shelby," she answered, barely awake. "Did you sleep well?"

"Like a babe in arms," Shelby fibbed. "Have Elena bring coffee to my study in about twenty minutes, and tell her I'll have breakfast in the garden room at 6:30. Ask Steve and Beverly to join me for breakfast."

"No problem, dear."

"And I need you in my dressing room at 6 to work your magic. It's Christmas Eve, and I need to look like a Christmas present for our adoring congregation this morning." Adrian had always insisted on a Christmas Eve morning service, no matter what day of the week it fell on, allowing his parishioners to spend Christmas morning with their families.

"Santa's little elf at your service," Theresa joked sleepily.

"Oh, and make sure Gordon and Sean are ready to fly at 8. This special service has a million details. I need to be at the sanctuary a little early to go over everything with Stan."

"The plane will be ready," Theresa assured. "Steve will take us to the airport at 7:30."

A carafe of coffee was waiting when Shelby entered the study after her shower. She was wearing faded sweats, and her hair was wrapped in a towel. She sipped coffee absently as she paced the spacious office rehearsing her memorized Christmas sermon.

Memorized sermons were one of Adrian's perfectionist idiosyncrasies. He insisted that all his preaching staff memorize their messages but make them sound extemporaneous. Shelby was good at both memory and delivery, as good or better than Adrian had been. Shelby's flawless preaching was one of the things that drew him to her at the Oklahoma Bible college where they met. She was attracted to his boundless energy and wild abandon for God and the ministry.

By 6:30 Theresa had styled Shelby's hair and helped her into a chic new holly-green worsted wool suit. On her jacket was a large pin, a cross formed of gold holly leaves. The tiny rubies sprinkled over the cross could be taken for holly berries or drops of blood. The pin had been a gift from Adrian.

Steve and Beverly Cashion, the young couple who managed Shelby's affairs at the villa, were waiting for her at the breakfast table, which Elena had tastefully set with place settings of Portuguese pottery, sterling, and linen. The diffused light of near sunrise in overcast skies streaked the hills misty gray beyond the large eastern windows. Elena had already delivered bowls of fruit compote to each place and a platter of steaming muffins to the center of the table.

"Let's have a last-minute check for tonight," Shelby said in a warm but get-down-to-business tone after pronouncing the blessing on the food. Her southwestern drawl was subtle and elegant.

"We're right on schedule, Mrs. Hornecker," Steve replied proudly, ignoring his breakfast. A tall, skinny twenty-eight-year-old, Steve was one of a number of young disciples tooled by Adrian Hornecker as minor but necessary cogs in the vast Victory Life teleministry machine. Steve had a good heart, but he had buckled too often under the rigors of minute-by-minute pressure in the Dallas office. So in the reorganization after Adrian's death, Shelby moved him and Bev to the villa for the less critical but necessary role of managing the small villa staff. The Christmas Eve Victory Life staff reception was the most ambitious project Shelby had allowed Steve and Bev to undertake.

Steve referred to a list Bev had given him. "The caterers will be here at 2 P.M. The charter flight with our guests from Dallas will arrive about 4:30. The vans will ferry them here from the airport. Hors d'oeuvres and wassail will be served at 5. The buffet—"

"Will anyone be offended by the wassail?" Shelby interrupted. It was an expression of curiosity, not criticism.

"Oh, no, ma'am," Steve assured. "These are our people. Upper-level Dallas staff and their families. A few former execs from the studio who are in town for the holidays. Those who don't drink alcohol have no problem with those who do. And we have sparkling cider punch for the children."

Shelby nodded, then ate a small spoonful of compote.

Steve continued. "The buffet will be open at 6—sliced smoked turkey and ham, molasses-baked beans with bacon, steamed garden vegetables, fresh breads. For dessert we have—"

Satisfied that the menu was adequate, Shelby interrupted again. "What about the program?"

"Just as you requested, Mrs. Hornecker," Bev spoke up. Steve's wife was small and rather plain, provoking Theresa to take on the project of tutoring her in charm and grooming. But Bev was sharp, the real brains in the couple. She managed the household while Steve supervised the building and grounds staff and ranch hands.

"Tiffany will open by leading a Christmas carol sing-along on her laptop keyboard. Then Mr. Cannon will perform one of his dramatic monologues of the Christmas story in costume."

"Not the same story he's doing in the service this morning," Shelby interjected while lightly buttering a muffin.

"No, ma'am. He's doing the innkeeper this morning. Tonight he's doing the one where he's Joseph."

Shelby nodded and motioned Bev to continue. Her mouth was full of muffin.

"After Mr. Cannon's presentation, you will give your message to the staff. Then Pastor Stan will be Santa Claus again this year. He'll distribute gifts to the children—Bible story holobooks for the little ones and those hand-held Bible adventure video games for the bigger kids. Then he'll present the Dallas office staff with their gifts, which are. . . ?"

"Already wrapped and tagged," Shelby filled in. "Theresa left them in a large basket by the fireplace in the den. And make sure there are additional wrapped gifts ready for any of the studio people who come down tonight—leather-bound Victory Life Bibles for those who don't have them already, whatever else we have available. I want everyone to

39

receive a gift tonight."

"Yes ma'am. I'll take care of it." Bev scribbled a hasty note in her organizer.

Bev completed her report by explaining that the vans would ferry the guests back to Mueller Municipal Airport for the return flight to Dallas between 10 and 11 P.M.

Assured that the evening was under control, Shelby relaxed her businesslike posture. She hadn't rehearsed her next words, but she had thought them over carefully, hoping not to sound maudlin or condescending. She had always found it difficult to express words of appreciation to those who served her so tirelessly, especially young devotees like Steve and Bev who regarded her almost as a goddess.

"As you both know, this has been a difficult year for me. Your loyalty and helpfulness here in Austin has greatly benefited me and our ministry at Victory Life."

The couple shifted nervously at their mentor's unexpected transparency. Bev started to reply, "Mrs. Hornecker, it's always our privilege—" But a slight gesture from Shelby's hand stopped her in mid-sentence.

"You both have worked very hard to keep things running smoothly here, freeing me to concentrate on the ministry in Dallas. I know you have sacrificed much of your personal time. If memory serves me, you haven't been away from Austin since late summer. Am I correct?"

Steve and Bev nodded in unison. "Yes ma'am, but—" Again Shelby's hand cut them off. She pulled a large, plain envelope from a briefcase beside the table and handed it to them.

"I want to express my sincere appreciation to you, Steve and Beverly, for all you have done this year, and I want to wish you a very merry and blessed Christmas."

Bev received the envelope with a look of innocent surprise.

"Go ahead, open it," Shelby urged.

Bev lifted the flap and pulled out a folder bearing the logo of Delta Airlines. Bev gasped. "Airline tickets, Mrs. Hornecker?"

Shelby couldn't keep a smug grin from her face. "I want you two to be home for Christmas. Those are round-trip tickets from Dallas to Chattanooga. You need to be packed and aboard the charter tonight when it leaves for Dallas. Your flight home leaves at 11:15. Go have a wonderful time with your families, and I'll see you back here after Unity 2000."

"But we can't leave you here alone for a whole week, Mrs. Hornecker," Steve protested.

"I won't even *be* here this week, Steve. I'm driving up to be with my parents in Waco. And everybody else is leaving tonight. Theresa, Elena, and the Welbourns will all be with their people for a few days. Stan will run the service on Sunday morning. Then on Tuesday Stan, Eleanor, Theresa, Jeremy and I will fly to L.A. for the big night at the

Coliseum. The house will be locked up, and the security system will be on. Julio and Edgar will feed the animals. Everything will be fine. Just go and have a good time."

Shelby felt only a small pang of conscience for telling a half-truth. She wasn't driving to Waco until the day after Christmas, not Christmas Day as she led her staff to believe. She was looking forward to spending Christmas Day alone at the ranch. She hadn't really been by herself since the plane crash. Well-meaning staff members had surrounded her constantly since that awful day, as if she would topple under the weight of the ministry without their help—which she probably would have.

But Shelby yearned for space to breathe, time to think and pray about the future, her future. To the staff, her decision to send everyone home for Christmas was a generous expression of appreciation, a quality in short supply in their former boss, Adrian Hornecker. Shelby *was* generous and appreciative. But the dark corners of her heart held the real motive for her action—time alone. Even the plane tickets to Chattanooga were part of her careful plan to make sure the devoted Cashions wouldn't be around to spoil her solitude.

Shelby had also been less than completely honest about Unity 2000. She really didn't want to go, and she hoped that somehow, perhaps at the last minute, she wouldn't have to. Yes, she had promoted the event enthusiastically and persuaded thousands of Victory Life faithful to attend. And she had publicly declared that she would be on the platform in the Los Angeles Memorial Coliseum on Millennium's Eve to link arms in Christian unity with Morgan McClure, Simon Holloway, and T.D. Dunne.

What choice did she have? Adrian had come up with the grand scheme several months before he died. At the conclusion of a nationally televised sermon on the need for oneness in the worldwide body of Christ during the Last Days, Adrian had rocked Shelby and the Christian world with a startling announcement. He challenged McClure, Holloway, and Dunne and their congregations to join him in Los Angeles on Millennium's Eve in a display of Christian unity that would launch the American church into the twenty-first century.

The master had given Adrian the vision for Unity 2000 during the sermon, he had stated, and commanded him to announce it then and there. Shelby had been trained never to doubt anything Adrian said about what God revealed to him. But he had never before announced a "revelation" publicly without discussing it with her and Stan first. Ever since Adrian had announced it, in a small, quiet place in her heart Shelby had been uneasy about Unity 2000.

McClure, Holloway, and Dunne had responded to the invitation enthusiastically on their national programs, of course. What choice did *they* have? Any one of them saying no to a publicly announced "revelation from God" from a man with Hornecker's clout in the Christian world would be branded a liberal or a heretic. People don't send their tithes and offerings to liberals or heretics for airtime, and a teleministry without airtime soon becomes a *former* teleministry.

Shelby had tried to talk to Adrian a few times about the revelation, but he would have nothing of it, as if he had been sworn to secrecy. Next to the film ministry, Unity 2000 became his driving passion. He appointed Darin Chaumont, one of Stan Welbourn's gifted administrative lieutenants, to handle the details and coordinate the program with McClure, Holloway, and Dunne. But wherever he was in the world, Adrian demanded daily updates on Unity 2000's progress. Shelby had never seen him so obsessed with a project.

Then, in a moment of time, Adrian Hornecker was suddenly and totally out of the picture. The leaders and millions of followers of the other three megaministries of the information-age church turned to his successor to see what would become of Unity 2000. Shelby had heard through the grapevine that none of the other three televangelists would be disappointed if she called off the big event. But how could she? It would appear to the world that God had changed His mind about the revelation to Adrian Hornecker. Such an announcement could seriously cut into Victory Life's share of the American television market.

So Shelby announced to the world soon after Adrian's funeral that Unity 2000 would proceed as planned. From her pulpit she warmly referred to Morgan McClure, Simon Holloway, and T.D. Dunne as "my brothers in the ministry of reaching the world at light speed through television." But she knew they were really her rivals for the loyalty and financial support of millions of Christians who were leaving their boring, traditional churches for the excitement and global impact of the information-age church. And she was sure that her rivals thought of her in the same terms. She secretly hoped that by some miracle Unity 2000 would be canceled, so she wouldn't have to go through with what she considered a meaningless, hypocritical performance.

After Steve and Bev had thanked her profusely for the plane tickets and hurried off to call their parents in Tennessee with the good news, Shelby sat back with a sigh. *In less than twenty-four hours the Christmas Eve reception will be over and everyone will be gone,* she thought, aware that her Lord was listening. *My retreat with You begins when the airport vans drive away tonight. Hagar found You in the desert. Jacob found You beside the Jabbok. Moses stole away to meet You in the crags of Sinai. Perhaps I will find You in the silence of a frosty Christmas morning in Austin, Texas.*

One hour later Shelby was buckled into her plush leather chair aboard the immaculate twelve-passenger Gulfstream Five. It was owned by an oil tycoon in the congregation and leased exclusively, along with the pilots, for $1 a year to the Horneckers. The sleek jet was housed and expertly maintained at Mueller Municipal Airport in Austin, less than a twenty-minute drive from the ranch.

The jet sat at the end of the runway while Gordon and Sean completed their preflight checks. Sitting across the aisle from Shelby, as she did every time Shelby traveled, was an elegant, matronly, fortyish figure in a royal purple designer dress. Theresa Bordeaux had been Shelby's personal assistant for four years. Even though Theresa was an employee, Shelby regarded her as the mature and wise big sister she never had. And since Adrian's death, she had depended on Theresa as much for emotional support and friendship as for the myriad of administrative tasks she performed to keep Shelby's schedule running efficiently.

"Are you sure you're going to be all right this week?" Theresa said above the steady whisper-whine of the jet's two idling engines. "I feel like a traitor leaving you here alone tonight."

"I won't be alone for long. You'll be with your family, and I'll be with mine." *I'm just not telling you exactly when I'm going,* Shelby added to herself. She didn't feel good about misleading her best friend. But the nearer her day of peace at the ranch drew, the more territorial she felt about it. *Theresa will understand later,* Shelby assured herself, *if I ever decide to tell her.*

"And you'll be back here by Monday night. Do you want me to come down Monday to help you pack up your last-minute things?"

"Yes, I'll be back Monday, warden," Shelby said with a slight laugh, poking fun at Theresa's propensity for mothering her. "And no, you don't need to come down. You've already packed more clothes and jewelry for me than I'll be able to wear in a month. And you've stuffed that cosmetic case you gave me with enough foundation and mascara and Q-tips to equip the Miss Texas pageant. I'm the only woman I know with an overnight case that has wheels of its own. If I can go to my mother's with just a toothbrush, a hairbrush, and a tube of lipstick, I don't know why I need an entire cosmetic store just for a few days in L.A."

Theresa took the ribbing good-naturedly, but she couldn't resist restating the obvious. "Unity 2000 is very important for us, dear. You can lie around Waco in your holey jeans without any makeup on all week if you want to. But I'm not about to take you into L.A. looking like a tumbleweed just blown in from West Texas. You are the honorary chairperson of Unity 2000. Millions of people will be watching you lead the nationwide television church into the twenty-first century. There's no way I'm going to allow even one soul among them to wonder, 'Don't dat po' preacher lady have nothin' decent t' wear?' "

Theresa's exaggerated "po' folk" accent made Shelby laugh out loud. "Theresa, you are a treasure. I don't know what I'd do without you." *But I'm still wishing for a miracle that will keep me out of L.A. altogeth-*

er, she added silently.

Sean Meara's voice over the cabin's speakers refocused Shelby's attention: "Good morning, ladies and gentlemen—well, ladies at least. Welcome to Rudolph's Red-nosed Airlines, Texas division. This is First Elf Meara, and it's my pleasure to introduce our captain today, Santa Cobb."

Shelby and Theresa exchanged amused glances. Sean and Gordon loved to revert to their commercial pilot personas for the entertainment of their passengers.

"We are number one for takeoff," Gordon informed in a raspy drawl. "Our scenic forty-minute flight to Arlington Municipal Airport today will take us over the bustling metropolises of Pflugerville, Schwertner, Lovelace, and Venus. Unfortunately, these stunning sights will not be visible due to cloud cover all the way. The weather in the Dallas-Fort Worth area today is overcast with light drizzle. Current temperature at the Victory Life auditorium is 72 degrees—indoors.

"We on the flight deck invite you to buckle up, sit back, and enjoy your flight with us today. And thank you for choosing Rudolph's Airlines."

The speakers clicked off, and the jet's engines began to rev up. Shelby and Theresa automatically reached out and joined hands across the aisle. Since the loss of Adrian and the film crew aboard the charter, the two had agreed that they should join in silent prayer for travel safety every time Gordon gunned the Gulfstream Five down the runway. Holding Theresa's hand also helped quiet the gnawing fear of takeoffs that had plagued Shelby ever since the accident.

As the jet hurtled down the runway, Shelby glanced out the window again. She was supposed to be praying for Gordon and Sean, but with the thought of Adrian's absence on Christmas Eve morning, a sudden swell of anger rolled over her, anger she hadn't felt in weeks, anger she thought had been dealt with.

It's Christmas Eve, Adrian, and you're gone again. You were rarely here when I needed you. And when you were here, you locked yourself in your office with your Bibles and theology books and charts. You ran to the four corners of the earth to make those films based more on your imagination and hair-brained eschatological interpretations than on Scripture.

This would have been our eleventh Christmas together, and the Christmas wish I shared with you on our first Christmas is still unfulfilled. "Next year there will be three of us for Christmas," you promised that December, and the next, and the next. But year after year something "vitally important" got in the way: "Let's wait until the new auditorium is finished"; "We need to get settled in at the ranch in Austin first." "As soon as I get the film ministry off the ground we'll start our family." Well, you're gone now, Adrian. You did everything you set out to do, but I'm still childless.

So here I go to church alone again. Today I'm supposed to convince God-only-knows-how-many millions of your followers that they should be filled with joy on this last Christmas of the millennium even if their world is falling apart. Well, mine is falling apart, Adrian, thanks to you. And God and I have only one day of solitude together to figure out what to do with everything you started but didn't finish. Merry Christmas, Adrian, you. . . .

Shelby wanted to finish by calling him a name, one that if uttered publicly would have provoked gasps of horror from most of the dear saints around the country who revered her. But she couldn't bring herself to add the word to her silent soliloquy. After all, it was Christmas Eve.

The Gulfstream Five lifted off, pulled in its gear, and disappeared into the low-hanging clouds.

Five

Dona Scibelli was thrilled to be attending Simon Holloway's Festival of the Nativity at Jubilee Village in Orlando, even if the arrangements were last-minute. But she was not completely comfortable with the idea of sharing a condo apartment with two women she'd never met. Fortunately, she had a private bedroom and bath. Yet she felt awkward walking into the kitchen in her robe for morning coffee to greet her new suitemates. The women were already asleep when she arrived at the Village and checked in eight hours earlier.

"Good morning," chirped a roundish woman sipping coffee at the counter. "I'm Patty Deering from Salem, Ohio. You must be Donna S*ka*belli, our suitemate."

"It's Dona, long *o*, S*he*belli, soft *c*," she replied, forcing a smile.

"Sorry, Dona," Patty said with an expression of mock embarrassment.

"That's okay. It happens all the time."

"And you're from Los Angeles, Dona?"

"Yes. Woodland Hills, actually."

"Please help yourself to the coffee." Dona did.

The third suitemate appeared from the living room to join in the introductions. She held a mug in one hand and an open, worn Bible in the other. "I'm Mavis Tebbetts from Raleigh-Durham," she drawled warmly, peering over the top of her reading glasses. She looked about sixty and well preserved.

"Patty and I are old friends," Mavis continued, overemphasizing "old." "We met yesterday when we checked in." They all laughed, and Dona felt instantly at ease. "I hope you slept well after your long journey, Dona."

"Yes, thank you, Mavis." Dona held her steaming mug with both hands, relishing the warmth. "Just a slight case of jet lag this time."

"You've been to the Village before, have you?"

"Oh, yes. My husband and I try to get back here at least three times a year. This is my first time alone. We hadn't planned on coming for the Festival, especially since we have Unity 2000 right in our backyard next weekend. But when—"

"Oh, Unity 2000!" Patty interrupted excitedly. "Won't that be a glorious evening! Welcoming the new millennium with so many believers. I wouldn't miss it for anything! I don't care what they say about the millennium not officially beginning until 2001. As soon as I start writing 2000 instead of 1999 in my checkbook, the millennium has changed for me."

Dona nodded agreement, then continued. "When Rev. Holloway announced a few last-minute openings for the Festival yesterday, Jack and I just felt one of us should come and support the ministry. Besides, I really enjoy the Festival. So I came, and Jack stayed home with our daughter who is visiting from Seattle."

"Isn't it difficult being away from your family at Christmastime?" Patty asked. "It's no problem for Mavis and me. Neither of us has a husband or children to leave behind."

"Jack really understands the importance of supporting Rev. Holloway, even if it means being apart for Christmas. Besides, we've had thirty-four Christmases together. As for Beth, she doesn't know the Lord, but she understands His work comes first in our lives. We're really praying that Unity 2000 will be a turning point in her life."

"Your daughter will be attending Unity 2000 with you?" Mavis' interest was sincere.

"Actually, Beth is a free-lance journalist who is covering Unity 2000 so she can write a book about it," Dona glowed with maternal pride. "You know, it's one of those paperbacks they sell in the grocery store checkout lines, that comes out just a week after a big event."

"I'm still amazed at how they print them up so fast," Patty exclaimed, pouring a second cup of coffee for herself and refilling Mavis' mug.

"You mean your daughter, who needs the Lord, has been assigned the task of writing a book about the most significant gathering of God's people in this century?" Mavis continued, pondering the irony. "Well, praise the Lord! Patty, I think we need to agree in prayer with Dona right now that God will do something miraculous in this girl's life next weekend."

Mavis and Patty were at Dona's side praying fervently for Beth before she could think of anything to say. It was as if they really were old friends, a phenomenon she and Jack had experienced with pleasure during every visit to Jubilee Village.

As Patty and Mavis prayed for her daughter, a collage of memories flashed before Dona's eyes. Beth, the precocious ten-year-old winning spelling bees and garnering extra credit composition points for her poetry and imaginative short stories. Beth, the athletic, five-foot eight-inch fourteen-year-old practicing hook shots and tip-ins with Jack in the driveway while her dolls gathered dust in the attic. Beth, Taft High School's all-time girl scoring and rebounding leader. Beth, the award-winning editor of the school paper. And in the same year, runner-up for senior prom queen, towering above her escort. How striking she looked that night in her deep California tan and white taffeta gown. Dona loved the strong features, dark eyes, and shining raven hair Beth inherited from Jack.

"And Lord, You know the investment Jack and Dona have made in Beth's spiritual welfare over the years," Patty continued. "We just pray that their investment will pay a great dividend in her life this week, as she is so near to what You are about to do in Los Angeles."

Sorry, Patty, Dona thought, as her new friends prayed on. *Our investment was rather puny in Beth's early years. Jack and I were busy building his business and filling Beth's world with everything we could to assure her success and happiness. We were religious, but God wasn't a priority in our lives, so we didn't make Him a priority in Beth's life. And by the time we joined Rev. Holloway's Crusaders, Beth was in college pursuing success and happiness with abandon, just like we taught her to.*

Dona realized that the images in her memory from Beth's college years were fewer and fuzzier than those from childhood. Rev. Holloway's dynamic radio ministry was just taking off in the early '90s. Jack's business success allowed them the freedom to follow their sin-fighting pastor to several of his early rallies around the country, picketing abortion clinics and adult bookstores with the evangelist's growing army of Crusaders.

The Scibellis attended Beth's basketball games at USC when they were in town, and they left plenty of food in the freezer for her when they were away during school breaks. When they did see Beth at home or at school, Jack and Dona bubbled about their exploits for God and righteousness, but Beth showed little interest.

Jack and Dona had promised to be home for the awards dinners and receptions involving Beth during her last week at the university. But ground-breaking for the national headquarters of Jubilee Fellowship in Orlando was delayed, and the Scibellis barely made it home in time to change clothes and get to commencement. Beth never seemed to forgive them for that.

Mavis and Patty concluded their brief intercession with several whispered amens. "Thank you for your prayers," Dona said, squeezing the hands of her two new friends. "I know God has our little girl in His hands." Patty and Mavis hummed their agreement.

Patty glanced at the clock. "Well, girls, if we want a good seat at the opening meeting for the Festival, we'd better get moving." An hour later the three smartly dressed women left the apartment and joined hundreds of Village guests and local worshipers streaming to the Tabernacle Worship Center.

Next to the sprawling Disney entertainment complex, central Florida's most popular attraction was Jubilee Village with its famed Tabernacle, occupying nearly 9,000 acres of reclaimed swampland east of Kissimmee. The Village and Tabernacle were the brainchild of Rev. Simon Holloway, the self-styled fundamentalist whose ringing denunciations of abortion, pornography, homosexuality, and, most recently, genetic engineering, and other "heinous affronts to the Creator" through the '90s had established greater Orlando as the capital of the religious right.

Of course, the popularity of the Jubilee Fellowship movement among conservative Christians was not discouraged by the fact that its national headquarters and 1,200-unit Village were within twenty minutes of Disney World's main entrance, and that the ministry's financial supporters could lodge there for about half the cost of the area's resort hotels. Continuous free shuttles ran to and from the area's attractions. While Holloway's Crusaders and Warriors stormed the country battling unrighteousness, Jubilee Village remained a safe, sane, and saintly vacationland for his loyal troops.

Holloway had patterned his Village after Israel's camp in the wilderness. Surrounding Holloway's Tabernacle on four sides, lined in neat rows and interspersed with parks, playgrounds, rec rooms, and swimming pools, stood over 200 modest yet comfortable, beautifully landscaped condominiums. The condos were laid out in twelve sections, three per side, and named after the twelve tribes that camped around Israel's worship center in the Old Testament. Guests parked in the huge lot surrounding the complex and were ferried throughout the Village by an efficient network of Disney-style trams.

Each condo contained four living units with two to three bedrooms per unit. And every unit was equipped for family fun and inspiration. Monitors were hooked up to the twenty-four-hour Jubilee Network, offering video tours of the Village and Tabernacle, a documentary of Simon Holloway's life and ministry, interactive children's programs and video games, and a complete menu of Christian programming and wholesome family films.

A children's ministry staff offered nonstop activities in each of the tribal sections: rallies, classes, games, contests, crafts, and swimming lessons. To thousands of children growing up in Holloway's television congregation, traveling to Orlando to shake hands with Mickey Mouse was almost as exciting as visiting the Village they viewed on the TV screen in their parents' house churches every Sunday morning.

Closest to the Tabernacle on three of the four sides were a number of spacious single-family units named for the Levite clans and reserved for the Warriors, Holloway's most generous and faithful contributors. Jack and Dona Scibelli were established Warriors in Holloway's army. But on this trip, Dona had to settle for a room with Patty and Mavis in a remote corner of the Manasseh section west of the Tabernacle.

On the east side, between the Issachar, Judah, and Zebulun condos and the Tabernacle's main entrance, were the Jubilee Fellowship offices and studios. Adjacent to headquarters were a shopping center and a gated community of luxurious homes owned by Holloway, his top executive staff, and the Tabernacle's board of directors.

The centerpiece of the complex, of course, was the Tabernacle itself. Holloway had built the huge, rectangular auditorium to the scale of the Mosaic Tabernacle courtyard, enlarged to accommodate 5,500 seats. The outer walls were textured and painted to simulate finely twined linen interspersed with gleaming brass poles. The entire structure was capped by a somewhat convoluted white dome ingeniously crafted to look like a cloud and engineered to keep refrigerated air in and rain and humidity out.

Dona and her two suitemates opted to walk the several blocks from Manasseh 46B to the Tabernacle instead of riding one of the many open trams snaking through the Village. It was already 70 degrees outside and sparkling clear—a beautiful Christmas Eve Day in Central Florida.

The trams and sidewalks were jammed with noisy worshipers chattering about the events of the two-day Festival of the Nativity. . . . Two morning services featuring soul-stirring Christmas music by the choir and orchestra, which was made up of regular attenders from the greater Orlando area. The afternoon pageant in the shopping center, an extravagant outdoor dramatic recreation of Joseph and Mary's journey to Bethlehem. . . . An evening carol sing in the Tabernacle, with a Christmas story and gifts especially for the children.

Then on Christmas Day, the morning services, another midday pageant—this time the arrival of the wise men—and evening vespers. And at every event, an inspiring sermon by Rev. Simon Holloway. Great music, stimulating messages, and heartwarming fellowship with believers. Dona could hardly wait. She only wished Jack were there to enjoy it with her. And Beth, especially Beth.

Dona, Patty, and Mavis ascended the wide, crowded steps to the Tabernacle and jostled through one of the many doors into the large foyer. They wound quickly through the milling throng to the sanctuary doors, received programs from smiling usherettes, and hurried to three open seats five rows from the platform.

In contrast to the glimmering white exterior, the inside of the Tabernacle was decorated in rich blue, purple, and scarlet, accented for the season with lush holly boughs, twinkling lights, and flickering candles on brass candelabra.

A broad, carpeted platform stood near the western end of the building, surrounded on three sides by seats. The front half of the platform featured a massive mahogany pulpit, fashioned to resemble the Ark of the Covenant, and a row of upholstered chairs. The back half of the platform contained an orchestra pit and an elevated loft for a choir of 200.

A canopy suspended high above the platform was stocked with remotely operated spotlights, floodlights, and retractable mikes, curtains, and backdrops. For the Festival, the outer edge of the platform and the canopy were swagged with fragrant evergreen garland and scarlet satin ribbon.

Six remote, wall-mounted TV cameras around the huge sanctuary swept the platform and arriving worshipers, and a man and woman with hand-held units discussed shooting angles near the front corner of the platform. Large windows to the control room glared down from the back wall.

Dona watched with excitement as the twenty-eight-piece orchestra, dressed in black tuxedos and gowns with red accents, took their places and quietly tuned. The house lights dimmed, and the processional commenced. The pastors and department heads of Jubilee Fellowship, eight men and two women also formally attired, stepped from an anteroom and marched single file to the platform. And in the center of the spotlighted procession were Rev. and Mrs. Simon Holloway.

Jack and Dona had seen Simon and Grace Ellen in person many times and had even talked with them briefly on a few occasions. They were an inseparable pair, totally devoted to each other, their children, and their ministry. But today, as she watched first Simon and then Grace Ellen pass within thirty feet of her, Dona was suddenly struck by how unsuitably matched they seemed. She marveled silently at how two opposite halves could comprise such a beautiful whole.

Simon was short, stocky, and muscular, not far from roly-poly at forty-six. He stepped heavily down the aisle, head down, stern-faced, like a general contemplating the casualties of a recent battle while plotting his strategy for the next. His straight, salt-and-pepper hair was swept back close to the scalp and neatly trimmed around the ears. His posture and gait seemed better-suited to military fatigues than the finery his staff no doubt insisted he wear for the Festival. Christmas seemed the farthest thing from his mind.

Grace Ellen Holloway, no shorter or younger than her husband but much slimmer, glided toward the platform offering Christmas greetings to worshipers left and right with her flashing eyes and cordial smile. As always, she was tuned to the moment. Her midnight-blue, sequined gown and gold jewelry shimmered in the spotlight. Her finely styled hair wasn't natural auburn as it had been, but it looked it. Everything about her radiated confidence and grace. Dona admired and respected Grace Ellen as deeply as she revered her husband.

The service began precisely on time with the choir's processional, a stunning arrangement of "Joy to the World." Carols were sung by the congregation. Christmas Scriptures were read by various staff members. The Cherub Choir hopped and skipped up the platform stairs for a touching and humorous rendition of "Santa, Won't You Kneel at the Manger?" The offering was received, after an eloquent challenge to generous giving. Worshipers in the Tabernacle and the vast television congregation were encouraged to attend and uphold in prayer the Millennium's Eve gathering in Los Angeles, Unity 2000.

The service moved at such a comfortable pace it was difficult to imagine that it was programmed to the minute to fit the one-hour television time slot.

All the while Simon Holloway smiled and nodded rather absently from his chair and fidgeted with his Bible, turning it over and over in his hands, picking at the cover. Dona had first noticed the curious mannerism years earlier and likened it to a restless bull pawing the earth, itching to charge. The more Simon fidgeted before the sermon, Dona observed, the more passionately he preached. She recalled that some of his best sermons followed occasions when he could hardly hold his Bible still on his lap. Today's fidget factor, Dona mused with anticipation, predicted an excellent message.

Finally, after a triumphant Christmas anthem from the choir that brought the audience to its feet in worshipful applause, Simon Holloway strode eagerly to the pulpit. His congregation sat down and quieted. Cameras zoomed in from all angles.

"Our beloved Christmas story begins with words we tend to overlook. In our haste to return to the warm and familiar phrases describing Mary and Joseph, the wondering shepherds, the angelic chorus, and the Eastern visitors, we miss the significance of the opening line of Luke chapter 2: 'In those days Caesar Augustus issued a decree that a census should be taken of the entire Roman world.'"

Simon's voice was strong, measured, compelling as always. Here was the spiritual leader of nearly half a million tithing Christians at his best. Not as a pastor. The extensive telephone counseling ministry and regional training of home-church lay pastors was all handled by his large, efficient staff. Nor as a programmer. Jubilee Fellowship's multi-million-dollar television ministry and the extensive, detailed operation of the Village and the Tabernacle were in other hands as well.

Simon was a visionary. Simon was a communicator. Jubilee Fellowship in Orlando and its national television ministry were the by-products of his passion. And there was no one on religious television better at pleading a cause and evoking a response than Simon Holloway.

"Into whose world was the Savior born? God's? Yes, ultimately. Mary and Joseph were created by Him. The fearful shepherds, the inquisitive wise men, the apologetic innkeeper, the lowing oxen and timid sheep in the stable, all were the products of His hand. Even the gentle Judean hills around Bethlehem and the star-spangled canopy above were spoken into existence by God Almighty, Ruler of heaven and earth. Make no mistake: This is our Father's world.

"And yet, as Luke 2:1 reveals, the world of the Nativity was in the hostile grip of a godless power whom the Creator, in His unsearchable wisdom, had allowed intermediate jurisdiction. Jesus was born into a Roman world. Jesus was born into Caesar's world. Think of the paradox: The sinless Son of God drew His first breath under the iron hand of a government which neither regarded His Father's existence nor obeyed His law."

Holloway continued for several minutes eloquently contrasting the purity of God's world and the evil of Caesar's world at the time of the Savior's birth. Point by point, phrase by phrase, paragraph by paragraph, the message grew in intensity, just as rivulets combine to form streams and streams merge to form a mighty river. Never a hesitation. Never a hollow cliché. Never so much as an "um" or "ah." Only steady, flowing, convincing words.

Holloway's clear blue eyes were as articulate as his verbal message. They panned the crowd slowly, penetratingly, never once glancing at the notes spread before him on the pulpit. The director in the control booth selected shot after shot, mixing close-ups and wide shots of the speaker and his enthralled audience. Holloway had an uncanny knack for turning the right way and making a point to the camera trained on him at the moment.

"As we celebrate Christmas for the last time in this the second millennium since our Savior's birth, be aware that you are living in the same kind of world He came to visit and redeem 2,000 years ago. God has set the eternal agenda for His world and His people; but Caesar, the human leadership God has afforded limited authority till He returns, still attempts to control our activities. Proud, godless Caesar is still in the business of issuing decrees, many of which are in direct conflict with the decrees of the Almighty Creator.

"Jesus, who was born in Caesar's world but lived by His Father's decrees, established for all time the critical difference between these two conflicting worlds when He said, 'Give to Caesar what belongs to Caesar, but give to God what belongs to God.' Hear me, Warriors. Hear me, Crusaders. Hear me, Jubilee Church: We cannot give to

Caesar what belongs to God, even if Caesar decrees it."

Holloway's message, though couched in a Christmas theme, was not new. It was vintage Holloway. It was the same fiery cause that had burned within him for the ten years of his national ministry. It was the same message that landed him and hundreds of his followers in jail in the early years and still provoked death threats from many dark corners of society. Yet as he thundered his convictions again this Christmas Eve, his voice rose steadily and his face flushed with holy ardor, and his congregation in the Tabernacle and in house churches across the country was stirred.

"God has decreed that human life is sacred, His alone to give and His alone to receive. Yet Caesar has decreed that human life is conditional. We can initiate life in the laboratory if it pleases us. And we can terminate life in the womb, in the critical care wing, in the suicide clinic, or in the nursing home if it inconveniences us. The unborn, the terminally ill, the maimed, the retarded, and the aged belong to God. We cannot forfeit them to Caesar!"

A murmur of amens fluttered through the crowd.

"God has decreed that men and women were created for each other and that sexual intimacy is to be enjoyed monogamously within the boundaries of holy marriage. Caesar has decreed that neither sexual preference nor marital fidelity is important in an individual's expression of his or her sexual urges. Male and female sexuality and the sanctity of marriage belong to God. We cannot forfeit them to Caesar!"

The amens were louder, accompanied by a smattering of light applause.

"God has decreed that mankind is to reproduce after his kind through procreation. Caesar has decreed that mankind can genetically engineer the sex, size, hair and eye color, and physical ability of his offspring to suit his whim. The human genome belongs to God. We cannot forfeit it to Caesar!"

This time applause rolled like thunder through the congregation. Cameras zoomed in on some of the most enthusiastic responders. One of them caught Dona's roommate Mavis Tebbetts wiping tears from the corners of her eyes with a lace-trimmed hankie and mouthing the words, "Praise the Lord."

Acutely aware of the timing of the service, Holloway skillfully turned his sermon toward conclusion. He committed himself anew to carry the fight against godless Caesar into the new millennium, and urged his Crusaders and Warriors around the country to stand with him with their prayers and financial support. He challenged every member of his vast congregation to consider making a special Christmas gift to the ministry above their regular gifts. He closed by reminding viewers that next week's Millennium's Eve morning rally would be broadcast live from the Los Angeles Convention Center where thousands of the

Jubilee Fellowship television congregation would gather prior to Unity 2000.

Dona left the Tabernacle inspired and challenged. She and Jack had been faithful followers and generous supporters for almost ten years. But had they done enough? Much had been accomplished in the fight against the evils of a rampantly godless society. But there was so much more to do.

She politely declined Patty and Mavis' invitation to brunch with them in the shopping center. Instead she rode a tram back to the condo, took out her checkbook, and wrote a $500 check to Jubilee Fellowship. She and Jack had already mailed in their contribution for the month of December, but she wanted to respond to Rev. Holloway's challenge to do something extra. Jack would no doubt concur if he were here, she thought. In fact, he would probably insist they give $1,000.

Six

Beth could hear the phone beeping from the family room even with the door closed and the covers scrunched up around her ears. She knew it was morning—probably late morning at that—without opening her eyes. The sunlight flooding the bedroom through the large bay window glowed against her eyelids. It was already a breezy, 55-degree Christmas Eve in L.A.

Dad will get the phone, or the machine will get it, she thought sleepily. She didn't care how late it was, she wasn't ready to wake up. The early morning welcome to L.A. by the Latin Barons and that boorish cop had polluted her waking thoughts like the brown haze that hung over the west San Fernando Valley most of the year. And she couldn't bear the thought of seeing her banged-up Star Cruiser in broad daylight.

Beep. Beep. Beth turned away from the bright window with an annoyed whine and pulled the pillow over her head. But the phone kept beeping insistently. Six times, seven times. "C'mon, Dad, pick it up," she groaned hoarsely. But she knew he must be outdoors or gone. He always answered before the third beep.

Nine times, ten times. *Why isn't the dumb machine kicking in? Beep. Beep.*

Realizing that if her mother was calling from Orlando, the beeping would continue forever, Beth pulled herself reluctantly out of bed and swept the hair out of her face. Instantly chilled in her thigh-length

Trojan T-shirt, she yanked up her wool socks as far as they would go, threw the comforter around her, and tramped to the family room.

As if planned by some unseen prankster, the remote telephone receiver wasn't in its wall-mounted cradle when she got there. By the time she found it under the Friday *Times* on the coffee table, the beeping had stopped. She flicked the dial tone on and off several times and swore at the phone before returning it to the cradle. "The dawn of another beautiful day in L.A.," she muttered sourly.

Beth stood by the coffee table a moment, tugging the comforter around her. She was tempted to complain again, this time about her father's stinginess with the heat in their spacious, hillside, ranch-style home. But her crabby attitude was suddenly derailed by the familiar scene around her, a scene she had missed at 4:00 A.M. when she let herself into the dark house and slipped quietly to bed without waking her father. She had found the key under the potted palm on the front step where it had been since her high school days.

Beth thoughtfully surveyed the room where she had enjoyed so many happy hours during her childhood. There had been some changes in decor over the years. The drapes and the sofa were new. And it looked like Mom had recently refinished the coffee table. But there was Dad's familiar swivel rocker with the TV/VCR remote holster slung over one arm. Mom's wingback recliner sat next to it. The oversized leather beanbag where Beth had fallen asleep so many times during family popcorn and video nights at home was still piled in a nearby corner.

And Beth couldn't help but smile at the sight of some of her favorite old Christmas decorations around the room. The lumpy clay Santa Claus figurine she had made in the second grade was the centerpiece of a collection of Santas on the hearth. Three large, colorful, knit stockings—one for "Daddy," one for "Mommy," one for "Beth"—hung from the fireplace. The exquisite terra cotta creche on the mantle was new.

The old bookcases were still there. Rows of religious books now occupied shelves where Beth's favorite childhood board games and storybooks were once stored. And the "wall of fame" still adorned the backside of the oak cabinets dividing the family room from the kitchen. A few professional photos and numerous snapshots, framed and mounted on the wall, chronicled the Scibelli family. Beth was obviously the star of the gallery. Being an only child, most of the pictures featured her: baby pictures, school pictures, team pictures, and framed enlargements of shots Jack had taken of Beth patting Shamu on the nose, Beth skateboarding down Adele Drive with the neighborhood boys, Beth shaking hands with Kareem.

Beth stepped closer to the wall to inspect the latest additions and then frowned. There were only three photos of her after her high school graduation picture, none of them taken by her father. One was an eight-by-ten glossy of her banking in two of her career high 27 points against Tennessee. She had bought the print from the *Times* and sent it to them. Another was her graduation photo from USC, the traditional cap and gown shot she thought her parents would like. The third was a picture of her talking with Mikhail Gorbachev—she knew a little Russian, he knew a little English—after his lecture at the University of Washington in '95. A friend working for the *Post-Intelligencer* got it for her.

These last three pictures were surrounded by several photos of her parents standing with a stocky, sober-faced man and smiling woman—autographed, "Rev. and Mrs. Simon Holloway"—or posed with friends on the steps of the Tabernacle in Orlando. There was even a UPI photo of her mother being arrested at a sit-in at a bioengineering lab near Irvine. Beth shook her head and sighed.

She shuffled to the bar at the end of the wall of fame. There was her father's note, right where he had left so many for her as a child. Except this one was on a computer screen instead of a scratch pad:

WELCOME HOME, SWEETHEART!
   I DIDN'T WANT TO WAKE YOU. I'M AT THE HARDWARE STORE. BE HOME ABOUT 12:30. THERE ARE DONUTS ON THE RANGE AND FRUIT IN THE FRIDGE. HELP YOURSELF TO COFFEE.
   LOVE, DAD

Beth glanced at the clock on the range. It was 11:27. Plenty of time to read the paper and get into her tights and Nikes for several laps of the track at Taft High School before going one-on-one with Dad about God or Rev. Holloway or whatever the cause was this week.

She shoved a mug into the Coffee-Quik and pushed START. As the coffee brewed and poured, she pulled a cake donut with sprinkles out of the box on the range, then returned it in favor of a cream-filled eclair.

It was a challenge to balance her mug and eclair in one hand and gather up the *Times* with the other while keeping the comforter draped around her with a chin-to-chest maneuver. She did it, but as soon as she took one cautious step toward the bedroom, the phone beeped again. She wondered if someone at the telephone company was playing a hidden video stunt on her.

She let the comforter and newspaper drop to the floor with an exasperated groan and returned her breakfast to the counter.

"Hello," she answered curtly.

"Mary Elizabeth *Ska*belli, please." It was a masculine voice.

Beth was tempted to say "Wrong number!" and hang up. Only strangers bungled the family name so badly, and only salesmen making cold calls asked for Mary Elizabeth *Ska*belli or Dona Margarite

*Ska*belli or Mr. John Antony *Ska*belli. But her parents often called her Mary Elizabeth, and she would never forgive herself if it was an emergency call and she hung up on a doctor summoning her to the hospital to hear her father or mother's dying words.

"This is she," Beth said, unwilling to waste "that's S*he*belli, soft *c*" on someone she might never speak to again.

"I hope I'm not disturbing you. I called a few minutes ago and no one answered."

So you're the one who woke me up, she grumbled to herself. "No problem," she said coolly.

The caller cleared his throat. "Ms. *Ska*belli, this is Reagan Cole with the Los Angeles Police Department."

The name *Reagan* meant nothing to Beth. *Cole* sounded only remotely familiar. But mention of the police department in such an official tone made her blood suddenly run cold.

"I'm sorry?" she responded, as if she had understood none of the caller's introduction.

"This is *Sergeant* Cole, the police officer who was involved in your altercation with the Latino gang members last night."

Beth stiffened as the name, the voice, and the incident abruptly merged into one bad memory. Her next words rushed out without her permission. "Oh yes, you're the *off duty* officer who so bravely rescued me, nearly got me killed in a car chase, then said the whole thing was my fault."

There was a pause, then a rather subdued, "Yes, ma'am."

His meek reply numbed Beth into surprised speechlessness. She expected opposition, not concession. Their last moments together in front of the CHP yard were a flurry of verbal jabs and hooks. They had been like a couple of amateur boxers flailing at each other in the last seconds of a match—a match he had won. Now Beth had taken the first swing in the rematch, and Cole, it seemed, had simply dropped his guard.

Unwilling to accept a forfeit, Beth remained cautiously on the offensive. "What do you want, sergeant, and how did you get my number?" She felt suddenly cold again and reached for the comforter.

"You left your parents' number with the investigating officer at the scene. You indicated to him your concern over the damage sustained by your rental car and personal belongings due to the pursuit." Beth thought she was going to gag on the cop-speak Cole used to distance himself from what had happened to her and how he had treated her.

"Officially, I'm calling to notify you that the city of Los Angeles will reimburse you for any claims not met by your insurance carrier."

"Oh, wonderful," Beth said sardonically, beginning to pace the family room as the residue of anger and humiliation from the night before rose within her. "It's bad enough that I have to claim the rear-end damage to the Galaxy car on my policy. As one officer so encouragingly put it, 'I'm sorry, ma'am, but none of the perpetrators was insured.' Now I get to claim a $2,000 computer, who knows what kind of damage to the struts and suspension, and maybe months of physical therapy for a back injury."

"Did you sustain a back injury, ma'am?" Cole sounded genuinely concerned.

She flexed her back hoping to feel just a little pain. There was none. She cursed under her breath. "It's a little too soon to tell, but it's possible."

"As I said, whatever your insurance fails to cover, the city will cover."

"Are you kidding me, sergeant?" Beth pressed, still irritated. "My auto insurance and medical premiums could go sky high for the next five years because of this. And you're telling me that all the city of Los Angeles can do is toss me a few bucks for a wheel cover that may not be covered?" Beth knew the money wasn't the issue. But her wounds from last night were still smarting, and she wasn't finished letting Cole know it.

"We regret any inconvenience the pursuit may have caused you, ma'am. And we appreciate your cooperation in helping us bring to justice—"

"Oh cram it, sergeant!" Beth spat. "The city of Los Angeles screwed me royally last night. Killers assaulting me on the freeway, the gestapo tactic of commandeering my car, and then a death ride with the rudest, most inconsiderate, most pompous public servant I've ever met in my life. I think L.A. owes me more than just a few bucks."

Beth poised her thumb above the off button. *At the first sound of cop-speak, this guy is gone,* she determined.

Cole's silent pause was longer this time. "Unofficially, I called to say I'm sorry for the way I talked to you last night."

Beth stopped pacing. Cole sounded disarmingly civilian and penitent. Was this an apology or a ploy? Beth wasn't ready to let him off the hook so easily.

"Oh sure. I can hear the talk around the station now." Her irritation had tempered slightly but was tinged with cynicism. " 'If she gets testy and threatens to sue, apologize for everything,' your superiors probably told you. 'Crawl on your belly like a reptile. Eat crow. Don't let some hotheaded chick journalist from out of town give the department a black eye.'"

"You're a journalist?" Again Cole's expression of interest sounded disarmingly real.

"Don't you have *that* in your big-brother files?" She tried to sound hateful. She still wanted to deck him verbally for last night.

Cole exhaled an unperturbed, one-syllable laugh. "No, ma'am. All I know about you is what turned up when the officers scanned your holocard last night: date of birth, height, weight, hair and eye color— and that you were cited twice this year in Skagit County, Washington for speeding."

Beth blushed. Her spiteful uppercut had missed and she had landed on the canvas face-first. Cole obviously wanted to forfeit the fight, and she realized that nothing she said could bait him into another verbal scuffle.

"Seriously, Ms. *Ska*belli, you have every right to feel angry about what happened last night. My procedures were by the book, but I know now I should have let the black-and-whites handle it all the way. I was angry at those hoods for what they *tried* to do to you and what they *would have* done to you. And I was scared and angry after they tried to run me down. If you want to file a complaint against me, I'll give you the number to call. I think I can defend my actions as a police officer under the circumstances, but I'm probably subject to a reprimand for endangering your safety in the process.

"What I can't defend is the way I treated you." Cole's throat began to constrict slightly. Beth was suddenly aware how difficult this was for him. He sounded unsure of himself, yet he continued determinedly. "I pride myself in controlling my emotions, and I get very embarrassed and defensive when I lose control. Last night I lost control. I was very rude. I was inconsiderate of what you had experienced and how you must have felt. I said some things I wish I could take back. I'm sorry. Will you please forgive me?"

Beth sank into her father's plush rocker. She wanted to believe the sergeant, but she didn't know if she should. Was he just setting her up for a sucker punch? For all she knew, Cole was in a roomful of cops who were rolling on the floor silently splitting their guts as he jerked her around with his alleged apology. Yet the guy was obviously having a hard time expressing his feelings. He even sounded like he was in pain.

On the surface, the sergeant's apology sounded so hokey to Beth that she could almost hear schmaltzy organ music in the background. Yet her instincts challenged her skepticism. Many men had done her dirtier than Cole, and of the few who *did* apologize, none sounded this sincere. If he was just amusing himself or trying to skate out of trouble with his superiors for his behavior, he was good at it. His con artistry would make him a great living if he ever decided to defect to the other side of the law.

But if Cole was as sincere as he sounded, and she laughed down his apology, she would be the bigger fool in this escapade. She usually trusted her instincts, and this time she decided to go with them against her suspicions.

"All right, sergeant," she said with a sigh of resignation. "I accept your apology." Her conscience urged her to apologize to him too. She had seriously remonstrated herself about being so foolish and careless on the San Diego Freeway, the very things Cole had scolded her so hotly about, the very things that had endangered both of their lives. But she had already gone out on a limb with her instincts by accepting Cole's apology. She wasn't about to yield to her conscience so haphazardly.

Cole exhaled a long sigh. "Thank you, Ms. *Ska*belli. I feel much better."

"Actually, it's *She*belli, soft c." Her tone was intentionally more corrective than informative.

"*She*belli," he repeated.

"Yes."

There were several seconds of uncomfortable silence. Beth was aware that the conversation was over—apology offered, apology received. Now what? *He started it,* Beth thought, *so he should end it with something appropriately gracious like, "Thank you again for your kindness and understanding. Have a nice Christmas, ma'am. Good-bye."*

But instead Cole said, "So you're in town on business and to spend the holidays with your parents."

Beth was ready for the conversation to end, but her curiosity about Cole's valid assumption wouldn't let her cut him off. "What makes you think I have business in L.A?"

"You rented a car instead of taking a shuttle from the airport. I figured you must have some business in town to write off the rental. You also brought your computer along. That looks like work to me. And you have a nice fold-over suit bag in your luggage. Professional wardrobe is my guess."

"You're very observant."

"Occupational hazard. The minute a cop stops asking 'Why?' he's liable to find a bad guy at his back."

"Hm." She noted that he said "bad guys" instead of "suspects" or "perpetrators." At least he was beginning to sound more like a person than some kind of law enforcement android.

"And I'm guessing that your business has something to do with the big religious deal in the Coliseum on Millennium's Eve. I'll bet you're writing something about Unity 2000."

"How did you. . . ?" Beth couldn't cover her surprise, so she just cut her question short.

"Your necklace—that beautiful, ornate gold cross you were wearing last night. You're obviously a religious person, so you probably jumped at the chance to cover an event that's of personal interest to you. Am I right?"

Beth tugged at the comforter around her as if trying to shield herself from Cole's uncanny, all-seeing gaze. She pulled the cross from beneath the neck of her T-shirt pajamas and fingered it. *Nice try, Sergeant Cole, but very wrong,* she gloated silently. *I was a religious person, many years ago, at my parents' insistence. The necklace was a First Communion gift from them, and it's been tucked in my jewelry box ever since I left home. I only wore it on this trip as a concession, hoping to keep them off my back about going to church and being a good little Christian girl.*

Beth decided not to confirm or deny Cole's errant guess about her religious life. Instead she said, "Yes, I have an assignment for the Unity 2000 event."

"I think it's great that you get to enjoy Christmas with your family and write off your visit as a business expense."

"I'm afraid Christmas in L.A. isn't my idea of a good time, sergeant. You see, my parents—" Beth thought about telling him the story, then quickly changed her mind, unwilling to drop her guard. "Let's just say that we've had better Christmases in the past. My mother is out of town. She won't even be home until the day after Christmas. Tomorrow's basically just another workday for me, that is, if I can find a decent computer to rent today."

"Well, that Unity 2000 deal is screwing up my Christmas too. There are no days off this week for the LAPD—not Christmas Eve, not Christmas Day, not Millennium's Eve. As you discovered last night, the city is crawling with out-of-towners here to kick off the new millennium. Every law enforcement agency in Southern California is working overtime to keep them driving straight and behaving themselves."

"You're on duty right now?"

"No, I work P.M. watch—2:15 to 11."

"So you're calling on your own time."

"Yeah, I'm at home."

"Couldn't your 'official business' have waited until you were on duty?"

"It could have. But I knew you were concerned about the car, so I called in to verify the department's position on compensation. Besides, my unofficial business couldn't wait. I had to get my feelings off my chest."

Beth warmed again at the reminder of Cole's sincere apology. "So will you get to spend any time with your family tomorrow?" Beth hoped she didn't sound too interested in him, but she *was* curious.

"No family in L.A. The folks retired to Tahoe twelve years ago, and Dad died there in '94. I have three older sisters living all over the country. I told Mom I'd be up to see her after the first. She understands. Dad was a cop too."

The conversation lagged again. Then the sergeant wrapped it up the way Beth had expected him to. "Thanks again for accepting my apology. I hope your Christmas works out all right." She responded in kind and they said their good-byes.

The moment she hung up Beth sensed an emotional letdown. She tried to prod herself into exulting a little over her successful standoff with the apologetic and obviously humbled cop. *But,* she thought, *it's like trying to celebrate a victory over an opponent who not only forfeits the match but hands you the winner's trophy and congratulates you. All you can do is admire someone who accepts defeat so gracefully.*

Yes, there is something admirable about Sergeant Cole, something genuine, something attractive, Beth found herself admitting. *Under any other circumstances . . . no, it isn't worth wondering about because I'm never going to see this man again.* But somehow Beth wasn't completely at peace with that reality.

The phone beeped again within thirty seconds. The receiver was still in her hand. "Yes?"

"I may be pressing my luck," Cole said as if the conversation had never ended, "but since Christmas looks rather bleak for both of us, I'd like to treat you to lunch tomorrow before I go to work. What do you say?"

Beth was as flattered as she was surprised—except she didn't want to feel flattered by Sergeant Cole, not yet anyway. A stream of reasons to refuse flooded her mind: *I don't even know you; I don't want to get involved with a cop; my father might have plans for tomorrow.* She felt herself digging in to resist Cole's invitation as she had his attempts to commandeer her car nearly twelve hours before.

"Well, ah, I, er. . . ." She was at a loss for a quick reply and felt stupid for it.

As if reading Beth's thoughts, Cole cut in, "All I'm talking about is a couple of hours. No hidden agenda. It would just make Christmas Day a lot nicer for me."

Beth sensed the same inner turmoil she felt on the freeway when offered the choice between getting out of the car or riding along with Sergeant Cole on the chase. The thought of spending Christmas at home was almost as foreboding as being dumped off in the middle of the freeway with the two wounded Latin Barons. Beth wasn't sure she wanted to say yes to Cole, but she was sure she didn't want to stay behind.

For the second time in twelve hours she opted to take a chance. "Okay," she said at last.

"Great! Meet me in the plaza at Olvera Street at 11. You remember Olvera Street, don't you?"

"Yes, but isn't 11 a little early for lunch?"

"There's something I want to show you at Olvera Street. Is that too early for you?"

"No, 11 will be fine."

"Remember how to get there?"

"I can find it okay."

"See you then. And don't forget to lock your doors."

Touche, she thought.

Beth hung up the receiver and released a long what-am-I-getting-myself-into? sigh. Then she picked up her mug of cold coffee, shoved it into the microwave, and punched WARM. *What kind of a ride does Sergeant Cole have in store for me this time?* she wondered.

Seven

Hodge stepped off the Metro at eight minutes till noon. He gripped the handle of his plastic picnic chest in one hand, and tugged his Dodgers cap low on his forehead with the other to deflect the bright sunlight of a chilly but brilliant day in L.A. He walked two blocks down Sixth Street and entered Pershing Square from the south as usual.

Pershing Square is a city block patch of palm trees, grass, and walkways spread atop an underground parking structure in the heart of the towering canyons of concrete, steel, and glass of the downtown Los Angeles business district. For decades the Square has been a shady oasis for city workers and shoppers as well as a rest stop, open-air motel, and toilet for many of L.A.'s derelicts and transients. At noon during the warmer months, it's not unusual to see the benches lined with lunching office workers and pigeon-feeding retirees, while the lawns are littered with glassy-eyed, foul-smelling vagrants and catatonic winos sleeping off an all-night drunk.

Not far away in any direction, utilizing old plastic milk crates or beat-up metal trunks for podiums, are members of the "Pershing Square Ministerial Association." At first glance, some of these self-ordained street preachers appear to have stepped right out of a downtown office. On closer examination, however, their jackets and ties are usually far from fashionable and often not even clean. Most of the Pershing Square prophets look to be only a few days removed from the rescue mission or detox center, as rough-cut, haggard, shabby, and dirty as the souls on the lawn they are trying to save.

On any given day, the Square is liable to be graced by the appearance of "Jesus Christ" himself, usually dropping in on his way from Mercury to Jupiter or Pluto. The "messiah" is always easily recognized by his striking costume: an old, soap-encrusted shower curtain fashioned into a robe with electrical tape, a crown of styrofoam and tinfoil, a broom-handle scepter, and GI surplus boots—no laces.

For all their different costumes and styles of delivery—from wild-eyed whisperers to nerve-rankling screamers—most of the Pershing Square preachers over the years have been fanatically fired by similar convictions. The angel Gabriel or the prophet Mohammed or the ghost of Billy Sunday or some other historical religious dignitary had appeared to them—personally, privately—and delivered a message of such monumental consequence that it could be entrusted to only one faithful soul. The message might be that God had changed His mind about the plan of salvation or revealed the true identity of the antichrist.

But in 1999, most of the preachers of the Square, reflecting an ominous mood running away with millions of religious souls across the world, gravitated toward apocalyptic themes. They trumpeted prophecies of gloom and doom, resurrection and rapture, the end of the world.

During the Spring, a shaggy-looking character from the hills around Sedona, Arizona appeared in the Square claiming to be the reincarnation of sixteenth-century French astrologer Nostradamus. He harangued the park population for several weeks that the seventh month would see the parting of the skies and the advent of the great King Angoulmois and his reign of terror, the very one he had predicted in his former life.

But July came and went. When the king failed to appear, "Nostradamus" and his computer-generated charts quickly disappeared from the Square.

He was survived, however, by numerous of his rivals for the parishioners of the park. The great Zantac—who insisted that he was centuries older than the gastrointestinal remedy of the same name—proclaimed that Pershing Square was to be the vortex for the catching away of the faithful to an invisible Doomsday Ark, presently orbiting Earth. The great rapture was to take place at the stroke of midnight on Millennium's Eve, seconds before the planet was ground to powder in the hands of God.

A trio of self-styled, loosely screwed New Age prophets relayed the countdown of the cosmos according to the Mayan calendar. And off-the-chart fundamentalists declared an impending nuclear holocaust, followed by thirty-seven days of world shock, followed by the emergence of the antichrist, followed in six years and 328 days by Christ's return to Jerusalem.

Every bizarre theory of cataclysm and chiliasm rampant in the last year of the first millennium eventually spawned a wild-eyed representative in Pershing Square.

As Hodge shuffled into the Square on Christmas Eve day, he noted that the weather and the holiday had taken a toll on the population. There were no secretaries or computer programmers sitting down with their bag lunches. A few old men scattered around the park were strolling the sidewalks absently or tossing bread crumbs to the pigeons. Significantly fewer street people than normal hunkered in patches of sunlight on the lawn swigging from brown-bag-wrapped bottles. A couple of them risked a park bench nap while the bike cops were elsewhere. Even most of the park prophets were missing from their usual corners, forsaking their missions from God for the comfort and warmth of a shelter on nippy Christmas Eve day.

It didn't matter to Hodge who was there or how many. His calling was to be there and to proclaim the truth every day as he had since the beginning of the month. Visitors to the Square gawked at him, and the regulars laughed or taunted if they didn't completely ignore him. The bike cops found Hodge and the other soapbox nuts in the Square a welcome source of amusement in their daily grind of policing the downtown riffraff.

A few souls in the Square *did* occasionally listen to Hodge, but they were the zombies of the streets with brains as empty as their eyes. They seemed to find as much spiritual inspiration listening to a palm tree or trash can. And those to whom Hodge's warnings were particularly directed had never even come to the Square. It didn't matter. It was Hodge's destiny to speak and theirs to listen if they would. And if they would not, so be it. Judgment was theirs alone to bear.

Hodge had his choice of locations today. He trudged into the park to a spot near the cement pond on the Sixth Street side. This spot was usually occupied by the Rev. Wingate, a sallow-faced man who wore the same urine-stained trousers every day.

Wingate's "ministry" was to stand silently in this spot for an hour at a time, glaring at passersby and bench-sitters sourly. Then precisely on the hour, like the tone of a giant clock gone berserk, he screeched at the top of his voice, "The kingdom of heaven is at hand!" Visitors to the Square caught unawares by the Reverend's sudden explosion jumped with fright. Then Wingate would lapse into another hour of judgmental glaring as startled visitors scurried away and old-timers chuckled. The bike cops tried to be in the area near the top of the hour just to watch the responses and enjoy the fun.

Hodge decided to make the most of Rev. Wingate's absence by taking over his choice location. He placed his picnic chest on the cement next to the pond. Then he folded the handle down, lifted the lid, and pulled out a tattered Bible. Replacing the lid, he carefully stepped up on the chest and turned to face the park. He positioned his feet for good balance, clutched the Bible to his chest, and closed his eyes. There was no one within 100 feet of him in any direction. And the scattered occupants of the Square who happened to notice him paid him no mind.

After several minutes of meditation, Hodge took a deep breath, exhaled, and opened his eyes. He turned to his preselected Bible text for the day—Psalm 53—adjusted the thick lenses on his splotchy nose, squinted at the white pages glaring up at him, and began to read in a loud, clear voice:

The fool hath said in his heart, "There is no God."
Corrupt are they, and have done abominable iniquity:
there is none that doeth good.
God looked down from heaven upon the children of men,
to see if there were any that did understand, that did seek God.
Every one of them is gone back: they are altogether become filthy;
there is none that doeth good, no, not one.
Have the workers of iniquity no knowledge?
who eat up my people as they eat bread:
they have not called upon God.
There were they in great fear, where no fear was:
for God hath scattered the bones of him
that encampeth against thee:
thou hast put them to shame, because God hath despised them.
Oh that the salvation of Israel were come out of Zion!
When God bringeth back the captivity of his people,
Jacob shall rejoice, and Israel shall be glad.

When Hodge looked up from the page, he was no nearer gathering an audience than when he started. He was not concerned in the least. For twenty-three days his fiery denunciations had been ignored or scorned. But he had been faithful, and he would remain faithful until he was rewarded as promised. *Then they will listen to me*, he consoled himself vengefully. *They will* all *listen to me.*

Hodge launched into the familiar diatribe that characterized his daily visit to the Square. His boisterous yet surprisingly articulate sermons were never exactly the same, but the theme was recurrent and relentless: Those who claimed to be for God were thoroughly evil; the cup of wrath was full; judgment was imminent.

Hodge seemed to take delight in enunciating at great length the outpouring of wrath upon the unrepentant. Being careful not to lose his balance, he alternately pounded on his Bible and flung his fist into the air to describe the impending fury. Had Lionel Whatley and Hodge's other co-workers seen him in action in the Square, they never would have believed him to be the same mousy, deferring concessionaire who stocked the food stands at the Sports Arena.

As Hodge pressed on with his tirade, a wino as ragged and homely as Hodge staggered along the sidewalk in front of him. The old man stopped to stare up at the street preacher on the picnic chest. He swayed unsteadily as he alternately squinted and blinked trying to focus on Hodge. Offended for no apparent reason, the man began muttering a stream of foul words toward Hodge, who continued his invective against unrighteousness as if he didn't see or hear him.

Being ignored only irritated the wino further. He sidled a little closer to Hodge, raising his voice and flailing his arms angrily. Hodge kept preaching while he unobtrusively slipped his right hand through the hole in his jacket pocket to touch the handle of his knife. He had never been provoked into using the blade in the Square, but he had come close on a few occasions. He had no qualms about cutting anyone who threatened him or his mission.

After a few moments the shaggy transient broke off his verbal attack abruptly and glanced around as if Hodge and the picnic chest had suddenly vaporized. His eyes were glazed and his head bobbed like it was on springs. Presently he wandered away without so much as another sneer while Hodge continued to preach.

Hodge always saved his choicest condemnations for last, and he addressed these bitter words to the same unseen audience. A few of the words were from his favorite book of the Bible: The Revelation.

> Woe to thee, rider of the white horse.
> Thou who wearest the crown of the conqueror
> shall thyself be conquered.
> May thy flesh be torn and thy bones be scattered
> and thy blood quench the parched earth,
> and may the beast from heaven
> take thy throne and thy inheritance.
>   Woe to thee, rider of the red horse, the great harlot.
> Thou who slayest thy fellow man shall be slain.
> May thy flesh be torn and thy bones be scattered
> and thy blood quench the parched earth,
> and may the beast from heaven
> take thy throne and thy inheritance.
>   Woe to thee, rider of the black horse, the prince of thieves.
> Thou who emptieth the purse of the widow
> will be turned inside out.
> May thy flesh be torn and thy bones be scattered
> and thy blood quench the parched earth,
> and may the beast from heaven
> take thy throne and thy inheritance.
>   Woe to thee—

Hodge broke off his thundering rebuke when he saw Officer Ochoa and Officer Scanlon peddling their mountain bikes into Pershing Square from the northwest corner. Without much action in the Square today, they would surely humor themselves by paying Hodge a visit. Like so many others who heard him, they thought his mission and message were a joke, a few minutes of comic relief in the midst of the tedium and tension of their jobs. *On Millennium's Eve they will realize,* Hodge thought as he watched them approach from the corner of his eye, *that who I am and what I have come to do is no laughing matter.*

Hodge quickly pulled himself together and continued as if he had not seen the approaching officers, even though their distracting presence always affected his delivery:

> Woe to thee, rider of the pale horse.
> Thou who beareth death and hell
> shall himself be thrown into . . .
> thrown into the grave and burn forever.
> May thy flesh be torn and thy bones . . . thy bones be scattered
> and thy blood quench the parched earth,
> and may the beast from heaven . . .
> may the beast take thy throne and thy inheritance.

The officers dismounted and applauded Hodge, their gloved hands making a thudding sound instead of a sharp clap. They were both young and muscular, with the black officer a few inches taller than the Hispanic. They wore LAPD regulation navy blue shirts and shorts and white bike helmets. In contrast to their lightweight attire their belts appeared cumbersome, encircled with holstered radios, handcuffs, DAB pistols, extra clips, and telescoping batons.

"Nice delivery, Rev. Hodge," Scanlon said with an amused grin, removing his sunglasses.

"Thank you, officer," he responded respectfully, stepping off his picnic chest podium. "But I ain't no reverend, sir. Just a servant of God." Hodge placed his Bible inside the chest. Had the officers not stopped to visit him today he would have expounded a little longer on the certainty and imminence of judgment on the four horsemen. But under the circumstances, he decided to appear finished for the day and move along.

"Well, anybody who can preach like that is a full-blown reverend to me, old buddy," Officer Ochoa grinned, nudging Scanlon to underscore his tongue-in-cheek comment. "Where's old Rev. Wingate today, Hodge? Are you taking over his congregation?" Hodge knew they didn't care about him or Wingate or their listeners. They were just passing time on a quiet holiday in the Square.

"Oh no, sir, this here is his spot. I don't know where the Reverend is today, sir, but when he's in the Square this is his spot."

"Oh, I remember now, Vince," Scanlon said to his partner with mock seriousness. "Rev. Wingate told me he had to pick up his dry cleaning and get his hair styled today for the holidays." The two officers laughed derisively. Hodge appeared not to understand. He picked up his picnic chest to be on his way, hoping the cops were done with their fun. They weren't.

"Say, Hodge, why do you preach such a bloody sermon?" Scanlon said with an amused grin. "Wingate is kind of fun to watch and listen to. But I don't think I'd want to come to your church with you always talking about death and hell and torn up flesh and bones. You make God out to be some kind of serial killer who loves tearing bodies apart."

"I'm just trying to be a faithful servant and proclaim the Word of God, sir," Hodge said apologetically. "I don't always understand what it means, sir, but I'm sure God ain't no killer like it sounds."

"Then are you the killer you're preaching about, Hodge?" Scanlon's expression was serious.

Hodge had thoroughly practiced his response to any suspicion that might be cast on him or his mission. The slightest misgiving about him in the eyes of the law could result in the discovery of his knife and a serious delay in his mission.

"Say, officer, I done some things I ain't proud of in my life," he said with a wounded look and tone. "But I ain't never—"

The two cops threw back their heads in laughter. "Old Rev. Hodge couldn't tear the wings off a moth, Tommy," Ochoa roared, slapping his partner on the shoulder.

Having amused themselves at Hodge's expense once again, they mounted their bikes without another word to him and peddled away, still laughing, toward the northwest entrance to the Square.

Hodge maintained his docile posture as he watched them go, exhaling his relief. It was just as he had been told. As long as he fulfilled his responsibilities, he would be protected. Hodge whispered a phrase of thanks, then picked up his chest and limped to the Metro landing.

Eight

The young man, not much more than a skin-draped skeleton, lay still in his bed, scarcely breathing. The late afternoon sun intruding through the window of the old Queen of Angels Hospital washed over his pasty-white face, neck, and shoulders, making the threadbare sheet pulled up to his chest appear dingy yellow by comparison. The harsh, jagged shadows of his fleshless brow, cheekbones, and chin cast on the pillow and mattress mingled with the swirling images of tubes and cords which surrounded his bed and kept him barely alive.

The young man had been comatose for two days as the ravaging virus devoured the last ounces of his life. He had been in what the staff called the "transporter room" for almost a week, a private corner room on the fifth floor where the most advanced cases were allowed to depart this life in peace. Sometimes the victims' loved ones were present to see them off. But the young man in the transporter room this Christmas Eve afternoon had never received a visitor during his two-month stay. He was dying alone.

A volunteer nurse, a short, trim Latino woman dressed in jeans, polo, and tennis shoes, silently glided into the room to check the young man's IV. Her shadow passing in front of his closed eyes somehow triggered a response. His stirring was barely perceptible—a slight wrinkling of his brow, a twitch of his bony fingers on top of the sheet. But the nurse noticed.

"Grant? Are you awake?" Her voice was soft and friendly, like a mother welcoming a child back from an afternoon nap. She placed a warm hand on his exposed shoulder and studied his face.

Grant labored to lift his eyelids, first one and then the other, enough to see her—at least she thought he could see her. His lips parted slightly as if to answer her, but no words came.

"It's good to see you awake, Grant. You've been asleep for awhile." She caressed his forehead and combed his long, stringy hair with her fingers. "I can't wait to tell Dr. No. Would you like to see him?"

Grant's eyelids raised another scant notch. The nurse wasn't sure he was cognizant but the flicker of response was good enough for her. "Okay, Grant, wait right here. I'll get him."

Queen of Angels Hospital, founded in Los Angeles in 1926 by the Franciscan Sisters of the Sacred Heart, was worn and cracked. It had survived several decades of Southern California earthquakes. What it couldn't survive was its location, the steadily declining Echo Park area. And in 1988, when Queen of Angels merged with Hollywood Presbyterian Medical Center, the aging facility overlooking the Hollywood Freeway became obsolete and was vacated. It stood empty, locked up tight, and was for sale for six years as the neighborhood around it was invaded and ravished by weeds, poverty, and crime.

Finally the old building was sold for pennies on the dollar to an unincorporated nonprofit affiliation of business people, medical personnel, and volunteers who, over a period of two years, spruced it up and turned it into a center of mercy for the hurting of Los Angeles. The group changed the name of the building from Queen of Angels to King's House.

Three floors of the main building were converted into a fully supervised homeless shelter, including facilities for job training and placement aimed at returning citizens to the mainstream confident, self-sufficient, and eager to contribute. The fifth floor became a hospice for the untouchables of the late twentieth century: victims of HIV, AIDS, and their always terminal complications. The west wing, formerly medical and dental offices, became a receiving, processing, and distribution center for food, clothing, household goods, and medical supplies for the poor. As funds and volunteers became available, the east wing was cleaned up and converted into a base of operations for contacting and befriending men and women incarcerated in the L.A. County jail system. The goal of the prison ministry staff was to prepare prisoners for release and then work with probation officers to assist ex-cons in going straight and returning to society.

King's House was headed by a slightly built, unassuming forty-two-year-old Vietnamese-American who had left his career as an electronics engineer to try to do something about the staggering number of needy Angelenos left unattended in a city immersed in drug wars and race riots. Thanh Hai Ngo was called Dr. No by almost everyone, but not because he was a physician. His training was in electronics engineering, and he was several course hours and a dissertation removed from a doctorate in that field. Yet his deeply caring manner and tireless work, especially among dying patients on the fifth floor where he spent much of his time, had earned him the title from both patients and associates. And he certainly looked the part in the oversized borrowed white lab coat he often wore.

It was not Dr. *No* because he was a negative person. Far from it. Few of his acquaintances knew anyone more positive and inspirational than the modest engineer turned missionary to L.A.'s down-and-outers. And Thanh Hai Ngo's moniker had nothing to do with the notorious Ian Fleming character, Dr. No, the fictional nemesis of arch spy James Bond. Rather his dubious title was simply a well-intentioned mispronunciation of his family name by non-Asians who understood how to end words with an *ng* sound but had no idea how to make them begin that way.

The nurse found Dr. No asleep on the thrift store couch in a waiting room several doors from the transporter room. Before stealing away for a brief nap, he had spent eleven hours on the fifth floor without a break.

"Dr. No." The nurse touched him lightly on the shoulder. He was instantly awake, as if thoroughly accustomed to his sleep being interrupted.

"Yes, what is it?" he said, sitting up and rubbing his face with both hands. Having immigrated from Vietnam with his family as a small boy at the beginning of the war and been educated in Los Angeles, he had practically no Asian accent.

"It's Grant, sir. I think he's awake. You asked me to call you if he came around. I don't think he'll last the night."

Dr. No quickly stood and raked his thick, straight black hair with his small fingers. He was barely taller than the nurse and several pounds thinner, but not skinny. "Thank you, Gloria," he yawned, arching his back. He tried to brush some of the wrinkles out of his shirt, then slipped into his baggy white lab coat. "Yes, I was hoping to talk to Grant once more. Thank you." His smile of appreciation was genuine.

Dr. No followed the nurse out of the office and down the hall past rooms occupied with dying patients who themselves were destined to spend their last hours in the transporter room in a matter of weeks. Simple Christmas decorations adorned the normally austere hallway. A music box in one of the rooms softly chimed, "O Come, All Ye Faithful."

Gloria turned into the C ward at the cry of a patient in pain. Dr. No nodded amiably to volunteers and a few ambulatory patients in the hall but moved resolutely toward room 540. The handmade sign on the door read GRANT KELLY.

"Hello, Grant," Dr. No said, as he eased quietly into a bedside chair. Grant's eyelids, which had drooped closed as soon as Gloria had left the room, slowly reopened at the sound of the voice. Dr. No tenderly grasped the patient's bony hand, and the young man painstakingly rolled his head until he could gaze into the compassionate eyes of Dr. No.

The ensuing conversation was silent because Grant was too weak to speak. But the communication flowing between their eyes was no less meaningful than it had been during their many visits in past weeks.

"How are you today, Grant?"

"Could be better, doc. Could be worse."

"Are you experiencing any pain or discomfort today?"

"Nothing Gloria and The Man and me can't handle."

"Anything I can do for you?"

"Yeah, check the newspaper and see if anybody discovered the cure for AIDS today. Then run down to the drugstore and get me a couple of bottles of the stuff."

"I already checked, Grant. Nothing new today. Sorry. But they're working on it. Getting closer to a cure every day. Anyone I can call for you?"

"I don't have nobody, doc, nobody but you and the others here in the House. I don't understand why you waste your time messing with throwaways like us. But I don't know where I'd be if you hadn't—"

"It's okay, Grant, I'm here for you. We all are. You just relax and let us take care of everything."

"Thanks, doc. I don't know what to say but thanks."

The sun began to slip behind the skyline out the window to the southwest, dissolving the hue in the room from flaming orange to drab rust. The dying patient's lids began to close again, so Dr. No continued the conversation aloud.

"It's Christmas Eve, Grant. I rather envy you because of where you may be by tomorrow." They had talked frankly in the past about the reality of Grant being in heaven by Christmas. Dr. No and the medical staff had been mildly surprised that Grant had lasted this long. "You're almost home, my friend. Home for Christmas, what a treat, huh?"

Grant's eyes were closed again, but Dr. No read what he thought to be a frail cry of pain or fear in the dark lines of the young man's colorless face.

"Are you afraid today, Grant?" It was a question Dr. No had asked hundreds of times in the transporter room and at other bedsides across the fifth floor of King's House. Sometimes he was answered with anguished screams, sometimes with broken whimpers. "We're here to help you with the pain and the fear," Dr. No always assured them. "We'll stay with you until the pain and fear are gone."

"Grant, are you afraid?" Dr. No asked again, searching the young man's face for the transfused hope that had sustained so many of the fifth floor patients during their last months and weeks.

Grant, with eyes still closed, slipped his hand from Dr. No's grasp and began moving it by fractions of inches up his sheet-draped torso. Dr. No was puzzled about what Grant was trying to do. "Can I get something for you, Grant?" he said, marveling at how the emaciated patient labored to move his hand, yet wondering why he was spending his last ounces of strength reaching for some unknown—

Then he saw it. Dr. No delicately lifted Grant's thin hand and moved it to the base of the dying man's neck. The bony fingers reverently closed around a small gold cross which hung around his neck.

It wasn't much more than a feeble breath as Grant barely mouthed the words, but Dr. No heard it, "No fear, doc." The slightest hint of a contented smile tugged at the corners of Grant's mouth.

Dr. No grinned broadly. "That's good, Grant. You've found the secret," he said, patting his hand gently. "Merry Christmas, my friend." But Grant didn't hear him. He had slipped back into a coma that would consume the last two hours of his life.

Dr. No found Gloria at the nursing station. "Grant won't be with us much longer. Is there someone who can sit with him when you're not in the room?"

"Yes. Keesha Green came in about thirty minutes ago to visit patients for a few hours. She has a tender heart for the ones in their last hours. She likes to be with them and read psalms to them and pray for them, whether they're conscious or not. I'll ask her to go to the transporter room."

"Perfect. Keesha's a real saint." Dr. No pulled Grant's chart and scribbled a few quick notes about their "conversation" next to the medical data entered by the physicians. "Anything else happen while I was resting?"

Gloria glanced at the bank of charts to refresh her memory. "Danny

Firmin tried to eat a bland lunch, but couldn't keep it down. He complained of nausea, so Dr. Triplett ordered an IV."

Dr. No nodded as he slid Grant's chart back into the rack. "Danny's failing fast," he sighed. "Probably won't eat again. He may be our next candidate for the transporter room."

Dr. No pinched the bridge of his nose between thumb and forefinger. He wasn't sleepy at the moment, but he was still weary. The weariness hardly ever left him. Nor did the gnawing drain of caring for patients who only got worse, never better. He and Dr. Alan Triplett, an internist in private practice in Beverly Hills before joining Dr. No's mercy team to head up the volunteer medical staff, talked about this occupational hazard often with the fifth floor team.

"We're here to provide physical, emotional, and spiritual comfort to many who are dying from HIV-related complications while being neglected by society, in most cases even their families," Dr. No constantly reminded his team. "It doesn't matter how our patients contracted the virus. We can't change the past. But we can make the present and future as positive and hopeful as possible for those given to our care. Only God can work miracles. Without divine intervention, every one of the men and women we welcome onto the fifth floor will eventually be moved into the transporter room and die. We will do whatever we can to prepare them for this eventuality and keep them as comfortable as possible while they await it."

Dr. No flashed on a mental gallery of wasted, hollow-eyed men and women who had entered the fifth floor on crutches or in wheelchairs and departed sheet-draped on gurneys loaded into black-windowed vans. Many had clung to him, begged his prayers, and welcomed his comforting words about God and heaven. Others had literally spit on him, called him every vile name in the book, and had thrown his God-talk back in his face with their dying breath venting their despair. He prayed for them and comforted them too.

How many had there been in the past forty-six months—no, forty-seven months as of December 15? Nine hundred? A thousand? And how many had been turned away simply for lack of space and supplies? Double that? Triple? It pained him every time he thought of it.

"If you're looking for an exhilarating, ego-massaging career in caregiving," Dr. No often told the volunteer doctors, nurses, and laypersons on the fifth floor, "you've come to the wrong place. The people who enter these crowded wards already reek with the stench of death. Barring a miracle, you will someday wheel every one of them to room 540 and hold their hands as they die. You will then wheel them down to the first floor loading dock and watch the undertaker drive them away. Most of them will be buried in cheap pine boxes, usually without a funeral. They are throwaways when they come here. And we will eventually throw them away too.

"For every corpse that goes out the back door there are five more near-corpses waiting on the front steps for the vacated bed. And no matter which ones we accept, they will be as haggard and helpless and hopeless as all the rest. You will feed them and bathe them, only to have them vomit and void all over themselves—and you too, sometimes. You will try to ease their pain and suffering with every vaccine and therapy available, but many of them will still curse you because you don't do enough, and their pain will rip you to shreds inside because you *can't* do enough.

"We take every precaution against the spread of HIV to the staff, but we issue no guarantees. By serving these dear people, you run the risk of contracting the very disease that is wasting them. Be as careful as possible, but don't be so careful that you forget how to be care-filled.

"In between these endless hours of suffering and stench and caring, if you're lucky you'll get to tell your patients something about your hope for heaven. A few of them may listen and find hope themselves. Others will laugh in your face. Still others will damn you to hell simply because you're part of the blankity-blank establishment that didn't warn them enough about dangerous sex or dirty needles.

"Some of the more philosophical ones will spin your head around demanding that you explain why a loving, just God would allow such a terrible disease to fester, and then cruelly hide the cure for two decades while millions worldwide waste away. And no matter how clearly you articulate free will, sin, consequences, grace, and mercy, many of them will flip you off and curse you because you don't know what they're going through. Then in the same breath they will ask you to clean their bedpans and wipe their bottoms."

"Your wife also called while you were asleep." Dr. No heard Gloria speaking to him but didn't catch what she said. He was embarrassed about being lost in thought. "Pardon me, I guess I was somewhere else."

"I said Mai called while you were asleep, about forty-five minutes ago. She asked me not to wake you, but she wants you to call her when you have a minute."

"Was she down in the apartment?" Dr. No and his wife, along with several others committed to the King's House vision, had sold their homes in Orange County, the San Fernando Valley, and trendy beach communities and moved into apartments constructed during the refurbishing of the east wing. They funneled most of the proceeds of their home sales into the ministries of the House.

"No, I think she was still at the office," Gloria said. "I could hear all that deadline chatter in the background." Dr. No smiled and nodded knowingly.

Gloria turned to go look for Keesha Green, but Dr. No's call stopped her. "Gloria, how late are you staying today?"

"Actually my shift ended at three. But if you don't mind I'd like to stay through the evening. It's Christmas Eve, and I'd like to spend it with my family and friends—and they're all right here." Gloria beamed and gestured toward the wards surrounding the nursing station.

Dr. No shook his head disbelievingly as he returned her broad smile. "You are an angel, pure and simple. For you, Gloria, I say, 'Gloria in excelsis Deo.' "

"Gloria a Dios, Dr. No," the nurse responded in her beautiful Latin accent.

Dr. No returned to his office by way of the staff lounge, where he pulled a diet Squirt out of the refrigerator and lifted the tab. After a couple of impromptu visits with patients, he settled into his couch with the hand-held phone and punched the memory button for the *Times*. He interrupted the electronic receptionist by keying the extension number before she could finish her spiel about touch-tone access to the various departments.

The phone rang several times. "Religion desk, this is Mai." The female voice echoing over a speaker phone sounded harried but courteous. Dr. No could hear the clack of a computer keyboard in the background.

"Is this the famous religion editor Mai Ngo, the delicate, fragrant flower of the *Times* editorial staff?"

The first response was a pleasant laugh. Then, "Wrong. This is the overworked, underpaid part-time assistant religion editor. And right now I feel more like a wilted weed." Mai's Vietnamese accent was more pronounced than her husband's.

"Having a rough day, dear?" Dr. No's voice was thick with mock sympathy.

"Oh, I guess it's not that bad, my darling," Mai responded with another little laugh. The background clacking stopped. "It's just that Serg was late transmitting his data on the Harmony series for the next two issues. And he left a bit of line editing for me on both stories. I'm trying to get them cleaned up and put to bed so I don't have to come in tomorrow. And I can't say I'm very inspired about working on the New Age millennial convergence on Christmas Eve."

"When do you think you'll be done?" Dr. No took a long sip of Squirt and relished the icy, burning sensation on his taste buds.

"What time is it now?"

Dr. No put the pop can on the desk and glanced at his watch. "Almost 5:30."

"I should be able to shut the computer off by 6:30. What about you?"

Dr. No sighed and pinched the bridge of his nose subconsciously. "Well, we're a little shorthanded tonight. I tried to give the night off to as many staff as possible, especially those who will be here tomorrow. I feel I need to stay around a few hours to help clean up and put patients to bed."

Mai hummed with understanding. "I guess that's our calling, my darling—cleaning up and putting to bed."

"Then I need to get down to the chapel ahead of time to collect my thoughts before the Christmas Eve service at 11. It sounds like most everyone who isn't working somewhere in the House or out on the streets tonight is going to be there."

"Then can you come home after the meeting? Can we actually go to bed together on Christmas Eve and enjoy Christmas morning with our children?"

"Yes, my dear one," Dr. No chuckled. "I have the night off. But I need to be back at the west wing at 9 in the morning to help the staff get Christmas dinner ready."

"You're pushing yourself too hard, Thanh. It worries me. You can't do it all, you know." Mai had delivered the same lecture before, with little result. Dr. No was a devoted husband and father, but he was also devoted to the hurting hundreds who lived in or passed through King's House each month. His vision and example had attracted a large number of skilled and loyal volunteers. But there was never enough help, and Dr. No wanted to do so much more. Mai's mild scoldings were met by a rather sheepish shrug that communicated, "I'm only doing what needs to be done."

She often chided him—lovingly but with some concern, "They should call you Dr. Yes instead of Dr. No. You can't say no to anyone in need."

"And I bet you haven't eaten anything decent all day," Mai continued with concern.

"Wait a minute, dear. I've had two diet Squirts today"—Dr. No spied the half-empty can on his desk—"make that three, a bag of low-fat corn chips, and an apple, er, actually a candy apple. What's wrong with that?" The couple laughed at the ludicrous menu.

"Listen, my darling," Mai said. "You come downstairs as much before 10 tonight as you can. I'll fix rice and vegetables and meat, and we'll have Christmas Eve dinner together with the children before the meeting. What do you say?"

"That, my dear, is an offer too good to refuse. I'll try to come downstairs by 9:30."

Two minutes later Dr. No was sipping the last of his Squirt when Kevin Gorman, a husky, black volunteer, stuck his head in the office. "I hate to bother you, Dr. No," he said with a perturbed look on his face, "but we're having trouble with Theta again."

Dr. No was quickly on his feet and following Kevin down the hall toward one of three wards of women patients on the fifth floor. Many were former prostitutes who came up losers at sexual roulette with the johns they serviced on L.A.'s street corners. Theta Breckinridge was one of them. Once a shapely, $500-a-night call girl, Theta fell victim to crack and then heroin, thanks to the generosity of one of her regular customers. In order to support her rapidly escalating habit, she became careless in choosing both her customers and her needles.

Theta's pimp worked her until she became sick, then continued to work her until even heavy makeup, peroxide, and figure-enhancing appliances couldn't doll her up enough to attract a $50 trick. Then one night he beat her up, stripped her, and threw her out on the street.

Volunteers from King's House found her in the gutter. They cleaned her up, clothed her, and gave her a bed. When she was diagnosed with AIDS, as many of the street people who ended up at King's House were, Theta was transferred upstairs to the fifth floor. While begrudgingly accepting the care offered at the hospice, she proceeded to make life miserable for everyone around her.

Theta Breckinridge was clearly the vilest-speaking woman Dr. No had ever known, and she regularly blistered the staff and fellow patients with her disgusting language. The more her health deteriorated and the more her drug-fried brain lost touch with reality, the more vile she became. The staff had joked privately that Theta's scathing verbal attacks could send a Marine drill sergeant crying to his mother. Next to Theta Breckinridge, a woman with Tourette's Syndrome had the vocabulary of a high society debutante. If a private room had been available, they'd have put Theta in it. But with the ward perpetually overcrowded, Theta just had to be dealt with—by everybody.

"Same old same old, doc," quipped Kevin, a former college football player, as they approached the ward where all the racket was coming from. "She complained about dinner again and started throwing green beans and those little boiled potatoes dripping with gravy around the room. Thank goodness she doesn't have much zip on her fastball anymore. She got most of the stuff on herself and her bed. When I tried to talk her down and clean up the mess, she went ballistic. Called me some names I've never been called before. Whew, what a command of gutter language!"

"I'm sorry, Kevin." Dr. No's apology was heartfelt and reflected genuine embarrassment at Theta's misbehavior.

"Hey, it's okay, doc. I don't let it bother me. I know Theta's playing on a short field. I'd just like to get her quieted down and cleaned up for the night."

Just as they reached the door a girl volunteer in her early twenties hurried out and stormed past them, followed by a few of Theta's shouted expletives. The girl's blouse was smeared with gravy, and her face was a dark cloud ready to explode in a torrent of tears.

Dr. No and Kevin were greeted with a stinging barrage of acrid curses and derogatory epithets from Theta, none they hadn't heard before. And the other seven bedfast women patients crowded into the small ward were almost as abusive, complaining loudly to the two men in dissonant chorus for making them put up with Theta's loud-mouthed belligerence day in and day out. As the two men later searched for some humor in the tragic situation, they agreed that had thundering Theta and her hostile roommates not been weakened by disease and confined to their beds, they would have probably had to run for their lives.

Dr. No stood with hands on hips in the midst of the din surveying the scene. Kevin stood behind him as if seeking protection, even though the young black man towered over him and outweighed him by seventy pounds. The eight thin, gaunt, wild-eyed women sat upright in their beds with their meal trays in front of them. Seven of the beds were crowded closely together, keeping as much floor space as possible between them and Theta. Theta's blanket was stained with the remains of a whole day's menu from the King's House kitchen, and the floor around the bed was littered with garbage from a dinner that obviously didn't meet her fancy.

She aimed a devilish stare and a stream of vulgar words at Dr. No while her bony hands searched the meal tray and the bed around her for something to throw at him. She had used up all her ammo, so she futilely flicked smudges of gravy toward him. All the while the other seven patients called him names and demanded to be moved to another room. One woman insisted loudly and repeatedly that she had a room waiting for her at the Ambassador Hotel.

Dr. No suddenly began to sing at the top of his lungs in a somewhat off-key voice.

Jingle bells, jingle bells, jingle all the way.
Oh what fun it is to ride in a one-horse open sleigh, hey!
Jingle bells, jingle bells, jingle all the way.
Oh what fun it is to ride in a one-horse open sleigh.

By the time he completed the first chorus the patients' raucous complaining had dwindled to openmouthed staring. Then he sucked in a quick breath and charged into another chorus, elbowing Kevin—who looked just as stunned as the patients—until he joined in but in another octave and key. By the third chorus the two men were clapping in time and Kevin was improvising a little choreography around some of the potatoes and green beans on the floor.

The lady from the Ambassador was the first to join in, clapping weakly while singing three or four words behind Dr. No's lead. But there was a smile on her face, and he hoped the distraction was infectious. "C'mon, ladies, it's Christmas Eve! Dashing through the snow in a one-horse open sleigh . . . " A few other volunteers curiously stuck their heads in the room and were commandeered by Dr. No for the chorale.

One by one the disgruntled faces around him were transformed by the holiday atmosphere as Dr. No led the group through "Frosty the Snowman" and "Rudolph the Red-nosed Reindeer." Even explosive Theta was defused and joined in. It was a contrived Christmas spirit, Dr. No mused, as he watched the hostility in the room melt away. He thought it was kind of like the manufactured snow on Mt. Baldy. It wasn't the real stuff, but you could ski on it to the bottom of the hill just the same. Similarly, his spur-of-the-moment, riot-control Christmas sing-along wasn't the most noble means of achieving a sense of peace and goodwill, but it was working.

As he slowed the pace and started into "The First Noel," Dr. No motioned subtly for Kevin and the others to join him in tending to the patients. They collected food trays and cleansed hands and faces without skipping a note or a word of the carols while Dr. No and Kevin picked garbage off the floor and wiped up gravy. Even Theta was docile as a couple of cautious female volunteers pulled a curtain around her bed and bathed her and changed her soiled gown and bedding.

As the volunteers gradually departed to other tasks, Dr. No remained to lead the eight dying women in "Silent Night." As he stumbled through the last verse, he was suddenly sobered by the realization that none of these women would live to see Christmas in 2000, and half of them, including Theta Breckinridge, probably wouldn't make it to Easter.

At the end of the song he spent a few minutes at the bedside of each of the women, encouraging them to consider the reason for the season and wishing them a Merry Christmas. Theta wasn't interested in Dr. No's "Christmas slop," but at least she didn't cuss him out.

He was standing in the lounge opening his fourth diet Squirt of the day when a slender, ebony-skinned high school girl in a light blue jumpsuit appeared in the doorway. Keesha Green's normally angelic face was clouded and tearstained. Dr. No immediately knew why. He opened his arms and Keesha fell into his fatherly embrace weeping softly.

"I can't get used to them dying, Dr. No," she said between quivering sighs. "I was holding Grant's hand and reading a psalm to him, and he just stopped breathing. I knew he was going to die. They all die. But it's still hard when it happens."

"I know, Keesha. It's hard for me too." It was all Dr. No could do to hold back his own tears.

Nine

The subtly muscular and artificially tanned man in the center of the room wore a calf-length, long-sleeved tunic of neutral-colored wool gathered at the waist by a strip of cloth the same color. Leather sandals were strapped to his bare feet and his head was uncovered. His thick, wavy black hair, flecked with gray at the temples, was thoroughly stylish, yet long enough to appear believable for the biblical character he was portraying, especially considering the rest of the costume. He was on one knee with his head tilted dramatically toward heaven. His arms tenderly cradled an imaginary infant. The well-dressed onlookers crowding the perimeter of the room were rapt and silent.

"And so, Lord God, I will call the boy-child Jesus in accordance with Thy will. I will raise Him as my own son. Yet I will never forget that I am only His earthly father, and that Thou, God of Abraham and of Isaac and of Jacob, art His true Father." The actor was American, but his crisp stage diction made him sound almost British.

"I will teach Him to work the wood with His hands as I have done and as my fathers before me have done. But I covenant before Thee now, that from His earliest years this lad will be about His Father's business." With the last few emphatic words Joseph slowly lifted the sleeping infant Jesus toward heaven as if offering a gift. Then the actor dropped his head dramatically and held the prayerfully submissive pose until the applause and hums of approval began. At that moment Joseph and his newborn son vanished, and Jeremy Cannon the actor stood erect with a flourish and bowed to his enthusiastically appreciative audience.

Televangelist Adrian Hornecker had found Jeremy Cannon—his stage name, of course—in Hollywood playing bit parts in B movies and teetering on the brink of starvation. At the time, Adrian was attempting to pull together a film company to produce his first movie for Victory Life Ministries, *The Doomsday Disk*, which he had written himself. The story was about a handsome, self-assured computer genius who stumbles onto a coded electronic data network secretly rallying the Arab states for an all-out war on Israel—the overture to Armageddon. The hero breaks the code, rushes to Tel Aviv, single-handedly disarms the plot, then flies away into the sunset with the Prime Minister's daughter.

Rugged, athletic, twenty-eight-year-old Jeremy Cannon perfectly matched Adrian's vision for Bren Becker, the hero in his story. He regarded Jeremy as an answer to prayer, though the actor's lifestyle was plainly unchristian. Undaunted, Adrian pitched Jeremy aggressively on the project, challenging him to become a Christian and accept the role of Bren Becker on the screen. Although unimpressed with—and even rather cynical about—Adrian's religious convictions, Jeremy desperately needed a job. So he professed to become a Christian at Adrian's insistence, signed a lucrative contract, and immediately began work on *The Doomsday Disk.*

About halfway through filming, however, the openly skeptical young actor claimed to have a transforming religious experience on location in Egypt. He had been drinking heavily one night—a habit Adrian threatened him about repeatedly—in an American club near the location compound, and was in the process of seducing one of the female makeup assistants. He had just lured her back to his trailer two blocks from the bar when a terrorist's bomb exploded less than fifty feet from where Jeremy had been plying the girl with gin fizzes moments earlier. One side of the building was reduced to kindling, but luckily the place was almost deserted, and no one was seriously injured.

When he realized what had happened, even in his fuzzy-headed state Jeremy knew he had been miraculously spared a horrible death. He dropped to his knees in the trailer (the terrified girl had run screaming and guilt-ridden to her quarters as soon as the bomb went off) and spent the night confessing every sin he'd ever committed and many he had only planned. Jeremy Cannon was a changed man.

When the film was finally "in the can," Cannon returned to Dallas with Adrian and gave his dramatic testimony—minus the parts about the drinking and the girl—in the packed Victory Life auditorium during a nationally televised Sunday service. Jeremy was unknown to the Christian world to that point. But after his testimony on TV, Jeremy Cannon became a Christian celebrity overnight.

When *Doomsday* was released, first to theaters and then to video, the name Jeremy Cannon became as well known in the religious world as that of Adrian Hornecker. The televangelist, seizing the windfall despite Jeremy's remaining rough edges, quickly signed Jeremy to portray Bren Becker in three more end-times thrillers, which later became known in the industry as the Doomsday Chronicles. Money flowed into the ministry like the Rio Grande into the Gulf of Mexico.

Out of the public eye, Jeremy still struggled with some of the "unspiritual" habits that had plagued him since before the bomb in Egypt drove him to his knees. Ironically, for the second time in his young Christian life, an incident of moral compromise probably saved his life. In late February 1999, Jeremy left Tel Aviv in first class on a commercial flight—ostensibly due to a virus—immediately after completing his scenes in Adrian's third film. Known only to Adrian and a silent few, Jeremy was being sent back to Dallas early to meet secretly with the Victory Life psychologist. The "virus" turned out to be an incident in Tel Aviv involving a Jewish girl, one of the location caterers, an incident Adrian had succeeded in keeping from everyone, even his wife. Had Jeremy waited to return to the States on the Victory Life charter

two weeks later, he would have plunged to the bottom of the Mediterranean with Adrian Hornecker and the rest of the Victory Life film
crew.

As with the rest of the Victory Life family, Jeremy was deeply shaken
by the tragedy, but even more so because of his second brush with
death. For weeks after the crash he lay awake nights begging God to
reveal to him why he had been spared *twice!*—despite his weakness.
He could only imagine that he had been chosen for something, cast for
a significant role in God's real-life last-days drama.

In the months that followed the crash, even though it seemed that
Jeremy's meal ticket, Bren Becker, had gone down in flames with the
film company, Jeremy once again landed on his feet. He parlayed his
success as Bren Becker and his sudden availability to the industry into
a supporting role in a major motion picture with Touchstone, and he
was in the running for another significant role with MGM. Other lucrative opportunities loomed on the horizon.

All the while, having bonded with the Victory Life staff and television
congregation as the only member of the location crew to pass through
the fiery furnace of the tragedy, Jeremy continued to support Shelby
Hornecker and the ministry with his periodic presence in the Dallas
services as a guest performer. And at Shelby's request, Jeremy, who
had been like a brother to her since the crash, would be on the platform with her in the Coliseum on Millennium's Eve performing one of
his captivating biblical monologues.

Shelby applauded heartily with the others as Jeremy continued his
curtain call bows for his portrayal of Joseph at the birth of Jesus. It had
been a wonderful party, Shelby acknowledged silently, as she glanced
across the glowing faces of her top-level Victory Life ministry staff and
their guests crowded into her spacious living room. Yet she had had
her doubts about giving this party. This year's annual Christmas Eve
reception was another in a year-long series of firsts without Adrian and
the others lost in the crash. *Will the specter of the tragedy dampen the
celebration?* she had wondered during the weeks of November and
December. *Will I be sorry that I pushed ahead with the party?* The
questions had nagged at her as recently as during this morning's flight
to Arlington.

But Christmas Eve morning at Victory Life had not only quieted
Shelby's doubts but had filled her with confident anticipation for the
evening and for tomorrow. The service had been the most moving one
in the auditorium since the tragedy. The congregational worship was
electric, unifying. Jeremy Cannon's dramatic monologue as the innkeeper of Bethlehem received a standing ovation. And Shelby's sermon
was flawless, prompting hundreds to crowd around the altar to renew
their commitment to Christ.

Even Shelby herself was inspired as the memorized verses and lines from her sermon seemed to penetrate her own somewhat calloused, resentful heart. She was encouraged to believe she was directly on course with what God was doing in her life, even by going ahead with the party.

And to top it all off, Stan Welbourn, her fatherly associate pastor, closed the service by presenting to her, on behalf of tens of thousands of grateful television partners across America, the keys to a brand new Lincoln Tour de Grace. Stan had assured Shelby, as she and the Welbourns and Theresa Bordeaux drove the 200 miles from Dallas to Austin after lunch, that the gleaming white Lincoln had been purchased with a love offering from the congregation, above and beyond regular tithes and offerings. The ministry's strained operating funds had not been tapped to fund the gift.

"What am I going to do with the de Ville Adrian bought me?" Shelby had wondered aloud as she piloted the fully loaded Lincoln at almost 70 MPH down Interstate 35. "It's a '95, but it only has 30,000 miles on it. And it's in mint condition—Adrian made sure of that. But I don't need two cars."

"I've been thinking about it, Shelby, and I have an idea," Stan had advanced. "You know the Honeycutts, the older couple in the counseling office, retired pastor and his wife?" Shelby recognized the names and nodded. "They work very hard answering letters for us, and we don't pay them very much. Their old car is on its last legs. How would you feel about selling the Caddie to them at a bargain price?"

"Sell it? I'll just give it to them," Shelby had said excitedly. "I'll be happy to do that. I don't need the money."

"I think they'd feel better about giving you *something* for it."

"Ridiculous. It's theirs. They can drive it home tonight after the party if they want to."

"Hiram and Marjory won't be here tonight. They're in Missouri with their children for Christmas."

"Then find someone else to drive it back to Dallas for them. And I won't take a dime for the car. Tell the Honeycutts it's just like salvation," she said, almost laughing. "They can't buy it. They can't earn it. They can only receive it."

"Okay, Shelby. I'll do my best," Stan acquiesced, chuckling. "I suppose they'll have a hard time refusing it if it's parked in their driveway with a big bow on it when they get home from Springfield." The mental picture, along with the excitement of her own new car, flooded Shelby with the Christmas spirit.

The feeling seemed to carry Shelby through the emotionally taxing evening of having her normally quiet villa swarm with nearly seventy people—including a dozen children under the age of ten. Shelby was a rather private person for someone in such a public role. She enjoyed being with people, but she readily admitted that, unlike extroverts whose batteries charge when they're socializing, she felt drained by prolonged social exposure.

Adrian had been the same way. To most everyone who knew them, the Horneckers appeared to be thoroughly people-oriented. After all, as the figureheads of a national television ministry, they were the center attraction wherever they went. People surrounded them constantly, so wherever they went Adrian and Shelby dutifully played their role and fulfilled the expectations of their devoted staff and adoring parishioners.

But when the last smiles had been smiled and the door of privacy had closed behind them, the Horneckers would collapse in silence, even toward each other. Adrian would retreat to his office and submerge himself—sometimes for days at a time—in studying and writing about end-times prophecies or reworking a scene for his latest movie thriller. And Shelby, grateful for the quietness but yearning for camaraderie with a husband who seemed to have time for everyone but her, would busy herself with the nest, decorating and redecorating the villa, plotting the purchase of new treasures. Shelby's busyness in Austin didn't really compensate her for Adrian's preoccupation with his preaching and films, or quiet her mounting concern that he was spending too much time in Hollywood for his own good. But at least her diversions consoled her somewhat.

When the applause began to wane, Shelby stood and embraced Jeremy appreciatively. With so many people catching her arm at the party, she hadn't said more than a few words to him all night. She looked forward to his frequent visits in Dallas. She loved to hear him talk about his budding film career, and he always seemed interested in her ministry and sensitive to her loss. She hoped they would be able to visit on the Gulfstream flying to Los Angeles for Unity 2000.

Jeremy sat cross-legged on the carpet with another cup of wassail, and Shelby stood near the arched adobe brick hearth to give the annual Christmas address to the staff gathered in her living room. As always, she was a vision of elegance and beauty, thanks to Theresa Bordeaux's eye for color and style. She wore a billowy silk pantsuit swirled with a large floral pattern of burgundy, rose, gold, and forest green. Her suit was accented by a large silk scarf tied in the back and matching low heels. Her medium-length naturally blond hair was neatly styled to highlight stunning gold and diamond earrings, which complemented the gold and jewels adorning her wrists and fingers. Theresa recommended only enough makeup to bring out the natural beauty of Shelby's powder blue eyes, long lashes, and small mouth.

In previous years Adrian spoke to the staff during their annual Christmas Eve gathering. His words of appreciation were usually brief and formal. He preferred to spend most of his time regaling the troops with the prophetic possibilities that "this next year could be the year of Christ's return" and challenging them to serve Him as if every day were this world's last.

Shelby had no such premonitions about the first year of the new millennium being the last year of the earth's existence, and she had no desire to deliver an Adrian-style pep talk urging her staff to look for the Second Coming behind every cloud. Instead of sermonizing, she simply and warmly expressed her appreciation to the staff for their support through the year, much like she had to Steve and Beverly Cashion at their early-morning breakfast meeting. She wondered if this would be both her first and last Christmas to address the staff. It all depended on what she and God decided tomorrow.

No one could have guessed the thoughts and feelings that were vying for Shelby's attention as she gazed around the room during her informal address. Pangs of loneliness pricked at her insides as she noticed several couples leaning against each other, linking arms, or squeezing hands as she spoke. In a few hours they would be in their homes, in their beds, sharing secrets words, making love. Spawning intimacy in their relationship hadn't been Adrian's strong suit, but Shelby had many good memories of closeness and loving with Adrian, mostly from their earlier years. She had no husband to snuggle up with this Christmas, and she wondered if all her chances for intimacy were buried in the Mediterranean with Adrian.

Shelby was also aware of how tired she was. She had had a restless night and an exhilarating but energy-sapping day. Driving the Lincoln home from Dallas instead of flying meant no afternoon nap before the reception, but the fun of being in her new car was worth it to her at the time. Now it was an effort just to keep the weariness from draining all the Christmas joy from her expression. Her back and legs begged her to sit down, as they often did after she had been on her feet and tense with people pressure.

Just two more hours, Shelby reminded herself as she concluded her words of thanks. *The party will be over. Everyone will be gone. I can soak in the spa till midnight and sleep till noon if I want. Then the Lord and I will get in that new Lincoln and spend Christmas Day touring central Texas and conferencing on where we go from here.* The thought suddenly energized her and brought a full, genuine smile to her lips as she said her final thank you.

As the party wound down, Shelby dutifully visited with several clusters of guests, adding snatches of small talk. The caterers quickly and quietly cleaned up and left.

Stan Welbourn caught Shelby's eye, so she excused herself to join him in the dining room.

"We have a small problem, Shelby, and I hope I haven't spoken out of turn." Stan's overemphasis of the word "small" aroused Shelby's suspicion that it might not be as small as Stan hoped.

"Earlier this evening I asked Jeremy if he would mind driving your de Ville back to Dallas tonight so we could deliver it to the Honeycutts on Tuesday. He said he's just going back to his condo anyway and he'd be happy to do it. But—" Stan lowered his voice to a near whisper tinged with embarrassment "—I'm afraid he's been to the wassail bowl once too often, and I don't think he should drive tonight. So I gave him the excuse about it being so late and him having to drive all that way in the dark. Then I suggested that you might allow him to spend the night in one of the cottages and drive home in the morning." Stan's eyebrows lifted as if to add, "Is that okay with you?"

Shelby looked across the living room and into the den where Jeremy Cannon, now smartly clothed in slacks, a long-sleeved dress shirt, and a loose-fitting, bulky-knit pullover sweater, was sprawled on the sofa talking animatedly with two of Adrian's former studio executives, now working elsewhere, who had shown up for the party. He wasn't drunk, she surmised, but he was clearly too happy to drive.

Shelby felt like strangling Stan. *Yes, you did speak out of turn*, she remonstrated him silently, still staring at Jeremy and drawing a long, slow breath. *Jeremy is a wonderful friend, but I want him out of here. I want everyone out of here. How dare you delay my retreat into solitude by inviting someone to stay in my cottage!*

The flash of irritation caught Shelby off guard and reminded her how tired she was. But by the time she turned back to Stan she had her words under control. "*If* you take Jeremy out to the cottage and get him settled in before you fly home, and *if* he leaves first thing in the morning, then it's okay."

Stan caught the subtle sharpness in his employer's reply. "I'm sorry for the inconvenience, Shelby. If you like, I'll just take him on the plane with us and drive him home myself."

"No, I said it's okay as long as I don't have to talk to him before he leaves. Put him in the Mesquite unit."

Am I being heartless, too selfish? Shelby interrogated herself as Stan left to hustle Jeremy out to one of three Spanish-style cottages across the back lawn. Adrian had built them to accommodate visiting dignitaries, mainly from the film industry. *After all, it's not like Jeremy is a skid row bum in need of a flophouse. He's a friend, like a brother. Despite his faults he's been good to me and loyal to the ministry, especially in the last nine months. He doesn't need us anymore for his livelihood, yet he continues to be one of our strongest, most visible endorsing personalities. I hope I'm not hurting his feelings by acting so detached.*

She watched Jeremy stand, say good-bye to the film people, and follow Stan toward the sliding glass door. Then he looked back across the room and, seeing her standing in the dining room, gave a boyish wave, mouthed the words "Thank you, Shelby," and stepped outside.

It was past 10:30 P.M. before the vans pulled away from the house and headed down the driveway toward the road. Shelby, bundled in a leather shepherd's coat, waved good-bye to a few faces peering out the windows, then hurried back toward the house. The absence of cloud cover would push the temperature near freezing tonight.

She glanced toward the cottages as she pulled the slider closed and locked it. The lights were off in Jeremy's cottage, and the de Ville was parked in the driveway outside the garage which now housed the new white Lincoln. Shelby had asked Steve Cashion to wash the Caddy and remove her possessions in hopes that someone would be able to drive it to Dallas after the party. Thanks to Stan and Jeremy, the de Ville would be gone when she awoke.

Shelby hung her coat in the closet, pulled the drapes in the den, activated the security system, and turned out the lights one by one on her winding path through the house to her suite. She was dead tired, thoroughly grateful that Beverly had insisted on caterers who served *and* cleaned up. She was out of her clothes and sliding into the steaming indoor spa adjacent to her bedroom in five minutes.

Shelby turned the water jets on low and positioned herself so one of them aimed squarely at her lower back. She laid her head back on a rubber pad and welcomed the rising steam with several deep, cleansing breaths.

She couldn't remember the last time she had been in the house alone at night. Elena's quarters seemed a mile away on the other side of the kitchen, but she was still under Shelby's roof—when she was here, which she had been all year until Shelby sent her home to Mexico for Christmas. And Theresa's apartment was detached from the main house, but only by a few steps and easily accessible by a covered walkway. Theresa should be touching down in Baton Rouge shortly, Shelby thought.

The Cashions lived in the renovated old house down by the barn. They would be in Chattanooga in a couple of hours. The ranch hands didn't usually stay on the property. Julio and Edgar would be coming out to the ranch for a few hours a day to tend the stock while the staff was away.

Suddenly Shelby realized—and she had never thought about it this way till now—how alone she was. *I'm the only living soul within a four-mile radius.* Then she remembered—*except for Jeremy Cannon sleeping off too many cups of wassail in Mesquite Cottage.* Despite her previous objections to lodging him, Shelby felt almost relieved that someone was nearby in case of an emergency, especially a trusted friend like Jeremy Cannon.

After a luxurious soak and water massage, Shelby toweled off and slipped into her floor-length, wraparound terry robe. She was just beginning to slather her face with cleansing cream when an electronic tone in the bedroom startled her. She dreaded after-hours calls. The sound still triggered a flood of negative emotions, especially after dark. She quickly dried her hands while breathing a prayer she'd prayed countless nights since March: "No more tragedies, Lord, please!"

When she reached the phone she saw that the call was on the in-house line—from Mesquite Cottage.

"Yes? Jeremy?"

"I hope I didn't wake you, Shelby."

"No, I'm still up. Jeremy, are you all right?"

"I couldn't sleep. I appreciate your hospitality, but I've decided to drive back to Dallas tonight."

"Do you feel well enough to drive tonight?" She avoided specific reference to Jeremy's drinking.

"I think Stan overreacted a bit about my . . . condition," he said. "I'm fine, really. But I could use some coffee before I go. Do you mind if I come in and fix a cup? I know where everything is. You don't have to bother."

But it is *a bother*, she thought, feeling a little ashamed for thinking it. "Sure, Jeremy," she acquiesced, reminding herself that he was a friend. "Give me a couple of minutes and I'll meet you at the slider."

Shelby wiped the cream from her face and wrapped the robe tightly around her. Jeremy was already at the glass door fully dressed when she deactivated the alarm and pulled back the drapes. "Your call really gave me a start," she said as she led him into the kitchen and pulled out the coffeemaker.

"Sorry," he said sheepishly. "I didn't feel right about driving away without saying anything."

Ignoring Jeremy's insistence to do it himself, Shelby loaded the brewer while he sat at the table in the nook. Jeremy was male-model immaculate as always, and she felt a little self-conscious about her appearance and kept tugging her robe around her and fluffing her limp hairdo.

When she placed his coffee before him, Jeremy said, "Thanks, but aren't you going to have a cup with me?"

Shelby was dead on her feet. But she still felt a little embarrassed about her selfishness for earlier banishing Jeremy to the cottage. It was not the way to treat a good friend on Christmas Eve. She at least owed him a few minutes of friendly conversation before he left. And there was something comfortable and inviting about a chat in the nook over steaming mugs. Had she paused to analyze that feeling, she would have remembered that late nights in the kitchen over tea was one of the few times when Adrian wasn't too busy to sit and talk with her, just to be with her. "Sure, I'll fix myself a cup of herb tea," Shelby agreed.

Jeremy was a great conversationalist. Unlike Adrian and many other men Shelby knew who needed to be constantly nagged to communicate, Jeremy seemed to have a gift for pleasant, evocative discussion. They sat in the nook sipping from their steaming mugs and talking about the holiday. Jeremy drew out of Shelby story after story about her childhood Christmases in Waco. His dark eyes seemed to absorb — and his warm smile approve — her every word. Time and her need for rest suddenly seemed unimportant to Shelby.

Jeremy was a pleasantly sanguine, tactile type — a natural talker, hugger, and toucher. Shelby knew that his propensity for touch and closeness, pushed over the line at times by his carnal nature, had landed him in trouble, even since his conversion. He had always been thoroughly proper toward her, but Shelby was acutely aware, as they sipped and chatted, of the disarming charm that had weakened the resolve of many young ladies in Jeremy's past. His attentiveness and gentle laugh warmed her. The occasional reassuring touch of his hand on hers energized her and subtly aroused her.

When Jeremy's mug was empty, Shelby quickly refilled it before he could think of leaving. This was what she hungered for. Someone to talk with who was sincerely interested in her, not just her ministry or her success. Someone to be with her and accept her just as she was — even in her bathrobe with no makeup and her hair coming undone. She found herself enchanted by Jeremy's allure, playing to his next smile, anticipating another touch on her hand.

Amber warning lights flashed steadily somewhere in Shelby's brain. *You are physically worn out. Your defenses are down. The pressures of the last months have sapped your inner strength. You are allowing yourself to be beguiled by a loving, desirable man. Your demanding need for intimacy is usurping control over your judgment. You are vulnerable.* But every entrancing moment across the table from Jeremy slipped another dimming filter over the insistent lights and trivialized their warning.

Jeremy glanced at his watch. "Wow, it's almost Christmas! Can you believe we've been talking for almost an hour? I'd better be getting out of here." He downed the last of his coffee and stood with a stretch.

The thought of Jeremy leaving suddenly pierced Shelby with a desperate sense of loneliness. "But I haven't heard about your childhood Christmases yet," she chided playfully. She felt herself blush slightly, realizing she was acting like a high school girl looking for ways to avoid saying good-night at the end of an enjoyable date.

In her school days, it wasn't as important *who* she was with but that she was with *someone* — someone who wanted to be with her. But tonight, the fact that the someone in her nook was Jeremy Cannon, an attractive, available man and a warm friend, deepened her distress at being left alone. She flashed on nights years ago when evenings of long talk and friendship with Adrian in the nook culminated in their bedroom with exhilarating lovemaking. Her desire to be enveloped in that warmth again was demandingly urgent.

Shelby was breathlessly aware that the dull amber lights in her mind were rapidly turning red. She ignored them. She had been cautious all her life, proper, perhaps even prudish at times. And what had it gained her? A marriage of diminishing intimacy and now, in her widowhood, an unquenchable ache for someone.

Jeremy quickly rinsed his mug, and Shelby followed him to the sliding glass door in the den, terrified of her feelings but desperate for one more understanding word, another loving touch. *Don't leave me, Jeremy,* she cried inside.

Jeremy turned toward her. "Thanks for the coffee, Shelby." As he said it he wrapped her in a gentle, brotherly embrace as he had done often during their friendship. "You're a wonderful friend. I don't know what I'd do without you. Merry Christmas."

Shelby wrapped her arms tightly around his waist, pressing her body closely to his, and nestling her head under his chin. She could hardly control her excited breathing. *Am I attractive to you at all, Jeremy?* she thought frantically. *Can you think of me as more than a sister or friend? I need more than a friend tonight.*

They held the embrace for several seconds. Shelby sensed the reassuring strength in Jeremy's arms and drank in the masculine fragrance in his sweater. His closeness intensified the searing feelings within her. When he made a move to release her, she tightened her grip and pressed herself closer. Without saying a word, she slipped her hands inside his sweater and caressed his lower back sensually. *Come on,* Jeremy, she pleaded silently. *Can't you recognize the signals of a lonely woman?*

Jeremy responded. His arms tightened around her, and he drew a deep breath of startled, pleased surprise. The awareness of Jeremy's sudden arousal intensified her longing for the intimacy she was beginning to taste. *He knows what I want now, and he wants it too.*

Jeremy kissed her lightly near the top of her head, then behind her ear, then on her neck above the collar of her robe. The electric shock that coursed through Shelby at the touch of Jeremy's lips on her bare skin made her gasp and shudder. Her brain immediately blared the pre-programmed, red-light response into her consciousness: *wrong, stop, break away, run.* Everything she had ever learned and believed and taught and counseled about purity screamed at her *No, No, No!* But like a runaway train, her ravenous desire hurtled her past the red lights and through the flimsy barricades. *We're alone. No one will know. I want this!* something cried within her.

Shelby moved her trembling hands to Jeremy's head and pulled his mouth toward hers. "I'm so lonely, Jeremy," she whispered. "Please love me and stay with me tonight." Then she kissed him deeply.

Jeremy returned her passion at first, smothering her mouth and neck for several moments with forceful kisses. Then he pulled away. "No, this isn't right!" he panted, almost whimpering. "Shelby, our friendship . . . this is wrong . . . I can't do this to you!"

He stepped away from her, an expression of disillusionment and pain clouding his face. He looked around as if searching for the right words. "I'm so . . .sorry. I shouldn't have stayed. But I never thought you would . . ." His voice trailed off to a sickly moan, his head shaking in disbelief. Then he quickly pushed open the slider and ran toward the de Ville.

An icy wind swept through the open door and snapped Shelby out of her stunned silence. Her fleshly fantasy evaporated before her eyes, and the horrifying reality of what she had done—of what she was—ripped through her like a shotgun blast at point-blank range. The same insistent voice that had encouraged her seductive thoughts and actions suddenly taunted her acidly: *How can you call yourself a Christian or a minister of the gospel? You're nothing but a slut, a whore. You've not only ruined your life and your ministry, you've destroyed that young Christian man.*

The de Ville started up, revved high, and squealed down the driveway toward the road. Shelby dropped to her knees and buried her face in her hands trying to smother a wrenching sob. "O dear God!" she wailed repeatedly. An avalanche of shame engulfed her. Tears and mucous flowed through her fingers and dripped to the floor. She could hardly breathe.

Behind her, the huge clock in the hall chimed midnight. It was Christmas. Shelby tried, stumbling and crawling, to reach the bathroom before she vomited. She didn't make it.

NOVEMBER 1999						
S	M	T	W	T	F	S
	1	2	3	4	5	6
7	8	9	10	11	12	13
14	15	16	17	18	19	20
21	22	23	24	25	26	27
28	29	30				

1999 DECEMBER 1999

S	M	T	W	T	F	S
			1	2	3	4
5	6	7	8	9	10	11
12	13	14	15	16	17	18
19	20	21	22	23	24	25
26	27	28	29	30	31	

JANUARY 2000						
S	M	T	W	T	F	S
						1
2	3	4	5	6	7	8
9	10	11	12	13	14	15
16	17	18	19	20	21	22
23	24	25	26	27	28	29
30	31					

6 Days
Till
Millennium's
Eve

Ten

Simon Holloway loved the early morning, waking daily at 4:30 without an alarm. This was his hour to bear his burden for the godless nation and his concerns for Jubilee Fellowship on his broad shoulders in prayer. His discipline was unflagging, as if the success of his church and the purity of the nation hinged on the hour he spent every morning on his knees in fervent supplication.

The last Christmas morning of the twentieth century was no exception. Simon slipped quietly from bed at his regular time, pulled on a velour warm-up suit and leather slippers in the darkness, and padded to his study next to the bedroom. Grace Ellen was used to her husband's early schedule and slept on undisturbed.

Simon closed the study door and switched on a small table lamp next to the brocade couch which faced his desk. The dark wood, drapes, and wall fabrics seemed to absorb the lamplight, keeping the study in dusky shadows except for a sphere of soft light around the lamp. Simon knelt beside the couch at the perimeter of the sphere and opened a notebook before him on the cushion. He began his earnest prayer in a low but audible tone.

Simon spent several minutes thanking God for the birth of His Son, Jesus. His alert, creative mind pictured his study as the stable, the couch as the manger. He was inspired to consider that the holy event could have happened at this very hour of the morning twenty centuries ago in Bethlehem. He imagined himself one of the privileged shepherds peeking in on the miracle of the ages while the world slept on unaware.

Simon's gift of language did not fail him in his hour of prayer. Simon Holloway prayed as he spoke—in rich prose, always original, always erudite. Sentence after sentence of gratitude and adoration rolled from his soul like waves to the shore. Occasionally he paused to write down in the notebook an idea or mental picture he might use later during the Christmas service in the Tabernacle.

He prayed for Grace Ellen and their two sons, Mark, almost twenty-one, and Timothy, eighteen, as he did every morning. Simon and Grace Ellen were thrilled that their sons were home for Christmas, and that they would all travel to Los Angeles Sunday afternoon for a brief family vacation before sitting together on the platform at Unity 2000.

Simon thought of Mark and Tim sleeping only steps away in their bedrooms. How many Christmas mornings had they interrupted his hour of prayer by bursting into the study with jubilant cries, "Daddy, Santa Claus came!" Moved by the pleasant memories, Simon surrounded his two grown sons with petitions for safety and guidance.

A junior at Jubilee Bible College in Georgia, Mark had planned since high school to finish college and join his father and mother in the ministry. The more pragmatic and less scholarly Tim was just out of high school and uncertain of his life's direction. Contrary to his parents' hopes, Tim did not matriculate at JBC or any other college that fall. "I'm not going to school until I know what I'm going to school *for*," he decreed flatly. Although several positions in the Village were available to him, Tim had opted for a job as an attraction operator at Epcot Center. He hoped to gain a new perspective on his parents' endeavors and his own future from the vantage point of the secular workplace.

Simon prayed for his top-level staff by name and other facets of Jubilee Fellowship by department. He spent more time praying for the research department than the others. The eighteen full-time employees in research traveled the country continuously reconnoitering prospective targets for Holloway's Crusaders and Warriors: principally, centers for genetic engineering (genetic *manipulation*, he preferred to call it). Simon blessed his research staff with keen minds and fearless hearts to identify the enemy and propose effective strategies for ridding the country of these ungodly practices.

He prayed earnestly for the ongoing Festival of the Nativity, then turned his attention to Unity 2000. As with the other three national Christian figures involved, Simon would have one hour at the pulpit in the Los Angeles Coliseum on Millennium's Eve. Their assignment was to challenge over 100,000 Christians gathered in Los Angeles and another 20 million viewing by satellite to come together and evangelize the world before Christ's return. Before his death, Adrian Hornecker had insisted that the "show of force"—the four leaders standing shoulder to shoulder on the Coliseum platform—would serve as a compelling statement of Christian unity to the world.

But to Simon Holloway, the true rallying cry for Unity 2000 was to purge the country of its unrighteous practices. Like watchmen asleep on the city walls, previous generations of Christians had allowed these enemies to infiltrate unchecked. Simon repeated his daily petition that God would send him 1 million new Warriors and Crusaders as a result of his presentation to the Christian world on Millennium's Eve.

He prayed for boldness for Dr. Francine McGowan, the noted Christian microbiologist, and Dr. Rudyard Motabwa, theology professor at Jubilee Bible College, who would share the hour with Simon at the microphone. Together they would cite the evils of society and dare the Christian world to join them in standing for righteousness. And Adrian Hornecker would not be there to stop them.

It was with mixed feelings that Simon prayed for those who would stand with him on the platform on Millennium's Eve: Rev. Shelby Hornecker, Dr. Morgan McClure, and T.D. Dunne. Holloway couldn't argue with the success or acceptance of their ministries, just the direction, or better, *mis*direction.

He gave thanks that Shelby Hornecker's emphasis on the Last Days wasn't nearly as intense and sensational as that of her late husband. Yet her ministry's focus on spiritual blessing, physical health, and material prosperity wasn't moving Christians any closer to ridding the country of the "Lucifer scientists"—biotechnicians who wanted to be "like God" by engineering the next generation's crop of superathletes, math, science, and music prodigies, and beauty queens.

And Chicago's flamboyant T.D. Dunne was obviously having a positive impact on the nation's youth with his music television network, called GoTown—short for God's Town. Dunne, a thirty-seven-year-old African-American with the physique of an all-pro linebacker, had been the most successful of the Christian crossover artists in the '90s. The singer/songwriter/producer had emerged from a background of black gospel to top the secular charts with hit after hit. They had all been songs with wholesome lyrics, an infectious beat, and arrangements that bordered on musical genius.

Once enthroned at the upper level of the pop music world, T.D. Dunne set about to infiltrate the industry with other top-flight Christian artists. His growing stable of solo performers and bands had injected pop music with tunes nobody was ashamed to sing or listen to. Some of these hits had religious themes, but most were simply catchy tunes, creatively videoed, celebrating life and love from a moral perspective. And in the process of storming the industry with great music, Dunne and his disciples had reached numerous secular artists with the Gospel.

T.D. Dunne didn't have a local congregation or auditorium in Chicago. But he had the popular GoTown network which deluged millions of homes with the slickest music videos going. And once or twice an hour GoTown presented an up-close-and-personal feature highlighting the Christian faith and lifestyle of one of pop music's brightest stars—a Dunne disciple, of course.

And Dunne had his concerts—trademarked "A Dunne Deal." GoTown promoted scores of them across the country every weekend, each one starring T.D. himself or one of his polished Christian music acts. The concerts were famous for great music, to-the-point testimonies and teachings, and invitations to come forward, receive a free CD, and talk to a counselor about becoming a Christian. And the merchandise tables in the foyer raked in megadollars nightly hawking CDs, music videos, T-shirts, and posters.

Dunne's organization was like a church without a sanctuary, constitution, or creed. Yet Dunne was adored as a spiritual leader by hundreds of thousands of people who had found a new way of life by listening to his music, attending his concerts, and making his songs their own.

But none of the songs on the GoTown network or label promote the sanctity of life or the rights of the unborn, Holloway thought, as he mumbled a halfhearted prayer for T.D. Dunne's enlightenment. *No*

catchy tunes celebrating the integrity of the human genome or railing on
those who tamper with it.

"He has such a widespread influence on the young people of the land, Lord," Holloway argued. "Oh that he would lend his God-given talents to fuel the torch for purity in this darkened land." Simon stopped to think about his last phrase. Judging it to be inspired and useful in a future public prayer, he quickly scribbled it in his notebook.

As Holloway turned his thoughts toward Dr. Morgan McClure, he grimaced and shifted self-consciously on his knees. He felt about praying for Morgan McClure as a defiant child feels when his parents stand over him with a paddle demanding that he apologize to a playmate for misbehavior. He had to comply or get swatted, but his heart wasn't in it. Simon prayed for Morgan McClure because he had to. God said to hate the sin but love the sinner. But in McClure's case, Simon continually chastised himself for lumping the sinner in with the sin and loathing them both.

Alleged sin. Holloway remonstrated himself for leaping so easily to judgment. But if the news media reports contained only a kernel of truth, Morgan McClure, esteemed spiritual guru of the mind-tripping, affluent Paradise Church of Paradise Valley, Arizona, had plenty to confess every night when his head hit the pillow. The headlines flashed before Simon's eyes unbidden.

TROUBLE IN PARADISE; McCLURE BILKS PARISHIONERS.
IRS, UNDERWORLD WANT McCLURE'S SCALP.
UPTHINK PREACHER HIDING HAREM IN DESERT?

Simon's articulate prayer suddenly stalled. As in recent weeks, his consternation over the enigmatic, wealthy psychotherapist-turned-positive-thinking-television-minister spurred him into a debate with God — one-sided as it was.

How can all these news reports be fiction? Certainly there is something rotten at the core of that man's life and ministry. He's always being accused of thieving and philandering. Why, he hasn't even been ordained. He doesn't preach the Bible; he preaches upthink: believe for the best, hope for the best, strive for the best. What kind of call to faith is that? How can You allow him to go on this way? Look how many millions he is leading astray, people who could be recruited for the real battle. If You will show me a highway into that congregation—

From the next room, the softly creaking floorboards alerted Simon that Grace Ellen had risen. He looked at the burnished brass quartz clock on the wall. It was quarter to six. His prayer time was over, and he felt both chagrined and relieved. His concerns for Unity 2000 had distracted him again, dulling the thrust of his supplication. He breathed an appropriate closing to his prayer in apologetic tones, grateful for God's patience. Then he rose and left his study to wish Grace Ellen a Merry Christmas and prepare for the busy day ahead.

Eleven

Shelby had feared she would not live through the night. She fully expected God to destroy her and everything she owned with a flaming meteorite of judgment hurled from heaven. Each time she awakened from an hour or two of fitful sleep she gasped at the shadows around her, thinking them to be death angels sent to snuff out her life with a touch. Then she would flee to another room in the large house and cry herself to sleep again in a chair, a couch, or on the floor.

During her frightful waking moments, the principle taught by Jesus pummeled her accusingly: "Whoever looks at a woman to lust for her has already committed adultery with her in his heart." Not only had she committed adultery in her heart; she had come within minutes of consummating her desire with Jeremy Cannon. And it hadn't been *her* physical restraint but *his* which kept Shelby from taking him to her bed.

Shelby judged herself worth no more to God than a pile of stones large enough to bury her. She was an adulteress, not in the flesh perhaps, but in the mind, which seemed to her infinitely worse. God would surely not let her eyes see the light of Christmas morning.

Shelby was curled in a ball in a corner of the dining room still draped in her terry robe when morning light aroused her. When she realized that she was still alive and that the grotesque scene haunting her consciousness was a memory instead of a nightmare, another tidal wave of despair crashed over her. *God is through with me,* she told herself. *I'm alive only because God turned His back on me last night. He doesn't care enough about me to judge me. He has walked out of my life and left me to fend for myself, just like Adrian did.*

She could almost see her husband leering at her condemningly from heaven. How Adrian used to harangue against immorality in the church, insisting that adulterers and fornicators be excised from the congregation and given over to Satan for punishment. How she felt his scorn just now.

Shelby Hornecker had never been unfaithful to Adrian. Thanks to her strict religious training as a child and youth, she was a virgin when she met Adrian at Bible college and still a virgin when they married two years later. Unlike some of her women classmates, Shelby had not been scarred by the heresy that sex is evil and that even in Christian marriage it was endured more than enjoyed. Sex is beautiful, she had argued with them, designed by God to be enjoyed within the bounds of marriage. Sex is evil only before marriage or during marriage with another partner.

Shelby had little difficulty living out her convictions while dating Adrian. There were, however, some moments when her firm "Good night, Adrian" probably kept his resolve for purity from melting away in the heat of college-aged male passion. Yes, Shelby had looked forward—with an appropriate amount of anxiety—to their wedding night and physical oneness under God. But the lust of the flesh had never been a serious opponent to her purity. Fantasizing about sex with Adrian or anyone else seemed a pointless waste of mental energy. The beauty of their relationship was that she and Adrian loved each other, were committed to each other, and would spend their lives together serving God.

"That's probably why Jesus addressed His comments about lust to men instead of women," she had often explained to her women friends at college. "Men need sex to enjoy closeness; women need closeness to enjoy sex. When men even think about meeting their needs, it's lust, and they commit mental adultery. But it's not lust or adultery for us to meet our needs by daydreaming about a relationship of closeness and belonging with a man."

Shelby had believed her bold dictum for the first five years of her marriage. Both closeness and sex with Adrian were good in the early years of their ministry in a rapidly growing Arlington pastorate. But when Victory Life Ministries mushroomed to a national enterprise through television, Adrian Hornecker spent more time in the office and less time at home. Shelby encouraged the purchase of their Austin ranch in hopes that the distance from the office and the church would provide them more privacy and time together.

But instead, the three-and-one-half-hour commute became the reason Adrian stayed in Dallas longer, sometimes a week at a time. The lease of their first private jet brought Adrian home faster and more often. But the conveniences of the jet age also allowed him to leave home for Dallas whenever a problem arose—often at a phone call's notice—and stay away longer.

As Adrian became increasingly absorbed in the church, the television ministry, and then films, Shelby watched in silent desperation as their close-knit friendship began to unravel. They both worked in the ministry office three or four days a week, but rarely did they work together. Adrian's burgeoning film ministry and travel schedule took him away from Texas more often, leaving Shelby to manage the office and their ranch. And when he was home, Adrian found diminishing amounts of time to invest in nurturing the closeness Shelby desired. Her hunger for intimacy deepened.

The more creatively Shelby tried to revive her husband's waning attention to friendship and intimacy with sex, the less interest he displayed in her. Although she never said a word to him or anyone, she began to suspect another woman. But Adrian's accounting of his days and nights away from Austin always jibed with the reports she had cunningly obtained from staff members who were with him. *The other woman*, she concluded sourly, *is his ministry. The energy he once poured into our life together is being diverted into his concubine, Victory Life Ministries.*

Shelby surprised herself with another sobering realization one Sunday morning several months before Adrian's death. She was on the platform trying to look attentive as her husband, via videotape, unveiled another end-times prophetic mystery for his rapt congregation. Shelby's eyes fell on one of the elders in their congregation, a handsome and distinguished oil company executive, sitting in the third row with his wife of twenty-seven years. The happiness of their marriage was legend in the congregation. As a young husband, he had committed never to spend more than two nights a month away from home on business. And when his international responsibilities grew and trips required him to be gone longer, he took his wife with him.

For several minutes that morning Shelby ruminated about how she might enjoy being that elder's wife. She saw herself traveling with him, visiting the world's most exotic ports, staying in five-star hotels. And every evening included an intimate, gourmet dinner and the kind of conversation enjoyed by the most committed friends. And every night ended with . . .

When Shelby had realized what she was thinking, and where she was thinking it, she was so appalled at herself that she had difficulty maintaining her placid expression on the platform. She had not pictured herself going to bed with the man, and the alarm in her head had sounded before her mind had formed the images. *But it's lust just the same*, she scolded herself brusquely.

Lust isn't just a man's problem, she admitted to herself with embarrassment after that Sunday morning. *Women can lust too, maybe not as much for sex as for intimacy. But what's the difference? An unhealthy desire to be close to a man other than your husband is just as bad as going to bed with him, especially when emotional intimacy so naturally precipitates physical intimacy.*

Shelby had copiously confessed her wandering thoughts to God that day, but neither her emptiness nor the pesky lustful thoughts it provoked left her completely. She knew many men who appeared to be more caring and sensitive toward their wives than Adrian. She tried to resist the temptations to fantasize about being with them. It seemed a constant battle.

After Adrian was gone, Shelby had hoped the new responsibilities thrust upon her would divert her attention from her aching need, just as Adrian had been distracted from her by his work. But Shelby's increased involvement at Victory Life only intensified her need to share her work, her triumphs, her stumblings, her doubts, and her dark fears with someone. Had she realized how insidiously demanding her need had grown, she never would have allowed Jeremy in the house for coffee on Christmas Eve.

Shelby lay on the dining room floor for several minutes wishing she was dead. The fiery dart of suicide entered her mind, but she quickly brushed it away. She wasn't about to put herself in the presence of the two individuals who had abandoned her—God and Adrian Hornecker.

An alternate plan dashed into Shelby's brain. It didn't include driving to Waco to see her parents, attending Unity 2000 in Los Angeles, or ever returning to Victory Life Center. She could never face them again, any of them—her parents, her staff, her congregation, and certainly not Jeremy Cannon. Her brutal conscience would never let her live at peace with them again. The solution was simple, she calculated, rising stiffly from the carpet. She would disappear.

Shelby returned to the spa—as she had after Jeremy left—not to soak luxuriantly but to wash. She had never felt dirtier in her life. But no matter how thoroughly she lathered herself, scrubbed, and rinsed, the grimy film coating on her soul wouldn't go away. She brushed her teeth and rinsed her mouth repeatedly, berating herself without mercy between mouthfuls of toothpaste and water for seeking Jeremy's lips so lustfully. A foul taste remained in her mouth.

She pulled on faded blue jeans, an old, white Texas Longhorn sweatshirt, socks, and white tennies. She found a nylon sport bag in the back of Adrian's closet and threw into it a pair of cords, a heavy shirt, a wool pullover, and a flannel nightgown.

Unwilling to look at herself in the mirror for long, Shelby quickly ran a brush through her damp hair and disregarded the blush, lipstick, and eye makeup on the counter. She started to reach for a small cosmetic case, then canceled the idea with a disdainful sigh and tossed only her hair brush, toothbrush, and a tube of Crest into the sport bag with her clothes.

Shelby's next stop was the library to get some cash. Adrian hadn't trusted banks or most other institutions that clamored to care for his money. He preferred to keep the Hornecker wealth in appreciatory commodities such as acreage, jewelry, paintings, and objets d'art. Even though he had also maintained a few liquid investments as a supply of ready funds, he always kept several thousand dollars in cash in a place he considered more secure than any bank: a cement safe hidden under the floor in his library.

When Shelby had checked the safe after Adrian's death, she discovered that he had cleaned it out before leaving for Tel Aviv. The missing money—nearly $9,000—wasn't the problem. Adrian's life insurance benefits plus the substantial investments he had left her assured her of a comfortable life whether the ministry flourished or waned. But, the fact that Adrian had taken the money without telling her cast another puzzling pall over his tragic death. Why had he taken so much cash to Israel? she had wondered. All his filming expenses were covered by the ministry. If he spent it on a gift for her, which she thought unlikely for such a large sum, it probably plunged to the bottom of the Mediterranean with the plane. Shelby had replenished the cash in the safe right after the funeral.

By pressing buttons hidden above the lintel of the door, Shelby disengaged two electronic alarms for the safe. A third button sprung a small door in the oak floor near the corner of the library, revealing a cement-encased safe anchored to the house's foundation. She worked the combination deftly and opened the platinum steel door. Three of the four lift-out drawers contained a variety of documents relating to her possessions. Shelby ignored them and pulled out the fourth. Eight $1,000 bundles of $20s were neatly stacked inside. She took them all, closed the safe, and reset the alarm on her way out of the room.

With pulse-quickening resolve Shelby stuffed the bundles of bills under her clothes in the sport bag. She rummaged through her purse for her small, burnished bronze phone and placed it on the counter. These days, personal phones were as compact as a cigarette case and as affordable as a newspaper subscription. Leaving home without a phone in your pocket or purse was as unthinkable as driving without a license. But Shelby dumped hers without a qualm. *There's no one I want to talk to, and no one who wants to talk to me*, she thought, giving in to self-pity.

She grabbed her leather coat and walked into the garage, pressing the opener to lift the door. The sight of the gleaming white Lincoln pierced her heart with suffocating remorse, provoking another outburst of tears. She was completely unworthy of this expensive symbol of the congregation's love and devotion. She had failed them as well as everyone else. She could never accept their gift now.

She threw the keys to the Lincoln on the garage floor and closed the door with a push of the button. She stepped from the garage through the back door into the clear, cold Christmas morning, striding purposefully down the gravel road to the barn. The ranch pickup—a mud-splattered old three-quarter-ton Silverado with four-wheel drive—sat under the carport next to the barn where Steve Cashion parked it. As always, it was unlocked and the keys were stuffed into the pocket in the door. Shelby tossed her bag and coat across the front seat of the cab and stepped in. The truck started on the first try.

It took Shelby ten minutes at 50 MPH on country roads to reach Austin's city limits and another ten minutes through town to the interstate. The sign approaching the onramps to I-35 simply contained an arrow pointing north and the words WACO and DALLAS, and an arrow pointing south next to the words SAN ANTONIO. She turned right and entered the interstate southbound.

Shelby Hornecker was running away for the first time in her life. She wasn't sure San Antonio was far enough, but if she decided it wasn't, she could be in Mexico before nightfall.

Twelve

Reagan Cole allowed himself several more minutes than usual under the pulsating jets of his hot shower. After all, it was Christmas. He considered the luxurious water massage a gift to himself. And with his next day off—his first in three weeks—still a week away, the sergeant felt he deserved the extra pampering. The overtime pay would easily cover the splurge on water and energy. So he leaned his forehead against the blue and white tile and welcomed the pounding streams of water aimed at his upper back.

Cole was also up earlier than normal for a swing-shift workday—9 A.M. instead of his customary 10 A.M. reveille. He owed his mother an unhurried Christmas call before work—ten minutes instead of his usual five. And then there was the matter of Mary Elizabeth Scibelli. Cole wrinkled his face in embarrassment at the memory of his ugly first encounter with the feisty, beautiful visitor from Whidbey Island.

He was surprised at how often he had thought of her in the last twenty-four hours. Her confrontation with the young hoods had been stupid—but gutsy. He had railed on her—more caustically than necessary, he had admitted to himself—for her brazen defiance of the Latin Barons. But there was something attractive about a woman who stood up to trouble instead of squealing in fear and burying her head. "Your fortitude is admirable, but your methods could be a little more diplomatic," he wished he had said to her instead of pummeling her with venomous criticism.

And her willingness to ride along with him on the chase was a sign of her reckless abandon, which Cole also found engaging in a woman. *Why didn't I tell her that?* he thought, drumming his fingers on his temple as if punishing his brain for misbehavior. *Why did I have to make an ass of myself by dinging her for what she did wrong instead of complimenting her grit?*

At least the apology went better than I hoped, Cole thought. *And her willingness to meet me at Olvera Street is nothing short of a miracle under the circumstances. Just another indication of her resilience, unpredictability, and spunk,* Cole mused as he reached behind him and tweaked the chrome handle a couple more millimeters toward HOT. *Spirited, that's what she is,* he thought, smiling. *And I like spirited women.*

Cole sat at the kitchen bar in a pair of baggy shorts and a T-shirt slurping his third mug of coffee as he dialed his mother in Lake Tahoe. The kitchen and living room of his modest second-story Santa Monica condo overlooked the promenade and shoreline across Ocean Avenue. The sky was overcast, and the thermometer outside the window had been stuck at 45 since Cole got up. Occasionally a jogger or skater on the promenade glided past the window, and there were a few bundled-up beachcombers trudging across the sand this morning.

The condo was devoid of Christmas decorations except for some greeting cards hastily propped up on the bookcase and parson's tables. Normally Cole, whose taste in furnishings and eye for color had impressed many of his woman friends, shunned seasonal decorations as mere folderol. But last year there had been an ornamented scotch pine, twinkling lights, and other splashes of red, green, and white around the home. His live-in had insisted, and Cole had willingly complied.

But in the late summer Cole's significant other changed her mind about his significance to her and left him, taking her box of Christmas decorations with her. *Just as well*, Cole had decided as the holiday season approached. *The Millennium's Eve splash is all but wiping out Christmas for me anyway. So no decorations, no parties, and only obligatory gifts to family members.* Even Cole's CD selection for Christmas morning—a Telemann trumpet concerto—bore no resemblance to the holiday being celebrated outside his walls.

Cole's ten-minute call to Lake Tahoe lagged into forty minutes. His mother kept him on the line while she conference-called two of his sisters whose families were, like himself, unable to be in Tahoe for the holiday. Cole tried several times to excuse himself from the conversation in order to get dressed to leave. But each attempt to hang up was foiled by the innocent voice of another niece or nephew coming on the line to wish Uncle Reagan a merry Christmas and thank him, under strict prompting, for the Christmas gifts he'd sent.

So Cole tucked the phone between his ear and shoulder and tried to sound cordial as he rummaged through the clean laundry for an appropriate shirt for his lunch date, pressed it, and got dressed. Finally, having spoken to everyone in the family at least once, Cole said his good-byes.

He was just ready to step into his nylon flight suit when the phone beeped again.

"Merry Christmas, 14." The instantly familiar, deeply resonant voice on the line brought a genuine smile to Cole's face.

"Hey, same back at you, 22," Cole answered. He set his flight suit aside and flopped into an armchair, suddenly unconcerned about the time.

"You keep forgetting, man," the deep voice was chuckling. "I've been number 23 since I moved to Portland. Drexler was number 22 when I got here, and when he retired so did his number. I haven't been 22 since UCLA days. That's ancient history, buddy. You've got to quit living in the past."

Cole laughed aloud, relishing the reminder of playing basketball and rooming with his UCLA teammate and longtime friend, Curtis Spooner. Curtis had accomplished what Cole and most other collegiate ballplayers only dream about. An All-American shooting guard in his junior and senior seasons at UCLA, Curtis was drafted in the third round by the Portland Trail Blazers. The same day Cole entered the academy, Curtis started training camp in Portland.

For the first few years of his NBA career, Curtis labored in the shadows as a backup to superstar Clyde Drexler. When the All-Star Blazer guard retired, Curtis moved into the starting five for two years. Then an all-everything rookie from North Carolina beat him out of a job and Curtis returned to a backup role.

"Where are you, Spoon, Portland?"

"Right. The Spooner estate in luxurious Lake Oswego," Curtis joked. "Natty's folks came up for Christmas since I have a couple of days off."

"Great game against Houston the other night, man," Cole said.

"Not bad, I guess. Played some minutes, canned a few good shots. You watch it?"

"I taped it off the satellite and watched it the next day. I'm working swing these days, remember? And with this big religious deal coming up in L.A., there's no rest for the wicked."

"Does that mean you won't be in the Arena when we play the Clippers Wednesday night?"

"Yeah, Spoon, I'm afraid that's what it means." Cole hated missing Curtis' games when the Blazers were in L.A. to play the Clippers or the Lakers. "But I should be cruising the Sports Arena area that night, so I'll plan on dropping in during the game—on any kind of semiofficial business I can drum up."

"What about after the game?" Curtis asked.

"By 11 or 11:30, I should be free. Do you want to grab a beer?"

"Yeah, great, Reag, but let me press my luck. How are you fixed for roommates these days?"

"If you need a place to crash, Spoon, you've got it. Anytime, you know that. I figured you would be heading back to Portland right away."

"The team flies home after the game, but we don't play again until Sunday night. I'd like to stay at your place for a couple of days, but I don't want to interfere with anything . . . or anyone."

Cole finally caught his drift. "She's been gone for about four months, man. I thought I told you."

"Yeah, I knew about that one," Curtis laughed. "But I kind of expected my man to have something else going by now."

The vision of a very tall, shapely, dark-haired woman journalist suddenly filled Cole's imagination. He glanced at his watch and realized he was cutting it close for meeting his date on time. "No, not much going on right now, Spoon," Cole said, hoping he was wrong. "You can stay as long as you want to. What's the occasion?"

"That Unity thing at the Coliseum. Brace yourself, man. I'll be on the platform standing up for T.D. Dunne. I may even say something in front of all those people."

Cole let out a groan of disbelief. "You're jiving me, Spoon. I'm your old roomy, remember? I know you. You're about as far from being a religious person as I am from playing in the NBA finals."

"I'm not as far as I used to be, Reag," Curtis said. Cole detected a note of sobriety in his friend's rich, baritone voice. "Dunne's an okay guy. I've been watching GoTown on the cable. I've hit a few of his 'Deals,' even talked to him a couple of times. There's something about that God music, Reag. I'm not sure what it is, but it's already doing some good for me and Natty and the kids. He asked me to stand up for him at the Coliseum. It's kind of like being in a commercial for his . . . ministry . . . I guess that's the word. So I said I would."

Cole was intrigued by a side of his friend he'd never seen before. He wanted to hear more. But the numerals on his watch urged him to end the conversation and hit the road for downtown L.A. in a hurry.

"I've got to get going, Spoon. When do you arrive in town?" Cole grabbed his flight suit and stepped into it as he talked.

"We play in Salt Lake tomorrow night and Phoenix Monday night. Then we fly over from Phoenix after the game. I'll stay with the team at the Hilton until after we play the Clippers."

"Maybe I can swing by the Hilton Monday night after work and we can have a beer."

"Hey, you're on."

"And staying at my place is no problem. I still have a king-sized bed in the spare room. Will Natty be down for your big Coliseum appearance?"

"No, I don't feel real good about her being in L.A. with the crowds and all. Besides, she can watch my religious debut on the cable. The kids love seeing their dad on our home theater screen."

"Well, it'll be great to have you around for a couple of days," Cole added, juggling the phone as he zipped up his suit.

"Hey, they don't have any problem with blacks in your complex, do they, 14?" Curtis was only half serious, as evidenced by his quiet laugh.

Cole laughed too. "No, Spoon, Santa Monica is cool with blacks — especially those with a 38-inch vertical leap who can drop three-pointers like you can."

Cole hoped his powerful Kawasaki and the light traffic on the Santa Monica Freeway would help him shrink a thirty-minute drive into twenty. But traffic wasn't so light. He knew he was pushing the envelope of legality even for a law enforcement officer as he roared between cars in a crouched position on his bike. He only saw one CHP cruiser on the Santa Monica and a pair of motorcycle officers on the Harbor, but they were both headed in the opposite direction.

The closer Cole got to the civic center, the more the coastal soup receded behind him. The emerging sun warmed his face behind the shaded visor, but the windchill of a 50-degree morning in L.A. stung him on the neck above the collar of his flight suit.

He exited the Harbor Freeway at Sixth and sped east on the practically deserted downtown street, making most of the lights with the exception of Hill Street. And he would have cheated on that one except for the small, scruffy-looking man in the crosswalk in front of him heading toward Pershing Square. He was wearing a dirty baseball cap and carrying a dinged-up plastic picnic chest.

It was Cole's nature and training to notice the oddballs on his inner-city turf, even when he wasn't on duty. The man looked like a thousand others who littered the downtown streets. But the picnic chest registered in his analytical brain as unique—and slightly familiar. Cole couldn't remember seeing the picnic-chest-toting tramp around Pershing Square before, but he was sure he had seen him somewhere on his beat. Figueroa Street came to mind. The sergeant subconsciously entered a couple of quick notes in his massive mental file headed, "L.A.'s Weird and Wacky."

Cole raced to Main Street and turned north, traveling the half mile to Olvera Street in less than a minute. Olvera Street is a quaint tourist trap near the heart of historic El Pueblo de la Reina de los Angeles. The pueblo was founded in 1781 as the first Spanish civilian settlement in Southern California. Eleven families, including twenty-two adults and twenty-two children, were recruited from the provinces of Sinaloa and Sonora in New Spain, now called Mexico, by an emissary of the governor of California, Felipe de Neve. Escorted by soldiers, they departed Los Alamos, Sonora early in 1781 and arrived in several groups during the summer of that year.

Their task was to provide food for the soldiers of the presidios and to help secure Spain's hold on the region. The settlers included farmers, artisans, and stock raisers necessary for the survival of the settlement. The original forty-four *pobladores* would have staggered at the knowledge that their tiny settlement would grow to a population of just over 9 million by the end of the second millennium. And the contrast in time periods is very obvious. The sleepy little pueblo sits just across the Santa Ana Freeway from L.A.'s sprawling, skyscraping civic center.

Cole slowed his bike crossing the overpass on Main. He rolled to a stop at the curb behind a banged-up, candy-apple-red GM Star Cruiser. He had already spotted the tall, dark-haired woman standing in the tree-lined plaza beside the bronze statue of Felipe de Neve. Olvera Street, behind the plaza, was deserted. But several people on the sidewalk across Main Street, mostly Latinos in family clusters, were streaming into the courtyard of the Old Plaza Church.

Cole dismounted and checked his watch, then berated himself for being a few minutes late. He saw his date staring at him and gave a slight wave, which she acknowledged with a nod and no change of expression. He wondered how long it would take to regain the ground he had lost playing the macho, know-it-all cop on Christmas Eve morning.

He removed his gloves and helmet and quickly smoothed his sandy hair. He unzipped and pulled off his nylon flight suit, unobtrusively transferring his DAB gun to the pocket of his khaki cotton slacks for a moment. He wished he had worn his leather loafers instead of his steel-toed motorcycle boots.

He lifted the Kawasaki's cushion, pulled a tan windbreaker out of the compartment, and stuffed his gloves and flight suit, which he had rolled up, inside. He donned the windbreaker over a dull plum-colored, long-sleeved shirt and slid his gun into an inside jacket pocket. He locked the bike's storage compartment, grabbed his helmet, and walked briskly toward the entrance to the three-foot brick wall surrounding the plaza.

"Thanks for coming," Cole said as he approached her. Beth looked striking in black wool slacks, black turtleneck, and a gray tweed jacket. Her hair was pulled back softly and secured with a silver clasp. She was even more beautiful than Cole had remembered.

"Merry Christmas, sergeant," Beth said with a thin smile. It was the kind of greeting an employer might offer to a subordinate: sincere, friendly, but lacking depth.

"Do you mind if I stash my helmet in your car? I don't have anywhere to hide it on my bike."

"It's okay with me," Beth said, "but I can't guarantee it or the car will be there when we come back." Cole expected a few subtle digs but had already decided, in the name of having a good time, to let them slide.

As they began walking back to the car, Cole said, "By the way, I'd like you to call me Reagan."

"Reagan," Beth repeated evenly, as if considering the origin of Cole's unusual first name.

"I was named after the former president," Cole said somewhat apologetically. "My parents were staunch California Republicans and supporters of Reagan when he was governor. He attended our church— Bel Air Presbyterian—when he was in town."

"Yes, I understand about the name thing," Beth said, sounding interested. "My parents were devout Catholics when I was born. If I had been a boy, they probably would have named me Jesus. As it was, I still got stuck being named after His mother and His aunt."

It took a second for the comment to register with Cole. "Oh, your name . . . Mary Elizabeth. I get it." They both enjoyed a comfortable laugh. Cole felt the tension of their second meeting begin to abate.

"So what do you prefer: Mary Elizabeth, Mary. . . ?"

"It's Beth," she said as she released the keyless door lock with a touch of the remote on her key chain. Cole tossed his helmet onto the floor of the back seat and closed the door. Another touch of the remote relocked the doors.

"Well, Beth, I hope you're not too hungry yet," Cole said as he checked the one-way traffic on Main Street. "I thought you might enjoy attending the Christmas Mass before lunch." He motioned toward the old Spanish-style church across the street. "But we'd better hurry. It's already started."

Beth hesitated and flashed a look of mild surprise. "Mass? But you said you're a Presbyterian, and I haven't been to Mass in years. I'm really not interested in religion—"

"I don't go for religious reasons, and I'm not a religious person," Cole cut in, gently grabbing her by the elbow to direct her across the street. "I go for the music. The mariachi band doing the Mass is better than most of the club bands in L.A."

Beth allowed him to hold her elbow for the first few steps, then coyly strode out of his grasp. Cole smiled away from her view. *Spirit, I love it,* he chuckled to himself.

The long, narrow sanctuary was packed. Cole found two open seats in a straight-back wooden pew near the rear. With a smile and some hand signals he convinced the worshipers to close ranks, leaving enough room on the aisle for the two of them to squeeze in, an inconvenience Cole found enjoyable and to which Beth didn't object.

The mariachis were spectacular. The thundering guitars and piercing brass resounded through the high-arched sanctuary. The powerful male voices saluted the advent with Hispanic songs Cole didn't completely understand but thoroughly enjoyed. He found himself caught up in the festive air of the Mass. There was a paradoxical simplicity and depth to the service of music, prayers, and liturgy. Cole found himself absorbed in the spirit of the celebration, as if Christmas had sneaked up behind him and suddenly surprised him. And he knew that part of the good feeling was because Mary Elizabeth Scibelli—beautiful Beth—was with him.

Hodge sat on his picnic chest catching his breath next to the Pershing Square pond. For the first time in twenty-five days he had occupied the Square alone. It was a cold Christmas Day, and none of the regular soapbox prophets or street people had chanced to visit during Hodge's hour-long Christmas oration. Even the bike cops had stayed away.

Hodge had held forth with gusto in the absence of distracting visitors. His text was Jeremiah 8, likening the backslidden to dung upon the face of the earth, those whose bones are left to rot in the sun because they ignore the Word of the Lord. Hodge's vehement denunciations of backsliders and declarations of bitter judgment echoed from the vacant office buildings ringing the Square. Only in the windows of the elegant old Biltmore Hotel, overlooking the northwest corner of Pershing Square, did a few curious faces appear at the height of Hodge's boisterous diatribe.

As usual, he had concluded his sermon by hurling dark woes at the Four Horsemen of the Apocalypse. His delivery today had been so fiery and animated that his voice became hoarse. Twice he nearly lost his balance on the picnic chest. But he had again successfully fended off another insistent cry in his soul: *Forsake your errant ways! Return to me now!* At the end of the hour he was panting and perspiring like he had run a marathon, and so he had sat down to rest before heading home.

Just as he rose to leave, Hodge saw two young men—an Asian and a Latino—enter Pershing Square from the southeast corner, the route he usually traveled to and from the Metro stop. The men were clean-cut and casually dressed with warm jackets—not cops, not street people. They strode purposefully toward the center of the Square with their eyes on Hodge.

Hodge lifted his picnic chest and headed toward the northeast exit as if he hadn't seen them. A casual glance over his shoulder revealed that the two men were walking faster and coming his way. Hodge slipped his hand into his jacket pocket and continued toward the corner, ears tuned to the footsteps behind him. When the two men were almost upon him, Hodge whirled and drew his knife in one fluid motion.

"Whoa, just a minute, sir," the Asian said as the two men stopped in their tracks. "We don't mean any harm."

Hodge scrutinized their faces, keeping them at bay with the blade. They were college age, and their eyes reflected surprise and a flicker of fear at the sight of the knife, but no malice. "Leave me alone or I'll cut you," Hodge growled hoarsely.

"We didn't mean to alarm you, sir," the Latino said, glancing between Hodge's wary stare and the tip of the blade pointed at him. "We're from King's House, you know, the old Queen of Angels Hospital off the Hollywood Freeway. We're just checking for anyone on the street today who has no place to go for Christmas dinner."

The young man pulled a folded flyer from his pocket and displayed it for Hodge from a respectful distance. "See, free turkey dinner at 4 o'clock today. King's House. We'll provide transportation if you need it. It's all free, sir. Would you like to—"

"Get lost, you punks!" Hodge barked fiercely with an impatient wave of his knife.

The two young men backed away, looking more disappointed at Hodge's refusal of their invitation than afraid of his threat. "I'll leave the flyer in case you want to look it over," the Latino said. "It's a good dinner, and it's free."

"We'll be praying for you, sir," his partner added. "Let us know if we can help you." The men dropped the flyer on a park bench and quickly left the Square by the route they had entered.

Hodge carefully sheathed his knife through his jacket pocket, glancing around to ensure that Officers Scanlon and Ochoa, wherever they might be, had not seen him threaten the young men.

Hodge walked to the park bench and retrieved the flyer. He crumpled it in his palm without reading it, then tossed it away. *Had those two kids known who they were talking to,* he thought with a wry smile, *they would have asked* me *for favors.* Then he hurried out of the Square bolstered with the conviction that his holy mission was right on schedule.

Thirteen

Cole held onto Beth's elbow as they left the church just to keep them together in the throng. This time she didn't pull away. Clouds were rolling in, and the temperature was dropping.

The chatter around them was mostly in Spanish, and laughter was abundant. Black-eyed Latino children gawked unashamedly at the white couple towering over them and their parents. Cole caught Beth coaxing a smile out of some of them with a playful wink or wave. He hoped this truer representation of L.A.'s Hispanic community was draining the poison of Beth's trauma with the Latin Barons from her system.

"Well, what did you think?" Cole asked as they emerged from the courtyard onto Main Street.

"You were right; great music. I haven't been to a Mass I've enjoyed more." She sounded genuinely pleased, and that pleased Cole.

"Do you like Mexican food?" he asked as they crossed Main and approached Olvera Street.

"Yes, very much. But we're not going to find any in here. I walked clear to the end before you arrived and all the restaurants are closed for Christmas."

"Closed to the *public*," Cole corrected her, suppressing a grin of triumph.

Beth's response was playful but on the edge of being sardonic. "What are you going to do, sergeant, break in and cook up a meal yourself?"

"You'll see—and I wish you would call me Reagan."

After a thoughtful pause she acquiesced. "Okay, Reagan."

Olvera Street is comprised of two rows of Spanish-style plaster, brick, and wrought iron stores and restaurants which face each other across a red brick walkway. A third row of small wooden kiosks stretches down the center of the walkway. Normally the stores and kiosks are draped inside and out with merchandise and souvenirs: hand-tooled leather purses, belts, and harachis, silk-screened T-shirts, serapes and sombreros, and jewelry. And by this time of day the restaurants and food stands usually bustled with tourists sampling some of L.A.'s finest Mexican cuisine. But not on Christmas Day. As Cole and Beth strolled down the brick walkway the stores were closed, the kiosks were folded up, and the restaurants were quiet.

Cole steered Beth into a patio which was separated from the walkway by a fence made of old wagon wheels. They walked past a row of empty wooden tables for outdoor dining to double, wood-framed glass doors under a red brick arch. The large, colorfully painted wood sign above the arch read, QUINTEROS. A hand-lettered poster hanging inside the glass door announced, CLOSED FOR CHRISTMAS. FELIZ NAVIDAD.

Cole rapped on the glass with his key while peering inside. Beth stood by, curious. Presently the round, brown face of a short, plump Hispanic woman appeared above the poster. The questioning expression on the woman's face quickly broke into a wide-eyed grin, and her excited exclamation could be easily heard through the locked doors. "Reagan!"

"Mamacita!" Cole returned, imitating the woman's accent.

The woman quickly unlocked the door and threw herself into Cole's arms. "Feliz Navidad, Reagan. We hoped you were coming." Her accent was thick, punctuated with strong rolling r's. Cole had to bend slightly to embrace her around the shoulders.

"I wouldn't miss Christmas dinner with you, Raphaela. Thank you for inviting me again. I hope you don't mind that I brought a friend."

The woman turned to Beth, obviously pleased.

"Raphaela Quintero, I'd like you to meet my friend—a new friend—Beth Scibelli. Beth lives in Seattle, on Whidbey Island actually. She's in L.A. for the holidays. Beth, this is my Mexican mamacita, Raphaela Quintero."

Raphaela grabbed Beth's hand and looked up at her appreciatively, as if in awe of a lovely fruit tree in full bloom. "She is so beautiful, Reagan, and so tall, like you. Welcome, Beth. I'm so happy you could be with our family today."

Nonplussed and a little embarrassed by the sudden attention, Beth could only respond with a broad smile and, "Thank you, Mrs. Quintero."

"Please come in, both of you. Dinner is almost ready. Luis will be so happy to see you, Reagan." Raphaela excitedly shooed them into the restaurant and locked the door. Then she hurried ahead of them through the main dining room, past the bar, and into a large banquet room off the kitchen to announce their arrival. The fragrance of a Mexican feast grew more inviting with every step.

"Raphaela and Luis are the owners," Cole told Beth as they walked. "I started coming in here for dinner during my shift when I was a rookie working Central Division, and they kind of adopted me. On Christmas they invite all their relatives to gather for a big Mexican dinner. The whole family goes to early Mass together, then they spend the morning cooking. It's a meal you'll never forget."

"But Raphaela didn't know I was coming," Beth objected mildly. "I really feel like I'm intruding."

"No way. I've had someone with me every Christmas . . . " Cole paused, wishing he hadn't brought it up. "They welcome my . . . friends . . . as much as they welcome me."

Those were the last words Cole and Beth were able to exchange in private for the next hour. When they entered the banquet room they were engulfed in a noisy, churning sea of happy brown faces and festive chattering and laughing. Cole introduced his guest to as many of the Quinteros as he could get to. And the favorite topic of conversation became Beth's heigh—"¡La señorita está muy alta!" the children exclaimed in innocent wonder when they realized that she was at least half a head taller than their fathers. Beth took it good-naturedly, enjoying the attention. Cole was glad.

Their plates were piled high with homemade tamales wrapped in corn husks, mounds of spicy carnitas and frijoles, and layers of steaming, handmade tortillas. When they had almost reached the bottom of their first heaping platefuls, Raphaela was there to pile them high again with delicious food. And there was hardly a moment when some members of the Quintero family weren't crowded around the table welcoming Beth and swapping stories with Cole about the activities in and around El Pueblo de la Reina de los Angeles.

Cole reluctantly turned down round after round of cold cerveza, reminding his hosts that he was on his way to work. Beth agreed that Mexican food and ice cold beer were made for each other. But she deferred to his predicament and drank Cokes as he did.

Conversation between the two was spotty and light in the noisy room. Cole wedged in a question between interruptions about Beth's visit with her father. She said it was going well enough. Later she asked if he had called his mother and wished her Merry Christmas. He said he had.

After another wave of visitors to their table Cole told Beth about his call from Curtis Spooner. He hoped she would be impressed, and she seemed so. Cole asked her if she might like to meet him. She was mildly interested. He said he could probably get a ticket for her from Curtis to the Clippers–Blazers game Friday night. Beth said she'd think about it.

At about 1:30 Cole made the appropriate comments to the Quinteros about the food never tasting better and him being full to the point of bursting. He excused himself and Beth after many exchanges of thank-you's and Christmas wishes. When they stepped outside Cole suggested a walk around the block in the fresh air. Beth readily agreed.

"Luis and Raphaela had a son about my age," Cole began after a few awkward moments of what-do-we-talk-about-now silence. "Clemente was a tough kid, I guess—gangs, trouble with the law. But he survived, turned around, even finished high school. He wanted to get into the folks' business, so he bussed tables and cooked, then tended bar for them. One night a thug with a score to settle from the old neighborhood walked into the restaurant and emptied a nine-millimeter clip into Clemente's chest."

"Oh, no," Beth groaned involuntarily. "Poor Raphaela."

"I was working that night—in fact, I had just eaten dinner in the restaurant a couple of hours earlier. There must have been twenty of us cops in the restaurant within five minutes. I wanted to go look for the guy, but Raphaela and Luis wouldn't let go of me. They were hysterical, and I didn't know what to do. So I just held them and let them cry. Probably a good thing. If I had caught the guy, I would have emptied a clip into him. And we weren't carrying DAB guns in those days."

"Did they catch him?"

"Oh, yeah, he was in jail before the coroner picked up Clemente's body."

"No wonder the Quinteros think of you as a son."

"I only see them every couple of weeks, but we're very close. When my dad died, I was in Tahoe for two weeks with Mom and my sisters. When I got back, Luis and Raphaela arranged a special Mass for my dad at the Old Plaza Church. I don't think it did any good for Dad, but just knowing the Quinteros did it—and it cost them some money— really made me feel good. After the Mass they hosted a big dinner in the banquet room for me and any of my friends who wanted to come."

"That's wonderful. You're lucky to have such friends."

The conversation lapsed again, and Cole wondered if Beth even cared. She seemed to enjoy the Mass and the dinner, but there was a line of tentativeness she hadn't crossed. She wasn't saying anything about herself. Cole was afraid that if he didn't keep the conversation alive they would go their separate ways in silence. He wasn't ready to let that happen.

"So you're a journalist, Beth. What do you write?"

"I'm a free-lancer. I specialize in those quick-turn news and feature paperbacks that hit the streets about a week after the event. Seven-day wonders we call them in the trade."

"Like that one about the eruption of Mt. Lassen earlier this year? That book was on the stands before the ash had settled."

"Yes, that's the kind. I didn't work on that one, however. The more sensational, unscheduled stories—like the Lassen eruption and the assassination of the Canadian prime minister last year—are handled by writers who thrive on middle-of-the-night phone calls and five-day deadlines. I enjoy a challenge, but I work better with a little lead time. So I only accept assignments I can plan for and research in advance.

"That's why I'm doing this Unity 2000 story. I've done a little reading about it already, and I'll be doing more research and writing during the week. In fact, I have an appointment tomorrow with one of the religion editors at the *Los Angeles Times*, hoping she'll give me some inside stuff on the 'big four.' Then after all the amens and hallelujahs have been pronounced, I'll finish the book at home and modem the final draft to the publisher by about the fifth of January. The book will hit the streets no later than the tenth."

"That's incredible," Cole said, thinking more about her willingness to open up than the information she was sharing. The more she talked, the less defensive and adversarial she seemed to him. He wanted to hear more.

"So how did you come by covering a big religious event?" he continued. "I take it that, in spite of the cross you were wearing the other night, you're not a deeply religious person."

"You're right, I'm not. My parents were devout Catholics. I played the role for awhile, but by the time I reached high school I bailed. Then shortly after I graduated, Mom and Dad ran away with Simon Holloway's circus."

"That televangelist guy from Florida, one of the 'big four' responsible for this deal in the Coliseum that's eating up all my days off?"

"The very same. My parents are overboard Holloway groupies." Beth wrinkled her nose and shook her head to underscore her dislike for the man and his radical movement. "They follow him all over the country. They've been trying to get me on the bandwagon ever since they walked the sawdust trail."

"So you're not a Catholic, and you're not a Holloway disciple. What are you?"

"A devout cynic, I guess."

Cole chuckled. "Does that mean you're an atheist?"

"Are you kidding? It takes more faith *not* to believe in the existence of God than to believe it. I'm not willing to work that hard."

"An agnostic, then?"

"Not really. There must be a God somewhere, and I think He's knowable. But with bigoted, money-grabbing people like Holloway, Hornecker, Dunne, and McClure as His first-string representatives, I just don't care to make His acquaintance. And with His children so busy chasing after His blessings and enforcing His laws instead of trying to alleviate the suffering in the world, I'd rather be a spiritual orphan."

Beth paused, then added in a softer tone, "I get a little acrimonious on the topic of religion. I hope I'm not offending you."

"Not at all. Actually, I share some of your feelings. I've thought of myself as a kind of a reluctant deist."

"God created the world, then wound it up like a clock and left it running while He went off to bigger and better things?"

"Yeah. I know too much from my Presbyterian upbringing to completely reject the concept of God. But the world is falling apart, and the people who say they belong to God are more interested in recruiting givers for their television ministers than in accomplishing something in the world. It makes me think God has taken an early retirement to some pristine planet on the far side of the galaxy."

"Amen, brother!" Beth sang emphatically. They both laughed.

"So I'm back to my question," Cole continued. "Being almost anti-religion, why did you take this assignment?"

"Good money—that's it. The publisher had to up the ante just to get a writer interested in coming to L.A. for this gig. It's a crummy job, but somebody has to take all that money. It might as well be me."

"So you write a best-seller, get your name in huge letters on the cover, and a fat royalty check every six months, right?"

"Sorry to disappoint you, Reagan. This is pulp journalism, not Pulitzer Prize literature. I simply write news stories; they just happen to be 160 pages long—including the photos. Like any reporter, I get a flat fee and a modest byline. The publishers and editors get the big bucks and the limelight."

"So why don't you settle in with one of those national dailies and work your way up to editor—or even publisher?"

"Not me. I like the flexibility of free-lancing. I like being my own boss, picking my own assignments. Only, after the other night on the freeway and the hassles of being home, I wonder if this assignment is worth it."

"I'm afraid you had a bad first impression on this trip," Cole consoled. "The L.A. I love is what I did today, the people I was with—including you. Today hasn't been so bad, has it?"

Beth was silent and thoughtful until they turned the corner. The Kawasaki, the Star Cruiser, and the end of their few hours together were only steps away. "No, it wasn't bad at all," Beth said finally. "In fact, I enjoyed today. I enjoyed it very much. Thank you for inviting me."

"I'm the one who should be thanking you," Cole said. "I still feel bad about—"

"Don't worry about it." Beth cut in quickly. She stopped beside her car to face him. "I must admit that I was a little hesitant about accepting your apology. But after today—well, you've proved your sincerity."

She dropped her head for a brief moment—not long enough for Cole to speak—then looked at him again. "Now I'm the one who needs to apologize. My foolishness on the freeway the other night put you in great danger. I deserved a chewing out. I'm sorry for being so defensive, so hostile. Will *you* forgive *me*?"

Beth's dark eyes, locked on his, would not allow Cole to avoid a response, even though he wanted to brush it off. "Okay, Beth. I forgive you."

Beth thrust out her hand, and Cole shook it. They smiled as if each had out-benefited the other in a shrewd business deal.

Cole helped Beth into the car, reminded her about the locks, then closed the door. She fired up the engine and rolled down the window. Her face was suddenly serious again. "Yesterday on the phone you said there was a number I could call to register a complaint with the LAPD. What was that phone number?"

Cole couldn't hide a look of confused surprise. But Beth's poker face quickly broke. "Just kidding," she said with a broad smile as she pulled away from the curb.

Cole watched the Star Cruiser disappear around Macy Street. He returned to his bike and mounted, deciding to forgo his flight suit for the short ride to the station. He had conveniently "forgotten" about leaving his helmet in Beth's car. He wondered, with high hopes, if her lapse in memory had been intentional purpose too.

Fourteen

It was like coming out of anesthesia. Shelby had been driving numbly for almost two hours, following I-35 south from San Antonio, allowing Nuevo Laredo, Mexico to reel her in without a fight. Then the freeway sign jogged Shelby fully alert. The sign announced an exit for Los Angeles. At least Shelby *thought* it said Los Angeles when she roared by it at 70 MPH. *Maybe I read it wrong*, she second-guessed herself. *How could there be a turnoff for Los Angeles in southwest Texas eighty miles from the Mexican border?* It seemed crazy. But then the last twenty-four hours had been anything but sane.

Next to Austin and Dallas, Los Angeles was the last place Shelby wanted to be. Her fleshly failure on Christmas Eve had instantly disqualified her from all spiritual responsibilities, including serving as honorary chairperson for Unity 2000 in L.A. She hadn't really wanted the job in the first place. It had been Adrian's brainchild, becoming Shelby's responsibility by default at his death. Los Angeles and Unity 2000 represented all the loneliness and suspicion he had left her with when he went down in the Mediterranean. Was this some kind of cruel joke for God to plant a sign beside the road—or a hallucination in her head—mentioning the very city she was running away from?

It was so ludicrous that Shelby had to check it out. She eased the Silverado into the right lane and gradually let up on the accelerator. The loud monotone hum of traction tires on pavement slowly dropped from tenor to baritone range. The highway exit sign approached and Shelby read it aloud: "469, Millett, Woodward, Los Angeles." Even seeing the words clearly on the sign, she couldn't believe it. The arrow on the sign veered to the right. She followed it down the off-ramp to a four-way stop.

She could see the entire community of Millett—five old houses and a couple of rusty mobile homes—from the intersection. Beyond them was the flat, dirty beige of mesquite, huisache, and stick brush merging at the horizon with an equally dirty gray sky. An ambitious wind buffeted the truck, and Shelby guessed it was very cold outside.

A green and white sign on the opposite corner bore the number 469, designating a Texas ranch road. Beneath the number was the information: Woodward 9 miles—with an arrow pointing west; Los Angeles 16 miles—with an arrow pointing east. Shelby had never heard of a town in Texas called Los Angeles. But for some reason the freeway sign had jarred her out of her distant thoughts, and now she felt a sudden urge to go see this place. Perhaps it was because Los Angeles, Texas, in the sprawling, dusty ranch land, sounded so very far away from Austin, Dallas, and Los Angeles, California, more remote even than Mexico.

Shelby couldn't think of any logical reason to drive the sixteen miles to Los Angeles. It was probably no more than a wide spot in the road in the middle of undeveloped grazing land. She could easily cross the highway and enter the freeway again, leaving Millett and Los Angeles behind her, and be in Nuevo Laredo in less than two hours. Or she could turn left and follow this strange prodding to find a remote little town in the middle of nowhere, as close to the backside of the world as she could imagine at the moment.

A truck horn blared loudly behind the Silverado causing Shelby to jump. The rearview mirror revealed a rickety old stake truck with a brown-skinned driver wearing a scowl of impatience. Shelby made a snap decision. Nothing else she had done in the last twenty-four hours had been logical. Why start now? She flipped on the blinker and accelerated the pickup left onto the narrow, two-lane road to Los Angeles. Her last view of the intersection in the mirror showed the stake truck turning away toward Woodward.

As the Silverado rolled eastward at 60 MPH along the deserted road, the overcast sky slipped to increasingly deeper shades of gray. Shelby turned the headlights on and glanced at her watch. It was 3:30. The reality of night approaching caused her to admit that, running away or not, she would need a place to spend the night. She doubted that the little town which mysteriously drew her onward would offer decent lodging. *After a quick drive through Los Angeles,* she thought, *I can still get to Nuevo Laredo and find a motel before it's too dark.*

As the miles slipped behind her, Shelby tried to remember where the last three hours had gone. Her trip from Austin was like a distant dream. She remembered crying most of the eighty miles from Austin to San Antonio. She thought of the curious stares of the children in a minivan, no doubt on their way to Grandmother's for Christmas dinner, who watched her weep as she slowly passed them on the freeway.

Shelby had agonized over the mental replays of the night before, desperately trying to edit her feelings and make them right, and berating herself cruelly for actions she could never recapture and change. Every thought of Jeremy Cannon had brought another sickening wave of humiliation. The same phrases pierced her repeatedly: *I tried to seduce him. I didn't just want him; I offered myself to him.* He *had to tell* me *it wasn't right—Jeremy, a man with a history of loose morals. What does that make me?*

Shelby remembered following I-35 through most of San Antonio before she even realized that she was in the city. With grief and shame still raining on her like a private thunderstorm, she had quickly decided that San Antonio wasn't nearly far enough away from Austin—or from herself. She had to keep going, perhaps clear to Mexico. After that, she didn't know—and she didn't care.

At least she had had the presence of mind to check the fuel gauges before she left the city limits of San Antonio. She had pulled into a freewayside station offering full service and filled both tanks with premium—Adrian had insisted on premium in all their vehicles. When she had paid for the gas in the minimart—wearing sunglasses to ensure that no one would recognize her from TV—the sight of snack foods and cold beverages reminded her that she had not eaten since the buffet supper in her home nearly twenty hours earlier. Unwilling to justify her right to eat in light of her behavior, Shelby had ignored her mounting hunger and walked out of the minimart without buying anything but gas.

It occurred to Shelby to telephone Theresa Bordeaux from the service station. She reminded herself, *That's what good friends do when they're in trouble: they call each other and pray for each other and encourage each other.* But humiliation loomed like an impenetrable barrier between her and the pay phone. *The best thing that can happen is for me to disappear without a trace,* she thought, returning to the truck.

Back on I-35 southbound Shelby had actually tried to pray. Momentary flashes of God's love and forgiveness—vestiges of a lifetime spent in Bible teaching and preaching—appeared like small patches of blue in the boiling dark clouds rolling through her mind. But each time she reached for the light, another menacing thunderclap of accusation caused her to cower in disgrace. The foreboding words had rumbled through her head: *If you regard iniquity in your heart, the Lord will not hear you. . . . Adulterers will not inherit the kingdom of God. . . . When desire conceives, it gives birth to sin; and sin gives birth to death. . . . The wages of sin is death.*

More than once a dark attack had concluded with the thought that she could do God a favor by aiming the three-quarter-ton Silverado at the cement abutment of an overpass at 70 MPH. But she kept the thought at bay in hopes that Mexico would provide a better answer.

Having failed to penetrate the steely clouds within her and reach the light she knew must be above them, Shelby had succumbed again to the mesmerizing drone of the tires and the featureless landscape of southwest Texas. She would probably have continued driving as if in a daze all the way to the border had the captivating sign to Los Angeles not enticed her off the freeway and onto lonely ranch road 469.

Shelby smelled the burning rubber and steam just seconds before the red temperature light began to flicker on the Silverado's dash. "Oh, no," she breathed, instantly alarmed. "Not a breakdown, not here." She glanced into the rearview mirror and gasped. Billows of steam poured out behind the pickup. She decelerated gradually, hoping the problem—whatever it was—would go away at 35 MPH or even 25.

She judged that she was still five or six miles from Los Angeles. *I have to nurse the truck into town,* she thought frantically. *I can't get stuck out here alone.* But the needle on the heat gauge was already in the red zone and the engine was beginning to misfire. Reluctantly she nosed the truck onto the shoulder, looking for space enough between the pavement and the brush to keep it well off the road. In less than fifty yards she found a spot—the entrance to a narrow, rutted road that wound away over mounds of dirt and brush.

With the engine off Shelby could hear the hiss of steam escaping in the engine compartment and the whistle of the wind over the corners of the truck. Advice Adrian had given her for responding to a break-down came to her like an instinct. She shut off the headlights to save the battery, then switched on the emergency flashers. *As if anybody is going to see them,* Shelby mumbled to herself cynically. *I've passed one car since I left the freeway, and there's not another one in sight—east or west.*

The most crucial step of Adrian's instructions, Shelby realized with a helpless sigh, was impossible: phone the Auto Club. The truck didn't have a phone—Steve always carried a portable with him on the ranch. And Shelby had left her phone in Austin. *Even if I did have a phone,* she thought, *who would I call?* She could imagine the Auto Club's 800 operator responding, "Sorry, ma'am, the nearest tow truck is in south San Antonio. It will be there sometime tomorrow."

Shelby stepped out of the truck to scan the road for signs of life. Dripping coolant had already formed a steaming pool under the engine. "Great, a punctured radiator or blown hose," Shelby growled. The cold wind stung her face and hands and slashed through her jeans and sweatshirt. She dragged her coat out of the cab, slipped it on, and jerked the collar up around her neck.

Shelby had never felt more isolated or lonely in her life. Standing beside the silent road with night approaching and the temperature dipping toward freezing, the events of the last twenty-four hours seemed to taunt her even more condemningly. She had fallen prey to an abhorrent temptation. She had destroyed her reputation and her relationship with a good friend. She had disqualified herself from ministry, and she could never face anyone she knew again. The heavens were indeed brass; she couldn't even pray; God had clearly turned His back on her. And to top it all off, she couldn't even run away right. What had possessed her to turn off the freeway so close to evening and risk being stranded in the boondocks just to see some no-account town?

In one black moment, Shelby's failure, frustration, and fear boiled into vindictive anger. "You did this, didn't You!" she abruptly cried toward heaven. "You weren't satisfied to sit by while I turned myself into a whore! It wasn't enough for You to leave me to sour in my own sin! You couldn't think of letting me run away in peace! No, You had to trick me into coming out here to the middle of nowhere so You could rub my nose in it!"

Shelby stormed up and down the pavement screaming at God and weeping uncontrollably. Feeling she had nothing to lose, she railed at Him bitterly for saddling her with such an uncaring husband and then taking him away altogether, leaving her to hold his empire together. "It's Your fault that I fell into temptation so easily last night," she bawled, waving her arms at Him. "You could have made Adrian more loving. You could have kept him from being seduced by the Last Days and Hollywood. You could have prevented that explosion over the Mediterranean. You could have kept Jeremy sober last night and sent him home before the others left. Why do I have to pay for what You didn't do?"

Her searing geyser of vented anger soon gushed up deeply buried hurt. Physically and mentally drained, walls of defense and propriety crumbling, she poured herself out beside the highway. Every mocking disappointment, every shadowy fear, the dark blots of her past, the torment of her present, the hopelessness of her future tumbled out in wails, groans, and sobs.

Feeling disgorged of everything but her next breath, Shelby slumped against the door of the truck and whispered, "God, I'm so lost. Please help me." Hoping beyond hope, she listened for an answer, hearing only the wind, the soft *clack-clack clack-clack* of the flashers, and — Shelby stood erect and held her breath — the sound of a slow-moving vehicle approaching.

She stepped quickly to the highway and searched both directions in the gathering darkness. No lights, no movement, nothing. Yet the sound of a car engine grew louder. It seemed to be upon her.

The flash of headlights in her peripheral vision spun Shelby around toward the dirt road. An old dusty red station wagon — as old as she was, Shelby guessed, from its boxy shape and clattering engine — emerged from the tall brush and stopped where the Silverado blocked the road. In the near darkness Shelby could make out several silhouetted heads inside the car straining to investigate the obstruction through closed windows. The car's engine continued to run.

A shiver of fear rippled down Shelby's spine as a terrifying scenario flashed before her. *Alone on a deserted road . . . robbed, raped, and murdered by a gang of thugs . . . my body dumped in an unmarked grave hundreds of yards off the highway, never to be seen again. Is this God's final answer to my plea for help?* She felt too lost to run, too weary to fight. With utter resignation to the chilling possibilities, Shelby walked around the truck to confront her visitors.

"You have trouble, lady?" The question came from the driver, a short, stocky Latino man with a heavy mustache who stepped out of the car to face her. He was wearing an oversized, faded flannel shirt and well-worn jeans. His Spanish accent was substantial, his tone of voice pleasant. He closed his car door and immediately stuffed his hands into his pockets against the cold.

"Yes," Shelby answered in her most self-assured voice. She could think of no reason to cover the facts of her predicament. "My truck overheated. I think there's a serious leak in the cooling system." She gestured toward the earth around the truck's front end which was still damp with escaped coolant.

"My wife saw your flashers half an hour ago from our house," the man said. Shelby chanced a look past him into the car. The passenger in the front seat was a woman. The four faces clustered inquiringly at the back window were children, all under the age of ten. "We thought you would come down the road to our house if you needed help."

The man jerked a thumb toward a gentle rise about a half-mile into the brush. A solitary light gleamed from the family's home, which Shelby had overlooked when assessing the area to be unpopulated. It occurred to Shelby, with some irony, that the family might have come out to the road sooner, except they were probably as wary of a stranger on the highway as she had been at first sight of them.

"I didn't see the house; I didn't know anyone lived around here," Shelby explained. Then, hopeful for safety and possible aid from the Latino family, she added, "Actually, I didn't know what to do."

The man opened the door to the station wagon and issued a terse command in Spanish. A flashlight was thrust out to him, and he closed the door again. He walked slowly around the front of the truck inspecting the spilled coolant and probing the front undercarriage with the flashlight beam.

"Where are you going, lady?" he asked as he walked and searched.

"I was heading for Los Angeles," Shelby said, trying to sound purposeful and confident.

"You know somebody in Los Angeles?" the man asked, disbelievingly.

"Well, no. Actually, I was going to Nuevo Laredo and decided to take a side trip. If I could get to Los Angeles tonight, perhaps I could find a motel."

"Motel? In Los Angeles?" the man asked, stopping to look at Shelby. "There's no motel in Los Angeles, lady. No gas stations, no mechanics, no stores either. Just a beer joint and a few ranches around there. Why do you want to go to Los Angeles?"

Shelby sighed, embarrassed about a quandary she didn't understand herself. "I don't know. I was just curious, I guess."

The man continued his circle of the truck, as if looking for clues to why a gringa would wander so far from the interstate on a cold Christmas afternoon. "The nearest motel is over at Cotulla—back out by the freeway. You have to go to Los Angeles and take 97 west—that's about twenty miles."

Following the man around the back of the truck, Shelby screwed up her courage. "I really must get to a motel tonight. Can you possibly fix my truck enough to get me to Ka . . . Katolla. . . ."

"Cotulla."

"Cotulla . . . I can pay you in cash, and I can pay you well." Shelby hoped her offer wouldn't bring out a hidden, devious side of what appeared to be a simple, good-hearted local resident.

The man trained his flashlight beam on the truck's rear bumper. "Lady, do you love Jesus?" he asked with animation. In the center of the beam was a reflective sticker featuring a red cross and a gold dove, the symbol Adrian had created for Victory Life Ministries. Shelby had forgotten that the sticker was there. She silently hoped that the man wouldn't recognize the symbol or her.

How should I answer him? Is he a religious man who is ready to help me if answer yes? Or is he a pagan, or even a satanist, who will walk away in disdain if I say yes, leaving me helpless beside the road? She opted for the former.

"Yes, I love Jesus," Shelby answered convincingly. She wasn't sure at the moment what her response meant to her, but she was hopeful that her confession would impress the man enough for him to help her.

"¡Lupe, vamos!" the man called out toward the car, beckoning his wife wildly with his hand. A barrel-bodied woman wearing a cotton dress and sweater and carrying a warmly wrapped infant climbed out of the driver's side door. She was closely followed by four stair-stepped children—one boy and three girls—excitedly chattering in Spanish. The noisy tappets of the idling station wagon continued to beat out a syncopated rhythm.

The man gestured toward the bumper sticker and rattled off several quick phrases in Spanish. The children clustered around the shiny sticker, tracing the cross and dove with tiny brown fingers, seemingly unfazed by the cold.

Shelby caught a few key words: señora—the woman, no doubt referring to herself, el Señor—the Lord. Thankfully, she did not hear her name.

After a few seconds the couple turned toward Shelby, beaming. "We love Jesus too, sister. I am Soledad Cruz. This is my wife, Lupe, and my children. Que Dios le bendiga." Then the two adults were upon her with warm embraces reminiscent of Shelby's visits to Latin American congregations. The wide-eyed, grinning children swarmed around her too, hugging her legs and mimicking their parents' greeting: Que Dios le bendiga—God bless you.

Shelby was overwhelmed, speechless. Minutes earlier, when the station wagon had surprised her out of the brush, she feared for her life. Now she was being embraced and blessed by a family of strangers simply because she said she loved Jesus. She felt their unbidden love, like healing oil, flowing into her aching soul, warming the icy caverns of bitter failure, lost hope, and shattered dreams. She struggled against a sudden swelling tide of emotion to remind herself that a loving embrace couldn't reverse the devastation of the past twenty-four hours.

But she secretly grasped and held onto a tiny glimmering promise of hope.

"You love Jesus, and we love Jesus, sister," Soledad repeated. "That is why your truck broke down in our road, because Jesus knew we are here to help you."

Feeling flustered for imposing on such a humble family, Shelby said, "Thank you, Soledad, but it's Christmas. You and your family have plans—"

"No, sister," Soledad interrupted. "We went to church this morning in Cotulla, and we have been celebrating the Savior's birth at home together. We only came to the highway to see if you needed our help. Now we know that Jesus sent us."

Disarmed by the couple's kindness, Shelby smiled broadly and genuinely—for the first time all day, she realized.

Soledad barked instructions in Spanish to his family, and they obediently scampered back into the warmth of the car. Then he strode to the driver's side of the cab and opened the door. Shelby quickly quelled a flash of alarm, thinking of the $8,000 in the bag on the seat. *Soledad Cruz is no thief*, she assured herself. *He's a Christian brother.*

Soledad pulled the hood release under the dash, then stepped up on the front bumper, lifted the hood, and sent the light in to investigate. Shelby watched over his shoulder.

"There is your problem, sister," he said, aiming the light at a jaggedly gaping, coolant-splattered heater hose. "That hose is split. You need a new one."

"But where can I get. . . ."

Soledad stepped down and walked to his car without acknowledging her. He held a brief, one-way conversation with his family—he spoke, and they listened and nodded.

"Sister, we must go to Cotulla to find a hose," he began when he returned to the front of the truck. "But everything is closed today. My family would be honored to have you stay with us tonight. Our home is clean and warm; our children are obedient. We have a room for you— a private room. I will go to Cotulla in the morning and buy a hose. Then I will put it on for you, and you will be on your way."

"Thank you, Soledad, but I can't trouble you—"

"Sister, you will freeze if you sleep in the truck. Or someone may come along and hurt you or steal your truck. It is no trouble for us to help you in this way. It is our service to Jesus."

Shelby was dumbstruck. She had no logical response, and she had no workable alternatives.

Soledad switched off his flashlight and dropped the hood. "The engine is cool now. You can start the truck and follow us down the road and park beside the house. The short distance will not hurt the engine."

Soledad looked up at Shelby as if daring her to resist their love. *If they knew who you were and what you have done,* a dark, inner voice mocked, *they would leave you out here to freeze.* But the guileless hospitality radiating from Soledad's eyes turned the taunt to tin. As unworthy as she felt to receive from these innocent saints, refusing them would only make her feel worse.

The Cruz home was a small 100-year-old ranch house, the original structure on the 3,000-acre spread where Soledad worked as the only resident caretaker. It had once been a cattle ranch, he explained. But the ranch had changed hands twenty years earlier and the cattle sold. Except for the Cruz place, the land had been allowed to return to its natural state. The owners, who lived in San Antonio, now rented the property out to hunters of white-tailed deer and wild hogs.

Soledad, Lupe, and the children welcomed Shelby into their home with the same deference to visiting royalty she usually received from her adoring parishioners—except these people had no idea who she was. They were satisfied when she gave only her first name—although they persisted in calling her Sister Shelby—and content to know that she was on her way from Austin to Nuevo Laredo. There was no television in the house, so she guessed they had never heard of Adrian and Shelby Hornecker, Victory Life Ministries, or even Unity 2000. Shelby relaxed in her anonymity.

After a meal of roast pork, beans, and bread—which Shelby devoured eagerly while trying to disguise her ravenous appetite—the family retired to the cozy living room for "Jesus stories." Lupe nursed the infant in a wooden rocker while Soledad and the other four youngsters piled up on the large woven rag rug near the fire. Shelby sat on the floor beside the hearth, leaning against an overstuffed chair dating back to the '50s. For the moment, the rest of the world and her problems seemed light-years away.

With strict instructions to practice their English, each child was allowed to select one story from a thick, dog-eared book of Bible stories for children. The two oldest—Magdalena, nine, and Ernie, eight—turned straight to the Advent section of the book and read aloud, with Soledad's gentle coaching, stories of the journey to Bethlehem and Jesus' birth in a stable. Six-year-old Maria Paula also selected a Christmas story, which her father read aloud with great drama to her delight.

Three-year-old Antonia was more interested in colors and shapes than text. When it was her turn to find a story, she flipped the pages furiously until her eyes lit on a picture that pleased her. But when Soledad took the book to read, Antonia objected, making known her special request in Spanish. After some coaxing from her patient father, Antonia flashed her large black eyes at Shelby expectantly and said in English, "Sister, read the story please?"

Shelby was charmed at being included. She scooted close to Antonia and, sitting cross-legged, took the child in her lap. The other children gathered around. She pulled the storybook close, hardly noticing the picture of a woman kneeling before Jesus with a crowd surrounding them.

Shelby read slowly and clearly, hoping at least the older children would understand. "There were some people in the city who hated Jesus. One day they brought a woman to Him who had done something very bad. 'We think this woman should be put to death with stones for what she did,' they said to Jesus. 'What do You think?'

"Jesus bent down and wrote in the dirt with His finger. Then He stood up and said, 'If anyone here has done nothing bad, he may throw the first stone at her.' One by one the people who hated Jesus walked away.

"When they were alone, Jesus asked the woman, 'Where are the people who wanted to kill you? Who is still here saying that you are a bad person?'

"The woman answered, 'No one, Sir.'

"Jesus said, 'I don't blame you either. Go now and stop doing bad things.'"

Shelby suddenly gripped the book as if an electric charge had welded her fingers to it. He was standing before her, right in the middle of the room. He was so real to her that she wondered why Soledad, Lupe, and the children didn't see Him. His gaze was one of empathy and love. His words were direct, personal, "Neither do I condemn you, Shelby. Leave your sin behind you. Walk on with Me."

"Muchas gracias, hermana," Antonia sang from Shelby's lap, then with encouragement from her parents added, "Thank you, sister, for the story."

"Thank you, sister," Magdalena, Ernie, and Maria Paula chimed in.

"But sister," Maria Paula interjected, gazing up at Shelby's face. "It was a nice story. Why are you crying?"

Fifteen

"Hello, Gregory." Dr. No gripped the homeless man's hand and shook it cordially. "Isn't this your third Christmas dinner with us?"

The unkempt man in threadbare coat and dirty stocking cap shifted from foot to foot, shoulders hunched up to his neck against the cold. Most of the 200 disadvantaged men, women, and children bunched in a straggly line from the main entrance of King's House around the corner onto Waterloo Street were also doing their best to stay warm. The late afternoon weather system predicted for Christmas Day was overtaking L.A. rapidly. The temperature had already dropped below 50. An overture of brief showers from the darkening sky announced the soon arrival of the full-blown storm.

"That's right, Dr. No," Gregory answered excitedly. "This is the best meal of the year at the House . . . except maybe for Thanksgiving and Easter." The broad, superficial grin on Gregory's unshaven face revealed a mouth full of broken and diseased teeth.

Dr. No leaned closer to the man so as not to embarrass him. "Gregory, didn't you see one of our dentists when you were staying here last month?"

Gregory snapped his mouth shut self-consciously, then answered as tight-lipped as possible, "Well . . . I had a . . . mm . . ."

"An appointment?"

"Yeah, I had an appointment, but . . . er . . . I guess it kind of slipped my mind."

"Something else must have slipped your mind, Gregory. You didn't come home one night. I haven't seen you for, what, three weeks? We had to give your cubicle to someone else. Are you doing all right out there?" Dr. No gestured vaguely toward the Hollywood Freeway and the city beyond.

Gregory cleared his throat nervously. "Well, now that you mention it, I'm kind of down on my luck, Dr. No. Maybe I should come back and give it another try."

"Gregory, let me tell you the rules again," Dr. No said straightforwardly but without condescension. His gaze tracked the disheveled man's darting eyes. "We're not just here to give you a bunk and a meal when you need one. We're here to help you find yourself and get your life together. We have eighty-eight bunks for men in the House and 800 men in the city who want them. When you came into our program, you agreed to work with our counselors to resolve your addictions and then go through the training and placement program. It's a good program, Gregory. You know some of the men who have been through the House— Sugar Ray Mazurski, the Bologna Man, Fernando Rijos, Wabash Willie They're working and paying their own way and helping others now."

Gregory nodded, still avoiding eye contact.

"We love you, Gregory—you know that. But we can't help you if you keep walking out on us. If you want back into the program, you come to the office over on the Coronado side of the building tomorrow morning and fill out another application with the housing staff. When there's an opening, we'll let you know."

Gregory had heard the lecture before. Head down, he grunted his comprehension.

The double glass doors at the main entrance swung open for the 4 o'clock King's House Christmas dinner, and the line began to surge forward.

"But remember," Dr. No pressed on, walking alongside Gregory as he climbed the steps toward the entrance, "you're always welcome for the public meals on Tuesdays, Thursdays, and Saturdays. And if you need anything—socks, a blanket, soap, medical attention—you know where to come, right?"

Gregory nodded again impatiently. His attention was being lured toward the open doors and the aroma of roast turkey and gravy.

Dr. No gripped Gregory around the shoulders with one arm. "God bless you, Gregory, and Merry Christmas." Gregory mumbled something similar as he passed into the building.

Dr. No stood by the door greeting the King's House dinner guests as they passed by him into the warmth of the hospital's refurbished cafeteria. His enthusiasm couldn't have been more sincere if he was welcoming God Himself, which is precisely how he had trained his large staff to view the poor, hungry, and hurting who came through the doors of King's House.

At each place setting in the dining hall was a small wrapped gift of assorted toilet articles. Children received new toys—balls or small plush animals. As guests were seated, kitchen volunteers served individual plates of turkey and stuffing, mashed potatoes and gravy, cooked peas and carrots, and a large dinner roll. Other workers circulated with pots of coffee and trays of half-pint cartons of milk. In the corner of the dining room a group of high school students stood caroling around a man playing at a keyboard.

When the tables were full, a platoon of cheery volunteers ushered the overflow guests into what was once the hospital's main lobby. There they were served hot coffee or cocoa and cookies as they awaited the second seating. As if on cue, when the tail end of the line stepped into the building the dark clouds released their cargo in torrents.

Satisfied that the guests had been properly greeted and the staff members and volunteers affirmed, Dr. No took an elevator to the third floor of the east wing and entered the spacious, modestly furnished apartment he and his family had called home for over three years. The aroma of roasting turkey mingled with traditional Southeast Asian spices provoked immediate hunger pangs.

"Hi, Dad. How's it going downstairs?" Fourteen-year-old David Ngo was slouched in a living room chair poring over a large book on whales, one of his Christmas gifts from his parents. He was wearing the Lakers T-shirt he had put on as soon as he opened the gift that morning, oblivious to the tags still dangling from one sleeve. A T.D. Dunne tune—from one of the singer's more forthright Gospel albums—was pouring from the stereo speakers. The CD was a Christmas gift from David to his sixteen-year-old sister, Wendy, who had volunteered with Mai in the fifth floor women's ward until 6 P.M.

"It's going well," Dr. No said, as he knelt beside his son and tousled his short black hair. "It looks like we'll serve over 200 guests today. By the way, Byron Sandoz said to tell you thanks for helping him set up chairs this afternoon."

David had not looked up from his book and seemed not to hear his father's last sentence. "Look at this breaching humpback." He tapped the picture emphatically. "It's just like the one we saw on the whale-watching boat, isn't it?"

Dr. No leaned closer to the book, scrutinizing the large photo. "I don't know, David. You're the zoologist in the family. I wouldn't even know that was a humpback without the caption."

"I keep telling you, Dad," David lectured playfully, "the humpback is the one with the large flippers—see—and this dorsal fin that looks like a hump."

"You're amazing, son—your knowledge about animals," Dr. No chuckled. "And speaking of animals, I'm supposed to check the turkey and then make the salad for dinner. Can you give me a hand?"

"Are the Tripletts and Danielsons eating with us tonight?" David asked, setting the book aside and following his father into the kitchen. It was an often-asked question in the Ngo household. Medical director Alan Triplett and administrator Will Danielson and their families had moved into their King's House apartments the same week the Ngos moved into theirs. The three families often shared meals together.

"Just the Tripletts. The Danielsons are spending the day with Will's parents in La Mirada." Dr. No tapped the range controls for a digital readout for the thermometer inside the turkey. "Mm, it's a little ahead of schedule." After a few errant tries he entered the proper command to slow the roasting process to coordinate with their guests' arrival.

"Are just Dr. and Mrs. Triplett coming, or are Ronny and Andy coming too?" David pressed.

"Your mother told me to set the table for eight. Sounds like the boys must be coming. I think the Danielsons are going to join us for dessert when they get home from La Mirada." As he spoke he pulled a large head of romaine out of the refrigerator and placed it in the sink to be washed. "You guys are getting along all right, aren't you?" With the three families living so closely in the House, Dr. No and Mai and their co-workers were diligent about monitoring the normal squabbles that arose between their teenage children, who spent more time together than cousins.

"Dad, Ronny's my best friend," David asserted emphatically.

This week, Dr. No added silently, marveling at the flux of allegiance and loyalty between the seven King's House kids.

"He gave me one of his old Darryl Strawberry baseball cards for Christmas—they're collector's items now," David said.

Dr. No hummed, sounding impressed.

Then he pulled an envelope of Caesar salad dressing mix and a cut glass cruet from the cupboard. "David, I have a chemistry experiment for you." David, an avid science buff, was immediately interested. "See this formula on the envelope?"

"Dad, that's no formula," David said, smirking. "It's the instructions for making the salad dressing."

"Yes, it is a formula," Dr. No insisted, repressing a grin. "The salad dressing company hypothesizes that if you combine these ingredients, you'll get a delicious dressing for Caesar salad. I need a dedicated scientist to test this theory for us. I think you're just the one."

"Why don't you just say, 'David, will you please make the dressing for the salad'?" the lanky fourteen-year-old said, unable to keep from giggling at his father's teasing.

Father began poking son playfully. "Because making salad dressing is such a mundane task for such a bright boy. You need to be challenged to scientific greatness. Just think how the company will feel when they receive a letter from you stating that their hypothesis was correct. They'll probably put your picture on the label."

Their father-son tickle-fest lasted only a few seconds, both of them mindful that horseplay in the kitchen was forbidden. Dr. No returned to the sink to wash the romaine as David retrieved olive oil from the pantry.

"Dad, we've been talking . . ." he said as he measured ingredients into a mixing pitcher.

"We?"

"Us older kids—Ronny, Skip, Summer, Wendy, and me," David specified. Dr. No noted that David had not included the two youngest children living in King's House—twelve-year-olds Andy Triplett and Tippy Danielson—who as preteens were often considered "too young" by the older five, who were more "mature" at fourteen, fifteen, and sixteen.

"What have *we* been talking about?"

"We want to go to the Coliseum New Year's Eve to hear T.D. Dunne." David thought his best chance for getting permission was to deluge his father with the facts, so he kept talking. "Dad, it's going to be really cool. T.D. is doing a one-hour concert in that Unity 2000 thing. His band will be there and he's bringing a choir of all the GoTown stars. This is a historical Christian event. They've never been together on the same stage before—and it's going to happen right here in the Coliseum. Do you think we could go?"

Dr. No had been expecting the question to pop up sooner or later. He and Mai, who were careful to screen the media coming into their home and discuss with their children any input of questionable value, had placed their stamp of approval on T.D. Dunne and his GoTown network. At least the music was wholesome—a quality in short supply outside Dunne's circle of influence in the music indus-try. And in addition to his "secular" tunes, Dunne continued to pro-duce CDs and music videos that promoted positive Christian values.

"It sounds like you were elected spokesperson for your 'associa-tion,'" Dr. No said, chuckling.

"Kind of."

"Mom and I haven't talked much with the Tripletts and the Daniel-sons about Unity 2000," Dr. No said, carefully tearing the romaine into salad-sized leaves. "But your request reminds me that we need to have that conversation."

"Tonight, maybe?" David added hopefully.

His father thought for a moment. "Maybe after dinner, especially if the Danielsons get home in time to have dessert with us," he said.

Father and son finished the salad preparations and moved to setting the dining room table. Buoyed with confidence over having successful-ly presented his request, David voiced a deeper concern as the two of them distributed plates, silverware, goblets, and napkins around the table.

"Dad, is there something wrong with Unity 2000?"

"Wrong? What do you mean?"

"Well, on television T.D. Dunne is pushing this meeting on Millen-nium's Eve as the biggest Christian event of the century. He says Christians from all over the country are going to pack the Coliseum and Sports Arena. And I've seen those other big preachers on TV—like that guy in Orlando and the lady preacher in Texas—telling all their people to come to L.A. But you haven't said much about it—except that you and Mom aren't planning to go. So I just wondered if there was something wrong with it—you know, unchristian or New Age or satan-ic or something. That's why we were a little nervous about bringing up the T.D. Dunne concert."

Dr. No hadn't really expected this question. David understood that the ministry at King's House was more than a job; it was a way of life for the three families who had undertaken it, leaving little time for outside involvements, including positive ones like Unity 2000. They were responsible for a staff—paid and volunteer—of nearly 200. They served the physical and spiritual needs of up to 500 hurting people a day. And they had a seventy-five-year-old hospital building to keep in one piece. King's House was their world.

As such, the Ngos, the Tripletts, and the Danielsons, as well as most of the staff, attended no other church. Worship services, Bible studies, prayer meetings, and evangelistic outreaches were available at the House throughout the week—day and night—to accommodate the schedules of staff and "guests" alike. Dr. No and his cadre of lay ministers and leaders maintained strict, transparent accountability to each other for personal integrity and the ongoing fulfillment of their call to serve others selflessly. And they made sure that everyone serving in the House took time for fun, family activities, and occasional escapes for "R and R." With such great needs in the city and such a full agenda for meeting them, Dr. No, his family, and his co-workers had time for little else.

"No, I don't see anything wrong with Unity 2000," he answered after a thoughtful moment. "For all I know, T.D. Dunne, Rev. Holloway, Rev. Hornecker, and Dr. McClure are doing what God has called them to do. If they feel they need to bring their congregations together on Millennium's Eve, that's fine. It sounds like it will be a very inspiring evening. Your mother and I decided not to attend simply because our work is here. Besides, we wouldn't want to take the seat of someone who really needs to be there."

"So you wouldn't mind if we went—us kids, I mean—if you and the other parents agreed on it."

"No, I don't mind, as long as we talk about it afterward like we do with other things you participate in."

David was silent for several moments, wheels turning in his head. "Dad, there's something else I don't understand," he said at last with a disturbed sigh, sitting down at the dining room table.

Dr. No sensed in his tone the onset of a wonderful and unpredictable and sometimes scary moment of transparency in his young son. He sat down at the table opposite David. "Tell me about it."

David searched a moment for the right words. "Why are we stuck in this old hospital? I mean, T.D. Dunne and those other TV preachers who are coming to L.A. have huge churches. Everybody wears nice clothes and puts lots of money in the offering. That lady in Texas has a big ranch, and I saw on TV yesterday that her church gave her a brand new Lincoln. T.D. Dunne has his fancy studio and TV programs and concerts and CDs and videos. All these other Christians are having so much fun. But look at the people who come to King's House. They're dirty, and some of them try to steal from us, and the people on the fifth floor are dying. Look how hard you have to work, and nobody gives you a new car or invites you to the Coliseum on Millennium's Eve. It just looks like God is blessing them and not us. Are we doing something wrong?"

David's concerned expression convinced Dr. No that his son's rough-edged thoughts had been painfully scraping at his insides for some time, and he felt his heart swell with compassion for his son. He silently lifted a word of thanks to God for the special moment and asked for wisdom to take full advantage of it.

Dr. No and Mai had often tried to explain to Wendy and David why they did what they did at King's House. But like so many of their words of parental wisdom and explanation, their comments answered a question the children weren't yet asking. Dr. No compared it to teaching Wendy and David about their Southeast Asian heritage. He and Mai had talked often with their young children about the color of their skin, the shape of their eyes, and their distant origins. But it wasn't until eight-year-old Wendy came home from public school spouting a stream of derogatory ethnic slurs thrown in her face by her classmates that she really heard what her parents said about being Vietnamese-American.

The same thing happened when teaching their children about sex. Dr. No and Mai had always satisfied their children's curiosity with honest answers on a need-to-know basis. Unprovoked lectures on the subject, no matter how thoroughly prepared or cleverly presented, were met with blank looks and responses like, "Yeah, okay, can I watch TV now?" But eleven-year-old David had riveted to his father's explanation after bringing home a pornographic magazine he had found in the street.

Standing on the threshold of another teachable moment, Dr. No suddenly received a flash of inspiration. "To answer your question, David, let's go for a little walk. There are a few people I want to look in on before dinner. Okay?"

David shrugged as if to say, "Do I really have a choice?"

Dr. No checked the digital readout on the turkey once more, and then he and David took the elevator to the first floor. The second seating of the Christmas dinner was in progress, and the director threaded his way between the crowded tables offering warm Christmas greetings and picking up empty plates and crumpled gift wrap. He shook hands, patted shoulders, and lifted children into his arms and nuzzled them until they giggled. David followed behind his father silently, trying to ignore the foul odor emanating from many of the guests.

Finally the pair drifted into an inconspicuous corner of the noisy dining room. Dr. No, arms crossed at his chest, silently surveyed the dirty, downtrodden people relishing the sumptuous meal. David, not knowing what he was supposed to do, did the same.

"David, how many of these people do you know?" he said quietly as they watched the guests eat.

"Not too many, Dad," David answered, wondering at the question.

"Give me some names."

David looked closer. "The man in the green and gold stocking cap and dirty blue jacket, third table from the wall, is Rocky. . . . The guy on the end with the crutches on the floor calls himself Bosco. . . . That big woman wearing a man's coat and pants is Mama Rosie. . . ."

Dr. No shook his head. "Nice try, son, but you're wrong."

"Dad," David objected with a puzzled expression, "you asked me their names. Those are their names."

Dr. No walked toward the elevator, motioning David to follow him. "Nope. Sorry."

He led his son off the elevator at the second floor and turned toward the men's living facility. They peeked into the day room where a King's House volunteer sat with four new arrivals explaining procedures and giving housekeeping assignments. Then they entered the dormitory and strolled between the cubicles. The residents were cleaner than most of the guests in the dining room, but they still bore the evidences of the hard life that brought them to King's House.

"Remember the names of anyone you recognize in here," Dr. No whispered as they walked. Several of the men they looked in on were napping. Others were reading or working on study assignments, which were mandatory for temporary residents. Still others were writing letters, folding laundry, or mending clothes. A few staff volunteers circulated, giving aid.

When they stepped out of the dorm, Dr. No asked, "Well?"

"The guy with only one eye and no teeth who was sewing his jeans is Alvin Johnson—I'm sure about that, Dad." David's confidence was tinged with defensiveness. "And the old man who can't get his back straight is Oklahoma. I know it is, because I've heard you call him that."

Dr. No shook his head. "Wrong again."

"Dad," David whined, exasperated. "What's this all about?"

"Hang in there, David," he said warmly. "I'm trying to show you something."

"Well, it's not fair. I'm giving you the right answers, and you keep telling me I'm wrong."

Dr. No gave him a squeeze around the shoulders. "One more stop, and then I'll explain."

They stepped out of the elevator on fifth floor and found Mai and Wendy in the central nursing station chatting with two volunteers. The mother and daughter were close enough in size to share each other's clothes. Mai's black hair was short and permed; Wendy's was long and braided.

After assuring Mai that Christmas dinner was on schedule, he led David into the men's wing of the hospice and to the bedside of Danny Firman. Danny was gaunt and yellow, ravaged by AIDS. His face was contorted into a constant grimace. An IV dripped nourishment into his arm, which seemed to have room for little more than bones and a vein. David watched as his father sat at the bedside holding Danny's face in his hands, leaning close and speaking words of encouragement.

They visited several other men, then stopped by the women's ward to see Theta Breckinridge, who was now isolated from her roommates by a standing room divider. She had been remarkably docile most of the day.

When they reached the staff lounge, David spoke first. "You want me to say that we saw Danny Firman, Moses Womack, Eddie Vicente, and Theta Breckinridge. But when I do, you'll shake your head and say I'm wrong. So what's the use of me telling you?" He wasn't as frustrated as he was curious about his father's motives for the bizarre guessing game.

"You asked me why we live in this place and take care of these people. The tour and my little game is half the answer. The other half is right here." Dr. No opened a Bible on the table desk and flipped pages to a well-worn section. He pointed David to his chair, and the young man sat down in front of the open Bible.

"Read this section out loud for me," he said, tapping an underlined block of verses. David began to read as his father settled into the overstuffed couch.

When I, the Messiah, shall come in My glory, and all the angels with Me, then I shall sit upon My throne of glory. And all the nations shall be gathered before Me. And I will separate the people as a Shepherd separates the sheep from the goats, and place the sheep at My right hand, and the goats at My left.

Then I, the King, shall say to those at my right, "Come, blessed of My Father, into the Kingdom prepared for you from the founding of the world. For I was hungry and you fed Me; I was thirsty and you gave Me water; I was a stranger and you invited Me into your homes; naked and you clothed Me; sick and in prison, and you visited Me."

Then these righteous ones will reply, "Sir, when did we ever see You hungry and feed You? Or thirsty and give You anything to drink? Or a stranger, and help You? Or naked, and clothe You? When did we ever see You sick or in prison, and visit You?"

And I, the King, will tell them, "When you did it to these My brothers you were doing it to Me!"

David looked up, puzzled. "What does this have to do with the names of the people in the House?"

Instead of answering, Dr. No asked, "Who were the righteous ones helping in those verses?"

David flashed a quirky grin, "Is this another trick question that I'll answer right, then you'll say 'wrong'?"

His father chuckled. "No, just read what it says."

David looked back at the page. "Hungry . . . thirsty . . . strangers . . . naked . . . sick . . . prisoners."

"Right. And who did the King say the righteous were really helping when they helped these people?"

David read for a moment. "The King Himself."

"Who is the King?"

"Easy. The Lord Jesus."

"So when we serve a meal to someone like Rocky, Bosco, or Mama Rosie, who are we really feeding?"

"I get it," David beamed.

"When we provide a bed and shower and job training for guys like Alvin and Oklahoma, who are we really doing it for?"

"Jesus."

"And when we tend to the physical needs of AIDS victims, we're not just helping Danny and Moses and Theta—"

"Daddy!" Wendy Ngo burst into the lounge screaming. Dr. No and David jumped up in alarm. A gob of brown goo ran down the front of Wendy's candy-striper smock. Mai was right behind her.

"Theta Breckinridge," Mai growled as she took her daughter's arm and escorted her daughter through the lounge toward the rest room.

"Didn't Theta like her turkey and gravy?" Dr. No called after them.

Mai's voice came back from down the hall, almost drowned out by Wendy's sobbing. "It's *not* turkey and gravy."

Just at that moment the odor of human waste wafted under the noses of father and son. They both groaned in disbelief, waving their hands trying to dissipate the stench in the air.

After a thoughtful moment, David said, "Dad, after Wendy gets cleaned up, I think you need to take her on the tour and play the name game with her."

Sixteen

Hodge left Union Station aboard a Metro commuter just after 6:30 P.M. He sat alone near the back of a nearly empty middle car with his picnic chest on the floor between his legs. A few noisy teenagers flitted between cars testing new short-range communicators—either Christmas gifts or trophies from a shoplifting adventure. Hodge leaned his head against the window feigning sleep.

The Red Line winds out of downtown Los Angeles to Wilshire Boulevard, then west and north to Hollywood with connections to the San Fernando and Santa Clarita Valleys and Ventura County. With his eyes closed and mouth agape to discourage interruptions by other passengers, Hodge listened carefully to the computer-announced station stops along Wilshire.

138

When the train turned north onto Rossmore Avenue, Hodge "woke up." At the Melrose Avenue stop in Hollywood, where Rossmore becomes Vine Street, he glanced eastward several blocks. Traffic was light in the steady drizzle from the departing storm. He hoped it would be even less populated when he returned in a couple of hours.

Hodge stepped off the train at Hollywood and Vine. He turned his collar up and buttoned the top button of his jean jacket against the light rain. The train snaked away past the Capitol Records tower and the Hollywood Freeway to the north.

In the decades of decline since its mid-century glory years, downtown Hollywood had stubbornly resisted most attempts to revive its glitz and glamour. The city of the stars, like so many of its famous residents, had allowed wealth, success, and acclaim to go to its head. It became careless in its vices and slovenly in appearance. Hollywood still held a magical attraction for millions with its studios, theaters, restaurants, and the famous walk of stars. But like an aging actress, all the cosmetics and gaudy trappings the politicians and merchants applied could no longer cover the wrinkles, warts, and age spots of a city well past its prime.

Hodge had some time to kill. He crossed Vine Street to the north side of Hollywood Boulevard. Once a fashionable shopping area, the stores along the boulevard had long since lost out to the megamalls. The name-brand establishments were gone, giving way to an odd assortment of ethnic clothing and jewelry stores, New Age crystal shops, occult bookstores, pawnshops, and musty bars. And on Christmas night everything was closed.

Hodge shuffled slowly along the sidewalk under awnings and close to the buildings to avoid the light rain. He stopped at a few trash bins along the sidewalk—especially when he saw a black-and-white cruising the boulevard—and pawed through them convincingly. His actions were carefully calculated to help him blend into his dismal surroundings and not attract attention. Hodge had practiced this skill over his last six months in Los Angeles and become very good at it. And tonight on Hollywood Boulevard he was as unnoticed as the puddles of rain on the sidewalks.

Hodge's picnic chest was in his left hand, and his right hand lightly gripped the handle of the knife inside his jacket pocket. Very few lost souls were roaming Hollywood Boulevard, which is why Hodge selected Christmas night for this strategic phase of his mission. But each dark doorway and blind corner could not be ignored as a potential hiding place for some derelict ready to assault a stranger for his picnic chest and anything it might contain. Hodge moved with the stodginess of a drunk, but his eyes and ears were sharply tuned to his surroundings.

He wandered as far as the Chinese Theater on the north side of

Hollywood Boulevard, then crossed to the south side and slowly worked his way back to Vine. The light rain had dwindled to a fine mist. Hodge's cap and jacket were damp, and he was cold. He encouraged himself to continue by acknowledging that his six-month-long ignoble lifestyle would soon come to an end. After Millennium's Eve, he would never be cold or shabby or dirty again.

He assessed that only about an hour had passed since he stepped off the train. *Still at least an hour to wait,* he thought. He walked two blocks south, then turned west again and repeated his act along the sidewalks and storefronts of Sunset Boulevard.

A hole-in-the-wall beer joint that happened to be open brought Hodge welcome respite from the cold and wet of the street. He sat alone at the bar slowly sipping three cups of bitter coffee—each paid for in advance—and enduring tinny country music on the radio and the gibberish of a pair of drunks at a table in the back. The owner/bartender, a stout, hairless Jew in his late fifties, bent Hodge's ear for the last twenty minutes. He explained, without Hodge asking or seeming interested, that the bar was open on Christmas because it was open 365 days a year. And except for the two weeks each year when he took his girlfriend to Belize, the man said, he was behind the bar himself—every day of the year.

"My brother-in-law takes over when I'm gone," he droned on. "He's nothing but a greasy goy, and I don't trust him any farther than I can spit. But how else can I get away with my lady friends? So I let Robert watch the bar and hope he doesn't screw me too bad. You know what I mean?"

Hodge watched the clock behind the bar while only pretending to listen to the obnoxious bar owner. In his mind he carefully rehearsed the task he must accomplish in the next two hours. He had been successful twice before. But tonight's attempt involved two critical additional steps. The fulfillment of his mission on Millennium's Eve hinged on his success tonight. A failure would nullify all other triumphs.

Hodge acknowledged the bothersome anxiety pecking away at his confidence and resolve. At every step of challenge in the past, Hodge's focus on the glory to come numbed his fear and anxiety about his mission like a powerful drug. Thinking about it now—the judgment of the evil ones and ascendancy of the chosen one in preparation for the glory of the new millennium—Hodge felt confidence surge through him like a river of fire.

At 9 o'clock Hodge slid off his stool, picked up his picnic chest, and walked out of the bar. The old Jew was still yakking away as the door closed.

As on his two previous visits to Hollywood, Hodge left Sunset for the quieter, darker side streets for his long walk toward Melrose Avenue.

He moved carefully between the shadows while acting the part of the harmless lost drunk for any eyes which happened to notice him. The streets of this commercial district were deserted except for an occasional passing car.

When Hodge reached Willoughby Avenue, he angled east for several blocks across Vine Street to where Willoughby dead-ended into Paramount Studios at Gower. He cut south again until he crossed well-lit Melrose, then he disappeared into a quiet residential area. Keeping to the shadows, he walked quietly east along Clinton Street until he reached a city-block sized complex of buildings which faced Melrose on the north. The buildings were dark as always, and the eight-foot, iron-bar fence which secured the entire lot from intruders was intact.

Hodge pulled a ring of keys from his pants pocket and, in the darkness of shadows, selected the key he wanted by touch. Assured that he could reach the complex unseen, he stepped out of the shadows and moved quickly across the street to the rear gate of the fence. He slipped the key into the lock, opened the gate, and stepped inside. Then he closed and locked the gate soundlessly before disappearing between the buildings.

The outdoor security lights Hodge had disabled on his first visit several months earlier were still out, as they had been during his second break-in. With the buildings in the complex unoccupied for the better part of a year, the missing bulbs had gone unnoticed. The center courtyard and walkways between the three- and four-story buildings were in complete darkness.

Hodge moved swiftly across the courtyard to the large building behind the main office facing Melrose. Another key on his ring gained him entrance through the locked glass door. Once inside he moved directly to the building's alarm panel and, with light from a tiny flashlight on his key ring, tapped in the disarm sequence.

He stood in the darkness for a moment, slowing his breathing and collecting his thoughts for the next step. This was the easy part. He had succeeded twice before without a hitch, but he cautioned himself against carelessness.

Hodge hurried up the stairway to a large supply room on the second floor. Another key on his ring opened the simple lock in the doorknob. He moved purposely between the shelves in the room selecting several cans and boxes of materials and a few specialized tools, stacking them inside his picnic chest. Within three minutes he was downstairs at the glass door. He checked the dark courtyard again before resetting the alarm and slipping outside.

Now for the hard part, Hodge reminded himself. He had practiced it repeatedly in his mind. He knew every door, lock, corner, and shelf he would encounter. But he had never dealt with them in the dark, and never under the jeopardy of detection or threat to the success of his mission. Again he called on images of the glory awaiting him and his master less than a week away to steel him against the anxiety of the challenge.

Hodge moved as silently as a shadow across the courtyard to a smaller building. The fireproof metal entrance door was windowless. He negotiated the lock, then disarmed the security system easily by entering the memorized code sequence on the keypad.

Immediately inside the entrance, just off the main hall, was a door. Once unlocked, the door opened to a stairway leading downward. At the base of the stairs was another metal door set into reinforced concrete.

Keys applied to two separate locks admitted Hodge to the small basement room. A sweep with the tiny flashlight revealed what he had expected: bare floors and empty shelves. He walked across the cold basement room and knelt before a rack of shelves bolted to the cement wall. He reached under the lowest shelf, groped for a few seconds, then smiled, finding the large screwdriver taped securely to the under surface of the shelf. He carefully pulled the tape loose and freed the tool.

Using the lower shelves like the rungs of a ladder, Hodge climbed the rack until he could touch the ceiling. He panned the flashlight along the wall just below the ceiling until the beam of light found the aluminum screen covering a small ventilation duct. With the tiny flashlight between his teeth and one hand gripping an upper shelf for support, Hodge loosened the four screws on the screen with the screwdriver. Then he removed the screws with his fingers and pried the screen away from the opening with the blade of the screwdriver.

Hodge's heart pounded with excitement as he reached into the vent and pulled out a thin plastic box a little smaller than a cigar box. He climbed down the shelf, holding the box carefully, almost reverently. Allowing himself only a minute to admire the prize and envision the strategic role it would play in his holy mission, Hodge placed the box gently inside his picnic chest with his other acquisitions, then mounted the shelf again to replace the vent screen and screw it down.

Hodge resisted the temptation to linger too long in the basement thinking about the box and its contents. He had yet to get safely out of the building, off the property, and back to Los Angeles. He rolled the screwdriver out of sight under a low shelf, picked up the nearly full picnic chest, and left the room.

One last, important step, he thought. Hodge sneaked through the darkness of the complex to a large storage building, admitted himself with a key, and disarmed the alarm. By the light of his key ring flashlight he found the room he wanted and entered. A sweep of faint light around the room revealed multiple thousands of dollars in professional sound equipment: amplifiers, mixers, miles of cable, mike stands, mikes, speakers, and metal boxes stocked with wiring and tools. The equipment was carefully wrapped against the dust.

Hodge placed the picnic chest on a work-bench and hung his tiny flashlight on a shelf above it to provide a weak but adequate shower of light. He removed from the chest two battery-powered electronic timers and other supplies he had brought from the bungalow, and also the plastic box he had recently removed from the ventilation duct in another building. It took him less than twenty minutes to wire one of the timers to a blasting cap and a small cylinder of plastic explosives from the box. It took less than ten minutes to assemble the second bomb.

Hodge quickly located the two six-foot speaker cabinets he knew would be in the room and pulled off their plastic shrouds. Using tools from the work-bench, he removed the rear panel to both speakers. Then he secreted a bomb in the dark cavity of each cabinet, secured it with duct tape, replaced the rear panels, and draped the speakers again with plastic.

As Hodge prepared to leave the storage room, he was jolted by another forceful inner plea. The silent message was as clear to his understanding as if it had been broadcast through the speakers he had recently worked on: *You are mine! You have been bought with a price! Forsake your evil ways! Return to me!*

Hodge gnashed his teeth against the assault on his soul. The appeal bored into him and gripped him as it had many times for many months, and he stopped in his tracks to consider it. But his master was immediately at his ear, inundating him with convincing lies about the glory and power awaiting his faithful servant. Hodge rallied to the convincing argument and scoffed at the warning, affirming again his choice to fulfill the master's plan for Millennium's Eve.

Hodge was aware that leaving the storage building and returning to the courtyard was the most difficult and hazardous step of his task. With no windows near the exit, he could not be sure the courtyard was secure without opening the door. After resetting the alarm, he had thirty seconds to crack the door and check for danger before stepping outside. Choosing to err on the side of caution, he used twenty-eight of those seconds before he was outside again with the door clicking closed behind him.

Hodge was between buildings on his way to the outer gate when he saw the sweeping beam of a flashlight near the street. With no time to think, he jumped off the sidewalk through the overgrown flower beds and into a wedge of dark shadows where a tall bay window jutted out from a building. The beam, which Hodge judged was shining from outside the fence, swept up the walkway precisely where he had been two seconds earlier. Hodge froze and stopped breathing. It was a powerful flashlight, he noted, like those carried by the police and security guards.

The light continued its probe while a male voice from the street talked in a low tone. Hodge could pick up only a few words: perimeter check . . . vacant studio on Melrose . . . heard something . . . check inside. The words were followed by a static snap and a louder voice on a portable radio speaker: "That's a ten-four, Benjy. Check in with me if you see something. Over."

A security guard, Hodge thought, pressing himself into the corner. *When did they start using security guards to watch this place?* Then he rebuked himself silently. *I should have known about this!*

Next he heard the jingling of keys, the click of key in lock, then the soft groan of metal turning on metal. The gate was open. The intruder was inside the fence, mere steps away. Hodge had only seconds to think. To escape he would have to dash for the courtyard in plain sight. He would be quickly seen, chased, and caught — or possibly shot as he ran. Hodge realized his only chance was to blend into the wall and hope the guard ignored his skimpy hiding place.

Slow steps came up the walkway. The powerful light beam swung from side to side. Suddenly the footsteps stopped. Though still tucked in the shadows, Hodge could see the beam aimed and fixed in his direction, trained near his feet. He glanced down to see the corner of his blue and white picnic chest illuminated by the strong light. In his haste, Hodge had left it in partial view. The guard would be upon him in seconds.

A shock of adrenaline raced through Hodge's body. His thoughts quickly turned again to the magnitude of his mission and the eternal glory of succeeding. He had assured himself and the powers directing him that he would do anything to fulfill his role and occupy his destiny. The thrill of the opportunity to prove his devotion seized him and energized him.

Hodge heard the guard leave the walk and swish through the tall, wet grass toward his hiding place with the light still trained on the picnic chest. The guard was making a stupid approach, Hodge thought, by coming straight to the picnic chest instead of swinging wide and illuminating the dark corner where Hodge waited. Probably an LAPD wannabe who was drummed out of the Academy for being too dumb and too slow.

The unwary guard was within a step of the chest when Hodge struck. Three flashing thrusts of his blade into the man's chest ended the threat. The guard, short and seriously overweight, groaned and crumpled, then lay still.

Hodge stood over the dying man for a few seconds, exulting in his triumph. "If you doubted my ability and willingness, my master, to execute your judgment on anyone standing in our path," he breathed excitedly, "behold the evidence. May your servant be as swift and sure on Millennium's Eve to deliver the blow and rise with you to glory."

Hodge had no time to waste. The guard's disappearance would soon be discovered, and the dispatcher would know exactly where to look for him. Hodge's mind grasped for a plan. Hiding the body would prolong the search and give Hodge enough time to escape to the Metro station and disappear into Los Angeles. *That's what I must do,* he thought.

Hodge clicked off the guard's flashlight and tossed it across the walkway into a weedy flower patch. Then he wiped his bloody knife in the wet grass and returned it to the sheath inside his jacket.

He dragged the body through the grass to the cover of a clump of bushes between buildings. He was walking away when he heard, "Benjy, this is Julius. Do you read me? Where are you, man? Did you fall into a hole over there?" Hodge returned to the body, ripped the radio from the guard's belt, and smashed it to pieces against the side of the building.

Hodge picked up the picnic chest and slipped quickly out the gate. The guard's pickup sat at the curb. Hodge seized the opportunity and climbed in. Finding the keys under the floor mat, he drove cautiously through back streets toward Vine Street and the Metro station. He ditched the truck in the parking lot behind a print shop and walked to the station two blocks away.

He waited on the bench beside the tracks. Just as the Red Line train to L.A. arrived, two patrol cars with sirens wailing sped down Melrose toward the buildings Hodge had recently left. *The dispatcher suspects trouble and has called in the law,* Hodge thought. *I'll be halfway to L.A. before they find the body.*

He climbed aboard the train and handed a wrinkled ticket to the conductor. He found a seat away from the two other passengers in his car, tucked the picnic chest between his legs on the floor, and reassumed the posture of a drowsy, noncommunicative passenger. The memory of his swift and deadly attack brought a smile to his lips, even if it was only an insignificant security guard. The story of his murder would amount to little more than a fifteen-second soundbite on the morning TV news.

Then Hodge recalled with pleasure a day nine months earlier when his unhesitating obedience triggered a news story seen around the world. *How much sweeter,* he thought, *will be my master's vengeance on Millennium's Eve.*

Seventeen

Beth knew Cole would call about his helmet. It happened at almost 7 o'clock, mercifully interrupting a discussion—on its way to becoming an argument—with her father about televangelist Simon Holloway's fundamentalist views.

"Beth, this is Reagan Cole."

"I didn't expect to hear from you tonight," she lied convincingly. "Aren't you on duty?"

"Dinner break, which tonight means about ten minutes to sit in my patrol car and eat a candy bar."

"Busy night?"

"A few fender benders, standard for a rainstorm. And I've been called out on two street fights. Some of our local drunks run a little short of the Christmas spirit as the day wears on."

Beth hummed sympathetically, then waited.

"The reason I called, Beth, is that I left my brain bucket in your car this afternoon—on the floor in the back seat."

"Oh, I guess you did." Beth purposely sounded surprised, but smiled at herself smugly for driving away from Olvera Street without reminding Cole about his helmet.

Beth had enjoyed her afternoon with Reagan Cole, even more than she had conveyed with her proper thank-you's. *There's something refreshing about a nonreligious man taking a nonreligious woman to Mass on their first date,* she had conceded while driving home from Olvera Street. *And there's something attractive in the way he immersed me in the noisy, delightful dinner with the Quinteros instead of stealing me away all to himself.*

Beth wasn't ready to admit to a romantic interest in Reagan Cole. But she *was* interested—enough to conveniently forget about his helmet in the back seat. She suspected that Reagan Cole was also the willing victim of a slight case of selective amnesia. The prospect was exciting to her.

"Would it be a problem for me to come by after work tonight and pick it up?" Cole said.

Beth hummed indecisively, masking her interest in seeing him again so soon.

Cole picked up quickly. "If that's too late for you, you could just leave it on your front porch and I won't disturb you."

"I don't think it will be a problem," Beth said tentatively. "Dad will be in bed by then, but I'm kind of a night owl myself. I'll probably be working late on my book assignment. Maybe we can have that cold beer we turned down at—"

"Can you hold a second, Beth," Cole interrupted in a more official tone. "There's a call on my radio." Beth could hear the official cop talk in the background before he put his phone on hold. The sound caused her to remember the danger and excitement of the chase with Cole. She was pleased that the harsher memories of the incident were being distanced from her by the positive qualities drawing her to him. No, she definitely was not ready to say good-bye to Reagan Cole.

"Sorry, Beth, I've got to go. A couple of my men are having trouble controlling a street fight down on Ninth and San Pedro. Later tonight then, for a beer?"

"Sure, I'd like that. You need directions?"

"I have the address. It may be close to midnight before I get there. Is that okay?"

"I'll be up."

"See you then, Beth. Over, er, I mean, good-bye." Cole was laughing at himself as he hung up. It made Beth smile.

Beth could hear the Kawasaki winding up Winnetka Avenue as soon as it left the stop sign at Wells Drive halfway down the hill. She stood in the well-lit driveway bouncing the basketball on the still damp cement and launching hooks and jump shots at the basket above the garage door. Her father had installed the backboard twenty years ago and meticulously maintained it for his "basketball princess."

The storm had passed, but some high clouds remained. It was still below 50 degrees. Beth dressed for her workout in expensive court shoes and loose-fitting sweats over her tights. Her hair was pulled into a competition ponytail.

The motorcycle droned louder as it climbed the hill above the Scibelli house, then quieted as Cole downshifted, approaching the turn at Adele Court. In a moment the single headlight was visible snaking down the quiet hillside street lined with large ranch-style homes. Cole, wearing his maroon flight suit and goggles instead of a helmet, parked his bike at the curb behind the Star Cruiser.

"Great neighborhood for skateboarding," he said, nodding toward the steep curves of Adele Court as he approached Beth.

"The best," she said, still dribbling the basketball. "I could roll down these hills almost before I could walk. The boys and I had a lot of fun on this street—and raised some serious blisters and scabs."

"Brothers?"

"No, the neighborhood boys. I'm an only child. When we were growing up, I was the only girl who would ride the hill with them." Beth hooked the basketball toward the backboard. It rattled the rim and bounced off to the right. Cole chased the ball down, his heavy boots thudding on the pavement. He threw up a shot from just clear of the eaves that missed everything.

"I bet you played some heavy-duty hoops in this driveway," he said, as he retrieved his errant shot and passed the ball to Beth on the free throw line—a seam in the cement driveway.

Beth twirled the ball in her hands, eyeing the basket. "The guys around here wouldn't play ball with me very often."

"You were too good?"

"Too tall. In junior high I was a head taller than every guy in my neighborhood. And being an early bloomer, I was better coordinated. By the time their bodies caught up to mine in high school, I was still a couple years ahead of them in skill development."

"You were the neighborhood champion of Horse and Tip-in."

"No question." Beth tossed up a free throw that skipped off the back of the rim. Cole rebounded and bounced the ball back to her.

"And when we played one-on-one for blood, the boys wouldn't guard me closely. I guess they were afraid they'd reach in and touch something they shouldn't. So I could drive the lane on them or score from outside. I almost always won, so they stopped playing me."

Beth sent another free throw toward the basket and it swished through the net without touching the rim. Cole caught it on the first bounce and threw it back to her. "Two in a row—let's see it, Ms. USC," he prodded. Beth sighted, shot, and swished again. Cole kept feeding her the ball, and she made seven out of ten free throws.

"Can you beat that, Mr. Bruin?" Beth challenged playfully, waving him to the line.

"Hey, I haven't shot the ball for awhile, and I'm a little out of shape."

"Funny, that's what the neighborhood boys used to say," Beth said with a devious grin.

Cole laughed. "Okay, okay, but I need a little warm-up."

"Take as many shots as you need," Beth said, settling under the basket.

Cole took five practice shots, making four, then confidently announced that he was ready. Then he missed his next three. Beth put a hand to her throat and made a choking sound. They both laughed, then Cole sank five of his next eight shots from the line.

"So how did you learn to play basketball?" Cole asked as they moved around the driveway attempting a variety of shots.

"My dad. He wanted me to be well rounded in the play department. So some evenings he played dolls with me, and some evenings he pulled me out here to shoot hoops with him. He didn't force me to be a jock. But when I really started to enjoy basketball and showed some promise, he gave me great coaching and encouragement."

"And you had some natural talent," Cole added.

Beth shrugged trying to convey modest agreement. "Being five-eight in junior high didn't hurt me either."

Cole walked the ball to Beth at center court. "Speaking of your dad, how was it around here today with him?" His voice was quieter, more serious.

Beth tried to look beyond the pleasant blue eyes into the mind of the handsome, intriguing man gazing at her questioningly. *Do you really want to know?* she wondered. *Or are you just putting a move on me? Are you as sincere and unclouded as you seem? Or is the warmth and sensitivity I see just your way to bait a wicked hook?*

Beth was convinced that the man who verbally humiliated her the other night in front of the CHP yard wasn't the real Reagan Cole. But she wasn't sure if his disarming affability on Olvera Street and interest in her family reflected the real Cole either. At this moment, she ardently hoped so. With all that was wrong about being in L.A. over the holidays, Reagan Cole seemed so very right. But how much was she willing to risk to plumb his true identity and motives? Her wager was increasing every moment she spent with him.

"My visits with Dad always start out all right," she said at last. "He asks how I'm doing, so I tell him about my work and my friends and my latest decorating project at home. That part usually goes well. But when I ask how he's feeling, how work is going—"

"His business is. . . ?"

"Accounting. He's a CPA. Owns a firm in West L.A."

"Mm."

"Anyway, whatever I ask him about, he always turns the conversation to Simon Holloway. Ever since they heard I was going to be here for Unity 2000 they've been saying, 'Beth, we want you to sit with us and listen to Rev. Holloway. He will change your life. We want to introduce you to him. Maybe you can write a book about him.'"

Beth sighed with disgust, then turned her back to the garage and walked slowly toward the street to make sure her sleeping father wouldn't hear her. Cole walked with her.

"Then this evening, after a pleasant afternoon looking through family photo albums, Dad baited me into an old argument. He asked, 'Are you going to mention in your book Rev. Holloway's stand on genetic engineering?' I said, 'No, my book isn't about what Holloway or these other religious leaders believe; it's about Unity 2000 and what people in Los Angeles think about it.'

"Then he said, 'Well, don't you think it's important that people understand the sacrilege of tampering with the human genome and reprogramming DNA?' I said, 'No, Dad, because I don't believe genetic engineering is sacrilegious or immoral or wrong.'

"If I would have just stopped there and walked away from him, it would have been okay. But today, like so many times before, I just couldn't leave it alone. I said, 'God gave us a brain to solve our problems. If we fail to use the technology we have discovered to help eliminate birth defects, reverse world hunger, and reduce crime, we're ignoring the gift God gave us. And that's what I consider sacrilegious, immoral, and wrong.' Luckily, you called before we got too wound up. I spent the rest of the evening working in my room."

"So this isn't a simple lifestyle conflict between you and your dad; it's philosophical."

"Exactly. And I get so steamed when he tells me about all the money he and Mom shove into Holloway's pockets to keep that hallelujah compound in Florida running and to fund his army of bigots and doomsayers. I've told him, 'Dad, think about what all those millions Holloway collects could do to help the homeless or find a cure for AIDS or relieve world hunger.'"

"And he says. . . ?"

"You won't believe it," Beth said with obvious disdain. "He says it's no good helping the disadvantaged when the world is so ungodly. He says it's like sending a leaky boat into the ocean to rescue a drowning man. 'What good is it to pull someone into a boat that's just going to sink anyway?' he says. 'We're helping Simon Holloway try to fix the boat.'"

Beth paced the length of the driveway and back to calm herself. Cole waited by the curb watching her, spinning the basketball in his hands, puffing steam.

"What about your mother?" Cole asked when she returned. "Is it just as difficult being around her?"

"Mom and I are as different in temperament as Dad and I are alike. She isn't a debater or a hothead like us. She just blissfully wanders through life doing whatever Simon Holloway says. She worships him like he's a member of the Trinity. Talk about blind faith! If Holloway ever goes completely over the falls and starts preaching at people to move to a monastery in Tibet or take a suicide pill, she'll be the first one in line."

"Do you talk to her about her beliefs?"

"Sure. I say, 'Mom, how can you accept everything Simon Holloway preaches as complete truth? Isn't there anything you wonder about or disagree with, especially when there are so many people around who hate Holloway for his radical stand on moral issues?' She just smiles and tells me that if Holloway—she always calls him *Reverend* Holloway—needs to be corrected, God will take care of it. Then she excitedly tells me about the next conference or seminar she and Dad will be attending at Jubilee Village."

"That's where she is now? Orlando?"

Beth flushed with anger at the reminder. "Yeah, can you believe it! They were so excited that I was coming home. Then Holloway announces on Christmas Eve that he has some vacant rooms for rent at the Village, and off she goes—checkbook in hand!"

Cole whistled in sympathy and disbelief.

The expression on Beth's face abruptly changed from consternation to chagrin. "Geez, I'm sorry, Reagan. I didn't mean to dump all this on you."

"I'm glad you did. You'll probably feel better. Besides, I'm interested in your life, Beth. I'm interested in you."

A magnetic charge passed from Cole's eyes into Beth's. The momentary attraction between them was strong, undeniable. Beth thought she should look away. It's too soon, you don't know him, her more cautious side objected. But she couldn't avert his eyes. She knew she was vulnerable to Cole's kiss, and she recklessly wished for it.

But he broke the spell with a nervous clearing of the throat. Then he said, "Say, I believe you promised me a beer."

Beth was silently amused at the glimmer of boyish innocence and reticence. *You're right, Reagan,* she thought. *There's no reason to hurry.*

"Dad doesn't allow any alcohol in the house," she explained. "But there's a twenty-four-hour market down on Ventura Boulevard." Then she snatched the basketball out of his hands with an impish grin. "How about a game of one-on-one to 20 points, loser buys the six-pack—imported, of course, in bottles."

"The Trojans against the Bruins," he said, returning her smile.

"Crosstown showdown, right here in the driveway."

"But you're wearing your Nikes; I'm wearing boots," he objected teasingly.

"You're six-five; I'm only five-eleven. I call that even."

"Okay, but I have to warn you. I'm not like your neighborhood boys. I'll defend you. I'll go for the ball, I'll put a body on you."

"That's the only way to play!"

"Twenty points, loser buys?"

"Right. And the winner drives the bike; loser rides on the back," Beth added tauntingly.

"You're on, lady!"

"UCLA is the visiting team," Beth said, shoving the ball in Cole's gut. "You have first outs, and you get outs every time you make a basket."

Cole squared with the basket and began dribbling in place. Beth took a defensive posture, limbs spread apart, eyes focused on the ball. Cole started toward the basket, faked left, rolled right, and pushed a short jumper toward the basket over Beth's extended arms. The ball spiraled through the net.

"Two-oh," Cole announced, returning to the back line.

This time he faked a drive to the hoop and pulled up for a long shot that went in. "Four-oh," he said, trying not to exult.

Next he tried to charge the basket, but Beth played him tight and bumped him, and his lay-up sailed over the rim. Cole was thinking about calling a foul as Beth grabbed the rebound, cleared the ball, and launched a twenty-two-footer before he could get back. The ball went in. "Two-four," Beth said, all business.

Beth's next shot, a hook over the leaping Cole, failed. But she out-hustled him for the loose ball and banked in a quick turnaround jumper. "Four all."

Beth hadn't really expected to win. But when she sank a shot to tie Cole at 16 after trailing by as many as 6 points, she became hopeful. Cole's boots were a greater liability to him than she had first thought. And even though he used plenty of hand-checking and body contact on defense, Beth was convinced he was holding back, trying not to hurt her or embarrass himself with a careless hand.

"Don't your neighbors get upset when you shoot hoops at mid-night?" Cole said, trying to catch his breath as Beth took the ball out.

"When I'm home," Beth answered, breathing hard, "the neighbors think there's something wrong if I'm *not* out here at midnight."

Cole stole the ball on Beth's next drive and made the shot. But he missed a game-winning opportunity when Beth batted the ball away as he drove to the basket. After clearing the ball, she backed Cole deep into the key, faked left, then dropped in a high-arching, left-handed hook. Cole couldn't move his clunky boots fast enough to recover from the fake and block the shot.

"Eighteen all," Beth said. "Next basket wins." They were both bent at the waist exhaling clouds of steam near the end line.

"I could sure use that beer," Cole puffed.

"Get your money ready," Beth returned, dribbling the ball into the street.

Cole stood in the driveway waiting for her to make her play. But instead she stopped in the middle of the street and turned toward the basket. When he realized she was sighting in a long shot, he charged her, boots clomping loudly, arms flailing trying to distract her. Beth's two-handed shot was away before he arrived, but momentum carried him into her, knocking her hard to the pavement.

"That's the game; Trojans win!" Beth exulted, lying in the street with arms lifted to the sky.

"I didn't see it go in. How do you know it went in?" Cole looked for the ball. It was bouncing underneath the basket.

"Because I've been making this shot since I was fourteen. And this isn't the first time I've won a six-pack with it."

"But you shot from the middle of the street. That's out of bounds," Cole objected playfully.

"Home court advantage," Beth chided with a laugh.

Cole extended an arm and helped her up, making sure she wasn't hurt. Their embrace was tentative, fraternal, like two teammates con-gratulating each other after a victory. But Beth felt the promise in Cole's arms.

"You aren't serious about driving my bike down the hill, are you?" Cole said as they returned to the driveway and collected the ball.

"Sure I am. I've owned a couple of bikes in my day. I even have my own helmet. A bet's a bet, Bruin."

Moments later the Kawasaki climbed Adele Court toward Winnetka with Beth at the controls. Cole sat behind her, one arm around her waist and one arm on her shoulder as he leaned close to refresh her memory on the bike's controls. They roared down Winnetka at almost 50, barely slowing to 15 at the stop sign at Wells Drive. Beth drove them to the market on Ventura Boulevard, and Cole paid for a six-pack of tall, dark green bottles.

"You've honored your wager, Mr. Bruin," Beth said as they returned to the bike and pulled on their helmets. "You can drive back."

"You're sure? You won the driver's seat fair and square—even though I never saw the shot go in."

"No, I'd like you to drive," Beth smiled up at him.

Cole strapped the beer to the short luggage rack behind the seat. Once he settled in place Beth slipped in behind him. Cole drove slowly up gently winding Winnetka. Beth wrapped both arms around him and pressed herself against him tightly, sheltered from the wind, relishing his warmth.

Enjoying Beth's closeness behind him, Cole added several detours to the return trip, extending a five-minute ride into a cozy twenty-minute tour of the hills above Ventura Boulevard.

"I really shouldn't drink a whole bottle," Cole said as he parked behind the candy-apple rental car with the strapped-down deck lid. "It's past midnight, and I have a few miles to cover yet tonight."

"Let's split one, and I'll hide the rest in the bushes—that's what I did in high school."

They huddled on the curb sharing sips from the tall bottle for a silent minute. Then Cole said, "I want to see you again this week, Beth. Very much." He slipped his arm around her and held her close. Beth didn't resist.

"I'm open to a rematch, maybe even a championship series," Beth said, smiling at him warmly.

"Best four out of seven?"

"I don't know. A match-up this good could go on for awhile." Beth blushed at her own forwardness. But she had no desire to take back the words—or the subtle meaning they conveyed.

After two more sips, Cole said, "So what's your schedule tomorrow? When can I see you?"

"It's a busy day, I'm afraid. I have that appointment at the *Times* at 11:30. I'm treating the editor to a long lunch in exchange for all the dirt she can dish me about Holloway and those other three religious kooks."

"But tomorrow is Sunday. You have a business appointment on Sunday?"

"The work of a good journalist can't be confined to banker's hours," Beth returned, exaggerating mock superiority. "Besides, her boss is out of town, so she's spending extra hours in the office getting ready for all the new millennium religious events. I arranged the appointment for tomorrow to get me out of the house."

"And after you play meet the press. . . ?"

"Dad wants me to pick up Mom at LAX—she gets in at 4:10—and meet him in Century City for dinner. Assuming I survive the freeway and family time, I'll spend the evening writing on my rented computer."

Cole gave her another gentle squeeze. "So shall I meet you here after work tomorrow night for game two of the series?"

"If you think you can handle the punishment."

"I'll bring the punishment; you bring the refreshments."

"The beer will be in the bushes."

"If you let me win, I'll take you for another ride on my bike."

"I'd like that. But a Trojan never *lets* a Bruin win. If you want it badly enough, you have to come and get it."

Beth's not-so-inadvertent double entendre caught them both by surprise. Their eyes locked again in a magnetic gaze. Only this time Cole did not back away. He folded Beth in his arms and gave her a long, fulfilling kiss.

NOVEMBER 1999						
S	M	T	W	T	F	S
	1	2	3	4	5	6
7	8	9	10	11	12	13
14	15	16	17	18	19	20
21	22	23	24	25	26	27
28	29	30				

1999 DECEMBER 1999

S	M	T	W	T	F	S
			~~1~~	~~2~~	~~3~~	~~4~~
~~5~~	~~6~~	~~7~~	~~8~~	~~9~~	~~10~~	~~11~~
~~12~~	~~13~~	~~14~~	~~15~~	~~16~~	~~17~~	~~18~~
~~19~~	~~20~~	~~21~~	~~22~~	~~23~~	~~24~~	~~25~~
26	27	28	29	30	31	

JANUARY 2000						
S	M	T	W	T	F	S
						1
2	3	4	5	6	7	8
9	10	11	12	13	14	15
16	17	18	19	20	21	22
23	24	25	26	27	28	29
30	31					

(5) Days
Till
Millenniums'
Eve

Eighteen

Shelby's familiar dream returned with several puzzling and discomforting twists. She squirmed fitfully in the narrow bed belonging to Magdalena Cruz, as the scenes unfolded in her brain.

She saw her late husband greeting the crowd at the gate of the film team's charter flight in Tel Aviv. Though shorter than most of the men standing around him, and trim bordering on skinny, Adrian's commanding presence burned through the images in Shelby's restless subconscious . . . expensive, fashionable clothes . . . perfectly styled, medium-length blond hair . . . the regal bearing of a vastly talented and successful motivator and communicator. With Adrian's cool, private, uncommunicative persona momentarily obscured by the dream, Shelby again saw her late husband as the strikingly handsome and desirable man who had won her heart as a college girl.

The scene quickly changed to a Boeing 767 lifting off, steeply ascending, gracefully banking over water. Eight thousand feet and climbing, a crew of six and seventy-eight weary filmmakers headed back to the U.S. after a grueling month-long location shoot. In the dream Shelby watched the plane depart from an outdoor observation deck. In reality she had been asleep in Austin when the fateful flight left Tel Aviv.

Then a blinding flash, a consuming ball of fire. Not a disabling explosion simply meant to knock the plane from the sky, eyewitnesses had said. But a disintegrating blast—actually three or four explosions occurring like a machine gun burst—clearly planned to blow the plane and its occupants apart. In her dream, Shelby saw herself, devoid of emotion, watching the fiery fragments fall, thanking God that poor Adrian and the film crew had died long before their remains reached the sea.

A new scene crowded into Shelby's subconscious, a scene she had never dreamed before. She stood before her congregation in the Victory Life Center auditorium in Arlington. The sanctuary was packed, with an overflow crowd spilling outside onto the grounds. TV cameras were aimed at her, televising her comments to Victory Life faith partners across the country. And in the front row, sitting tall and handsome, was Jeremy Cannon.

She stood on the platform breaking the sad news of her tragic loss to the world. But she didn't stop with the details of the crash. "In reality, Adrian has been dead a long time," she announced calmly as cameras zoomed in. The congregation gasped in shock.

"You saw us as the perfect, loving Christian couple. But Adrian has been a virtual stranger to me for five years. He's been married to the ministry, consumed by his End-Times studies, lost in his films. My loneliness has been so severe that I have fantasized about being with some of you." She pointed unashamedly to several of the men sitting around the room.

Shock and disbelief swept across the crowd like a chilling wind. Many rose to their feet and left the room shaking their heads.

"You can't expect me to run this ministry by myself," Shelby continued from the pulpit. "I need companionship, a man who will dream with me, plan with me, pray with me, and love me." She focused her gaze on Jeremy Cannon. "And you're the one I want," she said. Extending her arms toward Jeremy, she cooed seductively, "And I want you now." Another collective gasp washed across the room. Scores of people departed muttering their disgust, leaving large blocks of empty seats.

Shelby tossed restlessly on her bed, groaning at the painful image, burning with shame and powerless to alter the scene unfolding in her mind. Jeremy Cannon stood to speak to her in the sparsely populated auditorium. She recognized his voice and polished diction. But Shelby knew the words were from her Lord.

"Shelby, do you love Me?"

She was broken with remorse. "You know I love You, Lord. But I have ruined everything by—"

"Feed My sheep," the Christ figure in her dream interrupted, pointing to a crowd of people streaming into the sanctuary and finding their way to the seats vacated by disillusioned members. The new worshipers were not as nattily groomed and attired as those who had departed. Many were poor, downcast, forlorn. Shelby wanted to explain to Jesus both her unworthiness to minister and her uneasiness with people who obviously could not support the ministry financially. But the scene quickly dissolved to black.

Next Shelby found herself dreaming about the dark south Texas roadside where her Silverado pickup sat disabled, leaking coolant. As she stood watching, Soledad Cruz circled the truck with his flashlight, concluding his inspection at the rear bumper with the beam trained on the cross-and-dove bumper sticker. Soledad looked at Shelby with large, sensitive black eyes. It was Soledad's voice and Hispanic accent, but the words belonged to Jesus.

"Shelby, do you love Me?"

"Lord, You know I love You," she answered, ashamed and weeping softly. "But You also know what I've done. The problem is not my love for You. I have failed You and am no longer worthy—"

"Feed My sheep." Jesus, in the form of Soledad Cruz, turned toward his family huddled beside their ancient station wagon. Behind them wave after wave of poor Hispanic and Indian families materialized out of the stick brush, surrounding Shelby, Soledad, and the truck. They gazed at her expectantly, but Shelby didn't know how to help them.

In an instant the roadside scene was gone, and Shelby saw herself on a downtown city street, surrounded by skyscrapers, deluged by the

Five Days Till Millennium's Eve

noise of traffic, brushed and bumped by people on all sides. There were no distinguishing landmarks to the city, but she knew—as those who dream can know without learning—that it was Los Angeles, California.

A figure approached her in the throng, a tall man in a business suit, white shirt, and tie. His skin was of the blackest black. Had it not been for the man's winsome smile and guileless eyes, she might have been afraid of him.

Shelby didn't recognize the black man, but she knew he had come to speak to her just as Jeremy and Soledad had. She bowed her head contritely, her heart still clouded with reproach. Yet the words came again, as surely from heaven as anything she had been sure of in her life. The man's accent was crisp and pronounced—Nigerian, she thought—and his voice was melodic.

"Shelby, do you love Me?"

Her defenses were weakening against the onslaught of compassion she could not explain. She still felt she should argue the point, try to make God understand why He shouldn't love her and why she could no longer serve Him. But her objections were futile. God wasn't listening to her rationalizations. She suddenly knew how Peter must have felt sitting with Jesus beside Galilee as the Master forgave his cowardice and denial and called the despondent apostle into the yoke of ministry with Him again.

Shelby looked into the penetrating black eyes gazing at her. "Yes, Lord," she said with weary resignation and no opposition. "I do love You."

The black man glanced at the masses sweeping by them on both sides. Few looked wealthy or well schooled, and Shelby was aware she was standing in the inner city, not in the suburbs of Beverly Hills or Marina del Rey. "Feed My sheep," He said.

A small voice in her ear and a tiny hand on her cheek penetrated Shelby's unconsciousness. An instant of disorientation caused her to gasp with alarm. She opened her eyes to see the shadow of a tousle-haired three-year-old hovering over her in the predawn darkness.

"Hermana, estoy muy fría," little Antonia Cruz whispered sleepily, patting Shelby's cheek softly with a cool hand.

"O baby, you're so cold," Shelby whispered. "Your sister has taken all the covers in that small bed of yours, hasn't she?" Shelby felt instantly guilty for displacing Magdalena, who had then crowded Antonia out of her own bed. She pulled open a corner of her sheet and blanket. "Come in here, sweetheart, and get warm."

Antonia slid into the opening, snuggled close to Shelby's flannel gown, and was instantly asleep again.

Shelby lay awake in the darkness, warmed by the closeness of the little life lying beside her. Her dream came back to her in large segments, and she was amazed at the calm that attended each scene. The

sinister whispers were still there, rushing dark thoughts of condemnation for her failure. But another voice was strong and pervading, and
the truth was beginning to penetrate. Contrary to the bitter, turbulent
emotions and thoughts that had reigned since Jeremy raced out of her
house, Shelby was being pummeled by the message that God had not
left her, nor was He finished with her.

I know You didn't drag me into the wilderness or disable the truck, she
resigned silently. *I'm the one who ran away. You just followed me until
I came to the end of myself. You brought Soledad Cruz out of the brush
to help me. You offered forgiveness to me through a child's storybook.
And I heard You in my dream calling me to feed Your sheep.*

Shelby paused in her prayer. She was certain she understood what
God was communicating to her: compassion, forgiveness, restoration.
But she didn't know if she really believed Him or how she should
respond to Him—if she indeed decided to respond at all. How could
He wink at her attempt at adultery? How could He repair the breach
her failure had caused in her friendship with Jeremy? How could He
heal the disillusionment she had brought to the young man? How
could He return her to Austin, Victory Life Ministries, and Unity 2000
as if nothing had happened, when she had failed Him so badly? The
rankle of accusing taunts grew louder.

The voice of Christ pierced the inner din so clearly Shelby thought it
might wake the sleeping baby in her arms: "All I want to know right
now is, do you love Me? I can't lead you to the second step until you
take the first."

Shelby knew that. Obedience is a step-by-step operation. God can't
move you to square two unless you trust Him at square one. She had
taught it and preached it for years. And she had lived it in the green-
house environment of affluent, thriving Victory Life Ministries with
Adrian Hornecker securely at the helm. But she knew her past success-
es were hollow and trivial if she did not follow through at this painful
juncture of failure, fear, and faith.

Insistent "can'ts" and "won'ts" scraped through her mind like fingernails on a chalkboard. *God can't restore you to full fellowship with
Him; you sinned in the face of great spiritual knowledge. God won't
trust you with responsibility for ministry again; you acted irresponsibly
toward Jeremy and then childishly ran away instead of owning up to
your failure. You can't go to Los Angeles as honorary chairperson of
Unity 2000; you have forfeited your status as a national spiritual leader
through your wantonness. You can't return to Dallas as the head of
Victory Life Ministries; you are an adulteress.*

In the face of all she didn't understand about what God was saying,
Shelby knew she must act on what she *did* know or be swept away by
the devilish accusations haunting her. She must be decisive; she must
move now.

She carefully slipped out of bed without disturbing tiny Antonia and knelt in the middle of the dark bedroom with her face to the floor. Shivering as much from humiliation as from the cold, she silently and emotionally released herself to the love she could not escape.

Nineteen

Hodge stood at the sink in his tiny bungalow, painstakingly readying himself for a busy day. The glaring lightbulb dangled above him. He turned his face from side to side, carefully examining the image staring back at him in the mirror. During his first few weeks in Los Angeles, Hodge needed at least two hours every morning to complete his preparation. Even now it rarely took him less than ninety minutes. *No need to be hasty or careless so near to the end*, he reminded himself. *The rewards awaiting me on Millennium's Eve and beyond will more than make up for these hours of daily tedium.*

Satisfied with his effort, Hodge donned his jacket and retrieved his knife from the table in the center of the room. He paused to examine the long, sharp blade before sliding it into the sheath hidden inside his jacket. Dried blood was caked in the seam between the blade and the hilt. He took a small screwdriver from the table and scraped the seam clean.

There was a time, when Hodge abhorred the thought of taking a life even for a holy cause. But how far he had come, what great summits of understanding he had scaled in only a few years. How vital was his master's plan for the purification of the church and the preparation of the earth for a millennium of righteousness. And how incredibly splendid that he had been chosen to stand on the highest peak alone, entrusted with the fulfillment of the master's will. No task, including the necessary elimination of human obstacles, could be regarded as unpleasant, in view of the glory of the kingdom to come.

When the scope of the plan was first revealed to him, Hodge had been at once stunned at the responsibility and overcome with humility at the honor bestowed on him. His preliminary task, brilliantly planned and flawlessly executed, had galvanized his courage and commitment. Over eighty innocent souls sacrificed in a blinding, deafening flash to ensure that one would perish from the face of the earth. It had not been as difficult as he had imagined, and it had deepened his resolve for the greater judgment he had been called to execute on Millennium's Eve.

The security guard was obviously an eleventh-hour test of his devotion, Hodge had reasoned in the hours since he escaped Hollywood on the Metro. He had been commanded to arm himself with the sword of judgment, but in almost six months he had never done more than flash the blade to discourage dull-witted infidels who took him for an easy mark.

Sticking the man in the darkness last night had been a greater challenge than sabotaging the jet. Death was remote and sterile from almost two miles away. He had heard the explosions but hadn't seen the lifeless bodies and severed limbs tumbling into the sea. Nor would he let himself imagine the scene.

But the elimination of the hapless guard had been intimate, personal. Hodge felt the man's gut convulse against the hilt of his plunging knife. By the eerie light of the fallen flashlight, Hodge saw the terror in the guard's bulging eyes and the twisted grimace of his silent scream. And he heard the rattle of blood and air in the man's lungs and a final, desperate, dying breath.

But Hodge had accomplished the task without hesitation and without regret. He had proved his mettle, and his master had rewarded him with a clean escape. The countdown to Millennium's Eve was moving smoothly. With many strategic tasks yet to complete, Hodge's confidence and anticipation were rising by the hour.

Hodge arrived at Pershing Square at 11:45 A.M. Downtown traffic was Sunday sparse. With a Southern California warming trend pushing the midday temperature over 60 degrees, the Square had come back to life. Several out-of-town visitors were walking in the Park. And many street people loitered on the lawns, slyly sipping and comparing notes on the Christmas dinners they had sampled at the downtown rescue missions.

Hodge usually disdained fraternizing with the bums in the Square. But this morning he spent several minutes visiting with a small man known around the park simply as the Beetle. Far from being interested in the man's well-being, Hodge considered his visits with the Beetle every few days a kind of investment. He cultivated the simpleton's friendship solely because it might be useful to him in his mission.

Rev. Wingate, with whom Hodge had developed a similar relationship, was back at his regular place near the pond. So Hodge decided to set up shop near the southeast corner of the Square.

"Are you going to lay another blood-and-guts-to-kingdom-come sermon on us today, Hodge?" Bike cop Ochoa rolled up behind him as he dug in his picnic chest to retrieve his Bible. Officer Scanlon was shaking down a couple of drunks on the lawn nearby. *Ochoa sounds more businesslike than usual*, Hodge thought. *He has something more important on his mind than making jokes about my sermon material.*

"I'm just going to preach the Word of God like I always do, officer," Hodge almost whimpered. "This here is a free country, sir. I just praise the Lord that I can preach what the Bible says." He lifted up his Bible reverently and displayed it for Ochoa like it was a box of diamonds.

"You can preach the Gospel, Hodge, but don't cause any trouble in this Square," Ochoa said, his admonition plain despite his pleasant tone, "or Tommy and I will have to take you down to County Jail. You wouldn't like the congregation down there, Hodge, believe me."

Ochoa parked his bike on the sidewalk and joined Officer Tommy Scanlon, who was having trouble achieving the cooperation of one of the drunks.

Hodge bided his time until the two cops had rousted the drunks out of the Square, sending them in the direction of the nearest flophouse. Then Ochoa and Scanlon headed toward Rev. Wingate, who was only a couple of minutes from going off.

Emboldened by his late-night encounter with the security guard and by the mounting success of his mission, Hodge had chosen a special text for Pershing Square today. After a moment of meditation standing atop the picnic chest—during which he heard Rev. Wingate scream, "The kingdom of heaven is at hand!" from the center of the Square— Hodge opened his Bible to the Book of Judges and began to read loudly and dramatically.

Ehud made him a dagger which had two edges, of a cubit length; and he did gird it under his raiment upon his right thigh. And he brought the present unto Eglon king of Moab: and Eglon was a very fat man. And when he had made an end to offer the present, he sent away the people that bare the present. But he himself . . . said, "I have a secret errand unto thee, O king:" who said, "Keep silence." And all that stood by him went out from him.

Hodge looked up from the page. Two vagrants had wandered onto the sidewalk in front of him and appeared to be listening intently. Behind them stood an overweight man in a white shirt and tie—a tourist, Hodge guessed—stuffing his face with a sandwich. Encouraged that his audience was more than just pigeons, he continued reading.

And Ehud said, "I have a message from God unto thee." And he arose out of his seat. And Ehud put forth his left hand, and took the dagger from his right thigh, and thrust it into his belly: and the haft also went in after the blade; and the fat closed upon the blade, so that he could not draw the dagger out of his body; and the dirt came out. Then Ehud—

"All right, Hodge, what's all this stuff about a knife?" It was Vince Ochoa's voice, and he was serious. Ochoa and Scanlon had quietly circled behind Hodge on their bikes and been listening to him read. The vagrants and the chunky tourist hadn't been interested in Hodge's text, only in what the cops were going to do to him.

Hodge stepped off the picnic chest and turned to face the two bike cops. "It's right here in the Bible, officer. I ain't causing no trouble, sir. I'm just reading about a man who cut another man because he was evil."

"Well, we heard about a guy in the Square yesterday wearing a jean jacket and Dodgers cap just like yours and carrying a blue and white picnic chest just like yours." Scanlon was slowly walking behind Hodge as Ochoa talked. Several more curious onlookers gathered around at a safe distance. "This guy we heard about almost cut a couple of kids who were passing out invitations to a Christmas dinner. Do you know anything about that, Hodge?"

Hodge hoped they hadn't heard about another incident with a knife in neighboring Hollywood. As always, he knew cooperation was vital to maintaining an appearance of innocence.

"Yes, sir, officer. They came up on me so fast I thought they was going to jump me, sir. You know how it is downtown, sir. I didn't try to cut those guys, sir. I was just protecting myself in case they was trying to cut me."

"Now you can't go pulling knives on people, Hodge, just because you're a little paranoid." Officer Ochoa was unsnapping the strap securing his pistol as he spoke. "You know it's illegal to carry a concealed weapon. Now put your Bible on the sidewalk and very slowly take the lid off your picnic chest and step away from it." The cop's hand was resting on the butt of his DAB gun. Hodge imagined that Scanlon had taken the same posture behind him.

"Officer Ochoa, sir, you know—"

"Do it, Hodge, now!"

Hodge saw two black-and-whites pull up to the curb across the Square. Scanlon had called for backup.

Hodge slowly squatted and laid his Bible on the sidewalk. Then he reached out in exaggerated slow motion, lifted the lid on the picnic chest, and placed it next to the Bible.

"Now stand up, Hodge, and back away," Ochoa commanded. "Empty your pockets on the sidewalk." He complied, pulling out his key ring, a couple of Metro transfers, and a dollar and a quarter in change, laying them on the cement in front of him.

"Spread your hands and feet," Ochoa continued.

Hodge moved his feet apart and stretched out his arms at 45-degree angles to the earth. Four more uniformed officers stepped inside the wide circle of gawking tourists. Most of the transients had moved toward the park exits at the appearance of more cops.

"You don't have any needles on you, do you, Hodge?" Scanlon asked from behind, dead serious. "I get real upset when I find a needle that wasn't supposed to be there."

"No sir, officer. My pockets is empty, sir. I don't use no drugs, sir."

Scanlon, still wearing his riding gloves, removed Hodge's baseball cap and checked inside it. Then he began patting Hodge down from behind. He said, "If I find a knife on you, Hodge, you're going to jail. You know that?"

"'Yes, sir. I don't have no knife, sir," Hodge said, turning his head toward the cop.

"Geez, Hodge, don't you own a toothbrush?"

"Yes, sir. And I use it too, sir. I just don't have no toothpaste."

Scanlon cautiously frisked Hodge's torso, arms, and legs as Ochoa and the other cops looked on. Then Scanlon nodded at his partner, signaling that Hodge was clean.

"What did you do with the knife you pulled yesterday, Hodge?" Ochoa asked.

"Oh, I got rid of that thing, officer," Hodge said, dropping his arms slowly and shuffling his feet together. "I didn't want to hurt nobody, sir. So I just threw it away."

"Right," Ochoa muttered disbelievingly. "What's in the ice chest?"

"Just a sandwich and an apple and a can of pop, sir. That's my lunch kit, sir."

"If I find a knife in there, I'm taking you to jail, Hodge," Ochoa repeated, approaching the picnic chest while Scanlon stayed close behind Hodge.

"I understand, officer. I ain't got no knife in there, sir. It's gone, sir."

Ochoa stooped to the picnic chest and carefully lifted out a badly bruised apple, a tuna sandwich on hard bread wrapped in newspaper, and a warm can of Coke. The chest was empty.

"Okay, Hodge, you're off the hook today," Ochoa said, standing. "But if I ever hear about you pulling a knife again, you will go to jail. It's that simple. Got that?"

"Yes, sir, officer," Hodge groveled. "That knife is gone, sir. I don't need it no more, sir. I won't be no trouble to you officers again, I can guarantee it."

The crowd began to disperse, and the backup officers returned to their cars. Hodge put his lunch back in the chest, then said, "Officer, I ain't quite finished with my sermon today, sir. If you don't mind, I'll just stay and—"

"Sorry, Hodge," Ochoa cut in, still in a serious tone. "You're finished for today. I want you out of the Square until tomorrow. And I don't want to hear any more of that blood and guts, broken bones and torn flesh crap you've been preaching. If you're going to preach in my Square, you can't talk about people getting wasted by God, whether it's in your Bible or not."

"But it's the Word of God, officer. I'm only preaching what—"

"Don't push it, Hodge. We'll be watching you. Now, adios."

Hodge reluctantly slid his Bible underneath his sandwich in the picnic chest and replaced the lid. With the two officers watching him, he walked slowly toward the southeast exit of the Square.

Hodge was perplexed as he rode the Metro south to Twenty-third and walked to his bungalow. For the first time in twenty-five days he had been unable to deliver the judgments he had been sent to Pershing Square to announce. He locked the door behind him, turned on the light, and placed his chest on the table. And Ochoa had forbidden him to declare God's judgments in the Square again.

Yet it had also been a day of uncanny foresight. He lifted the lid from the picnic chest and laid it top-down on the table. Then he ran a small screwdriver between the plastic lining and the lid until the lining popped loose, revealing a six-inch knife sheath wrapped in plastic bubble sheeting.

Hodge had been uncertain about his premonition to hide his knife before leaving for the Square today. He felt vulnerable without the sword of judgment tucked close to his side under his jacket. However, the omen was strong, and Hodge had obeyed. But was he saved from going to jail only to be banned from preaching God's judgment in the Square? Why would the master warn him to hide the knife but fail to prevent the cops from kicking him out of Pershing Square?

The answer came to him in glorious revelation. The Pershing Square pronouncements had been fulfilled. He had been faithful through Christmas Day as he had been commanded. Now it was time for the final push, a more focused statement of the judgment to be delivered on Millennium's Eve. He had been specifically directed away from the Square to a new medium for his message, and enthusiasm surged through him like fire.

He returned his knife to the cloth pocket he had prepared for it inside his jacket. Then he sat down and began scribbling a new set of messages as fast as they came to him.

Twenty

Times-Mirror Square occupies a full city block in the heart of downtown Los Angeles, bordered north and south by First and Second Streets, and east and west by Spring and Broadway. Home of the *Los Angeles Times* and the expansive Times-Mirror media empire, the massive cement fortress is perched like a vigilant watchdog across First Street from the sprawling Los Angeles civic center. This three-block-wide conglomeration of city, county, state, and federal offices stretches for nearly a mile between First Street and U.S. Route 101, the Hollywood Freeway.

During her years as a journalism major at USC, Beth had visited the *Times* building occasionally, so she had no trouble locating the editorial floor. Today the building was much quieter than it would be tomorrow, but a receptionist was there to serve the small weekend staff. She buzzed associate religion editor Mai Ngo and announced her. Beth paced the carpeted lobby as she waited, missing the familiar sounds rising from the maze of open cubicles stretching far across the floor— softly clacking keyboards, beeping phones, and occasional bursts of chatter and laughter.

Beth didn't know what to expect from the editor she had spoken to briefly by phone two weeks earlier when she set up the appointment. Mai Ngo had seemed cordial enough, agreeing to meet with Beth to share information about Unity 2000 and its principle characters—information Beth previously hadn't exercised much initiative to collect.

Beth first imagined that Mai Ngo might be the classic strictly business, you-scratch-my-back-and-I'll-scratch-yours professional. Mai had been so willing to give her time that she suspected an ulterior motive. Beth had offered her a free lunch, but she wondered what additional tariffs the pleasant-sounding associate editor was going to levy for "professional services rendered." *Is she going to touch me up for free copies of the book, data files on other topics I have researched and written about, comp time helping her in the* Times *office? Whatever deal she hopes to cut,* Beth thought, *Mai Ngo will discover that I drive a hard bargain.*

Then Beth wondered if Mai Ngo was some kind of religious nut. Beth understood that religion editors didn't have to be religious any more than obituary editors have to be licensed in embalming or entertainment editors have to own a virtual reality module. Case in point, here she was, a very unreligious writer contracted by an equally unreligious publisher to write the story of Christian television's clash of the titans. Similarly, Mai Ngo could just as easily be a fellow cynic, an atheist, a crystal-gazing New Ager, or a priestess in a satanist cult who just happened to be available when the religion desk was accepting resumés for an associate.

But what if she is *deeply religious?* Beth pondered. *She may be a disciple of Morgan McClure, Shelby Hornecker, T.D. Dunne, or—*the thought iced her spine—*Simon Holloway. Mai Ngo may be as giddy about the gathering at the Coliseum as Jack and Dona Scibelli. Her sweet disposition over the phone and ready compliance with my request may just be bait dangled before a prospective convert.*

In order to get what I want, Beth thought uncomfortably, *I may have to dig through a mountain of religious manure: an emotional "testimony" of Mai's rescue from a life of sin or a memorized presentation of God's "spiritual laws."* (At USC Beth just cursed and walked away whenever a fellow student whipped out a religious booklet.) *This woman may try to buttonhole me into a heavenly network marketing scheme that promises health, wealth, and wisdom for those climbing the ladder of spiritual success.*

No matter what her religious pitch may be, Beth assured herself, *I can handle it. After ten years of keeping Dad, Mom, and Simon Holloway at bay, I could kiss off a pitch by the Pope himself.*

"Hello, Beth. I'm Mai Ngo." The petite woman approached her with hand outstretched and a winsome smile. Her round, pleasant face was framed by softly curled black hair. She wore a flowing black and turquoise print dress, matching earrings and necklace, and black flats. The outfit was both stylish and comfortable. Beth felt overdressed in her expensive gray suit and low heels.

"Good morning, Mai," Beth said, grasping her hand and returning her smile. She had to look down on the diminutive Vietnamese-American, as she did most women and many men. "I'm pleased to finally meet you in person. I have enjoyed your background series on Unity 2000 in the *Times*, and I'm anxious to hear more. Thanks for fitting me in today."

"It's my pleasure, Beth. From what you told me about your assignment, it sounds like we have a lot in common. I've been looking forward to swapping stories with you."

Beth glanced at her watch, not to see the time but to transition from pleasantries to the task at hand. "Are you ready to go? I thought we might eat and talk on Olvera Street, that is if Mexican food sounds good to you." Being out of touch with the restaurants around the civic center and feeling responsible to take the lead, Beth had opted for Quinteros for lunch. It was close and reasonable, and the pleasant memory of being there with Reagan Cole might take her mind off Mai Ngo if the meeting turned out to be a dud.

"Mexican would be great," Mai said. "I need to get my purse and phone. Would you like to walk back with me and see our little corner of the *Times* world?"

"Yes, very much," Beth said enthusiastically, though she was only casually interested. *What's so great about another desk, computer, and phone?* she thought.

Mai led Beth on a winding path through five-foot-tall office cubicles into an enclosure simply marked with a laser-printed sign: RELIGION. Beth surveyed the cramped quarters and a desk top crowded with a keyboard and stacks of diskette files, but thought better about making a negative comment.

Mai seemed to read her mind. "As you can see, I barely have enough room in here to turn around. That's nanotechnology for you. The machines keep getting smaller and faster, so every time we rearrange the floor—which is a couple of times a year—the brass think we can get along with less space."

Beth smiled and nodded understandingly.

"This is my boss' office—Serg Buonoconti," Mai said, pointing to the work station directly behind hers. "Did I tell you that he's on the

East Coast all week covering that New Age harmonic convergence on New Year's Day?"

"Yes, you mentioned he would be back east. Why did your senior editor take a traveling assignment over the holidays instead of sending you?" Beth hoped the answer might give her a clue about Mai's personal involvement in Unity 2000.

"Serg is single, and with me having a family here, he volunteered to go east and let me cover the Unity event. Serg has been very good to me that way. I don't have to travel often."

Logical, Beth thought, *but it doesn't answer my real question.* "Is Serg into the New Age lifestyle or just a professional observer?" she asked.

"He's a devout Catholic, a lay minister in fact, very active in the Los Angeles archdiocese. He doesn't have a personal interest in Harmony 2000. He went back strictly to get a West Coast perspective for *Times* readers."

"It's very confusing that the two events are called Unity 2000 and Harmony 2000. Who came up with the name first?"

Mai laughed. "Nobody's sure. The Harmony people say they came up with it first, and the Unity organizers contend that the New Agers stole the idea from them. Neither was willing to back down and change the name. And yes, it's been very confusing for everybody. At least two or three times a day I'm changing 'Unity' to 'Harmony' and 'Harmony' to 'Unity' in the new millennium data coming through our computer network."

"I've discovered the same problem in my research on Unity 2000," Beth said, hoping to convince Mai that her research had been extensive. "I wonder how many travel agents have booked New Agers into L.A. and sent Bible-thumpers to Myrtle Beach, South Carolina by mistake." They both laughed at the humorous possibilities. Beth noticed that Mai took no visible offense at her term "Bible-thumpers."

"Will you be at the Coliseum Friday night to cheer on your favorite televangelist?" Beth asked. *If you're a flag-waving disciple, Mai, now's your chance to tell me,* she added silently.

"Actually, my husband and I are still discussing whether or not we will attend. I have two excellent writers covering the event for the New Year's Day edition, so I don't have to be there. But our kids have never seen anything like this before, so they're bugging us to take them or at least let them go with friends."

Mai, you're either cleverly noncommittal or you don't give a rip about what's happening in the Coliseum, Beth thought. She decided to take one more stab at discerning Mai's religious position. "Would you rather be standing beside the Atlantic Ocean with the New Agers welcoming the first sunrise of the new millennium?"

Mai smiled. "No, I'm not into New Age. Are you?"

"Oh, not me either," Beth said, wishing Mai would tell her what she *was* into. She was sure it would come out sooner or later, hopefully not in the form of a sermon. "I like some of the music and art, but I can't handle the mindlessness and the spirit guides and the crystals and all that."

"Excuse me for just a moment, then I'll be ready to go," Mai said. She quickly recorded a fresh voice-mail message. Then she picked up her purse and black felt jacket and the two women left the building for a five-block walk in the pleasant sunshine to Olvera Street.

As they walked along First toward Main, Mai kept the conversation centered on Beth. Flattered by Mai's interest, Beth related a brief and carefully edited personal history, focusing on her education, athletic achievements, and career. She purposely omitted her family until Mai asked about them. Even then Beth said nothing about her parents' religious peculiarities and her difficulty tolerating them.

Mai's interest in Beth's personal life, flowing through her evocative questions and attentive comments as they walked, warmed Beth to her immediately. *This is no brassy, territorial professional,* she thought. *She's a nice woman treating a casual business encounter as an opportunity to make a new acquaintance. And she shows no signs of sizing me up for a pitch about feel-good, solve-all-your-problems religion. But the meeting has just begun.*

When Mai asked how Beth was enjoying her visit to Los Angeles this time, the story of the harrowing assault on the freeway and her rescue at the hands of an off-duty police officer tumbled from her mouth. She enjoyed talking about Reagan Cole; he had scarcely left her thoughts since they were last together. Yet she told Mai only about the rescue and the chase, and nothing about her feelings for Reagan, which had plummeted to the pits and then soared to the pinnacle in less than twenty-four hours.

When they entered Quinteros, Raphaela spied Beth immediately and rushed to greet her. After introductions, Raphaela bubbled to Mai about how much she and Luis enjoyed having Beth and Reagan as their guests for Christmas. Then she personally escorted Beth and Mai to a table.

The busboy delivered glasses of ice water, a basket of tortilla chips, and two small bowls of fragrant salsa. "So you and the police officer are seeing each other?" Mai asked with a twinkle.

Beth blushed, wishing the conversation hadn't drifted so far from the reason for their meeting. "He's a very nice man," Beth said finally, hoping her tone of voice conveyed her desire to close the subject. Mai got the message. After they ordered, she asked Beth about some of her latest writing projects, and Beth reveled in the kind attention.

When their entrees were served, Mai said softly, "Thank you for the delicious food and the delightful company."

Admiring the chicken tostada salad before her, Beth was about to say, "My pleasure." But looking up, she had the sinking feeling that Mai's comments weren't directed at her. The woman's head was bowed over her plate. *She's not scrutinizing her taco salad for bugs; she's praying,* Beth thought sourly. *I knew it. She'll probably pull out the little booklet any time now.*

Hoping to delay that eventuality, Beth turned immediately to business. She pulled a tiny digital recorder from her purse, set it on the table between them, and pushed RECORD. As soon as Mai reached for her fork, Beth said, "What do I need to know about Unity 2000?"

"Where would you like to start?" Mai showed no signs of launching into a religious monologue, for which Beth was grateful.

"Who came up with the concept?" Beth had a sketchy idea of how the event came about, but she was eager to have Mai fill in the details.

"Originally, Adrian Hornecker, the founder of Victory Life Ministries in Dallas."

"The televangelist whose plane exploded over the Mediterranean in March?"

"Yes. He reportedly received a vision for Unity 2000 back in September of '98 while preaching one Sunday."

"You say 'reportedly.' Do you think he just made it all up?"

"I don't know, Beth. It could have been a vision. It could have been something else he interpreted as a vision. I can't make a judgment on it. Whatever it was, Hornecker announced it to the world at the end of the service and publicly invited—or should I say challenged—the other three, McClure, Holloway, and Dunne, to throw in with him. Then he gave the whole project over to one of his administrative associates, Darin Chaumont, to organize. The man has done a miraculous job putting it all together on such short notice."

"Then Hornecker was killed in the crash. I heard that the so-called vision almost died with him."

Mai drizzled a spoonful of dressing on her salad. "Officially, his wife and successor, Shelby Hornecker, picked up the baton as the honorary chairperson for the big event, and the other three televangelists fell in behind her enthusiastically."

"And unofficially?"

"Serg told me—and he isn't prone to perpetuating unfounded rumors—that neither McClure, Holloway, nor Dunne were very excited about Unity 2000 in the first place. There's stiff competition among the four of them for television market shares and freewill offerings. As you probably know, each of the TV ministries needs several million dollars a month just to operate. The televangelists saw Unity 2000 as something like a debate between presidential candidates. They each feared losing followers to their rivals if they appeared on the same platform together. But none of them was willing to pull out of the event, thinking it would be seen as factionalism or exclusivism in the face of a call to Christian unity."

"You pull out of Unity 2000, you look bad to the religious world, your support takes a heavy financial hit," Beth interjected.

"Yes. So with Adrian Hornecker's death, the other principal characters held their breath, hoping Mrs. Hornecker would cancel the event."

"But she couldn't do it, because it would make *her* look bad for not following through with an alleged heavenly vision."

"That's what Serg believes."

Beth paused for a bite of salad and a sip of mineral water. "So you have four televangelists and at least 100,000 people coming to L.A. for a convocation on unity. But the leaders couldn't be less interested in joining forces. The whole thing is a farce."

Mai put her fork down and looked away from the table thoughtfully. Then she said, "In all fairness, I believe the rank-and-file followers in these four groups have high hopes for unity. Despite what we know about the rivalry between the televangelists, these people have been hearing their spiritual leaders promote this gathering for months. They're coming to L.A. expecting to experience a dramatic sense of oneness as Christians. And if the program goes as planned, about 100,000 people will return to their homes greatly encouraged to face the new millennium together."

"In other words, Holloway, Hornecker, Dunne, and McClure will put on a show of unity, and all the people will be happy. The problem I scc is, within a week it will be back to business as usual. The four leaders will be doing their own thing again, urging their television 'partners' to have more faith, expect more blessings, and send more money. So for all this hollow hoopla, nothing changes." Beth couldn't help thinking about her gullible parents being blindly jerked around by the charade. She felt indignation steaming around the collar of her designer blouse.

"I see your point," Mai said, unruffled by Beth's mild tirade. "And I agree that much more could be accomplished at Unity 2000 if the four leaders were more open to one another. All I'm saying is that I believe this event can produce a positive effect in the people who attend, regardless of what the leaders do. And who knows? Maybe something good will happen among the leaders that wouldn't have happened without Unity 2000."

"So you think Adrian Hornecker's vision for Unity 2000 was really from God, but his widow and the other televangelists are botching the job?"

Mai flashed an easy smile. "As I said, Beth, I don't know about the vision. But however this event came about and whatever the motives are in the leaders and the people who are coming, I think God will use it to accomplish something good. At least I'm praying to that end."

Beth was momentarily distracted by a confusing glimpse into Mai's soul. Were the comments of the woman sitting across from her reflecting laughable naiveté or quiet wisdom, groundless optimism or well-anchored faith? Was she talking out of her hat, saying that something good could come of this convocation of hypocrites called Unity 2000? Or was she drawing from a deep well of insight and understanding about the event, a well hidden from Beth's view?

Beth felt both attracted to and a little threatened by the warmth, peace, and self-assuredness Mai exuded. The woman obviously had some opinions about Unity 2000, but Beth admired how Mai resisted the opportunity to lock horns with her over them.

Unwilling to allow the interview to lag and give Mai the opportunity to launch into a religious pitch, Beth pressed on.

"What can you tell me about each of the televangelists?"

Mai touched the linen napkin to her lips demurely. "I have extensive profiles on all of them in my computer at the office, the same material the writers and I used for the background series. I'll be happy to make disk copies for you. You can use whatever you want."

"I would appreciate having whatever you can give me. But I'm also looking for the story behind the story on these four charac—, er, personalities. I know that they're all rich—or at least very comfortable—while many of their television supporters live at or below poverty level. I've heard that Morgan McClure is a womanizing crook and that T.D. Dunne is gay. Shelby Hornecker is proving herself incompetent to run her late husband's empire. And Simon Holloway is a narrow-minded, red-necked, bigot-extremist who is probably on the hit lists of a dozen political, human rights, and activist groups. I'd like to know what Serg's unimpeachable sources have to say about all that."

Beth hoped the animosity she felt toward the stars of the Unity 2000 drama wasn't too evident in her words. Had she been pushed into a corner, Beth would admit that her primary interest in Holloway and the others wasn't for her book. The more warts she could uncover on her parents' pastor, the better prepared she would be to discredit Holloway and his organization to them. And the more dirt she could dig up about all four televangelists, the easier it would be to justify her conviction that Unity 2000 was at best a religious circus and at worst a sinister con job.

"It sounds like either you're planning to write an exposé or you have a vendetta against televangelists," Mai said straightforwardly but without malice or condemnation.

Beth was momentarily speechless, stunned by Mai's uncanny perception and by the concern in her voice.

"Well, no," she said, trying not to sound defensive or apologetic. "It's just that the more I know about the principle players, the better prepared I am. . . ." Her words trailed off as she realized how illogical her backpedaling sounded.

"Beth, I'm very happy to make the *Times* data files available to you on the four televangelists. In fact, you could set up shop in our office and work on Serg's PC while you're in town. You would have instant access to everything we have, and you can draw your own conclusions about these people from what you find. But it's my personal and professional policy never to write or pass along unsubstantiated fact, even if I'm inclined to believe it.

"For example, there were some strong allegations leveled at Morgan McClure last year for misuse of funds at the retirement village his church operates. But he hasn't been indicted, tried, or convicted on any counts. I've studied the allegations and interviewed some of the complainants. We printed their stories, and I fully expect McClure to be indicted in the next few months. But I won't call him a crook until it happens, and I won't fabricate anything from my feelings and opinions and promote it as fact."

There was nothing in Mai's tone to suggest she was reprimanding Beth for the rumors she had voiced. She was simply explaining her code of ethics, a code Beth subscribed to theoretically, but which sometimes was overlooked in the emotion of a potentially hot story. Still, Beth *felt* reprimanded and reluctantly admitted to herself that she needed it.

"On the other hand," Mai continued, "when I run across a rumor that's just begging to be reported as juicy news, I track it to the source so I can print the truth. What you heard about T.D. Dunne being a homosexual was a vindictive lie. Dunne fired one of his band members for refusing to give up his immoral lifestyle, so the man started the rumor to get back at him. I talked to both of them. Dunne told me the story and the ex-band member eventually confirmed it. I was especially glad this rumor turned out to be false, because my kids are crazy about T.D. Dunne's music."

Ordinarily Beth never apologized to her professional peers. She hated appearing weak or giving anyone an advantage. But she somehow knew Mai wouldn't throw it back in her face or use it against her.

"I guess I sounded a little like I'm on a witch-hunt," she said sheepishly. "I'm sorry." Then she thought, *Mai, you seem to be someone I could vent my real concerns to about Simon Holloway and the others—someday, maybe.*

"Oh, no offense taken, Beth. Not at all."

Beth knew she was right.

Twenty-one

It was almost noon before Soledad Cruz returned from the auto parts store in Cotulla with a new heater hose and a gallon of coolant for Shelby's disabled Silverado pickup. By then it was time for the midday meal, which was a festive family event with a guest in the home. Sister Shelby was again afforded the honored place at the table. Ernie and Maria Paula were allowed to sit beside her, since Magdalena and Antonia had enjoyed that privilege during the evening meal.

Sister was asked to pronounce the blessing. Beans, rice, and tortillas were passed to Sister first. And Sister was the last to finish her meal because of an endless stream of questions from the children about her large ranch in Austin. "How many horses do you have, sister?" "Do you ride your Brahman bulls, sister?" "When I come to visit you in Austin, can I ride your tractor, sister?" "Will you send me a picture of your ranch house, Sister?"

When the children were finally shooed from the table, Soledad and Lupe continued the questions without prying. They were satisfied knowing only that Shelby was a widow who owned a large ranch and managed her late husband's business interests in Dallas. She remained purposely vague on the source of her wealth, the kind of business she was involved in, who her husband was, and how he had died, and Soledad and Lupe respected her distance.

Although the children had chattered excitedly about someday visiting Sister in Austin, Shelby had not extended an invitation and her hosts did not attempt to secure so much as a phone number.

It also sounded logical to them that Shelby had been on her way to Nuevo Laredo for a "brief vacation" when she turned off to investigate Los Angeles, Texas on a whim. Having been delayed by the truck's breakdown, she told them, she would now forgo the trip to Mexico and drive back to Austin and then on to Waco, where her parents were expecting her.

Shelby had considered telling her kind hosts that God had used them to rescue her in the midst of a foolish, Jonah-like attempt to flee Him. But she felt checked about it in her spirit. Such a confession would require her to disclose details that would only confuse and possibly discourage the Cruzes. Feeling checked by God was another encouraging sign that the fellowship with Him she had feared to be lost forever had been reestablished during her private moments of humility, confession, and restoration in the predawn darkness.

Though she could not fully explain to Soledad and Lupe how pivotal, how seemingly angelic their intervention had been, Shelby had decided on a way to thank them—a way that would rival in surprise value their sudden, helpful appearance at the roadside in her darkest moment.

With Soledad outside installing the truck's heater hose, and Lupe and the children tending to cleanup chores in the kitchen, Shelby excused herself to the bedroom to change clothes. Among the toys and art supplies in the closet she found the things she needed: blank sheets of paper, tape, and crayons. It took her only a few minutes to complete the task. She couldn't help smiling broadly, imagining the expressions on the faces of Soledad, Lupe, Magdalena, Ernie, Maria Paula, and Antonia when they discovered her handiwork. A silent, secret visit to each bedroom finished the deed.

It took Soledad about an hour to replace the hose and refill the cooling system with a mix of coolant and water. Shelby offered him $100 for the repairs, but he firmly refused everything but the cost of the parts—as she expected.

It was almost 2 P.M., and Shelby needed to leave quickly to be home by dark. The farewells and embraces were brief. Shelby and Antonia cried, and Magdalena and Maria Paula sniffled. As she watched the Cruz family waving good-bye in the rearview mirror through the swirling dust, Shelby was deeply touched again by the profound love and acceptance of this family and the providential care they had rendered so selflessly.

Los Angeles, Texas held no more allure for Shelby. She accepted that whether God or her curiosity had caused her to turn off at that Los Angeles sign alongside the freeway, breaking down in front of the Cruz's place had worked out for her good. So Shelby followed ranch road 469 back to I-35 and turned north for the three-hour drive to Austin.

She would stop at the first exit promising a pay phone, she decided, and call her parents. She knew they had expected her to arrive at their home in Waco around noon for the post-Christmas visit she had promised. She would explain to them her delay inexplicitly—without lying, of course—and tell them not to hold supper for her. Then she would head home, clean up, and drive on to Waco this evening, a ninety-minute trip from the ranch.

Then what? As the miles of interstate rolled beneath the truck, Shelby really didn't want to think about "then what?" Twenty-four hours earlier she had been a basket case. Like a person running in panic when his clothes catch fire, she had tried to escape the inner flames of her humiliating failure by dashing away. But her frantic flight had only fueled the blaze, as she discovered while standing helplessly beside her broken-down truck as darkness and fear engulfed her.

Then, the sudden safety and acceptance of the Cruz family. The unexpected redemptive encounter with God through a child's storybook and a hope-filled dream. The fire had been quenched and her inner wounds mercifully numbed as the Physician skillfully treated the burns and promised recovery. Shelby had awakened at first light intensely aware of the flames she had vainly tried to escape, but remarkably free of the pain.

Now, with every mile closer to Austin, the reality of what awaited her loomed larger. *It's one thing to sense God's touch in the desert,* she thought, *and quite another to return to the scene of the pain and make it right.*

She didn't have much time to plan for it. On Tuesday morning Gordon and Sean would pick her up at Mueller Airport and fly her to Dallas. There they would pick up Theresa, the Welbourns, and Jeremy Cannon for the trip to L.A. and Unity 2000 on Friday.

The thought of facing Jeremy sent cold fear down her back and weakened her knees. *I have to talk to him—even before Tuesday,* she lamented silently. *I have to apologize, confess my sin, beg his forgiveness. But he may not even want to see me. He may have already dumped his plans for attending Unity 2000 with me. Please, God, don't let him kick over the traces on account of me and return to his old life.* Shelby bit her lip at the vexing thought.

The prospect of facing Theresa, Stan, and Eleanor was no less discomforting. *Should I tell them what happened? I would be less than honest if I didn't. And I would be mortified if they found out from anyone else. Has Jeremy told them already? Have they been out to the ranch or called Mom and Dad looking for me already? Perhaps they have met with the Board of Directors and drummed me out of the ministry on charges of immoral behavior. I may be returning to Austin and Dallas only to find that my life there is over.*

Shelby wanted to turn around and race back to the Cruz's and hide forever behind the sagebrush and huisache, cuddling precious Antonia and reading stories to the children. But there was no escaping that what had happened to her near Los Angeles, Texas was fruitless if she did not return to her loved ones and co-workers, confess her weakness and failure to them, and submit to their counsel and nurture.

She started to weep again, but recognized immediately that these were not tears of desperation and hopelessness like those that attended her flight from Austin. New layers of life were being grafted into her damaged soul, and it hurt. But it hurt *good,* not bad.

This is the healing process, she reminded herself as she wept. Paragraph after paragraph came back to her from memorized sermons—sermons she had preached on the very ordeal she was experiencing. Verse after verse of Scripture flowed into her soul like a balm. A wave of confidence swelled within her. She rubbed a wet trail of tears from each cheek, and, with a cleansing sigh willed away her apprehension about returning. The restoration process would begin tonight, she decided firmly. She would tell everything to the only two people in the world she knew would hear her out and love her without judgment:

her parents.

A sign announcing the exit to Derby, Texas was approaching, and Shelby could see a gaudy blue and orange service station sign standing like a sentinel near the off-ramp. There would be a telephone there. She moved the Silverado into the right lane.

She thought about the surprises she had left hidden in the Cruz home, and her smile returned. Would it be bedtime before Soledad, Lupe, and each of the children discovered the small wrapped packets of bills under their pillows? Or would one of the children see the curious-looking treasure, colorfully labeled in crayon with his or her name and simply, "Love, Sister," during playtime when a pillow was tossed playfully at a sibling?

The packets for Soledad and Lupe each contained $600 in $20 bills, and each of the children would discover a packet of ten bills totaling $200. *Soledad will be aghast, thinking he is accepting payment for service to Jesus. But he won't know where to return it.* Shelby almost laughed at the thought. *It's just like salvation, Soledad,* she encouraged him silently. *You can't buy it and you can't earn it. All you can do is receive it.*

Twenty-two

"Everything we have published on Unity 2000 is filed in the directory I have named UNITY." Mai Ngo was standing behind Beth, who sat at the keyboard of Serg Buonoconti's computer. Beth entered the word UNITY at the prompt and a list of file names, mostly numeric in nature followed by a line of descriptive text, filled the monitor screen.

"See, the stories are filed by the date they were published and the section they appeared in," Mai said, pointing to the growing list of characters. "For example, 021599.G indicates that the story appeared in Section G—that's the ARTS AND ENTERTAINMENT section—of the February 15 edition this year. The long-display entry to the right is either the actual headline for the story or a summary of its contents. For this one, PLANNING COMMITTEE BIOS indicates that the article is an up-close-and-personal feature on the people behind the scenes, the representatives from the four organizations who are putting Unity 2000 together."

Beth glanced down the list of long-display summaries and saw the names Holloway, Hornecker, Dunne, and McClure appearing repeatedly in dozens of articles. She hummed to herself, appreciating the vast treasure trove of material at her fingertips that she hoped would make up for her meager research on Unity 2000 to date.

Contrary to what she had led Mai to believe, Beth had read very little of the *Times* year-long coverage leading up to the Coliseum event planned for Millennium's Eve. She didn't even sign the contract to do the book until September, and for several weeks afterward she was still working long hours on a local project, the story of the Puget Sound Superferry system.

Then, realizing that Christmas would be anything but a vacation for her because of Unity 2000, Beth took a couple of weeks off in October to sail the San Juans with an old flame who was intent on rekindling their romance. More interested in the respite than the relationship, Beth had a great time poking around Friday Harbor, Orcas, and Port Stanley. Meanwhile, Brad's efforts at warming her to intimate nights aboard his yacht fizzled and died.

Even after the trip Beth had found it difficult to concentrate on Unity 2000. She read a little and wrote a little, but was easily distracted from her research by almost anything that seemed more relevant. But her Christmas wish for a gold mine of data for the big writing push before Millennium's Eve was being granted before her eyes as she sat at Serg Buonoconti's computer.

Mai reached over Beth's shoulder and scrolled the screen data downward with two quick taps on the keyboard. "You'll see that most of the early work we did on Unity 2000 is filed under G. That's the section where our general religious news usually appears. But by summer and early fall—see the dates?—we have an increasing number of articles running in Section C, CITYSCENE, and even in Section A, including a few front-page articles on the preparations."

"So if I wanted to review everything you have on Holloway or Mc-Clure. . . ."

"You simply perform a search-and-file function in this directory, say for example, on Simon Holloway. The program will assemble a complete file of stories on him. Same with the others. However, you won't be able to get into the original documents without the code. That's so someone won't open and edit the originals by accident. So just make copies and use the disks. That way you can take them with you when you work on your rented computer."

Beth whistled to underscore, for Mai's sake, her amazement over the resources before her. "Mai, this is tremendous. I don't know how to thank you."

"That delicious taco salad and the chance to meet you today, Beth, is thanks enough. If you have any questions, just ask." Beth needed no help with the busywork task of copying files from the *Times* system onto one tiny, high-density diskette Mai had loaned her.

Mai worked at her own terminal for ten minutes, then was summoned to the office of the weekend city editor. She apologized for leaving Beth alone, and Beth assured her she would be fine.

Actually, Beth welcomed the opportunity to be in the cubicle without being monitored. She was curious about other files in Serg's computer that might answer her questions about Holloway, Hornecker, Dunne, and McClure. Mai hadn't issued carte blanche permission for Beth's use of the computer, but neither had she mentioned any specific prohibitions. This was her chance to copy anything and everything she could find that might beef up her book and confirm her suspicions about the lack of credibility of her parents' guru, Simon Holloway, and the other clowns in the religious extravaganza called Unity 2000.

She worked her way back to Serg's root directory and snooped into any electronic drawer that looked promising. Few actually were worth her time. Then she stumbled onto a directory simply named BIOS and pried it open. Bingo! Serg kept a detailed file of historical, biographical, and background information for most of the world's major living religious figures: the Pope, influential cardinals, bishops, and archbishops from Eastern and Western religions, the Dalai Lama, high priests and ayatollahs of every description, denominational presidents and other grand poobahs of Protestantism, and the heads of a number of oriental religions whose titles and names Beth couldn't begin to pronounce.

Beth opened a file at random—for one Demetrius Alexis, seventy-five, a bigwig in Greek Orthodoxy she'd never heard of. She scrolled through the text and viewed some of the integrated photos and video footage. This was nothing more than an obituary in progress, she thought wryly. Old Demetrius' life history was reduced to 400,000 computer bytes, ready to be edited into a stirring tribute for instant publication the moment he dropped dead.

Beth's eye fell on a typo that made her chuckle aloud: Geek Orthodox instead of Greek Orthodox. *I've dated some orthodox geeks in my day*, she snickered to herself, *but most of them were quite unorthodox. This will give Reagan a laugh.* She paused for a moment to savor the delectable thought of being with him again later tonight.

She ran the cursor to the misspelled word and tried to insert an *r*, then realized that she was restricted by a look-but-don't-touch mode in the program. She could not edit Serg's originals without a code. No matter. She wasn't interested in Geek Orthodoxy or some Geek named Demetrius anyway. She just hoped, for Serg's sake, that the error was corrected before Demetrius' obit was published.

She returned to the list of names and searched for the ones she *was* interested in: Simon Holloway, Shelby Hornecker, T.D. Dunne, Morgan McClure. There were extensive subfiles on each one indicating an abundance of photos and video documentation. McClure had the largest file, followed by Holloway and Dunne, with comparatively little on Shelby Hornecker. She pulled up one or two sections for each and read them quickly.

180

Beth realized that the stories she had already copied probably contained much of the same information stored in the bio files. But she wanted to see it all. She wanted to uncover the hidden flaws, foibles, and failures of these holier-than-thou supersaints. There just might be something—

Beth heard Mai's voice in conversation coming toward the cubicle. Her meeting was over, and so was Beth's secret foray into Serg's files. She quickly starred the four master bio files, copied them to the disk, and returned to the UNITY directory in case Mai happened to look over her shoulder.

Adrian Hornecker? Where is his bio? she thought. *There may be something about him in Shelby's file, but I need to see his life story.* Then it hit her: *Adrian Hornecker's data is no longer in the obits of the living; he's been dead nine months. His file has already been moved to another directory.* Beth made a mental note to snoop around for the late Adrian Hornecker the next time Mai left her alone at Serg's terminal.

"Are you finding anything that will help you?" Mai asked, breezing into the cubicle.

Beth scrolled through the list of files, looking busy. "Yes, I have copied a number of stories I need to review. I have some reading to do tonight."

"I just learned something I think you might be interested in," Mai said. Beth looked up to see her displaying a microcassette tape.

"What is it?"

Mai sat down in her chair and swiveled around to face Beth across Serg's desk. "Have you heard of our VoiceLink feature?"

"That's the old 'Letters to the Editor' page, isn't it, except readers call in their gripes and leave them on voice mail instead of writing?"

"Right. The good ones we publish right away. But Sammy, our VoiceLink monitor, has to wade through a lot of verbal garbage to find something worth printing. Sometimes it's just one obscene call after another. I wouldn't want to be responsible for screening those tapes."

"Nor would I," Beth said, imagining what people might say anonymously to get attention or create a stir.

"Well, this call came in while you and I were at lunch, and Jeff wanted me to see it." Mai held up the tape again. "It's a religious message, like many of the calls we get on VoiceLink, especially in the last few months with the new millennium approaching. Most of them are gloom-and-doom, turn-or-burn warnings. But lately the eleventh-hour chiliasts have been on the phone in force."

"The who?"

"Chiliasts—people who believe in the literal biblical millennium, the 1,000-year reign of Christ. Many conservative Christian groups believe that Christ's return to earth will initiate a literal 1,000-year reign of peace and righteousness. But most of the chiliasts we hear from on

VoiceLink are convinced that the biblical millennium corresponds with the third millennium."

"Okay, these are the kooks I've read about who have quit their jobs, given away their possessions, and moved to the mountaintops, hoping to be 'beamed up' at the stroke of midnight on Millennium's Eve?"

"Right."

"That's been happening for centuries—nuts predicting the end of the world and the beginning of the millennium. But the day of doom always comes and goes, and the poor saps have to go back to work until somebody comes up with another formula."

"The hard-core chiliasts are adamant about this one. They can't resist all those nines turning to naughts in one moment; they *know* it's going to happen this time. There's even a group of them in San Francisco—about 100 or so—who have purchased an old jet and staffed it with a crew of their own kind. They plan to take off Friday evening, purposely low on fuel, and fly toward Hawaii. They're confident that when the plane runs out of fuel and plunges into the Pacific they'll be long gone, among the first to be 'translated' into the millennial kingdom. And they're betting their lives on it."

"Is that what you have on the tape there, somebody offering last-minute reservations on the Doomsday Express?"

Beth expected her droll comment to provoke at least a chuckle from Mai. It was laughable to Beth that people were stupid enough to book passage on a doomed flight. If they crashed, they got what they deserved. But the editor was subdued, as if wrestling under the weight of a planeload of people dying because of misplaced hope. Beth was momentarily touched with chagrin. Mai's example chided her for being so flippant toward the misguided souls who would perish in the crash.

"No, this call has nothing to do with that group," Mai said, characteristically overlooking Beth's insensitivity. "In fact, it's similar to many of the chiliast-type calls we have received lately heralding imminent judgment on the faithless and the onset of millennial peace. But this one is unique, more specific. It states—well, why don't you listen for yourself?"

Mai pulled a compact microcassette player from a desk drawer and slid the tiny cassette inside. She placed the player on Serg's desk between herself and Beth and pushed PLAY. The tape began with the tail end of another call, someone insisting that California and Hawaii secede from the Union and form an independent state. Mai used the last two sentences as a sound check, adjusting the volume so she and Beth could hear clearly without blasting the neighboring cubicles.

"This is it," Mai informed as a recorded click opened the incoming line.

Thus saith my lord and master
to the four horsemen journeying to the city.

The voice was masculine, measured, dramatic, and articulate. The caller had a distinctly Slavic accent. Beth's first impression was that he was doing a polished impression of Count Dracula.

Woe to thee, rider of the white horse.
Thou who wearest the crown of the conqueror
shall thyself be conquered.
May thy flesh be torn and thy bones be scattered,
and thy blood quench the parched earth,
and may the beast from heaven
take thy throne and thy inheritance.
  Woe to thee, rider of the red horse, the great harlot.
Thou who slayest thy fellowman shall be slain.
May thy flesh be torn and thy bones be scattered,
and thy blood quench the parched earth,
and may the beast from heaven
take thy throne and thy inheritance.
  Woe to thee, rider of the black horse, the prince of thieves.
Thou who emptieth the purse of the widow
will be turned inside out.
May thy flesh be torn and thy bones be scattered,
and thy blood quench the parched earth,
and may the beast from heaven
take thy throne and thy inheritance.
  Woe to thee, rider of the pale horse.
Thou who beareth death and hell
shall himself be thrown into the grave and burn forever.
May thy flesh be torn and thy bones be scattered,
and thy blood quench the parched earth,
and may the beast from heaven
take thy throne and thy inheritance.

The caller paused. Beth said, "The Four Horsemen of the Apocalypse—even I've heard of them. What's so unique about that?"
Mai's gaze was fixed on the slowly spinning tape. "There's more."

Though inscribed upon the scrolls for an age and an age,
this word shall be confirmed
before the dawn of the age breaks forth.
The riders shall fall, the beast of heaven shall arise.
Four thrones shall become one,
four peoples shall be a heavenly nation.

This city shall know that the master is nigh thee,
even within thy gates. *Click.*

Mai and Beth stared at the microcassette for several seconds. Then Mai touched REWIND. As the tape whined back to the beginning she returned the player to her desk and interfaced it with the TRANSCRIBE port on her computer using a length of slender cable. Then she opened a blank document on the screen and activated the transcription function.

She advanced the rewound tape to the space between calls and pressed PLAY. As the caller's message began again, bursts of transcribed text appeared on screen.

Beth spoke first. "Sounds like a bona fide loony to me, at least two tacos short of a combo plate. And that spooky voice . . . he could be the reincarnation of Bela Lugosi."

Mai smiled thinly at Beth's humor, preoccupied with the white cursor dragging phrases across the blue background. "Yes, and we've had our share of them lately, especially on VoiceLink. 'The world is coming to an end on Millennium's Eve'; 'The antichrist will appear in the east and sway many to his heresy'; 'God will simultaneously detonate the world's reactors and warheads and destroy the earth by nuclear fire.'

"Most of the messages we get are from total crackpots. You can tell they are drunk or loaded or flipped out just from their tone of voice, gutter language, and slurred speech. But listen to this guy." Mai tapped the cassette player with her finger as the transcription continued. "His diction is clear. He has a radio/TV voice. Even if he's reading a script, he sounds like a college-trained communicator."

"So he's a well-educated crackpot," Beth advanced in jest. "A guy doesn't have to be dumb to be crazy."

"That's possible, but 99 percent of our doom-and-gloom callers don't have the authoritative presence and command of the language you hear on this tape," Mai said. "Furthermore, the people we hear on VoiceLink usually talk in vague, disjointed generalities about a coming global apocalypse and Christ's return. Much of it is contradictory or nonsensical. This caller not only sounds better educated and articulate, but he's more specific about his prophecy."

The transcription ended and the player clicked off. The full text of the caller's message stared at them from the screen.

Mai continued, pointing to the text. "The woes directed at the four horsemen may sound like a quotation from the *King James* Bible. But it's little more than Bible-sounding gibberish. The Book of Revelation says nothing like this about the four horsemen. And the opening and closing statements are not from the Bible either. Look at this: 'to the four horsemen journeying to the city.' In light of what we have been talking about today, who would you say—"

"The four televangelists coming to L.A. for Unity 2000," Beth interjected the answer Mai was fishing for. She wasn't convinced it was the right answer. "But he could be referring to any four people headed to any city. There's a lot of journeying going on around the world this week."

"Then this phrase at the bottom: 'Four thrones shall become one, four peoples shall be a heavenly nation.'"

"That sounds to me like a slick marketing pitch for Unity 2000. 'Let's come together, bury the hatchet, and charge into the new millennium united.' I'll bet the ad man for the steering committee put this campaign together." Beth knew she sounded cynical, but she felt a little defensive about Mai's advantage at interpreting the religious mumbo jumbo on the tape.

Mai was unfazed by the cynicism. "The problem the editors had is with these biblical woes sandwiched between the caller's statements. Flesh torn, bones scattered, blood spilled—it sounds like a series of brutal assassinations, but it could be nothing at all. In fact, the odds are that it's no more than a sensational bid for attention from a rather intelligent, articulate weirdo. But it could also be a death threat by a psychopath so confident that he isn't afraid to toss out a few veiled clues."

"But who would want to knock off four televangelists?" Beth flashed on her dislike for religious extremists in general and Simon Holloway in particular, but quickly acknowledged that her strong negative feelings for them were light-years from wanting to harm them or kill them.

"That's just it. The whole thing is probably a hoax or a hollow threat. But there's always a chance that the turn of the millennium has pushed a would-be messiah over the edge, someone crazy enough to think he can assassinate Holloway, Hornecker, McClure, and Dunne and merge their kingdoms into one."

Beth stared at the prophecy on the screen for several moments. "That's sick."

"You're right, very sick. There are a lot of people in L.A. crazy enough to threaten it, and I suppose there are even some crazy enough to think they could get away with it. Let's just pray that this guy isn't one of them, or if he is, that he's not clever enough to pull it off."

"So what does the *Times* do with a tape like this?"

"We turn it over to LAPD. In fact, Parker Center, LAPD headquarters, already has a copy by now."

"Aren't you going to run a story on it?"

"No, because if it's a hoax, the publicity will only encourage the guy."

"And if it's a genuine threat?"

"The police will handle it, and they don't want us alarming the public or tipping off the assassin in the process."

"Will they warn the big four?"

"Probably not. This is only the first hint of a death threat on the televangelists we've heard about. That's unusual for L.A. But maybe there's so much new millennium activity going on that the crazies aren't going to bother with four harmless church leaders. The only thing the LAPD may do at this point is step up security for the visitors. You can probably ask your sergeant friend about that."

Yes, and I'll see him later tonight, Beth thought with anticipation. She glanced at her watch. It read 3:40. "Oh, geez!" she exclaimed, jumping up from Serg's executive swivel chair. "I'm supposed to be at LAX in thirty minutes!"

Mai asked why with her surprised, questioning look.

"Oh, my mother has been out of town for a few days, and Dad asked me to pick her up." Beth was glad there wasn't time to explain why her mother had been away from home on Christmas. She scooped up her purse and stepped around the desk. "Thank you very much, Mai, for the help today," she said, offering her hand quickly.

"You're most welcome, Beth. Feel free to use Serg's work station whenever you want to."

Beth thanked her again and darted out of the cubicle, only to dart back in again in five seconds. "My disk," she said, shaking her head. She pulled the diskette from the B drawer, then whisked past Mai again with a quick wave. She slipped the diskette into her purse as she wound between cubicles toward the exit. *I have some great reading ahead of me tonight,* she exulted.

Twenty-three

Sergeant Reagan Cole hated ride-alongs, especially kids. One of the pluses about making sergeant was the authority to pawn civilian riders off on the rank-and-file officers. *As a sergeant, I have enough on my mind,* Cole reasoned. *I'm responsible for the men and women on my shift, not to mention watching my own back. Besides, I signed on to catch bad guys, not to do public relations. Ride-alongs distract me from police work, cramp my style. They ask too many questions, and they usually expect that dinner comes with the deal. No more ride-alongs. No way.*

But the city councilman had been adamant. He wanted his teenage son to ride with a sergeant. He'd be safer with a more experienced officer, he insisted. So Councilman McBirney had leaned on Lieutenant Arias, and Lieutenant Arias had leaned on Sergeant Cole.

"Why can't he ride on day shift like other civilians?" Cole had countered.

"Because the kid doesn't get up before noon for anything during Christmas vacation, and his dad won't make him," the lieutenant had explained. So the upshot of the discussion was now sitting in the passenger bucket of Cole's Ford police car, chain-eating a bag of Hershey's candy kisses and dropping the red and green foil wrappers on the floor.

Fifteen-year-old Philip McBirney was curly-headed, pimply-faced, and chubby-cheeked with a snot-nosed attitude. Big for his age, Phillie—as he insisted on being called—had tried out for quarterback on his high school football team in the fall. Possessing the agility of a cement block and the throwing arm of a freshman rally girl, Phillie sat on the bench all season.

When his pushy father pestered the coach about Phillie getting some playing time next year, the unpushable coach said that the only way he'd put him on the field is if the kid bulked up thirty or forty pounds and played line. It was a goal Phillie embraced with gusto. He had been stuffing his face ever since and was well on his way to his target weight of 240.

"I need another Coke, Sergeant Cole," Phillie whined. "And I'm getting hungry for dinner."

Cole was seething inside. It was 4:30. They had only been on the road two hours, and Phillie had already downed a quart of pop and half a bag of candy kisses. Lieutenant Arias had reminded Cole that Phillie's old man was an influential member of city government, then added sternly, "So show the kid a good time." But Cole wouldn't allow civilians—even a councilman's kid—to bring food or drink inside his car. The computer and communication array occupying the dash and center console was too sensitive. One spill could knock him off line or off the air, and Cole despised anything that kept him out of action on the streets of downtown L.A.

So Phillie had sucked down his first Coke standing outside a minimart, while the sergeant waited impatiently in the car. Cole decided to let the candy slide. He was afraid if he didn't let Phillie eat Hershey kisses in the car, he would spend his whole shift in the parking lot of the minimarket.

"What would you like for dinner, Phillie?" It was all Cole could do to sound civil.

"Taquitos. I always eat taquitos on ride-alongs."

Takeout taco joints were as common on L.A. streets as hot dog stands in Dodger Stadium. But they were a novelty for a white kid from suburban Valencia. Cruising west on Adams Boulevard, Cole remembered a greasy taqueria near the corner of Adams and Figueroa, six blocks ahead. *Let's get it over with,* he resigned with a sigh.

Cole turned into a corner shopping center and parked in front of a run-down taqueria that used to be a run-down donut shop that used to be a trendy espresso bar catering to USC students. Three Latinos hunkered on their haunches to the right of the door, talking and smoking cigarettes. *A little worn out to be Latin Barons,* Cole surmised.

To the left of the door was an older, scruffy-looking white guy in a jean jacket and Dodgers cap eating taquitos out of a brown paper bag. The man was sitting on a blue and white picnic chest with the handle folded down. Cole recognized him from Figueroa Street and remembered seeing him near Pershing Square yesterday. *This old boy gets around,* Cole mused.

"I want eight taquitos and a large Coke—a 32-ouncer," Phillie announced. He knew Cole would pay for his dinner. His dad said it was a professional courtesy to other civil servants and their dependents.

Cole stepped out of the car and approached the takeout window. He received a nod from the old guy on the picnic chest and only stares from the hunkering Latinos.

Five minutes later he came to the passenger window of the car with Phillie's dinner—eight taquitos, which are corn tortillas wrapped tightly around shredded beef to about the size of a cigar and deep fried. The bag also contained two plastic cups of spicy guacamole, a 32-ounce Coke, and a fistful of napkins.

"You'll have to stand outside to eat, Phillie. Police regulations, remember?"

"Sergeant Cole regulations," Phillie sneered. "All the other cops let me eat in the car."

"You eat outside my car or you don't eat," Cole retorted curtly.

"I'm not eating next to those Mexicans. Besides, it's cold out there."

Cole took the greased-stained brown bag to the back of the car and placed it on top of the deck lid. He paused to slowly and silently count to ten, noticing as he did that the old man with the picnic chest had moved on. Then he climbed into the driver's seat and said with remarkable control, "Phillie, we have to leave in ten minutes. If you want any dinner before we leave, you'd better step to the back of the car."

Phillie glowered at the sergeant with a wait-till-I-tell-my-dad-the-councilman-about-this look. Then he climbed out muttering and began devouring taquitos and slurping his Coke.

Phillie had been outside less than two minutes when the call came. A foiled robbery and possible hostage situation at a dry cleaning place on Pico.

"Phillie, dump your dinner and get in now; we have to go!" Cole yelled, starting the engine. He saw in the side mirror that the wide-eyed kid was stuffing taquitos into his mouth two at a time and washing them down with huge gulps of Coke which dribbled past the corners of his mouth down his neck and into his shirt.

"Now, Phillie, now!" Cole hit reverse and backed slowly away from the building. Phillie shuffled alongside the car, cramming taquitos and guzzling Coke like an animal. Then he dived into the car with his cheeks bulging, and Cole squealed out of the parking lot, leaving behind a trail of fluttering napkins.

Phillie had never experienced a code-three run, so Cole decided to give him one he would never forget. Perhaps he would think twice about riding along with the LAPD again.

They flew east on Adams dodging many motorists who simply stopped in their tracks at the flashing red lights and yelping siren instead of pulling far to the right. A hard, fast turn at San Pedro threw the chunky kid against the passenger door. He was hanging onto his seat belt like it was a lifeline.

Weaving through the traffic on San Pedro and then Pico required deft steering, accelerating, and braking, a challenge Cole always welcomed. *The best thing about this high-speed run*, he thought, *is that it has shut up Phillie McBirney.*

Cole couldn't help flashing back to his last high-speed adventure—driving a candy-apple red GM Star Cruiser with a tall, dark-haired beauty in the passenger seat. Thinking about being with Beth again tonight helped him believe he could endure anything—even six more hours with Phillie McBirney.

"Stay in the car," Cole commanded as he pulled up behind two other black-and-whites a few doors down from Kim's Dry Cleaning. He secretly wished Phillie *would* ignore his strict orders. A civilian rider who wouldn't follow instructions lost his ride-along privileges on the spot.

Cole jumped out of the car just as two other uniformed officers led a handcuffed Asian man out of the store. The robber had given himself up to the proprietor at the first sound of approaching sirens. Cole was disappointed that he missed out on the arrest, but he hid it well as he interviewed his officers on their tactics and commended them for good work.

In less than five minutes he was back to the car. He smelled the foul odor immediately and turned to Phillie suspiciously. The chunky kid wore a deflated, hangdog expression. At his feet, a dozen foil candy wrappers were swimming in a pool of regurgitated soda pop, taquitos, and chocolate.

"It's your fault, sergeant," he said with a sickly quaver. "You told me to stay in the car."

While his car was being cleaned up in the maintenance garage by an unlucky Explorer Scout who said he'd do anything to earn his law enforcement merit badge, Cole sat at the keyboard in the Southwest Division station. The sergeant logged his comments on the robbery attempt while he waited for Councilman McBirney to arrive. Throwing up in a police car wasn't a direct violation of ride-along regulations, but it was good enough to convince the councilman that Phillie was too ill to complete his shift. Cole felt little pity for the forlorn-looking kid slumped in a wooden chair at the conference table.

"Cole?" Lieutenant Arias was standing in the doorway. Except for a deviated septum from his brief boxing career, the lieutenant looked like a Hispanic Dick Tracy: slick black hair, square jaw, muscular frame.

"Yeah, skipper."

"Can I see you for a few minutes before you head out again?"

"Sure, as soon as I hand our friend Phillie over to his dad."

The handoff went smoothly enough. McBirney coddled his pale-faced son and talked about the flu going around. Cole thought he would gag. Phillie whimpered and whined about his car sickness, but said nothing about the eight greasy taquitos, two quarts of pop, and half-pound of chocolate he'd consumed. Cole decided not to delay their departure by clarifying the story.

"Sorry about that kid blowing chunks in your car," Lieutenant Arias began as Cole sat down in his cubicle.

"Could have been worse. Thank God he missed my computer, my radio, and me."

"I feel kind of responsible, pushing him on you like that," Arias said. "But you know old man McBirney. . . ."

"Don't sweat it, skip. I should have known Phillie was a ticking time bomb after all the junk he ate. I didn't realize that a tame code-three run would set him off."

The lieutenant picked a couple of fax memos off his desk and studied them briefly. "This could have waited until briefing tomorrow. But since you're here and I have a couple of minutes. . . ."

Cole sat back in the wooden side chair. Arias didn't sound overly serious, and Cole was certain he wasn't due for a dressing down.

"We received this fax from Hollywood Division homicide detectives late this afternoon. They're looking for somebody who stuck a security guard last night near Melrose and VanNess."

"Needle in a haystack. They're always looking for someone who stabbed someone. That's Hollywood."

Arias hummed agreement. "But this guy was cut pretty deep—it wasn't a boy scout knife. And after the deed, the suspect apparently swiped the guard's pickup. It was found this morning a couple of blocks from the Melrose Metro station. They think the bad guy might have hopped a rail into downtown. They want us to keep our eyes open for serious blades."

Cole grunted his disbelief. "Bigger haystack, smaller needle. If I had a nickel for every pig-sticker in Southwest and a dime for every sleazebag that's crazy enough to use it on someone, I could buy the city."

Arias hummed again, then set the memo aside. "Well, you know detectives. They want everybody in the haystack looking for their needle. I just bring it up because you know the streets of our division as well as anyone. If you come up with any names they can check out, let me know."

Arias perused the second fax memo. He had already read it several times, but he scanned it in Cole's presence to assure the sergeant that he hadn't come up with the assignment by himself. "If you liked the Phillie McBirney caper," he said wryly, "you're going to love me for this one."

Cole braced for the worst.

"Today the *Times* received a possible death threat on their VoiceLink line, supposedly directed at the four religious leaders attending the big deal at the Coliseum Friday night."

"Unity 2000."

"Right. It's probably a prank—some religious nut spouting off. But the chief is very sensitive about all these religious people coming into the city for this thing. He wants to ensure the safety of their leaders. So he has offered twenty-four-hour LAPD 'escorts' to all four televangelists, plainclothes officers who will—"

"You can't be serious, Al," Cole cut in. "Baby-sitting preachers? Please, man, not me."

"It's only for four or five days, Cole. We keep our eye on them, drive them wherever they need to go, and get them safely to and from the Coliseum on Friday night. On the bright side, you can dress in civvies, and you'll be driving a clean, unmarked car. and you'll have an assistant: Jayne Watanabe."

"Central should take care of them." Cole grasped at anything.

"Central *is* involved. They're taking one of the two preachers who is staying downtown. We're taking the other one. West L.A. is taking the two staying at the Century Plaza."

"There must be some other guys on this shift who are into escort duty. What about Candy Diaz? Or better yet, Tollefson? He's a religious guy. He would love being in the middle of Unity 2000."

"I have no problem with Sergeant Diaz or Sergeant Tollefson. But the chief wants Southwest's best on each shift, Cole. That's Jarrett on A.M.s, Nguyen on days, and you on P.M.s."

Beth is not going to believe this, Cole mouthed silently. *First, she has to write a book about them; now I have to baby-sit one of them. There's got to be a way out of this for both of us.*

For a moment he saw himself with Beth boarding a Mexicana flight to Cozumel. Hours after walking off their jobs they could be snorkeling in the crystal water and sipping piña coladas on the white sand. They could welcome in the new millennium together—alone—in a candle-lit villa overlooking the shimmering bay, seemingly continents away from the Los Angeles Memorial Coliseum.

The bubble burst as quickly as it formed. Dumping their careers to escape an unpleasant assignment was ludicrous. Flights to Mexico for the holidays had been overbooked for months. And there wasn't a room available anywhere on the Gulf coast, let alone a romantic villa with an ocean view. Besides, Cole wasn't sure Beth would agree to go with him. Things were definitely looking up, but there's a big difference between a lingering kiss in the driveway and a week together in Mexico—or anywhere else.

Cole released a long breath. "Okay, skipper. But if you tell me I've been assigned to Simon Holloway. . . ." Cole stopped short, realizing he had no viable threat.

"Why? What's wrong with Holloway?"

Cole sighed again. "It's a long story. Let's just say that if I ended up baby-sitting Holloway this week, I would not be very popular with a certain lady I'm seeing."

Arias smiled. "Well, you lucked out. Central got Holloway. He's staying at the Bonaventure. Your preacher will be at the Biltmore. Or should I say 'lady preacher.' You'll be escorting the Rev. Shelby Hornecker of Dallas."

Twenty-four

Hodge ambled through dark Exposition Park toward the Los Angeles Memorial Coliseum, swinging his picnic chest at his side. The greasy taquitos he had just eaten were burning a hole in his stomach. Between sour belches he vowed that after Millennium's Eve he would never eat inferior food again.

It was a little after 5 P.M., still more than two hours before tip-off of the Clippers–Knicks game in the neighboring Sports Arena. Hodge didn't have to be on duty with his mop and broom until 7. That's when the careless early arriving fans began spilling popcorn and beer in the concourse and on the stairways to the Arena. But he purposely arrived at Exposition Park early to continue his reconnaissance of the Coliseum being readied for Unity 2000.

Hodge crossed the park using the better lit walkways between the Arena and the Coliseum. Clusters of punks loitered in the darker corners of the park ready to threaten unwary basketball fans out of their cash, or their tickets which they would sell for cash on the other side of the Arena. Hodge wasn't afraid of them. In fact, sometimes he purposely walked through their turf just to show them his knife. But there were only five days till Millennium's Eve, and he had no time to waste hassling young hoods over the contents of his picnic chest.

Hodge walked across the plaza in front of the main entrance of the Coliseum at the east end of the seventy-year-old stadium. He paused briefly between the elevated statues of the headless man and woman and the tall arch leading into the stadium. He had often stood here beside the main gate, imagining the scene that would unfold beyond the arch on Millennium's Eve. He was momentarily breathless, captivated by the utter reality that the culmination of his quest and the glory of his reward were a scant five days away.

Hodge continued around the Coliseum to Gate 14 on the west end. Maintenance workers were exiting through the open gate in twos and threes after another full day of preparations for Unity 2000.

"'Evening, Mr. Bailey, sir," Hodge called out as he walked into the bright overhead light at the gate entrance.

"Yeah, hi, Hodge," Bailey called back from under the surrey of his electric golf cart parked next to the entrance. His hands were jammed into the pockets of his uniform jacket as he wiled away the last boring hour of his shift.

Security man Bailey, a retired L.A. fireman, hardly gave the disheveled Hodge a second glance when he approached the gate for the first time more than a month ago. Even when Hodge displayed his concessionaire's holocard and said he was sent from the Arena by Lionel Whatley on official concessions business—which was a lie—crusty old Bailey was barely civil.

But after several evening visits, Hodge's sick-cow deference had worn the old man down. Being called "mister" and "sir" so gratuitously, always with "please" and "thank you," was too much for a thirty-six-year veteran who had failed every attempt at promotion within the fire department and had to address a fireman his son's age as "captain." Hearing someone afford him a little respect, even someone as homely as Hodge, was a welcome boost to Bailey's flagging self-esteem.

Bailey didn't view Hodge, the Sports Arena janitor, as a friend by any stretch. But Hodge's persistent groveling had at least warmed the old guard to tolerate him and trust him inside the fence—which had been Hodge's intent since the beginning.

"Is Paddy still here, Mr. Bailey?"

"Aw, he's around here somewhere, Hodge. He's always the last one to leave, even though he don't have nothing to do."

"Mr. Whatley said I should come see Paddy before work tonight and talk to him about the big event Friday night." It was a sketchy excuse for getting inside, and Hodge was prepared to fabricate more of a story if he needed to.

"Whatever, Hodge," the old man said distantly, nodding permission for Hodge to pass through the opening.

"Thank you, Mr. Bailey," Hodge said, entering. Bailey grunted.

"I'll bet this'll be a busy week for you, sir," Hodge said, pausing by the golf cart to stroke the old man's ego with a little attention. "You have an important job, sir, being in charge of security for the big event."

Bailey was not in charge of security for the Coliseum or for Unity 2000, and Hodge knew it. But the old guard didn't know Hodge knew it, so he quietly reveled in the bliss of Hodge's apparent ignorance.

Bailey swore and spat like a head of security might. "Yeah, we'll all have plenty to do, won't we, Hodge?"

"But my job ain't as important or as dangerous as yours, sir," Hodge said with artificial admiration and respect. "There's nothing special about mopping up spilled soda pop. But you have the safety of all them people to think about, sir." Hodge swept a hand toward the huge bowl of seats inside the ivy-covered concrete walls above them. "I admire your courage, sir."

Bailey shrugged and shook his head slightly as if to say, "It might be a tough job for you but not for me."

"Do you think Paddy will be in his office, sir?" Hodge said.

Bailey snorted a laugh. "I told you, Hodge, Paddy ain't had an office for years. For all I know he's sleeping out there on the 50-yard line stone drunk." He swore and spat again.

"Thank you, Mr. Bailey. I'll find him all right, sir," Hodge said. He headed toward the nearest tunnel leading through the stadium to the dark playing field within. Hodge was quietly pleased that Bailey trusted him enough to no longer search his picnic chest at the gate.

"Don't forget, Hodge," the guard called in his most authoritative tone. "I lock up tonight at 6 sharp. Don't make me come looking for you and that soused friend of yours."

"No sir, Mr. Bailey," Hodge called back over his shoulder. "Paddy and me, we'll be out at the gate before 6, sir. You can count on me, Mr. Bailey."

Hodge knew exactly where he would find Paddy Duckett. He walked through the narrow tunnel, emerging in the darkened stadium at a point one-third of the way from the grassy field to the upper rim of the concrete bowl. Pausing only a moment to gaze at the 70,000 empty seats draped in the dark gray and black of evening, he descended the long stairway to field level.

Hodge hopped over the low railing designed to separate the spectators from the players. He followed the railing toward the southwest corner of the field to where a concrete ramp angled up into the huge mouth of the main tunnel. The tunnel curved upward through the bowels of the Coliseum to the tunnel gate entrance and Menlo Street on the west end of Exposition Park.

Hodge ascended through the gently curving, dimly lit cavern toward the two doors in the center of the tunnel leading into the dressing rooms. The air in the corridor was heavy. The pores of the concrete seemed to exude the body odor of multiplied thousands of athletes — from professional and college football players to daredevil motorcyclists to Olympic runners and jumpers — who for seven decades had trudged this broad thoroughfare, spent and sweaty.

He purposely passed by the lower door into the complex and continued up the tunnel to a second door. Entering, he stepped down a short flight of cement stairs to a long hallway parallel to the tunnel. Several doors opened off the hallway to team rooms and showers.

Hodge turned hard to his right to face a door at the base of the stairs. Light appeared underneath the closed door. He slowly opened it and stuck his head inside. "Hello, Paddy."

"Well, it's my friend Hodge." The sleepy voice, Irish-tinged like Hodge's, came from a lower shelf in a small room completely lined with metal shelves. A man well past seventy and barely five feet tall was stretched out on a bed of folded and bundled white towels. He wore a rumpled khaki shirt and trousers and white socks. His worn work boots had dropped to the cement floor. His glasses sat on the tip of his nose, and a dog-eared paperback lay on his chest where it had fallen when Paddy last dropped off. A half-empty bottle of port was wedged between two bundles of towels near his right hand.

At one time Paddy Duckett had been head groundskeeper for the Los Angeles Memorial Coliseum. In his younger days, he had meticulously groomed the turf for the gridiron gladiators of the Trojans, Bruins, Rams, and Raiders. His supreme glory was achieved in 1984 when the staff under his direction prepared the Coliseum floor for the Olympic Games.

But in the mid-'90s, when age and intemperance cruelly ganged up on him, Paddy was eased out of management and offered the meaningless position of maintenance consultant at a criminal cut in pay. The Coliseum Commission expected him to retire, of course. But Paddy wasn't about to leave his beloved Coliseum. He remained on, contentedly doing odd jobs nobody else even knew needed to be done. And when his tasks weren't pressing, which was most of the time over the last two years, he found plenty of time for rest and "refreshment."

Hodge stepped fully into the towel room. "I'm sorry to disturb you, Paddy, but I brought your Christmas present." He opened his picnic chest, lifted out a small brown bag, and handed it to Paddy, who remained prone. Paddy received the bag and opened it, pulling out a half-pint of bourbon.

Hodge had cultivated Paddy's friendship as a fellow Irishman with spirits, just as he had ingratiated himself to Bailey at the gate with ego-stroking flattery. He needed both relationships for his holy mission to succeed. Bailey was his legitimate passport into the Coliseum during certain hours, and Paddy was an unsuspecting pipeline of information about the inner workings of Unity 2000.

In his younger days, Paddy had been more discriminating in his social life and had never hobnobbed with the likes of Hodge. But over the last few years his taste in friends was strongly influenced by his appetite for cheap wine and those who enjoyed it with him. Ugly, smelly Hodge had become a true friend with the first bottle of port he presented to Paddy nearly a month ago.

"Jim Beam!" Paddy exulted proudly, sitting up. His head barely cleared the shelf above him. "This is very special, my friend."

"Yesterday was Christmas," Hodge said, pulling a metal folding chair beside Paddy and sitting down. "Christmas is the time for special gifts between friends."

"Then we'll drink to friendship," Paddy announced. He twisted the cap expectantly, saluted Hodge with a nod, then took a healthy swig. His face screwed up in pain as if he had just swallowed a mouthful of broken glass. "Argh! That's good!" he roared, smacking his lips and catching his breath. "Help yourself."

Hodge took the bottle and feigned a drink, keeping his tongue over the bottle's opening. He mimicked Paddy's sour expression. "Yes, great stuff."

For several minutes the men drank and extolled the virtues of good bourbon and other vices. Then Hodge turned the conversation to Paddy's "work." Hodge had endeared himself to Paddy not only with an occasional bottle, but by displaying a seemingly genuine interest in Paddy's first love, the activities at the Los Angeles Memorial Coliseum.

"So, Paddy, how are you coming with preparations for the big night?" Hodge said "you" knowing that the old man was regarded as little more than a gofer by the current maintenance staff, who weren't allowing Paddy to do much of anything. Paddy used "we" in the same way.

"We got the folding chairs today—25,000 of them to set up in rows across the football field. They're out there in big racks right now, all around the perimeter of the field."

"Where did the chairs come from?" Hodge already knew most of what he was asking Paddy to explain.

"Oh, that committee rented them from somewhere in Orange County."

"The Unity 2000 committee?"

Paddy took another sip of Jim Beam. "Yep. One of the drivers today told me those chairs out there have been reserved for months just for Millennium's Eve."

"I guess you'll be setting up the chairs tomorrow."

"Oh no, Hodge. We can't set up the chairs until we erect that huge platform."

"A platform?"

"Yep. It's a monster. Ten feet high, 1,800 square feet of surface. They'll have twenty to thirty people sitting on top of it down there at the open end of the stadium, right under the video screen."

"Well, how are they going to get such a big thing in here?" Hodge hoped he wasn't overacting his feigned ignorance.

"It comes in pieces, Hodge," Paddy said with a tone implying that anyone with half a brain would know it. "They say it's like a giant Tinker Toy set with interconnecting steel tubes, joints, and braces. Light and easy to transport but solid as a granite slab."

"You ever seen a platform like this before?"

"Of course not, Hodge. The thing was specially made for this shindig." Paddy's words were coming slower and running together as the Jim Beam seeped into his brain. "I heard it was designed by the guy who planned this big party—that Hornecker fellow who made all those religious movies and then was killed in the plane crash."

Hodge cocked his head and lifted his eyebrows as if receiving new information. Then he asked, "So when does this big Tinker Toy platform arrive, and when do you set it up?" He leaned slightly closer to Paddy. The information he needed from him tonight was near.

"The platform kit arrives Tuesday all wrapped up in one of those piggyback containers that goes from boat to train to flatbed trailer. It'll take us all day Wednesday to put it together."

Arriving Tuesday! Excellent! Hodge exulted silently without so much as a twitch changing his expression. *Another sign that the master's will is unfolding on schedule.*

Paddy continued, "On Thursday the committee's people will hook up all the video and audio equipment. And we'll have a crew in here to line up those folding chairs."

"So with all that expensive equipment around, you'll need extra security on duty, won't you?" Hodge probed.

"Naw, nothing special. All the TV and sound stuff is locked up at Hornecker's old studio in Hollywood. The committee's doing all that. It won't even arrive till Thursday morning. The chairs and the platform kit will be safe in their containers on the field—who'd want to steal them anyhow? So we'll have our regular night watchman coming on duty at 6 when old Bailey leaves. Burt usually lets himself into the press box and sleeps."

The plan congealed quickly in Hodge's brain as Paddy spoke. It would be as easy as child's play. Everything was falling into place. Hodge could hardly contain his excitement.

The two men drank and talked until quarter to 6. Then Hodge helped Paddy to his feet and steered him through the tunnel, up the stairs and out Gate 14. Bailey locked it behind them.

"Thank you, my friend, for the Christmas present and the delightful chat." Paddy's words were slurred and he swayed slightly on his feet.

"You're welcome, Paddy. Are you sure you'll make it home all right?"

"Listen, my friend," Paddy said, waving a proud but shaky finger at Hodge. "In seventy-three years I've never failed to make it home all right."

"I'm sure you will, Paddy. And I'll see you again soon—maybe Tuesday afternoon." Hodge's seemingly spur-of-the-moment idea for his next visit with Paddy had already been carefully planned.

"Wonderful, my friend," Paddy said, starting toward Figueroa Street on unsteady legs. "Our big box of Tinker Toys will be here by then. I'll have to show them to you."

"I'm anxious to see them, Paddy," Hodge said, waving good-bye. Then he added at a whisper, "You have no idea *how* anxious I am to see that platform kit, old man."

Twenty-five

Phillie McBirney's "deposit" had been cleaned up and the floor mats thoroughly scrubbed, but Cole swore his police cruiser still smelled of upchuck. He hadn't been back on the road more than fifteen minutes before he stopped at a drugstore and bought a can of disinfectant spray with "refreshing country scent." Every twenty to thirty minutes he pulled the can from under the seat and sprayed the passenger side of the car thoroughly. But by 8 P.M. the country scent was getting to him almost as badly as the odor it was blanketing. So he hailed dispatch on the radio and cleared himself for a dinner break.

Cole pulled into a hole-in-the-wall Thai restaurant on Jefferson. He winked at the children ogling him as he walked to his table. He was used to the stares attracted by his uniform and his size, which was slightly exaggerated by the bulletproof vest under his long-sleeved navy shirt.

Cole propped his radio on the table and ordered his favorite dish and a cherry Coke. Then he pulled a phone from his shirt pocket and tapped two keys to dial a number he had recently stored in the phone's memory.

"Yes." Beth's cool, businesslike tone didn't seem to fit the background noise: the tinkle of china and crystal, festive conversation, and a piano rendition of "Volare." Cole had expected Beth to be holed up somewhere quiet working on her story.

"That's the noisiest library I've ever heard," he said.

"Will you hold, please?" Beth said, sounding like a recording. She didn't wait for him to say "Okay" before she said "Thank you," and the phone went silent. Cole poked at the ice chips in his Coke with a straw while he waited, wondering about Beth's odd response.

After almost a minute Beth was back. "Hello, Reagan." The background noise was gone. So was the cool distance in her voice. "Where are you?"

"I'm at the Bangkok Terrace on Jefferson. It's my dinner break. Where are you?"

"I'm at Zaffino's in Century City. It's my dinner break too—with my parents. I've made it through the soup and salad. I'm gearing up for the main course." She didn't sound like a happy camper.

"That bad?"

"Oh, it's the same old thing. Simon Holloway. Jubilee Village. The sacrilege of biotechnology." She punctuated her repugnance with a curse. "I'm so glad you called. I'm in the ladies' lounge. They think I'm talking to my publisher. Please don't hang up, Reagan. If I can stay in here for an hour, maybe they'll leave."

Cole suddenly wanted to be with her. Not because Beth was a helpless female who couldn't survive without a man fawning over her. He'd had his fill of women like that. Spirited Beth was anything but helpless, and he was captivated by her for it. He wanted to be there to take her mind off her unpleasantness and show her a good time. *You're a wonderful person, Beth*, he thought. *You deserve better.*

A flash of inspiration tinged with mild lunacy burst upon him. "Then let's have dinner together. Put me on hold and go find your waiter. Tell him to bring your entree to the ladies' lounge. Then have him take a message to your folks—'you're arguing with your publisher over the contract, it may take an hour, go ahead and eat,' something like that. Then we can eat dinner in different restaurants together—you there and me here."

There was a moment of silence, followed by, "Reagan, you are . . . I can't believe you want me to. . . ." Then Beth laughed. "What a wonderful idea! Just a minute."

While Beth was off the phone, Cole's dinner arrived. He ordered a refill of cherry Coke.

Beth came back on. "I caught him just in time. He was leaving the kitchen with our order. This is a first, Reagan. I've never had dinner with a man by phone in the ladies' lounge of a fashionable restaurant." Beth sounded pleased.

"What are you having tonight, Beth?"

"Tortellini d'aragosta. It looks and smells good."

"Sounds delicious . . . and expensive. I'm glad I'm not paying."

"Dad's buying, he always does. And since they're in the other room, I also ordered a nice glass of dry white wine. What are you having?"

"Good old number four on the menu. They whack the daylights out of a chicken with a cleaver, then fry it up greasy and spicy and serve it on a bed of rice. I call it 'cave man chicken.' The wine steward recommended a chilled bottle of Thunderbird, but I went for Coca Cola, vintage 1999."

Beth laughed again. Cole loved hearing her laugh, and he loved being the one to make her laugh.

"Cheers, I'm sure," Beth said with an exaggerated high-society inflection. Cole imagined her sitting on a lacy divan in a ladies' lounge balancing a plate on her knees, holding a phone to one ear, and lifting her wine glass toward downtown.

Cole lifted his glass, returning her invisible salute while ignoring the curious stares of nearby diners. "Yes, cheers. Or as we say in the city, rubba-dub-dub, thanks for the grub, let's eat."

Cole took a gulp of Coke and envisioned Beth sipping her wine demurely.

"I thought you were supposed to eat three hours ago," Cole said between mouthfuls of cave man chicken.

Beth released an audible perturbed sigh. "We *were* supposed to eat three hours ago. First, Mom's plane was late, almost an hour. Next—I can't believe this happened to me—she just had to introduce me to Simon Holloway. He was on her flight from Orlando with his family—flying first class, of course. So she drags me through a horde of hymn-singing groupies and reporters and lights and TV cameras around him, grabs him by the coattail and says, 'Rev. Holloway, I'd like you to meet my daughter, the author.'"

"Geez," Cole groaned in sympathy. "What did Holloway say?"

"He didn't have a chance to say anything. His goons jumped between us and whisked the family away. The cops asked us a lot of questions. I think Mom was a little disillusioned by the snub. I told her we were lucky not to get arrested."

"You *were* lucky. We were put on alert today because of a possible death threat against Holloway and the other Unity 2000 leaders."

"I know," Beth said with a hint of one-upmanship.

"You know what?"

"About the death threat. I was at the *Times* today just after the call came in on VoiceLink. I heard the guy on tape—a real wacko. Mai said the LAPD would probably keep a low profile on the threat because—"

"Who?"

"The editor I interviewed at the *Times*. Her name is Mai Ngo—Vietnamese, I think. Anyway, she says the cops don't get too excited over calls like this. Is she right?"

"Yeah, basically. But the chief is hair-trigger this week with all the out-of-towners crowding into the city for the circus at the Coliseum. He wants the tourists to have a good time, spend lots of money, do their religious thing Friday night without incident, and go home happy. And he's not about to let a publicity-seeking nut with a messiah complex steal his thunder with an assassination attempt. Which brings me to tonight's really big news."

"What could be bigger news than *me* being one of the first to hear the nut on tape and almost meeting Simon Holloway in person and almost getting arrested for it?" There was a subtle can-you-top-this? dare in Beth's voice. It reminded Cole of her brazen challenge to a game of one-on-one for a six-pack in the driveway last night. It was the same zesty spirit that attracted him to her in the beginning.

Cole gloated silently for a moment over the news he knew was going to knock Beth off her pins. He wasn't any happier about his assignment, but he relished the shock value of announcing it to the woman who had beat him at one-on-one with a lucky shot from the middle of the street. "The really big news is that the LAPD is providing personal escorts for the four televangelists this week, and that I have been assigned to cover the lady preacher from Texas."

Beth swore in amazement. But the words didn't seem adequate, so she swore again. "You're going to be guarding Shelby Hornecker?"

" 'Guarding' is an overstatement. Another officer and I are assigned to 'escort' the Rev. Mrs. Hornecker wherever she goes during our shift."

"But if there really is a mad killer somewhere in L.A. stalking Hornecker and Holloway and the others . . ." Beth left the thought dangling.

Cole might have laughed at what he considered an implausible danger. But hearing what he thought was concern for his safety in Beth's voice, he said, "Okay, on the outside chance that the message to the *Times* reflects a genuine threat, we're ready. We'll have a beefed-up, unmarked, bulletproof car—except it looks like an ordinary sedan. We don't want to alarm Hornecker or anyone else. The black-and-whites will be nearby, geared to a thirty-second response to our call. And Jayne and I are professionals. We can handle ourselves."

"Jayne?"

"Officer Jayne Watanabe, my partner in this assignment," Cole clarified.

"You mean a girl Jayne, not a boy Jayne?"

"Yes, Jayne is a female officer." Then with a playful taunt in his tone, Cole added. "She's pretty cute too . . . short, like a little point guard. Too bad for her I'm attracted to statuesque power forwards who can shoot three-pointers from the middle of the street."

Beth brushed away his compliment with a self-conscious laugh, then said, "So when do you and Officer Jayne go on duty? When does Shelby Hornecker arrive in L.A.?"

"We meet her at LAX Tuesday afternoon about 4 and deliver her to the Biltmore."

"When can I meet her and get an exclusive interview?"

"Hey, I haven't even met her myself yet. Besides, this is official police department business."

"I could make it worth your while, officer."

"You just bribed a peace officer, lady. But I may be persuaded to overlook it. What's an interview worth to you?"

"And I believe that's called graft, Sergeant Slick—peddling your influence to a private citizen."

"So we're at an impasse. I guess we have to settle this on the court tonight—one-on-one."

"You already lost a six-pack to me, Mr. Bruin. Can you handle another crushing defeat?"

"Lucky shot. It can't happen again. I'm putting up six more green bottles and an opportunity to meet and talk to Shelby Hornecker. What are you putting up?"

"It's a moot point. You won't collect because you won't win."

"C'mon, Ms. Trojan. It's not a wager without stakes. Put up or shut up."

Beth was thoughtfully silent. Then, "Okay, here it is. Dinner for two at the location of your choice. Millennium's Eve, after midnight, after the Coliseum thing. And if you beat me by more than 10 points—it's ludicrous for me to even think it could happen—I'll also buy you breakfast."

Cole took a deep breath and released it slowly. The tantalizing possibilities buzzed through his brain. A dozen retorts leaped into his mind, most of them brash and suggestive. *Don't blow it with this girl,* he cautioned himself. *This one is special.*

Finally he said, "Then I'll see you tonight, and you'd better be ready to play." He silently congratulated himself for bringing his best Nikes to work with him.

Twenty-six

The three directors of King's House gathered in Will Danielson's office on the first floor at 9 P.M. for staff meeting. Their normal 10 A.M. meeting had been rescheduled to 1 P.M., then to 3:30, then to 4, postponed each time due to minor emergencies demanding the attention of one or more of them. With so much happening at King's House, daytime staff meetings were often pushed through the day that way.

But by 9 each night, the patients on the fifth floor were bedded down and initial preparations for the next day's breakfast service in the dining hall were complete. The distribution center for the poor, called the free store, was closed. All entrances to the building were secured for the night. A volunteer "butler," tonight a college student enjoying time for light reading during his Christmas break, was stationed inside the glass front doors to admit residents returning late from work assignments. Another student stayed on duty near the rear loading dock, in case King's House volunteers on the street found someone in need of immediate care and shelter. But for most of King's House, 9 o'clock was a time for calm, perfect for postponed staff meetings.

Will Danielson leaned back in his chair with his legs crossed on the desk top. He had been a successful CPA in affluent Irvine before coming to King's House as administrator in 1995. In his late thirties and of medium build, Will was fair-colored with distinctly African facial features and hair, reflecting his mixed parentage. While upstairs for dinner, he had changed out of his normal business attire into jeans, a sweater, and fleece-lined slippers.

Dr. Alan Triplett took his usual place on one end of the large couch opposite Will's desk. He was a year younger than Will but looked ten years older. The King's House "surgeon general," as he was affectionately and respectfully called, was tall and lean. His close-cropped beard and receding hair were more gray than brown. Though his shift had concluded three hours earlier, Dr. Triplett still wore his lab coat with two or three sealed pairs of rubber gloves stuffed into each pocket.

Dr. No took the other end of the couch. He slipped out of his shoes as soon as he sat down, as usual, and propped his stockinged feet on the cushion.

Though he resisted titles and preferential treatment, and consistently acknowledged Will and Alan as the rulers in their realms of expertise, Dr. No was undeniably the leader of King's House. Had the operation been a for-profit business, it would have been a three-way partnership with Dr. No being the majority shareholder, if only by one share. Had it been a church, all three men would have been considered ministers, with Dr. No being senior minister. Though King's House was neither a business nor a church, it often functioned as both. And with the three men equally sharing responsibility for its success, Dr. No was first among equals.

Staff meetings generally began with a review of the current activities at the House, especially matters of concern that required prayer and action. Each man spoke freely about the daily triumphs and trials within his sphere of responsibility. Every concern was shouldered corporately, and each man faithfully checked back with the others, offering encouragement and providing accountability.

The triumvirate was in the midst of discussing volunteer staffing needs when the butler on duty rapped softly on the door, then stuck his head inside the office.

"I'm sorry to bother you, Dr. No, but there's a man at the door who wants to see you."

Seemingly every bummed-out ex-con, strung-out prostitute, and zoned-out transient showing up on the doorstep at night wanted to see Dr. No. For that reason, the night butlers were trained to discern which visitors, if any, really *needed* to see him.

The physically wounded coming to the door were directed to the walk-in trauma clinic a few blocks west on Alvarado. Substance abusers were referred to a rehab center in nearby Westlake. The destitute were given a small boxed snack and written instructions for receiving aid at the House's distribution center and free store during business hours.

Visitors judged to be in dire physical emergency were assisted to Alan Triplett's small clinic near the loading dock for overnight lodging and care. Each case was evaluated in the morning and handled accordingly. Some were shuttled to hospitals or to the homes of family members. Others were admitted to King's House for care, rehabilitation, and job training.

Dr. No eventually saw all of them. But thanks to the screening and response system devised by Will Danielson, he rarely saw any of them first, despite their demands. So when a night butler interrupted a staff meeting saying someone needed to see Dr. No, it was usually a valid need.

"What do you have, Casey?" Dr. No said, standing and slipping into his shoes.

"He says he's with the Unity 2000 committee—even has a fancy plastic ID card with his holograph on it. He wants to talk to you for a couple of minutes about Unity 2000 business."

"At this hour?" Dr. No wondered aloud. He glanced at his partners as if asking, "Do you know anything about this?" Alan shrugged innocence and Will shook his head.

"Is he inside?" Dr. No asked.

"Oh no, sir. I never unlock the door without authorization. He's on the front step."

"Well, let's have a look. Excuse me for a minute, guys." Dr. No followed Casey down the hall from Will's office toward the front entrance. He could see the man standing outside the glass doors. Very tall, very black. His high forehead ended with a thin layer of curly hair the color of his skin. He wore a fashionable suit and coordinating shirt, tie, and jewelry. His hands were thrust into the pockets of his slacks in the chilly night air.

When the visitor saw Dr. No approaching, a broad smile illuminated his face. Dr. No immediately felt at ease, as if reuniting with a long-lost friend—except he had never seen the black man before.

When they reached the door, Casey stepped aside and allowed Dr. No to deal with the visitor.

"Good evening, Dr. Ngo," the man called through the locked door, smiling winsomely. "I am William Malachi serving with the Unity 2000 committee."

Dr. No recognized the accent as coming from the African continent, the most lucid, precise, melodic English he had ever heard. The man even pronounced Dr. No's last name perfectly.

Malachi pulled the holocard from his jacket pocket and displayed it in front of the glass with fingers that seemed as long as new pencils. The white card bore the familiar blue Unity 2000 logo, a holographic image of the bearer, and the large, laser-printed words WILLIAM MALA-CHI.

Dr. No unlocked the door and pulled it open. Malachi remained outside as he explained his presence. "I am sorry to trouble you so late, Dr. Ngo. My schedule today prevented me from telephoning for an appointment. But I happened to be traveling near King's House this evening, so I have stopped by hoping you might spare me two minutes of your time."

Dr. No realized the man was not going to enter without an invitation. Convinced that he must be for real, Dr. No said, "Come in, please, Mr. Malachi," and extended a hand.

Malachi swept through the door, and his large hand swallowed Dr. No's in a friendly grip. "Thank you, Dr. Ngo, and God bless you." Then he turned to Casey with a gracious bow. "And thank you for your kind help, sir. God bless you." Flustered at the unexpected courtesy, Casey blushed, smiled, and said nothing.

Malachi turned to Dr. No. "I do not want to infringe on your time, Dr. Ngo, so I will come right to the point. I have a favor to ask of you and your associates, Dr. Triplett and Mr. Danielson."

"Do you know Alan and Will?" Dr. No asked, surprised that Malachi had mentioned their names.

"No, I have not met them personally. But, as with yourself, their reputation of service to God and to the community is known and appreciated by many of us who have observed your ministry from afar."

Dr. No was almost distracted by the black man's precise diction. Every vowel, every consonant, every diphthong was perfectly pronounced and clearly enunciated. He had never before seen such respect for the language from an obviously foreign-born individual. He had to introduce Mr. Malachi to Alan and Will.

"Well, if your request involves my associates," he said, "perhaps you would like to meet them and speak to all of us at once."

Malachi's eyes widened with pleasure. "If it is no imposition, I would be delighted to meet them."

Dr. No led Mr. Malachi down the hall and into Will's office. Alan and Will rose to their feet at the sight of the striking figure following their leader in the door.

Introductions were brief and cordial, with Malachi adding a warm "God bless you" to each greeting. An upholstered oak side chair was provided for the guest.

"One of my responsibilities for the Unity 2000 committee," Malachi began, "is to oversee the activities of the four leaders — Dr. McClure, Rev. Hornecker, Rev. Holloway, and Mr. Dunne — in Los Angeles prior to the event in the Coliseum on Millennium's Eve. Our particular interest is to expose them to noteworthy local ministries, places like King's House. With your permission, I would like to bring them to King's House this week so they may tour your facility."

"The four big televangelists here?" Alan said with an expression of incredulity.

Will added, "They have congregations in the tens of thousands and budgets in the millions. What will they find noteworthy about our little mission in run-down Echo Park?"

Dr. No sat in thoughtful silence, pinching the bridge of his nose and studying William Malachi.

"Gentlemen, you are too modest. You are performing a significant service to the less fortunate in Los Angeles. The Gospel of Jesus Christ is not only proclaimed here, it is demonstrated here. We believe the four leaders will find your facility and your scope of operation inspiring."

Finally, Dr. No said, "How did the committee learn about King's House? We don't really advertise our ministry."

Mr. Malachi laughed a warm laugh. "Yes, your anonymity to the secular media, which I assume you prefer, has been well guarded. But many key business and civic leaders in the city have spoken very highly of your ministry, so many, in fact, that the committee was unanimous in choosing King's House as a site our guests should visit."

Dr. No shifted uncomfortably as he envisioned a troop of dignitaries, reporters, and assorted hangers-on swarming the facility and disrupting the routine.

"Mr. Malachi, we're flattered by the committee's interest. But we're really not prepared for a crowd of people and all the media attention—"

"O Dr. Ngo, please do not worry," Malachi interrupted, lifting a long, slender hand to banish Dr. No's concern. "We do not in any way wish to upset for a moment the tranquility of this facility. The visit will be private, limited to the four ministers and their families. The media will not even be informed. We want our guests to be able to visit with you and see King's House without distraction, and we also want you to be free of the inconvenience which attends a large crowd."

Mr. Malachi had thoroughly defused Dr. No's objections, as much with his demeanor as with his answers. "When would you like to bring them here?" he asked.

"Each of the leaders is occupied with appointments during the day," Malachi said. "Wednesday evening at 7 o'clock would be ideal for us."

Dr. No looked at Alan and Will for possible objections. There were none. "I guess that will be fine."

"Excellent!" he sang, obviously elated. "I am sure this will be an experience Dr. McClure, Rev. Hornecker, Rev. Holloway, and Mr. Dunne will never forget." Then he stood quickly. "But I have already taken too much of your time. I must be going."

The King's House trio stood in unison and followed Mr. Malachi out the door and down the hall. The elegant black man seemed anxious to leave. Dr. No unlocked the glass door as Malachi bid a warm farewell to Alan, Will, and even Casey.

"Dr. Ngo, it has been a pleasure meeting you. I look forward to seeing you again Friday evening."

"Thank you, Mr. Malachi. I'm glad we can be of service."

Malachi said, "Good night, and God bless you," then stepped through the door. "Oh, one more item," he said, turning to face Dr. No from the top step. "I would like you to prepare a devotional message to deliver to our four guests on Wednesday evening during their visit."

"Me? A message? For them?" he answered in shock. "But I'm not a minister, I'm just a—"

Mr. Malachi again raised a comforting hand. "Not a sermon, Dr. Ngo. Just a simple message from your heart. God will give it to you, I am sure." Malachi disappeared into the darkness with a smile and a wave, leaving Dr. No standing at the door with his mouth open.

Twenty-seven

"If you play in your Nikes, you have to spot me 6 points; home court advantage."

Beth had made the rule when she saw Cole pull his white high-tops out of his gym bag before their second game of midnight one-on-one basketball in the driveway of her parents' home. Cole gave her the 6-point advantage, quietly delighted that she hadn't asked for 10. Then he proceeded to beat her, 20–12.

Cole played much better in his Nikes than he had in his motorcycle boots the night before. But the main reason for the lopsided victory was Beth's ankle. She turned it slightly on a spin-move to the basket while scoring her first earned points after being spotted to a 6-0 lead.

She hobbled around the driveway grimacing during a brief time-out, and Cole offered to cancel the game.

"No chance," she insisted, snatching the ball from his hands and limping to the end line to begin her next drive. "I'm 8 points up, and I have a lot riding on this game."

So do I, Cole judged silently, thinking especially of the romantic bonus Beth had inferred for a 10-point victory. Then he thought, *But our Millennium's Eve date won't be much fun if you're in a cast due to an aggravated sprain.* "I'll introduce you to Shelby Hornecker," he said, trying to convince her to ice down her ankle and forget the game. "You don't have to beat me for it."

Beth responded by driving quickly past him, bad ankle and all, and scoring an easy layup while he stood watching flatfooted. Cole was suddenly down 10–0.

"If your leg was broken in five places, would you play?" he prodded, still wishing she would give up.

"I could beat you even if one leg withered up and fell off." She was joking, but there was a cutting competitive edge to her voice that warned Cole to play defense on her next drive.

She isn't going to quit; she wants an all-out game, bum ankle or not, Cole thought, squaring to defend her. "Okay, Beth, take your best shot," he challenged.

Beth's intense competitive fire couldn't make up for her bad "wheel" or for Cole's quickness, strength, and height. He reeled off 18 straight points despite Beth's valiant hand-checking, ball-swatting, body-blocking defense all over the driveway. Cole played hard and played to win. And the moment he began to feel sorry about Beth's ankle and let up in the slightest, a sharp elbow in his ribs or a stinging slap on his arm from an attempted steal quickened his resolve.

As he dribbled the ball and eyed the basket for what he hoped would be his final shot, Cole was aware that his next goal would secure a 10-point margin of victory. He wasn't exactly sure what Beth meant when she offered him breakfast as well as dinner for a 10-point win, but it was a delicious thought. It was precisely during Cole's moment of fantasy that Beth swiped the ball off his dribble, faked him one way, and limped in for another easy layup.

Cole finally made his winning basket, but Beth couldn't keep a devilish grin from her face as she offered him a congratulatory handshake. "Nice game. I owe you dinner on Millennium's Eve—and that's all."

Cole used the handshake to pull her into an embrace and kiss. Beth didn't resist. "I guess breakfast is on me, then," he whispered.

Her dark eyes pierced his deeply, then her frisky smirk returned. "You can always hope."

Beth pulled two bottles of beer from the carton in the shrubs and waved Cole toward the house. "Let's go into the family room," she said, puffing clouds of steam in the midnight chill. "I taped the Blazers–Jazz game tonight from Salt Lake. Let's watch it."

"But you told me your parents don't allow beer in the house," Cole said, pointing to the bottles.

"Aw, don't worry. Mom and Dad have been asleep for over an hour, and the family room is on the other side of the house from their room. I'll hide the empties in the bushes, and if Dad finds them and puts me on the rack, I won't squeal on you."

Portland and Utah played a close, seesaw game for most of the first half. Cole sat in Jack Scibelli's swivel rocker, while Beth lounged in her old leather beanbag with an ice bag on her sore ankle. She used the remote to fast-forward through time-outs and commercials.

Cole quietly cheered for the Blazers and his friend Curtis Spooner while Beth pulled for the Jazz just to be playfully obstinate. But by halftime Utah had built a 17-point lead that ballooned to a complete blowout midway through the third quarter. With the game out of reach, Beth muted the sound. She sat cross-legged on the beanbag, favoring her ankle, and turned the conversation to thoughts which had been loitering at the fringes of her consciousness all day like a dull headache.

"Reagan, what if the message at the *Times* today is a real threat? What could the guy get away with?"

"What did he say?" Cole asked, watching the action on the screen out of the corner of his eye.

"Mostly he talked about the Four Horsemen of the Apocalypse, you know, the red horse, the black horse, whatever. From the guy's comments, it sounds like he's threatening the four televangelists."

"How could you tell?"

"He mentioned four horsemen journeying to the city and four thrones becoming one before the dawn of the new age."

"You have to swing pretty far out to make that apply to the televangelists. He could be referring to any four people coming into L.A."

"That was my impression too. But Mai and the other editors felt it was a reference to Hornecker, Dunne, McClure, and Holloway."

"Of course they would. They need a hot story to finish off the old millennium, something to panic the city and spook the herd of religious kooks grazing here this week waiting for the big event."

Cole was silent for a moment as he watched a strong defensive effort by Curtis Spooner in a game that had already been lost. Then he said, "What did the mystery caller threaten to do to the Four Horsemen?"

"He mentioned something about the riders' flesh being torn and blood flowing into the earth."

"Sounds like a slasher. There's always an alleged slasher on the loose somewhere in L.A.; we're briefed about them nearly every day. The lieutenant told me about another one tonight. A security guard in Hollywood got himself disemboweled by someone with a big knife. We're supposed to keep an eye out for 'serious blades.' That's about as easy as rounding up all the bootleg fireworks in L.A. before Millennium's Eve."

"The caller also mentioned something about bones being scattered," Beth continued.

"So he's also going to dismember his victims and throw the pieces around," Cole said cynically. "This is no killer on the loose; this is a scriptwriter for a horror movie."

"You really don't think anything is going to happen, do you?" Beth's question was issued more as a challenge than an inquiry.

"I'm not saying there isn't someone out there who wants to make chopped liver out of the televangelists. But, number one, I'm saying it's highly unlikely that it's a serious threat, that the guy actually plans to do the job. He probably gets high just thinking about scaring the crap out of important people.

"Number two, normal security precautions make it nearly impossible for anyone to get close enough to stick a knife into one of the four, let alone all four of them. And, three, with police escorts assigned now, even if he's lucky enough to get close to his intended victims, we'll be there to stop him."

Beth couldn't argue with Cole's logic. She agreed that any odds favoring a mad slasher getting to the four televangelists were dubious at best. Then another dark possibility surfaced in her thoughts. "What about a bomb?"

Cole was momentarily distracted by a fast break that ended with Spooner jamming the ball through the net. "A bomb?" he said at last.

"Yes, a bomb. In the Coliseum on Millennium's Eve. Kaboom! Torn flesh, spilled blood, scattered bones, just like the caller predicted."

"You've been watching too many spy movies," Cole said with a smirk, his eyes still on the game.

Beth clicked off the VCR abruptly and came up on her knees in front of Cole's chair, frowning. "Reagan, I'm serious. I realize that the threat on the tape today may be as phony as a pro wrestling match. It's easy for me to be skeptical about this kind of thing. But what if it's not a hoax? Mai said this guy didn't sound like the other zoned-out doomsday prophets who call the *Times*. You don't seem to believe that a psychopath somewhere in L.A. might have the guts and the goods to blow the televangelists and God only knows how many other people to kingdom come on Millennium's Eve."

Beth's sudden seriousness stopped another sarcastic remark in Cole's throat. He leaned forward and reached for her hand. "I'm sorry, Beth. I didn't mean to make fun of you or the potential danger. I know there are nuts out there and that some of them are capable of doing nasty things. I hope I don't sound too cocky, but we're ready for anything that comes down. We have contingencies in place for the safety of any VIPs in the city, such as the escorts for the big four.

"The Coliseum has its own security staff. And our terrorist experts will probably scour the place thoroughly with bomb dogs before Friday night—they can sniff out an ounce of Semtex from twenty feet away. I'm not saying our system is foolproof, but most bad guys aren't clever enough to slip through it."

Beth gazed at Cole admiringly. "Well, your explanation makes me feel a little bit better—for the moment at least. But I may need to have you explain it to me again."

"It will be my pleasure, ma'am," Cole said in an affected condescending tone while lifting a comically cockeyed salute. "I'm here to serve, protect, and—"

With a rascally grin, Beth grabbed him behind one knee and squeezed hard. Cole stifled a surprised yelp and flew out of the upholstered rocker to defend himself. The tickling and wrestling match on the family room carpet and beanbag lasted several minutes. The kissing and caressing continued a few minutes longer.

"It's getting late, I'd better be going," Cole said, trying to calm himself.

"Yes, you need to go," Beth cooed, then pulled him into another long kiss.

"What about tomorrow?" he said, sitting up.

Beth glanced at her watch. "Tomorrow is now today."

"So what are your plans today?"

"Research and write, I guess. Except right now that sounds terribly dull." She grabbed his hand and held it.

"Will you be at the *Times?*"

"Yes, all morning. Mai's boss is on the East Coast this week, and she invited me to use his work station if I want to. She's given me a golden key to all the *Times'* files. And I like the idea of being close to the VoiceLink line, in case our mystery hoaxer calls again. I'll probably spend the afternoon working in the library downtown."

"And tonight, after 11?"

"Mm, I think I have an opening at that time. Make me an offer."

"The Blazers fly into L.A., after their game in Phoenix. I told Curtis I'd meet him at the University Hilton when I get off work. I'd like to introduce you to him. How about meeting me at the Hilton a little after 11?"

Beth gasped in mock horror. "You've known me for all of two days and you're asking me to meet you at a hotel?"

"At *the bar* in the hotel," Cole clarified. The Trojan Horse Saloon.

"Yes, but you know where one or two drinks can lead," she said temptingly.

Cole stood, pulled Beth to her feet, and pecked her on the forehead. "You can always hope," he said as he turned to leave.

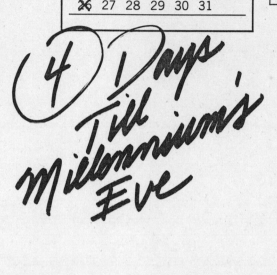

NOVEMBER 1999						
S	M	T	W	T	F	S
	1	2	3	4	5	6
7	8	9	10	11	12	13
14	15	16	17	18	19	20
21	22	23	24	25	26	27
28	29	30				

1999 DECEMBER 1999

S	M	T	W	T	F	S
			1	2	3	4
5	6	7	8	9	10	11
12	13	14	15	16	17	18
19	20	21	22	23	24	25
26	27	28	29	30	31	

JANUARY 2000						
S	M	T	W	T	F	S
						1
2	3	4	5	6	7	8
9	10	11	12	13	14	15
16	17	18	19	20	21	22
23	24	25	26	27	28	29
30	31					

(4) Days Till Millennium's Eve

Twenty-eight

The man sitting behind the large, antique oak desk wore a cotton print shirt, neatly pressed cotton pants, and new canvas loafers. He was too thin for his six-foot frame, and his sparse straight hair was too dark for his sixty-two years. Small, cold eyes surveyed his guests from the shadow of a protruding brow, and his narrow, hawkish nose was aimed at his meaningless mechanical smile, like a directional arrow pointing to a dead-end road.

The four men sitting stiffly around the desk were twenty to twenty-five years younger than their host and, despite the early morning hour of the hastily called meeting, formally dressed in business suits and ties. Dr. Morgan McClure was within minutes of leaving for Phoenix's Sky Harbor by limo and then for Mazatlan by private jet. Though they didn't know it yet, his attorneys were within minutes of scurrying to their offices in Phoenix for five of the most grueling, stressful days of their careers.

The four guests desperately needed coffee, but the mogul of Paradise Church and Sunny Haven Retirement Resort hadn't offered any.

"Have you been to Mazatlan before, Dr. McClure?" The newest junior partner embarrassed himself and his colleagues by asking it.

"Of course I have, Roberti. I own a villa there." The smile only thinly veiled McClure's inference that Roberti was a dolt.

"I enjoy the golf, snorkeling, and shopping in Mazatlan, Dr. McClure, don't you?" another man offered, trying to be cordial.

"I go for the tranquility and personal renewal. I rarely leave the villa."

"Will Mrs. McClure be going with you this year, Dr. McClure?"

"No, Mrs. McClure always spends the holidays with her sister in Columbus. I'm going to Mazatlan alone."

McClure mercilessly interrupted the plastic pleasantries by standing and turning toward the large window behind his desk. The view was spectacular from the rocky knoll where the McClure's $6 million home stood. Below him sprawled the modern worship, education, and media complex of Paradise Church. From this center Dr. McClure's popular psycho/theology of upthink was disseminated across the country.

Surrounding the church, a string of luxurious, two-story retirement residences snaked through the verdant fairways and manicured greens of an 18-hole golf course. The view from the living room window was similar: 18 additional holes, like a string of emeralds on the desert floor, set in a chain of opulent homes. And at the outer limits of the retirement resort, slashing at the golden December dawn, stood rugged and starkly beautiful peaks sprayed with dried brush and dotted with saguaro.

"Gentlemen, I have called you here in order to clarify for you the issue once again," McClure began, absorbing the view. "This is my life: a thriving national ministry, a very profitable living center for retiring baby boomers swimming in principal and interest from lifetime investments, and a dream home for Mrs. McClure and myself. I have poured thirty years of my life into this effort, and I intend to spend the next thirty years enjoying the rewards I deserve."

McClure turned away from the glorious scene with reluctance to grace his guests with his ever-present prefab smile and subtly hostile eyes. "But the District Attorney for the state of Arizona and the United States Department of the Treasury want to take it all away from me. The Honorable Darlene Davis contends that our Sunny Haven residents are not getting what they paid for. And the Internal Revenue Service insists that our guests have paid more than I have reported. All indications are that these allegations, based on months of investigation, will crystallize into formal indictments in the next month."

McClure paused, the smile receding slightly. "Unfortunately for me, my detractors have in their favor the bothersome technicalities of the law. But, unfortunately for them, I have in my favor more resources for my defense than they have—or are willing to use—for my prosecution. Public servants are so woefully scrupulous and underpaid, which helps me understand why you gentlemen have not aspired to state or federal appointments."

The four men didn't know whether to laugh or take offense at McClure's comment, so they remained stoic.

The full smile returned to McClure's face, but it was overpowered by his icy stare. "But for all the money I have poured into this august law firm, I am no nearer a plausible defense than when we first met in October. The reports you have sent, the strategies you have outlined—pure rubbish. Any intern could stand up for the state and the feds and get a conviction against me."

McClure stepped around the desk and hovered menacingly over the four attorneys like the craggy peaks hovered over Paradise Valley, Arizona. Roberti embarrassed himself again by clearing his throat nervously.

"I didn't retain this firm because you're famous or cheap. You're neither. I retained you because our mutual associates in Illinois assured me that you could get me off. Now in two minutes I am walking out that door, riding to the airport, and flying to Mexico for five days. Then I will be in Los Angeles on Friday night for that ridiculous event in the Coliseum. I will try to convince the Christian world that my religious beliefs and practices as well as my personal life as a minister are being attacked by a godless government. I'm doing my damnedest to sway the popular vote.

"But I will return to Phoenix on Sunday morning. And, if you are not waiting for me in this room with a foolproof strategy for defeating the state and the feds—by whatever means, I'll see to it that you won't get so much as a divorce or child custody case for the rest of this firm's existence."

McClure waited until he had burned his icy, grinning stare into the eyes of each man. Then he brushed past them toward the door.

The senior member of the attorney team tried to reply. "Dr. McClure, you can be assured—" But he was cut off by McClure telling his burly Navajo bodyguard, "Tony, show them to their car." The attorneys scurried out the door with Tony at their heels.

As McClure strode toward the bedroom to retrieve his packed luggage, his pocket phone sounded. He stopped on the black slate floor in the center of the huge house and answered.

"Dr. McClure, this is Tanner. I have just one matter to talk to you about before you leave." Richard Tanner, an associate, was calling from home.

"Make it fast, Tanner. My car is waiting." McClure continued toward the master suite.

"Yes, sir. I received a call last night from someone on the Unity 2000 committee about a special meeting you have with Hornecker, Dunne, and Holloway in Los Angeles on Wednesday night. His name was William Malachi. Do you recognize the name?"

"I've never heard of William Malachi, and I don't know anything about a meeting on Wednesday night in L.A."

"Well, you have one now. According to Malachi, the meeting was scheduled recently for—"

McClure stopped in the hall outside his suite and interrupted. "I don't care who scheduled the meeting. It's not on my calendar, and I will not leave Mexico early for any last-minute meeting."

"But the other three will be there, sir. I told the man you had prior plans, but he strongly insisted that you change your—"

"Tanner, I will not be in L.A. on Wednesday night!" McClure boiled into the phone. "Do whatever you have to do, tell whomever you have to tell. I won't be there." Then he snapped the phone shut and returned it to his shirt pocket.

"Can we go now, Morgan?" She was stretched across his bed reading a magazine when he walked into the bedroom. Melanie was thirtyish with a model's figure and mounds of cascading auburn hair. She had been ready to go for half an hour, only to be confined to McClure's room while he dispatched his four attorneys in the 7 A.M. meeting.

McClure stopped to admire her stunning beauty, his anger suddenly diffused. They had stolen many nights together over the last few months, pleasantly distracting McClure from the vultures circling ever closer and his loveless marriage to Wanda McClure. How much more tempting Melanie would be beside the pool at the villa. He could hardly wait to be with her there for five uninterrupted, sun-drenched days.

Morgan McClure had dealt with the guilt from his adultery just as he had dealt with the guilt from living a lie and lining his pockets with tens of thousands of dollars in extorted funds and unpaid taxes. He ignored it, buried it, told God to get out of his life, and kept doing what he wanted to do. In his moments of uneasy solitude, McClure only hoped he was clever enough to stay steps ahead of the women he had hurt and the residents and government he had cheated.

"Yes, my lovely one," he hummed with anticipation. "It's time to go to Mexico."

Twenty-nine

Jimmy Tuggle was born, raised, and educated a Baptist. As a fourteen-year-old, he went forward in Lakeside Baptist Church in Waco, Texas to shake the pastor's hand, signifying his decision to accept Jesus Christ as his personal Savior and join the church. He went on to serve as president of his Baptist Youth Fellowship group all three years of high school.

Confident—but somewhat disappointed—that God had not called him to be a pastor or missionary, Jimmy pursued his second love. He majored in history at Baylor University, the world's largest Baptist University, where he met and married Evelyn McCleary, the daughter of a Baptist minister in Amarillo. After teaching history at the high school level in town for seven years and pecking away at advanced degrees, Jimmy returned to Baylor as assistant professor of history.

Thirty-five years later, Dr. Jimmy Tuggle was head of the history department at Baylor and chairman of the deacon board at Lakeside Baptist Church in West Waco. Evelyn Tuggle hosted the weekly Women's Bible Study and the Missionary Sewing Circle in their spacious home off Lake Shore Drive, overlooking Lake Waco. Two of Jimmy and Evelyn's sons were Baptist missionaries in Europe. A third was a production supervisor at the M & M / Mars plant in town and a volunteer youth leader at Lakeside Baptist.

The only disappointment in their storybook Christian family—and Jimmy and Evelyn would insist it was not a disappointment, only an unexpected challenge to their understanding of God's will—was their daughter. And if they could have changed only one thing about the way they raised her, they would have said no instead of a reluctant yes when sixteen-year-old Shelby Tuggle asked if she could attend church camp with a Christian girlfriend from school instead of going to Baptist camp with the Lakeside youth group.

Shelby came home from camp changed. She had not only enjoyed six of the most fun-filled days of her life, but she'd had an "experience" with God. Like her parents and three brothers, Shelby had walked forward in the Baptist church as a young teen to shake the pastor's hand. But at Maranatha Camp, she explained to her parents through tears of joy and wonder, she had walked forward and been embraced by Jesus Himself.

Though Jimmy and Evelyn had insisted that Shelby continue attending the Baptist church and BYF activities, the girl's heart was not in it. "BYF meetings are boring, and our church services are so lifeless and predictable," Shelby contended overdramatically. "Megan's church is alive and exciting. Their services are directed by God, not by a schedule printed in the bulletin. Sometimes they get so wrapped up in worshiping God, the pastor just cancels his sermon. And that's never happened at Lakeside," Shelby emphasized.

Neither had Jimmy and Evelyn recalled a sermon being canceled in church because people were caught up in the song service, nor could they imagine such a thing. But they said nothing. They didn't want to discourage Shelby's spiritual enthusiasm. Still, they were quietly concerned that their daughter was elevating her spiritual experience above biblical exposition and Baptist tradition.

Young Shelby attended Lakeside so willingly at her parents' insistence that they couldn't refuse her requests to attend youth events and special services at Megan's church that didn't conflict with Lakeside's schedule. Jimmy and Evelyn secretly hoped their daughter's "hallelujah hot flashes" would cool over time. But immediately after high school graduation, the point at which her parents had said she was free to choose her own church, Shelby transferred her membership to Maranatha Community Church and mailed her final application papers to the church's Bible college in Bethany, Oklahoma. That August she moved north to the small campus with her parents' financial support and concerned prayers.

Although Jimmy's dream that his daughter become a Baptist pastor's or missionary's wife had been thwarted, his love for Shelby was undimmed by her choice for a charismatic Christian lifestyle. When she married Adrian Hornecker in college and the starry-eyed youngsters started their noisy little church in Arlington, Jimmy and Evelyn visited their services often. They were uncomfortable with the informal, emotional worship style and the almost fanatical emphasis on Bible prophecy and prosperity in Adrian's preaching. But the Tuggles always slipped a generous check into the offering pouch and were among the first contributors when the growing church established a building fund.

As good Baptists, Jimmy and Evelyn knew that lovingly accepting their daughter and her husband was more important than converting them into good Baptists. Their warm and positive attitude remained an inviting welcome mat for Shelby and her husband as Adrian's ministry burgeoned from a successful local church to a high-impact national ministry through television and films. Though Shelby's demanding schedule did not allow her to visit her parents often, she was on their doorstep for reassurance whenever problems in the church or personal pain slashed at her sometimes fragile self-confidence.

She was there when Adrian's reluctance to give her a child had nearly decimated her sense of purpose. She returned when his film ministry jammed days and weeks and thousands of miles between them every month. She was in her parents' arms within hours of the tragic crash. Now she was here again, realizing that her parents could never understand everything about her or her lifestyle, but confident that their love and listening was the medicine she needed.

When Shelby had arrived at the Tuggles' home at 10 P.M. on Sunday, Jimmy and Evelyn came outside to greet her and admire the beautiful new car. They had watched the presentation on TV Friday morning. Shelby beamed, and they were happy for her.

But as soon as they stepped inside the house, Shelby's tears began to flow and the whole story poured out—her loneliness, her failure, her futile attempt to run away, her rescue by Soledad Cruz and his family, her predawn surrender on the cold floor of a child's bedroom near Los Angeles, Texas.

Shelby and her parents talked and wept and embraced and prayed together into the night. Shelby drew on their strength and silently thanked God for the undergirding of her parents' love. She felt the jagged pieces of her soul come together and bond in the warmth of Jimmy and Evelyn's quiet, rather formal prayers.

They talked about Shelby's need to seek out a godly, trained counselor to help her deal with the emptiness the enemy had used to twist a friendly conversation with Jeremy Cannon into dark moments of lust and temptation. And when Shelby wondered aloud about quietly stepping back from responsibility at Victory Life, such as taking a few months for "study leave" to pray, saturate herself with God's Word, and seek extensive counsel, Jimmy and Evelyn agreed that the idea had merit.

They discussed a number of strategies for Shelby's personal restoration. Jimmy suspended the conversation periodically to offer another brief prayer. When they finally turned in after 2 A.M., exhausted Shelby was engulfed in dreamless sleep.

Shelby's brother Lance and his family were due in half an hour for a midmorning brunch. They would exchange gifts and phone her two missionary brothers and their families in Europe. The family get-together had been postponed a day when Shelby called after leaving the Cruz ranch.

The emotional tide from the previous night had receded to allow comfortable conversation about other topics. But as Shelby helped Jimmy and Evelyn prepare the food, she found herself struggling with a missing piece in her puzzle. She needed more of her parents' wisdom before the rest of the family arrived.

"What should I do about Jeremy?" she asked. "I know I have to seek his forgiveness, and I'm planning to call him tonight to apologize— that's going to be very difficult. But then what? He's supposed to fly to Los Angeles with us tomorrow and stand beside me on the Coliseum platform Friday night. Should I tell him not to come? Should I sever all ties with him?"

It was silent for a moment, and then Evelyn gave the floor to Jimmy with an affirming glance. "What would you like to happen?" he asked as he mixed a pitcher of frozen orange juice.

"You mean besides making last Friday night disappear?" Shelby responded wryly.

"In God's eyes, sugar, it *has* disappeared," Jimmy reminded her encouragingly. "What happens between you and Jeremy now is up to you—and Jeremy, of course. Do you want a romantic relationship with him, I mean a wholesome relationship that may someday lead to marriage?"

Shelby shook her head firmly. "No, Daddy, he's not the one. That's what makes my adolescent behavior Friday night so absurd. Jeremy is a good man, but he isn't the one I want to share my life with. I was hurting, I was tempted, I was deceived, he was there, I. . . ." Shelby saw her parents nodding. She didn't need to explain further.

"So what do you want your relationship with Jeremy to be?" Jimmy pressed.

"The best possible end to this nightmare would be for us to remain friends and for Jeremy to continue growing in his faith and ministering through our church. I hope I haven't ruined those possibilities."

"What has to happen to achieve this end, sugar?"

Shelby sighed heavily at the seeming mountain of impossibility looming over her. "Well, first I must confess my sin to Jeremy and sincerely apologize for my actions. That's what I intend to do tonight when I get home."

"And if God is working in his heart as well as in yours, he will receive your apology and forgive you. What else?"

Another sigh and silence, then finally, "This is hard for me, Daddy."

"I know, sugar. I'm just trying to help you think through the answers to your question."

Shelby nodded and flashed her appreciation with a quick smile. "Our friendship was healthy until I was alone with him Friday night and allowed my emotions to run away with me."

"So to minimize the possibility of Friday night happening again. . . ?" Jimmy's train of thought was obvious to Shelby, but she knew she had to take the logical steps her father was leading her through.

"I need to promise Jeremy that I will never put him in that position again—being alone with me. And I also need to assure him that I have not abandoned my morals, that Friday night happened because I foolishly allowed several volatile elements to come together in a moment of loneliness. And I suppose it wouldn't hurt to let him know that I will be submitting to counseling in order to defuse these elements."

"Anything else?" Her father's gentle prodding reminded Shelby of her school days. He used to help her prepare for tests by quizzing her. "Anything else?" always meant she was on the right track and doing well, but had omitted one or two important facts.

"I need a hint, Daddy," she said after a pause. Jimmy had always been generous with hints during his quizzes.

"You told us that Jeremy responded to your advances at first, then broke away and ran. What would have happened if he hadn't broken away?"

Shelby was thoughtful for a full minute as she contemplated the sobering possibilities and searched for the hint in Jimmy's question. Finally it appeared to her. "I need to thank him," she said. "What I did was bad enough, but if he hadn't run out when he did. . . " Shelby didn't need to finish the thought.

"Very good, sugar," Jimmy affirmed. "You put that young man in a dangerous position Friday night, but he eventually did the right thing. He needs to know that you appreciate his self-control."

Shelby was satisfied for the moment. She carried silverware and napkins from the hutch in the dining room to the table. Evelyn worked in the kitchen preparing her homemade cinnamon rolls for baking, and Jimmy assembled the ingredients for his specialty, huevos rancheros. Soon Shelby was back in the kitchen with another question.

"Can you think of any reason why Jeremy shouldn't go with me to Los Angeles and participate in Unity 2000?" Shelby had never mentioned to her parents her misgivings about participating in the big event or confided in them about the strong, behind-the-scenes rivalry that existed between the nation's four leading Christian television personalities.

Evelyn spoke first. "Has Jeremy's effectiveness been diminished to the point that he shouldn't appear at Unity 2000?"

"No, not unless—Lord forbid—he has fallen back into his old lifestyle because of me. If anyone's effectiveness has been diminished, it's mine. But I know God is restoring me and wants me in Los Angeles. So I don't know why He wouldn't want Jeremy there too."

"And you have already determined that you will guard against being tricked by the devil into another compromising scenario with

Jeremy?" Jimmy continued.

"Yes, Daddy. I will never be alone with him again. Theresa and the Welbourns will be flying with us to L.A., and Theresa will be at my side twenty-four hours a day in Los Angeles. I've learned my lesson. I will never again allow myself to be isolated with any man," then she added sheepishly, "unless God brings me another husband."

Evelyn said, "Then the only reason I can see why Jeremy shouldn't go to Los Angeles with you is if he doesn't want to. Have you considered that possibility?"

Shelby had. She wanted to believe that Jeremy had cried out to God for himself and for her all the way home to Dallas Friday night, and that God had mercifully ministered forgiveness to him just as He had to her. She hoped that Jeremy would receive her apology cordially and that their friendship would be restored. But he could have just as easily given up on her, Victory Life Ministries, Unity 2000, and God. The thought turned her stomach.

"From what Shelby has told us about that young man, Mother," Jimmy interjected, "I don't think she has much to worry about. He had an immoral past, but God saved him. And when he had a chance to fall back into his old ways Friday night, he ran like Joseph out of Potiphar's house—and, sugar, I don't mean to imply that you're anything like Potiphar's evil wife."

Shelby appreciated her father's sensitivity to her feelings. In reality, during her darker hours over the last three days, she had bitterly taunted herself with the very comparison Jimmy had carefully avoided.

Jimmy continued. "I think Jeremy has developed moral fiber over the last few years, perhaps greater strength than he realized he had. I believe God is going to honor your contrition and restore your relationship with your friend. We'll be praying that Unity 2000 will be a new step for both of you."

Always the optimist, Shelby thought, deeply appreciating her father. *I hope you're right, Daddy. I'll find out when I call Jeremy from Austin tonight.*

Thirty

Hodge delivered his memorized message in less than forty-five seconds and hung up. He was confident that neither the *Times* nor the police would try to trace the call. He had walked almost a mile from the bungalow to find a pay phone he'd never used before, just off the corner of Washington and Main. He also judged that being outside would be good for him on such a pleasant winter morning. A long walk in the fresh air would clear his head for the critical task awaiting him at the bungalow.

Trudging west along crowded Washington Boulevard toward home, Hodge contemplated the increased traffic in the city with Millennium's Eve drawing nearer. L.A.'s teeming thoroughfares resembled a vast network of interconnecting rivers and streams approaching flood stage. Inflow to the city had been exceeding outflow since well before Christmas, and the ratio increased daily.

It seemed that rush-hour traffic had stretched into midmorning—except that half the cars clogging Washington Boulevard were not even from California. License plates bore the colors and slogans of states and provinces all across North America. And bumpers were littered with stickers advertising the local attractions the tourists were patronizing during their Christmas vacation in sunny Southern California: The Tournament of Roses, Disneyland, Knott's Berry Farm, Sea World, the Queen Mary, and Magic Mountain.

A disproportionate number of visiting cars bore plates from Oregon and Ohio. Many of these cars were decorated with pom-poms, streamers, and handmade signs—green and gold for the Oregonians, red and gray for the Ohioans—in celebration of the two teams clashing New Year's Day in the first Rose Bowl game of the new millennium: Oregon and Ohio State.

As he viewed the parade of fun-seekers, Hodge noted smugly, *the Rose Parade, the Bowl games, the Millennium's Eve parties, and all the other attractions in Southern California this week will seem as inconsequential as hopscotch compared to the fireworks and glorious revelation at the Coliseum on December 31.*

Hodge could easily distinguish the out-of-towners who were including Unity 2000 in their itinerary to Southern California. Prominent spaces on their bumpers and back windows were occupied by blue and white Unity 2000 stickers. Most of these vehicles also displayed a variety of decals featuring crosses, doves, fish symbols, Bible verses, and obnoxious religious slogans. A few cars from Texas passed by bearing the familiar logo of Victory Life Ministries. A minivan with Florida plates was plastered with stickers and posters condemning genetic engineering. Hodge smiled. *How the factions will evaporate and the people will come together as a result of my mission on Millennium's Eve.*

Entering the bungalow and locking the door behind him, Hodge slipped out of his jacket and cap in the darkness. He stepped to the eight-foot table dominating the center of the room, found the naked bulb hanging from the ceiling, and pulled the chain. The tabletop was flooded with light.

The table was empty except for a stack of old newspapers on one end and a mismatched collection of household tools: two screwdrivers (one medium and one small), needle-nose pliers, wire cutters, crescent wrench, small hammer, chisel, electrical tape.

Hodge set about retrieving a number of other items from around the bungalow and placing them on the table. He moved deliberately, almost solemnly, like a priest setting a table for the sacrament of Holy Communion.

First he found two empty cardboard egg cartons, lids torn off, stored on the shelf in his kitchen corner. He laid them upside down and end to end at the opposite end of the table from the tools. Next he brought ten one-foot lengths of PVC pipe and a roll of duct tape to the table from a box under his bed. He had purchased the pipe at a hardware store in Florence several days earlier.

He laid the pipe sections horizontally across the inverted egg cartons, one section resting in each of the ten notches on the two cartons, as if on display at a plumbers convention. He set the duct tape next to the tools.

Hodge reached behind the dishes on his kitchen shelf and produced a brand new electric soldering kit, still in its plastic carrying case. He opened the case and ran the cord from the soldering gun to the socket on the overhead light fixture. Assured that the soldering gun was switched off for the moment, he laid it next to the tools and duct tape.

Then he pulled a shiny, red and yellow plastic bag from its hiding place among the layers of old insulation crudely stapled between the beams of the low ceiling. The bag bore the words A AND I COMMUNICATIONS. Hodge emptied the contents onto the table: a small, cellular pocket phone packed in a box and handful of assorted micro-circuitry supplies.

Finally, Hodge stepped to the mirror hanging from the Sheetrock wall over his sink. Distracted for a moment by the homely face reflected in the mirror, he touched his splotchy nose, scabbed lips, and ruddy cheeks. He watched an unbidden smile reroute the deep lines in his face. *Just a matter of days,* he reminded the image staring back at him, *and you will be changed, in the twinkling of an eye. This mortality will put on immortality. The cocoon will be stripped away, and the butterfly will emerge.*

Hodge lifted the mirror from the wall, revealing a large, square hole roughly chiseled through the Sheetrock with a two-by-four stud running through the center of the hole. He reached into the hole to the left of the stud and removed a cardboard box the size of a deck of cards. The box was marked with caution symbols. Hodge had stolen it during a late-November after-hours trip to the complex in Hollywood where the security guard had fallen on Christmas night.

At the table he opened the box and picked out a metal capsule no larger than a .22-caliber shell, cushioned in foam and wrapped in plastic.

Hodge stood over the table for a moment, hands on hips, admiring the array of supplies. He felt deeply humbled. Once again he would serve as his master's hands to execute judgment in preparation for a new kingdom. He silently prayed for the skill and patience he would need for the next several nerve-testing hours.

Sitting down at the table with a clear work space before him, Hodge opened the box containing the phone and pulled the instrument out. It was a moderately priced model with a built-in answering device. Following the instructions carefully, he programmed the answering unit for remote playback by entering a test code number: 22.

Then he dialed the clerk at A and I Communications and asked her to call him back to test his new number, the phone, and the answering device, a service the store offered to new customers. The instrument worked perfectly. When he tapped off the call after the test, he reprogrammed the answering device to the remote number he intended to use but did not want known to anyone: 666.

Next, he dismantled the phone, stripping away the plastic case, speaker, and receiver, down to its essential mechanism and tiny, five-year power source. The electronic guts of the phone took up little more space than half an emery board.

Sweeping the useless phone parts aside, Hodge switched on the soldering gun and began to assemble the detonating device. The memory of his triumphant success with the telephone bomb in Tel Aviv swelled him with confidence.

He was reaching for the tiny, plastic-wrapped switch when the unbidden voice tormented him again, causing him to flinch with alarm. The drumming impression in his mind was importunate and compassionate, but Hodge's stubborn refusals over the years had turned his heart to granite. To him each startling, earnest appeal was no more than a nuisance: *Forsake the way of death! Choose again the path of life! Return to me!*

Hodge leaped from his chair, incensed. "I will not return!" he cried aloud, thrusting a fist toward the heavens. He had taken this stand many times in the past. But in view of his immediate, delicate task, he was especially vehement in his response. "Your ways are an abomination to me! Your words are anathema to my mind! I serve a new master! Leave me, I say!"

Again, silence greeted his denunciation of the interrupting force. Hodge stood motionless for several seconds awaiting a rebuttal, which he was prepared to denounce with curses and oaths. The rebuttal never came. He shook his fist once again in spite and triumph, then sat down to work.

It took the better part of an hour to meticulously reroute the circuitry and link the telephone playback feature to a small, burnished metal blasting cap through a bipolar power switch. Satisfied that the connection was solid, he reviewed the procedure in his mind: *The call is received, the answering circuit is activated, the code sends the signal to the switch which detonates the blasting cap.*

Excellent! he hummed to himself. *One final critical element to be added.*

Hodge stepped again to the hole in the wall above the sink. Using his left hand, he reached behind the Sheetrock to the right of the stud until he touched a cold plastic box, the same box he had retrieved from the ventilation duct during his Christmas night visit to Hollywood. Hodge gingerly withdrew the box from its resting place and took it to the table.

The box was olive drab with black symbols stenciled on the lid. The inscription was Middle Eastern in origin, but Hodge didn't know the language or the precise meaning of the words. Nor did he care. Having seen the contents in action and having tested them personally over the Mediterranean, Hodge felt words were superfluous.

Drawing a long breath of anticipation and holding it, he lifted the lid. The box contained twelve black plastic cans, a little smaller than 35MM film cans, snuggled into appropriately sized cut-outs in a bed of gray foam rubber. The inside of the lid was similarly lined with gray foam, assuring that the cans remained firmly in place during transport.

Hodge pulled one can from the foam, lifted the lid, and emptied the contents—a small, mottled gray cylinder that looked like modeling clay—into his palm. He massaged the clay gently in his hand, working it into a slightly longer, narrower shape.

Hodge laid the mass of odorless, high-impact, moldable explosive next to the detonating device he had assembled. Then he inserted the blasting cap into one end of the gray clay and molded the pliable substance around the cap until it was almost surrounded. Completed, the linked chain of telephone mechanism, bipolar power switch, and blasting cap merged in plastic explosive measured about six inches in length and less than three-quarters of an inch in diameter at the widest bulge of the gray clay.

Hodge again traced with his eyes the trail of the split-second, deadly synapse: phone, switch, cap, explosives—boom—welcome to the new millennium. Hodge sat in breathless awe staring at the simple instrument of destruction lying before him.

He slipped a sheet of newspaper under the apparatus and gently rolled it into a long, skinny sausage of newsprint. Taking one of the PVC casings, he inserted the sausage and found the fit to be a trifle loose. An additional half-sheet of newspaper added just the right thickness. He slid the package into the PVC and stuffed the protruding newsprint tails snugly into each end. A short strip of duct tape served as a cap for each end of the pipe.

Hodge wiggled the white baton gently in his hand. No movement inside, just as he had planned. Then he wound duct tape around the length of the PVC. It wasn't neat, but it secured the two end strips and covered the white plastic with a layer of easy-to-grip silver-gray tape. The primary instrument of judgment was complete. Nine more pipe sections would be stuffed with plastic explosives and newspaper. The explosion of the first would trigger the rest.

Three hours after he began, with no time allowed for food, drink, or other distractions, Hodge carefully laid the last of the ten assembled, tape-wrapped bombs in its egg carton cradle. One or two would be sufficient to destroy the platform and everyone on it. But the master had called for ten bombs for Millennium's Eve just as surely as he had mandated five for the jet leaving Tel Aviv. *One bomb cripples and maims. Two bombs kill. Five bombs disintegrate and dismember. Ten bombs fulfill the the word of my master: "May thy flesh be torn and thy bones be scattered and thy blood quench the parched earth, and may the beast from heaven take thy throne and thy inheritance."*

Hodge stood over the table, transfixed at the sight of the ten strokes of judgment lined neatly on the table. The work being done, an ecstatic utterance bubbled within him like molten lava in the fiery bowels of the earth.

He circled the table slowly with his eyes on the ten silver-gray batons of destruction. His pulse and breathing quickened as the master flooded his brain with garish visions of judgment and conquest and the new kingdom.

Finally, Hodge stretched out trembling hands over the ten bombs, lifted his head, and cried out, "The ten horns which thou sawest upon the beast, these shall hate the whore, and make her desolate, and naked, and shall eat her flesh and burn her with fire. For God hath put it in their hearts to fulfill his will, and to agree, and to give their kingdom unto the beast, until the words of God shall be fulfilled."

Then he swooned and collapsed to the cot.

Thirty-one

Beth scolded herself for arriving at the *Times* after 11:30. She had planned to be at work at Serg's computer by 10 at the latest. Reagan Cole had kept her up late again last night—something she neither regretted nor intended to avoid on her remaining nights in L.A. The tall police sergeant with those disarming boyish eyes was no longer merely a diversion from her uninspiring assignment. He had replaced Unity 2000 in priority. Before falling asleep at nearly 3 A.M., she had specifically thanked God—whoever and wherever He was—for Unity 2000, because it had brought her to Reagan. Then she cursed the event for keeping them from seeing each other more often.

Beth had only herself to blame for lying in bed after the alarm sounded at 8, toying with feeble excuses for not getting up: *I don't do my best work without at least seven hours of sleep. My ankle is slightly sprained, and I should rest it longer. Thanks to the* Times' *files, the book won't take as long, so I don't have to start as early. If I stay in my room until 9,*

Dad will be off to work, and by 10 Mom will have left to help the other local Holloway Warriors plan Friday's luncheon for him at the Convention Center. In between excuses, she had snoozed half the morning away.

You're letting your love life tamper with your professional life, something you vowed never to do, Beth had lectured herself while fighting the Hollywood Freeway on her way to Times-Mirror Square. But then Reagan had called, and she suddenly forgot why she was in such a hurry. They treated the topics of their conversation—the Lakers' current losing streak, the prospect of a 78-degree afternoon for the Rose Bowl game, their mutual pleasure at being together last night—as world-impacting issues they must discuss in detail. Only after she pulled into the parking garage and said good-bye did she reawaken to the disgusting reality that it was almost lunch time and she had accomplished nothing on her story.

Beth hobbled into the cubicle carrying her computer. Mai was inputting furiously at her keyboard when Beth came into view.

"Hello, Beth. I was hoping you would come by this morning." Mai's greeting was as friendly as Reagan's had been. They both had a way of making her feel like the star of the moment. Beth was sure she understood Reagan's motivation for such attention. But she felt like little more than an imposition on Mai; her presence at the *Times* was surely an intrusion into the editor's schedule. Why Mai should be so genuinely affable toward her, Beth hadn't a clue. But she welcomed the warmth of the woman who treated her like a friend.

"Good morning, Mai. I won't be in your way for long today. I just came to copy a couple more files; then I'm going over to Central Branch and find a quiet carrel to work in."

Mai commented on Beth's limp. Beth explained how she received a minor injury playing driveway hoops, but she didn't mention Cole being there. Mai was discreet enough not to ask about him.

As Beth settled into Serg's work station, Mai said, "Before you get busy, I have some hot news you may be interested in—professionally speaking, of course."

"Hot news? I'm all ears," Beth said, facing Mai across Serg's desk.

"First, our mystery caller phoned VoiceLink again this morning."
Beth leaned forward with interest. "Same guy?"
"Unmistakably."
"Same message?"
"Not exactly. Actually, it's kind of a continuation or an amplification of yesterday's message."
"But you still think that this guy is more dangerous than one of your local spaced-out Klingons or reincarnated Elvises clogging up VoiceLink with nonsense?"
"Let's just say that I'm still *not* completely convinced that it's a joke

or a hoax, even though I'm praying that it is."

After an expectant pause, Beth said, "Well, when can I hear it?"

"I didn't get a copy of the tape yet. But I do have the transcribed text." Mai picked a sheet of paper off her desk and handed it to Beth. "Tell me what you think."

Beth scanned the sheet quickly and noticed poetic couplets within the message. "He's waxing lyrical today, isn't he?" she chuckled.

Mai nodded with no change of expression.

Beth read the message aloud, imagining how the mysterious caller with the Count Dracula voice might sound.

> Woe to thee, rider of the white horse.
> Thou who wearest the crown of the conqueror
> shall thyself be conquered.
> Thus saith my lord and master to thee:
> King from the East, champion of might;
> Thy Crusaders and Warriors fight for the right.
> Hear words of wisdom, hear truth from the sage;
> Thou wagest a battle thy Lord doth not wage.
> Thy kingdom is dust, thy crown is tin;
> Thou lookest without instead of within.
> Thine end is near, thy crown will fall;
> The beast from heaven is all in all.
> May thy flesh be torn and thy bones be scattered,
> and thy blood quench the parched earth,
> and may the beast from heaven
> take thy throne and thy inheritance.

Beth studied the words silently for another moment, then looked up, her face ashen with concern. Suddenly the nonsensical words of a nameless, faceless nut were no longer laughable. "He's after Simon Holloway," she said slowly.

Beth felt personally threatened. Her parents idolized Simon Holloway. They wanted to be as close to him as possible this week. An attempt on Holloway's life could hurt them . . . kill them.

"Yes, the reference to Holloway is obvious," Mai said. Unaware of how much Beth knew, she went on. "He's from the east—Orlando. He's known as the champion of right-wing fundamentalism. He refers to his supporters as—"

"Yes, I know," Beth cut in, still processing the frightening possibilities. She felt stupid for covering up her parents' involvement with Holloway before. At the moment, transparency with Mai seemed completely appropriate.

"My parents are rather fanatical followers of Simon Holloway—Warriors, I believe they call themselves. They donate a lot of money and travel to some of his sin-fighting campaign sites. My mother even went to jail once during one of his anti-genetic engineering sit-ins. And yesterday, when I left here to pick her up at the airport, she was coming in from spending Christmas at Jubilee Village. I didn't want to tell you about it, because I'm a little embarrassed about their involvement with someone I think is coming from left field."

Beth's embarrassment did not distract Mai from the anxiety she perceived in the tall, dark-haired young woman. Mai reached out to touch Beth's hand. "Are you a little worried that your parents may be in danger?"

Beth tried to brush off her concern. "I know there have been death threats on Holloway's life before, and nothing ever came of them. This caller is probably just another harmless fruitcake. But I must admit that today's message gives me a completely different perspective on all that torn flesh and scattered bones stuff. Suddenly it's up close and personal."

"Yes, the caller probably *is* a harmless fruitcake. Most of the maniacs we hear from are all talk and no action, thank the Lord. But even if this guy intends to do something, he will have a hard time pulling it off. The police are very good. They have already located the pay phones the caller used yesterday and today from the ID numbers logged in our receiver. And they have both tapes. The two messages are being studied by detectives."

"Where were the phone booths?" Beth asked.

"The call yesterday was placed from a phone in Union Station. Today's came from South Central L.A., not far from the Coliseum."

"Our telephone nut gets around," Beth quipped.

"The police are still questioning people at the South Central pay phone," Mai said. "But a lot of people used that phone this morning. And without a description of the guy, the cops don't really know what to ask for."

"They can run digital voiceprint analyses on these calls, can't they, and identify the caller's voice?" Beth asked hopefully.

Mai shook her head. "Unfortunately, the frequency band on a telephone is so narrow that they can't get an accurate voiceprint. But the police will continue to study the message. Maybe the guy has given himself away in something he said."

Beth studied the transcript again. "What do you think he means by 'Thou wagest a battle thy Lord doth not wage'?"

"One of the concerns about Holloway among some Christians is that he's majoring on minors, spending a disproportionate amount of time, energy, and money on secondary issues."

"Such as . . . ?"

"Such as biotechnology. As you probably know, Holloway's organization spends hundreds of thousands of dollars tracking developments in genetic engineering, publishing and distributing antibiotechnology literature, and picketing labs. Many Christians question the morality of experimenting with the human genome, especially when it comes to determining the physical and mental features of the unborn. But others are concerned that Holloway's militant approach does more harm than good, that he's more adversarial on this issue than God is. That may be what the caller means by that phrase about looking without instead of within. Holloway's detractors insist that he's so consumed by these issues on the periphery that he has lost sight of the essentials at the center."

Beth was quietly pleased to learn that not all Bible-thumpers were as gullible and misguided about Holloway as her parents. She wondered if Mai was one of them. "What do you think? Is Holloway in left field?"

Mai smiled. "I don't feel it's my place to judge him. Just like everyone else, Simon Holloway has to answer to God for his actions."

"Now that was a political answer, if I ever heard one," Beth laughed. Then, emboldened by her own recent self-disclosure, she pressed the issue. "What I really want to know is, do you support the ministry of Simon Holloway, or are you one of the 'many Christians' you referred to who, like the caller, think he's majoring on minors?"

Mai didn't seem offended by the pointed question. Beth was glad, because she didn't *want* to offend the woman who had shown her such kindness. But she did want some answers.

Mai thought a moment about her response, then said, "My family and I pray for Simon Holloway, Shelby Hornecker, T.D. Dunne, and Morgan McClure, just like we pray for numbers of other people. We ask God to govern their choices and direct their steps. And we ask God to empower them to do His will and to enlighten them if they have strayed off His path in any way. If you call that support, then I guess we support them."

"Do you attend one of Holloway's house churches or go to his sit-ins?" Beth was sure Mai didn't, but she had to ask.

"I've covered a couple of his protests for the *Times* but, no, we're not Crusaders or Warriors or what you might call followers of Simon Holloway."

Beth pressed in, "Do you send money to Holloway?" then in the same breath added, "Oh geez, that's none of my business. I'm sorry."

Mai signaled "no offense" with a wave of the hand. "We have never felt led to send money to Holloway or the others, but it's possible that God may direct us to at some time."

"But how could you send money to someone who majors on the minors?" Beth's tone was tinged with exasperation.

"I hope this doesn't sound like an oversimplification, Beth, but Simon Holloway will have to answer to God for every penny he receives and spends. If God ever leads us to do more than just pray for his ministry, then what Holloway does with that money is between him and God. I am not his judge."

Beth realized that if Mai was itching for a chance to preach at her, Beth was giving her every opportunity. Beth didn't know whether to respect her new friend for her restraint or pity her for a lack of fortitude.

"Well, it's for sure *somebody* thinks he's Holloway's judge," Beth sighed, waving the transcript.

Mai nodded. "That's the scary part. Whenever anybody tries to take over for God, all hell can break loose."

Beth blinked in surprise and almost laughed at the word "hell" coming from the obviously God-fearing editor. But Mai's facial expression divulged that she was entirely serious and not at all flippant.

"Speaking of *all* hell breaking loose," Beth said, leaning back in Serg's chair and perusing the transcription again, "yesterday's message mentioned all four horsemen. But today's little poem is only about the first one. Our diabolical caller may have additional messages for the others."

"Yes, we were discussing that possibility this morning with the police," Mai said. "The caller did mention four horsemen journeying to L.A., four thrones becoming one, four peoples becoming a heavenly nation. The detectives believe the caller has something against all four of them and that today's may be the first of a series of calls."

Beth thought aloud. "He gave his initial message yesterday—kind of a blanket condemnation of all four. Then on each of the next four days—today, Tuesday, Wednesday, and Thursday—he zeroes in on a different personality. And Friday is Millennium's Eve. Interesting timing. He may have big plans for all four of them during Unity 2000—or at least he wants everybody to think he does."

"A detective will be here tomorrow morning in case he calls again. They can pinpoint the caller's location in about thirty seconds unless he's smart enough to use a cellular phone tomorrow instead of a hardwired instrument. Today's message took about forty seconds. If he gives us that much help tomorrow, they should be able to find him."

"Maybe they won't find him. Maybe he's too clever for the cops." Beth was thinking not only of the safety of her parents but of Reagan Cole. She pushed away the sudden taunt that a vindictive God would bring Reagan into her life only to allow him to be blown away defending Shelby Hornecker from some demonic, Bible-spouting mass murderer.

"In the meantime," Mai continued, "Rev. Holloway and the others will have police escorts twenty-four hours a day from the moment they arrive in L.A. until—" Mai stopped abruptly as Beth flashed a Cheshire-cat grin that she hoped covered any anxiety in her countenance. "What?" Mai asked. "Did I say something. . . ?"

"That's *my* hot news of the day," Beth beamed, relishing the scoop on her fellow journalist. "Reagan—I mean Sergeant Cole, my policeman friend—has been assigned to escort Shelby Hornecker while she's in L.A.—at least during his P.M. shift."

"You're kidding!"

"He's supposed to pick her up at LAX tomorrow afternoon and take her to the Biltmore. I've already leaned on Reagan to introduce me to her. I may even get a personal interview with Shelby Hornecker out of this deal."

"This is too funny and too strange," Mai said with a mischievous grin of her own. "Believe me, I'm not trying to outdo your brave sergeant or outscoop you. But how would you like to meet all four televangelists in person?"

"Mai, what are you saying?" Beth begged, intrigued.

"You may not believe it, but this is the rest of the hot news I couldn't wait to tell you. This Wednesday night at 7 o'clock, Simon Holloway, Shelby Hornecker, T.D. Dunne, and Morgan McClure are coming to visit my husband and me. And Thanh said I could invite you too—strictly as a mouse in my pocket, not as a journalist—if you want to come."

Beth's first thought seemed oddly funny to her. She hoped Simon Holloway wouldn't remember her from the crowded LAX terminal when her mother tried to force an introduction. The idea of meeting Holloway as the daughter of two of his rabid supporters turned Beth cold. But the opportunity to meet him and the other televangelists on neutral turf was too good to pass up. It could be great material for her book. But, more importantly to Beth at the moment, she wanted to soothe her own curiosity about what made these religious superheroes tick. Maybe she could also find out how they felt about the mystery caller's threats.

"The televangelists are coming to visit you?" Beth said, trying to control her elation at her windfall. "There's a story behind this, Mai, and I need to hear it."

Mai gave Beth a *Reader's Digest* history of King's House and the Unity 2000 committee's surprising interest. "We really don't understand why the committee wants to bring America's top religious leaders to see our struggling little effort in run-down Echo Park," Mai concluded. "But they're coming, and I thought you might want to be included."

Mai had spoken so modestly about King's House and its need-meeting endeavors that Beth wasn't offended by her straightforward references to the motivation behind their work: serving Christ. To the contrary, Beth was piqued at the idea that somebody was doing noble, people-serving work in the name of religion, something she didn't see in Simon Holloway or his peers.

Aside from her surprise at Mai's disclosure about the ministry of King's House, Beth was relieved that Mai hadn't asked her to volunteer, donate money, or kneel beside the desk and make some kind of commitment. But the more she knew about Mai, the less she expected such a crass invasion of her privacy. *If this is the extent of the religious pitch I've been dreading,* she thought, *I have nothing to worry about.* If anything, Mai's story left Beth curious to know more about a converted hospital where ordinary laymen take care of L.A.'s throwaways.

"So are you interested? Would you like to come Wednesday night?" Mai asked.

"You can count on it."

Thirty-two

Beth turned down Mai's invitation to lunch, pleading her late start on the day and her need to get to the library. As soon as the editor left for lunch, Beth scoured Serg's directories until she found what she was looking for: the complete bio and obit of the late Rev. Adrian Hornecker. Beth had again "neglected" to tell Mai that she would be reaching a little deeper into Serg's data files than Mai had originally suggested she might. Beth quickly made a copy and left the building, alternately assuring herself that Mai wouldn't mind and chiding herself for not asking specific permission.

The weather was nice enough to walk the three blocks from Times-Mirror Square to the library on Spring Street, and Beth would have preferred the exercise. But her bad ankle discouraged her from trying. Instead, it took her almost as long to drive the short distance and find a new parking place.

Beth had her choice of study carrels on the third floor of the Los Angeles Public Library, Central Branch. She selected a large one away from the traffic pattern and switched on her computer. It took her only seconds to load the *Times* diskettes onto the computer's hard drive and arrange all the data into four directories: DUNNE, HOLLOWAY, HORNECKER, and MCCLURE.

Beth knew what she *should* do. She should work through the background histories of the four televangelists and prepare the biographical sketches that would be woven into the book's early chapters. But that's not what she *wanted* to do. Try as she might, she couldn't prod her thoughts away from Adrian Hornecker. She acknowledged to herself that, although Unity 2000 was originally Hornecker's idea, she would write little about him. The book would center on the living—the four principal players—and the event itself.

But she also acknowledged a strong curiosity about Hornecker's life and, more particularly, his death. She couldn't resist the temptation to browse through Hornecker's files, even though she knew that virtually none of it applied to the final content of her book.

Beth plugged in the computer's headphones and slipped the speakers over her ears. She opened the HORNECKER directory and scrolled through screen after screen of files until she reached those with the suffix A, for ADRIAN. *Forget the boring text files,* she thought. *Let's go right to the video files.* Beth electronically linked a series of video files that promised an overview of the late televangelist's life, including television footage taken directly before and after the fateful crash.

Beth cued the string of files and tapped ENTER. *All right, Rev. Adrian Hornecker,* Beth hummed to herself as the screen flooded with color, *this is your life.*

The first series of clips opened on a college soccer game in progress. Picture quality was mediocre at best, considering the amateur photography—probably a student shooting the game. But it was not difficult to identify the star of the clips, a short, wiry, blond midfielder wearing sports goggles with thick corrective lenses. The agile athlete dribbled through the defense setting up goal after goal. *So this is Adrian Hornecker, the college jock,* Beth thought as she fast-forwarded through the highlights of several matches.

The next series of clips featured Adrian Hornecker, wearing unsightly thick glasses, speaking at college commencement—as valedictorian, Beth surmised. He was articulate and fiery; even faculty members on the platform were weeping with conviction. Hornecker was clearly a televangelist in the making.

Wedding videos showed Hornecker in a white tux and tails. And there beside him, radiant yet deferring to her groom, the obvious star of the event, was the young Shelby Hornecker. "Did you have any idea you were getting a tiger by the tail, lady?" Beth found herself mumbling to the demure bride.

Beth moved rapidly through what originally must have been miles of videotape featuring the Rev. Adrian Hornecker behind a pulpit. Racing through the young evangelist's career as in a time machine, Beth watched the preacher's congregation mushroom from a handful to hundreds in a suburban Dallas church, and then from hundreds to thousands in the Victory Life auditorium.

As his life rolled by, compressed into fast-forward video minutes, Adrian Hornecker was transformed before Beth's eyes. Invisible contacts replaced his ugly glasses. His suits were more expensive and his jewelry more ostentatious with every passing year. He grew more imperious in bearing, more authoritarian in demeanor, bordering on arrogant domination.

Beth was repulsed by the metamorphosis occurring in Adrian Hornecker. She wondered how such a haughty leader managed to attract such a large and devoted following. *I can't believe so many people crave a domineering father figure for a spiritual leader,* she thought. *What kind of people really want to follow someone who shouts at them what to believe and castigates them in God's name when they fail to believe it?*

Beth also realized that she was viewing over a period of minutes a transformation that occurred so gradually that Hornecker's mesmerized parishioners probably didn't notice it. *You should have been paying attention, folks*, Beth sneered at the screen. *This guy sold you a bill of goods.*

Occasionally in the clips, Shelby Hornecker took the pulpit. She appeared to be just as refined and competent as her husband in her communication skills, but less demanding and controlling. Beth's dislike for Adrian Hornecker continued to grow. But she found herself fascinated by Shelby who, though excessively submissive to her husband in Beth's opinion, seemed the more winsome leader of the two. *That's the difference*, Beth suddenly realized, seeing the Horneckers side by side on the Victory Life platform. *Adrian drives, pressures, pushes. Shelby has the skill and grace to lead. The Victory Life crowd is probably healthier without Adrian Hornecker*, Beth determined.

The sound of Beth's phone startled her. It was Cole checking in from the station before beginning his P.M. shift. She gushed excitedly to him about being invited to meet Holloway, Hornecker, Dunne, and McClure on Wednesday night at King's House. He was amazed that Beth knew more about Shelby Hornecker's schedule than her police escort did.

"I told you that Spooner could get you tickets to the Blazers–Clippers game at the Arena Wednesday night," Cole said. "You would turn down free tickets for a meeting of religious stuffed shirts?"

"Ordinarily I'd take the game, no question. Call this a career move. Getting up close and personal with the big four Wednesday night could ice this book for me."

Cole said he was late for roll call and hung up. Beth wanted to discuss the VoiceLink message about Holloway, then realized he was probably in the dark about that too. Her connection with Mai seemed to keep her a couple of steps ahead of him. She would talk to him about it tonight when they rendezvoused at the Hilton.

About halfway through the video files of Adrian Hornecker's reign at Victory Life, Beth watched another transition evolve. The theme of his preaching, easily discernible in the clips from the video graphics highlighting Bible verses and key statements from Hornecker's sermons, began to change. In the early years, his emphasis was on mining the unlimited wealth available to God's children. "You're a child of the King, and God expects you to live like one," Hornecker pounded into his flock persistently.

From what Beth could determine from the pictures flitting across the screen, Adrian Hornecker's emphasis had been well received. Victory Life Center, with its pretentious furnishings and appointments and state-of-the-art video and sound equipment, looked more like a center for the performing arts than a church. The parishioners in the pews, as well as the Horneckers and their staff members on the platform, were dressed and accessorized like royalty.

But Adrian Hornecker's emphasis began to shift subtly. The mysteries of the Last Days, the Great Tribulation, the Rapture of the Church, Christ's Millennial Reign, and Hornecker's formulas for deciphering them, having run a close second to his prosperity message, now eased into prominence. Hornecker's pithy axioms governing the believer's mandate to possess his rightful abundance diminished from the on-screen graphics. They were replaced by colorful diagrams, charts, and timelines decorated with bizarre renderings of angels, beasts, and devils.

Whenever Beth slowed the clips to normal speed—which she had neither the time nor the stomach to do for long—Hornecker's sermons were riddled with terms like scrolls, seals, plagues, bowls, Babylon, chains, and the pit. It sounded like so much mumbo-jumbo to Beth. *That religious space cadet on the* Times *VoiceLink would have loved this preacher,* she mused sardonically.

Then Adrian Hornecker launched his film company and endured another personal metamorphosis. Increasing amounts of video footage showed him designing and overseeing construction of the Victory Life studio in Hollywood and controlling all facets of the location shooting and production of his end-times thrillers. National network clips showed Hornecker hobnobbing with major studio executives, technicians, and stars in some of New York and L.A.'s trendiest nightspots.

As the video images flashed before her, Beth noted two anomalies in Hornecker's lifestyle with the onset of his role as a filmmaker.

First, his appearance changed. Hornecker looked less like an evangelist and more like an entertainment mogul. He wore his hair a little longer, dressed casually in fashionable, expensive wools and leather boots instead of silk suits and alligator loafers. Like a chameleon, Adrian Hornecker had blended into his surroundings and looked for all the world like he belonged in Hollywood.

Second, Shelby was rarely at his side. During the glory years of Victory Life Ministries, Beth noted from the clips, Adrian and Shelby were inseparable. When Adrian preached, Shelby was visible in the background listening respectfully and taking notes. When Adrian traveled to special crusades around the country, Shelby was there to do her part by supporting him in the general sessions, organizing women's luncheons, and kneeling beside him during each pre-service prayer meeting.

But Adrian Hornecker the film producer and director appeared not even to have a wife. In approximately forty minutes of clips, which Beth skimmed in less than ten, Shelby was seen with Adrian only once—attending a Hollywood gala feting the completion of Victory Life Studios. On his location shoots in Israel, Egypt, Turkey, and Iran, Adrian was always prominent and active in all phases of the process. There was Adrian rigging lighting, adding his nitpicking touches to set decoration, and working with a makeup artist on a latex face for a burn victim. But Shelby was nowhere to be seen, nor did it appear that she was even missed.

Adrian's frenetic activity and intense absorption in his work apparently left little room for a tagalong wife. Shelby Hornecker, Beth learned eventually, had been left home to mind the store while Adrian pursued his dream of preaching his end-times gospel through film. Beth thought cynically, *And if that rascal didn't have a sweet young thing waiting for him in the trailer every night, I'll eat my keyboard.*

The file continued with cuts from each of Adrian Hornecker's three films, known collectively as the Doomsday Chronicles. Beth had never seen the films, and she was surprised by the quality of the cinematography and the obvious size of the budget. *Hornecker is blowing up cars and helicopters in these movies, hiring thousands of extras, and probably paying Jeremy Cannon and the other stars a handsome sum*, she thought in amazement. *These movies are into tall piles of dollars.*

The next scene on the monitor, near the end of the chain of video files, sobered her. She had seen some of this footage before, nine months earlier. Inside the Tel Aviv air terminal, Adrian Hornecker and his film crew were boarding their chartered 767 for an ill-fated flight to Dallas. Beth watched the scene unfold at regular speed.

Adrian was one of the first to arrive at the terminal. He greeted well-wishers graciously, thanked his Israeli hosts, and disappeared down the jetway.

At that point the clip became boring again. Beth fast-forwarded through a long segment of video, none of which had been included in the national news, showing other members of Hornecker's crew arriving at the terminal and boarding the charter. The video cameraman, from Israeli television, Beth guessed, apparently received permission from Adrian's people to board the plane for last-minute shots of the departing filmmakers. Again Beth slowed the video to normal speed.

Inside the plane, the camera panned the front section of the luxuriously appointed main cabin where passengers, mugging for the camera, collected pillows and blankets and settled into their extra wide seats in preparation for the long flight home. Beth's stomach turned thinking that the happy people on her monitor screen, who were joyously toasting each other a bon voyage with orange juice and champagne, were dead — literally blown apart — within thirty minutes of this scene.

The cameraman continued toward the rear of the plane and Adrian Hornecker's custom executive compartment. The door was shut and locked. The cameraman asked a flight attendant if Rev. Hornecker could come out for a moment and say farewell to the Israeli people. No, said the female attendant. Rev. Hornecker had asked not to be disturbed until meal service. He had come on board with a headache, and he was resting quietly.

Do we really believe he's in there alone? Beth thought skeptically. Then she chided herself for being so cynical and disrespectful toward the dead televangelist. *Even if he wasn't alone*, she thought, *what does it matter now?*

The flight attendant proceeded to shoo the cameraman toward the front exit so the flight could depart. The last inside shot captured a caterer, an older man, exiting the plane through the service door in the rear galley as the flight attendant secured the hatch from the inside.

The next jumble of clips were obviously shot after the takeoff and fatal explosion: stunned, grief-stricken Israelis in the Tel Aviv terminal and Americans at DFW grappling with the reality of the tragedy; rescue vessels futilely combing the Mediterranean for survivors; network anchors theorizing about the possible motives and methods of a variety of alleged Arab perpetrators.

The final seconds of the video file showed a tearful Shelby Hornecker addressing the overflow crowd attending the memorial service at the auditorium in Arlington. She praised God for Adrian Hornecker and his ministry. She assured the weeping congregation that God's work at Victory Life Ministries would continue undaunted. She pledged herself to serve the flock in whatever way God directed her. She asked the people for their continued prayerful and financial support.

The video file completed, the screen automatically reverted to the menu in the directory headed HORNECKER.

Beth stared at the characters frozen on the screen, but gazing far beyond them to the images she had absorbed during the last hour. She felt little sympathy at the loss of Adrian Hornecker. Nothing she had seen today convinced her that he was anything more than a brilliantly opportunistic high-tech religious huckster. Beth wouldn't have trusted Adrian Hornecker any farther than she would trust a man in a plaid suit selling snake oil on a downtown street corner.

But Shelby Hornecker had surprised her. Beth had concluded the hour with a higher regard for Shelby than when she began.

Granted, Shelby had been Adrian's most loyal supporter and was now his successor. And, granted, she apparently still espoused many of the same religious tenets her husband championed so forcefully. But they are not out of the same mold, Beth insisted silently. *Adrian was forever going for the jugular—pounding people with his dictums and squeezing them until they conformed. To Adrian, the message was the end, not the hearers.*

To her credit, Shelby lacks a killer instinct, Beth thought. *Despite her training and the influence of Adrian Hornecker on her life, Shelby has a softer edge. I'll bet she has struggled over the last nine months trying to maintain Adrian's kingdom without his heartless fanaticism and outright gall. I can't wait until Reagan introduces me to her.*

Thirty-three

Shelby sat at the curb at Mueller Municipal Airport in Austin for ten minutes before Theresa emerged through the automatic doors. She was followed by a skycap with a two-wheel dolly stacked high with suitcases and several parcels. Shelby watched her personal assistant and friend approach the car, exquisitely dressed as always, gliding with the grace of a debutante, and wondered again why she hadn't been swept away by some rich, southern widower years ago.

Shelby pressed the automatic trunk release, and the skycap transferred his burden from the dolly to the Lincoln's spacious trunk. Theresa tipped the young man generously, and he gladly opened the passenger door for her.

"Hello, dear," Theresa bubbled. Both women leaned to the middle of the front seat for their customary exchange of pecks on the cheek that never landed.

"Nice flight?" Shelby asked, as she watched for a window in the airport traffic.

"I'm afraid I'm too accustomed to riding in our own plane. Commercial flights are never nice."

Shelby maneuvered the Lincoln toward the airport exit. "I see that you managed to buy out another Baton Rouge mall on this trip home," she said, chuckling.

"Only half a mall." Theresa joined in the laughter. "Mother bought the other half. We have more fun at the after-Christmas sales than at the symphony."

"Mrs. Bordeaux is feeling well these days?"

"Mother is doing fabulously well for a seventy-three-year-old, thanks to prayer, her doctors, and a medicine chest full of vitamins, enzymes, and dietary supplements, most of which I've never heard of."

Shelby successfully exited the airport complex and headed toward downtown. "Thank you for coming in tonight, Theresa," she said in a more serious tone. "I hope I didn't curtail your visit with your mother."

"Not at all, dear. I just knew you wouldn't be able to pack without me. Besides, your call this morning was a lifesaver. Mother was threatening to serve turkey leftovers again for dinner tonight." They both laughed. "And I really wanted to spend a night at home before going on to L.A. I only stayed in Baton Rouge to afford you more time alone with the new love of your life."

Shelby felt the color leave her face. *She knows! . . . Or does she?* Shelby kept her eyes on the road. "What do you mean?" she asked calmly, playing dumb.

Theresa patted the leather armrests between their seats. "This new man in your life, of course—Mr. Lincoln," Theresa chirped, oblivious to Shelby's sudden discomfort. "I have to hand it to you, dear. You snagged a companion who will take you anywhere you want to go and never complain a peep. My idea of the strong, silent type."

Shelby forced a small laugh at Theresa's humor, relieved that her friend was still in the dark. She had planned to tell Theresa everything tonight, and then ask her to hold her hand as she telephoned Jeremy to apologize. But she couldn't start the story yet. She had to keep herself together until she could talk without the distraction of Austin traffic at rush hour.

Shelby quickly changed the subject. "Speaking of dinner, did you eat on the plane?"

"Are you kidding? At the prospect of a nice dinner on you, do you think I would be tempted by institutional chicken a la jet fumes?"

"Did I say I was buying you dinner?" Shelby said, playing along.

"Not exactly. But it's the least you can do after tearing me away from my dear, aged mother and her inimitable turkey-bone soup."

"Does barbecue sound good?"

"As long as it's not turkey."

Shelby and Theresa liked eating at the Branding Iron for three reasons. The barbecue and homemade slaw were superb. The booths were well spaced—allowing normal-level conversation without the concern of nosy eavesdroppers. And the clientele had enough class not to interrupt one of Austin's most recognized citizens to beg autographs or share prayer requests.

Shelby succeeded in fending off Theresa's "so how was your Christmas on the ranch?" inquiries until Terrance had delivered two orders of brisket, beans, slaw, and potato salad to the table. Following their custom of "you pay, I pray," Theresa invoked God's blessing on their food. Then, as if on cue, she said, "Shelby, I've told you all about my holiday. Now I want to hear about yours."

For the next two hours Shelby poured out the whole story: Christmas Eve and Jeremy, her frenzied, futile attempt to run away, the angelic Cruz family, and the divine intervention that had turned her back toward Austin. Aware of being in a public place, Shelby kept her emotions largely in check, pausing only a few times to dab at her eyes and nose with a tissue.

Theresa was every bit the friend Shelby knew she would be. She listened courteously, compassionately, reaching across the table every several minutes to take Shelby's hand and comfort her. Their dinners were removed barely touched. Terrance kept their coffee mugs full.

"So where do we go from here, dear?" Theresa's look-on-the-bright-side attitude, always an encouragement to Shelby, had never been more welcome. More than anyone Shelby knew, Theresa had a way of cutting through the fog, finding the highway, and getting people moving again.

"First, I need to call Jeremy—tonight. That's one reason I wanted you here. I couldn't bear to do that alone."

"You shouldn't have to do it alone. I'll be right by your side."

"Second, as much as I don't feel like it, I have decided to follow through with our Unity 2000 activities as scheduled."

"With or without Jeremy?"

"With or without Jeremy. We have too much invested at this point. Despite the mountain of guilt I have to work through, if I don't show up our ministry may suffer serious damage. Lord knows we can't survive another financial setback."

"Not to mention the others."

"I beg your pardon."

"If we bail out of Unity 2000, especially with you being chairperson—"

"*Honorary* chairperson," Shelby corrected. "Darin and Stan have done all the work. I'm just the figurehead."

"Nevertheless, if you don't follow through, the other three ministries may suffer as well. I don't think we want that on our conscience."

Yes, conscience, Shelby mused sourly. *If I had a conscience, we wouldn't be having this discussion.*

"You're right, of course," Shelby sighed. "I don't believe Holloway or Dunne or McClure want to do this any more than I do. But Adrian, in one of his passionately dramatic moments, convinced the Christian world that we want to do it. I guess we have to bite the bullet so we can all go home and get on with the new millennium."

Theresa leaned toward Shelby with a familiar look—not that of an employee kowtowing to her employer, but of a big sister about to lovingly but firmly pull her kid sister into line.

"Shelby Hornecker, it's high time that you let go of the notion that Unity 2000 is a big mistake. I understand your misgivings about Adrian's prophetic utterance which placed it on the calendar. And I fully realize that you and your colleagues in ministry feel pushed into something none of you would choose to do on your own. But I also believe—because you and your late husband taught me to believe it—that God can turn something untimely, unpleasant, or even evil—including your Christmas Eve experience and Unity 2000—into something worthwhile and good."

Shelby nodded respectfully. When Theresa exercised her big sister authority, she was rarely off base in her observations or advice.

"Therefore, only one of two options is open to us. One, God was behind Unity 2000 from the beginning, and your late husband was His instrument to set it in motion. Or two, Adrian was mistaken or deceived, or he purposely misled everybody about Unity 2000. It may not have been divinely inspired at all. And yet Almighty God, for reasons we're not privy to at this time, allowed it to stand, meaning that He is prepared to redeem this human effort for His divine purposes.

"Whichever option you choose, Shelby, I believe God desires to do a good thing in Los Angeles this weekend. But if you persist in viewing yourself as worthless and Unity 2000 as a bothersome, embarrassing wart you can't wait to have removed, you may miss the good thing God wants to do in you and through you. And you may spoil it for everyone else in the process."

The words were harsh in Shelby's ears, but the love pouring from Theresa's eyes disarmed any temptation to feel attacked.

"I hate it when you preach my sermons back to me," Shelby said finally with a tongue-in-cheek grin, "especially when you're right. Seriously, I can hardly fathom it, but I know God has been trying to reassure me since Christmas Eve that He isn't through with me. I know He wants me to go to Los Angeles—why, I don't know. But your rebuke is well taken. I need to go with my heart turned the right way. Thank you."

Theresa patted Shelby's hand as a big sister might. "Speaking of going, it's getting late. You have a phone call to make, and I need to make sure you're all packed." She moved to collect her purse.

Shelby stopped her with a raised hand. "Just one more thing I need to tell you in the where-do-we-go-from-here department."

Theresa gave Shelby her full attention.

"After Unity 2000, I'm going to take some time off—perhaps as much as three months. I'll announce it as a study leave or a sabbatical or something. Stan will run the ministry—I'll tell him all about this and everything else tomorrow on the plane. He can preach once or twice a month, and we'll show reruns the rest of the time. Darin Chaumont has really blossomed with his Unity 2000 assignment. I will ask him to pick up some of the administrative load."

"And you, dear?"

Shelby paused, pondering the mountain before her. "For one thing, I must submit to counseling. Something very basic inside me broke down on Christmas Eve, and I wasn't myself for almost twenty-four hours—at least I *hope* that wasn't the real me. It frightened me, Theresa. I need to find out what happened and take steps to prevent it from happening again."

"Do you have any ideas for a counselor?"

"Not really. I'd appreciate your prayers about that."

"Of course."

"Next, I have to find out what I'm doing here."

"Here?"

"At Victory Life Center. In the ministry. In the world. These were the issues I was planning to bring to God at the ranch on Christmas Day. After nine months in Adrian's shoes, I don't know if I'm cut out to head up Victory Life Ministries. Then after my experience on Christmas Eve, I doubted that I was fit for *any* kind of ministry.

"For the last two days now I've been hearing God say to me, 'Feed My sheep, feed My sheep.' But I have no idea what He means. I don't know if I should stay where I am or seek a successor. If I stay, I have to decide what to do with Victory Life Films. The studio is sitting there vacant at $12,000 a month, and all that expensive equipment is rotting away in storage. Should I revive that ministry? Or should I cut and run?

"On the other hand, if I'm supposed to move on, what will I do? Start another church? Go to Uzbekistan as a missionary? Work in a soup kitchen? I know it seems a little late to decide what I want to be when I grow up. But I've never answered that question for myself; Adrian always answered it for me. I need some time alone to get my own answer."

Theresa shook her head in wonder. "I have never met a woman who showed the courage you have shown over the last nine months—the way you held yourself and the ministry together after Adrian left. But I see now that you have only begun. I admire you, Shelby."

"It's a lot easier for me with someone like you holding my hand, Theresa."

"Well, I'll hold your left hand. But, Ms. Courageous, you need to use your right to call Jeremy. No more stalling."

Shelby and Theresa left the Branding Iron hand in hand.

Thirty-four

Rev. Simon Holloway and his wife and two sons had enjoyed a wonderful day on Catalina Island despite the inconveniences associated with being "celebrities." They had departed their luxurious suite at the Westin Bonaventure at 6:45 A.M. for San Pedro harbor in an unmarked police van chauffeured by their LAPD escort, a female sergeant. Since they were on vacation, the Holloways would have preferred renting a car and being on their own. But the police chief had personally insisted on providing the courtesy. He called it "a routine precaution," and purposely avoided mentioning the telephone call to the *Times* threatening Rev. Holloway's life.

Mark and Tim Holloway had requested that the family cross the twenty-six miles of ocean aboard a water taxi instead of flying to the island. Once aboard their chartered boat—which had been thoroughly inspected before their arrival by an LAPD bomb squad—the family anticipated complete privacy. But as luck would have it, the captain and his wife who owned and operated the charter service were big fans of the Jubilee Fellowship broadcast. They were full of questions about Rev. Holloway's ministry. Grace Ellen kept them occupied on the bridge while her three men escaped to the bow to enjoy the ride.

The Holloways' morning shopping tour in Avalon had been pleasant, except for periodic interruptions by adoring parishioners seeking autographs and photos. Occasionally detractors recognized Simon Holloway and verbalized their dislike for him and for his unbending, bigoted conservatism with taunts or obscenities. Accustomed to such mistreatment, the Holloways simply offered strained smiles of Christian beneficence and separated themselves from the distraction.

After lunch the family rented a jeep and escaped the locals and other tourists for a leisurely tour of the island, which recharged their batteries for the return to the big city. They hoped the flight to San Diego tomorrow, aboard one of their local Warriors' planes, and the trolley ride to Tijuana, Baja California for shopping would produce a similar result.

With their bodies still on East Coast time, the Holloways were back in their suite by 7, ready to eat and retire. The hotel chef and two of his assistants had just delivered a feast of stuffed halibut, rice pilaf, and steamed vegetables to their suite when the telephone sounded. By design, all incoming calls were routed through Simon's administrative assistant in another suite, and the Holloways' hotel phone could be accessed only by her.

Holloway answered as the rest of the family sat down at the table. "Yes?"

"I trust that you had a refreshing day at Catalina."

"Yes, we did, Virginia." Being more interested in dinner than chitchat, Simon hurried to add, "Do you have something for me?"

"Yes, actually he's holding on the other line, Simon. One of the local coordinators from the Unity 2000 committee. He apologized for the interruption and requested a minute of your time."

"Concerning. . . ?"

"He said the committee has arranged for you to visit a local ministry—a house that cares for the disadvantaged, I think he said. He wants to discuss a few details of the visit with you."

Simon Holloway hated surprises. "I know nothing about such a visit," he said, irritated. "Why wasn't I informed about this sooner?"

"According to this gentleman, the visit just came up, but the provision for it was included in the guidelines we agreed to months ago. I checked with Ron Baker about it just now. He confirmed that the guidelines allow the committee to schedule you for a couple of goodwill visits in the city this week. Ron didn't think they would exercise their option on it, but apparently they have."

Simon rubbed the stubble on his cheeks absently while his insides churned. Apart from enjoying a time of respite with his family, he had only one purpose in Los Angeles: to convince the Christian world on Millennium's Eve that God's agenda for America in the year 2000 is righteousness. Thousands of Crusaders and Warriors must be recruited and dispatched into the battle. Strongholds of evil in the land must be toppled. Simon had no time for good-will visits to flophouses or soup kitchens. He wished for the thousandth time he had never allowed Adrian Hornecker to bully him into Unity 2000 in the first place.

Finally he said, "When is this visit supposed to take place?"

"The man said Wednesday evening at 7."

Simon sighed, relieved. "I can't do it. I'm booked, right? Dr. McGowan and Dr. Matabwa are having dinner with us here to finalize our preparations for the rally."

Virginia's tone was apologetic. "Well, as it turns out, Dr. McGowan can't make it Wednesday night. She called today while you were out. Her daughter is flying in from London that night. We rescheduled the meeting for breakfast Thursday. Your Wednesday night is now open."

Simon groaned aloud, then scolded himself for sounding negative before his subordinate. At the same moment, a quiet impression wafted through his consciousness like a cool draft through a warm house. It was a warning without words, just as the touch of the breeze on the skin alerts that a door or window has been left ajar. Simon recognized it as a subtle reminder from God not to kick against an unpleasant circumstance that might be marked with a divine fingerprint. Simon didn't feel like altering his agenda at the whisper of God. But he knew better than to feel the cool wind and not investigate why it was touching him.

Simon waved at his family in the dining room to start eating without him. Mark took the hint and delivered a prayer for the food as Simon walked the phone into the living room.

"Okay, Virginia, what's the man's name?" Simon said.

"William Malachi. He sounds a little like Rudyard—that lovely accent you hear in the Caribbean or on the African continent."

"You checked out his credentials, of course."

"Yes, he faxed me his ID immediately upon request, and he knew all the code words the committee has established. Seems like a lot of James Bond tactics for a convocation of Christians."

"There are a lot of crazy people in Los Angeles, Virginia. You can't be too careful." Then after a pause, "All right, put Mr. Malachi on."

"Yes, sir."

There was a brief pause, a click, and then, "Good evening, Rev. Holloway, and God bless you. I am William Malachi, coordinator of local affairs for the Unity 2000 committee."

"Good evening, Mr. Malachi."

"I apologize for interrupting your evening with your family."

The warmth, charm, and respect evident in the pleasant voice put Simon at ease. But his fatigue and hunger prodded him to push the conversation right to the point. "No problem. What can I do for you?"

"The committee has taken the liberty to arrange for you to visit one of our local ministries to the poor. It is called King's House, located in

Echo Park, one of our more impoverished areas. I want to introduce you to the director of the mission, a most humble and dedicated servant of God. His name is Thanh Hai Ngo—affectionately called Dr. No by many at King's House. I am sure your presence there will be a great encouragement to Dr. No and his staff."

"I'm happy to be of service, Mr. Malachi." Simon hoped he sounded more sincere than he felt.

"You may be pleased to learn, Rev. Holloway, that your visit to King's House is not being announced to the media. You will be able to tour the facility and visit with the staff without interruption."

"Yes, I am pleased to hear that, Mr. Malachi. Sometimes the media is more of an obstacle to our ministry than an instrument in our service." *And if I had a dollar for every time the media misquoted me or misrepresented my ministry,* Simon grumbled silently, *I could fund our efforts for the next century single-handedly.*

"One more item, Rev. Holloway. Feel free to bring your family and your top aides with you to King's House. The committee is hopeful that this quiet, informal gathering will provide a pleasant atmosphere for your first official meeting with your three colleagues and their people."

Simon felt his fragile, tenuous sense of goodwill suddenly crack. He didn't want to ask, but the slim chance that he misunderstood the implied message pushed the question out. "What three colleagues, Mr. Malachi?"

There was a moment of silence followed by an embarrassed laugh. "Oh, I am sorry, Rev. Holloway. I neglected to inform you that Dr. McClure, Rev. Hornecker, and Mr. Dunne are also being invited to visit King's House on Wednesday evening. The committee feels it will be a grand time for the four of you to get better acquainted in preparation for Millennium's Eve. Don't you agree, Rev. Holloway?"

To his own surprise, Simon remained cordial and agreeable through the last three sentences of the conversation. But when he hung up the phone, he was glad to be in the living room alone. At the moment he felt toward God the way he had felt toward Adrian Hornecker for more than a year: quietly seething about being tricked into something he didn't want to be part of.

What do You want from me, Lord? he demanded silently. *You know that Morgan McClure is a thief and a lecher. Shelby Hornecker cares more about her furs and her jewels than preaching the Gospel. All T.D. Dunne wants to do is make music and sell records. Why are You forcing me to relate to these people when my calling is to establish Your righteousness as the standard in our land? And what does a visit to a rundown rescue mission have to do with Your call on my life to fight against Your enemies?*

The only answer Simon received was another soft, wordless whisper of warning he knew he must not ignore.

Thirty-five

During any other weekday of the year, the Trojan Horse Saloon at 11:30 P.M. was populated by a few traveling business people celebrating a signed contract or commiserating over the big one that got away. But with only four days till Millennium's Eve, every night at the lounge adjacent to the Hilton was party night. Early arrivers for L.A.'s many festivities lingered over their drinks, swapping predictions about the next 1,000 years. Raucous boosters from the University of Oregon and Ohio State taunted each other across the room with fight songs, then treated each other to rounds of beer.

Cole scanned the crowd and determined that Beth was not in the lounge. The presence of a number of eager, opportunistic young women in the lobby had indicated that the Portland Trail Blazer bus, with Cole's friend Curtis Spooner aboard, had also not arrived.

Cole waited until a table became available near the TV monitor tuned to the sports channel. He placed his helmet on the chair next to him to discourage potential visitors. He ordered a bottle of imported beer and was immediately engrossed in the NBA highlights on the tube, even though the noise in the lounge completely obliterated the audio.

After summarizing four Monday night games in the East and Midwest, the TV report turned to the game between the Blazers and the Suns in Phoenix. Stung by their previous night's loss in Salt Lake City, Portland charged out to an early lead, then played defense well enough to hold on for a 119–114 win. The delegation from Oregon in the lounge cheered wildly when the score was flashed on the screen.

Curtis Spooner wasn't featured in any of the highlight clips, but the game summary showed that he had represented himself well off the bench with 11 points and 2 steals. *With a victory under his belt, Spoon should be in a decent mood tonight,* Cole thought.

Cole was engrossed in the highlights of the Knicks' rout of the Sonics in Seattle when the noise level in the lounge abruptly increased several decibels. He turned to see a tall, dark-haired woman weaving between tables, headed in his direction, accompanied by good-natured roars and whistles of appreciation from the uninhibited male patrons. Beth was wearing a red jumpsuit which flattered her long, graceful legs. Her open black jacket revealed that she was as shapely above the waist as below.

A rowdy contingent of Oregon Ducks offered Beth a pitcher of beer if she would join them, and a table of Buckeyes quickly raised the bid to two pitchers and a ticket to the Rose Bowl game. Cole read in Beth's expression her unabashed pleasure at the attention, yet she continued to walk resolutely toward his table. He couldn't believe his luck at finding such a treasure in the middle of Interstate 405. He silently begged any gods who might be listening not to let him foul up a relationship with such mouth-watering promise.

Cole stood as Beth reached the table. Playing to her audience, Beth greeted him with a kiss on the mouth that banished any hopes among the onlookers that she was his sister. The crowd went crazy, many cheering, some booing, everyone having fun. Cole tried to cover his sudden embarrassment by quickly seating Beth and helping her remove her jacket—which only encouraged another round of wolf-whistles.

Cole flagged a waitress and ordered Beth a bottle. "You sure know how to make an entrance," he said, after the lounge patrons returned to their preoccupation with beer, football, and new millennium predictions.

"Yeah, I used to love the roar in the Sports Arena when I was being introduced in the starting lineup. Wasn't that a kick for you, hearing your name over the loudspeaker at Pauley Pavilion?"

"I wouldn't know," Cole shrugged, still feeling upstaged. "I never started at UCLA. Came off the bench all four years."

"I know. I'm just rubbing it in, Bruin," Beth said playfully. "Where is your Blazer friend?"

"Haven't seen him yet. Judging by the hoop nymphs swarming in the lobby, the team bus hasn't arrived from LAX."

Beth flashed Cole a sultry look, then said in a low, gravelly voice, "I'll bet you had plenty of hoop nymphs waiting for you in hotel lobbies around the PAC-10."

Cole ground his teeth, wishing he had never brought it up. "No, I was second string, remember? The only people waiting to see me on the road were basketball nerds with shoe boxes full of trading cards and old alums bidding for my complcmentary game tickets."

Not completely true, Cole admitted silently. *He flashed on the woman he met in a hotel lobby in Palo Alto who looked too good to be true, then proved it by stealing his wallet and disappearing while he slept.*

Beth's beer arrived. Cole was about to ask if she had had a good day of writing, but Beth spoke first. The concern in her voice hinted that the topic was lodged in the forefront of her thoughts. "Did you hear about today's VoiceLink call?"

"Yes, at roll call this afternoon, right after I called you. You obviously heard it."

"I read the transcript," Beth informed, slowly rotating her bottle on the tabletop. "The message was about Holloway, and there may be more messages about the others. I really think this nut is serious about getting the televangelists."

"He may *sound* serious. But I doubt that he can do what he is threatening to do."

"He may be planning something for the Coliseum, like setting off a bomb that could injure or kill hundreds of people . . . perhaps thousands."

"He may be planning it, but he'll have to be more clever than Houdini to pull it off. Trust me, Beth. We know how to handle terrorists, even those who quote the Bible."

Beth paused for a sip. A wrinkle of anxiety interrupted the smooth line of her brow. "Reagan, this isn't fair. I came to L.A. this week to write a book, say 'Merry Christmas and Happy New Millennium' to my parents, then get out of here. I didn't plan on a lunatic assassin running amok in L.A. threatening the people I care about. If this psycho tries to kill Holloway, who's to say he won't also hurt Dad and Mom?"

"If you're so worried about your folks, tell them to stay away from Holloway. Tell them to stay home Millennium's Eve, drink hot cocoa, and watch Unity 2000 on TV."

"I plan to, but fat chance," Beth huffed. "They won't stay away from the Coliseum unless Unity 2000 is canceled."

"Well, the chief won't cancel it. Neither will the mayor. Can you imagine the havoc in this town if we cowered to every threat to a public servant or celebrity? The crazies could shut down events all over the city with just a phone call: the Coliseum, the Sports Arena, the Forum, Dodger Stadium, the Hollywood Bowl, the Universal Amphitheater. No, if anybody cancels Unity 2000, it will be Holloway and the others."

Beth whispered a curse, then added, "That's an even fatter chance. Can you imagine Holloway saying, 'God told us to have this meeting in the Coliseum, but some demonic killer is threatening to blow us up and the Almighty can't figure out how to stop him, so we have to cancel the meeting'? It will never happen. To those Bible-thumpers, canceling Unity 2000 is the same as surrendering to the devil."

"So we're back to point A," Cole said, on the edge of impatience. "Unity 2000 goes on as scheduled. In the meantime, we take every precaution with the visiting preachers, and our detectives track down the guy who's making the calls and lock him up. Believe me, Beth, the quack making these calls probably doesn't know how to explode a paper bag. And if by some miracle he is able to build a bomb or load a gun without offing himself in the process, we'll catch him before he hurts anyone."

Beth still wasn't convinced. "You're so sure the police are going to catch this guy before he tries something. They probably said that about Jack the Ripper and the Boston Strangler. They say it about Arab terrorists all the time, and yet two or three planes go down every year. Ask Adrian Hornecker how he feels today about terrorist threats and airport security."

The touch of Beth's hand on his assured Cole that her frustration was not aimed at him. The anxious edge was gone from her voice when she sighed and said, "Mayhem on Millennium's Eve isn't what I signed on for this week, Reagan. They always say if you're not completely satisfied with the product, you can exchange it for something else. Well, I want to exchange this week for one in Rio. Where do I go to do that?"

Cole smiled at Beth's refreshing humor in the face of her frustration. He wrapped his hand around hers. "I won't tell you where the complaint window is unless I can go with you to Rio."

Beth looked at him wistfully. "A week in Rio together sounds magnificent," she hummed. Then a pouty frown clouded her face. Cole could tell it was manufactured. "No, you can't come until you catch the bad guy," she said, overacting the pout until Cole smiled. "If you don't catch him, he may follow us to Rio and Aruba and St. Thomas and the Riviera. . . ."

"Okay, I'll catch him, I'll catch him!" Cole laughed, leaning across the table to buss her cheek. Again the crowd in the lounge roared with excitement. Cole felt flushed with self-consciousness until he realized that the party people weren't reacting to him and Beth but to the presence of another head-turning figure in the room.

Curtis Spooner stood just inside the entrance to the lounge looking for Cole while the sports fans in the room, especially those from Oregon, greeted the Trail Blazer guard with cheers and offers of free beer.

Cole stood and waved Spooner to their table. The crowd yelled and hooted as the six-foot, seven-inch black man wearing an expensive sports jacket crossed the room. They couldn't believe that both the lovely lady in red and the veteran NBA player were guests of the same lucky guy.

Cole greeted Spooner with a fraternal handshake and casual embrace. As the two men hovered over Beth at the table, Cole said, "Spoon, I'd like you to meet my friend, Beth Scibelli. Beth, this is my good friend and former roomy, Curtis Spooner."

Beth thrust a hand up at Spooner. "I'm pleased to meet you, Curtis. I've enjoyed watching you play with the Blazers."

Curtis' large hand engulfed Beth's like it was a child's. "The pleasure is mine, Beth," he said warmly. "You must be a woman of great charm and tolerance to put up with an old, temperamental ballplayer like Reagan."

"Beth is quite a ballplayer herself," Cole bragged as the men sat down. "She started for SC when you and I were playing together."

"Scibelli . . . of course!" Spooner's face brightened with recognition. "Power forward with a nice outside shot. You had that great game against Tennessee."

Beth looked at Cole, amazed. Cole said, "Spoon doesn't just play the game; he's a student of the game. I swear he's going to coach an NBA team someday."

The trio talked basketball while Spooner signed several autographs for fans who were bold enough to interrupt the conversation. The Blazer player seemed relieved when a couple of his teammates, both starters, entered the lounge and found stools at the bar. Most of the sports freaks in the room turned their attention to the higher paid, more popular players, leaving Spooner free to talk to his friends.

Spooner asked Beth about her career, so she told her story, including her assignment for Unity 2000, the assault by the Latin Barons, Cole's brave intervention, and the hell-on-wheels chase through West Los Angeles. Cole was relieved to hear Beth laugh about the chase and speak about him in complimentary terms. The sparkle in her eyes telegraphed her affection for Cole so clearly that even Spooner could read it.

Beth filled Spooner in on the threatening calls to the *Times*, and Cole assured him that T.D. Dunne would be adequately protected by the LAPD. Spooner agreed with Cole that the mysterious caller was likely a harmless kook who would be quickly traced and hustled off to the funny farm.

"How did you get involved with T.D. Dunne, Curtis?" Beth asked.

"Yeah, Spoon," Cole added, "you blew me away on the phone telling me you were one of Dunne's missionaries."

"I kind of came in through the back door, I guess," Spooner said. "For four or five years I've been hanging out with a couple of musicians in Portland. I used to jam with them in a jazz club. A couple of years ago they 'saw the light,' I guess you could say, at one of Dunne's gigs in Seattle. They've been recording and doing concerts with him since then, and they give me all Dunne's new CDs. I like the music — good beat, a lot of creative instrumentation. But it was the lyrics that really started getting to me. Dunne does a lot of tunes about listening to God and living straight and doing right by your woman and your kids.

"Now, Reag here will tell you that I wasn't exactly the Salvation Army's man-of-the-year type in my college days. And when I turned pro, it didn't get better; it got worse. Even after I married Natty and the kids started coming, I . . . well, let's just say that I've done a lot of things I'm not very proud of.

"Then this spring when we were in Chicago for the playoffs against the Bulls, my musician buddies dragged me over to Dunne's studio and introduced me to him. I spent about an hour with him, and he didn't waste a minute of it. He hit me square between the eyes. He said, 'You're either living for God or for the devil. It's pretty easy to tell where you are: If your life is a little bit of heaven, you're probably living for God; if your life is hell on earth, you're living for the devil.'

"For me, it was an easy call. I was stepping out on Natty, especially on road trips, and she knew it. She was ready to bundle up the kids and split. I was getting pretty casual with some of the 'mood enhanc-

253

ing substances' available to people with money. I was gambling big and losing even bigger. And everything was affecting my game. I figure I was about six months from being on the streets as a junkie or at the bottom of the Willamette River with a bullet in my head. My life was hell.

"Dunne challenged me to give myself to God and let Him turn my life around. It was the same message I'd been hearing in his music for over a year. But that day it hit home and I decided to give it a try. Since then I've been praying a lot, and we go to church in Portland when I'm in town. I'm not using or gambling anymore. I cleared the decks with Natty—told her everything—and, thank God, she forgave me. And now on road trips"—Spooner glanced over his shoulder at his teammates and the starry-eyed young women clinging to them—"I do a lot of reading. I'm no angel, but my life is sure more like heaven than it used to be."

Cole and Beth sat in silence, both wishing the other would think of something appropriate to say. Finally, Cole said, "Well, if you're happy, Spoon, I'm happy for you. I guess everybody has to find out what works for them." Then he lobbed the conversation to Beth with a glance.

"Yes, that's what I always say," she added awkwardly. "Whatever works."

Thirty minutes later as Cole walked Beth to the Star Cruiser in the parking garage, he purposely steered the conversation away from Curtis Spooner's story. He was still sorting through the feelings his friend's disclosure had prompted.

There was embarrassment, of course, at hearing a 'sawdust trail' testimonial he couldn't identify with. Cole knew he wasn't living for the devil, at least compared to some cops he knew. But he couldn't tell Spooner he was living for God either. Spooner knew him too well.

There was also an uncomfortable poking and prodding in Cole's gut—guilt was the only term Cole could think of, but he didn't want to use it. Something about what Spooner said rang true, like the pure tone of a tuning fork being struck. But Cole had never heard that clear, free tone sounding within him. Even on his best days, all he ever heard was a semimelodious *clunk*. In the light of Spooner's story, Cole was again aware that something wasn't completely right, and it bothered him.

Then there was the conflict he felt over his relationship with Beth. They were moving steadily toward the physical intimacy he wanted and needed in a female companion. His hunger for her grew every time he looked at her or heard her voice. And hadn't she delivered an unmistakably clear invitation for Millennium's Eve? Dinner *and* breakfast? Cole didn't know if he wanted to wait until Millennium's Eve to be with Beth.

Last night, he reasoned, *if I had stayed with her twenty minutes longer, we would have ended up in her bedroom. But tonight, with Spooner talking about walking the straight and narrow and remaining faithful to Natty, what does that make me for even thinking about sex with Beth? And what will I look like in her eyes for suggesting it or intimating that I'm interested?*

Yeah, I'm real happy for you, Spoon, Cole thought wryly. *But you sure just complicated my life.*

As they reached the Star Cruiser, Cole said, "Did you make some headway on your book today?"

Beth shook her head, hissing at herself. "I would have done much better if I had pulled my butt out of bed this morning." Then with a mischievous grin, she added, "Of course, it's all your fault for keeping me up so late last night."

"Hey, don't lay that on me," Cole laughed. "It wasn't my idea to stay and watch the Blazer game."

"You and those devilish blue eyes of yours tricked me into asking you. And because of it I'll probably do a lousy job on the book, miss my deadline, and get fired. Then I'll be blackballed as a free-lancer, and since I have no other marketable skills, I'll end up walking the streets of Whidbey Island the rest of my life pushing an old shopping cart full of junk. The Bag Lady of Oak Harbor, that's what they'll call me. And it's all because of you. I hope you can handle the pressure, because I want you to keep me up late again tonight and tomorrow night. . . ."

Beth pulled him close and kissed him longingly. It occurred to Cole with delight that her response to Spooner's religious testimony was quite different than his.

NOVEMBER 1999	
S M T W T F S	
1 2 3 4 5 6	
7 8 9 10 11 12 13	
14 15 16 17 18 19 20	
21 22 23 24 25 26 27	
28 29 30	

1999 DECEMBER 1999
S M T W T F S
✗ ✗ ✗ ✗
✗ ✗ ✗ ✗ ✗ ✗ ✗
✗ ✗ ✗ ✗ ✗ ✗ ✗
✗ ✗ ✗ ✗ ✗ ✗ ✗
✗ ✗ 28 29 30 31

JANUARY 2000	
S M T W T F S	
1	
2 3 4 5 6 7 8	
9 10 11 12 13 14 15	
16 17 18 19 20 21 22	
23 24 25 26 27 28 29	
30 31	

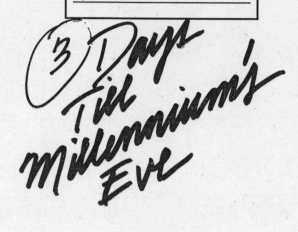

3 Days Till Millennium's Eve

Thirty-six

T.D. Dunne rarely did anything before 10 A.M., let alone compose music. He operated on what he called Entertainers' Standard Time: sleep till noon, conduct business till dinner, then perform concerts, tape shows, write and record music till dawn. Dunne felt displaced sitting at his electronic keyboard at this hour, like a mailman might feel who was forced to start his delivery route at midnight.

Adding to the confusion of the hour was Dunne's location: 37,000 feet above snow-blanketed Iowa in the first-class cabin of United Flight 1021 from Chicago to Los Angeles. He had his customary window seat, with his wife, Valerie, on the aisle ready to intercept autograph hounds sneaking through from coach. A headset jacked into the keyboard straddled his balding black pate, and full-sized, noise-attenuating earphones covered his ears.

Dunne's eyes were tired and grainy from lack of sleep. He blinked often against the harsh midmorning glare of clear sky above scattered clouds. His fingertips wandered among the white and black keys aimlessly as if looking for someplace to lie down and rest.

His laptop piano was programmed to memorize every keystroke so that a suddenly inspired chord progression or original melody could be captured for future use. But nothing came. Ever since the plane lifted off from O'Hare, Dunne had been playing snatches of everything from John Williams to André Crouch to Quincy Jones to Andrew Lloyd Webber to Chopin, searching for inspiration. Three simple chords, six or eight melody notes strung together in a novel way, that's all he wanted. He could do the rest.

Dunne had written over 300 songs in his career. He could sit down and dash off a potential Grammy-winning tune as easily as some people write a letter to their mother. But it wasn't happening today.

I can't write in the daylight, I can't write on a plane, Dunne muttered to himself. *Why did I put this off to the last minute?*

He already knew the answer. Unity 2000 had been a low priority to him and his GoTown Productions since the day Adrian Hornecker had conceived it and arm-wrestled Dunne into it. Hornecker had boldly asserted that God had called the four renowned shepherds and their flocks together. Dunne wasn't so sure. But any hesitation on his part might alienate him from thousands of Christians who attended his concerts, watched his cable programs, and bought his CDs. Snubbing Unity 2000 could seriously hamper the steady growth of T.D. Dunne's national music ministry.

So Dunne had agreed to bring his music and some of his famous converts to Los Angeles on Millennium's Eve. Dunne's troupe of all-star musicians had been recruited and supplied with music. They would rehearse together for the first time on Thursday afternoon. And they would perform Friday night as advertised.

Dunne was far from inspired, however, because a live concert in the acoustic hell of the Los Angeles Memorial Coliseum seemed a pitiful waste of talent. The best sound system in the world—and the Unity 2000 committee had settled for far less than the best—couldn't make up for all the negative dynamics of an open-air bowl crammed with people.

The funny thing is, Dunne thought as he fingered the keyboard absently, *the throng in the Coliseum will probably leap to their feet, applaud wildly, and scream for an encore no matter what it sounds like. Most people can't tell the difference between good music on a quality system and the noise of walnuts being chopped in a blender. But they'll be blessed anyway,* he acknowledged, shaking his head slightly at the thought. *The testimonies of Curtis Spooner and others will inspire them, and God may even use this fiasco to turn somebody in the right direction for the new millennium.*

But what a price to pay in dollars and man-hours just to get Christians together for a spiritual buzz. I can think of a lot better places to invest my money and time.

The thought of time brought Dunne back to the frustrating task at hand. The one item that should have been the easiest—which is why he had put it off till last—had him stymied. A simple, original song for everyone in the Coliseum to sing on Millennium's Eve—that was the committee's request. Something catchy, moving, unifying. A theme chorus Unity 2000 delegates will take with them into the new millennium to motivate them to do what God has called them to do.

That's the problem, Dunne sighed. *How am I supposed to know what God wants them to do? Everybody has his own opinion of what God wants. If Simon Holloway has his way, thousands of participants will charge out of the Coliseum ready to storm the gates of Gunnison Biotech Labs in Topanga Canyon. Shelby Hornecker will no doubt challenge the crowd toward greater faith and promise them prosperity—as long as they share their increase with Victory Life Ministries. And McClure just wants everybody to think happy thoughts, even though it sounds like he will need more than a few happy thoughts to outrun the Arizona DA and the IRS.*

Dunne glanced at his watch. Only two hours until they touched down in L.A., then nonstop appointments, receptions, and rehearsals until Millennium's Eve. A knot of anxiety began to form in his stomach. Dunne rarely tried to force inspiration to meet a deadline, but he knew if he didn't get something started in the next two hours, he would be in trouble.

Dunne suddenly realized that he had never actually asked God to give him the tune he needed. He accepted his musical ability and creativity as a gift from God. He always seemed to have two or three new melodies playing in his brain. When he was ready to compose, he simply grabbed one of them and hammered out an arrangement. Then he turned the music over to Valerie or one of his gifted performers for lyrics—T.D. Dunne rarely wrote the words to any of his songs.

But today the jukebox in his head was maddeningly quiet, so a moment of silent prayer seemed appropriate.

He had just acknowledged the idea in his mind when his phone signaled an incoming call. He nodded to Valerie to take it, thinking it was probably her mother in Joliet, who was caring for their two small children for the weekend. Only close family and immediate staff had access to the Dunnes' personal number. And most of his staff was on the plane with him.

Valerie answered, then passed the phone to her husband with a look that communicated, "I don't know who it is, but he asked for you by name."

Dunne removed his headset and took the phone. "Yes," he said.

"Good morning, Mr. Dunne, and God bless you. My name is William Malachi, coordinator of local affairs with the Unity 2000 committee."

It upset T.D. Dunne when his personal number was leaked outside the inner circle. He flashed Valerie a look of displeasure about the call.

"This is a private phone, Mr. Malachi. Any items of business concerning Unity 2000 are to be handled through my representative in L.A., Steve Nickerson."

"I am terribly sorry for interrupting your flight, Mr. Dunne. Mr. Nickerson supplied me with your private number and informed me that you are personally handling your schedule while in Los Angeles."

Dunne made a mental note to tighten the screws on Steve Nickerson for being too generous with his number.

"I'm working right now, Mr. Malachi. Can we make this brief?"

"Precisely my intention, sir," Malachi returned pleasantly. Then the coordinator quickly described a private meeting—unannounced, no press allowed—planned for the four televangelists on Wednesday night at a place called King's House, a ministry to the poor. Malachi briefly explained the ministry and insisted that Mr. and Mrs. Dunne's presence at the meeting would be a great encouragement to the director and his staff.

The meeting sounded more like a contrived social event than a visit to caretakers of the poor—and Dunne didn't much like the idea of socializing with Holloway, Hornecker, and McClure. They weren't gathering in L.A. to be chums; they were coming together to do a job. They would put on a lavish, emotionally charged program planned to give their constituents a spiritual boost into the new millennium. All four leaders had a role to play, and they would sit together on the platform as one big happy family. But they didn't need to socialize beforehand to make it happen.

Still, a "mandatory" meeting on Wednesday night would relieve Dunne of one bothersome responsibility he had agreed to in a moment of weakness. Professional basketball player Curtis Spooner, who was an important ingredient in Dunne's part of the program on Millennium's Eve, had invited him and Valerie to be his courtside guests at the Blazers–Clippers game in the Sports Arena on Wednesday night. Dunne deplored sports and disliked being in crowds he could not control with a keyboard and microphone.

And all the people who bothered him for autographs wherever he went, he didn't feel comfortable subjecting himself and Valerie to three hours among 15,000 strangers. The Wednesday meeting, though still not Dunne's idea of a wonderful night out, seemed the perfect solution.

"We will be happy to join you, Mr. Malachi," Dunne responded, suddenly affable.

"Splendid, Mr. Dunne! We will be praying with you that your presence will be a blessing to the fine people who operate King's House."

Dunne hung up and told Valerie about the change in plans. She was equally relieved.

When Dunne slipped his headset on again, it was as if the tune had been patiently waiting for him. It was there inside his head—the complete first line—the moment the earphones shut out the dull, monotonic *whoosh* of the cabin pressurization system. He fingered it on the keyboard, adding the appropriate chords. The second line came automatically, and the third and the fourth.

Dunne played the four lines again. It was beautiful. It was perfect. It was a miracle. He remembered that he had been on the verge of asking God for a tune when William Malachi called. He still hadn't prayed, but the answer was already here. *"Before you call, I will answer," says the Lord,* Dunne recited to himself in awe.

He added another four lines of music, an echo of the first section with a slightly different ending, since it needed a bridge. The notes and chords were suddenly clear in his mind, as if printed on a score in front of him.

In less than twenty minutes the music was complete: four lines—an entreaty, a call of some kind repeated once, relieved by a dramatic bridge, and then concluded with a reprise of the original theme. It was a simple tune, easy to remember, and, considering the frustrating block Dunne was facing only minutes earlier, heaven-sent.

The music was a message in itself; it didn't need lyrics, Dunne judged. But the committee had specifically asked for a song that the congregation assembled in the Coliseum on Millennium's Eve could sing together. So Dunne recorded a final version and passed the headset and keyboard to Valerie, his primary lyricist, with a pleased wink and nod. Then he reclined his chair and was asleep almost instantly.

The announcement that Flight 1021 had begun its initial descent into Los Angeles International Airport pulled Dunne back from an hour of hard sleep. When he opened his eyes, the laptop keyboard was packed in its leather carrying case and lying on his tray table. On Valerie's table was a yellow note pad with several lines handwritten in pen.

Seeing that her husband was awake and eyeing the pad, Valerie said, "Easiest lyrics I've ever written. The tune is marvelous, honey. I could almost hear the words in the melody. All I did was write them down."

Dunne picked up the pad and read as the tune, fully orchestrated, played in his mind.

> Let's begin again, brothers, Let's begin again, sisters,
> Let's begin again today To love the Lord our God.
> Let's renew our first love, Let's walk in God's new way;
> Let's begin again today To love the Lord our God.

> BRIDGE:
> As the Father has loved us, So we must love each other,
> Lay our lives down for our brothers, As a service unto Him;
> And whatever we may do, In His name for one another,
> For the least of these, His brothers, We do it unto Him.

> Let's begin again, brothers, Let's begin again, sisters,
> Let's begin again today To love the Lord our God.

Dunne looked up from the pad and flashed Valerie a look of amazed appreciation. Then he gripped her hand and said, "What a team!" quickly adding, "Thank You, Jesus!"

Thirty-seven

The Victory Life Ministries Gulfstream Five touched down at the Dallas-Fort Worth Airport shortly before noon after a forty-minute flight from Austin. Stan and Eleanor Welbourn and Jeremy Cannon, who were waiting in the Terminal 2W, boarded immediately and were welcomed at the door by Maureen Scott, the attendant who served Shelby Hornecker and her guests on all flights other than commuter hops between Austin and the Dallas area. The boarding trio found Shelby and Theresa waiting for them at the conference table near the front of the plane.

Preoccupied with the trip and their responsibilities in Los Angeles, Stan and Eleanor had been unfazed by the fact that the usually affable Jeremy didn't sit and visit with them in the private lounge as they awaited the plane's arrival. Instead, he engaged the bartender in small talk over a Perrier when he wasn't standing at the window stoically watching private aircraft come and go. Nor did it appear unusual to the Welbourns that Jeremy and Shelby greeted each other aboard the plane with a handshake instead of their customary brother-sister embrace. Yet these anomalies would come to mind and make perfect sense to Stan and Eleanor before the plane touched down at LAX.

The telephone conversation between Shelby and Jeremy the previous evening had gone surprisingly well. Contrary to Shelby's fears, Jeremy had told no one about Christmas Eve, nor did he give any indication that Shelby's behavior had prompted him to doubt his faith or abandon his pursuit of moral purity. Rather, he had answered Shelby's confession with one of his own. It was wrong for him to have stayed at the ranch and put their relationship in jeopardy, he said. It was wrong for him to have responded lustfully, if only for a moment, when she was clearly weak and vulnerable.

Apologies were humbly extended and graciously received by both sides during the conversation, even though Shelby emphatically insisted that Jeremy would have had nothing to apologize for if she had not acted so foolishly and irresponsibly in her moment of delusion. Both acknowledged the presence of God's mercy in the incident. And they expressed a wish for their friendship to continue as long as guidelines of propriety and accountability were established to prevent even the appearance of evil from tainting their relationship again.

Shelby was relieved that Jeremy still intended to stand with her in Los Angeles and continue his participation with Victory Life Ministries within the new guidelines of their friendship. And Jeremy was relieved that Shelby still wanted him to be involved. Shelby had closed the forty-minute conversation by assuring Jeremy that she would explain everything to Stan and Eleanor Welbourn as they all flew to Los Angeles.

Once the plane lifted off and approached cruising altitude, the five passengers swiveled their chairs to face each other. Maureen served a luncheon of tomato bisque and sesame rolls followed by large gulf prawns stuffed with crab. Stan assumed leadership of the informal lunch meeting, as was his place, intending to update everyone on accommodations and schedule for Los Angeles.

He wasn't into his agenda more than two sentences before a nervous Shelby said, "Excuse me, Stan, but I have an urgent personal matter to bring up before we get into our Unity 2000 business. Will you please ask Maureen not to interrupt us?" Then she began to cry softly. Puzzled, Stan conveyed the message to Maureen in the galley, then returned to his seat.

Shelby related for the third time in as many days her story of Christmas Eve and Jeremy and her momentary, aborted flight from God. The Welbourns listened in shock and disbelief, but with the same compassion and stability of spirit which had endeared them to Shelby and Adrian since Stan joined the couple in the early days of their ministry.

With the attention to detail of an attorney before a magistrate, Shelby explained her failure and sin. Then, as the defendant, she confessed her irresponsibility and acknowledged her guilt while exonerating Jeremy of complicity and releasing Stan from guilt for suggesting that Jeremy spend the night in Mesquite cottage. Finally, as judge Shelby pronounced sentence on herself by stating her plans to take a three-month sabbatical from the ministry immediately following Unity 2000 and seek counseling. She expressed her desire to restrict the knowledge of the incident to her parents, the Welbourns, and Theresa, and be held accountable for future actions by them.

Jeremy soberly confessed his thoughtlessness for agreeing to spend the night in the cottage and for wavering at the moment of temptation by first taking advantage of Shelby instead of immediately refusing her advances. Shelby reiterated that she had caused Jeremy to stumble, and that his moral resolve had prevented an even greater disaster. Jeremy also declared his hope that his friendship with Shelby could continue under the scrutiny of Stan, Eleanor, and Theresa.

When Shelby and Jeremy had finished, Stan Welbourn, whose wisdom, spiritual maturity, and sense of propriety had been a rock to Shelby in the past nine months, assumed his priestly role, just as she hoped he would. "Shelby and Jeremy, on the authority of 1 John 1:9, I affirm to you that, in response to your confession of sin, God has forgiven you and cleansed you of your unrighteousness. Furthermore, in keeping with James 5:16, since you have confessed your faults before us, it is our responsibility to pray for you that you may be healed in this area of your weakness."

Shelby and Jeremy nodded compliantly.

Stan continued. "Let me remind you that God may choose to perform an instantaneous work of healing, or He may choose to work supernaturally during the months ahead to effect your healing through the counseling and teaching you receive. What He does is His business; our responsibility is to lay hold of Him and His provision through prayer. And that's just what we are going to do."

At Stan's direction, all five of them unbuckled their seat belts and slipped to their knees in front of their chairs. Stan and Eleanor prayed long and fervently, releasing their grief and imploring God's intervention with many tears.

Then Stan, Eleanor, and Theresa clustered first around Shelby and then Jeremy with specific prayers for healing of soul and spirit and a petition for a hedge of protection against future temptation. Jeremy wept contritely, quietly. But Shelby, whose sense of grief and guilt had been all but expunged in the previous two days, merely sniffled.

When the five passengers were seated again with tears wiped away and nasal passages cleared, Stan continued with his agenda. Shelby marveled at how he had taken her news in stride, dealt with it maturely and sensitively, and was now ready to move on. His confidence in God's forgiveness bolstered her own against the pesky doubts that continued to buzz at her as the plane neared Los Angeles.

The team and their guests would be staying in a wing of suites in the stately Biltmore Hotel in downtown Los Angeles, Stan informed them. Their plane would be met at a private terminal at Los Angeles International Airport by escorts from the Los Angeles Police Department—Sergeant Reagan Cole and Officer Jayne Watanabe—courtesy of the Chief of Police. Twenty-four hour police escorts would provide transportation for Shelby and Theresa anywhere they went in the city.

Stan discussed the rumors of death threats circulating in Los Angeles against the four church leaders. The information had been forwarded to him by Darin Chaumont, Adrian Hornecker's personal appointee to head the organizational committee responsible for planning and orchestrating Unity 2000. Zealous Darin had been concerned about the threats, but Stan had not. Harassment, opposition, and threat were part of the package everywhere Shelby went. But the assurance of the Los Angeles Police Department's voluntary involvement in their security allowed the group to dismiss the concern with the usual warnings.

Stan further reported that he had been contacted in Dallas during Shelby's absence by another member of the Unity 2000 committee regarding a previously unscheduled gathering on Wednesday night, December 29. It was a visit to a church for the disadvantaged in Los Angeles, or something like that, Stan recalled from the brief conversation. All four leaders were invited, and no media people were involved.

Anticipating Shelby's objection to one more meeting during a very busy weekend, Stan had called Darin to confirm the event. Yes, Darin had said, the committee possessed the authority to schedule such goodwill visits. Darin didn't recognize the name of the committeeman who had contacted Stan, a William Malachi, but he assured Stan that if the subcommittee on local affairs had scheduled the event, it was official.

Just before Maureen arrived with beverages and dessert, Stan concluded the meeting with wise words that had been forming in the back of his thoughts since the group's prayer session, "My friends, I cannot believe it's coincidental that the enemy mounted such a potentially disastrous attack on us on the threshold of Unity 2000. God has something in store for us—for you, Shelby—in Los Angeles. He has already announced it to your heart, hasn't He?"

Shelby answered with a nod and a hope-filled smile.

"In my judgment, then, it is imperative that we continue in prayer, both in our private prayer closets and as we gather daily at the Biltmore, to lay hold of God's best for us, for our people, and for God's people at large."

"Amen," the others responded in unison.

Shelby pondered what the answers to their prayers might be.

Thirty-eight

The caller had hung up less than two minutes earlier. Beth scanned the hard copy of his latest message, which was still warm from the printer.

Woe to thee, rider of the red horse, the great harlot.
Thou who slayest thy fellowman shall be slain.
Thus saith my lord and master to thee,
Queen from the south, prophet from hell;
Entice thy people to be rich and well;
Tempt them with fatness and lust to be whole;
But fat in the flesh bringeth death to the soul.
Thy kingdom is dust, thy crown is tin;
Thou lookest without instead of within.
Thine end is near, thy crown shall fall;
The beast from heaven is all in all.
May thy flesh be torn and thy bones be scattered
and thy blood quench the parched earth,
and may the beast from heaven
take thy throne and thy inheritance.

"Shelby Hornecker this time, obviously," Beth said softly to Mai. The two women and a handful of *Times* employees were huddled around Sammy Chan's workstation. The VoiceLink editor was conferencing by phone and computer with an LAPD detective and an official from Global Communications to trace the caller's telephone number, which flashed like a warning light from Sammy's monitor.

"Mm," Mai agreed, at the moment more interested in the process of attempting to track the caller than in the message he had recited over the VoiceLink. No one in the circle of onlookers held much hope for success, because no one expected the caller to use a traceable hard-wired phone again.

Every incoming call in the late '90s left a clear electronic "finger-print" on the receiving unit: the telephone number of the instrument from which the call originated. But with the proliferation of portable telephones came the proliferation of portable telephone *snatching*. Even a mediocre thief could swipe a carelessly unguarded remote phone, run up several hundred dollars worth of calls—selling drugs or sex, placing bets, planning gang hits—then lose the instrument in a dumpster before the owner alerted the phone company to deactivate his number.

Sammy covered the mouthpiece on his phone and relayed the infor-mation he was receiving in short bursts between listening pauses. "The sending unit today belongs to a student from Ohio State—a female, name of Sandusky. Must be here for the Rose Bowl. . . . They ran her ID. No prior arrests, no warrants, not even a parking ticket. The small group laughed quietly at the ludicrous thought. The phone was stolen and everyone knew it. Ms. Sandusky was the innocent victim.

After almost a minute Sammy called above the murmuring, "Now they're going to contact her home in Huntington, Kentucky, to see if her parents know where . . . oh, wait. Ms. Sandusky is on the line to Global right now." Then after thirty seconds of listening, Sammy thanked the detective and the phone rep and hung up.

"Stolen, of course," Sammy said finally to his waiting audience. "It seems the girl was eating breakfast at a Denny's on Washington Boule-vard. She left her phone on the table when she and her friends went to the rest room and—*shazzam!*—when they came back, it was gone."

"Welcome to L.A., Ms. Sandusky," someone quipped sardonically, as the knot of curious workers unraveled and dispersed to their cubicles.

Beth was silent as she followed Mai back to her work station. Mai perceived an uneasiness in her silence. "The police will analyze and reanalyze the calls from yesterday and today," Mai said, hoping to bolster Beth's flagging spirits. "And if our perverted poet strikes again tomorrow or Thursday, the LAPD will have even more data to help them identify him and find him. In the meantime, Sergeant Cole and many more of L.A.'s finest law enforcement officers will keep our four visiting leaders safe. Everything is going to be all right, Beth. No harm will come to them or your parents or your friend."

Beth believed Mai . . . in her head. It was difficult to argue against such logic. *For openers,* Beth reasoned silently as she followed Mai into her cubicle, *the death threats are veiled at best. The caller never says, "I'm going to blow Holloway, Hornecker, McClure, and Dunne to bits in the Coliseum Friday night." In fact, he never mentions one name or place or heinous deed he is plotting. No crime has been committed. And there's barely enough evidence in these three tapes to bring someone in on suspicion.*

It's religious gibberish—cleverly written and delivered, to be sure—

intimating, through some kind of self-appointed spokesman, God's displeasure with people who have obviously fallen out of His favor. But if hellfire-and-damnation messages are a crime, the police will have to pick up every street-corner evangelist in the city and half the preachers pounding the pulpit on Sunday mornings. It's not a misdemeanor or a felony for someone to tell people that he thinks God is going to punish sinners. It's only a crime, as Mai said, when that person takes it on himself to execute God's punishment. And so far, the caller on VoiceLink has done nothing but hiss and blaze about God's wrath.

All this worrying will seem very childish in a few days, Beth told herself. *As Mai and Reagan keep insisting, it's probably a joke, a hoax, or at best a cruel but harmless threat. And if there is someone out there crazy enough to try something, it's extremely doubtful he can penetrate a security system that has protected popes, presidents, and rock 'n roll legends for decades. Millennium's Eve will probably come and go without incident.*

But that's the problem! Beth argued with herself. *Unless someone locates this kook and trots him off to Camarillo State Hospital, we won't know for sure it's a hoax until Millennium's Eve. And if by the wildest chance it's not an idle threat, Millennium's Eve may be too late for the big four—and for Jack and Dona Scibelli and Reagan Cole.*

Someone—the police, the Unity 2000 committee, someone—should be doing more to find this nut. I should be doing more. But what?

"Do you understand the allusions to Shelby Hornecker in the poem?" Mai interrupted Beth's mental debate. She was pointing to the transcript of the message Beth still held in her hand.

Beth sat down in Serg's chair. She was glad she had spent enough time in Adrian Hornecker's video files to recognize some of the themes the caller had addressed in his message to the rider of the red horse. Beth was pleased to respond to Mai with more than a blank stare.

"The word 'queen' makes it pretty obvious that the subject is a woman," she said, scanning the printed message again. "But this emphasis on health and wealth really tips it off. Adrian and Shelby Hornecker preached a gospel of prosperity and abundance. As Adrian used to say, 'You're a child of the King, and God expects you to live like one.' Mrs. Hornecker must have taken her husband's preaching to heart. She has the fattest bankroll of the big four, doesn't she?"

"She used to. It's difficult to tell anymore. Morgan McClure and T.D. Dunne are right up there. Even though Shelby's ministry has suffered financially since her husband died, Adrian did leave her a small personal fortune. She's comfortable, to say the least."

Satisfied that she hadn't embarrassed herself on the subject of Shelby Hornecker, Beth asked, "Why do you think the caller identifies Shelby Hornecker as 'thou who slayest thy fellowman'?"

"That's a puzzle to me too. It may not have a specific application at all. Remember, we're dealing with a crazy man here. He may be clever, but he may not always make sense."

"Maybe it's a reference to a woman in a man's game," Beth advanced, thinking out loud. "Maybe our man is a real man's man who can't stand a woman who exercises authority and enjoys success when so many men are out of work."

Mai shrugged in agreement. "Could be."

Beth studied the message again. "What do you think he's getting at with all this flap about wealth and health?"

"One segment of evangelical Christianity teaches that all Christians are destined to be materially prosperous and free from illness. They claim that the Bible guarantees these benefits, and they insist that if Christians are poor or diseased, they simply aren't believing what the Bible says."

"In other words, if you have the faith, you have the funds; no funds, no faith." It was another motto Beth remembered from the video files on Adrian Hornecker.

"That's how some of them might put it. Victory Life Ministries is one of the more prominent moderates in this camp. Some churches are more militant on the point; some are less. Apparently our caller takes issue with this view."

"Do you have a problem with this view?" Beth enjoyed putting Mai on the spot because she admired how this gracious woman could express her opinion without putting down those who believed differently.

Mai sat thoughtfully for a moment, contemplating her response. "I think the segment of the church represented by this view has been instrumental in reminding all Christians of God's ability and willingness to meet our needs. And I think many Christians suffer unnecessarily in many ways because they fail to ask God to supply their needs. I have no problem with Christians asking God for health and wealth. I think God wants to bless His children in many ways. But I am concerned when spiritual success is equated with these two qualities.

"Some of these groups say—and I'm not sure Shelby Hornecker lives at this extreme—'If you're healthy and wealthy, you must be a good Christian; when you're sick or poor, there's something wrong with your faith.' But by that standard most of the first-century believers would have to be judged failures, because of the poverty and pain they endured under persecution. And yet the church grew during the first century like no other time in history."

"But *somebody* has a problem even with Hornecker's moderate views," Beth said, waving the transcript.

"Yes, many people have objected to the Horneckers' health and wealth message over the years, and some have been verbally abusive about it. The 'haves' are often the target of criticism of the 'have nots,' even among people who are supposed to be known by their love and tolerance for others."

Beth remembered something else from the video files that suddenly puzzled her. "Adrian Hornecker seemed to drift from his 'live like a king' message during the last several years of his life. He became excited about the Tribulation and the Rapture and bowls of judgment being poured out, and spent millions making those apocalyptic movies. He hardly preached anything but the Book of Revelation in those last four or five years. Why do you suppose our caller is railing on Shelby for a doctrine that has taken a back seat to the Victory Life emphasis on end times?"

"Mrs. Hornecker never was the end-times enthusiast her husband was," Mai said. "Since he's been gone, she's been slowly turning the focus of Victory Life Ministries back to an emphasis on faith and prosperity. The Victory Life Studio over on Melrose has been closed since the plane crash. I talked to Darin Chaumont the other day— Darin is one of Shelby Hornecker's up-and-coming associates—and he said they're thinking about selling the film division."

Mai snapped her finger and blinked with recollection. "That reminds me, there was a brief story in Sunday's edition about the studio that I didn't get a chance to read. You may be interested in it. I believe someone was killed over there Christmas night."

Mai swung around in her chair to the keyboard and called up a copy of the *Los Angeles Times* for Sunday, December 26, 1999. She tapped in a search command and entered VICTORY LIFE FILMS at the prompt. Within seconds a three-paragraph article materialized on the monitor. Beth stepped around Serg's desk to read it with her.

GUARD SLAIN OUTSIDE VACANT STUDIO; KILLER AT LARGE

A 32-year-old security guard was stabbed to death late Christmas night by an unknown assailant on the grounds of the vacant Victory Life Films studio in Hollywood. The guard, Benjamin R. Olivares, an employee of Filmland Security, was discovered inside the fenced perimeter of the studio by a dispatcher, Julius F. Rathman, 47, after Olivares failed to resume radio contact during a routine security check of the vacant studio. Olivares was pronounced dead at the scene from stab wounds to the abdomen and heart.

Police investigators suspect that Olivares was attacked by a would-be burglar he may have surprised on the grounds. No signs of forced entry were found on any of the studio buildings. The assailant is thought to have used the victim's company pickup to flee the scene. The truck was later discovered parked behind a print shop eight blocks west of the murder scene.

Victory Life Films is owned by Victory Life Ministries of Dallas, Texas. The studio has been vacant since shortly after its founder and president, Rev. Adrian Hornecker, and his location film crew were killed when a terrorist bomb disintegrated their plane above the Mediterranean near Tel Aviv.

Beth felt suddenly cold. L.A. might be used to violence and murder every day, but she was not.

"That's terrible," she said, staring at the screen. Mai nodded her agreement. "And so many of these tragedies are preventable. If the guy had just been more alert, more careful—"

A tall, youthful intern leaned into Mai's cubicle and interrupted. "Lunch in the conference room, Mai. You're late."

Mai jumped up from her chair. "Oh, I forgot!" she squealed, chagrined. "Thank you, Kent. I'm on my way."

Mai grabbed her purse and phone. "Sorry to run out on you again, Beth."

"Don't worry about it. I need to get to the library and write anyway. I'll see you tomorrow morning for—what's next?—the message to the rider of the black horse."

"Yes, and I think that's supposed to be McClure," Mai said, sweeping past her and out the door. Then she called back, "Unless they catch our caller first."

How is anyone going to catch him? Beth thought grimly. *Nobody's really looking for him. He is using stolen phones now, so we have to wait to see if he will make good on his threats.*

She looked again at the story still glaring at her from Mai's monitor. *If the guard had just paid better attention, looked closer, maybe he would have found the burglar before the burglar found him and became a killer. At least the guard's adversary was there in person, not just a faceless voice on the phone. The VoiceLink caller is more than a voice too. He's somewhere in L.A. right now. But where do you look for a Revelation-spouting religious nut who—*

Suddenly, with heart-stopping, hold-your-breath surety, Beth knew where to look. It was a long shot for sure, but she had to check it out.

She should go to the library and work, and perhaps she would later. But the book had to wait for now. It was noon, the best possible time to investigate the one place in Los Angeles where the Great Tribulation, the Second Coming of Christ, and the Four Horsemen of the Apocalypse were discussed as openly and easily as the weather.

Beth grabbed her purse and hurried toward the door.

Thirty-nine

Jack Scibelli had taken Beth to Pershing Square many times when she was a child and young teen. At the time, Jack's accounting office was in a twenty-eight-story office building only three blocks from the Square. Once a week during summer vacations, Beth rode into the city with her father and spent the morning reading or playing quietly in a vacant office while he worked.

The highlight of young Beth's day downtown with her father was lunchtime. At 11:45, the two of them picked up the sack lunches Dona had prepared for them and walked hand in hand to Pershing Square. Eating lunch was merely incidental to everything else there was to experience in the Square on a warm summer day. There were flocks of waddling, ill-mannered pigeons and darting sparrows to feed with crusts of dried bread Dona always included in Beth's lunch sack. And there were people to watch—white-shirted computer programmers telling jokes; secretaries flirting with sales managers; fat old men in undershirts, Bermuda shorts with suspenders, and Panama hats playing checkers or gin rummy; garishly dressed ex-debutantes from the '40s and '50s walking their poodles and pretending to be movie stars.

But Beth was most enthralled watching the winos—grown men, disheveled and smelly, sprawled on the grass and snoring in broad daylight, or furtively nipping at concealed bottles. Once she even saw one of them urinate on the lawn without trying to cover himself. Beth was both aghast and saddened.

"Don't stare at the bums, Mary Elizabeth," her father would reprimand. "Just pretend they aren't there." But they *were* there, and she couldn't ignore them. They were so foreign to her life in upper-middle-class Woodland Hills. So she learned to steal glances at "the bums" when Jack wasn't looking.

The best part of being in Pershing Square with her father came after lunch. Jack and Beth played a game she called simply "the sidewalk game"—strolling the sidewalks which crisscrossed the Square, trying not to step on any lines. Beth especially liked the game because it allowed her to walk within a few feet of the most fascinating and sometimes terrifying occupants of the park: the Pershing Square preachers.

These were often desperate-faced, wild-eyed men—many looking as unkempt as the winos on the lawn—who stamped the sidewalk, flung their fists in the air, and shouted harsh words about God and heaven and sin and hell and ominous events to come. Beth had never heard this kind of talk in catechism or confirmation classes.

Beth would walk slowly past each one, holding her father's hand tightly, pretending to play the sidewalk game. But she always listened intently, sometimes sneaking a look into eyes that burned with passion, snarled with vengeance, or crackled with evil. Occasionally Jack would concede and allow Beth to toss a couple of quarters into the hat or cigar box of one of the more harmless looking preachers. She wondered what these enigmatic, seemingly fictional characters in the Square knew about the future that the priests and sisters at her parish had withheld from her.

Beth walked the five long blocks from Times-Mirror Square to Pershing Square expectantly, almost forgetting the mild pain in her ankle that hampered her long stride. She was also grateful for the Southern California weather that allowed her to be outdoors in slacks and a light wool jacket. At home on Whidbey Island the temperature would top out at 40 degrees today. L.A.'s TV weathermen had promised 65 degrees downtown and 75 degrees in the valleys. *For all its faults,* Beth hummed appreciatively, *Southern California still has the best winter weather on the West Coast.*

Pershing Square had been refurbished since Beth had last walked its sidewalks as a university student in 1989. But the people occupying the park looked the same as when she first came here with her father as a wide-eyed eight-year-old: retirees with their poodles and cards, office workers with their bag lunches, winos with their brown-paper-wrapped bottles, and several soapbox preachers holding forth for any who would listen. And around them all, sparrows darted and pigeons waddled after morsels of food people tossed to them or discarded.

During her walk to the Square, Beth formulated a three-tiered strategy for uncovering information that might lead to the identification of the VoiceLink caller. If the caller was stupid enough to think he could deliver the same threatening message in the square that he had so cleverly delivered to the *Times,* she would find him.

First, she would circulate casually through the park, blending in with the office crowd, listening carefully to the themes being sermonized. Anyone who preached in rhyming couplets or alluded to the Four Horsemen or proclaimed a particularly violent divine judgment would require closer scrutiny and perhaps a casual interview by a "serious inquirer after the faith."

Second, if none of the preachers in the park today sounded suspicious, she would ask among the lunching office workers and card-playing old folks for anyone who might have heard someone preaching in the Square about the Four Horsemen.

Third, if she exhausted all her leads on the walkways and park benches, she would get out onto the grass and ask some of the winos about a vengeful preacher who recited the demise of the riders of the white, red, black, and pale horses.

Beth entered Pershing Square from the corner of Fifth and Hill, fully expecting to turn up nothing. *It's like looking for a pearl in a hailstorm, but at least I'm doing something,* she encouraged herself.

She bought a hot dog and a warm can of Pepsi from a sidewalk vendor and found a bench within earshot of two vociferous sidewalk evangelists, one of them facing Fifth Street and the other facing Hill. Beth sat down and nibbled at her lunch as she listened and evaluated them.

The Fifth Street evangelist was a screamer with a speech impediment, kind of a lisp. Every sentence began with an explosive "Jee-shush!" and ended with the well-practiced "ah" of a holy roller on the brink of losing emotional control: *Jee-shush wants to shave you-ah! Jee-shush wants to shet you free-ah! Jee-shush wants you to put a dollar bill in my cup-ah!* He had an audience of two winos and a dozen pigeons.

The Hill Street preacher wasn't even speaking English. It was a Middle Eastern dialect, Beth guessed. A casual glance revealed the speaker to be small, dark, and swarthy with a black brush of a mustache and two days' stubble. *He could just as easily be preaching from the Koran as from the Bible,* Beth surmised. *But his inflection is nearly identical to that of the lisping screamer.*

Nobody paused on the sidewalk to listen to the Middle Eastern preacher, so he aimed his unintelligible sermon at cars passing the Square on Hill Street.

Beth discounted these first two as possible suspects. She quickly finished her hot dog and drink and set off on a leisurely stroll of Pershing Square to hear more. As she walked, she caught herself playing the sidewalk game, watching for cracks in the walkway and stepping over them. She remembered with fondness those summer days in the Square with her father.

All the more reason to find this religious nut, she prodded herself. *Dad and Mom have their blind spots, and religion may be the largest one. But they don't deserve to get hurt because of it.*

From the east corner of the Square to the center there was one other sidewalk preacher, a robed New Age guru crooning about stars, moons, and spirits. He urged his listeners—two young office girls who were flirting with him—to mind-merge with the crystal-gazers on the East Coast who would welcome the new millennium at sunrise by joining hands along the shore from Bar Harbor to Miami.

The center of the Square was humming with activity. A row of metal picnic tables hosted a dozen old gentlemen playing cards, chess, and checkers. Half a dozen people were crowded around a taquito vendor. A guitar-twanging beggar entertained a small cluster of would-be music lovers. And business people in knots of two to five sat on benches eating, or strolled through on their way back to the office.

Near the cement pond stood a pencil-thin, sickly looking man in dirty, rummage-sale clothes. His hands were clasped piously at his belt. Patches of hair were slicked back on his head as if with lard. When Beth noticed him from halfway across the Square, he was glaring at her cruelly, lasciviously. The icy finger of a chill traced her spine as she felt his eyes rake her body. He looked like the soapbox preacher type to Beth, but except for the vulgarities he telegraphed with his dark, evil eyes, he said nothing. Beth couldn't have felt more violated if he had physically grabbed her and manhandled her. She quickly turned away.

Beth's walk to the west corner of the park, then along Olive Street to the north corner and back to the center, proved fruitless. None of the half dozen preachers she passed, or their sermons, even remotely reminded her of the VoiceLink caller. Beth began to feel discouraged, but she decided to follow through with the tour just to play out her hunch.

She glanced again at the man by the pond. He remained motionless and silent while his eyes wantonly pawed the women and men who crossed his line of sight.

As Beth walked toward the south corner and turned up Sixth Street, Cole called. They exchanged warm greetings and expressed their eagerness to be with each other again.

"What are you doing today?" he asked.

Beth made a snap decision not to tell Cole her mission. She was afraid he would laugh at her if she said she was wandering around Pershing Square trying to solve the case of the mysterious VoiceLink assassin. The thought embarrassed even her.

"I'm working at the library, Central Branch," she lied cheerily.

After a silent pause, Cole said, "It doesn't sound like a library. It sounds like you're outside."

"I'm sitting by an open window," she answered without hesitation. "It's such a nice day today, I decided to let some sunshine in."

"You're in the library?" Cole pressed, sounding unconvinced.

Beth felt twinges of guilt for lying so pointedly, but she was stuck in it now. "Yes. I'll probably spend the afternoon here." *I will spend the afternoon at the library*—when *I get there*, she added silently, trying to quiet her conscience. *Besides, I'm almost at the library. It's only four blocks away.*

"Where are *you*?" Beth directed the attention away from herself.

Again Cole didn't answer immediately. Finally, he said, "I'm heading into work early. The lieutenant wants to brief Jayne and me before we leave for LAX to pick up Shelby Hornecker."

There was a subtle distance in Cole's voice. *He must be preoccupied with his big escort assignment*, Beth judged.

"So you're still at home?" Beth said.

"I'm . . . on the way into town."

"Will I get to meet Shelby Hornecker tonight?" Beth asked playfully, hoping to buoy a conversation that seemed to be sinking on Cole's end.

"No, I'm told she has a full schedule tonight. Tomorrow night you'll meet her, at that King's House deal."

Beth was uncomfortable with the vibes being transmitted through Cole's informative but markedly cool tone. It reminded her of their first conversation shortly after the chase. He answered her questions, but his heart wasn't in it. Beth suddenly wondered where Cole's heart was at this moment.

Cole promised Beth he would meet her at the Trojan Horse again after work, then hung up and slipped his phone into his jacket pocket. He continued to stare out the window from the third floor of the library. He had walked come to the library hoping to surprise Beth and take her to Quinteros before he went to work.

When he didn't find her, he pulled out his phone and called her.

Cole felt sick at heart. Beth had just lied to him . . . and with a cheery lilt in her lovely voice. *She isn't in the library. Why would she lie to me?*

A flood of answers deluged him immediately, all of them negative: *She's been stringing me along all this time; She's nothing more than a flirt, a game-player; She's not interested in me, she's just using me to find an inside edge for her book; She's still getting back at me for the chase and my harsh words on Christmas Eve.* Cole's heart wanted to rebut every charge. But his head reminded him that he had only known Beth Scibelli for four days—not enough time to get inside her head and know what made her tick.

Cole searched the building again, hoping he had somehow missed Beth. But she wasn't anywhere in the library. He was sure she never had been.

Cole stood beside his motorcycle and cursed as he pulled on his helmet and gloves and mounted. *What are you into, Beth? What's your game?* he pondered bitterly. *I don't like being lied to. I don't like being played with. But I can play this game too. And if find out that you're working some kind of con on me or your parents or Unity 2000, I'm going to break it open and let the world see it.*

Lunch hour was almost over. Beth stood in the center of Pershing Square watching business people wad up their paper sacks and leave the park for their offices. She had listened to a total of twelve would-be Simon Holloways—not counting the silent skeleton of a man still leering at her from near the pond—proclaim their twisted, ludicrous, or laughable versions of God's truth. None of them could be suspected as the VoiceLink caller. The hour had been a waste of time.

And now with the mass exodus of business people from the park,

Beth's backup strategy was in jeopardy. She had only a limited number of "normal" citizens left to interview. And she really didn't want to stoop to Plan C: interviewing winos.

Beth was in the midst of rethinking her strategy when she saw two police officers ride bicycles into the Square from the eastern corner. *Fantastic!* she exulted silently. *If anyone knows what's being preached around here—*

"The kingdom of heaven is at hand!"

The verbal explosion forty feet to her right caused Beth to jerk with alarm and let out a small squeal. She whirled to the right, thinking the sallow-faced, hollow-eyed lecher might be charging her. But the man, who continued to burn away Beth's clothes with his lustful stare, hadn't moved from his spot near the pond. Beth couldn't believe that such a booming, terrifying voice had come from such a gaunt shadow of a man.

"Don't worry, ma'am, he's basically harmless."

Beth turned around to find the two bike cops behind her. She was the same height as the black officer and three inches taller than the Hispanic. They were still smiling from the entertainment the vagrant had provided for them at Beth's expense.

"I'm not so sure he's harmless," Beth retorted, catching her breath from the fright. "He has the most wicked, diabolical stare I've ever seen."

"It's all show, ma'am," said Tommy Scanlon, the black officer, from behind his shiny dark glasses. "Old Rev. Wingate there is half blind. If it wasn't for your long hair and my dark skin, he probably couldn't tell the three of us apart from where he's standing. He puts on that face to keep people from hassling him."

Beth turned to look at Rev. Wingate again. The stare looked no less maniacal, despite the officer's explanation.

"You obviously don't visit the Square often," Vince Ochoa said when Beth turned back to face the policemen.

"No, actually I'm from out of town. I'm in L.A. for the holidays, visiting my parents."

"So what brings you to Pershing Square?" Ochoa asked, removing his shades. Beth couldn't tell if the officer was asking for himself or for the department. Either way, she was counting on her feminine charm to squeeze what information she could out of the two young officers who had her undivided attention.

"I'm looking for someone . . . a man . . . an older man I think." Beth added just enough of a lost little girl lilt to her voice hoping to evoke a helpful response.

"Describe him; maybe we know him," Scanlon offered.

"I've never seen him, and I don't even know his name. All I really know about him is that he's kind of a sidewalk preacher like some of these men." Beth waved a hand toward some of the Pershing Square preachers who were still thundering their message.

"If you've never seen the man and don't know his name, how are you going to find him?" Ochoa asked, adding "you dumb broad" with the tone of his voice. It steamed Beth a little inside. If she hadn't been so desperate for a clue, she might have walked away.

"His sermons. That's why I came down here today to listen to the men preaching in the park. The man I'm looking for preaches about the Four Horsemen in the Book of Revelation in the Bible. He really likes preaching about scattering their bones, tearing their flesh, and pouring their blood into the earth."

The look that Scanlon and Ochoa exchanged, subtle though it was, ignited a blaze of hope in Beth. *They know something!* she cheered inside, hiding her sudden excitement behind a mask of stoicism.

"Ma'am, why do you want to find this man?" Ochoa's question was abruptly police interest and no personal interest. *Another good sign*, Beth thought.

Beth had fabricated the story in her mind as she was walking around Pershing Square. She didn't plan to use it unless she had to. She surely didn't want to use it on the cops now for fear they might check it out and discover her to be lying. But she sensed she might be close to the information she sought. In an instant she decided to take the risk.

"This man and my father served in Vietnam together almost thirty years ago. He saved Dad's life. After the war Dad's buddy took to drinking and street preaching. Dad lost touch with him over ten years ago.

"Now Dad is dying of cancer, and he wants to see his buddy one more time. Dad says he owes the man his life, and he asked me to try to find him. He says he is somewhere in L.A., maybe around Pershing Square. He says I will know him from his sermons about the Four Horsemen in the Book of Revelation. Do you know of such a person around here?"

Beth retained steady eye contact with the Hispanic officer hoping to convince him of her truthfulness.

"If the friend was so important to your father, why doesn't he know his name?" Beth read the same "dumb broad" inference in Ochoa's question.

Beth was ready for him. She dropped her head and blinked away a wave of feigned sadness. "Since Dad's been sick, his mind is. . . ." She let the words fall away, as if suddenly choked by grief. "He may have mentioned his name years ago. I might recognize it if I heard it. But all Dad calls him is 'my buddy' "

Ochoa hesitated, but Scanlon took the bait. "Does the name Hodge sound familiar, ma'am?"

Beth looked up hopefully. "Hodge? Hm. I don't know. That could be him. Do you know someone by that name who preaches around here, someone who preaches about the Four Horsemen?"

Ochoa glanced at his partner to rein him in, but Officer Scanlon was helping a lady in distress.

"A guy named Hodge—that's all I've ever heard him called—has been hanging out here since early December. Ugly as the devil and crazier than Wingate over there. Always wears jeans and a Dodgers cap and carries a blue and white picnic chest for a briefcase. He used to show up every day and scream and holler about four horsemen and brimstone and torn flesh and broken bones. Not the kind of sermon that would inspire me to spiritual peace."

"He *used* to show up every day?" Beth pressed.

Ochoa took over. "Ma'am, I'm not so sure this is the man you're looking for. Hodge has been known to carry a knife and pull it on people in the Square."

Scanlon continued with information that Ochoa preferred not to release. "All that blood and gore in his four-horsemen sermons was bad enough. But when he started reading from the Bible about stabbing people in God's name, we ran him off and told him he couldn't preach that stuff in the Square."

Beth's heart was racing. "When?"

"A couple of days ago—Sunday, I guess," Scanlon said. "We haven't seen him since."

"But he preached about the four horseman—white horse, red horse, black horse . . . ?"

Scanlon answered authoritatively. "He preached about a lot of things, ma'am—most of it death and punishment, God-is-going-to-get-you kind of stuff. But he always ended with something about each of the four horsemen: 'May thy flesh be torn and thy bones broken and thy blood poured out'—something like that."

Excitement, apprehension, and raw fear had reached the boiling point within her, making it difficult for Beth to remain cool on the surface. She directed her key question to Scanlon, who had been the most cooperative. "Where can I find Mr. Hodge?"

Ochoa cut in, "Ma'am, Hodge is a potentially dangerous man. I'm not sure you want to go looking for—"

"Officer, I *must* do whatever I can to find this man. It's my father's last wish. Mr. Hodge may not be the right man, but maybe he knows the right man. It's my only lead. I must talk to Hodge." Beth hoped she looked on the verge of tears. It was a cruel, sexist ploy, but she was desperate.

Ochoa and Scanlon glanced at each other with resignation. Again Scanlon came first to her aid. "We don't know where Hodge lives, but *he* might." Scanlon waved his thumb toward the skinny, soiled, beady-eyed man glaring at them from his station near the pond.

"Wingate knows where Hodge is?" Beth asked, wincing at the prospect of talking to the dirty old man.

Scanlon and Ochoa said nothing. Rather, they were tuned to a call being received through the radio earbuds nestled in their right ears. After a few seconds Ochoa acknowledged the call with a few words directed toward a tiny mike pinned to his lapel.

"We have to go to work, ma'am," Ochoa said, slipping on his shades hurriedly. "Wingate may be able to tell you where to look for Hodge. But don't go anywhere with Wingate, no matter what he tells you. And don't go looking for Hodge alone."

"Oh, don't worry," Beth said, glancing nervously at Wingate as the cops mounted their bikes to leave. Then another convenient lie jelled in her brain. "I have a brother—a *big* brother. He's checking out Union Station right now. I won't be alone when I find Hodge. My brother will be with me. Thank you, officers."

Ochoa and Scanlon sprinted away on their bikes toward the east corner of the park. Beth turned to face the waiting Wingate, standing still and silent as a statue. The lunch hour crowd had dispersed, and many of the preachers had left the park to spend the coins they found in their offering cups on the sidewalk. But there were still several old men at the picnic tables, so Beth felt reasonably safe approaching Rev. Wingate, although she abhorred the thought of moving near enough to talk to him. *I can't give up now,* she reasoned.

Beth crossed the concrete square to within twelve feet of the man where the odor of stale tobacco and urine stopped her like a brick wall. His creepy, unrelenting gaze made her feel naked. *If he's half blind,* she thought coldly, *his evil imagination is more than making up for what he can't see.* Beth self-consciously pulled her jacket closed and buttoned it.

"Rev. Wingate, I'm looking for a friend of my father. I believe his name is Hodge. The officers told me you know Mr. Hodge. Can you tell me where to find him?"

Wingate didn't move, didn't blink, didn't twitch. Beth decided to try the sympathy angle again.

"My father is dying, Rev. Wingate. His last wish is to see his friend again. Will you please help me?"

Still no response. Beth sighed heavily, then opened her purse and pulled out her wallet. "I have a $20 bill here," she said, trying to display the bill for Wingate without waving it for the whole park to see. "I would be happy to contribute $20 to your ministry if you can just tell me where to look for Mr. Hodge."

Beth thought she saw Wingate's gaze shift from other parts of her anatomy to the hand holding the $20. He ogled the money for thirty seconds before his eyes released their grip and returned to Beth's figure.

Beth breathed a silent, bitter curse at the man. *He knows*, she hissed under her breath. *He's just holding out for more money*. The ploys had been useless. It was down to a simple business transaction.

Beth pulled another $20 from her wallet. "This is all I have, Wingate," she said sharply, snapping the two bills with her finger. "I'll give you $40 right now if you tell me where Hodge is."

Wingate's eyes widened as they labored to focus on the bills. Then a greedy grin creased his dark face, and he stretched a bony hand toward Beth, palm side up.

Forty

Bill Fawcett was a six-foot, six-inch, 250-pound sequoia of a man. When he lowered his frame into a dining room chair in Dr. No's apartment, sixteen-year-old Wendy, watching from the kitchen, cringed for the chair.

Bill had spent thirty of his fifty-seven years in jail—as a jailer with the Los Angeles County Sheriff's Department. If Deputy Fawcett had a fault as a jailer, it was being too helpful to his prisoners. He was a hard guy when he had to be—he wouldn't have lasted thirty years in the jails otherwise. But big Bill also had a big heart. He spent many hours each week on his own time counseling young offenders—especially first-timers—and helping released prisoners get settled and find jobs. He loved his work, and he was committed to doing everything he could to make sure his prisoners left and never came back.

Bill's pedal-to-the-metal devotion to his career had cost him plenty. Two wives and numerous girlfriends had left him because his work always came first. Twice he was shot during attempted jail breaks, losing his spleen and a chunk out of his neck in the process. And on three different occasions he spent a month drying out in an alcohol treatment center. Whenever one of his rehabilitated "projects" turned up dead in a gang fight or was arrested for a repeat offense, Bill's discouragement drove him to the bottle. Unfortunately for Bill, his projects disappointed him often.

Dr. No met Bill Fawcett at the Los Angeles County Jail two years before the deputy's retirement. Dr. No and a few volunteers visited prisoners in the jail regularly and worked through channels to qualify King's House as a halfway facility for work-release inmates.

Discovering someone on the outside who shared his passion for inmate rehabilitation, Bill wanted to learn more about Dr. No and King's House. So Bill spent many evenings snooping around the old hospital and interviewing volunteers. He was astonished at the commitment he found in Dr. No and his staff, not only to befriend prisoners but to feed the hungry, clothe the poor, shelter the homeless, and comfort the terminally ill. And Dr. No was doing it all without begging for money or skimming for personal gain the charitable contributions he received.

Big Bill Fawcett began attending Bible studies at King's House and soon became a humble servant of Jesus Christ and a King's House volunteer. Upon his retirement from the Sheriff's Department, he was a natural to assume leadership over the King's House prison ministry.

For two years Bill had coordinated the work of seventy part-time volunteers who visited the County Jail and conducted Bible studies with the inmates while they were incarcerated and after they were released. He also worked directly with twelve full-time paid staff who maintained the King's House job-training and placement office and the temporary residence facility for ex-cons.

During these two years, Dr. No and Bill got together every Tuesday for lunch to catch up on the ministry and nurture their friendship. Today's lunch had been prepared by Wendy Ngo. Fourteen-year-old David, who was also at the table, had mixed the lemonade.

"You welcomed some new arrivals this morning," Dr. No said, after praying over the first round of tacos Wendy had delivered to the table.

"Yes, three," Bill replied. Then he hungrily engulfed half a taco in one bite, unconcerned about the fragments of hamburger, lettuce, and cheese that rained from his mouth to his plate. After a gulp of lemonade he added, "We're full again—all thirty beds. We could fill another thirty beds tomorrow if we had them."

"Yes, I know," Dr. No said. "We need to keep praying that God will show us when and how to expand the second floor. Do you have any more residents ready to graduate?"

Bill waited to answer until he had devoured the rest of his first taco. Wendy brought him another, happy to be cooking for someone with a horse's appetite. "Two next month—Ricky Avila and Fiona Washington—and maybe another two in February," Bill said.

"Ricky's ready to go?" Dr. No asked with surprise.

"He is doing beautifully," Bill beamed, as he attacked his second taco. "His performance reviews at the machine shop are coming in very high. He's now the assistant leader in his Bible study group—and his group will stay together even after he moves in with his aunt. And he's already on a jail team. He goes to County Jail twice a week to visit his old gang members awaiting trial. Ricky says the gang just blew these guys off, gave up on them. But he's going to stick with them all the way through the system. He says that's what saved him—somebody from the House coming twice a week, being a friend to him, and praying for him after his gang buddies threw him away."

"Bill, when can I be on a jail team?" David piped up. "I'd like to help people like Ricky."

"The county won't let you visit in the jails until you're eighteen, Dave. But we can always use letter writers, people to send birthday cards to inmates, stuff like that. There are several ways you can visit inmates without actually going into the jail."

"Who can I write to? I don't know anybody in jail."

"Maurice has a list of names and a sheet of guidelines for what to say and what not to say in your cards and letters. He would love to set you up with an inmate pen pal, maybe someone in juvenile."

Dr. No affirmed David's willingness to get involved in letter writing, then steered the conversation back to the upcoming graduates of the former offenders' residence program. "What about Fiona? Where is she going?"

Bill leaned back in his chair to rest up for his third taco. "Fiona is a tough one," he said, shaking his head. "She almost bailed on the program. Her old boyfriend keeps hassling her at work, wearing her down. She wants to go back to the old neighborhood, but I don't think she's ready. I think she knows that too.

"So I worked out a deal with a friend of mine in Fresno, another ex-cop. He found Fiona a job cleaning houses, and there's a family in his church who will take her for at least a year, until well after the baby is born. I presented the package to Fiona just before Christmas. I said, 'The Apostle Paul went away from home for a while after he became a Christian to get his head straight, and he came back real strong. I think you will too.' She bought the idea. She'll be leaving for Fresno on the tenth. But we need to keep her on our prayer list."

"That's wonderful, Bill," Dr. No said, smiling. Then he added wistfully, "I wish—and I pray—that more of our King's House guests turned out as well as Ricky and Fiona."

"Just remember, Dr. No," Bill interjected, sounding like a parent trying to bolster a discouraged child, "like you keep telling us, our part is to house them, feed them, clothe them, and teach them. But we can't change them. That's God's job."

Dr. No winked his appreciation for the timely reminder.

Several more topics relating to Bill's second-floor ministry were addressed—and almost as many tacos were consumed—by the time Dr. No's next group of invited guests arrived. By 2:15 P.M. the overseers of meal service, food and clothing distribution, the homeless shelter, and building maintenance and security were seated with Dr. No, Bill Fawcett, and David Ngo around the dining room table. Like Bill, all of them had a story of how God prepared them and directed them to their places of service at the House.

Wendy offered lemonade and coffee to everyone and placed a platter of Christmas cookies and fudge in the center of the table.

"Wendy, would you join us for a minute," Dr. No called to his daughter, who had begun to load the dishwasher with lunch dishes. "I know you and David will be interested in what I have to talk about."

Wendy and David Ngo were rarely excluded from King's House business. Their parents tried to expose them to the variety of experiences, opportunities, and problems they faced in the House's extensive and varied ministries. But being invited to sit in on a meeting of overseers was a rare treat.

"You all know about Unity 2000 in the Coliseum Friday night," he began.

The group around the table nodded in unison. Unity 2000 had been a popular topic among staff members and guests in the House. Some who had Friday night off were planning to attend.

"And you're all familiar with the four leaders who are coming to Los Angeles for this event."

This time the group responded audibly, mentioning the names and accomplishments of Simon Holloway, Shelby Hornecker, T.D. Dunne, and Morgan McClure. Young David Ngo proudly announced that he owned five of T.D. Dunne's CDs.

Dr. No continued. "The local organizing committee for Unity 2000 is responsible for entertaining these four ministers while they're in L.A.— you know, giving them a taste of the city, acquainting them with local activities, and so on." He released a long sigh, still grappling with the reality of what he was about to disclose. "Well, I don't understand the whys and wherefores of it all, but the committee wants to bring all four of them here to King's House tomorrow night."

The reactions ranged from gasps of shock to hums of surprise to David's nearly ecstatic, "You mean T.D. Dunne is going to be in our building tomorrow night!"

After a burst of comments and questions had rippled around the table, Dr. No resumed his explanation. "The committee member who talked to us said that the ministers and their families and aides will arrive here about 7. They will tour our facility, have a brief meeting with us, and leave. I didn't mention it to you sooner because their visit is supposed to be low-key. They don't want the media here with lights and cameras. So I thought it best to be quiet about it until now, and I request that you restrict this information to your immediate families only. They don't want a crowd of people around; they just want their guests to see a local care-giving ministry in action."

The small circle of heads nodded compliance.

"This low-key mode also means that you don't need to make any special preparations. All of you do a wonderful job of loving and serving people here every day. The building is always clean. We don't need any extra spit and polish or red, white, and blue bunting. The food is always good. If they want a snack, we'll serve them what the rest of us eat for dessert tomorrow night.

"If any of the residents are unruly while our Unity 2000 guests are here, don't be embarrassed. Just deal with them the way you usually do. I want our guests to see the way we really are, because, thanks to you and those who serve with you, I'm proud of what we are."

When the last staff member had left the apartment, David and Wendy were in their father's face with excited questions. "Does this mean we can go to Unity 2000 Friday night and hear T.D. sing in person? After all, how would it look for T.D. to visit us—I can't believe he's going to be here!—then he asks us if we're going to his concert, and we say we can't or we don't know or Dad and Mom haven't decided yet? Wouldn't that be embarrassing?"

Dr. No wrapped an arm around each child and squeezed playfully. "My children, you have an excellent point. What kind of father would allow his children to be so humiliated in front of a big star. How heartless, how cruel, how utterly . . . parental. I think we should call Mom right now and make our plans for Friday night at the Coliseum."

Wendy and David cheered wildly.

Forty-one

Sergeant Cole sat with his partner in the silver gray, electric-powered Bolt 700 on the tarmac near the Imperial Terminal on the quiet south side of Los Angeles International Airport. A medium blue electric passenger van with another uniformed officer at the controls was parked behind him.

The gleaming white Gulfstream Five rolled to a halt in front of them. The engines were still winding down as the motorized passenger staircase jockeyed into position at the plane's front door.

A gaggle of Shelby Hornecker's fans waved excitedly from behind a fence near the small auxiliary terminal. An even larger crowd awaited her appearance at LAX's main terminal, unaware that Shelby's private plane was better served by the smaller remote Imperial Terminal.

"Remember," Officer Jayne Watanabe reminded Cole with a tongue-in-cheek grin, "it's a lady's prerogative to initiate a handshake. If you stick out your hand before she sticks out hers, you'll look like a real toad."

"Got it, Miss Manners," Cole smiled. "Thanks." He adjusted his tie and checked his appearance in the mirror. He had worn a sport jacket and tie only four times since graduating from the academy—for awards ceremonies at Parker Center. He hoped his ensemble hadn't drifted too far out of style in eight years.

Cole, Watanabe, and Officer Tizeri from the van were standing at the foot of the stairs when Shelby Hornecker and her entourage emerged from the plane and descended to the tarmac, waving graciously to the handful of cheering fans.

"Welcome to Los Angeles, Rev. Hornecker. My name is Sergeant. Reagan Cole, and this is Officer Jayne Watanabe and Officer Ron Tizeri." Cole didn't like all the folderol and formality of protocol, but he was good at it when he had to be.

"It's a pleasure, sergeant," Shelby said with a warm smile and an easy-as-a-rocking-chair Texas drawl. She extended her hand for a firm but friendly handshake. Then she presented her personal assistant, Ms. Theresa Bordeaux, her associates at Victory Life Ministries, Rev. and Mrs. Stan Welbourn, and Mr. Jeremy Cannon, an actor and friend of the ministry. The peace officers and visiting dignitaries exchanged thoroughly proper greetings all around.

The female preacher was younger and prettier than Cole had anticipated. Shelby's face and figure, though understandably not adorned for sex appeal, were nevertheless utterly feminine and attractive. *How did such a fine-looking woman end up selling eternal life insurance on TV?* Cole wondered, sensing the loss for thousands of single, more worldly men her age.

Shelby's hand, which Cole held briefly during the handshake, was soft and cool, obviously pampered and unaccustomed to physical labor. Her voice was cultured and honey-smooth. Rev. Shelby Hornecker was no Dallas Cowboys' cheerleader, Cole assessed. But she was a long way from being the "Sister Hester T. Salvation" type with a potato-shaped body, foghorn voice, and stringy hair wound into a bun. Despite the fact that Rev. Hornecker was closer to forty than to his thirty-one, under any other circumstances, he would be looking for an opportunity to ask her out.

The fact that the beautiful widow's entourage included an unattached actor with the good looks and bearing of a male model seemed suspicious to Cole. He understood that religious leaders were no less susceptible to sexual temptation than anyone else. The media ravenously exploited for public consumption every slip committed by a figurehead of the religious/moral minority. Who was the guy from Arizona—was it that tax-dodger McClure?—who allegedly left his wife at home while he flitted from crusade to crusade with a plaything half his age?

Cole eyed Shelby Hornecker and Jeremy Cannon, who stood on the tarmac separated by the Welbourns and Theresa Bordeaux, as the hired baggage handlers transferred luggage from the plane to the van. *The evidence is entirely circumstantial,* he thought. *But I wouldn't bet against the probability that they exchange spare room keys wherever they go together.*

Cole explained to the guests in dignified cop-speak that the Los Angeles Police Department was providing twenty-four-hour escort service for Rev. Hornecker only. Once Officer Tizeri delivered the remainder of the staff to the Biltmore, they were on their own. Stan Welbourn acknowledged that he had been thus informed. The ministry had made adequate provisions for transportation and security. He thanked Sergeant Cole for his kindness.

Once the baggage was loaded, Cole said to Shelby in the group's hearing, "Ma'am, we have room in the Bolt for you and another passenger. Would one of your colleagues care to ride with us?"

He was mildly surprised when, without a word from Shelby, Jeremy Cannon and the Welbourns climbed into the van and Theresa Bordeaux stepped toward the Bolt. "Theresa accompanies me wherever I go, sergeant," Shelby informed pleasantly.

I guess it would *be a little obvious for the preacher and the actor to ride in the same car*, Cole thought, as he and Jayne opened the back doors for their two passengers.

Cole drove through the runway security checkpoint and exited the airport onto Imperial Boulevard headed north. "Is there anything you would like to see on the way to the hotel, ma'am?" he asked. "Rodeo Drive? Avenue of the Stars? We're into afternoon rush hour. The traffic between here and downtown will be a challenge any way we go, so if you have a preference...."

"Thank you, sergeant, but we've been to Los Angeles numerous times, and I can't think of anywhere I care to visit on this trip."

Theresa whispered something to Shelby. "You're right, of course, Theresa!" Shelby chirped excitedly. Then they both laughed.

"Come to think of it, sergeant," the lady preacher said, "we are a little hungry. Theresa reminds me that we try to get to one of our favorite restaurants at least once when we come to L.A. Maybe this would be a good time, if it's okay with you."

"Of course, ma'am," Cole replied. "You name it, and we'll get you there. If you need reservations, we can call from here." Cole was sure they were headed to Century City or Beverly Hills.

"No reservations needed," Shelby said. "Where is the nearest In-N-Out Burger?"

"In-N-Out? The drive-through?" Jayne Watanabe exclaimed.

"I can drive you to the finest place in the city, ma'am, and you want to get a hamburger at In-N-Out?" Cole clarified in disbelief.

"Sergeant, I eat sensibly most of the time. But once in a while a body just needs to break down and enjoy a good greasy hamburger—a 'gut bomb,' as my daddy calls them. Don't you agree?" Shelby and Theresa laughed as if they hadn't enjoyed a good, hearty laugh in a long time.

"Yes, ma'am. If you like, I can have you at an In-N-Out in ten minutes," Cole said, enjoying the surprising break from the stifling formality he had expected.

"I'm buying hamburgers for everyone," Shelby said cheerily. "Keep the van in sight, sergeant. They need the In-N-Out experience too."

"Jayne, I think we're going to like this job," Cole quipped, loud enough for his guests to hear.

Forty-two

Hodge chose a quiet back-street route from his bungalow to the Coliseum, away from the teeming, late afternoon rush hour traffic on Figueroa Street. He could not afford to be seen and delayed now. Later, Hodge had decided, he would return home via Figueroa so he *could* be seen and delayed. The master had apparently ordained another test of Hodge's loyalty and perseverance, and he was prepared to meet that challenge head on. But all in good time. His appointment at the Coliseum was vital and preeminent, requiring his indirect but less noticeable approach.

Hodge cut through the peaceful University of Southern California campus and emerged onto busy Exposition Boulevard. He walked half a block west to avoid crossing at the signal in front of three dozen watching drivers. But then he had to wait several minutes for a break in the traffic, allowing him to hustle across the street—cradling his picnic chest carefully in both arms—unnoticed.

He passed through Exposition Park by circling to the east side of the Natural History Museum and approached Gate 14 to the Coliseum. The gate, which on most days stood wide open, was closed.

"Good evening, Mr. Bailey, sir," Hodge called pleasantly toward the golf cart near the gate. "Or maybe I should say afternoon, since it ain't quite evening yet."

"Yeah, Hodge," Bailey called back.

"I'd like to see Paddy for a few minutes, Mr. Bailey, if you don't mind, sir." Hodge flashed his concessionaire's holocard to remind the sullen guard that he had been cleared for access to the Coliseum and Sports Arena.

Bailey climbed out of the cart unenthusiastically and came to the gate. "I know who you are, Hodge," he said, lifting the latch and opening the gate, "but they don't." Bailey waved over his shoulder to two uniformed Los Angeles Police officers—a black woman with sergeant's stripes and a baby-faced white man fresh out of the academy—approaching the gate from the shadows of the nearest Coliseum tunnel. "So you'll have to show them your card and let them look in your box."

Hodge stepped through the gate. "You know I don't have nothing in my picnic chest, Mr. Bailey, nothing that would cause any trouble."

Bailey cursed and spat gratuitously, putting on a show of toughness for the two cops. "I know you didn't have anything in there before," he said gruffly. "But today's different, and we have to check everybody coming inside."

Hodge didn't fully expect the LAPD on duty at the Coliseum so soon. He breathed a prayer to the master as he anticipated inspection.

The sergeant eyed Hodge apprehensively. She had a short haircut and the tough appearance of someone who had fought her way out of Watts to the police force. Her name badge was inscribed L. WITT. Except for her womanly figure, she looked more like a man than the wimpy, soft-skinned rookie whose badge read T. COYLE.

"Good evening, officers," Hodge said, placing the picnic chest on the asphalt between himself and them. Then he thrust out his holocard.

Both pairs of eyes opposite him flitted from the image on the card to Hodge's face. Coyle's eyebrows lifted in disbelief at Hodge's homely appearance.

"Thank you, Mr. Hodge," Sergeant Witt said, unfazed. "What's your business in the Coliseum today?"

"I work here, ma'am, er, actually I work at the Sports Arena, but I'll be working here Friday night at the big convention. Me and Paddy have been making plans for keeping things shipshape around here on Millennium's Eve."

The sergeant looked at Bailey questioningly.

"Paddy Duckett is one of the maintenance men here," the guard answered, "the short, lazy old guy. You met him earlier today."

Both cops nodded. Then Witt said, "As a security precaution, Mr. Hodge, we need to pat you down and check your picnic box."

"Yes ma'am, officer," Hodge said, spreading his arms in a display of cooperation.

Coyle stepped behind Hodge and ran his leather-gloved hands systematically down his arms, around his torso, and down his legs. Then he lifted Hodge's Dodgers cap, checked inside, and returned it to his head. "He's clean," the rookie said, wrinkling his nose to clarify that he wasn't referring to Hodge's smelly, unwashed clothes and foul breath.

Hodge pushed the handles of his picnic chest aside and lifted the dingy white lid before either of the officers moved to do so. The weight of his knife hidden inside the lid may not have been discernible to the cops, but Hodge didn't want to take the chance.

"Anything in here we need to know about—drugs, needles, live animals?" Sergeant Witt asked, assuming a masculine squat to inspect the contents.

"No ma'am, officer. Just a bit of dinner for me and Paddy, and that old Bible of mine—I'm a very religious person, ma'am."

Witt snooped around the dog-eared Bible, two packages of freeze-dried vegetable beef soup, a small box of crackers, and a dented, stainless-steel thermos bottle. "What's in the thermos?" she asked.

"Hot coffee, ma'am."

Bailey snorted his disbelief, giving Witt cause to lift the bottle out of the box and unscrew the chrome lid and plastic stopper. The escaping steam and aroma of strong coffee testified to the bottle's contents.

"How long do you expect to be on the premises this evening?" Witt asked, as she returned the thermos to its place in the plastic chest and stood.

Hodge replaced the lid. "I'll be leaving with Paddy about 6, officer, after we've had us a bowl of soup and a chat about Millennium's Eve."

"The Coliseum floor is off limits tonight," Witt warned. "If we find you out on the field, you'll spend the night in jail."

"Yes ma'am. I'll be with Paddy in his office until we leave, ma'am."

The sergeant waved him inside. "OK, Mr. Hodge."

"Thank you, officers, thank you, Mr. Bailey," Hodge said as he headed for the Coliseum's inner caverns. Bailey grumbled his standard warning about getting back to the gate on time, and Hodge promised that he and Paddy would be there by 6.

Paddy was in the towel room as usual, finding late afternoon comfort in a bottle of wine and a bloody detective novel. He beamed at the sight of his friend Hodge as he sat up on his couch of bundled towels.

"I brought you some hot coffee, Paddy, and I'll make us each a bowl of soup in a little while," Hodge said.

Paddy, who was only half drunk, jabbered about the happenings of his day around the Coliseum as Hodge pulled the thermos bottle out of the picnic chest. The old janitor was especially excited about the arrival of the "Tinker Toy kit," the custom-designed platform for the Unity 2000 dignitaries. He was so preoccupied with his news that Hodge was able to slip two tablets of chloral hydrate into Paddy's cup of coffee undetected. The sedative dissolved almost instantly with the two sugar tablets Hodge stirred in.

"It's out there right now in a big chrome container," Paddy said, receiving the steaming cup. "They drove it through the tunnel on a flatbed truck this morning and laid it on the field with a big forklift. There's a crew coming in tomorrow to help us put it together."

Hodge nodded with feigned interest as he poured himself a cup and lifted it toward Paddy in a salute, encouraging him to drink. They both took long, slurping gulps of the hot liquid.

"That container must be locked up tight, eh, Paddy?" Hodge probed.

"Yes sir, tighter than tight."

Hodge encouraged Paddy to another sip of coffee by example. "But they left the key here so the crew could get into it tomorrow, no doubt."

"Of course, Hodge," Paddy said, taking Hodge's cue and downing another two ounces of coffee.

"So who holds the key until the work crew arrives?"

Paddy blinked hard twice as mesmerizing gremlins from the alcohol-aided sedative began marching before his eyes. He took another healthy drink, expecting the caffeine to chase them away. Instead, their numbers only increased, and Paddy's eyelids began to droop heavily.

Paddy's last words were delivered slowly, as if he had a golf ball in his mouth, "They gave the key to the only guy they could trust: me."

Paddy was reaching toward the large key ring clipped to the side of his belt when he blacked out. He toppled forward from the stack of towels like a log going over a waterfall. If Hodge hadn't jumped for him and broken his fall, Paddy would have hit the cement floor nose first.

Both cups went flying at the collision of bodies, splashing coffee over Hodge's pant leg. It was hot enough to smart but not to burn.

With difficulty Hodge wrestled Paddy's limp, dead-weight body back atop the towels to his normal position of repose. He wiped up the spilled coffee and propped Paddy's book in his hands. Hodge was unconcerned about the large wet spot on his pant leg. It would dry and blend in with the other stains before Paddy awoke.

Hodge had arrived expecting Paddy to know where the key to the platform container was, and he knew the stumpy old drunk couldn't keep from blabbing about it. But finding the key dangling from Paddy's belt was an added bonus. Hodge didn't have to go looking for it. That meant more time to place the bombs, to do it right.

Hodge located a small ring with two shiny keys clipped to Paddy's larger ring jammed with old keys, most of which no longer unlocked anything in the Coliseum. Hodge separated the smaller ring from the larger and slipped it into his pants pocket.

With Paddy sleeping peacefully, Hodge prepared for the next dangerous step in his mission. He locked the towel room door from the inside as a precaution. Then, using a screwdriver from Paddy's tool belt, he popped open the inner lining from the lid of the picnic chest and removed his knife. He slipped the sheathed blade into its resting place inside his jacket pocket.

Next, Hodge emptied the picnic chest and jimmied its plastic liner until it snapped free and was easily lifted out. There, taped five to a side where the foam insulation had once been, were the ten horns of the beast—enough latent firepower, Hodge reminded himself with awe, to tear the flesh, scatter the bones, and spill the blood of the four infidels claiming to be from God.

There is only one master—my master, he mouthed silently, touching each tape-wrapped bomb reverently. *All others will be silenced, as will their prophets, on Millennium's Eve.*

Hodge checked the watch on Paddy's slack wrist. It was 5:05 P.M. *For the next forty minutes Bailey, Witt, and Coyle will be occupied at the gate by departing workers, and two harmless old sots telling stories in the towel room will be out of their thoughts. Perfect!* Hodge thought. *Just enough time to complete this mission.*

Hodge set the inner shell of the picnic chest aside, leaving the bombs exposed. He lifted a bundle of clean white towels from a shelf above Paddy and set it on the floor beside the picnic chest for a chair. Then he pulled down another bundle of towels, dropped it beside his chair, and snapped the twine around it with his knife.

Sitting down, Hodge took a towel and cut the hem in several places. Then he tore the towel apart, dropping the strips of white terry cloth into the picnic chest. He repeated the process with a dozen towels.

After ten minutes the chest was nearly full of cloth strips. He nestled a few of Paddy's tools into the bed of terry cloth. Then he sheathed his knife and put the lid on the chest. Bits of cotton fuzz littered the cement floor like a light dusting of snow. Hodge swept them under the bottom shelves with a small push broom. Then he unscrewed the handle of the broom from the bristle end and leaned it next to the picnic chest. Meanwhile, Paddy slept on, motionless as a felled tree.

Hodge opened the door and casually checked the hallways outside. They were empty as he had expected. He returned to the towel room, picked up the chest and broom handle, and crept stealthily through the darkened halls toward the tunnel and the field.

Forty-three

During her days at USC, Beth Scibelli had spent a lot of time on Figueroa Street. It was a great place to walk and people-watch when cabin fever hit in the dorm. There were a couple of good coffee bars where students could sit and watch some of L.A.'s most entertaining weirdos stroll by. And it was a relatively safe activity—in broad daylight, as long as she was with friends and some of those friends were football players or weight lifters.

Beth enjoyed none of these advantages this Tuesday evening. It was nearly dark, she was alone, and the coffee-bar sanctuaries of Figueroa Street had become Latino gang hangouts and drug drive-throughs. And cabin fever hadn't driven her to Figueroa tonight; spooky Rev.

Wingate had. He wouldn't tell her where Hodge lived or worked; he said he didn't know. But for $40 Wingate directed her to Figueroa Street near the University where, according to him, Hodge could be found most evenings after dark.

"How near the University?" she had pressed. "A block? Six blocks? A mile? On the west side of Figueroa? East?"

Wingate was vague. "Somewhere along Figueroa. He moves around. We all do."

"After dark, but what time? After 5? After 9? After 11?"

"Hard to tell. We like the dark."

Beth ventured that had she offered Wingate $100—which she didn't have—he probably wouldn't have given her anything more specific.

Beth sat in the Star Cruiser in front of a liquor store near the corner of Figueroa and Adams, only three-quarters of a mile from the USC campus. The numerals 4:45 glared back at her from the dash display. *All I have to do*, she thought wryly, *is walk up and down Figueroa from now till dawn, eluding rapists, thieves, and murderers. If I'm lucky and don't get attacked, I may run into a man wearing a Dodgers cap and carrying a blue and white picnic chest. And with a ton more luck—make that a miracle on a par with picking all the numbers in the lottery—the guy will turn out to be the VoiceLink caller.*

Beth growled at herself for thinking that her amateur sleuthing would amount to anything. *Let the professionals handle this*, she goaded herself. *They can tell if someone is a quack or a killer, and they have all the high-tech toys to catch him and put him where he belongs. You're a writer, you're alone after dark on Figueroa, and you're overreacting. Pack it in and wait until the next phone call tomorrow. The cops will probably nail him by Thursday at the latest anyway.*

She slid the key into the ignition and prepared to fire up the engine and drive back to the library. But she couldn't do it. *I pursued a hunch at Pershing Square and, amazingly, it panned out*, she objected, in her own defense. *The bike cops tipped me off to Mr. Hodge, and Rev. Wingate told me where to look for him. I may have only lottery odds, but if I don't play them and something terrible happens, I'll never forgive myself. I must play out this hunch.*

Having made that decision, Beth had another question to answer: *Should I tell anyone what I am about to do?* She imagined calling Reagan Cole: "I just wanted you to know I'll be cruising Figueroa on foot tonight for a few hours looking for the religious nut who wants to assassinate the four televangelists. If I'm not in the Trojan Horse at 11:30, I'll still be walking."

She could almost hear his reply—which would most certainly be preceded by an expletive: "Don't you so much as talk to a panhandler on Figueroa or I'll have my men pick you up and run you in. That's no place for a woman alone after dark." No, she couldn't tell Reagan.

Beth thought about calling Mai, but anticipated the same negative response. Besides, finding the VoiceLink caller would be a tremendous scoop. She could write another book on her own experience in L.A. tracking the demented killer and saving the televangelists. It might be a bestseller. The last person you want to share a hot book idea with is another journalist, even if she is your friend.

The only other people in L.A. Beth knew to confide in were her parents, but she nixed that idea immediately. *They would call the cops on me too*, she speculated, *or even worse, they might come down here and get jumped looking for me. Better that I try to keep the killer away from them and their beloved Simon Holloway without them even knowing there is—or may be—someone stalking them.*

Beth rummaged in her purse and pulled out the little can of pepper mace she had purchased after her experience with the Latin Barons on Christmas Eve. The label promised that the lipstick-sized canister would release a blast of searing pepper mace with a touch of the button.

"I guess it's just you and me tonight," Beth said, holding up the little red and black metal canister.

Then she was surprised by an odd, almost embarrassing thought: *I should pray.* Beth hadn't prayed in years—not *really*, not *seriously*. She saw prayer as the exercise of making spiritual purchases from God. If you wanted something from God, you offered some of the equity you had accrued from good living.

But ever since she had left the church as a teenager, Beth carried only spare change in her soul. She was no flaming profligate, she knew, but neither was she a beaming saint. She expected most petitions she lifted to God to be thrown back in her face stamped INSUFFICIENT FUNDS, so she rarely prayed.

But this occasion is different, Beth reasoned. *It's top-heavy with religious overtones. The alleged attacker—and Hodge, my number-one suspect—both quote Bible verses. The intended victims are the primary religious leaders in the land. Thousands of God-fearing people will be in the Coliseum on Millennium's Eve, and they are automatically implicated in the danger. And Mai is involved, a very religious person. If God is interested in anything down here, He must be interested in this. And I'm just trying to help Him out, so why wouldn't He hear my prayer? It's certainly worth a shot.*

Beth slipped the pepper mace into her jacket pocket, closed her eyes, and crossed herself. *"Our Father, who art in heaven; hallowed—"* She stopped, and her eyes snapped open. It didn't seem right. It was too . . . mechanical. She decided to wing it.

"God, I know You're up there. I'm not a very good Christian, but I remember from somewhere in my training that You can see me anyway. I have a problem here, and I need some help solving it. I don't want anything to happen to my mother or father or Rev. Holloway or the others. But I'm worried that something bad will happen if somebody doesn't find this guy Hodge or whoever is making these phone calls. The police aren't having any luck, and I had this crazy idea about Pershing Square. So maybe I'm the one who is supposed to find him. Help me do it, God, and I will—"

Beth hesitated, trying to think of what she should promise God in exchange for His assistance. She wasn't about to promise Him anything she knew she wouldn't follow through on. And the things she *did* feel she could give—"I'll start attending mass again, at least once a month;" "I'll hang a crucifix over my bed at home;" "I'll donate part of my fees from this book to charity"—seemed cheap in comparison to what she was asking for.

After a silent moment, Beth concluded, "Help me, God . . . please. Amen." Then she crossed herself again, slung her purse over her shoulder, and stepped out onto Figueroa Street.

The faint light of the half-moon rising slowly over the rim of the empty Coliseum was sufficient for Hodge to reach the steel container quickly while affording him the privacy of near darkness. The two locks on the door of the container responded to the keys he had lifted from Paddy's belt.

Once inside with the door closed, Hodge used the flashlight borrowed from Paddy's tool kit to help him locate the 400 hollow steel tubes—each being four or six feet long and two inches in diameter—which would serve as struts for the platform. Ten of the steel tubes would receive the bombs he had prepared.

The tubes were secured to the sides of the container in disposable wooden racks, ends facing out. Each one was capped by an interlocking end piece that would be joined and secured to others to form the sturdy undergirding of the platform. Paddy's analogy was appropriate. The platform kit was like a man-sized Tinker Toy set that simply snapped together. It would take several hours for a crew of six to assemble all the pieces and erect the huge platform, Hodge calculated, but less than a second for one man to blow it apart with the tap of a button.

Hodge used Paddy's oversized vise grips to unscrew the end pieces on ten randomly selected six-foot tubes, careful to cushion the teeth of the grips with a scrap of towel so as not to leave marks. Into the first opening Hodge stuffed two or three wadded-up towel strips, ramming them midway into the tube with the broom handle. Next, he untaped one of the pipe bombs from the picnic chest, wrapped a strip of towel around it several times for a snug fit, and inserted it into the tube. A gentle push with the broom handle nestled the bomb into the center of the tube against the first wad of toweling. Hodge pushed in another wad to bookend the bomb in place, then replaced the tube's end piece. He repeated the procedure with the remaining nine uncapped tubes.

Once all the end pieces were back in place, Hodge paused a few seconds to admire his work, although now he couldn't identify which of the 400 steel struts stacked in the rack contained the lethal inserts. *The assembly crew won't be able to tell either,* he assured himself. *They probably won't even realize that the end pieces screw off, and there's no reason to remove them anyway. The bombs are well cushioned; they won't shift or rattle inside during the assembly of the platform. And the weight difference between a "loaded" tube and an empty one is negligible.*

By tomorrow night at this time the platform will be erected, and no one will suspect that it is armed for destruction, Hodge gloated. *Even LAPD's finest bomb dogs sniffing between the struts won't be able to detect the odorless explosives hidden inside the PVC, the duct tape, the toweling, and the tubes.*

Hodge slipped cautiously out of the steel container into the pale moonlight and locked the door. Moved by his success, he whispered a prayer of dedication to his master for the ten-horned beast now safely in repose inside the metal box.

Paddy awoke with Hodge shaking him brusquely. "Wake up, my friend," he heard Hodge calling. The voice seemed to come from the end of a long hallway. "Old Bailey will have our hides if we don't get to the gate in two minutes."

"Where's my coffee and soup? What happened?" the old man mumbled, disoriented, as Hodge pulled him to a sitting position on the towels.

"You dropped off, Paddy. You must have had a hard day, because you've been sleeping like a stone for almost an hour. I didn't want to disturb you, so I just sat here and read a little of your book."

Paddy squeezed his head between both palms hoping to keep his throbbing brain from exploding his skull. He tried to verbalize his confusion, but his mouth refused to operate intelligibly.

Hodge helped Paddy into his boots and hurriedly tied the laces. "You can have these soups to take home—one for tonight and one for tomorrow." Hodge stuck the two packets into the pockets of Paddy's khaki jacket and threw it over his shoulders. Then he pulled the man up onto his wobbly legs.

It was a challenge for Hodge to bolster Paddy with one arm while carrying his reassembled picnic chest with the other. But they made it to the gate and bade farewell to the grumpy guard and two cops. Hodge could hear Bailey explaining to Witt and Coyle that the two old bums often left the Coliseum "snockered." Hodge was grateful for Bailey's help in deflecting suspicion of his secret mission.

The cool night air in Exposition Park awakened Paddy so that he appeared normal: slightly drunk but functioning. "I wasn't very good company tonight, Hodge," he said, working hard to master his language.

"It's all right, Paddy. You go on home and have some soup. We'll get together again soon." Hodge sent Paddy on his way, then headed through the park toward Figueroa Street.

Forty-four

If Lieutenant Arias had not specifically instructed Sergeant Cole and Officer Watanabe to schmooze Shelby Hornecker and her staff, they would have refused the invitation for tea after they had delivered them safely to the Biltmore Hotel. "Be cordial, show them a good time, offer to take them places—that's what the chief wants," the lieutenant had said. "You're an escort on this assignment, an ambassador for L.A. You're also a cop, so carry your weapon and radio—out of sight, of course—and keep your eyes open. But try to show our guests some fun."

Driving through In-N-Out on Sepulveda Boulevard for burgers and fries was fun, even though Cole had to lighten up about food in his car to fully enjoy it. But sitting in the charming French Provincial living room of Shelby Hornecker's Biltmore suite with a room full of strangers sipping tea from a dainty china cup wasn't Cole's idea of fun. He would have preferred waiting in the Grand Avenue Bar downstairs or in the Bolt until Rev. Hornecker wanted to go somewhere. But Shelby had invited the two officers in for tea and to meet other members of her staff. So Cole put on his most ambassadorial expression and tried to look like he was enjoying himself.

The Welbourns and Ms. Bordeaux were there, but the actor was absent. Shelby explained that Mr. Cannon had hired a limo to visit friends in Hollywood. Despite the distance between the actor and the preacher since they stepped off the plane—obviously a ploy to keep up appearances—Cole still suspected that they had a secret and very personal agenda in Los Angeles.

Rev. Hornecker introduced Cole and Jayne to Mr. Darin Chaumont, "an MBA and the *real* brains behind Unity 2000," she said proudly. Cole noticed that she clearly introduced him as *Mr.* Chaumont instead of *Rev.* Chaumont, delineating him from several other ordained staffers in the room.

Darin Chaumont was in his middle thirties, small but muscular, with dark, commanding eyes and a Marine's bearing. He was immaculately dressed in a suit and accessories that Cole assumed must be at the cutting edge of style and the top end of the price scale. Chaumont displayed a huge Texas A & M class ring on his left hand—instead of a wedding band—like it was the medal of valor.

When he shook Cole's hand, Chaumont gripped hard and stared deeply into the policeman's eyes as if reading his thoughts and evaluating his spiritual state. After holding his intense pose for a full five seconds, Chaumont said with conviction in a strong southwest accent, "It's a real pleasure to meet you, sergeant." Cole was relieved, having expected the man with the soul-searching eyes to say something like, "How are things between you and God, sergeant?"

Cole survived several minutes of small talk in the large group. But when telephone calls and staff discussions began to break the group into smaller clusters, Cole and Jayne saw their chance to escape. They caught Shelby's eye long enough to mouth their thanks and wave goodbye. Shelby and her team were apparently in for the night, so their escorts were free to sit out the remainder of the P.M. shift drinking coffee in the Grand Avenue Bar.

They had just reached the entry of the suite when an authoritative voice intercepted them. "May I have a minute of your time, sergeant?"

Cole turned into the penetrating eyes of Darin Chaumont. "Of course, sir," he answered crisply, as if to a superior officer.

Chaumont motioned them into the hall, then dismissed Jayne cordially but pointedly with, "It was a pleasure to meet you, Officer Watanabe. I hope to see you tomorrow."

When they were alone in the hall, Chaumont spoke softly. "I have been in Los Angeles for most of this month preparing for Unity 2000, and I have made some fine friends among the local media. A few of them have hinted to me, strictly off the record, that a series of death threats targeting Rev. Hornecker and the other ministers has been received through the VoiceLink line at the *Los Angeles Times*. Is that true, sergeant?"

Cole was stunned by Chaumont's directness. *No wonder he's heading up Unity 2000 and climbing the ladder with Hornecker's church. This is a man on a mission.*

"Sir, in a city this size, death threats against anyone in the public eye are, unfortunately, quite common. It would not be unusual—"

"You're speaking in generalities, sergeant; I'm speaking in specifics," Chaumont pressed urgently. "I know that you and Officer Watanabe wouldn't be here unless your chief was concerned. Our organization has already lost its founder to an unknown violent and unconscionable faction. I am not going to allow that to happen again here.

"I've tried to get the story about these threats, but the *L.A. Times*

299

won't talk to me and the LAPD won't talk to me either. Please answer my question, sergeant. Are you aware of telephone calls to the *Times* threatening injury or death to Rev. Hornecker and the others?"

Darin Chaumont's eyes bored into Cole, not in anger or vengeance, but in a resolute effort to mine the truth.

Cole had been cautioned against revealing too much about the VoiceLink calls to Shelby Hornecker or her people. But Darin Chaumont had already heard too much, and he wasn't about to be deterred from the full truth by abstract pleasantries.

Cole returned Darin Chaumont's scrutinizing gaze. "Mr. Chaumont, I'm not in the inner circle on this matter, but I will tell you what I know. In return, I want your assurance that you won't do anything without talking to me or to one of the other officers who have been assigned to Rev. Hornecker. The last thing we need is a state of panic in your organization or in our city that provokes counterproductive actions."

Chaumont studied Cole a moment longer, measuring, calculating, and evaluating his offer. "All right, sergeant," he said finally, relaxing his posture. "That's fair enough."

Chaumont invited Cole into his suite and offered him coffee and Coke, which Cole declined. Once the two men were comfortably seated in the living room, Cole related what he had learned about the VoiceLink caller from briefing and from the *Times* through Beth Scibelli, to whom he referred simply as "a contact with the *Times*."

It crossed Cole's mind as he spoke that some of the information he had received from Beth was now suspect in light of the lie he had caught her in earlier in the day. So he shared with Darin Chaumont only the information from Beth he had substantiated through the LAPD.

Cole discussed the poetic nature of the last two messages, the violent overtones in the biblical-sounding content, and the fact that the caller appeared to be in the middle of a morbid series of calls condemning and threatening the four religious leaders coming to Los Angeles. To his knowledge, Cole clarified, no names had been mentioned in the calls, only inferences which the police and the *Times* linked to the four leaders.

Finally, Cole stated his conviction that the caller was a religious nut who was getting his jollies raising a ruckus over the phone instead of on a street corner. He assured Chaumont that LAPD detectives were tracking the calls and analyzing the messages. *The suspect is a clever but presumably harmless amateur,* Cole stressed. *The police will nail him long before the festivities at the Coliseum begin on Millennium's Eve.*

Chaumont drank in the information, and Cole could almost hear the man's MBA brain dissecting and processing it.

"Tell me more about the biblical content of the messages," Chaumont said.

Cole related what he remembered. When he mentioned the term "four horsemen," Chaumont pulled a thin leather New Testament from his inside coat pocket and flipped quickly to a passage near the back of the book. Then he traced his finger rapidly across sections of text and read snatches aloud describing the four horsemen.

Cole pointed to the New Testament. "Is there anything in those verses about torn flesh, broken bones, or blood? And doesn't it say 'Woe to thee'—or something like that—about each of the riders?"

"No, there's nothing like that in this passage."

Cole's expression reflected puzzlement. "In the phone messages he says 'Woe to thee' to the riders and then he says the same thing about each one: 'Thy bones will be broken . . . smashed . . . or something, thy flesh will be torn, and thy blood will pour into the earth.' That's not in there?"

Chaumont shook his head. "I don't recall that kind of phraseology anywhere in the Bible. The man has probably concocted his message from different sections of the Bible or out of his own head." Then he hissed in disdain. "That's how religious nuts *become* religious nuts, sergeant. Instead of accepting the Bible the way it is, they cut and paste phrases out of context, do away with some sections, and stir in their own heretical ideas in order to make it say what they want it to say."

"That proves my point about this guy being a crackpot," Cole interjected. "He's just like all the other kooks in the advanced stages of millennium fever who predict that the world is going to end at the stroke of midnight on Friday night. They're not planning to *cause* the end of the world; they just expect it to happen based on their hairbrained calculations or drug-induced hallucinations.

"The VoiceLink caller has fabricated this horrendous vision of God's judgment directed at Mrs. Hornecker and the other three. But I don't think he's planning to *make* something horrible happen. Rather, in his twisted little brain or in his tea leaves or in his cockeyed version of the Bible, he has found something causing him to *expect* something to happen, and he has come up with this cute little method of predicting it. When Unity 2000 is over, he'll probably walk away scratching his head, wondering why it didn't happen."

Chaumont nodded thoughtfully. "So you assume that our caller expects this bloody judgment to fall on Friday night in the Coliseum."

"Considering that all four leaders will be there together and that the world will be watching, yes, it seems a logical time and place—even though nuts like this don't always subscribe to laws of logic."

"And you think he will attend the gathering at the Coliseum Friday night hoping to see the sword of judgment fall, as it were."

Cole was ready for the discussion to end. He was tired of debating the probabilities of destruction on Millennium's Eve. He was tired of Darin Chaumont's persistence in blowing the situation out of proportion.

"If we don't find him first," Cole said with a sigh, "yes, I suppose he will be in the crowd somewhere. No offense intended, Mr. Chaumont, but your deal on Friday night is going to bring all kinds of creeps out from under the sidewalk." *Well, maybe I intended a* little *offense,* Cole mused.

"I'm aware of that, sergeant," Chaumont replied. "We are well prepared to deal with street-corner prophets seeking a hearing, religious demonstrators of every stripe, and the general rabble that is attracted by something promising free admission. We have a well-trained corps of lay ushers and a battalion of security police to back them up. We're prepared for everything from one person delivering an ill-timed ecstatic utterance to a thousand people conducting a sit-in on the Coliseum floor.

"What we're *not* prepared for, sergeant, is a mad bomber who intends to kill at least four people and who could kill and injure hundreds or thousands more. That's what it sounds like, don't you think? This person is expecting to see—if not plotting to detonate himself—an explosion that will fulfill his prophecy of people being reduced to torn flesh, broken bones, and spilled blood."

Cole ran a hand through his thin sandy hair, thinking it a more acceptable expression of his frustration than swearing or slamming his fist on the mahogany table next to his chair. He would get a grip on himself and go over it once more, but that was all.

"Mr. Chaumont, I repeat: The chances that the caller is actually planning harm to Mrs. Hornecker, Mr. Holloway, Mr. Dunne, and Mr. McClure, are slim to micro-slim. And the chances that he can pull it off, even if he is planning it, are infinitesimally slim.

"In order to reduce those chances to zero, first, we are monitoring his calls, and we'll probably catch him before he gets anywhere near the Coliseum.

"Second, we will be running a full bomb team through the Coliseum Friday afternoon. If there's a bomb in there, we'll find it and get rid of it.

"Third, your security officers are going to screen everyone coming into the Coliseum on Friday. The sneakiest crook in the world won't be able to get so much as a water pistol past that equipment.

"Granted, a guy could always launch a missile from a few miles away or fly an attack helicopter over the Coliseum or—"

Darin Chaumont halted Cole mid-sentence with a raised hand, signaling that Cole had made his point and that his absurd digression was unnecessary.

"What about tomorrow night?" Chaumont asked.

"Tomorrow night?"

"I have been informed by the local affairs subcommittee that all four leaders have been invited to visit a mission in the area—I believe it's called King's House—located in an old hospital. Three of the four have confirmed their intention to attend, and Dr. McClure may also show up at the last minute. What's to prevent someone from trying to harm them there?"

Cole knew of the meeting, of course. It was on Shelby Hornecker's printed itinerary given to him at briefing. And Beth had gushed to him about how she had been invited to attend with her friend from the *Times*. But Cole hadn't considered the meeting a potential danger to Hornecker, Holloway, Dunne, and McClure.

"Me, I guess," Cole answered, "along with Officer Watanabe and the other police escorts. It's a private meeting—no media allowed, no public announcements about it. As I understand it, the meeting was arranged at the last minute, just this week. I doubt that our mysterious caller knows anything about it.

"Besides, the old Queen of Angels Hospital is in a pretty rough area, not the kind of place people congregate to catch a glimpse of their favorite religious leader. If you're concerned about Mrs. Hornecker, you can always keep her locked up here. But I think the eight cops on site will be able to handle anything that comes down."

Chaumont sat silently for a moment, then said, "Yes, I think so too."

He stood, signifying that the meeting was over. Cole stood with him, grateful to be going. "Sergeant, I apologize for annoying you with my questions and worst-case scenarios," Chaumont said, walking Cole to the door. "I take Rev. Hornecker's security very seriously; it's my job. But sometimes my concern comes across as nitpicking. I'm sorry."

Cole said nothing, surprised at Chaumont's transparency but feeling that he deserved an apology.

They reached the door and Chaumont turned to face him. "I know you're right about the unlikelihood of these threats being carried out. But I would appreciate your keeping me informed of any developments toward apprehending the caller. And you can be assured that I will keep it confidential."

"I'll let you know if I hear anything," Cole said.

Chaumont thrust out his hand and again gripped Cole's firmly. "Sergeant, I'm very pleased to have you with us. Thank you for taking the time to help me work through my concerns." There was no doubting the sincerity in his strong eyes.

Riding the elevator down to the bar, Cole thought about Beth again. He regretted that he had recoiled suspiciously from her on the phone. *I should have confronted her right then*, he chastised himself for the umpteenth time since he had talked to her. *There's probably a logical explanation, and when she tells me I'll feel pretty stupid.*

He thought again about calling her, and even reached for his pocket phone as the elevator slowly descended. *No,* he thought, *I need to do this in person. I need to look Beth in the eye when I ask her why she lied to me. I'll do it tonight when I meet her at the Trojan Horse.*

Forty-five

Beth stood at the busy corner of Figueroa Street and Martin Luther King Boulevard waiting for the light to change. She was tired and discouraged, and her ankle hurt from walking. She had spent an hour snooping in liquor stores, bars, and greasy diners on the west side of the crowded four-lane street. She had even peeked into a few darkened doorways and alleys, guardedly keeping the traffic on Figueroa in view and gripping the tube of pepper mace in her pocket. But she had not seen a blue and white picnic chest or a man matching the cops' description of the mysterious Mr. Hodge.

There was no reason to go farther south, she figured. She would cross Figueroa here and double back to her car investigating the one-mile stretch on the east side of the street. Maybe the man with the picnic chest—or someone who knew something about him—would turn up. But Beth's hopes were again beginning to flag.

Trying to talk to people about Hodge had been as fruitless as looking for him. Many of the men and women she questioned wrinkled their brows and responded in a Hispanic or Oriental dialect. Many others simply ignored her. Some leered at her or propositioned her. Repulsed by the seedier types she encountered, Beth quietly amused herself by imagining how they would respond to a blast from the little canister in her pocket. Then she kept walking.

A few people on the street had allowed her to state her concern in full. "I'm looking for a friend of my father, an older man wearing a jean jacket, a Dodgers cap, and carrying a blue and white picnic chest. I must find him; it's a matter of life and death. Have you seen him?" But these people responded only with blank looks and negative shakes of the head. Beth was beginning to wonder if weird old Wingate had fleeced her of $40 only to send her on a wild goose chase.

Beth had considered leaving Figueroa to investigate Exposition Park. She knew the shadowy paths around the Coliseum and Sports Arena well from her college days. *It's possible,* she conjectured, extrapolating her flimsy theory, *that Mr. Hodge could be spending a lot of time around the Coliseum in preparation for Millennium's Eve.*

But Beth also knew the dangers of walking those dark, quiet paths alone. One can of pepper mace wasn't enough protection, so she stayed on the main drag, convincing herself that if Figueroa Street *was* Hodge's turf, he would come out of the dark sooner or later.

It had occurred to Beth shortly after she began her sweep down Figueroa that she had no idea what she would say to Hodge—or do with him—if indeed she found him. *That says something about your hollow expectations, Beth,* she derided herself. *If you really hoped to find him, you would have thought about some ways to stop him or turn him in.* She played out a ridiculous scene of unpreparedness in her head: *"Are you the VoiceLink caller, the man who is prophesying mayhem for the four televangelists?"*

"Yes, I am."

"Are you really planning to carry out this threat, I mean, blow them up or something?"

"Yes, they will all be dead before the new millennium dawns."

"Well, I was right then. My premonition about Pershing Square wasn't groundless after all. Thank you, Mr. Hodge. I just needed to know that. Have a nice day."

But maybe she wouldn't even get to the "have a nice day" part. *The guy may hear the words "VoiceLink caller" and snap. Realizing his plot is foiled, he may whip out a gun and wreak mayhem on me.*

Chilled by the thought, Beth had decided early in her walk down Figueroa that she would play out her hunch without attempting to play the hero. As far as Mr. Hodge was concerned—if, God helping her, she was lucky enough to find him—she was simply looking for a friend of her father who preaches about the four horsemen and judgment to come.

When Hodge declined to know her father—as he surely would since the story was pure fiction—Beth would try to get him talking, about his religious background and beliefs. Then she would ask him what he thought about Unity 2000 and Shelby Hornecker, Simon Holloway, T.D. Dunne, and Morgan McClure. She might even ask if he had heard anything about the disturbing calls to the *Times*.

But she would keep her distance, remaining on the street in plain view of busy Figueroa. If he seemed at all suspicious, if he sounded anything like the VoiceLink caller, she would play dumb and pull back. She would thank him for his help, give him $20 for his trouble, and excuse herself. Then she would keep him in sight and call Reagan—no, she would call the detectives working on the case and surprise Reagan with the news after they picked him up.

She would finally be able to breathe easy about her parents' involvement in the big rally on Millennium's Eve. And she would walk away from the experience with a juicy side-bar for her Unity 2000 book.

But everything hinges on finding Mr. Hodge, she thought, as the light finally flashed WALK, inviting her to cross. *And so far the Pershing Square tramp hasn't materialized.* She had already wasted valuable writing time playing Ms. Detective. She was leaving far too much work for the precious few days she had allotted herself to finish the book at home. She had to get back to the library tonight and make serious headway.

Beth crossed Figueroa in the glaring beams of an idling field of cars poised behind the crosswalk ready to resume the race for home when the light turned green. She would check out the east side of Figueroa as she had the west. If she still turned up a blank, she would go back to Pershing Square tomorrow and lean on Wingate a little harder—if he hadn't disappeared with her money. And, if need be, she would be back on Figueroa as soon as it turned dark.

Twenty minutes later Hodge walked out of the shadows of the park and crossed Exposition Boulevard with the light. He ambled up the west side of Figueroa past a few store fronts until he came to the hole-in-the-wall taqueria where he ate once or twice a week. He laid his money on the counter and flashed two fingers, the only communication the Latinos behind the counter needed to serve their English-speaking patrons.

Hodge sat on his picnic chest in front of the taqueria slowly munching his dinner. He had been told to expect a curious visitor. "Sit and wait, and the inquisitor will appear," he had been instructed. So he waited and watched the passing cars and occasional pedestrians chancing a walk down Figueroa.

The visitor is an infidel, an enemy of the cause, no doubt, Hodge pondered with anticipation. *How the master loves to test me, and how I love to prove myself worthy of his call.*

After forty-five minutes he bought a can of pop and returned to his seat to drink it slowly. No one came. After another forty-five minutes he stood. He chanced a look inside the taqueria, focusing on a tiny booth in the back where another customer sat in semidarkness. The man in the booth caught Hodge's glance and shrugged almost imperceptibly. Hodge picked up his picnic chest and headed home.

Forty-six

Shelby Hornecker sat at the bedroom table in a pink satin robe and slippers staring at her computer screen. She was supposed to be adding the finishing touches to the keynote address to be memorized and delivered Friday evening at Unity 2000. But her mind, like a fidgety horse resisting a bit and bridle, kept jerking away from her duty. Jeers of unworthiness, which had been muted all day by the whirl of activity, echoed through her soul in the quiet of her room.

With each taunt she mounted a counterattack by silently reciting a doubt-defeating statement Adrian had taught her before they were even married: "By faith I confessed my sin; by faith I received my forgiveness; evil thoughts be gone." It worked. But instead of returning to her task each time the doubts were quieted, she found herself reliving the hours of grace and wonder that followed her fall.

She saw saintly Soledad and Lupe Cruz and their cozy haven out in the stick brush of South Texas. She felt the warmth of innocent, cherubic Antonia, the symbol of God's acceptance and forgiveness in the early morning hours of her surrender. And she heard God's command, clearly but curiously conveyed in a dream through the voices of Jeremy Cannon, Soledad Cruz, and a tall, black African stranger, "Feed My sheep."

These three words, which recurred in her brain as if cued by an automatic timer, further distracted Shelby from her sermon notes. She reflected on how the words powerfully and poignantly burned into her subconsciousness as she slept that night at the Cruzes. But she also remembered with distaste the backdrop of each scene: the Victory Life auditorium infiltrated by bedraggled, nontithing parishioners; the South Texas range land and countless numbers of impoverished Hispanics and Native Americans adrift like flotsam and jetsam on a sea of brush; and the cold, gray canyons of this city—Los Angeles—teeming with the human refuse of a society which had learned to recycle everything except its noncontributing citizens.

That's not my calling, Lord; those aren't my sheep, she objected at the recurrence of each scene. Then she tried to force herself back to the message of unity and hope for the American church she was struggling to compose. But her ideas, capsulized by a screen full of notes on her computer, seemed so hollow, so contrived—like Unity 2000 itself.

There must be something more significant about all these believers being in L.A. There must be something more inspiring I can say than, "We really need to cooperate better; now God bless you, and have a nice millennium."

That's when the accusations would start up again. *"You? Provide something significant for all these Christians? After what you have done?"*

Shelby had been through the cycle half a dozen times in an hour's time when she released an exasperated sigh, switched off her computer, and tapped three numbers on her bedroom phone.

"Would you like to go for a ride?" she asked. "I need to get out of here for awhile."

"But it's almost 9 o'clock, dear," Theresa answered from her bedroom. "Isn't it a little unsafe riding around L.A. at this hour?"

"We have a police escort, for heaven's sake," Shelby countered. "And I'll bet you a dollar to a donut hole that the sergeant's car is even bulletproof."

"Are you . . . okay?" her assistant probed.

Shelby knew Theresa was referring specifically to her emotional state. "Yes, I'm fine. But writer's block has me by the throat. I need some air. I'm so antsy, even being out in the brown air of the city sounds good to me."

"Okay, I'll call Jeeves the chauffeur and have him meet us in the parking garage in ten minutes."

Sergeant Cole and Officer Watanabe were on time. Shelby and Theresa had agreed on slacks and sweaters—nothing fancy or flashy. They persuaded the sergeant to remove his tie so as not to look so official.

"Where to?" Cole inquired, driving up the garage ramp and turning east on Fourth Street.

"Just a little drive please, sergeant," Theresa said. "We're in the throes of an attack of cabin fever."

"And writer's block," Shelby added.

"Sounds like a soothing, hot latte to go might be a good place to start," Jayne suggested.

"Bravo, Officer Jayne!" chirped Theresa. "Would you and the sergeant be interested in a full-time escort job? Dallas is a lovely city. And Rev. Hornecker's congregation just presented her with a new Lincoln Tour de Grace."

"Very tempting, ma'am," Cole said, chuckling, "especially if all the people there are as nice as you two ladies."

Shelby laughed. "I think we're out of luck, Theresa. The sergeant is obviously headed for a successful career in politics."

Two minutes later Cole pulled to the curb in front of a dive called Ugly Frank's and brought out two large steaming lattes in disposable cups. The officers had declined drinks, having spent the last three hours in the Grand Avenue Bar swilling coffee.

Sergeant Cole drove his charges through Chinatown, the garment district, and a few areas CityLine Tours usually omits. When he drove them around Olvera Street, Shelby asked if he knew of a good Mexican restaurant where her staff could eat in reasonable privacy before the King's House meeting. It took Cole less than a minute to get Raphaela Quintero on the phone and reserve the banquet room for 5:30. But it took another five minutes for him to wrap up the conversation with his excited Mexican mamacita.

Shelby whispered an idea to Theresa, then Theresa said, "Sergeant, may we make a request?"

"Of course, ma'am."

"Do you know where that old hospital is, the location for the meeting tomorrow night?"

"Queen of Angels Hospital? Yes, ma'am. It's in the Echo Park area, overlooking the Hollywood Freeway."

"Is it close—close enough to drive by?" Shelby asked.

"It's close enough, but Echo Park is not exactly on the Chamber of Commerce's list of showcase sites for out-of-town dignitaries. It's a pretty shabby neighborhood."

"We've seen all the showcase sites, sergeant," Theresa chimed in. "We're ready to see the rest, especially since we have a meeting there tomorrow night. May we please drive by King's House, and then perhaps take a quick loop around the Coliseum?"

"No problem, ma'am."

Cole took the Hollywood Freeway west to Alvarado, then turned north. At Kent Street he plunged into the old, run-down neighborhood surrounding the complex of dirty white Spanish-style buildings that a half-century earlier was one of Los Angeles' premier health care facilities.

Shelby and Theresa stared out the window as Cole drove slowly through the front parking lot on Bellevue between the main entrance to King's House and the westbound lanes of the Hollywood Freeway. Then he proceeded around the other three sides of the block-square facility. The two officers kept a wary eye out for any problems on the street.

King's House looked anything but asleep at 9:30. Many lights were on, and there was a trickle of foot traffic in and out at the front and rear of the main building.

"This place is enormous," Shelby breathed in awe. "This is not the hole-in-the-wall skidrow mission I expected."

Theresa was equally impressed. "Where do they get the money to keep a facility of this size going? It must cost thousands of dollars a week just to keep the doors open. I mean, this is an entire hospital!"

After circumnavigating the facility once, Cole began to drive out of the neighborhood. But Shelby asked him to return to the front of the building.

"Do either of you know anything about this place?" Shelby asked, as the Bolt sat idling in the parking lot.

Cole began, "The hospital was built in the '20s by one of the Catholic—"

"Not the building, the organization that operates it now—King's House. Is some church doing this? Is the Salvation Army involved?"

Cole glanced at his partner for help.

"Don't look at me, sarge," Jayne said with a grin. "I'm new to downtown. Besides, I have a Shinto and Mormon background. I don't know much about your evangelical Christian organizations."

Cole mentally assembled the scraps of information he had collected on King's House over the last few days, most of them from talking with Beth. "From what I've heard, it's run by a nonprofit organization headed by a Vietnamese guy and his wife. They take in hard-core down-and-outers, hoping to turn them around. I think they also work with ex-cons, trying to get them jobs and providing housing if they need it. And they have some kind of a hospice for AIDS victims who are near the end."

At that moment a black minivan eased into the parking lot and pulled closely alongside the Bolt on the sergeant's side. The front windows of each vehicle slid down soundlessly. "Well, Sergeant Huntley," Cole said to the woman in the front passenger seat of the van. "It looks like King's House is a popular attraction for our guests tonight."

It took a few seconds for the comment to register with Shelby. Then she looked into the back window of the van and found herself locked eye to eye with Simon Holloway.

A flash of anxiety coursed through her. She was surprised and embarrassed at the involuntary defensive reaction. *Anxiety may be appropriate for a boxer who happens to run into his opponent in a back alley a few days before the big fight,* she thought, wincing, *but not for two Christian leaders meeting by chance for the first time.*

Since eye contact had been made, there was no way Shelby could avoid speaking to Simon Holloway. Nor did she feel right about avoiding him, even though she would have preferred waiting until tomorrow night. Shelby pulled down her window with a tap of her finger. Simon Holloway did the same.

"Rev. Hornecker," Holloway greeted her with a businesslike tone and expression.

"It's a pleasure to meet you, Rev. Holloway. But please call me Shelby." Had the two vehicles been a foot closer, Shelby would have extended her hand to him through the open window.

Holloway appeared startled by Shelby's friendly approach. But his expression quickly turned to guarded acceptance. "And I'm Simon," he said.

As their police escorts talked shop through the front windows, Shelby and Holloway introduced their fellow-travelers through the back windows: Theresa, Grace Ellen, and the Holloway's two boys, Mark and Tim.

Grace Ellen Holloway immediately took over the conversation for her reserved husband. As if greeting an old friend, she asked Shelby about her trip and her accommodations at the Biltmore. Then she told about the family's day on Catalina Island and their sobering excursion to Tijuana, from which they had returned only an hour ago.

"It wasn't at all what we expected," Grace Ellen explained. She leaned across her husband's lap to talk. Simon Holloway listened halfheartedly to the women chat, looking like he would rather be some-where else.

"We went to Tijuana for the shopping, but we could hardly buy anything because of the poverty . . . the children begging at the border and in the streets . . . the hovels of tin and cardboard in the riverbeds . . . it's difficult to think about buying a new leather coat when the children at your elbow don't have anything to eat."

Shelby responded with the appropriate remarks, then changed the subject, which didn't bother Grace Ellen at all. Shelby didn't want to talk about disadvantaged people. Wherever she turned, thoughts and pictures and memories of them found her, and with them came the puzzling command: "Feed My sheep." *I have not been called to be Mother Teresa to the poor of Tijuana or Echo Park or Cotulla, Texas or even Dallas*, she objected again to the persistent thought.

Despite the discomfiting topic Grace Ellen had unwittingly brought up, Shelby liked her. Here was someone who was ensconced in the thick of Unity 2000 with her husband and aware of the tensions be-tween its principle players. But she was totally unfazed by it all. In four minutes of conversation with Shelby, Grace Ellen's agenda was simply to extend a hand of friendship. And Shelby found that gesture by the wife of a powerful Christian leader irresistible.

Just before the windows were raised, the two women expressed their delight at meeting each other and their hope to visit longer at King's House tomorrow night.

As the Bolt left Echo Park and headed toward the Coliseum, Shelby leaned close to Theresa and spoke for her ears only, "Maybe she's the one."

" 'The one' what?"

"I need a spiritual mentor—a peer, an equal—who identifies with the kind of life I lead, someone who will hold me accountable, some-one I can meet with four or five times a year for counsel, advice, and prayer."

"Mrs. Holloway? Your spiritual mentor?" Theresa gasped.

"Theresa, it must be someone from outside Victory Life, an objective observer."

"But Simon Holloway is—"

Shelby stopped her by placing a calming hand on her arm. "Don't worry, dear. I'm not saying she *is* the one. But Grace Ellen Holloway looks like the kind of person I could open up to. Let's just make it a matter of prayer, okay?"

Theresa smiled thinly and agreed, but her eyebrows communicated a you-never-cease-to-amaze-me exclamation.

The drive to the Coliseum took fifteen minutes. Shelby watched in prayerful silence while the Bolt circled the park clockwise, giving her a clear view of the Coliseum from Exposition Boulevard, Menlo Avenue,

Martin Luther King Boulevard, and Figueroa. She was struck by the thought that Unity 2000 was bigger than the sum of its parts. *God may have more planned for Friday night than anyone can imagine*, she mused. It was a frightful and exciting thought.

"I'm ready to head back, sergeant," she said after one loop. "Thank you."

Cole turned the Bolt north on Figueroa to head back downtown. Traffic was moderate, and Shelby was surprised at the numbers of street people, mostly men, dotting the sidewalks and doorways along the route toward city center.

These were the kinds of people she saw in her dream, when the black man confronted her on a downtown street and said, "Feed My sheep." Her heart went out to these people, but she had no idea how she could help them.

She focused on several individuals on the street as the sergeant drove on . . . a long-haired Native American man without a coat sipping from a bottle, leaning on a building for support . . . a black kid no older than nine hanging out with a couple of has-been gang members high on drugs and hustling change from a few tourists on the street . . . a bona fide bag lady dressed in layers of clothes and pushing a shopping cart full of valueless possessions.

Shelby didn't want to look anymore. But just before she leaned back in the seat, she noticed another man on the street who stood out from the others. Not in appearance. He was also forlorn-looking, an older man in a baseball cap walking briskly along Figueroa, probably carrying all his worldly goods in the picnic chest swinging at his side.

But he seemed different in attitude. Others on the street were lolling, loitering, waiting for a scrap of good fortune to blow their way in the breeze. But the man with the picnic chest was moving purposefully. The scene reminded her of a sermon illustration Adrian had often used: God's people are like ships on the sea. He will direct us through life, but He can't do it unless we run up the sails, catch the breeze, and start moving.

So many of these souls on the street are dead in the water, Shelby thought. *They're not going anywhere because they don't put out the effort to start moving. But this man is moving. He will probably amount to something someday*, she judged, as she sat back for the ride.

Forty-seven

Reagan Cole had hoped to talk to Beth before the two of them met Curtis Spooner in the Trojan Horse. The more he thought about her blatant lie, the more he wanted get to the bottom of it. Earlier in the day he had doubted his wisdom in getting involved with Beth, but he couldn't escape his attraction to her and his deep feelings for her. Cole didn't like playing games, however, pretending he didn't know something when he did. He had decided that the best way to reconcile his feelings with Beth's actions was to confront her before Spooner showed up.

But it didn't happen. When Cole walked into the bustling lounge at 11:20, Beth and Spooner were already at the table talking. Cole reluctantly resigned to play dumb until he could speak to her alone.

Cole sat down and ordered a beer. Spooner was talking animatedly about the Blazers' good practice and how they were ready to tear the Clippers apart tomorrow night. He offered two VIP tickets to Beth, explaining that T.D. Dunne and his wife had cancelled their plans to attend the game due to a high-level Unity 2000 meeting. Beth regretfully declined the tickets, citing that she had been invited to the same meeting. Cole chimed in that he would also be at the meeting as the police escort for Shelby Hornecker.

"If this is such a hot meeting, why wasn't I invited?" Spooner joked.

Cole and Beth laughed, and then the conversation began to run thin. Spooner noticed that his two friends seemed strangely quiet, especially toward each other. Beth talked a little about the VoiceLink caller's latest message, but said nothing about how she had spent the rest of her day. And Cole didn't ask. Cole seemed especially reserved, mentioning only that he had picked up Shelby Hornecker at LAX and had spent most of the evening drinking coffee with his partner.

Spooner tried to keep the conversation alive by talking about basketball—the Blazers' chances in the Pacific Division, the recent trade between the Lakers and the Knicks. But soon he picked up the hint that a three-way conversation wasn't working tonight.

"Well, I'm going to let you two close this place by yourselves," Spooner said, taking a last sip of beer. "I need my beauty sleep tonight. Tomorrow is game day, and I have an early appointment with Dunne at the Century Plaza to talk over the game plan for Friday night at the Coliseum."

"Meet us here after the game tomorrow? Same time?" Cole asked.

"Sure."

"And you're moving into my place tomorrow night?" Cole asked.

"If it's still okay with you, Reag."

"Fine, no problem. Do you have a car?"

"Yeah. Rented a nice, big Caddy today. I didn't like the idea of riding around L.A. all weekend on the back of your Kawasaki."

Cole and Beth wished him a good game. Spooner said good-bye and left the lounge, signing a few autographs on the way out.

Beth took a breath to speak, grateful for Spooner's early departure so she could ask the details about Cole's day with Shelby Hornecker. But Cole spoke first.

"I have to ask you a question, Beth, and I need a straight answer." Cole's tone was serious but free of accusation. "When we talked on the phone today, you told me you were at the library. But I happen to know that you were *not* at the library when we talked, because that's where I was. I thought we had something good going, Beth, but after that call today, I'm perplexed. I need to ask you: Why did you lie to me?"

Beth cringed inside and cursed at herself for her foolishness. *So that's why he sounded so cool on the phone today*, she thought.

Beth considered for an instant covering up with another story. But she couldn't think of another story. She could try to joke her way out of it, but Cole's expression predicted that he would not be amused. She felt terrible about jeopardizing her relationship with Reagan Cole. But she couldn't tell him about Pershing Square and Wingate and Hodge — not yet, anyway.

She let out a sigh of surrender. Her head was down, and she picked nervously at the paper coaster under her glass. "I feel very stupid. You're right. I lied to you. I wasn't at the library. But — and I hope you understand this — I can't tell you where I was or what I was doing."

Beth looked into Cole's eyes, searching for an accepting glimmer that communicated, "It's okay; no problem; I forgive you." But all she saw were more questions.

"It's nothing about us," she continued, laying her hand on the back of his. "I'm not seeing anyone else this week; I don't want to see anyone else. It's just that I have some things to do in relation to my work — call it research — that I can't discuss yet. I know I should have told you that over the phone instead of . . . lying. It was a spur-of-the-moment decision — a bad choice — and I'm really sorry."

"Are you involved in anything illegal?" Cole asked, more from concern than to confront or accuse.

"No, nothing illegal."

"Are you doing anything foolhardy or dangerous, like the other night?"

Beth knew Cole was referring to her experience with the Latin Barons on the San Diego Freeway. She didn't want to lie again, but she realized she had to stretch the truth to the limit with her answer.

She thought of the caution she had taken during her search of Figueroa Street — staying close to the street, keeping the canister of mace at the ready. Her evening on the street may have been a *little* foolhardy and a *little* dangerous. Reagan Cole would surely consider it so. But Beth knew her capabilities and her limitations, and she felt she was acting within them.

"I've learned my lesson, Reagan," she said, looking into his eyes. "I won't put myself in that position again."

Reagan returned Beth's gaze and gripped both of her hands in his. He didn't know whether to believe her or not. He knew of the many dangers lurking in L.A. for beautiful young women like Beth. *She is smart, strong, and spirited—so much so that she isn't about to let a man coddle her overprotectively. But is she wise enough to stay out of trouble? O God, I hope so,* he thought.

At Beth's prodding, Cole gave his account of meeting Shelby Hornecker at the airport, driving through In-N-Out, enduring the tea party in her suite, getting the third degree from Darin Chaumont, and taking the late-night drive to King's House where they bumped into the Holloway family.

Beth talked in detail about the VoiceLink message aimed at Shelby Hornecker and carefully avoided mentioning anything about Pershing Square or her suspicions about a soapbox prophet named Hodge. Cole reminded her that the caller would give himself away before long and be caught. Beth glowed inside at the prospect that the caller had already given himself away in Pershing Square and that she might have a hand in catching him.

After midnight the crowd in the lounge began to thin. With their hands interlocked and heads close together, Cole and Beth found their conversation turning to more intimate subjects: their bizarre meeting on the freeway, their laughable first impressions, the magnetism they felt playing one-on-one at midnight, their first kiss, the dreamy prospects of being together Millennium's Eve. Captivated by each other's presence, they adjourned to the privacy of the parking garage to say good-night properly.

NOVEMBER 1999						
S	M	T	W	T	F	S
	1	2	3	4	5	6
7	8	9	10	11	12	13
14	15	16	17	18	19	20
21	22	23	24	25	26	27
28	29	30				

1999 DECEMBER 1999

S	M	T	W	T	F	S
			1	2	3	4
5	6	7	8	9	10	11
12	13	14	15	16	17	18
19	20	21	22	23	24	25
26	27	28	29	30	31	

JANUARY 2000						
S	M	T	W	T	F	S
						1
2	3	4	5	6	7	8
9	10	11	12	13	14	15
16	17	18	19	20	21	22
23	24	25	26	27	28	29
30	31					

(2) Days Till Millennium's Eve

Forty-eight

Dr. No moved soundlessly between the cubicles on the vacant fourth floor. In an hour the training center would be vibrating with activity—keyboards clacking, copiers humming, telephones beeping, voices reverberating above the work cubes, and the noise of constant traffic from King's House residents shuffling to and from classrooms and counseling appointments. But for the moment, at just past 7 A.M., the floor was as peaceful as a garden. The head of King's House often visited the training center alone in the early morning to walk, think, and pray.

In other parts of the old hospital, the machinery of care-giving was already in high gear. In the first floor kitchen and dining room, meals were being prepared and served for early departers for work assignments. On the Coronado Terrace side of the building, volunteers were readying the free store for a hectic day of distributing staple foods, clean used clothing, and household wares along with invitations to job training classes, crisis counseling sessions, and Bible studies.

On the second floor, staff members were rousing scores of residents in the dorms of the homeless shelter and halfway hotel and encouraging them into the disciplines of cleanliness and planning their next steps of recovery.

Life on the third floor at 7 A.M. resembled a miniature urban neighborhood. Families in the resident staff apartments—such as the Ngos, the Tripletts, the Danielsons, and Bill Fawcett—and others, were rising and preparing for the day. While many third floor residents walked or took the elevator only a few hundred feet to job sites in the building, their spouses and children left the building for offices and schools across the city.

The fifth floor hospice never quieted to total inactivity. Day and night, patients cried and moaned, tormented by pain and terrified by the black tide of death ebbing ever nearer. And at all hours, trained, compassionate caregivers ministered to them with drugs, prayers, a calming touch, or a sympathetic ear.

Dr. No cared about all the activity in King's House. But for a few more minutes at least, the fourth floor would be his sanctuary. And he cherished the solitude. A nonstop day awaited him, capped by the bewildering occasion of the four central personalities in Unity 2000 paying a visit to King's House.

What do I have to say to them? He prayed silently, walking along the carpet in the semidarkness. He clutched a thin, worn Bible, folded in half. He was too mature in the faith to think he could argue God out of whatever it was He intended to do tonight. But he was also mature enough to know that his doubts and questions would not be viewed by

Him as rebellion.

I feel foolish addressing these people, he prayed. *They are trained ministers; I'm an ex-engineer who just talks to people—other laypersons like myself—about what You put on my heart. I'm not sure that Mr. Malachi understands this. I'm not sure I'm the one who should speak to these people tonight. And if I am, why have You waited so long to give me something to say?*

He wandered between the darkened work cubes, continuing the one-way discourse—questions without answers, debate without rebuttal. At moments, the vision of standing before T.D. Dunne, Morgan McClure, Simon Holloway, and Shelby Hornecker and their associates tempted him to anxiety. Yet he persisted in presenting his case, certain that his Confidant would respond at the proper time and that the answer would be sufficient to the occasion.

He paused at a counselor's desk where a tiny cone of brightness shining from an overhead security light encouraged him to sit down, open his Bible, and read. He had already decided that he was not going to dig something out of his files for tonight's devotional—an old Bible study talk he had used with his staff or a group of patients or residents. *This is such an extraordinary situation,* he had told God a number of times since Mr. Malachi's visit, *that I expect You to give me something extraordinary to give to them—something fresh, brand new.*

Dr. No had stolen several extra moments over the last few days to open his Bible and give God ample opportunity to awaken him to an extraordinary message—or to supernaturally relieve him of the responsibility Mr. Malachi had foisted on him. But so far he had not felt relieved of either his assignment or the need to continue in prayer for a message.

He steadfastly avoided the lottery approach to searching the Scriptures: opening its pages at random and stabbing at the contents with eyes closed to find the winning verse. *If God has something extraordinary for me,* he affirmed, *He can direct me to it in the course of my ordinary daily reading.*

He sat on the edge of the armless swivel chair, not intending to stay longer than to read a few verses, then resume his prayerful pacing of the fourth floor during his last minutes of solitude. The Bible-reading schedule he had been following all year specified that today he read Genesis 32:22-30. He opened to the passage and read quickly and expectantly:

That night Jacob got up and took his two wives, his two maidservants and his eleven sons and crossed the ford of the Jabbok. After he had sent them across the stream, he sent over all his possessions. So Jacob was left alone, and a man wrestled with him till daybreak. When the man saw that he could not overpower him, he touched the socket of Jacob's hip so that his hip was wrenched as he wrestled with the man. Then the man said, "Let me go, for it is daybreak."

But Jacob replied, "I will not let you go unless you bless me."

The man asked him, "What is your name?"

"Jacob," he answered.

Then the man said, "Your name will no longer be Jacob, but Israel, because you have struggled with God and with men and have overcome."

Jacob said, "Please tell me your name."

But he replied, "Why do you ask my name?" Then he blessed him there.

So Jacob called the place Peniel, saying, "It is because I saw God face to face, and yet my life was spared."

Dr. No pinched the bridge of his nose and pursed his lips in a silent whistle of dismay. *How on earth does this passage fit my distinguished guests?* he wondered, almost chuckling at what seemed to him to be a story suited for anyone but the four most successful Christian leaders in the land. *If any people in God's kingdom have been blessed, they certainly have,* he thought. *They have large, loyal, and generous congregations. What more can I tell the leaders of Unity 2000 about seeking and receiving God's blessing? They're already abundantly blessed.*

He remained at the desk a few moments longer scouring the words and phrases in this tiny pool of truth for a pearl of wisdom from which to create a simple talk. He had discarded several ideas by the time he heard Mai's footsteps approaching. She stepped into the cube where her husband was sitting tentatively, bent down, and kissed him on the cheek. He remained staring at the page as if he hadn't noticed her.

"Good morning, my darling," she said, putting her arm around his shoulder. "Wendy has your eggs almost ready. Are you at a breaking point?"

"Mm, breaking point—interesting choice of words, dear," Dr. No answered, still scanning the text.

"Nothing yet?" she asked sympathetically, fully aware of her husband's dilemma.

"Well, take a look," he answered, trying to keep discouragement from his tone. "Jacob wrestling with the angel; 'I will not let you go unless you bless me.' Do you see anything here the four televangelists haven't already mastered? I'd say all four of them are Olympic champions at wresting blessings from God. *I* could learn some techniques from *them.*"

Mai used the occasion of peering over his shoulder to snuggle her cheek close to his encouragingly. Her eyes flitted over the verses, then a first impression popped out of her mouth. "Can you imagine the gall of someone grabbing God by the throat and saying, 'Give me what I want or I'll beat you up'?"

Dr. No hummed his appreciation for her insight. "Sounds rather presumptuous, doesn't it? But then I have caught myself praying something like that on occasions when Will tells me that our needed outflow for the month is greatly exceeded by the anticipated inflow. Jacob's pushy demand—and my occasional panicky prayers—don't sound very grace-filled, do they?"

"So if Jacob were living today, knowing what we know about God's grace," Mai advanced as an almost humorous challenge, "how do you suppose he would pray?"

Dr. No held his breath as inspiration burst in his mind like an exploding skyrocket. His eyes raced across the words repeatedly, "I will not let you go unless you bless me." There it was. He had found it—or at least, thank God, he had found *something*.

He turned to kiss his wife's warm cheek. "You're a genius, Mai," he chuckled gratefully.

"What? What did I do?" Mai said, still in the dark.

"Give me a couple more minutes to make some notes and I'll tell you over breakfast."

Mai walked away shaking her head as Dr. No switched on a PC and began tapping keys excitedly.

Forty-nine

Mai Ngo, Beth Scibelli, and others who waited around Sammy Chan's VoiceLink communication center weren't surprised. The Friday morning call from the familiar, sinister prophet rained rhyming words of judgment upon the rider of the black horse, the prince of thieves who empties the widow's purse. Though the subject was again unnamed, all agreed that the first four lines of the crude poem pointed to Dr. Morgan McClure of Paradise Valley, Arizona:

> Western King in the desert of sin,
> Thou wilt soon lose what thou strivest to win.
> Robber of widows, hoarder of gold,
> Thou hast grown rich, but thou wilt not grow old. . . .

A female LAPD detective assigned to the case had picked up the phone while the caller was reciting and, in her best imitation of a reporter, tried to interrupt. She said, "Sir, we at the *Times* are really moved by your messages. We would like to do a series about the four horsemen. What is your name, sir? May we set up a time to get together? Sir? Sir?"

But the caller was undeterred. He calmly completed his message and clicked off. The detective cursed, referring to the unresponsive caller as a blankety-blank pea-brained blankety-blank nutso.

Global Communications traced the sending number to a cell phone that had been reported "lost" even before the VoiceLink caller used the instrument to deliver his latest message. "The phone belongs to a couple from Oklahoma City who are in town for Unity 2000," Sammy relayed as he listened to Global's rep explain. "They're staying at the University Hilton and 'misplaced' their phone at a donut shop on Exposition Boulevard this morning."

University Hilton? Exposition Boulevard? Beth thought anxiously. *That means the last three calls—two on stolen remotes and one on a pay phone—can be traced to near the Coliseum area, Hodge's alleged turf. And the first call had been made from a pay phone near Pershing Square on the last day he was seen there.* In Beth's mind, the odds of Hodge's involvement with the calls soared far beyond coincidental.

Beth was dying to tell Mai how her premonition about someone from Pershing Square making the calls was materializing into a flesh-and-blood suspect. But she restrained herself. *I still must find this man named Hodge,* she cautioned herself. *I must verify that he really exists. Better yet, maybe I can catch him in the act of placing his call tomorrow. Then I'll summon the cavalry and we'll find out if the mysterious man with the blue and white picnic chest is a kook or a potential killer.*

"Are you still planning to come over to King's House tonight?" Mai asked as the two women ate an early lunch in the *Times* cafeteria.

"Are you kidding?" Beth exclaimed, trying to gush appreciation. "I gave up VIP tickets to the Clippers game tonight in order to attend this meeting. You bet I'll be there. I'm grateful to you for the opportunity."

"How about coming early to eat dinner with us—say 5:30? I'd like you to meet my family. I could fix a Vietnamese meal."

"I'd really love to, Mai." Beth was serious. There was a winsomeness about this warm, uncomplicated, unpretentious journalist that was reeling her in. And she was intrigued to meet the man Mai had married, a man who had given up a successful engineering career to run a hotel/hospital for the untouchables of Los Angeles.

What motivated this couple to walk away from cushy suburbia and battle crime and disease in Echo Park to help people that many so-called Christians didn't even notice? How could Protestants be so different in their priorities? She wanted some answers before she left L.A.

Beth continued, "But I can't tonight. I have to work all afternoon at the library, and then I have an appointment at 5 that may take me right up to the meeting."

Hopefully I will find a way to rendezvous with the nut making these calls, she added silently, fingering a copy of the caller's latest message, which was lying on the table between them. *Then you and I will* really *have something interesting to talk about.*

"But I want a rain check on that dinner," Beth said. "I love Southeast Asian cuisine."

"Perhaps Thursday night then," Mai offered.

"Let's plan on it."

"You may bring a guest if you like." There was no mistaking Mai's smiling reference to Beth's new policeman friend.

"Thank you, but I'm afraid Sergeant Cole has a standing date with Shelby Hornecker through midnight Friday."

The two women returned to Mai's work station. Beth picked up her computer and sweater to leave for the library, with an intermediate stop at Pershing Square and another secret tete-a-tete—likely an expensive one—with the disgusting Rev. Wingate. Beth had withdrawn $100 from the cash dispenser on her way into town this morning. She was prepared to spend it all if Wingate would tell her precisely where to look for Hodge on Figueroa Street between 5 and 7 P.M. She wanted to find him tonight and be done with her search.

"You know how to find us tonight?" Mai asked as Beth headed for the door of the cubicle.

"Yes. Take Kent Street off Alvarado, then look for the big white buildings."

"Right. Just remember: You'll be in Echo Park after dark, so keep your doors locked. Park on the Bellevue side near the front entrance. Honk until one of our security people comes to escort you inside. It's not as bad as it sounds, but there's no sense taking chances."

"Taking chances is one thing I don't do, Mai," Beth assured her as she left.

Beth reached the Square in time to observe from a distance as Rev. Wingate "chimed" 1 P.M. with his seven-word screaming pronouncement: "The kingdom of heaven is at hand." The frightened reaction of a few tourists would have amused her, except she found nothing amusing about the despicable, soiled lecher of Pershing Square.

"Good afternoon, Rev. Wingate," Beth said coolly, as she approached him near the pond.

Wingate's cloudy eyes frisked Beth roughly as she stood at a respectful distance. "Did you find Rev. Hodge, dear lady?" he said in a sickeningly syrupy tone.

"No, and I don't think I got my money's worth yesterday," Beth replied, trying to keep her desire for vengeance from escalating to self-defeating anger. "I spent at least two hours on Figueroa last night. I didn't see anyone with a picnic chest, and nobody else I talked to had either. I'm wondering if you took my money knowing full well that I wouldn't find Rev. Hodge." She unobtrusively gripped the tube of pepper in the pocket of her cardigan, almost wishing Wingate would try something.

"He was there, dear lady. You must have missed him."

"I need to find him tonight, Wingate . . . my dying father, you know." She doubted that he bought her hokey story, but she decided to hold onto a semblance of the ruse. "I want to know where Hodge will be between 5 and 7 P.M. I need to know exactly. I'm not wandering Figueroa again tonight like a streetwalker."

Wingate just stared at her, obviously savoring the image she had carelessly introduced into his warped mind.

"I suppose you want more money," she growled. "Well, here's the deal: I'll give you more money—$100—but only if I find Mr. Hodge and talk to him tonight." She lifted the flap on her purse with her left hand and furtively showed the corners of five $20 bills, keeping her right hand in her sweater pocket. "I'll bring the money here tomorrow at noon—if I find success tonight."

Wingate hungrily fondled the bills with his eyes, but wouldn't respond.

"This is it, Wingate," Beth said icily. "Take it or leave it. I'll find him eventually without you. I'm just giving you the opportunity to save me some time."

After another long pause, Wingate said, "Rev. Hodge likes to eat taquitos for dinner."

"You're telling me I will find Hodge at dinner time in a taqueria on Figueroa?" she clarified.

"Rev. Hodge likes to eat taquitos for dinner," Wingate repeated.

"But there are half a dozen taquerias between Washington and Exposition. Which one?"

Wingate was silent. Beth waited, asked again, then waited, and asked again. Wingate had said all he was going to say.

"If it takes me half an hour to find him, you only get $50," she spat. "If it takes forty-five minutes, it's $25. And if I don't find him by 6:30— zilch."

She jammed the money back into her purse and stormed off. Wingate stared after her until she left the Square.

Fifty

Reagan Cole was late for roll call. It began when his fashion-conscious partner caught him stepping out of his flight suit in the station's parking garage.

"Same slacks, jacket, shirt, and tie as yesterday, sarge?" Jayne said, shaking her head. "The fashion police are going to pull you over. You could get thirty days for failure to display a decent wardrobe."

Jayne's smart business ensemble was different in color and style from yesterday, from her earrings to her shoes. She was only half joking about Cole's unimpressive tan jacket, brown slacks, and plaid tie in brown tones.

"Hey, this is a clean shirt," Cole objected.

"But it's the same color as yesterday, sarge—and white, of all things. Who wears white shirts anymore?"

"So it's an escort's uniform. Nobody complains when I wear my blues three days in a row."

"But you're escorting a wealthy, nationally known personality. You need to look sharp, sarge. Your jacket is . . . okay, for one more day. But at least change the tie. And tomorrow, different slacks and jacket. Maybe something in blue or gray, with matching tie, belt, and shoes."

Cole trusted Jayne's advice, but he grumbled as he mounted his bike and roared out of the garage to find a tie, leaving his flight suit crumpled in his parking place.

When he hurried into roll call five minutes late, the tie he was knotting into place beneath his up-turned collar was a vivid blue and orange print. His uniformed fellow officers, to whom Jayne had reported her partner's fashion problem in detail, saw him and released a merciless corporate groan.

"Hey, I wasn't going to spend $25 for a tie," Cole argued, "so I found this one on the sale rack for $9." The good-natured razzing continued until Lieutenant Arias called the meeting back to order.

The VoiceLink caller and the stolen phones he used in the Coliseum area were a major topic of conversation during the briefing. Street patrols were instructed to squeeze their most productive informants for tips on active phone-snatchers. An additional team was assigned to work with Witt and Coyle on Coliseum security to thoroughly screen unauthorized personnel. Two separate dog teams, one from the Sheriff's Department and one from the LAPD, would search the Coliseum Thursday and Friday for explosives, the lieutenant reported. And Cole and Watanabe were reminded to keep alert, seeing that their charge, Shelby Hornecker, had been clearly implicated in the messages.

"Chief Robinson and our detectives still regard these telephone threats as an imaginative hoax perpetrated by a mental case," Lieutenant Arias continued. "But, as you all know, we must err on the side of caution. So keep your eyes and ears open out there. If we can find this guy today, he will be one less thing to worry about on Millennium's Eve."

The officers murmured at the reminder of having to work an extended shift—2:15 P.M. to 1 A.M.—on Millennium's Eve.

An officer spoke up from the back of the room. "Lieutenant, is it possible that the event at the Coliseum may be canceled if we don't turn up the VoiceLink caller?"

"Not likely, Anderson. There over 100,000 people in town for this deal—Bible-believing people. This is a big religious experience for them. Even if they hear about the threat—and so far the media has helped us keep it to an unsubstantiated rumor—they won't back down. They believe that God is on their side, that they are somehow invincible to evil plots. Chief Robinson expects them to fill the Coliseum and Sports Arena, no matter what we do or don't do."

"What about the big guns—the four preachers coming in?" another policeman said. "They're the ones being threatened. Maybe they will call it off."

"Again, not likely," Arias said. "By the way, the preachers don't know it yet, but the chief and Captain Thomasson will be meeting with them tonight at the old Queen of Angels hospital."

Cole and Jayne exchanged looks of surprise.

Arias continued. "The brass will fill them in on the telephone threats and review our security precautions. But nobody expects a cancellation. After all, these are high-visibility spiritual leaders. They preach at their people to believe and hope and pray and go forward and so forth. How would it look if they bailed out at a threat from a religious crank?

"No, I think we have an event on our hands, folks. I don't know if God is going to help them out or not, but we're sure going to do our best. Now let's get out there."

Jayne begged Cole to make a quick stop at Ari's Men's Shop two blocks from the station and exchange his horrid tie before they relieved the day watch at the Biltmore. But he insisted that since Jayne was his fashion consultant, she make the exchange. While she was inside, Cole sat tieless in the silver Bolt and called Beth.

"You're *really* at Central Branch today?" Cole asked, enjoying a playful dig.

"Yes, Reagan," Beth answered with a tinge of scorn. "And I'm rather busy."

"How do I know for sure you're at the library?" he pressed.

"Just listen," Beth said defiantly, and then she was silent.

Cole listened for several seconds, wondering if she had put him on hold. "I don't hear anything," he said at last.

"Of course not. I'm at the library, and libraries are quiet. Case closed."

Cole laughed, and Beth finally joined in with a chuckle.

"I thought you might be interested in some hot gossip about the party at King's House tonight," Cole said.

"Tell me; I'm interested," Beth replied expectantly.

"Chief DeShea Robinson has been added to the guest list."

"The L.A. police chief? Are you kidding?"

"The very same."

"What's the deal?"

"He wants to have a fireside chat with the big four about the phone threats—clear the air, smooth the waters, impress them with his security measures. I guess he thought a quiet gathering out of the spotlight would be the perfect place."

"Who knows about the chief's plans?"

"It's being kept quiet for the same reasons the meeting of the big four has not been publicized: privacy, safety, absence of media."

"This is turning out to be some kind of top-secret summit conference."

Cole could hear the soft *clack* of Beth's keyboard in the background. *She really* is *working,* he thought.

"Here's another tidbit," Cole continued. "I'm taking Shelby Hornecker and her staff to Quinteros for dinner before the meeting. I reserved the banquet room for them. Can you join us?"

Beth paused. "I'm sorry, Reagan, but there is . . . something I have to do before the meeting."

"I'll introduce you to Shelby—let you sit right next to her," Cole said, deliberately enticing her. "I'll even buy your dinner."

"I'd love that, Reagan, especially being with you. But—"

"Carnitas, chiles rellenos, frijoles refritos . . ." he tempted.

"I know it will be delicious. But I already turned down a home-cooked Vietnamese dinner at King's House because of my . . . assignment. It's something I can't put off, something I have to finish before the meeting."

"And that's all you're going to tell me about tonight's 'assignment,' right?" Cole probed, feeling put off by Beth's secrecy.

"Tonight at the meeting I hope to tell you *everything* about it," Beth advanced, trying to sound positive. "And I think you'll be very surprised . . . and pleased."

Cole hummed thoughtfully. "It must be something special for you to turn down two free meals."

"It is. What I have to do this evening is very important to me. I don't like keeping it from you, but I must for now. Will you please trust me?"

"What choice do I have?"

"Reagan, that's not really the vote of confidence I was hoping for."

"All right, I trust you. But please keep your head in the game. Be careful. I really feel . . . I mean, I just want you to remember. . . ." Cole didn't want to sound maudlin, but he did want to express his true feelings. He thought it might make her think twice about doing something foolish.

But at that moment Jayne jerked open the door and slid into the Bolt. She tossed a subdued print tie over the shoulder of Cole's jacket. It improved his outfit considerably.

Cole concluded quickly. "I just want you to remember that you owe me dinner on Millennium's Eve. Got to go to work now. See you at King's House tonight. Bye."

"Sorry to interrupt," Jayne said.

"No problem. What do I owe you for the new tie? You didn't get this off the sale rack." Cole flipped up his collar and hastily tied the tie.

"My treat. It's worth it to me not to be embarrassed in front of our clients."

"What a pal," Cole chuckled. Then he tugged his collar into place, stuffed the tail of the tie inside his jacket, and aimed the Bolt toward the Biltmore.

Fifty-one

Beth left Central Library at 4:45 P.M. feeling accomplished. In three hours she had made significant headway toward finishing the biographical sketches of Holloway, Hornecker, McClure, and Dunne for her book. She had also pieced together a short chapter on Adrian Hornecker, the instigator of Unity 2000.

Concentration had been a challenge. Every thought of Figueroa Street induced another distracting shot of adrenaline as she considered actually finding Hodge in one of the taquerias there. But she had persevered doggedly at the keyboard, reminding herself that she couldn't even start looking for him until after 5:00 P.M. She was pleased about making the most of her afternoon in the library.

Congested downtown traffic made Beth's drive to the University district a stop-and-go ordeal. As soon as she crossed Washington Boulevard, she pulled to the curb and slipped into PARK. She checked her watch. It was 5:14—supposedly dinnertime for the elusive Mr. Hodge.

She reviewed her plan. She would drive slowly along Figueroa, hugging the curb where possible. When she came upon a Mexican food place, she would stop, check it out from the car, and, if necessary, step into the restaurant to look for the blue and white picnic chest.

She reached into the pocket of her bulky knit cardigan. The canister of mace was ready and waiting.

Beth eased the Cruiser into gear, then crossed herself. She thought about saying a prayer, but instead she crossed herself again and started down the street.

The first two places were hole-in-the-wall taquerias with most of the patrons hunkering outside, eating various combinations of tortillas, meat, rice, and beans. Each shop had a few chairs inside, so Beth parked and walked cautiously to the doorway to make sure she hadn't overlooked a man in a Dodgers cap and jean jacket.

The third place was a sit-down Mexican restaurant just past Adams. It was tiny and dingy in comparison to Quinteros. The Spanish-speaking host, a boy in his mid-teens, didn't understand why Beth refused to sit down. Finally he gave up and let her wander between the customers until she was satisfied and left.

The fragrant aroma inside reminded Beth how hungry she was. *You could be sitting down with Reagan and Shelby to enjoy a Mexican feast at Quinteros right now if it wasn't for your obsession to find Hodge,* she taunted herself. But she quickly recalled the importance of her contribution to the search for the VoiceLink caller. Beth couldn't escape the conviction that finding Hodge was the key to ending the threats against the Unity 2000 four—and the key to her peace of mind about her parents' and Reagan Cole's safety.

Beth was two blocks from Jefferson Boulevard when she saw a tiny, storefront food stand in what had once been a small, bustling shopping center. She pulled into the parking lot. As the Cruiser's headlights swept in front of the taqueria, Beth's heart stopped. There, sitting on a blue and white picnic chest just outside the doorway, was a small, bedraggled man. He wore a jean jacket and a shabby Dodgers cap. The stylistic white letters LA were almost obliterated with grime. Thick, wire-rimmed glasses were perched crookedly on his discolored, misshapen nose. He was reading an old Bible by the faint light streaming out from the taqueria.

Beth nosed the Cruiser into the diagonal parking space directly in front of the man. Even though the car stopped only three feet from him, he kept on reading unperturbed. The brightness of the headlights highlighted his homely, soiled appearance. It looked to Beth like he had lived on the streets all his life.

Beth switched off the headlights, and the scene faded again to dim light. The man on the picnic chest read on, tilting his Bible toward the doorway of the taqueria. She could hear her heart pounding above the noise of the traffic on Figueroa.

Beth quickly surveyed the rest of the scene. Five of the ten little stores in the center were vacant. Boarded windows and cracked stucco walls were sprayed with lewd or unintelligible graffiti and gang symbols. Windblown trash littered the corners and doorways.

There were only two other cars in the twenty-space parking lot. One of them was a total beater that looked like it had been there six months. The other looked drivable, but only barely.

Two Latino men hunkered in front of the taqueria eating. Beth could make out a Latino man and woman cooking in the kitchen area near the front window of the shop. The only two booths in the store, near the rear, appeared to be empty.

Beth fought off pangs of apprehension, crossed herself again, and stepped out of the car. The doors locked with a soft electronic *chirp* in response to a touch on the key ring. She slipped the keys into her purse and stood beside the door a full ten feet from the man.

"Mr. Hodge?" she called.

The man on the picnic chest looked up. "Yes, ma'am," he answered in a submissive, almost defeated tone. Beth brushed away the first impression that the mousy-looking man before her couldn't even imagine a harmful threat, let alone deliver one. She knew that no one living on the streets of L.A. was harmless.

"Is that your name, sir — Hodge?"

The man looked at her timidly. "Yes, ma'am. But I don't believe I know —"

"No, you don't know me. My name is Beth . . . Johnson. May I ask you a few questions?"

The man recoiled slightly. "Are you with the police, Ms. Johnson?"

"No, I'm not with the police."

"Well, if you're one of them county people, I don't want to move into no shelter, ma'am. I get along just fine. I don't cause no trouble." Beth took note of the Irish tinge in the man's voice.

"No, Mr. Hodge, I'm not a social worker. I'm a . . . writer . . . and like yourself" — she gestured toward the Bible resting on Hodge's knee — "I'm a deeply religious person."

The man relaxed slightly. "That's good, ma'am. We need more religion in the world today. After Friday, times is just going to get worse and worse on this old earth." He tapped his Bible reassuringly.

Then his expression clouded. "But, Ms. Johnson, I ain't no educated man. I don't know if I can answer your questions about religion."

"My questions aren't about religion. I'm looking for someone you may know." Without moving any closer to the man, Beth related her fabricated story about a dying father and his long-lost army buddy. She emphasized the friend's preoccupation with God's judgment and the four horsemen from Revelation. She said nothing about the *Times*, VoiceLink, or the threatening calls.

Beth concluded with the vital question, "Rev. Wingate at Pershing Square tells me that you sometimes preach about the Four Horsemen. Are you the man I'm looking for, or can you tell me where I might find him?"

"Paddy Duckett," Hodge answered without hesitation.

"I beg your pardon."

"I ain't the man you're looking for, ma'am. I was never in the army. I don't know if Paddy Duckett was in the army, but he taught me everything I know about religion. He understands Revelation backwards and forwards, preaches about it every day in the Park there." Hodge aimed a finger toward Exposition Park.

Beth was perplexed. Suddenly she had two suspects: the disheveled, spineless man in front of her and another soapbox preacher named Paddy Duckett who called Exposition Park his parish.

The wheels turned rapidly in Beth's brain. *This Duckett guy — if he truly exists and lives around here — could just as easily have stolen those phones near the Coliseum and made the VoiceLink calls. And he could also have been at Pershing Square the day the first call registered from a phone booth near there. If it's this easy to turn up new leads, how many more possibilities can there be?*

Beth took one step toward Hodge, then said, "I'd like to hear more about your friend's preaching. Maybe he is the man I'm looking for."

Hodge eyed her meekly, "Well, I was just about to have some dinner," he said, nodding toward the taqueria's open doorway.

Beth recognized the subtle pitch for a handout. *At least he's not holding out for $100,* she thought.

"If I buy you some dinner, can we talk about your friend and the four horsemen?" Beth asked.

"That would be very kind, ma'am," Hodge returned, bowing in thanks. "And don't you worry, ma'am. I don't eat much—just a couple of taquitos and maybe some rice and beans in a tortilla." He rose and respectfully laid his Bible inside the chest. Then he picked up the plastic chest and stepped into the little restaurant.

Beth didn't like the idea of going inside. It was too confining; there appeared to be only one way out. Furthermore, entering the taqueria would take her farther away from motorists and passing cops on Figueroa who might be able to help her if something went wrong.

On the plus side, Beth calculated, *the taqueria is a public place, and public places are supposed to be safe. It's empty except for the two employees. I'm bigger, stronger, and in better shape than wiry little Hodge. He doesn't look like a threat, but if he tries something, I could probably mace him and hold him down until the cops arrive.*

Unwilling to take any chances, Beth pulled the small canister from her sweater pocket. She decided to keep her only weapon right in the palm of her hand until she was safely outside again. She didn't care if Hodge saw it; she rather hoped he did and behaved accordingly.

The pungent odor of hot grease greeted Beth as she stepped into the taqueria. The couple behind the counter looked at the two customers eagerly. With hand signs and a couple of key words, Hodge ordered two taquitos, a large corn tortilla stuffed with rice and beans, and a can of Coke. Beth nodded and pointed to Hodge, indicating she wanted the same. To pay for the food, she broke out one of the $20 bills she had begrudgingly promised to Rev. Wingate.

"What do you and your friend Paddy believe about the four horsemen?" Beth asked as she slid into the booth.

Hodge didn't speak until he had mouthed a silent prayer over the simple meal piled on the paper plate. Beth wasn't very thankful for the food before her, so she decided she would give it to Hodge later if he wanted it.

Hodge folded a greasy taquito and stuffed the whole thing into his mouth as if he hadn't eaten in a week. He chewed and talked at once.

"Paddy says it's a secret."

"What's a secret?"

Hodge whispered dramatically, spraying food particles as he did so, "Them four horsemen coming to Los Angeles this week."

"The four horsemen? Here? What does he mean?" Beth asked, feigning ignorance.

With much of the taquito still in his mouth, Hodge took a massive bite of his bean and rice burrito. "Didn't your father tell you?" he said while chewing. "Paddy's been preaching it for years."

Reminded of her phony story, Beth backpedaled. "Mm, yes, Dad did mention something about the four horsemen. But who is your friend talking about?"

Hodge looked around wide-eyed, as if searching the empty room for spies. "Paddy says I ain't supposed to tell, but with you being a religious person and all, I guess it's okay." Hodge leaned in, and Beth leaned backward. "It's them preachers coming to the Coliseum on Millennium's Eve. Paddy says they're the four horsemen from the Book of Revelation. He says they're antichrist, and God Almighty is going to bring them up short on Friday night. That's what he told me to preach in the Square."

Beth was trying to evaluate Hodge's voice despite his perpetually full mouth. He didn't sound at all like the VoiceLink caller, even though the message he related was suspiciously parallel. Nor did Hodge seem capable of the cold aggression conveyed in the VoiceLink calls. The story of a vengeful Exposition Park preacher named Paddy Duckett sounded increasingly convincing.

"Does your friend really believe something is going to happen to the four horsemen Friday night?"

Hodge stuffed his mouth full of rice and beans again. "He *knows* it will happen. 'May thy flesh be torn and thy bones be scattered and thy blood quench the parched earth.' That's what Paddy's been preaching, and that's what he told me to preach. Doesn't that sound like something's going to happen?" Hodge challenged.

Beth had listened to the macabre phrase before in Mai's office, but Hodge's voice still didn't fit her memory of the articulate, impassioned VoiceLink caller.

One more question may be enough, Beth assessed. *If I receive the answer I expect, I'll ask Hodge where I can find Paddy, then leave the taqueria and call the detectives.* She felt she was as close to the caller as she dared to be.

She bit her lip and clutched the canister tightly beneath the table. She would have crossed herself again if Hodge wasn't looking straight at her. "Mr. Hodge, has your friend been preaching his message about the four horsemen outside the park, like on the telephone to the *Los Angeles Times*?"

Hodge's bulging eyes conveyed, *How did you find out, ma'am?* But at the same moment a gasp of surprise caught in his throat. He coughed a violent gagging cough, and a mouthful of food and saliva exploded from his mouth onto the table. He tried to inhale, but couldn't. He panicked. He jumped up, spinning and beating his chest beside the table. He was choking.

The proprietors peered out from the kitchen at the ruckus. "Call an ambulance!" Beth yelled at them. They looked puzzled at the command. "Ambulance! Paramedics!" she shouted, cursing at their ignorance.

Beth had administered the Heimlich maneuver successfully twice in the past. But Hodge was not cooperating. He rolled along the wall toward the back of the building, alternately beating on himself and grasping at his clogged windpipe. Whenever Beth tried to grab him from behind, he lurched or spun violently, pushing her away.

Hodge reached the back wall and fumbled for the handle of the service door. As he flung himself against it, it opened into the alley, and Hodge fell heavily to the asphalt, writhing. In an instant of selfless, unthinking compassion, Beth followed the choking man out the door into the night and the door closed behind her.

A strong arm slammed across Beth's throat from behind and held her fast while a fist crashed down on her forearm, dislodging the canister before Beth could use it. The attacker grabbed her flailing right arm and wrenched it behind her. Like a steel bar, the arm across her neck jerked her backward against his body. The stench was unmistakable. She was in the clutches of the demon of Pershing Square, Rev. Wingate.

Beth's terrified scream was stifled in her throat by the stranglehold across her windpipe. She instinctively grabbed for his face with her free hand and threw her heel back at his shins. But Wingate yanked her off the ground by the neck and right arm, choking her and wrenching her shoulder, elbow, and wrist into blinding pain.

Hodge was immediately in her face. "Do not resist the master's will, lady." It was not the voice of an uncouth, downtrodden old man from Pershing Square who seconds earlier was choking on his dinner. It had all been a ploy, an act more clever and fiendish than her own. The measured, articulate, Dracula-like voice speaking to her now was the same one she heard in the offices of Mai Ngo and Sammy Chan at the *Los Angeles Times*. Beth knew she was looking into the shadowy eyes of the VoiceLink caller.

Beth continued to struggle and gag and whine in pain. "Be still, or I will hurt you more," Hodge warned coolly.

Beth had programmed herself to go down fighting if she was ever attacked. She jerked hard against Wingate and mounted another attempt at a scream, which turned into a muffled cry of pain as Wingate again bounced her off the ground.

Hodge pulled the large knife from his pocket and waved it in front of Beth's eyes. Then, with a ferocious scowl, he pressed the point into her left side until it sliced through her sweater and blouse and punctured the skin. Beth recoiled in pain as she felt a warm trickle of blood run down her side to the waistband of her slacks.

"Be still, or I will hurt you *more*," Hodge hissed. Convinced and terrified, Beth held still.

Suddenly a stab of pain seared Beth's right shoulder. She strained her tear-filled eyes to see Hodge's other hand at the end of a hypodermic imbedded in her upper arm. He had jabbed the needle through her sweater and injected its contents with the plunger, a huge dose of Halothane 3IM.

"Don't let her move," Hodge instructed Wingate, tossing the spent needle aside. "I'll bring her car around."

Hodge disappeared into the taqueria to collect Beth's purse and quiet the anxiety of the Latino proprietors. Wingate squeezed Beth harder to affirm his intention to obey.

This was the nightmare Beth had narrowly escaped at the hands of the Latin Barons on Christmas Eve, the danger Reagan had repeatedly warned her about. She thrust away the specter of what could happen to her in the hands of these two men. *O Jesus! God!* she cried inside. Wingate's iron forearm choked a sob of fear before it could be heard.

Every flinch of resistance only encouraged Wingate to apply greater force to her arm. Every attempt to utter a cry brought more pressure to her throat. She feared that he could easily strangle her, separate her shoulder, or dislocate her wrist or elbow. Unable to struggle, she forced herself to think.

I will resist them and fight them when I can, she resolved, wincing. *They will not get any pleasure out of me. But I won't be foolish. I can outsmart them. I can buy time. I'll think of a way out.*

The first wave of the powerful sedative flooded Beth's system, blurring her thoughts and relaxing her limbs. She was aware of the Star Cruiser approaching with its lights off. Feeling his captive's rapid transition from taut resistance to dead weight, Wingate gradually released his grip. Beth was powerless to take advantage of her freedom.

With the next wave, Beth's eyes dropped shut and her knees buckled. She was distantly aware of Wingate catching her around the midriff as she crumpled toward the pavement. There were curt, hushed instructions. A car door opened. Beth smelled the leather as she was dragged prone and face down onto the back seat. A musty blanket was thrown over her. Then the door slammed and the Cruiser accelerated.

The murky tide of unconsciousness swept over her and Beth plunged headlong into darkness.

Fifty-two

Reagan Cole turned into the visitor's parking lot in front of King's House at 7:15. Two unmarked police vehicles were among the half dozen cars in the lot. Cole recognized the black minivan assigned to Simon Holloway's entourage. Another Bolt sedan, identical to his own except for its pale blue exterior, was parked next to the van. *McClure's or Dunne's escorts also beat us here,* he surmised.

There was no sign of the media. Cole was grateful for the committee's apparent success at keeping the meeting out of the spotlight. He expected, however, to find two other vehicles in the lot: Chief DeShea Robinson's official car and Beth's crumpled candy-apple red Star Cruiser. But, curiously, both cars were missing.

Cole had informed Rev. Hornecker when they must leave Quinteros to arrive at King's House on time. But the festive staff dinner in Luis and Raphaela's banquet room had evolved into a lengthy discussion of tasks and assignments leading up to Millennium's Eve, so they were already late for the 7 o'clock meeting.

Cole parked in the space next to the van, and the rental car driven by Stan Welbourn pulled in next to him. Eleanor was his only passenger. Darin Chaumont had declined dinner and the tour of King's House, citing a mountain of last-minute details for the Friday night mega-gathering.

Jeremy Cannon had attended the dinner, but from what Cole could tell, the actor hadn't been invited to King's House. *If they are carrying on an affair in Los Angeles*, Cole smirked to himself, *I'll have to give them an A+ for intrigue but a D- for excitement.*

"Well, at least we're in time to make a dramatic entrance," Theresa joked as the four guests followed their police escorts quickly to the door.

"Yes, but I fear the onions and salsa we just ate may make our entrance more dramatic than we desire," Shelby added. "The dinner was excellent, sergeant. But does anyone have a breath mint?" Eleanor Welbourn passed around a roll of LifeSavers.

"Will your journalist friend be here tonight, sergeant?" Shelby asked.

"Her car isn't here, but I expect her. She's looking forward to meeting you."

The group was greeted at the front door by a cheery college girl who led them down the hall to the cafeteria. Cole and Jayne lagged slightly behind, dreading another insipid tea party and hoping to remain invisible.

As Shelby's team entered the spacious dining room, three clusters of people turned to them with the eagerness of misery welcoming company. Cole quickly perceived from the grumbling body language that this was not a naturally homogeneous group.

A handsome, exquisitely dressed African-American couple stood alone, looking tentative. Three glum white males in business suits, whom Cole recognized as the Holloway men, appeared to be hiding behind the dignified but quietly effusive Grace Ellen. Four plainclothes police officers—Huntley and Goldman, escorting the Holloways, and two others Cole didn't know—formed the tightest knot. Cole guessed that they were discussing their preference for a gun battle with L.A.'s deadly Grave Warriors over escort duty.

A Vietnamese couple and a few other staff members moved between the clusters trying to keep the conversations, which wobbled like china plates on sticks, spinning. Two Vietnamese teenagers dutifully circulated with cups of coffee and tea, which the stilted guests dutifully accepted.

This isn't a reunion of old friends or war buddies, Cole observed quietly. *This is contrived congeniality, like that exhibited by rival players at center court before a game. They tap fists and wish each other a good game, then moments later they're hacking each other, throwing elbows, and trash-talking like mortal enemies.*

Cole imagined that the religious leaders would just as soon get the party over with so they could return to their bunkers and prepare for the big clash on Millennium's Eve.

Seeing Shelby's group enter, the Vietnamese man stepped forward. His wife followed him. "Welcome, Rev. Hornecker. I am Thanh Hai Ngo, the director of King's House. This is my wife, Mai, and those are our children, Wendy and David." He pointed to the teenagers filling cups.

Shelby introduced her small team to the couple, including the police escorts.

Cole had hoped to remain anonymous, but Mrs. Ngo brightened at the mention of his name. While Shelby, Theresa, and the Welbourns were being served beverages by the children, she approached him.

"Sergeant Cole, I'm very happy to meet you finally," she said, gripping his hand warmly. "I've been working with your friend, Beth, at the *Times*. What a delightful girl. And she's told me so much about you, the dangerous rescue and all."

Cole hoped his blush wasn't too conspicuous. "Yes, ma'am. Beth has mentioned how helpful you have been to her."

Mai's expression turned to one of curiosity. "Did she change her mind about coming tonight?"

Cole glanced at his watch. "No, ma'am, not to my knowledge. In fact, I expected her to be here by now. When we talked this afternoon she was still planning to come." A pinprick of concern distracted him for a second. He was still uneasy about her unspoken late-afternoon activity.

Dr. No's voice interrupted his thoughts. "Ladies and gentlemen, welcome again to King's House. We are very honored to have you here. I know you are all very busy preparing for the big gathering Friday night, so we had better start."

Mai turned toward her husband, who was addressing the scattered clusters from near the coffee urn. Wendy and David put down their serving pitchers to gawk at their hero, T.D. Dunne, from across the room. Cole drifted toward the group of police officers that his partner Jayne had already joined.

"I'm sorry that Dr. Morgan McClure was unable to join us for the meeting tonight. His staff informed the committee that important matters have kept him from flying into Los Angeles until tomorrow afternoon."

Cole had his own lurid interpretation of the "matters" the famed womanizer might be dealing with at the moment.

Dr. No continued, "When Mr. Malachi from the Unity 2000 committee told us that all of you were coming to visit King's House, my first question was, 'Why?' "

Quiet, sterile laughter fluttered between the clusters. Each of the leaders present or their representatives had posed the same question to Mr. Malachi.

"I explained to him that we are just a collection of ordinary people trying to perform the Lord's work in a needy city. We're not a big church, and we're not on television. Our ministry is rather insignificant compared to the millions of people touched by your ministries. But Mr. Malachi *insisted* that you would enjoy seeing what we're doing."

The word "insisted" provoked another ripple of knowing laughter. Mr. Malachi had been just as insistent that Shelby Hornecker, Simon Holloway, and T.D. Dunne come to King's House.

"Mr. Malachi was planning to be here by 7, but he has been detained on other committee business. He requested that I get things started. He hopes to join us before you leave this evening."

Dr. No explained that he would lead the group on a walking tour of the old hospital, which would be followed by dessert in the cafeteria. During dessert he would answer any questions the group might have about the ministry. Finally, he announced that Mr. Malachi had asked him to conclude the evening with a brief devotional.

"Doesn't he know that the chief and the captain are going to be here later to talk about the caller?" Jayne whispered to Cole.

Cole shrugged. "I don't know. Maybe the chief wants to keep his visit hush-hush. Maybe he changed his mind about coming."

"Maybe the detectives have turned up a suspect since we clocked in," Jayne advanced.

"I couldn't be happier," Cole said, wondering again about Beth.

The visiting dignitaries, like a flock of reluctant sheep, followed Dr. No out of the cafeteria and down the main hall to begin the tour. Cole's LAPD colleagues filled their coffee cups and found a comfortable corner in the cafeteria to sit down and wait. Cole stepped into a quiet corner of the cafeteria, pulled out his pocket phone, and tapped Beth's memory code.

After five unanswered tones, a synthesized voice invited the caller to leave a message. "Beth, this is Reagan." He checked his watch. "It's 7:30. I'm at King's House, and I'm wondering where you are. Call me." He tapped the phone off.

Cole was torn between feelings of concern and anger. He decided to be angry, because he didn't want to unleash the dark thoughts that provoked his concern. *This is the second time you've lied to me, Beth*, he thought. *You said you were going to be here tonight. I don't like playing true-or-false games.*

Mai, who was collecting empty coffee cups, saw him with the phone. "Are you trying to locate Beth?" she asked.

Cole nodded. "No answer, though. I left a message."

"Maybe she's at the library, away from her phone. Or maybe she went home to change clothes and left her phone in the car. Do you have her parents' number?"

"Yes. But I'll wait awhile. I'm sure she'll hear my message and call."

"Well, then, why don't you come with us on the tour. Beth will catch up when she gets here."

Cole eyed his five fellow officers swilling coffee and talking shop in the corner. "Really, I—"

"Oh, come on, sergeant," Mai prodded. "Beth speaks of you so highly, and I'd like to get to know you better. Besides, you might be interested in what we do here. You can fill Beth in on whatever she misses."

Cole felt trapped between two lousy choices. He had a beautiful new lady in his life, but he was stuck between raising callouses on his rear end with a bunch of cops and touring an Echo Park flophouse. He would rather be on his way to the Clippers game with Beth right now to watch his friend Curtis Spooner play, then top off the evening with a cold beer and a little romance. But neither his schedule nor his lady was cooperating.

Of the two remaining choices, rehashing stories of drug busts and gang sweeps suddenly sounded dull. Cole didn't expect that walking the halls of King's House would rival the county art museum for entertainment, but it could be fun seeing how these stuffy religious big shots handled being crowded into the same elevator.

"Why not?" Cole resigned, trying to sound a little enthusiastic.

Hodge circled Exposition Park slowly in the Star Cruiser looking for a parking place. The game between the Clippers and the Trail Blazers had already begun, and he was late for work. It couldn't be helped. The test at the hands of the prying lady journalist had been a priority. She had to be dealt with effectively. But he still had to show up at the Sports Arena or risk losing his access into the Coliseum on Millennium's Eve.

Hodge anticipated the scenario when he walked in the employee entrance. Whatley would curse at him for being late and threaten to fire him. Hodge would grovel and whimper and make up an excuse. Whatley would give him "just one more chance" and send him scurrying after his mop to clean up spilled beer and pop in the Arena while the crowd roared at the game.

Hodge steeled himself to endure Lionel Whatley for one more night. *On Millennium's Eve I will disappear,* he thought, *and Whatley will never curse at me again.*

Parking near the Arena on game night seemed impossible, but Hodge knew the master had prepared a place for him. He would like to have used the employee lot—something he had never done before since he didn't own a car. But he couldn't get into the lot without being seen by an attendant, who would later link him with the car he intended to abandon. Millennium's Eve was only forty-eight hours away, and he couldn't take the chance of being associated with what would soon be the very suspicious vehicle in a missing persons investigation. He would leave the car somewhere on the street.

For the fourth time in ten minutes, Hodge turned down Menlo Avenue on the west side of Exposition Park. Cars were lined nose to tail on both sides of the street. Then, 100 yards ahead, the lights of a pickup truck flashed on, and the driver, a Coliseum workman leaving late, squealed away from the curb. Hodge smiled. Again the master had provided. Hodge nosed the Cruiser into the vacant space.

He waited until a few late-arriving fans walked past on the sidewalk. Then he stepped out with his picnic chest, closed the door, and locked it with a touch on the key ring.

He walked north on Menlo past the Coliseum, then entered Exposition Park through an open gate. He glanced at Gate 14 from the shadows where he walked. Bailey and Paddy Duckett were long gone by now, Hodge knew. He saw Witt and Coyle with two other cops and a police dog inside the fence, passing time. They did not see him. Circling the Coliseum, he approached the Sports Arena from the north so no one would associate him with a car parked to the southwest of the Arena.

Your will is being fulfilled to perfection, he breathed to his master as he walked the dark sidewalk toward the employee entrance. *By now the huge platform has been assembled on the Coliseum floor. The ten horns of the beast are ready to unleash your vengeance and purge the land of the infidels. In barely forty-eight hours your plan will culminate in righteous judgment and the revelation of a new order. And the threat of a journalist who was too smart for her own good has been defused. Nothing can stop us now.*

Hodge tossed the Cruiser's keys deep into a clump of oleanders and entered the Arena.

Fifty-three

Reagan Cole wasn't prepared for what he saw—and expected to see but didn't—on his tour of King's House. In his eight years on the force, he had visited many downtown flophouses, soup kitchens, and rescue missions, usually to stop a fight, subdue a drug-crazed resident, or interrogate witnesses to a stabbing or shooting. Most of the facilities looked the same: drab, neglected, overcrowded, helter-skelter. And most of them smelled the same: a strong odor of industrial-strength disinfectant that never completely masked the stomach-turning pungency of rancid tobacco, alcohol, and human waste.

In contrast to what Cole had seen elsewhere, the second floor shelter at King's House was the Beverly Hills Hotel. The eighty-eight-bed men's wing, the thirty-eight-bed women's wing, several small family apartments, and the thirty-bed wing for prisoners in transition were adequately monitored by live-in staff and volunteers.

Residents were required to bathe daily, wash and dry their own clothes, and keep their living space tidy. When they weren't attending job counseling or tracking down leads for outside employment and lodging, residents worked in shifts washing and folding bedding; sweeping, mopping, and polishing floors; working in the kitchen; or performing a myriad of maintenance and caregiving tasks throughout the complex.

The training center and counseling offices on the fourth floor looked like any other office building across the city. Functional and tastefully decorated, the work cubicles and classrooms seemed suitable to the task of transforming undisciplined, uncared-for rejects of society into self-respecting contributors to society. Cole couldn't believe that such a well-organized, efficiently managed facility was operating in such a shabby neighborhood.

The sergeant was also surprised at the change that took place in the visiting dignitaries as the tour progressed. They were like strangers on a plane who end up exchanging business cards and phone numbers before they land. The parties of the three religious leaders found the walls of reserve and indifference crumbling as they explored the unique ministry of King's House together.

Shelby Hornecker and Grace Ellen Holloway were talking like old friends before they left the first floor. Soon they coaxed Valerie Dunne into their conversation while Wendy and David Ngo and Simon Holloway's two sons, Mark and Tim, surrounded T.D. with questions about the music scene.

Stan Welbourn forced himself to strike up a conversation with the withdrawn Simon Holloway. The chat was strained and tenuous until an offhand comment on the health of an indoor plant on the second floor uncovered a mutual interest in gardening.

At 8:30, Cole stepped away from the group on the fourth floor to dial Beth again. She did not respond, so he left a second message. He tried to remind himself that Beth was a smart, capable woman who, having almost been burned on the San Diego Freeway, would use her head and stay away from trouble. But concern for her grew within him like a cancer.

By the time they reached the fifth floor, the group's collective attitude toward what they were experiencing had been transformed from impassivity to curiosity to rapt interest. Cole had also been captivated by what he saw, though Beth's absence dogged his conscious thoughts.

The group huddled around Dr. No while he described the care given to AIDS patients on the floor. Then they walked in respectful silence past room after room where men and women clutched their last weeks of life like sand slipping through their fingers.

From a nearby door, a sudden moan from a male patient mounted to a cry of pain. The intensity of the cry startled the small tour group. Theresa Bordeaux and Grace Ellen Holloway gasped in unison. T.D. Dunne and Holloway's sons stepped away from the door as if expecting a monster to charge out at them.

A volunteer male nurse rushed past the group into the room, pulling on rubber gloves as he went. The patient's cry was choked off by a convulsive sob, then the gurgling, retching sound of vomit being expelled. Eleanor Welbourn covered her face.

"Doctor!" the nurse pleaded loudly from inside the room.

The group stood frozen in the hall. A young intern hurried into the room followed by Dr. Alan Triplett, who had left the tour earlier in response to a summons from the fifth floor. Wendy Ngo also stepped into the room, swinging the door half-closed behind her. Cole read the name taped to the door: DANNY FIRMAN.

"Danny is one of our advanced patients," Dr. No explained quietly. "His digestive system just doesn't work anymore. These attacks happen two or three times a day."

"How did he . . . ?" Grace Ellen didn't know exactly how to ask about the origin of Danny's condition.

"We don't know how Danny was infected, but he was in San Quentin for armed robbery and assault when his AIDS was discovered," Dr.

No said. Everyone leaned close to listen. "They gave him an early parole, but he has no family. He came back to L.A. hoping his gang buddies would take care of him. They didn't. Somehow he survived on the street for a year and a half until he could no longer take care of himself. We found him eight months ago, and he's been here ever since. He won't be with us much longer."

The group stood mute, listening. Soft but urgent commands from Dr. Triplett could be heard behind Danny Firman's groans and coughs. The man in a nurse's smock rushed out with a wad of soiled sheets and returned moments later with clean sheets and a handful of supplies.

As Danny's sounds of pain subsided, the group could hear a soft feminine voice. "It's okay, Danny. We're here with you. Jesus is right here too. We love you, Danny, and we won't leave you."

Intrigued, Cole moved to where he could see her through the half-open door. Wendy Ngo stood near the head of the bed as the intern patched the hole in Danny's arm where he had ripped out his IV in a fit of pain. Wendy was bent close to the patient's face. She stroked his forehead gently while anointing him with soothing words of assurance and encouragement. Danny's eyes were locked on hers as if the peace he so desperately craved was being transfused through her gaze.

The doctors and nurse finished their task and left the room, but Wendy remained. Other members of the group took turns peering in the door as Wendy caressed Danny's face, recited Bible verses, and prayed for him. Dr. No looked on, mirroring fatherly pride.

"I've never seen anything like that before." The voice at Cole's ear belonged to Stan Welbourn. "Look at the compassion pouring from her eyes. You can almost see the fear leave the man."

"But isn't she going to catch something standing that close to him and touching him?" Simon Holloway asked no one in particular, peering over Cole's other shoulder. No one answered.

"That was beautiful the way you calmed that man, young lady," Grace Ellen Holloway said as Wendy emerged from the room drying her hands, leaving Danny asleep. The rest of the group nodded their agreement. Dr. No stepped alongside his daughter and wrapped his arm around her shoulder. He said to the group, "Dr. Triplett and his staff are medical specialists, and we need them. But you don't need a doctor to do what Wendy just did. She has taught us all a lot about loving the unlovely."

Cole rode down the elevator with the group. Impressed as he was with what he had seen, he was unable to give King's House his full attention. *Where is Beth?* he asked himself repeatedly. *Why doesn't she call? What's wrong?*

As the group turned into the dining room for dessert, Cole walked to the front door to survey the parking lot, nodding to the young woman maintaining door security. Chief Robinson and Captain Thomasson were just stepping out of the chief's chauffeured black Bolt. But Beth's car was nowhere to be seen.

Before greeting his superiors, Cole sought a quiet corner in the hall and dialed Beth once again. Same five unanswered rings; same tone for leaving a message. The urgency of Cole's concern came out in his voice, "Beth, this isn't funny, not returning my calls. I'm . . . I'm worried about you. I just need to know where you are. Call me right away, Beth . . . please."

The room was as black as blindness except for a barely perceptible glimmer near the center. A tiny, silent, amber light—flashing *blip-blip, blip-blip, blip-blip*—illuminated a spot no larger than a nickel on its source—a compact telephone styled for a woman's hand. Surrounding the phone were the contents of a woman's purse.

The phone came to life again. Five soft tones called out. An even, synthetic voice answered and recited instructions. Another tone sounded. Then through the tiny speaker, "Beth, this isn't funny, not returning my calls. I'm . . . I'm worried about you. I just need to know where you are. Call me right away, Beth . . . please."

A faint *click* sent the message to memory. The minuscule amber light changed its pattern: *blip-blip-blip, blip-blip-blip*.

For the third time in ninety minutes, the only presence in the room, lying motionless a few feet from the table, had seen and heard nothing.

Fifty-four

The questions began flying before all the visitors had picked up their squares of chocolate sheet cake and found seats at two large tables in the cafeteria. Chief Robinson and Captain Thomasson took seats with the other police officers in the back of the room to await their opportunity to discuss the death threats and assure the leaders of their commitment to provide ironclad security at the Coliseum on Millennium's Eve.

"How many people are served at King's House each month?"

Administrator Will Danielson, who had joined the tour group in the cafeteria for cake and questions, gave a statistical breakdown of each of the House's ministries: meal service, overnight shelter, clothing distribution, job training, counseling, medical treatment, and prisoner visitation and counseling. "And on average," he concluded soberly, "five people die in King's House every month."

"How were you able to purchase this old hospital, and how do you finance your day-to-day operation?"

Dr. No told the story of his vision for King's House and how scores of people had volunteered large sums of cash toward the purchase of a facility. In response to pressing questions, he reluctantly admitted that he and his co-directors, Will Danielson and Alan Triplett, had contributed the lion's share toward the purchase of Queen of Angels Hospital by cashing in IRAs and liquidating other investments.

"You rolled all your personal assets into the ministry?" young Mark Holloway exclaimed more than asked.

"Most, but not all," Dr. Triplett interjected.

"But what about your children, doctor?" Simon Holloway cut in. "Don't you feel responsible to provide for them after you're . . . gone?"

"Rachelle and I have set aside a small amount for our children's education—with a little left over for emergencies. But what you saw Wendy do on the fifth floor a few minutes ago, that's the real inheritance my wife and I want to leave for Skip, Summer, and Tippy." Standing in the back of the room, Wendy lowered her eyes demurely.

Dr. No broke into the conversation to change the subject. "As for the ongoing need for operating funds, we purchased King's House thinking we would solicit support from churches in the city. But we found that most churches were already deluged with worthy opportunities. It didn't seem fair to us to ask them to move their support from other ministries to ours.

"Since King's House was God's idea, we began to ask Him if He had a plan for its operation. Then Will came up with an idea that we believe is providential." With a nod, he invited Will to speak.

"Early on, the business sector, especially downtown, was very supportive of our efforts to help people off the streets and encourage them back into the mainstream. They understood that what we were doing was good for the community and good for business.

"One day a jeweler on Hope Street called me and said, 'Mr. Danielson, I think your organization is doing a fine job in our city. If I were a grocer, I'd send over fifty pounds of potatoes. But I'm a jeweler, and I don't suppose a gold necklace would help.'

"We laughed about his comment. Then I said, without even really thinking, 'No, but if you sell that necklace and send us your profit, we could put it to good use.'

"He said, 'I'll tell you what I'll do. I have a particular necklace in stock that hasn't sold well. It's not a popular style, and I think it's overpriced. If I sell one this month, I'll be happy. If I sell two, which will be a miracle, I *will* send the profits to King's House.'

"I told Dr. Triplett and Dr. No about it, so we began to pray that someone would come in and buy Mr. Detweiler's necklace. The first one sold in a week. By the end of the month, Detweiler had sold four of them. He was so overwhelmed that he sent us the profits for all four."

Half the mouths in the room dropped open.

"Since that time we have been systematically contacting businesses around town to explain what we do. To those who seem appreciative, we make a simple proposal."

Will held up one finger for each point. "First, designate one product you sell or one service you provide as a King's House project. Second, determine a reasonable sales goal for that product or service for the coming month or quarter. Third, dedicate any profits you receive above and beyond your goal to the ministry of King's House.

"Then every month we distribute to our volunteers and friends a prayer list of companies who have set project sales goals. We ask people to pray for the success of those businesses in general and especially for the items they have targeted as King's House projects. The monthly contributions we have received since instituting this program have covered all our operating expenses and provided a base for expanding our work."

A whistle of amazement from Tim Holloway aptly expressed the feelings of the captivated listeners.

"For example," Will continued, "we found a car dealer in town who sells about eight Zap Runabouts a month. After hearing our presentation, he set a goal to sell twelve Zaps last month. We put the dealership on the prayer list, and fifteen Zaps sold in November. The dealer was thrilled because he met his sales goal and also gained a tax write-off. And we were thrilled because the proceeds from the last three cars he sold nearly paid for a month's worth of groceries.

"This month there are people all over the city praying for computer stores, machine shops, restaurants, attorneys, plumbers—you name it. And you would be amazed at how often these businesses exceed their sales goals for their King's House projects. Now we have companies *coming to us* hoping to set up projects and get on that prayer list."

T.D. Dunne asked, "Is your staff salaried?"

"Not completely. Apart from free rent and utilities, Dr. Triplett, Dr. No, and I receive nothing—by our choice. A couple of our wives work outside the building. And we each have a number of friends and relatives who have supported us generously and faithfully since King's House began. We don't live at the levels we used to, but then we don't really care to anymore.

"The House maintains a salaried staff, twenty-six full-time people who coordinate our services—although about a third of them insist on working for the grand sum of $1 per year. Then we have a volunteer staff—200 or so, I've lost count: doctors, nurses, aides, maintenance engineers, custodians, cooks, dishwashers, counselors, secretaries. . . ."

Will's comment trailed off in mid-sentence when Shelby Hornecker stood. Ever since she had begun the tour of King's House, a coil spring of anxiety had been winding tighter and tighter within her.

The sight of street-weary residents throughout the building had summoned strong images from her recent dreams. A Latino family on the second floor reminded her of Soledad and Lupe Cruz and their precious children. A cluster of impoverished residents gathered in a fourth-floor conference room for a Bible study recalled the stream of needy souls filling the Victory Life sanctuary in her dream. And the haggard faces of the AIDS patients on the fifth floor . . . Shelby had seen them before too in her dream scene of the streets of Los Angeles where she encountered the black stranger.

And from every corner of the building, inaudible but no less perceptible, she had heard again the seven words thundering in her consciousness like seven driving drumbeats, *Do you love Me? Feed My sheep.* Then as Shelby had listened to Dr. No and Will Danielson unfold the amazing story of King's House, another word—an appallingly unthinkable word—added a heart-stopping counterpoint to the rhythmic reprise from her dream: *Sabbatical.*

Oh no, dear God, she had pleaded silently, *You wouldn't direct me to spend my sabbatical here. You wouldn't pluck me from a deserted highway near Los Angeles, Texas only to sentence me to three months penance in a rescue mission in Los Angeles, California! What would my family think? What would my congregation think?*

Do you love Me? Feed My sheep. Sabbatical.

Shelby had risen to her feet intending to break the momentum of what she desperately hoped was not a message from God. Then she asked a question hoping that the answer given by the King's House directors—their motivation for leaving a normal, comfortable life for the squalor of Los Angeles' dark side—would somehow disqualify her from the command pounding within her. "Why did you gentlemen decide to do this?"

Shelby sat down expectantly, and Alan and Will yielded the floor to Dr. No with a glance.

He began, "Mrs. Hornecker, your question leads into the devotional thought I had prepared to share with all of you tonight. I'm not a gifted speaker like yourselves, but Mr. Malachi asked . . . so I trust you will bear with me."

He called for a Bible, which his son David supplied. Then he read aloud the passage from Genesis describing Jacob's wrestling match with God.

"Ten years ago, my relationship with God was a lot like Jacob's in this passage. I was holding onto God for all I was worth, begging Him to bless me. My needs and wants were the focus of the relationship. I sought material success. I craved recognition in my work and authority in my church. I wanted my prayers answered my way. I wanted God's work done my way. Basically, I was a follower of Jesus for what

I could get out of Him to make my life more rewarding, more comfortable, and more significant.

"Like Jacob, I paid a high price for my stubborn self-centeredness. I didn't get my hip knocked out of joint, but my heart was out of joint, and my family was out of joint. I was spending too much time at work and at church trying to get the blessings I felt I deserved. But for all the money I earned and prestige I acquired, I only wanted more. My whole life was consumed with Jacob's cry, 'I won't let You go until You bless me.'"

Dr. No stared at the page in his Bible for almost a minute, ordering thoughts, choosing words. His tiny congregation was respectfully silent. Even the eight police officers in the back of the room sat quietly, waiting.

"Then I made a discovery—something so fundamental that I'm embarrassed to mention it in a group of mature Christian leaders. I discovered that it is more blessed to give than to receive. I discovered that God has already given us everything we need in Christ, and that life as a child of God is to be an experience of giving back to God what He has given us. Maybe it was okay in the Old Testament for Jacob to wrestle God for a blessing. But if Jacob lived today, I think he might say to God, 'Thank You for everything You have provided for me. I won't let You go *until I bless You.*'

"King's House came into being when several of us realized there was something specific we could do to be a blessing to God, something He has already told us about. In the parable Jesus gave about the sheep and the goats, He said that those who feed the hungry, shelter the homeless, clothe the naked, and care for the sick and imprisoned are doing it for God. So when we wrap our arms around the poor, diseased, and directionless people who come to us and say to them, 'We won't let you go until we bless you,' we know that we are blessing God. We can't think of anything more worthwhile to do. So that's why we do it."

"Thank you, Dr. Ngo, for your helpful explanation, and God bless you."

The hauntingly familiar voice from the back of the room stunned the already shaken Shelby Hornecker. The instant charm and congeniality, the crystal tone, the melodic accent recalled another poignant image from the puzzling dreams of only days ago.

Looking beyond the group seated before him, Dr. No smiled and said, "Good evening, Mr. Malachi. We have been expecting you."

All heads turned to see the tall, gleaming black man striding regally toward Dr. No's outstretched hand of welcome.

Shelby's eyes instantly filled with tears of awe and holy fear. *It's him!* she gasped inside. *The African man in my dream!*

The drumbeat within her reached a deafening crescendo: *Do you love Me? Feed My sheep. Sabbatical.*

Fifty-five

Had there been an opportunity at the conclusion of the King's House meeting, Cole would have taken Mai Ngo aside and confided to her his mounting concern over Beth's puzzling nonappearance. If anyone would be willing to share his burden, he thought, Mai would. She had exuded a big sister's interest in the visiting journalist for whom Cole discovered such deep feelings.

But the director of King's House and his wife had been surrounded by their appreciative guests from the moment the suave African Unity 2000 committeeman pronounced the benedictory amen. So Cole paced quietly at the outer periphery of the talkative knot of Christians, wondering what more he could do than to keep trying to contact Beth by phone.

And had Shelby Hornecker seemed more sociable in the Bolt as Cole and Jayne and their passengers left Echo Park to return to the Biltmore, Cole might have said something to her about Beth. Nothing portentous, of course. Just a comment like, "I'm sorry you didn't get to meet Beth tonight; I don't know why she wasn't here." To which Shelby or Theresa could have responded reassuringly, "Don't worry. There must be a dozen places in Los Angeles an active young woman like your friend would rather be than at a homeless shelter."

But neither Shelby nor her assistant had spoken a word since Cole pulled out of the parking lot. The sergeant was convinced that the two women had a lot on their minds. The sights and sounds of King's House had arrested *his* attention; how much more had the poignant caregiving ministry intrigued those committed to caring for the poor for religious reasons. Shelby had seemed completely absorbed in the tour and especially captivated by Dr. No's presentation in the cafeteria. Then she seemed struck dumb at Mr. Malachi's appearance. Cole wasn't about to break the pensive silence in the Bolt to talk about Beth.

And as if she didn't have enough on her mind, Shelby also had to deal with the sobering details of the VoiceLink caller, as presented by Chief DeShea Robinson in terse cop-speak at the conclusion of the meeting. Robinson had decided that since the department had yet to turn up a suspect, full disclosure of the known facts was appropriate.

The chief had read aloud the three chilling messages of judgment directed at Holloway, Hornecker, and McClure. Then he added flippantly, "Mr. Dunne, don't feel left out. We expect this loony to add you to the hit list in tomorrow's call." No one laughed.

Lacking the full measure of tact his position required, the chief had graphically extrapolated "torn flesh" and "shattered bones" to imply the mutilating and dismembering capabilities of a number of sophisticated modern plastic explosives, some even defying detection by bomb dogs. He shocked the group by describing the utter simplicity of concocting a lethal explosive from such common elements as nitrate and diesel oil. "Any eighth-grader could do it," he almost bragged.

Chief Robinson's tactlessness reached its apex when he used the fated Victory Life Films charter as an example of the death and destruction effected by half-brained nuts and terrorists. From his chair in the back of the room, Cole could see Shelby and her team cringe at the reminder of the carnage.

Having unnerved his audience with the possibilities, Chief Robinson proceeded to dismiss any likelihood of an attack. "This caller likes to think he's capable of something terrible, and he wants *us* to think it too," he stated. "But in our experience, the nuts who make the most noise don't know a blasting cap from a thimble."

He assured the leaders that the Coliseum was "clean" and that extra security teams were on duty to guarantee that it stayed that way through the end of the program on Millennium's Eve.

Simon Holloway had been the first to respond to the chief. He said he was prepared to go through with Unity 2000, whether or not the VoiceLink caller was apprehended. T.D. Dunne voiced his confidence in the LAPD's security force at the Coliseum and also voted to go forward. Stan Welbourn, speaking for a subdued Shelby Hornecker, agreed that the show must go on. Ebullient Mr. Malachi had applauded the group for its courage and commitment, then closed the meeting in prayer.

"May we drive around the Coliseum again tonight please, sergeant?" Shelby broke the silence as Cole accelerated up the on-ramp of the eastbound Hollywood Freeway. "Then I will be ready to turn in for the night."

"Of course, ma'am," Cole agreed. He appreciated her commitment to another silent prayer vigil after such a trying evening. But he dreaded the traffic that clogged the streets around the Sports Arena and Coliseum on a game night.

He switched on the AM radio and tuned to the Clippers' broadcast. The Trail Blazers were leading the game by 8 points with four minutes to go. *Perfect timing*, Cole thought wryly. *The game will end about the time we arrive at Exposition Park, plunging us into gridlock as the streets flood with departing fans.*

By the time the Bolt left the freeway at Exposition Boulevard, Cole could see the cars and foot traffic beginning to stream away from the Arena. He turned left onto Figueroa in order to circle Exposition Park in a clockwise direction, avoiding left turns in the swelling traffic.

"I'm sorry, sergeant," Shelby said as the Bolt crept down Figueroa and eased onto King Boulevard. "I didn't realize this would be an ordeal."

"It's okay, ma'am. It won't take too long to get around the block. Then we'll be out of here." Cole quietly assessed that being stuck in Sports Arena traffic was better than spending the last hour of his watch in a booth with Jayne at the Grand Avenue Bar.

Rivulets of jaywalkers coursed between the cars, slowing traffic further. A knot of rowdy teenagers swept past the Bolt, thumping the hood and trunk with their hands and ogling the three women inside. Cole inched the car ahead steadily, encouraging his passengers to ignore the distraction.

Traffic was even slower on Menlo Avenue along the west side of the Park. Had the Bolt been traveling much faster, Cole would have missed the sight that caused him to stop abruptly in the middle of the street, provoking a series of tire chirps from the braking cars behind him. He had stopped alongside a candy-apple red Star Cruiser parked at the curb.

"What's up, sarge?" Jayne asked, scanning the crowd on the sidewalk for trouble.

Cole didn't answer. He quickly stepped out of the Bolt to get a better look at the Cruiser. The driver of the Mercedes behind him angrily jumped out to confront Cole about nearly causing an accident. The sergeant stopped the approaching man mid-stride by flashing his badge and stating crisply, "Police business, sir. Shut up, and get back into your car." The man apologized and hastily obeyed.

It's Beth's car, all right, Cole determined from his vantage point in the middle of the street. *The scrapes on the door, the crumpled trunk tied down with nylon cord are dead giveaways. But what is it doing here?*

The cacophony of horns and curses from angry motorists hastened Cole back into the Bolt. "That's my friend Beth's rental car," he announced to his passengers as he resumed his circle of the Park. "I know she wanted to go to the game, but I can't believe she didn't tell anyone about her change of plans."

Crawling down Menlo, Cole searched the throng on the sidewalk for Beth, welcoming a tentative measure of relief. *No wonder I couldn't reach her,* he thought. *The crowd in the Arena was so noisy she couldn't hear her phone, or the game was so exciting she didn't want to answer it. She is somewhere in this horde of people. When she's seated safely inside the Cruiser, she'll check her messages and return my calls.*

He couldn't wait. He found his pocket phone and tapped Beth's number with his thumb. No answer. He muffled a curse.

Shelby spoke up. "Sergeant, would you like to drive around again to see if she shows up?"

Cole was suddenly embarrassed for allowing his personal life to interfere with his assignment. "That's all right, ma'am. I need to get you back to the hotel. I'm sure she must have been at the game. She's in this crowd somewhere. Besides, we're meeting a mutual friend after I get off work tonight. It will all make sense then."

He hoped he was right.

Cole psyched himself up all the way from Southwest Division headquarters to the University Hilton. He would walk into the lounge and find Beth and Curtis Spooner waiting for him at their favorite table. Beth still hadn't returned his calls, nor did Cole see her Star Cruiser in its usual space in the Hilton garage. But after parking the Kawasaki and removing his helmet, Cole took a moment to comb his hair in hopes that Beth would be inside to appreciate it.

Spooner was not alone in the lounge. With the rest of the Trail Blazers already on a plane back to Portland, the muscular reserve guard was the celebrity of the hour. A quartet of flirty females hovered over him at the table, pestering him for attention and an autograph. But Beth was not one of them, nor was she anywhere in the room.

Cole invaded the huddle around Spooner and dismissed the women curtly. "Has Beth been here, Spoon?" he asked, without greeting his friend.

"This *must* be love, my friend," Spooner chuckled. "I didn't hear, 'How are you, Spoon?' or 'Good game,' or 'Let me buy you a beer.' First thing I hear is, 'Spoon, have you seen my woman?'"

"I'm serious, man," Cole said, sitting down. "I was supposed to be with her tonight, but she didn't show. And she's not answering her phone. Has she been here?"

"No, Reag, I haven't seen her yet tonight," Spooner answered, taken aback at Cole's brusque manner.

"Did you see her at the game? Did she use your tickets?"

"No, man. They sold my seats to a couple of Iranians. If she was at the game, I never saw her. What's going on?"

Cole swept aside the question with one of his own. "Is your Caddy here?"

"Yeah, but what—"

There was an edge of panic in Cole's voice. "Drive me over to the other side of the Arena and I'll explain."

Traffic around Exposition Park had thinned to near normal for a Wednesday night at almost midnight. The street corners were dotted with winos sharing bottles and youths selling drugs and hustling change. Post-game litter swirled in the gutters and doorways prompted by a mild Santa Ana breeze.

At Cole's insistence, Curtis Spooner cheated a couple of yellow lights as he raced his rented Cadillac Excelis coupe from the Hilton on Figueroa toward King Boulevard. As they drove, Cole explained Beth's sudden disappearance and vented his trepidation that she had fallen into something she couldn't handle.

"She said she was doing something late this afternoon that she couldn't tell me about—research for her book or something. She said she'd explain it to me when we met at King's House." Cole cursed angrily at himself. "Like an idiot I trusted her judgment. She's been away from L.A. too long, Spoon. She doesn't know how easy it is to find trouble here, even when you're not looking for it."

"There's probably a logical explanation for all this," Spooner said, trying to shore up his friend's flagging spirits. "Have you called her parents?"

"Beth is not on great terms with her folks, Spoon. She's only at the house long enough to sleep and change clothes. And she couldn't have been home tonight, because her car was parked on Menlo next to the Coliseum. But if she wasn't at the game, where was she? I just hope the car is gone now. There's nothing worthwhile to do in this part of town at midnight."

Most of the cars on Menlo Avenue had disappeared since the end of the game. But as Cole feared, the red Star Cruiser was still parked where he had seen it over an hour earlier. He directed Spooner to pull up behind it. The southwest rim of the Coliseum loomed above them just inside the fence.

"Something's wrong," Cole said, eyeing the Cruiser and shaking his head.

"Are you sure this is her car?"

"Spoon, I was there when the Latin Barons rammed her trunk. I know this car." Cole was climbing out of the car as he spoke. Then he stuck his head back inside. "Does this rig have a beam? I have to look inside."

"It has everything else. It must have a beam." Spooner searched the dash until he found the pop-out, rechargeable, cordless beam. He ejected it from its recessed storage panel, handed it to Cole, then stepped out to watch his friend search.

The doors were clearly in lock position. Cole shined the beam into the front—the bucket seats, the floor, the dash, and around the center console. Nothing seemed unusual.

Cole moved to the back door and aimed the beam inside, leaning close to the window and shading his eyes from the glare. There was a moment of silent inspection, then, "O dear Jesus, no!"

"What's wrong?" Spooner stepped to his friend's side and leaned near the window, following the bright beam to the floor. An old drab army blanket had been hastily thrown over an irregular form on the floor between the seats. The blanket was spotted and streaked dark red. Faint smears on the white leather seat looked like blood. "O God, help us," Spooner whispered.

"I've got to get in there," Cole said resolutely. He took a step back from the car and launched three violent kicks at the window with the heel of his boot. He failed to break the glass.

Spooner grabbed him by the shoulders and pulled him away from the car. "Get a grip on yourself, Reag. You don't need to see this. Call the station. Get some cops over here to open the car. They'll know what to do."

Cole struggled free. "I *am* a cop! I *know* what to do!" he shouted angrily. Then he took a calming breath. "Here," he said, handing his friend the beam and his phone. "You can call 911, but I have to look inside before they get here."

While Spooner dialed, Cole hurried to the trunk of the Cruiser, pulled out a pocket knife, and slashed through the nylon cord securing the lid. Lifting the trunk floor, he removed the lug wrench from the clips securing it to the trunk well.

It took several hard blows on the safety glass to punch a hole large enough for Cole to reach in and manually release the rear door lock. He opened the door and squatted at the curb. Having completed his call, Spooner stood over his friend.

Cole reached out a hand and felt along the top of the blanket, avoiding contact with the many glass fragments. He hoped to prove wrong his suspicion about what was underneath. After a moment he said, "It's a body—a knee and ankle at this end." There was a slight quaver in his voice.

Cole paused, breathless. Sirens wailing in the distance signaled approaching black-and-whites.

"You don't have to do this, Reag," Spooner assured.

"Yes . . . yes, I do. Give me some light."

Spooner aimed the beam over Cole's shoulder at the bloody shroud on the floor. After another deep breath, Cole slowly pulled the blanket away.

"Oh, geez," he muttered. Then he dropped his head in his hands.

Spooner groaned at the sight and turned away. When he turned back, he gripped Cole by the shoulders. "Thank God, it's not her," he breathed.

The body was that of a man—a tall, skeleton of a man folded up and awkwardly wedged between the front and rear seats. His dirty clothes were soaked with blood. His pasty-white face was contorted into a grimace suggesting that his final thought was one of betrayal.

A worn leather wallet stuck half out of a hip pocket. Cole carefully removed it. The wallet was empty except for a dog-eared social security card.

"What's his name?" Spooner asked.

Cole's hand was still shaking. He squinted to make out the name. "It says Gideon L. Wingate."

Fifty-six

Cole and Spooner watched in stunned silence as two attendants transferred the sheet-draped corpse from the back seat of the Star Cruiser to the coroner's van. The preliminary examination had revealed several deep stab wounds to the chest and abdomen, any one of which could have killed the unfortunate street person.

Gaudy red and amber lights splashing the scene from two black-and-whites and the animated chatter of four uniformed cops belied any semblance of respect for the dead. A tow truck driver waited impatiently beside his rig, which was poised to drag the Cruiser to an LAPD impound lot. Several small clusters of street people gawked from a respectable distance.

Sergeant Epstein from Southwest Detective Division had concluded a hasty crime scene investigation. The detective cursed repeatedly about being called out in the middle of the night to investigate "a bag of bones worth no more than gum stuck to the sidewalk."

The Star Cruiser showed no signs of forced entry or jimmied ignition. But the keys, which had obviously been used to drive the vehicle to the Menlo Street location, were missing. An ID scan of Gideon L. Wingate turned up only a date of birth and the address of a fleabag hotel on Grand Avenue downtown. At Epstein's request, a unit from Central Division checked the hotel and found that Wingate hadn't lived there in two years.

Cole had encountered Epstein at a few of crime scenes in the past and didn't like his calloused attitude toward innocent victims. "It was his own fault for being in the wrong place at the wrong time," Epstein had said more than once about a victim of assault, robbery, or homicide—as if the poor soul had made an appointment to be mugged or killed.

When Cole tried to explain to the surly detective that the woman who had rented the car could be in great danger, Epstein nodded with a smirk and said, "You bet your life she is. A severely perforated bum is found in the back seat of her rental car. She's wanted for questioning in a homicide and has disappeared. Yeah, I'd call that pretty great danger."

Seething at Epstein's insensitivity, Cole took a step toward grabbing him as the detective sauntered toward his car. Spooner held him back. "Don't get yourself kicked out of the game, Reag," he warned. "You have to channel your feelings toward something positive. You won't do Beth any good from a jail cell."

Cole didn't need much encouragement to refocus his thoughts on Beth's disappearance. He relaxed his posture while glaring after the departing detective. "You're right, Spoon," he sighed. "Thanks."

Cole called Beth again. As he waited through the five unanswered tones, the coroner's van, Epstein's Runabout, and one of the black-and-whites left the scene. Cole was not surprised when the same leave-a-message-at-the-tone spiel came through the receiver.

He switched off his phone and looked toward the black sky. "Where are you, Beth?" he asked at a whisper, as if bouncing his concerned plea off an unseen satellite to wherever she was. "I can't help you if I don't know where you are."

The grip of Spooner's hand on his shoulder brought Cole back to earth. "You've got to call Beth's parents, Reag," he urged, as they watched the tow truck operator attach the Cruiser's front wheels to his rig. "If Beth happens to be at home, you'll save yourself a lot of grief. And if she's not, well, her mom and dad deserve to know what's going on."

Cole reluctantly agreed. They retreated to the front seat of Spooner's Cadillac to escape the noisy strain of the tow truck lifting the Cruiser.

Cole accessed the Scibelli residence in Woodland Hills. He winced as he read the numerals on the dashboard clock: 1:07 A.M.

After several tones, a sleepy feminine voice answered, "Hello."

"Mrs. Scibelli?"

The woman on the phone cleared her voice. "Who is this?"

"Ma'am, this is Reagan Cole, a friend of your daughter," Cole said, trying not to sound like a cop. "I'm very sorry to bother you at this hour, but I'm trying to reach Beth. It's rather urgent, and she's apparently away from her phone. Can you tell me if she's at home?"

"It's very late, Mr. Cole," the woman said, annoyed. "She is probably in bed by now. Perhaps you should call back—"

"I know this is an imposition, Mrs. Scibelli, but would you please see if Beth can come to the phone?"

There were muffled conversational tones in the background, then the woman said curtly, "Just a moment."

Cole held the phone away from his mouth. "She's going to look for her," he whispered to Spooner. Then he added wistfully, "I just hope to God she's there."

While Cole waited, the tow truck pulled away from the curb with its candy-apple-red burden in tow. The sight of Beth's Star Cruiser being towed away brought another twist to the anxious knot which had been turning in his stomach since early evening.

Again Cole heard hushed tones in the background. Then a man's voice spoke to him over the phone. Any sense of irritation over the late call had been replaced by mild apprehension.

"Mr. Cole, this is Beth's father."

"Yes sir."

"Beth is not here. As near as I can tell, she hasn't been home since she left this morning. Do you know where she might be?"

Cole paused, pondering how much to reveal of what he knew. "No, sir, I was hoping *you* might tell *me*. Beth was supposed to meet me this evening near USC, but I guess she made other plans. I'm sure she'll be home eventually. After all, it's a holiday week—party time. Please have her call me tomorrow."

Spooner urged his friend with a mild scowl to get to the point of Beth's strange disappearance. But instead Cole apologized again to Mr. Scibelli for the inconvenience and hung up.

Spooner started to scold him for not telling the Scibellis more about the grisly circumstances surrounding the discovery of Beth's car, but Cole cut him off. "I can't tell them over the phone that Beth has been missing for almost eight hours and that a bloody corpse was just found in her abandoned car." Cole bit his lip. "If she's still missing by tomorrow morning, I'll ride out there and tell them about it in person. Then I'll stand on Epstein's throat until he starts looking for her."

Spooner read the worry in his friend's face and laid a comforting hand on his shoulder. "In the meantime, how can I help you, Reag?"

Cole sighed heavily. "Drop me off at the Hilton, then you can drive out to the house and get some sleep. I'll give you my security card."

"What about you?"

"I can't just wait around. I've got to do something. I think I'll ride the bike over to King's House and talk to the *Times* editor Beth has been working with. She'll want to know what we found tonight. She may have an idea where I can look for her."

"Hey, man, it's almost 1:30 in the morning. You go knocking on their door at this hour and they're going to shoot you."

"No, these people are . . . different," Cole said thoughtfully. "Strange as it may sound, I think they'll be happy to see me. They're not just good religious people, Spoon. They're deeply caring people. There's something genuine, something . . . substantial . . . about them. Besides, from what I heard earlier tonight, Dr. No and his wife seem to know a lot about making miracles happen. I need to talk to them about what happened tonight. Maybe they have a direct line to the Big Man upstairs."

"Well, then, let's go wake them up. Where is this King's House place?" Spoon fired up the Caddy, tapped on the lights, and selected DRIVE on the console control panel.

"Hey, Spoon, you don't need to do this," Cole said. "Go home and get some sleep and I'll—"

"Forget it," Spooner interjected. "I can sleep anytime. I'm going with you. Now where is this place?"

Cole gave directions, then he dialed King's House to tell the Ngos that he was bringing news about Beth.

The Caddy roared away from the curb, leaving behind the last disbursing cluster of curious street people. Watching the departing white vehicle from the shadows with particular interest was a man wearing a shaggy jean jacket and Dodgers cap and carrying a picnic chest.

Dr. No and his wife met Reagan Cole and Curtis Spooner at the front door of King's House. Smiles of welcome momentarily brightened the pall of concern on their faces.

Cole introduced Spooner and apologized profusely for visiting at such an unthinkable hour. But the Vietnamese couple assured him that they were anxious to hear the latest developments in Beth's strange disappearance.

The Ngos ushered Cole and his friend to the cafeteria and brewed coffee while Cole related the discovery of the Star Cruiser and Wingate's body and expressed his fear for Beth's safety. Shaken at the news, Mai dabbed at her eyes and nose with a tissue. Dr. No mirrored Cole's concern in his furrowed brow. Spooner sat beside Cole in silent support.

"And the worst thing is not knowing," Cole concluded, wringing his hands in front of his untouched cup of coffee. Then looking at Mai, "Can you remember anything Beth said about what she was going to do yesterday? Did she mention any names or places?"

Mai thought for a moment, then shook her head. "She said only that she was going to the library for the afternoon and that she had an appointment at 5. I invited her to dinner, but she said her appointment would involve her right up to 7. She said nothing about the place or the people she was meeting at 5."

Cole said, "She also turned down dinner with me and Shelby Hornecker's crew."

Then he asked Mai, "What did she talk about when you were together at the *Times*?"

"A little about her project. But she seemed especially interested in the threatening calls coming in on the VoiceLink line. She wanted to be there when each message came in. She was obviously concerned for the safety of her parents, especially after the first specific threat appeared to be aimed at Simon Holloway."

Cole nodded. "Yes, she was worried—almost paranoid—that we wouldn't catch the nut making the calls and that her parents might be caught in the cross fire in an attempt on Holloway's life."

"And she was afraid for you too, sergeant, after you were assigned to escort Mrs. Hornecker," Mai added. "No wonder she was concerned. Three people very important to her were implicated by those calls on VoiceLink."

Spooner spoke next, addressing both Cole and Mai. "Was Beth worried enough or afraid enough to do something . . . crazy . . . to try to find the maniac and stop him herself?"

"Or stupid enough," Cole added, huffing.

Mai asked rhetorically, "Even if Beth wanted to find the caller herself, what chance would she have when the police haven't been able to turn a clue about his identity?"

"What I'm getting at is this," Spooner said. "Could Beth have possibly stumbled onto something about the caller's location or identity and simply kept it to herself while planning to do something about it?"

Cole answered, "When I talked to her this afternoon she promised to tell me all about her appointment when she arrived here for the meeting. She said I would be impressed with what she had to say—actually, 'surprised and pleased' were her exact words. Maybe she *was* on to something."

Spooner continued, "If she thought she was on to something, would she have the gall to go after the caller without telling either of you or her parents?"

Mai shrugged ignorance. Cole said quietly, "After witnessing her confrontation with the Latin Barons on Christmas Eve, I'd say Beth has the attitude of a Pekingese picking a fight with a pit bull. She definitely has the gall but not the common sense or respect or fear—and that's a dangerous deficit in L.A. I had hoped she learned a lesson on the freeway. And today I warned her again. . . ." Cole let his words trail away, suddenly flooded with the same feelings for Beth that had prompted his caution to her several hours earlier.

The others at the table respected Cole's inner struggle with a moment of silence.

Then Spooner said, "Maybe this Wingate guy was connected with the guy making the phone calls. Maybe Beth got tangled up with Wingate in her search for the caller. Maybe they both got too close to the bad guy and. . . ." Spooner didn't want to speculate further.

"Maybe the man you found tonight is—or was—the VoiceLink caller," Mai advanced, thinking aloud.

The thought had already crossed Cole's mind. He wanted to believe that Gideon L. Wingate was the voice on the VoiceLink line and that the death threats to Shelby Hornecker and her colleagues—whether real or a cruel hoax—had died with him. But the sorry-looking, foul-smelling transient appeared completely incapable of such a clever strategy. Spooner's chilling premonition seemed more likely: that Beth had stumbled across Wingate on her foolish solo venture into L.A.'s dark side, and Wingate—and possibly Beth—had paid the price for their folly.

Cole's frustration with the unknown abruptly boiled into an angry eruption. He had the presence of mind to stifle the expletive forming on his lips. Instead he slammed his fist on the table, launching a wave of cold coffee from his mug onto the table. Then he pushed himself away from the table and stood to pace.

"So what did she know—or think she knew—that separated her from her car and phone? How did she get involved with that disgusting Wingate character? How do we know she's not just as dead as he is, stuffed into a trunk or closet or storm drain somewhere? And how are we ever going to find out what's happened to her?" Cole paced the length of the cafeteria and back as he vented a sense of futility.

When he returned to the table, Dr. No, who had been thoughtfully silent during the discussion, cleared his throat and spoke. "Sergeant, I don't know much about police work, but I've learned a few things about solving problems since I have been operating the House. It sounds like we have a major problem here. I wonder if I might make a suggestion."

Cole anticipated a religious pitch about standing in the need of prayer. Ordinarily, he walked away from anyone who hinted at a lecture about human inadequacy and an individual's need for God. But the respect he had gained for Dr. No and his mission during the tour several hours earlier prevented him from tuning out. Cole desperately needed a miracle, and he was ready to try almost anything. He looked at Dr. No expectantly and nodded.

"We have encountered obstacles of Mount Everest proportions in our work over the last few years—financial needs, staff needs, interpersonal conflicts, difficult residents. I don't mean to trivialize the danger Beth may be in by equating it with our occasional need for 500 pounds of potatoes or 100 bed sheets. But when you consider the seeming impossibilities we faced in solving those problems, there is a definite correlation.

"For example, earlier this year we needed $18,476 to place an order for medical supplies for the fifth floor. Dr. Triplett told us, 'We need that order in seven days or we will have to start putting our AIDS patients out on the street.' But Will Danielson said, 'We don't have $18,476, and we have no prospect of receiving anywhere near that amount in the next seven days.' We had a specific need that looked impossible."

Spooner interrupted. "You prayed, right?"

Dr. No nodded. "We invited our staff to an impromptu prayer meeting that same night. We got down on our knees and told God exactly what we needed—$18,476. We wrote the number down on a sheet of paper and laid it on the altar in our chapel. Then we thanked God for His love and generosity and went back to work."

Dr. No sat back as if there was nothing more to tell. Cole and Spooner leaned in. "And?" Spooner pressed.

"Two days later, a man drove up to the House in a bread delivery truck. He said he worked for the bakery where we buy our bread. They were getting rid of a couple of older trucks, and this man convinced his boss to donate one of them to us as a tax write-off. The truck was worth well over $20,000, so we had Mai list it in the *Times* classifieds the next day—for $18,476 exactly. It sold for cash in two days. We faxed the medical order and wired the money, and the supplies arrived exactly on time."

"Geez!" Cole whistled in amazement.

"Amen!" Spooner exclaimed. "T.D. Dunne talks about prayer too, and Natty and I have been doing more praying lately. But I've never heard anything like that before!"

Dr. No continued. "Mai and I learned years ago that many things are impossible for us, but nothing is impossible for God. And the bridge between our impossibility and His possibility is prayer—stating our specific needs to God and inviting Him to make a specific response. When that bread truck came to us and sold for exactly what we needed, there was no doubt that the answer to our prayer came from God, not from circumstances. Sometimes God's answers aren't as dramatic or as prompt as we would like. And sometimes, for whatever reason, He answers 'No.' But if we don't ask for God to meet our needs, they will surely go unmet.

"Sergeant, God is just as concerned for Beth as He is about anything we're doing around here. He knows where she is. He knows what she needs. How would you like us to pray for her?" Dr. No pulled a pen from his lab coat and poised it over a napkin, ready to write.

One side of the tall, muscular policeman wanted to bolt and run from the slight, humble man sitting across from him. Cole felt uncomfortable, self-conscious, out of his element. But another side, despairing at the ominous prospect that his new love had been snatched from him, controlled his response.

He spoke at just above a whisper. "Wherever she is, I want her to be safe. I want her to be alive."

Dr. No wrote a few words on the napkin.

After a thoughtful moment, Cole continued, "And if somebody is holding her against her will, I want her to be able to escape or to contact me so we can find her and help her."

Dr. No scribbled another note. "Anything else?"

Cole was silent, but Spooner spoke up. "I think you should pray about the VoiceLink caller. He's got to be found and stopped."

"I agree," Mai said. "Whatever his plans are, God can foil them and bring him out into the open."

When Dr. No finished writing on the napkin, he said, "All right, let's tell God what we need." He slipped out of his chair and knelt beside it, as did Mai.

Cole and Spooner looked at each other. Then they eased their large frames out of their chairs and lowered their knees to the floor.

Scenes ebbed and flowed through Beth's drugged brain like a restless tide. Each incoming swell of images swirled and mingled with the retreating wave to form a continually changing collage of places, faces, and events.

Beth saw the Star Cruiser being rammed by the Latin Barons' truck. The faces in the van were those of Simon Holloway, Shelby Hornecker,

T.D. Dunne, and Morgan McClure. A Latino gang member dived into the car and grabbed at her. She screamed an empty scream and battled futilely. The man's snarling face was transfigured into that of the devilish Mr. Hodge.

The terrifying image was washed away by a scene from the driveway of her parents' home. She and Reagan Cole were playing a midnight game of one-on-one. They played hard, bodies colliding, until they fell into a passionate embrace. Beth's parents, Mai Ngo, and the neighbors looked on disapprovingly.

Then Rev. Wingate's powerful arm closed around Beth's neck and ripped her from Reagan's grasp. As Wingate painfully twisted Beth's arm behind her back, Hodge herded the handsome police sergeant and Beth's parents and the four televangelists into the Los Angeles Memorial Coliseum, which was filled with people. While Beth watched in horror, a blinding blast reduced the huge concrete bowl and its occupants to smoldering gravel and shredded corpses.

The macabre scene dissolved into another and another and another: Olvera Street, Pershing Square, Figueroa Street, the Trojan Horse Saloon. In every scene Beth was assaulted and dragged away from her parents, Mai Ngo, or Reagan Cole by the same two sinister figures. When she tried to scream, nothing came out. When she tried to run from Hodge, her legs seemed encased in cement. When she tried to fight back, her arms would not move.

Scene after scene ended with Beth bound and helpless, tormented with pain, and paralyzed with fear as Hodge carried out his murderous scheme against the leaders of Unity 2000.

At some point in the night, reality began to steal into Beth's dreams. In her first frightful seconds of hazy consciousness, she was aware that she was flat on her back in total darkness. Her limbs seemed leaden, immovable. She sensed a subtle pressure on her face. She rolled her throbbing head—which seemed as large and heavy as a wrecking ball—slowly to one side and then the other. The puzzling constricting sensation across her brow and cheeks remained.

Beth's sluggish attempts to determine where she was and what had happened to her were quickly immersed in a residual wave of drug-induced stupor.

When Beth awoke again, the terror of total darkness was exacerbated by the realization that she was physically restrained. She could move her fingers, but her wrists were securely strapped down. She wiggled her toes but could not lift or turn her ankles. In her semiconsciousness, the pressure on her face seemed like a giant bandage across her eyes. She could see and hear nothing. With great effort she formed the questions: *Where am I? What's happening to me?*

Beth's lethargic imagination struggled to advance a response: *You're in a recovery room in the hospital. Your arms and legs are in restraints because you just had surgery. You awoke with the same sensation after your appendectomy in high school, remember? They tied you down so you wouldn't rip out your IV or tear away your bandage.*

But why am I in the hospital? Was I in a wreck? Did I suddenly become ill?

Sharp pains in Beth's right arm from her shoulder to her wrist injected a recent, terrifying memory into her tenuous consciousness: *I was tricked by Mr. Hodge. I was assaulted in the alley behind the taqueria and abducted by Hodge and Rev. Wingate. I must have been injured in the chase or the rescue. Thank God I'm in the hospital. Thank God I'm safe. I need to rest . . . to rest.*

The next time Beth awoke was in response to a door opening and closing. Soft noises in the room alerted her to someone's presence. She imagined that she must have been moved into a private room, although she was still in the dark and still restrained.

The urgent message was clear in Beth's mind: *Nurse, I need to use the toilet, please.* But when she tried to speak the words they were garbled and unintelligible. She worked at it until the word "toilet" became clear enough to prompt a response.

Beth's silent aide released the restraints and practically carried her to the toilet and back to the narrow bed. Beth whimpered in pain whenever she tried to use her right arm. Her feeble attempts to touch the bandage across her eyes were firmly thwarted. Her aide's steadying grip around her waist painfully reminded her that Hodge had sliced into her side with his knife.

Within seconds of returning to the bed Beth was out again. She didn't feel her wrists and ankles being retaped to the frame of the metal cot. Nor did she feel the needle plunge into her arm, engulfing her in several more hours of deathlike slumber.

NOVEMBER 1999
S M T W T F S
1 2 3 4 5 6
7 8 9 10 11 12 13
14 15 16 17 18 19 20
21 22 23 24 25 26 27
28 29 30

1999 DECEMBER 1999

S	M	T	W	T	F	S
			1	2	3	4
5	6	7	8	9	10	11
12	13	14	15	16	17	18
19	20	21	22	23	24	25
26	27	28	29	30	31	

JANUARY 2000
S M T W T F S
1
2 3 4 5 6 7 8
9 10 11 12 13 14 15
16 17 18 19 20 21 22
23 24 25 26 27 28 29
30 31

0 Day Till Millennium's Eve

Fifty-seven

Simon Holloway found Mark and Tim seated on the couch in their sweats and drinking coffee when he emerged from the suite's spare bedroom after prayers. Mark and Tim greeted their father as if they had been waiting anxiously for him—which they had.

Simon blinked with surprise. "It's barely 6 o'clock, lads; I can't believe you're up. Do you have an early workout this morning?"

"We're doing a lap swim at 7," Mark said, "but we were hoping to talk to you before we go over. Care for some coffee?" Mark poured a cup for his father without waiting for an answer.

"Talk? You two? At 6 A.M.?" Simon prodded disbelievingly. Then his amazement turned to suspicion and concern. "Why? What's wrong?"

"Nothing's wrong, Dad," the younger Tim said. "We just have something on our minds. Can you spare a few minutes?"

Simon noted the expectancy in his sons' faces. "Of course," he said, warmed at the prospect of a father-and-sons moment. He sat down in a chair next to the couch and received the steaming cup of coffee from Mark.

Tim looked to his older brother to break the ice. Mark began, "Dad, what do you think about King's House?"

Simon searched Mark's eyes for the inevitable question behind the question. Whatever it was, it eluded him. He decided to give a vanilla answer until he could ascertain Mark and Tim's point, although misgivings about the ministry in the old hospital had been on his mind ever since last night's tour. "Well, they appear to be doing a good work. The director seems compassionate and resourceful. The place is clean, well-organized. Why?"

Tim ignored his father's question to ask one of his own. "Did you see anything wrong with what they are doing, Dad?"

Unsure of his sons' direction, Simon opted for honesty. "Frankly, I was a little concerned about their location. They are vulnerable to gangs in the area who would think nothing of breaking in and hurting people to get food and drugs. If I were them, I'd think about—"

Mark cut him off with the next question. He was sitting on the edge of the couch. "What Tim means is, do you think King's House is a valid Christian ministry? Is there anything unbiblical about them that you can see?"

Mark's pointed question prompted Simon to verbalize a silent concern about King's House that had been gnawing at his insides since the tour. "For one thing, Dr. No doesn't appear to be as evangelistic as he could be. For example, King's House helps hundreds of people with their physical needs, but I didn't see much evidence that these derelicts are being converted to Christianity. I believe in soup *and* salvation. They're serving plenty of soup, but where's the salvation?

"What's more, King's House certainly doesn't share our emphasis of standing against the moral compromises of society. Dr. No seems to be doing a good job at what he does. My question is whether he is doing enough to combat the real adversaries of the faith."

"But you agree that King's House is doing ministry, I mean, they are meeting basic needs in the name of Christ," Mark clarified.

Simon's patience with the verbal game was wearing thin. "Mark, you have an agenda behind these questions. Why don't we just get to the point."

Mark fidgeted with his coffee cup, and the two boys exchanged nervous glances. Finally Mark said, "Dad, if a Christian young person wanted to get practical, hands-on ministry experience, don't you think King's House would be a good place to volunteer?"

At last Simon knew. "Are you talking about a young person like yourself, Mark?" he asked.

"Actually, both of us, Dad," Mark answered. "Tim and I were talking and praying last night and—"

"We hardly got any sleep at all, Dad," Tim cut in excitedly. "It was really cool, right Mark?"

Mark nodded, then continued. "We were talking about how great it would be to volunteer in a place like King's House some day, you know, work on the kitchen staff, do maintenance, take care of street people or AIDS patients. Working in a mission would be so down-to-earth, so fulfilling."

"We prayed about it too, Dad, for a long time—twenty minutes, maybe even half an hour," Tim interjected proudly.

"Dad," Mark concluded, "about 3 this morning Tim and I decided that we want to serve the Lord by signing up as volunteers at King's House. We'd like to start as soon as possible—if you and Mom agree."

Mark and Tim exchanged congratulatory looks, then turned to receive their father's response.

Simon Holloway's gut was a battlefield of conflicting emotions. His and Grace Ellen's prayer since the boys were born was that they would choose the ministry as a full-time vocation. It was always gratifying when they made a step in that direction. Their interest in King's House showed that their hearts were headed in the right direction.

But Simon's great desire was that his two sons would join him at Jubilee Fellowship and that one of them would eventually succeed him at the helm. He foresaw a dynasty of Holloway men continuing the fight against the ungodly army of biotechnicians and genetic engineers tampering with God's creation. Simon was nervous about anything that delayed their preparation to ascend the throne.

Simon tried not to sound disappointed. "What about your schooling,

Mark? You're only a junior."

"I still want to get a degree at JBC," Mark assured. "But I feel that I should delay it for at least six months to work at King's House. To be honest, I've been really bored at school. It's all theory with little practical application. I think a break will do me good. It will be a chance to practice what I've been learning about ministry. I've been praying about taking a break. I think King's House came along at just the right time."

Simon studied his elder son, flooded with pride at his maturity and stung by apprehension that his long-held fatherly goals for Mark might be in jeopardy.

"Once you drop out of school, it may be very hard to start again. You may lose your momentum, your drive to finish what you started."

"I'm aware of that temptation, Dad. I still believe it's God's will for me to graduate, and, thanks to your teaching and example, I am committed to do God's will. But Tim and I also believe that He brought us to Los Angeles this week—and to King's House last night—to discover another facet of His will. There is a great opportunity to serve here, and we feel that God is calling us to take this opportunity."

"How will you support yourselves?" Simon objected. "Volunteers don't receive a paycheck, you know."

Tim spoke first. "Disneyland isn't too far from downtown. I can transfer to Epcot West. I'll work part-time and volunteer part-time."

Mark followed. "I told Tim last night that I want to volunteer full-time. I can't explain it other than it's what I believe God is calling me to do. I'm not sure how I will cover my expenses. But, like you've taught us, where God leads, God provides."

"It won't cost us much to live here, Dad," Tim threw in. "I was talking to one of the volunteers last night, and he said that some of them live at King's House, you know, proctors in the shelter. Room and board is only a couple hundred a month."

Simon stiffened. "Living at King's House? Well, I don't think your mother will be too happy about your living in a gang-infested neighborhood," he said, poorly disguising his own discomfort with the idea. "And what about the diseases all those people bring in with them? She would be devastated if you contracted AIDS."

Mark said, "Mom isn't very happy when you picket a biotech lab where people pelt you with eggs and bottles and threaten to rearrange *your* genes. But you still do it because you know you're called to do it. We've heard you preach a hundred times, 'God never promised to take us *out of* tribulation, but He did promise to keep us *through* it.' Doesn't that apply to us?"

Simon shuddered at being fed his own medicine, but he was defenseless against it. His sons had done their homework.

"You know, lads, there must be places in Florida and up the East

Coast where you can get the same experience. We have homeless people and AIDS victims there too."

Mark and Tim glanced at each other knowingly. "We talked about that last night also," Mark said. "We thought, 'Wouldn't it be great if there was a King's House in Central Florida or even Miami?' Who knows, Dad, after our experience at King's House, maybe God will use Tim and me to establish a similar ministry at home someday. Maybe we will even have a King's House right there at Jubilee Village."

The concept sounded so foreign to Simon that he was momentarily speechless. He tried to envision the unsightly old Queen of Angels hospital standing beside his massive Tabernacle or among the luxurious condos. *It wouldn't look right*, he thought. He imagined with distaste street people and former convicts mingling in the Village with his Crusaders and Warriors. *Some of our people would stop attending; some would stop giving; the ministry would suffer.*

Mark interrupted his thoughts. "I know you need to talk to Mom about us spending a few months at King's House. But what's your first impression?" Mark and Tim leaned in eagerly.

For all the opposition he felt toward the idea, Simon knew not to say much until he and Grace Ellen had talked and prayed together. But he couldn't stifle his one pressing concern. "My heart's desire, lads, is that any ministry you get involved in now won't detour you from God's call on our lives at Jubilee Fellowship. There is so much we need to—"

"Dad," Mark interrupted, "there's something I need to say about God's call. This has been on my heart for several months, and I've been waiting for the right time to bring it up. I think that time is now."

Tim looked at his big brother quizzically, convincing Simon that his sons had not talked together about what Mark was preparing to discuss.

Mark released a deep breath. "I want to say this as respectfully as I can. Dad, *you* have been called to Jubilee Fellowship, but up to this point in my life, *I* have not been similarly called. I know that it's your great hope that Tim and I follow in your footsteps, and, for my part, I will gladly do so—if that's what God wants me to do. But I don't know that yet. In reality, over the last several months I've been wondering if God has something else for me to do. My roommate at school has been praying with me a lot about it."

Simon stroked his unshaven face with his hands, hoping to cover the disappointment he felt inside.

"I believe in what you're doing, Dad. But I also believe there's more to be done—inside the Village and out. God may call me to be the next Simon Holloway, but he also may call me to be the next Dr. No. I just want to be open to what God has in mind. I know that's what you want too, Dad, right?"

Simon nodded, perhaps a little too eagerly to be convincing.

Fifty-eight

For all the work Theresa Bordeaux put into securing a gourmet breakfast from the Biltmore kitchen and finding flowers for the table at the last minute, it seemed a shame that Shelby Hornecker and her guest barely noticed the food and decorations.

On a whim, Shelby had invited Grace Ellen Holloway to her suite for breakfast, as they had walked to their waiting cars after the meeting at King's House. Grace Ellen expressed genuine delight at the prospect since, "like long-lost sisters, we have so much to talk about." This eagerness confirmed Shelby's expectation that Grace Ellen might be the personal counselor, confidante, mentor, and minister of healing she yearned for.

But what would Grace Ellen think of such a role? Shelby had awakened several times during the night wondering. *Grace Ellen's alacrity for friendship may in reality be little more than her public persona. She may be an introvert like myself. Grace Ellen may just be looking for someone "in the industry" with whom to pass the time while in Los Angeles for Unity 2000.* With each awakening, Shelby wished she had not scheduled the breakfast.

However, the moment Grace Ellen had stepped into her suite, Shelby's fears were allayed. After they embraced warmly, Grace Ellen said, "Dear, I feel like I've known you all my life. I may be wrong, but my sense is that we have come together for a divine purpose." Shelby wept at the comment without giving an explanation, and Grace Ellen held her like a loving sister without probing for one.

As they had picked at their quiche and crepes, Shelby talked about the pressures and indecision she had faced in the nine months since Adrian's death. She alluded to her "recent, personally devastating experience" without mentioning Jeremy Cannon or Christmas Eve or her attempt to run from God. *There will be plenty of time to go into detail later,* Shelby told herself, *if Grace Ellen proves to be the confidante I need.*

Grace Ellen listened to, sympathized with, and consoled Shelby without judging or prying. She related her own stories of fear and self-doubt as the wife of a powerful national religious leader. The bond that began to form between the two women during that first hour was more than Shelby had dreamed possible.

"You mentioned a divine purpose for our friendship," Shelby said, as the two women took fresh cups of herb tea from the table to the ornate French provincial settee. "I must admit that I've had a similar sense since we met in the parking lot at King's House on Tuesday night. I have a specific concern in mind. May I tell you about it?"

371

"Of course, dear."

"Ever since my recent . . . problem . . . I have felt the need for a mentor, a confidante, someone to hold me accountable. This person must be a woman, for obvious reasons. Theresa is a capable assistant and a dear friend, but I need a mentor from outside my organization, someone who will remain totally objective. Yet she must be my peer in many ways, someone who understands the inner workings of an organization like Victory Life Ministries, someone who can empathize with the pressures and . . . temptations . . . I face.

"I would like to meet with this person once or twice a quarter for prayer and counsel over perhaps a year's time. I would like her to help me set goals for my personal life and ministry and then call me into account for my progress. Everything we share would be held in strictest confidence. I might be able to serve a reciprocal role for my mentor, but not right away. I have some rather sticky issues to deal with, and I don't know how much help I would be until I get on my feet again."

Shelby took a long sip of tea, as if drawing from the cup the courage for her next statement. "Grace Ellen, I know you may need to think and pray about this, but will you consider being my spiritual mentor?"

Grace Ellen first smiled then broke into a soft, friendly laugh. "So you *are* the one," she said.

Shelby looked at her questioningly. "I beg your pardon."

"Several nights ago in Orlando—on Christmas Eve, actually—I was awakened in the middle of the night by a strong urge to pray for someone. All I knew was that it was a woman who was alone and in deep inner pain. I slipped out of bed and prayed fervently for about half an hour. Then I went back to sleep.

"The next night I was called to prayer again for the same unknown subject, as I have been every night since. With each prayerful encounter, I gained a mounting sense that I was to do more for this person than pray. I kept asking God, 'How can I help this person? I don't even know who she is.' The only direction I received was to pray and wait.

"When I met you in the parking lot Tuesday night, I liked you immediately. But I thought, *This can't be the woman I'm praying for. She's the head of a national ministry. She's the chairperson of Unity 2000. Why would she need my prayers and help?*"

By this time Shelby's eyes had filled with tears of awe and humility at yet another evidence of divine providence since Christmas Eve. Grace Ellen took her hand and blinked away a few small sympathetic tears of her own.

"Then in the meeting last night I saw the hint of a struggle in your eyes. I wondered, Maybe this woman is carrying more hurt than she lets on. Maybe she *is* the one I've been praying for. Then, when you invited me to breakfast, I knew I had the perfect opportunity to find out. And here you are asking for my help.

"So you see, Shelby, I'm not surprised at your request, nor do I need to pray about it further. You have been in my prayers every night since Christmas Eve. I would be privileged to serve you as a mentor, a sister, and a friend."

Moved with gratitude, Shelby embraced Grace Ellen and cried softly. Then she wiped her eyes and nose and said, "You may change your mind after you learn what you're dealing with." She was only half joking.

Shelby refilled their cups with tea. Then she told again her story of loneliness, vulnerability, failure, despair, and restoration. As she poured out the details to Grace Ellen, she cringed that an unscrupulous mentor could use the information to ruin her ministry forever. And even if Grace Ellen proved to be as blameless and reliable as she seemed, would she leak the story to her husband, and would Simon use it against her in the competition for ministry support among America's Christian television viewers?

Shelby could only trust that God had led her to the right person and that her story—indeed, her life—was safe in Grace Ellen's hands.

Then there was the matter of Shelby's persistent inner call: *Feed My sheep*. She related the dreams to Grace Ellen, including the almost other-worldly appearance of William Malachi in her dream—before Shelby had ever met him! She agonized as she revealed to Grace Ellen something she had not even told Theresa: the unwelcome impression that she was to spend her sabbatical—at least three months of it—serving as a volunteer at King's House.

Again, Grace Ellen laughed her gentle, knowing laugh. She said, "It's amazing how God seems to be putting our lives together. Just this morning my sons, Mark and Tim, announced to their father that they feel called to volunteer at King's House. They're ready to go home after Friday night, pack their things, and come back as soon as possible."

"What did your husband think?" Shelby asked.

"Simon was flustered when he told me about it. He's afraid that the boys are abandoning him and our ministry. He envisions them getting beat up or kidnapped and held for ransom or shot here in L.A. And he's sure that the AIDS virus is a monster with a life of its own that will creep through the hospital at night and infect Mark and Tim where they sleep."

"Judging from your laugh, you don't share Simon's concerns?"

Grace Ellen reflected on her answer as she sipped tea. "Yes, I'm concerned. What mother wouldn't feel some anguish about leaving her 'babies' to fend for themselves in a place like Los Angeles? But I learned years ago, Shelby, that the safest place to be in all the world is where God puts you. If I didn't believe that, I would be a basket case by now, after all the danger Simon has been exposed to."

"So you are disposed to let Mark and Tim volunteer at King's House?"

"Yes, and Simon will come around in a day or so. Serving at King's

House will be a marvelous experience for them. You have seen what they are doing there. Dr. No's ministry is a shadow image of Jesus' teaching in Matthew 25. He is feeding the hungry, housing the homeless, clothing the naked, looking after the sick, and visiting prisoners. How much more basic can ministry be?"

Grace Ellen checked her watch and explained that she must leave in a few minutes to meet Simon and the boys to inspect the auditorium in the Convention Center for Friday morning's rally.

Shelby added a few more grains of sweetener to her cup, stirring her thoughts as she stirred her tea. Finally, she said, "Before you go, tell me: As my mentor, how would you advise me concerning spending my sabbatical at King's House?" Before Grace Ellen could speak, Shelby added emphatically, "I can't believe I'm even considering it!"

Grace Ellen said, "I agreed to serve as your mentor, but I can't be your conscience. God will tell *you* what He wants you to do, not me. I will be happy to hold you accountable for how you decide to respond to God; but God's will for your life is between you and Him."

Shelby nodded. "I have already determined that it would be best for me to take at least three months off to seek God's direction for my life and my ministry."

"That sounds healthy to me," Grace Ellen said.

"But ever since Christmas night at the Cruzes, I've had this strong impression to express my love for Christ by serving the underprivileged. I've never done anything like that before. But last night as we toured King's House, it was as if God pointed a giant neon arrow at the place and said, 'Feed My sheep *here and now!*' Does God really want me to spend my sabbatical as a volunteer at King's House?"

Grace Ellen thought for a moment. "Short of physical harm, what's the worst that can happen if you do?" she quizzed.

"Three months of hard work in a dangerous location that may bring me no closer to understanding my role at Victory Life Ministries," Shelby answered glumly.

"Three months of hard work *serving people*," Grace Ellen clarified. "The hungry will be fed, the homeless and the sick will be cared for. If that's all you accomplish in the next three months, will it be a waste of time?"

Shelby's countenance brightened with insight. "No, not at all."

"And what's the best that can happen?" Grace Ellen pressed.

Shelby nodded knowingly. "In the process of serving, my soul can be healed, my faith can be revitalized, my goals as a child of God and a minister of the Gospel can be clarified. . . ."

"And you will be right here to keep an eye on Mark and Tim for me," Grace Ellen added with a twinkle as she stood to leave. "Besides, your being in Los Angeles will make it convenient for us to get together every couple of months when I fly out with home-baked cookies for my babies."

The two women laughed together. Shelby thanked Grace Ellen profusely as they walked to the door. Then they shared a farewell embrace and Grace Ellen left.

Moments later, Theresa appeared. Shelby glowingly related the highlights of the visit and explained, in confidence, her decision to apply as a volunteer at King's House during her sabbatical. It took several minutes for the shock and disbelief to drain from Theresa's face.

"Just look what that innocent visit to King's House last night has accomplished," Theresa thought aloud. "It brought us together with Simon Holloway and T.D. Dunne, and we discovered that neither of them are the antichrists we suspected them to be."

Shelby laughed at her friend's ridiculous overstatement.

Theresa continued, "And this morning you and Holloway's two boys are ready to give three months of your lives to King's House. Only twenty-four hours ago that was the farthest thing from your minds. Who knows . . . maybe T.D. Dunne will sign on as minister of music for Dr. No."

Shelby was thoughtfully silent for a moment. "It wouldn't have happened except for Mr. Malachi. He's the one who set up the meeting with Dr. No. He's the one who insisted that we all come."

Theresa began stacking the dishes on the table for pickup by the hotel staff. "If I hadn't seen him with my own eyes," she said, "I might think he was some kind of angel."

"Captivating thought," Shelby mused aloud.

Fifty-nine

Reagan Cole had been awake so often that he wondered if he had slept at all. Through the night he had replayed the previous twelve hours repeatedly, upbraiding himself for everything he didn't do to keep Beth from getting into trouble. And when he wasn't mentally editing the past he was plotting the future, thinking whom he could talk to and where he might look for clues to Beth's whereabouts.

Dr. No's moving early-morning prayer at King's House had touched Cole deeply. *Perhaps God* is *big and caring enough to do something specific about returning Beth to me,* he had thought on the lonely motorcycle ride from L.A. to his condo in Santa Monica. But as the minutes crept by in the darkness of his bedroom, Cole's inactivity mocked him. *Beth may be in grave danger, and I'm just lying here,* he agonized. *How do I know God is doing His part? I have to do something to find her. But what?*

After thrashing restlessly on the bed for four hours, Cole arose dog tired at 7 A.M. He phoned Beth's number again with the same disheartening result. He left no further message.

Cole showered quickly and dressed in a clean shirt, slacks, and sport jacket, stuffing a tie into an inside pocket. He did not expect to return home before beginning his shift at 2:15.

He downed a cup of coffee as he tapped a note to Spooner into his kitchen computer. He explained that he would be around the Coliseum rousing street people out of their bedrolls and asking questions. He added the number of his pocket phone to the end of the note and requested that his friend call him when he got up. Then he swiveled the monitor toward the coffee machine, zipped into his flight suit, and left.

The coastal fog along Interstate 10 prevailed from Santa Monica to Culver City where it was replaced by low, dewy overcast. Cole's waterproof flight suit kept him dry but not warm enough in the cold, heavy air. Thursday morning traffic into the city was moderate and slow.

Cole arrived at Exposition Park at almost 8, stopping first on Menlo Street where the Star Cruiser had been abandoned. The street was deserted. Cole hadn't been satisfied with Sergeant Epstein's cursory investigation of the crime scene. But after twenty minutes of scrutinizing the sidewalk and street around the Cruiser's parking space, he turned up nothing new.

He remounted his bike and rode into the park itself. Using the paved roads and cement walkways, he circled each of the museums, the expansive, walled rose garden, the Coliseum, and the Sports Arena. He checked every out-of-the-way cranny for a telltale mound of blankets, plastic sheeting, newspaper, or cardboard.

For every sleeping vagrant he found, Cole peeled away smelly layers of mummy wrap until a head was visible. "I'm a Los Angeles police officer. Do you know a man named Gideon Wingate?" he said loudly — sometimes several times before getting a response. In an hour's time Cole had roused and interrogated eight men and a couple sleeping together across the two-and-a-half square mile park. No one admitted to knowing anything about Wingate.

Mai Ngo had invited Cole to meet her at the *Times* at 9:30 to await what would surely be the final message from the VoiceLink caller. So Cole left Exposition Park at 9 and cruised slowly up Figueroa Street toward downtown. He stopped occasionally to question anyone on the street who looked like he could be one of Gideon Wingate's fraternity brothers. Nobody he talked to responded to the name.

By the time Cole reached Times-Mirror Square the sun was breaking through the soup, giving promise for the 68-degree day the weatherman had predicted. Cole pulled into the visitor's parking structure at 9:30. He draped his damp flight suit across the bike to dry and propped his helmet on the handlebars, asking the security guard to keep an eye on them. The guard's call to the editorial department cleared Cole into the building.

Mai greeted him as he stepped off the elevator.

"How did you sleep, sergeant?" she asked as she led Cole through the maze of cubicles toward Sammy Chan's corner. She was cordial but not jovial.

"Who slept?" Cole quipped sarcastically.

"Yes, there were also many lights on at King's House through the night."

"You were up late worrying too?" Cole asked, surprised.

"Not exactly. After you left, we organized a round-the-clock prayer vigil. Someone from our staff will be in the chapel praying for Beth's safety until she is found. We're also praying that any harmful plot against the leaders of Unity 2000 will fail."

"Well, prayer isn't exactly my strong suit," Cole retorted, masking his self-consciousness about the subject with toughness. "Pray all you want; I hope it does some good. But I'm going to keep looking for Beth until I find her."

"Diligent prayer and diligent work: both are necessary, sergeant," Mai said affirmingly.

Entering the VoiceLink cubicle, Cole and Mai found editor Sammy Chan and two casually dressed LAPD detectives from Metro Division, a lady detective named Cisneros and a man named Steerman. Cole had never met either of them. Detective Steerman was holding an open line to Global Communications, ready to trace the caller's instrument. Cisneros was on a hot line to central dispatch, which was ready to roll patrol units in case a stationary location was identified.

Mai introduced Cole and explained his personal interest in the investigation: a possible connection between the mysterious caller and Beth Scibelli's disappearance. Cisneros had been present for the Friday morning call and remembered Beth. She breathed a curse, adding, "If this guy is snatching citizens off the street, we're dealing with more than your everyday religious nut."

"Are you going to be able to locate this guy today?" Cole asked the detectives anxiously.

"Don't count on it, sergeant," answered Steerman matter-of-factly. "Obviously we can't pinpoint the location of a remote. The best we can hope for is that he can't find a cell phone to steal today and has to use a hard-wired instrument—a pay phone. If he does—and if we're lucky—we might get a black-and-white to the location in time to find someone who saw him make the call."

The small group passed the next thirty minutes sipping coffee, straining at conversation, and waiting. With every new tone signaling an incoming call on VoiceLink (on average, one call every six minutes, the cubicle fell dead silent. Employees from nearby cubicles scrambled to the VoiceLink corner like sharks to a wounded albacore as the electronic voice announced, "You have reached the VoiceLink line at the *Los Angeles Times*.

Our editors welcome your comments on any issue impacting our city, state, or nation. Some contributions will be edited and published in the *Times*. At the tone, please state your name and telephone number. Then you have one minute to speak. Thank you for calling, and have a good news day."

But the crowd groaned in disappointment and quickly disbursed each time the caller turned out to be someone fed up with crime on L.A.'s Metrolink System or decrying the construction of a double-decker freeway in the earthquake center of the United States.

Shortly after 10, Spooner checked in on Cole's pocket phone. He apologized for not accompanying his friend into town. "No problem; you needed your rest," Cole said, unoffended. "As soon as I learn something here, I'll beep you."

At 10:18 the long-awaited call came. With Sammy Chan and the two detectives huddled over the machine and the phones, Cole and Mai could only listen from behind them.

As with the previous messages, the caller coldly recited a crude poem of vengeance in biblical verbiage. And, as expected, the message was directed at "the king from the north," a veiled reference to T.D. Dunne of Chicago, "who playeth music from the devil's hole, which shrinketh the heart and wasteth the soul."

As the caller concluded with his chilling signature lines about torn flesh, scattered bones, and spilled blood, Cole heard Steerman relay a seven-digit number to his contact at Global. Cole repeated the number to himself, then a shock of recognition iced his blood. He pushed his way between Chan and Cisneros to stare at the number displayed on the receiving console.

"You don't need to check that number with Global," he said. Shock had blanched his face and dismay had weakened his voice. "I know that number. It's a remote phone. It belongs to Beth Scibelli."

Beth awoke with a dull headache and pain throbbing the length of her right arm. But her attention soon turned to the troubling awareness that she could not open her eyes. She tried to lift her hands to investigate but discovered that they were tightly strapped down. She fingered a cold metal rail on each side of her to which her wrists were attached. She also felt the seam of the thin mattress beneath her. Beyond the metal rail on her right, her extended fingers touched a wall.

An earlier, fuzzy explanation returned: *I was abducted and drugged. I was injured in the rescue. I'm now in the hospital recovering from my injuries. I've had surgery of some kind, perhaps on my face or my eyes, which feel bandaged. My limbs are being restrained to keep me from . . .*

Beth's increasing consciousness and awakening senses objected. She began to question her earlier reasoning. Her thoughts came grudgingly, as if all her neurons were firing in superslow motion. *This isn't a normal hospital bed; it has the mattress of a cot. It doesn't sound like a hospital: no voices from the nurse's station, no pages or canned music over the intercom, no sound at all. And the fragrance of disinfectant and flowers is missing; the room smells like a musty locker room with an open trash can standing in the corner.*

The suffocating drug-induced stupor lurking at the borders of her consciousness tugged Beth back toward dark sleep, but she resisted. She groped at the metal rail within her restricted reach for a nurse's call button. There was none. She summoned strength to call out, but her muddled brain and dry throat and mouth could barely produce the sound she wanted, "Nurse? Doctor? Dad? Reagan? Where am I?"

She waited for a response. Nothing. Turning her head one way and then the other to listen, she felt the large bandage pull at her hair. She struggled again unsuccessfully to open her eyes. *Why is the bandage wrapped so tightly?* she pondered.

She called out again, "Nurse? Someone? I need water. And my hands, please let—"

A door opened to her left, then closed. Someone had entered her room. Beth mustered as much voice as she could. "Sir? Ma'am? Please call the nurse or doctor for me." Then she listened.

She heard someone shuffle toward her. She turned her head toward the sound. She willed her eyelids to lift under the bandage, but they would not. "Who's there? Will you help me please?"

A Slavic masculine voice, cold and raspy, replied, "Look, master, our guest is awake."

Beth gasped, then instinctively jerked at the restraints trying vainly to free her hands and defend herself. "Who are you?" she demanded.

"You should know, Ms. Mary-Elizabeth-prying-journalist. You're the one who came looking for *me.*"

Comprehension crashed down on Beth as if the building around her had collapsed on her. *This is no hospital. I have not been rescued. I am still with Hodge. Wingate must also be in the room. And this is no bandage across my eyes; it's a tight, sticky blindfold wrapped around my head and pressing my eyelids shut. I recognize the smell: it's duct tape. My arms and legs are not in restraints; I'm in bonds, I'm taped to this metal cot at the wrists and ankles. He's been through my purse; he knows who I am.*

With every painful movement of her body, Beth remembered what Hodge and Wingate had done to her. Her neck and throat burned from Wingate's death grip, and her arm ached from his vicious arm lock. The stitch in her side recalled the painful, threatening flick of Hodge's knife point. Soreness in her upper arm reminded her of the plunging hypodermic. Her head pounded with the aftereffects of some kind of knockout drug.

Beth searched her clouded memory for other offenses. She gasped with alarm, thinking, *After they dragged me in here, did they. . . ?* A sour, sickening wave rolled up Beth's throat. *No! Please, God, no!* She moved enough to assure herself that, except for shoes, she was still fully clothed, including her hose and cardigan sweater.

Relieved only for an instant, Beth flashed back to a blurred moment in the darkness of her imprisonment when a "nurse" assisted her to the toilet. The contemptible thought of being seen and touched in her vulnerable state provoked a scream of anguish and defiance toward her unseen captors.

A strong hand gripped Beth's throat, choking off her scream. Hodge said in an unmerciful tone, "Mary Elizabeth, you are an intelligent, clever woman, too clever for your own good, as it turns out. In your snooping you have roused the master's wrath. You could easily be but a spirit by now. But for reasons known only to him, the master has temporarily spared you from the same judgment which fell upon greedy, lustful Rev. Wingate."

Beth's heart pounded. Hodge's inference was clear even to her numbed mind. Wingate was dead at the will of "the master"—obviously carried out by Hodge's hand. Beth felt no sympathy for Wingate, but was gripped with fear for her own life. Hodge was as diabolical and unconscionable as he sounded on the VoiceLink line.

He continued, "This room is soundproofed, Mary Elizabeth. No one outside these walls can hear you, and I am not disposed to listen to your futile cries. If you persist in your belligerence, the master wills me to sedate you again. And at his command, I will gladly commute his judgment and put an end to your untimely and very unwise interference in his plan."

Hodge released his grip, and Beth heard him take a step back. The fire in his voice tempered slightly. "On the other hand, if you are convinced to acquiesce to the master's will, I may be persuaded to withhold the needle. Perhaps the master has spared you for a purpose. Perhaps he wills me to enlighten you concerning his message of judgment which you have so astutely traced to me, his vessel.

"Yet if you play the fool, I have no alternative but to neutralize your interference with this." Beth stiffened at the sensation of a needle being dragged lightly across her cheek. "Or this." She gasped and held her breath as the cold steel of Hodge's blade touched her bare neck for at least five seconds.

Beth forced herself to think. She would be unable to discern Hodge's capability and plan for carrying out his VoiceLink threats if she was unconscious. Nor could she attempt an escape to warn her parents or Unity 2000 without her full mental faculties. She could not afford to defy her captor, even though seething hatred urged her to lash out at him to her last breath.

Beth's thoughtful silence lasted only a moment. "May I have some water please, sir," she requested in feigned submission.

Hodge stepped away without a word, and Beth heard the sound of the knife and hypodermic being laid on a wooden surface. A few steps took him to a place near the head of the cot. She heard water run and then stop. Drops of cold water splashing on her face startled her, but she instinctively turned her mouth toward the source, a trickle being poured from a cup far above her, and welcomed it.

"Thank you," she said, noting that a sink must be within arm's reach. She wished for more than the half cup of water she caught but was unwilling to press her luck. She was surprised when Hodge wiped the excess water from her face. The cloth smelled of spoiled milk.

It took great effort for Beth to say it convincingly, but she knew she must, "Please don't sedate me, sir. I will cooperate with you . . . and learn from your master."

Jesus, help me, Jesus, she added silently, wishing she could cross herself.

Sixty

Reagan Cole's angry urge to telephone the VoiceLink caller who used Beth's remote was immediately quelled by Sergeant Cisneros. "If he has the young lady, Cole," she said, "any tip-off that we know about her may put her in greater danger. Let us take care of it." Cole reluctantly acquiesced and stepped back while Cisneros entered the details of the incident on her computer.

But when Cole pressed the detectives about how they were going to find her, they proved no more helpful than Sergeant Epstein. "First, we don't know for sure if this guy has your lady," Steerman said. He was irritated at Cole's inference that they should drop everything to canvas the city for Beth. "All we have is a stolen car, which happened to be recovered with a body in it, and an apparent stolen phone. And at this point the two crimes are unrelated, except that the property can be traced to Ms. Scibelli.

"Second, even if we knew that this nut has done something to her or is holding her, the best way to find *her*—if she is alive—is to find *him*, which is exactly what we're trying to do. The only other thing you can do is have her parents report her as missing."

Cole walked away from the VoiceLink cubicle upset and frustrated. His head grasped that Cisneros and Steerman were acting by the book. But his gut knew that Beth was in trouble and that finding her by the book might not be fast enough. He remembered countless numbers of citizens whose loved ones had been victimized. He now knew how ill-assured they felt when he issued a meaningless platitude like, "Don't worry; the LAPD can handle it."

Mai caught up with him. "You know they're doing the best they can," she consoled.

"Yes, but I work for this organization, and I know too well that the best isn't always good enough," Cole retorted.

"That's why we're praying, sergeant. God knows what the police don't know, and He can do what they can't do. You'll see."

More than ever, for Beth's sake and for his, Cole wanted to believe that she was right. "Well, if you have an extra prayer to spare, I think Beth's parents are going to need it," he said. "I have to go out to Woodland Hills now and tell them that nobody has seen Beth since yesterday afternoon— except maybe Wingate and the quack on the telephone."

"I *will* pray, sergeant. Please let me know how it goes."

Cole promised that he would.

On his way downstairs he called Spooner with an update. His friend offered to go along for moral support, but Cole declined. It would be better if he went alone.

It was a Chamber of Commerce day in Los Angeles. Pleasant wester-ly breezes had pushed most of the smog across the basin to the moun-tains, leaving the city clear and warm. Cole threaded through the late morning freeway traffic on Interstate 405 northward through the pass and into the San Fernando Valley. Under any other circumstances he would be spending the few hours before going to work sunning himself on Santa Monica Beach. And today he might have challenged Spooner to a game of one-on-one on an outdoor court—providing Spooner spotted him 10 points in a 20-point game.

But the confrontation with Jack and Dona Scibelli was heavy on his mind, pushing the sun and the sand far into the background. He had anticipated meeting Beth's parents before she returned home to Wash-ington, but never under circumstances like these. He wished he could leave this unpleasant job to on-duty officers. Technically, he could, but his conscience urged him to validate his feelings for Beth by taking personal responsibility for informing her parents. And since meeting Mai and Dr. No, Cole was beginning to listen to his conscience.

"Mr. Scibelli, I'm Reagan Cole. I'm the one who woke you last night with a telephone call."

Jack Scibelli was tinkering at his work bench in the open garage when Cole approached. Jack stepped into the sunshine on the driveway to greet the stranger. Cole immediately recognized Beth in his features: dark eyes, a full head of dark hair streaked with gray, a tall, lean frame.

"Reagan, I'm pleased to meet you," Jack said, acting more cordial than Cole had anticipated. "Beth mentioned your name once, but she's been so busy this week that she hasn't been able to sit down and tell us about you."

Cole had wondered if Beth had told her parents about Christmas Eve and the wild chase through West Los Angeles. It appeared that she hadn't. "Did Beth come home last night?" he asked.

"No, I'm afraid she didn't, and her mother and I are concerned."

Cole's flimsy hope that he might find Beth safe at home instantly evaporated. "That's what I have come to talk to you about, sir," he said. "I don't mean to alarm you unduly, but I have some disturbing news about Beth. Is Mrs. Scibelli at home?"

Jack Scibelli's face mirrored anxiety at the ominous statement. "Yes, won't you come in, please."

Dona Scibelli was equally cordial when meeting Cole and equally apprehensive when Jack informed her why the young man had come. The couple led their guest into the family room.

Cole was tempted to sidestep the emotion of the confrontation by resorting to the standard stoic police approach he used when communicating bad news with citizens—cop-speak, Beth had termed it. But he knew that such an approach would belie his feelings and distance him from people he felt responsible to comfort and help.

He began, "I come to you first as Beth's friend. We met by chance the night she arrived in town, and we have been seeing each other since as our schedules have allowed. But I haven't been in touch with her since yesterday afternoon, and I share your concern over the fact that she hasn't returned home.

"I also come to you as a Los Angeles police officer—though not on official business—with information that I'm sure will trouble you even more than it does me." Cole breathed deeply, wishing he didn't have to say more. "The police department has reason to suspect that Beth's sudden disappearance may be the result of foul play."

Jack and Dona reached for and found each others' hands without taking their eyes off their guest.

Cole summarized Beth's failure to meet him at King's House and answer his repeated calls. He explained that her book research may have taken her to a number of dark corners in the city which were more dangerous than she expected. He decided not to add an unnecessary burden to the story by relating Beth's narrow escape from the Latin Barons on Christmas Eve.

He described as gently as possible the discovery of Beth's rental car with the slain vagrant in the back seat, quickly assuring the Scibellis that cars are stolen and used in crimes every day in Los Angeles without the owners being involved or harmed. Jack and Dona sat holding each other, faces lined with dread.

Cole continued by citing the evidence of Beth's phone being stolen, but he did not discuss the VoiceLink caller or reveal his strong suspicion that Beth may have found trouble while looking for him.

He said, "Officially, the police can't do much to find her. But I advise you to call West Valley Division anyway and ask for an officer to come out and take a missing persons report. Once we have a picture and description, we can keep an eye out for her.

"In reality, however, hundreds of missing persons reports are filed in L.A. every week. I wish I could tell you that we actively look for these people. But with only 9,500 officers in a population of 9 million, we spend most of our time trying to keep the bad guys from burning down the city. Missing persons reports are seldom consulted except to identify John and Jane Does in the morgue."

Mrs. Scibelli began to weep at the thought, and her husband valiantly fought against tears. Touched as much by their anguish as his own, Cole apologized for his bluntness. Jack assured him that they appreciated his honesty and directness.

Cole shifted self-consciously in his chair about what he wanted to say next. "Unofficially, I have a suggestion. Beth has told me that you are deeply religious people. If you know any prayers that work really well, I think now is the time to use them. I'm not much of Christian myself, but the people at King's House are sure that if anyone can find Beth, God can. If it's any comfort to you, they're holding a prayer vigil for Beth around the clock. Let's just hope it does some good."

Cole rose to leave, aware that he could do little more for the Scibellis and anxious to do something more himself to find Beth. Mr. Scibelli grasped his hand to say good-bye, then held on as he mouthed a simple prayer in his quavering voice. "Dear Lord, keep our Beth safe wherever she is. And help this young man and the other officers to find her."

Cole gave Jack and Dona his personal number and promised to keep them apprised of any progress. They expressed gratitude for his visit as they walked him to his motorcycle and said good-bye, making Cole feel uncomfortable. *How can they be so gracious after I brought them such bad news?* he wondered.

Winding down Winnetka toward the freeway, Cole noted that he only had two hours before going on duty. He chided himself about being such a lousy host for his houseguest, Curtis Spooner; but he had to use his free minutes wisely. The last time he had talked to Beth by phone she was at the library on Spring Street downtown—or at least she claimed to be there. *Maybe one of the employees saw her there,* he thought. *Maybe they noticed her leave with someone. It's a feeble lead, but at the moment it's all I have.*

Cole roared up the freeway on-ramp at 60 MPH headed for downtown and Central Branch.

Sixty-one

Theresa Bordeaux stepped into the room where Shelby was organizing her thoughts on the computer. "Your call is ready, Shelby. Everyone's on the line."

"Even Dr. McClure?" Shelby returned, surprised.

"Even McClure," Theresa answered, with a hint of triumph in her voice. "We found him aboard his jet en route from Mazatlan to Los Angeles. He's a little testy. I think we interrupted his lunch."

"And the others?"

"Rev. Holloway is at the Convention Center preparing for his rally tomorrow morning. T.D. Dunne is getting ready for rehearsal at the Coliseum."

"Nicely done, Theresa. Thank you."

Shelby picked up her phone. "Good afternoon, gentlemen."

Simon Holloway and T.D. Dunne responded in unison with a warm, "Good afternoon." One evening together at King's House hadn't melted all the armor between the three spiritual leaders. But having been equally awestruck and humbled by their experience, the three had found a patch of level ground where they could stand together. Their commonality was reflected in their cordiality.

"Dr. McClure, are you there?" Shelby probed.

"Good afternoon, Mrs. Hornecker," came the cool reply.

"Thank you for taking a few minutes to touch base. I know we all have important things to do, so I'll make this as brief as possible."

"Yes, please do," McClure said.

Shelby continued undaunted, "By now you have received from Mr. Chaumont your agenda for the Millennium's Eve service. Let me go over it quickly to make sure we all understand the timing."

Shelby scanned the agenda displayed on her monitor. She began the talk-through by explaining that the security scanning gates around the Coliseum and concession stands inside would open at 6 P.M. The actual program would begin at 7 with Rev. Stan Welbourn serving as master of ceremonies for the evening.

"I want to know about those security gates," McClure interrupted. "My people in L.A. have told me about the rumors. If we don't have ironclad security, I'm not setting foot inside the Coliseum."

"We have the full cooperation of the Los Angeles Police Department, Dr. McClure," Shelby assured. "Chief Robinson met with us last night and apprised us of his efforts to apprehend the suspect, even though he is convinced that the threats are the idle babble of a harmless mental case. All the same, our security system is tighter than at an international airport, though quite a bit less conspicuous."

McClure grunted, sounding unconvinced.

Shelby continued with the agenda. From 7 to 7:30, T.D. Dunne and his band would lead the congregation in singing, including the debut performance of the Unity 2000 theme song. Then, beginning at 7:30, each of the four ministries represented would have an hour to challenge the gathered throng and viewing audience to unity and righteousness in the coming millennium. Shelby requested that each one use the last five minutes of his hour to allow participants to stand and stretch.

"When do we take the offering?" McClure cut in again.

"As the agenda states, we will receive the offering at 10:30, just before my segment begins."

"I'm on vacation; I didn't bring my agenda," McClure said curtly. "When do we distribute the proceeds?"

Shelby was becoming irked at McClure's attitude. She silently willed not to allow his adversarial bent to dampen the goodwill developing between herself, Simon Holloway, and T.D. Dunne.

"Next week, after expenses are paid, the proceeds—if there are any—will be equally divided between the four ministries. If there is a shortfall, we will share equally in making it up."

Apparently satisfied for the moment, McClure fell silent. Shelby pressed on with the schedule.

After the congregational singing, T.D. Dunne would stay on the platform and take the first hour beginning at 7:30. His presentation consisted of a live concert featuring an ensemble of acclaimed GoTown recording artists.

"We will open with two solo music acts plus testimonies by four-time Grammy winner, Jodell Blue, and NBA star, Curtis Spooner," Dunne clarified. "I'll sing a song or two and give a brief talk. The program will conclude with a big number by a band and choir made up of GoTown all-stars. The Coliseum will by rocking by 8:30."

Shelby reminded McClure that he had the next time slot. He complained that many people in the audience would probably leave for the hot dog stands and rest rooms after the concert, instead of listening to his opening remarks. Simon Holloway impatiently rebutted that because the event lasted five hours, people would be moving around the Coliseum all night. "We're all in the same boat, Dr. McClure. We just have to deal with it."

Shelby added that the Coliseum's tunnels and concourses—and even the rest rooms—were equipped with loudspeakers, so no one would miss a word.

When asked about the details of his program, McClure reluctantly reported that he would be filling the hour himself, since both of his platform guests had canceled on him due to sudden illnesses.

It sounds like the rats are deserting McClure's ship, Shelby quipped silently. Then she quickly chastised herself for the response.

Simon Holloway informed them that he would share his 9:30–10:30 slot with Drs. Francine McGowan and Rudyard Matabwa, speaking to the need for moral unity in an age of godless science and technology. McClure butted in acidly with, "And you'll have an altar call to sign up Crusaders and Warriors, right, Holloway?"

To Shelby, McClure sounded like a man on the run who had nothing left to lose. She felt sorry for him. Holding his cool well, Simon Holloway explained to McClure that he was prepared to challenge people to action and to inform them of the opportunities his ministry offered.

"To open the last segment," Shelby said, "I have asked actor Jeremy Cannon to present one of his dramatic monologues. He will portray Christ addressing the disciples during the forty-day period between His resurrection and ascension. I expect it to be a poignant challenge to revival and unity, just as it was for the early church."

Shelby paused to appreciate that she could talk about Jeremy without the crushing humiliation and bitter remorse of only days ago. Occasional pricks of self-doubt persisted, but they were waning, especially as she aligned herself with the inner impulse to spend the next three months as a humble feeder of sheep.

"I had originally intended to follow Jeremy Cannon with a major address on the need for unity in the Christian church," she continued. "But in the last few days I have sensed the need for a slight change in direction."

Shelby didn't know how transparent she should be with Morgan McClure listening in. He seemed particularly uncharitable toward his three colleagues in ministry. She feared that he might laugh her to scorn. But she decided to risk it.

"I will be sharing my time on the platform with a man whose unpretentious life and selfless ministry has made a significant impact on me. I spent the last hour persuading Dr. No of King's House here in Los Angeles to speak Sunday night. He finally agreed."

"Who?" Maxwell snapped.

"Thanh Hai Ngo—called Dr. No by most everyone—operates a ministry to the poor and homeless, former law offenders, and AIDS victims here in the city. I think he will bring a pivotal perspective to our people for the coming dawn of the twenty-first century."

"If you want to share the stage with a rescue mission preacher, that's your business," McClure said dourly. "Just make sure he doesn't take any of my time."

"I think it's a wonderful idea, Shelby," T.D. Dunne exclaimed. "I agree that Dr. No is something of a spiritual hero. In fact, the song I wrote especially for Unity 2000 fits in beautifully with what we saw last night."

Shelby noted with satisfaction that Dunne had used her first name. *The barriers are coming down,* she thought. *But instead of feeling threatened by it, I'm enjoying it.*

Simon Holloway's response was less animated, but it sounded genuine. "Dr. No's example has already touched my family, and I think he should be heard. Thank you, Mrs. Hornecker, for asking him to speak."

"And the last half hour before midnight is Holy Communion, right?" McClure pressed impatiently.

Shelby said, "Yes, and I would like us all to stand together on the platform as the congregation partakes. After the closing song and prayer, which should be right at midnight, the fireworks display will commence."

"There better not be any fireworks *before* midnight," McClure inserted. "Just make sure maximum security is in place, Hornecker." Then he excused himself abruptly and hung up before asking if Shelby had more to say.

"There's a man in a world of hurt," Dunne said with a sigh.

"He has sown the wind; he's about to reap the whirlwind," Holloway offered, with little compassion.

"I think he needs a good psychologist and a good lawyer," Shelby chipped in. As soon as she heard what she had said, she recanted. "I'm sorry, I didn't mean that. I think Dr. McClure needs prayer. We should be in prayer for him."

Holloway and Dunne sheepishly agreed.

"One more thing before we hang up," Holloway said. "I would be pleased if both of you would take part in our televised rally in the Convention Center tomorrow morning. Mrs. Hornecker, it would be an honor to share the pulpit with you. And Mr. Dunne, we would appreciate very much a song or two from you."

Shelby felt the old ingrained rivalry stiffen within her, like a platoon of bodyguards snapping to attention around her at the appearance of an intruder. But what did she have to defend? Had it not been for providential intervention, she would have no ministry at all. Quietly she commanded her fears to stand at ease.

"Would it be possible to pick up your television coverage for our network?" she asked.

"Of course, and we can introduce the program as a joint service so your people will know right away that you are participating."

Shelby considered the opportunity for only a moment. "The honor would be mine, Simon. Thank you."

"And you, T.D.?"

"You obviously haven't heard me sing in the morning," Dunne said, laughing. "But if you're game, let's do it."

After discussing a few key details, Simon Holloway concluded the conversation with a prayer for the rally, for Unity 2000, and for Morgan McClure.

Sixty-two

Beth found it difficult to pretend she was mostly asleep while trying to keep herself awake and will her brain to clear. Lying still with her eyes taped shut invited the residue of drugs in her system to put her out again. She dug her nails into her palms and bit the inside of her cheek trying to shock herself toward greater consciousness without appearing to move. Hoping mental gymnastics would help, she even tried to piece together the catechism she had memorized as a child.

Hodge had been silent for what Beth guessed to be an hour or more. She could hear the occasional creak of a wooden chair, the rustle of pages, the scrape of a drawer opening and closing, and the scratch of a pencil on paper. Periodically Hodge would mumble something unintelligible to himself. Beth imagined that he was sitting at a desk nearby, engrossed in paperwork.

Beth's sense of time was totally adrift. Her best guess was that it was Thursday, perhaps late morning. A gnawing hunger communicated that many hours had passed since she was abducted.

The increasing soreness in her back and limbs from inactivity on the sagging cot begged Beth to ask Hodge to let her up. And as much as she loathed the thought, she had to use the toilet again—soon.

But she needed a plan, an idea, an edge she could use to free herself from Hodge. She was at a disadvantage for using her physical strength; she would have to use her mind.

Hodge duped me by being a clever actor; I will have to out-clever him, she challenged herself. *He has obviously burned out a few of his forward gears, so I must find a way to take advantage of his mental instability. But first I must get up and also have something to eat.*

Beth steeled herself for the unknown and slowly began to "wake up," rolling her head and moaning sleepily.

"Sir, are you here?" she said, purposely garbling her words. A creak of the chair told her that Hodge was turned in her direction. "Sir, I need to use the toilet please."

Beth waited and listened. She heard Hodge stand and step to the bedside, then she felt the knife cutting through the tape holding her left arm to the frame. The bond relaxed and she cautiously pulled her wrist and elbow free of the tape, which remained stuck to the metal. After similar cuts beside her right arm and both legs Beth was free.

Still lying on her back, she instinctively reached her left arm to remove the blindfold. She was stopped by a startling and painful slap on the wrist with the flat side of Hodge's blade. "You will not touch your face," Hodge warned sternly. "The master wills you to remain sightless until the eyes of your understanding are opened."

A hand grabbed Beth's elbow and pulled her to a sitting position. She cringed as the dried blood on her blouse pulled away from the superficial knife wound on her side. She moved cautiously, confident that Hodge would not hesitate to cut her again.

"Please, sir," she said plaintively, "if you will just direct me, I can take care of myself." To Beth's surprise, Hodge agreed, and even returned to his creaking chair. Beth stood on shaky legs, swallowed her modesty, and fumbled her way past the sink to the toilet.

Returning, Beth bumped into a straight-backed wooden chair and a table in the center of the room. She did not want to be strapped to the cot again. And she needed something to eat. *But how can I gain his confidence?* she thought. The idea was suddenly there. Sensing Hodge's eyes upon her, she pulled the chair out from the table in a slow, deliberate motion as if she had been given permission to do so. Sitting down, she asked in Hodge's direction, "Sir, will you please teach me about the master?" She kept her hands in plain sight on the table top. She felt nothing on the surface within reach.

She heard Hodge move in his noisy chair. "The master will teach you what he wants you to know."

"Perhaps he has already begun to enlighten me," she said. "I had . . . a vision . . . while I was asleep."

"And what did you see in your vision?" Hodge asked in a skeptical but interested tone.

"I saw that the master has appointed you to execute judgment on the queen of the south and the kings of the east, north—"

"Flesh and blood revealed that to you, not the master," Hodge interrupted. "You heard the messages on the VoiceLink line at the *Times*. You told me so last night."

Beth's mind logged the information excitedly. *He said "last night." It really is Thursday. There's still time to find out what he is planning and stop him.*

She continued, "It has also been revealed to me who the four rulers in your message are: Shelby Hornecker, Simon Holloway, T.D. Dunne, and Morgan McClure."

"A simple deduction for a journalist," said the unseen Hodge from across the table. "What else?"

Beth decided to venture a calculated guess and hope she was lucky. "The master also revealed to me that you have prepared powerful explosives to rid the earth of the infidels in Los Angeles just—"

"Child's play!" Hodge growled. "Anyone could suspect explosives from the prophetic message."

Beth picked up where he had cut her off, "—just as you rid the earth of Adrian Hornecker by planting explosives aboard his charter."

Hodge was silent for several seconds. Beth held her breath, hoping she had not incurred the master's judgment to be administered through Hodge's knife.

"So, the master has chosen you to bring to light what once was hidden." Hodge's skepticism was tempered by mild surprise. "What else do you see?"

Beth grasped for a response, clinging to the hope that her act was beginning to work. "My strength is failing, sir, and my vision of the master is clouded. Perhaps if I have something to eat. . . ."

Beth felt Hodge's gaze studying her, weighing her answer. For the moment she was glad her captor could not see her eyes. She had never possessed much of a poker face.

After a few moments Hodge rose. Listening carefully, Beth heard him walk past her on the left and stop somewhere behind her left shoulder. She could almost feel the cold steel of his ever-present knife in the disturbed air as he passed.

In a moment came the familiar sound of an old can opener grinding the lid off a tin can. The smell reached her almost immediately: tuna. Hodge dropped the opened can, a spoon, and a small cup of water in front of her. "Eat quickly," he ordered. Beth heard him return to the creaky chair and the work on his desk.

It hurt when she tried to use her right hand to cross herself. So she ate her meal with her left, using the fingers of her right hand to guide the spoon under unseen chunks of meat.

As she ate, Beth plotted a mental map of the room from what she had noticed. Arbitrarily designating the direction straight ahead of her as north, she pictured the metal cot along the east wall near or in the northeast corner. She had been strapped on the cot, with her feet to the north.

The sink and toilet were also on the east wall in the southeast corner with a wooden dresser between the head of the bed and the sink. Hodge had retrieved the tuna and utensils from behind her and to the left: the southwest corner. Hodge's creaky chair and writing surface was then somewhere near the northwest corner.

Beth pictured the table where she was sitting to be near the center of the room. By subtle touch she had determined it to be a narrow wooden table running north and south in the room.

The door to the room was somewhere on the western wall, she judged. But she had no idea where it led or where in Southern California she would be, if and when she ever passed through it alive.

Immediately after Beth's last swallow, Hodge escorted her back to the cot without a word and strapped her securely to the frame with duct tape. Then he checked the security of her blindfold, pressing the tape against her eyes.

Beth tried to engage him in conversation about the master, but he would not respond. Other frantic urges tempted her to lash out at her captor with one arm as he worked to tape the other to the frame. But the sobering vision of Hodge's knife lying within his reach dissuaded her. *I can beat this guy with my brain*, she reminded herself. *Think, think, think.*

"I'll be back in twenty minutes," Hodge said at last. He opened what sounded like the famous blue and white plastic picnic chest, stuffed something inside, and closed it again. "If I find you anywhere in this room except where you are right now, it will be a sign to me that the master's patience with you has expired." Hodge again laid the flat side of his knife on Beth's neck for emphasis.

But she was thinking ahead. *The room may be soundproofed, but in a moment Hodge will open a door and my scream may be heard....*

Beth's flicker of hope was quickly doused as Hodge ripped a short length of duct tape off the roll and slapped it firmly across her mouth. Then he left. Beth heard the dead bolt click into position.

Lying alone in perpetual darkness, arms and legs strapped so tightly that she feared for her circulation, Beth fought back a wave of hopelessness. Her clear mind had brought her more bane than blessing. The numbing effects of the drugs having dissipated, she could again clearly define the grave danger poised over herself, the leaders of Unity 2000, her parents, and Reagan Cole. But her restored mental faculties had yet to propose a viable escape.

A small memory suddenly sparked in her consciousness like a match light in a black cavern. It was something her father often told her as a child, as he sat on her bed for bedtime prayers. "If a nightmare wakes you up, sweetheart, just say the Our Father." How often she had taken his advice after bad dreams disturbed her sleep, even into her teenage years. She would silently recite the Our Father in the darkness of her room until she was calmed and asleep again. She could almost feel her father sitting beside her now encouraging her, "Recite the Our Father, sweetheart."

Her lips were tightly sealed by the tape, but Beth made her tongue form the silent words phrase by phrase:

Our Father which art in heaven,
Hallowed be Thy name. Thy kingdom come.
Thy will be done on earth, as it is in heaven.
Give us this day our daily bread.
And forgive us our trespasses,
As we forgive those who trespass against us.
And lead us not into temptation,
But deliver us from evil.

The last phrase lit up the darkness like a torch. *I'm in a prison of evil,* Beth thought. *My parents are probably worried sick by now. Reagan, Mai, and even Curtis Spooner may be looking for me. But they can't*

deliver me because they don't know where I am. Only You know where I am, God. You can see me in this prison. Dear God, deliver me from evil.
Beth didn't need to cross herself. She knew she had been heard.

Sixty-three

Cole parked the Bolt in the garage underneath the Biltmore to begin his shift, but his mind wasn't on his work. Driving from the station to the hotel, he had bent his partner's ear with the details of how Beth's Star Cruiser had appeared with a dead body in the back, while she had vanished. In Jayne's hearing he cursed his inability to find a shred of a clue about her in Exposition Park or in the library where she had last worked on her book.

The last thing Cole wanted to think about today was an additional security risk for his responsibility, Rev. Shelby Hornecker. But she greeted him with, "Sergeant, it's such a nice day, and I've never been through the park across the street. Theresa and I would like to take a walk."

The park was Pershing Square, and Cole was nervous about allowing his charge a leisurely stroll through a place frequented by unsavory characters, especially with death threats hanging over her. But, as Lieutenant Arias had reminded him repeatedly, she was the boss. So he radioed for additional units to cruise the area. Then he and Officer Watanabe warily escorted Shelby and Theresa across Olive Street and into the Square.

A few Unity 2000 delegates who happened to be visiting the Square recognized Shelby and followed her from a distance, snapping pictures. A couple of them ventured close enough to ask for autographs, which Shelby graciously supplied. The shabbier looking patrons of the park saw the well-dressed visitors as worthy marks for their begging. But Cole and Jayne kept them at a distance, directing them instead toward the local missions. Since visiting King's House, Cole had a new appreciation for people in the city who fed, clothed, and housed the destitute.

Occasionally Shelby stopped to watch and listen as a member of the "Pershing Square Ministerial Association" harangued and harassed passersby in the name of God. Cole noted that she appeared saddened by the characters he regarded as laughable.

As the group circled the pond and walked between the shade trees, Shelby asked Cole, "Did you find out why your journalist friend didn't meet us at King's House last night?"

It was all the encouragement he needed. He poured out the story of Beth's strange disappearance, the discovery of the body in her car, and the use of her telephone by the VoiceLink caller. Shelby and Theresa were alarmed by the report and moved by Cole's concern. They promised their prayers for Beth's safety.

Walking through a corridor of palms near the northeast corner of the Square, the group was joined by two officers on bike patrol who had been dispatched to the Square in response to Cole's request for support. The patrolmen correctly pegged the civilian-dressed Cole and Watanabe as police escorts. They introduced themselves as Officers Ochoa and Scanlon out of Central Division.

"Are there always so many street-corner preachers in the Square, officer?" Shelby asked Scanlon while Cole, standing nearby, radioed his position and status.

"On a nice day like today they come out of the woodwork, ma'am," Scanlon joked. "A few of them are troublemakers, but most are rather harmless. Vince and I have heard so many sermons down here we could open our own church."

Scanlon pointed to several of the preachers within view and described some of their humorous idiosyncrasies. Then he said, "One of our favorites didn't show up today. You would have enjoyed him. Old Wingate stands over there by the pond as silent as a statue until the top of each hour. Then he screams like a banshee, 'The kingdom of—' "

"Did you say *Wingate?*" Cole was in Scanlon's face, eyes wide with interest.

"Yeah, Wingate," Scanlon said. He was disarmed by Cole's sudden intensity, as were Shelby, Theresa, and Jayne Watanabe.

"First name of Gideon?" Cole pressed.

"Wingate, that's all he goes by around here," Ochoa cut in. "Do you know him, sergeant?"

"Give me a description," Cole drilled as if interrogating a star witness.

"Tall, real skinny with straight, slicked-back hair," Ochoa began.

"Real smelly clothes, Dr. Death look in his eyes," Scanlon added.

"When did you last see him?" Cole jabbed at the two officers with his question.

Ochoa and Scanlon looked at each other. Then Scanlon said, "Yesterday, about this time, wasn't it, Vince?" Ochoa nodded.

"Where?"

"Over by the pond—his regular spot," Scanlon answered.

"Did you see anybody talking to him—a woman, I mean?"

Ochoa remembered immediately. "Yeah, a real nice-looking woman. Tall, black hair pulled back. She asked us about one of the other regulars in the Square. Said she was looking for a long-lost buddy of her father. We told her to talk to Wingate."

Cole spun completely around, pounding his fist into his palm angrily. Shelby and Theresa stepped back in alarm.

Cole spit out the facts of finding Wingate's body in Beth's car and hearing the VoiceLink death threat originating from her phone. Ochoa and Scanlon had heard of the VoiceLink threats, but not in detail. And news of Wingate's murder had been lost in a sheaf of reports of violent crimes their superior had breezed through during morning roll call.

When Cole summarized the content of the VoiceLink messages, the bike cops responded in unison, "That's Hodge." Ochoa explained that a preacher named Hodge had preached every day in the Square until they shook him down after a knife complaint had been lodged against him. "Then we ran him out of the park for preaching that 'scattered bones and torn flesh' stuff."

"What does he look like?" Cole said, pulling out his phone.

Scanlon supplied the description. "Small build, homely as a gargoyle, simple-minded. Wears a dirty jean jacket and Dodgers cap. Carries a lunch box kind of thing."

"A picnic chest," Ochoa inserted. "Blue and white plastic with—"

"I've seen that guy on the street!" Cole blurted. "Figueroa, around the Coliseum!"

"Could be," Scanlon agreed. "We've only seen him between the Square and the Metro station."

Cole was immediately on the phone to Southwest Division alerting Lieutenant Arias to locate and apprehend Hodge on suspicion of murder. He gave a full description, emphasizing the picnic chest.

When Cole was off the phone, a downcast Ochoa said, "I'm sorry, sergeant, if we gave your woman friend any information that resulted in her getting hurt."

Cole nodded and hummed acceptance without really hearing. His thoughts were three miles south, somewhere along Figueroa Street, searching the alleys and doorways for the small man with a picnic chest who could possibly lead him to Beth. Ochoa and Scanlon excused themselves and continued their tour of the park.

"Maybe we'd better take the ladies off the street, sergeant," Jayne encouraged.

"Yeah, right. Let's get back to the hotel," Cole said distantly.

Shelby studied Cole's face as they angled through the Square toward the northwest corner to cross the street. She read the anxiety and tension in his clenched jaw and silent preoccupation.

Finally she said, "Sergeant, I would like to drive down by the Coliseum, please. I know you want to be there in case your colleagues find the man."

Cole looked at her. "Ma'am, I appreciate your concern. But I can't endanger your life just because I have a special interest in this arrest."

"Sergeant," Shelby responded almost sternly, "you may forget that I also have a vested interest in the arrest. This man is suspected of issuing threats against my life. He may be capable of committing grievous harm to many attending Unity 2000. I want to see him brought to justice."

Cole nodded, recognizing his self-centered shortsightedness.

Shelby continued, "Now I believe that you are at my disposal to drive me where I want to go. Am I correct?"

"Yes, ma'am."

"Well, then, I want to drive down Figueroa Street toward the Coliseum, and I want to do it right now." Shelby's demand would have sounded tyrannical except for the vein of good humor obvious in her attitude.

Cole looked at her appreciatively, then gave a mock salute. "Yes, ma'am. Right away. And thank you."

They crossed Olive Street hurriedly, entered the Biltmore, and took the elevator immediately to the parking garage.

Cole steered the Bolt out of the Biltmore garage onto Olive Street, maneuvered through heavy traffic to Grand Avenue, and turned south. It was 4:45, and the lazy shadows of near twilight in the city's concrete canyons prompted him to turn on the headlights. It seemed that all the tourists visiting L.A. for Millennium's Eve weekend had chosen Thursday to explore downtown. Rubbernecking motorists stopped and started along Grand Avenue, gawking at the skyline and staring at the sideshow of vagrants on the sidewalk.

Cole fumed for two blocks behind a knot of slow-moving cars. When he cut over to Flower Street hoping for clearer sailing, the traffic was equally congested. He sounded his horn and tried to wave cars along, but it didn't help. He considered going to code three but grudgingly conceded that even flashing lights and screaming siren couldn't make the cars move aside when they were jammed curb to curb.

The Bolt was inching between Seventh and Eighth Streets on Flower when the first response came over the radio from a female officer in a patrol car. Cole recognized the voice of one of his co-workers from Southwest Division: "I have the possible picnic chest suspect in sight. White male, approximately five feet, six inches, slight build. Wearing a dark baseball cap, jean jacket. Carrying a dirty plastic chest, blue and white. Suspect is walking west on the south side of Exposition Boulevard, presently in front of the Aerospace Museum."

"Way to go, Pollard!" Cole cheered. "That's him. Keep him in sight." Shelby and Theresa leaned forward with interest to listen to the radio chatter.

The dispatcher, also a female, spoke next. "What is your location?"

"I'm stopped at the curb on the north side of Exposition, approximately 100 yards behind the suspect."

"Hold your position," the dispatcher instructed. "Wait for backup and air cover."

"Roger," Pollard answered.

Cole had reached the end of his patience. He touched the dash panel, igniting red and blue lights recessed in the Bolt's grille and triggering the siren. Befuddled drivers unable to pull over stopped dead still. "Get out there and move those cars!" Cole ordered Jayne.

Jayne jumped out and jogged ahead several cars, flashing her badge and vigorously directing cars to merge in order to open a lane for the Bolt. By the time Cole caught up with her, the cars ahead were squeezing to the left and right. With Jayne back in the car he gradually accelerated as an open path appeared. By the time they reached Eleventh Street, they were up to 20 MPH.

Cole swerved west onto Eleventh Street to reach Figueroa, then south toward Exposition Park two miles away. Traffic yielded to the wailing siren, and Cole picked up speed, easing Shelby and Theresa back into their seat.

"He saw me. He's taking off!" Pollard reported suddenly over the radio. "The suspect just tossed the ice chest. He's running into the park."

The crisp reports emanating from the converging units chronicled the action as Cole raced frantically toward the scene. He recognized each new voice joining the chase.

Pollard: "He's heading toward the rose garden."

Takaguchi: "I'm coming north on Menlo. I'll cut him off in the middle of the park."

Air unit: "I see him. He's going west along the garden wall."

Royce: "I'm three blocks away on Exposition. I'll seal off Menlo."

Air unit: "He hears the chopper. He's really spooked. Now he's turning back toward Exposition."

Cole visualized the view from the helicopter circling the fleeing suspect. He had ridden along with the "eye in the sky" a number of times.

Pollard (running): "I'm out of the car. I'll cut him off when he hits the sidewalk."

Air unit: "He's almost there. He'll hit the street about forty yards ahead of you."

Pollard (running): "I see him! I have him! Freeze, mister! Freeze!"

Two sharp reports from a DAB gun convinced Cole that Pollard *didn't* have him. Her expletive at the missed shots was embarrassingly clear over the radio.

"Don't lose him, Pollard! Move in, Takaguchi!' Cole growled to the radio as the Bolt sped to within a mile of the scene.

Air unit: "He's running into traffic, he's crossing Exposition. Geez, a car just missed him. He's running like a crazy man. He must be wired. He's running into USC."

Royce: "I'm at Vermont. I'll seal off the west end of the campus."

Cole listened anxiously as other ground units converged and reported in. The campus was quickly surrounded. The helicopter reported, "He's running straight through the campus on University Avenue toward Jefferson. Get ready on the north side."

Cole braked sharply as he approached Jefferson from the north, then cranked a hard right turn. Three black-and-whites with lights blazing were angled into the curb at the north entrance to the University. Street traffic was moderate, slowing only slightly. The roar of the helicopter was directly overhead.

Air unit: "He sees you at the entrance. He's turning west."

Pollard (running): "I'm closing in from behind."

Takaguchi (running): "I'm behind him on the south too."

Royce: "We're ready on Vermont."

Air unit: "He's turning north on McClintock. He's coming out! He's coming out!"

Cole raced down Jefferson past University Avenue He saw a figure dart out of the campus at McClintock and onto the sidewalk. Several voices on the radio yelled "Freeze!" at once. Directly ahead of Cole two civilian cars braked severely. Tires screamed as cars skidded violently.

"Oh, geez, he's hit!" the air unit exclaimed. "The suspect ran in front of a car. He's down in the street. He's down and hurt."

Cole parked behind a cluster of civilian vehicles. "Stay with these two, Jayne," he ordered as he jumped out. He brushed past Pollard and Royce comforting the hysterical USC coed who was driving the wrecked BMW that butted the escaping suspect into the path of another car, which also hit him. Cole stepped into a circle of four officers surrounding a figure lying face down on the pavement with his limbs at grotesque and unnatural angles. A pool of blood under his head was enlarging rapidly. Another uniformed officer was bent over the still form. The victim was wearing jeans and a jean jacket. A soiled Dodgers cap was lying in the street several feet away.

Cole squatted beside the attending officer. "What are you getting, Nuñez?"

"Weak pulse, sarge," said Nuñez. "His head's split open. This guy is hanging by a thread."

"We've got to keep him alive," Cole said, with a trace of desperation in his voice. "He's holding information I need."

"Rescue is rolling, sarge," Nuñez assured. "There's not much we can do until they get here."

Cole whispered an acrid curse at the unconscious victim. "Don't you dare die, Hodge, until you tell me what you've done with her," he hissed.

Cole desperately wanted to search the pockets of the jean jacket before the unconscious vagrant was life-flighted to Los Angeles County General Hospital. But the paramedics insisted that the man's clothes not be touched until they were cut away from him in the emergency room.

The code three race across town to County General took fifteen minutes. Cole didn't ask his passengers if they wanted to go or apologize for taking them, and they didn't object.

In response to Cole's radio inquiry, Officer Pollard reported the contents of the fleeing suspect's jettisoned picnic chest: a few dried crusts of bread and an orange peel in a sandwich bag, several small baggies containing a white powdery substance thought to be a popular hallucinogen, and a well-worn Bible with the section of Revelation profusely dog-eared and underlined.

By the time Cole reached the emergency room, shortly before 7, the victim had been hurried upstairs to be prepped for surgery. Cole had to get nasty with an equally nasty ER aide to obtain the plastic bag containing the man's personal effects. While Jayne occupied Shelby and Theresa in the waiting room, Cole found an unoccupied examination table in the noisy ER and anxiously emptied the contents of the bag onto it.

The grimy, blood-stained pair of jeans had been cut into three sections. A quick search of the back pockets revealed no wallet or ID. In one front pocket Cole found a wadded-up scrap of paper: a pay stub from the Los Angeles Sports Arena. The name of the payee was R. Hodge. In the other front pocket he found a wad of currency more befitting the weekly income of a low-management drug dealer than a Sports Arena employee or a sidewalk preacher.

Cole pulled out the remnants of a dark sweatshirt and the sleeves of a ratty-looking jean jacket, which had been cut away from the body. The torso of the jacket had been sliced in two. Cole retrieved both halves from the plastic bag.

He carefully reached into the first pocket he came to and pulled out several sheets of lined notebook paper folded together in fourths. Opening the papers, he read at a whisper the words scrawled in pencil: "Woe to thee, rider of the white horse. Thou who wearest the crown of the conqueror shall himself be conquered." Cole stopped reading and held his breath as his eyes quickly scanned the rest of the first page and the three pages which followed. *The four horsemen! The VoiceLink messages!* he exulted silently. *This is the caller!*

His interest quickly turned back to the handwritten sheets. *There has to be more*, he insisted, as he scoured the sheets front and back . . . *an address, a clue of some kind about what happened to Beth.* But apart from the dooming prophecies scrawled on the four sheets, there was nothing, not so much as a doodle in the margin.

Cole set the sheets aside and returned to the pocket. Empty. He reached for the second half of the jacket and explored the pocket, finding a smaller sheet of folded paper. Cole's heart sank again as the crude pencil scratching on the paper suggested nothing that might guide him to Beth—or her body—no numbers, no words, nothing more than a simple line drawing that looked as if it had been done by a kindergartner, or perhaps by an adult in a great hurry.

There was a large oval filling the page, like the outline of an egg standing upright, and another oval inside it. Near the top of the inside oval was a rectangle with a small square drawn in each of the two bottom corners. The two squares were marked with an X. That was the extent of the drawing.

Cole stared at the drawing while his imagination scrambled for an interpretation. A mask with two eyes but no nose or mouth. An elongated tire with a box suspended inside. Nothing made sense. He turned the sheet upside down and sideways. After several minutes, the best Cole could come up with was that it was a diagram of the Sports Arena showing areas where Hodge must have had work responsibilities.

He laid the drawing on top of the other sheets and continued to examine the pieces of the jacket. The pockets were now empty and the outside bore no other ornamentation. But on the inside of the jacket, the half that would have covered the left side of the wearer's torso front and back, Cole found another pocket. It was a long, narrow strip of denim hand-sewn at an angle with the opening near the metal snaps. The pocket was empty.

A pocket for a knife—a large knife in a leather sheath perhaps, Cole quickly deduced. He inspected the pocket more closely. Specks of dried blood from a hastily sheathed blade dotted the inside of the jacket near the top of the pocket. *Dear God,* he breathed as a chill traced his spine, *please let that be Wingate's blood, not Beth's.*

This is no garden-variety low-life or drug pusher, Cole reviewed soberly. *This one has stepped over the line. This one is a killer.*

Suddenly the diagram made sense. He picked it up in one hand and held the pencil-scrawled threats in the other, glancing between them. He took each logical step slowly. The oval isn't the Sports Arena; it's the Coliseum. The rectangle is clearly the platform set up for Unity 2000 at the east end of the field. And the two small boxes marked with X's must be the bombs.

The voice from behind startled Cole. "Still looking for your doll in the middle of all this, Cole?"

Sergeant Epstein was a throwback to the TV detectives of the '50s, his style deeply influenced by his video library of episodes from *Dragnet* and *Sam Spade.* Cole assessed that Epstein's controlling "just give me the facts" demeanor was his way of compensating for being stuck with the size of a jockey.

"Yes, she's tied in here somewhere, Epstein, not that you would care," Cole said, his tone and expression devoid of any regard for the man.

Epstein ignored the comment and pulled the sheets out of Cole's hand. "What do you have here?"

Cole relished knowing first what Epstein would probably claim credit for later. "The guy they're cutting on upstairs is named Hodge. Here's a pay stub from his pocket. He's the nut who has been threatening the TV preachers on the *Times* VoiceLink line. You're holding the last four messages he called in. I'm guessing they're the originals."

Then Cole pulled the diagram out of the stack and placed it on top. "It also looks like he had more in mind than scaring people. If I were you, I'd call Metro and have them send a bomb team over to the Coliseum to look for these two boxes." Cole tapped the two X-marked squares on the diagram.

Next he laid the piece of jacket with the knife pocket across the papers Epstein was holding—blood-spattered side up. "These blood stains may prove to be Wingate's . . . or my girlfriend's."

Cole added the wad of bills to the stack. "And this was in his pants pocket, drug money probably."

"Or a payoff from somebody using your street rat to do his dirty work," Epstein asserted self-assuredly. "You just go back to your babysitting. If he knows anything about bombs or Wingate or your doll, I'll get it out of him."

Cole bored in on the little man, incensed at his arrogance. "Listen, Epstein. When you find out whose blood is on the jacket, you call me. And if that guy wakes up tonight and is able to talk, you call me."

"I don't have to call you, *patrol* sergeant," Epstein spat, clearly asserting his superiority as a *detective* sergeant. "This is not your investigation."

A half-dozen demeaning comebacks flew into Cole's mind along with several specific places he wanted to target with his fist on Epstein's little body. But Spooner's wise warning from the previous night held his response to a punishing glare. Then he turned and walked away.

At the doorway of the ER, Cole looked back. "Don't even think of skimming beer money off that stack of bills, Epstein," he said loudly enough for two nurses and an intern to hear. "I counted it and phoned it in." He knew it would take someone smarter than Epstein to figure out that he was lying.

Sixty-four

It was good news, but it wasn't nearly as good as it could be—or needed to be—for the nine people crowded into Dr. No's office.

On the up side, the group agreed, the VoiceLink caller had been captured, although his life still hung in the balance after four hours of brain surgery. Little had been learned about R. Hodge, however. Hospital staff had prohibited investigators from fingerprinting the patient for at least twenty-four hours due, to his tenuous condition. A call to the Sports Arena had produced from his job application only the name "R. Hodge" and a home address—which turned out to be false. The Arena official admitted that background checks validating age, address, previous work history, etc. were seldom performed on applicants for menial jobs.

Also on the up side, the telephone threats against the leaders of Unity 2000, which proved to be frighteningly substantial, were defused. The simple diagram of the Coliseum found in the caller's jacket pocket had prompted a cautious investigation of two six-foot speakers installed near the front corners of the platform on the Coliseum floor. The search had uncovered a small but powerful plastic bomb hidden in each speaker. The bombs were rigged to battery-driven electronic timers set to detonate at midnight on Millennium's Eve.

Bomb experts estimated that the double-barreled blast would have killed everyone on the platform, as well as most of the people sitting within 100 feet of it. Both bombs were successfully defused and removed.

On the down side, Beth Scibelli was still missing. Wingate had taken to his grave anything he knew about her. And R. Hodge, if indeed he held the keys to Beth's fate or whereabouts, wouldn't be talking again for days—if ever.

So Cole had emerged from the emergency room at County General full of promising news about the threat being ended, but agitated and depressed over the lack of information about Beth. It was Shelby's suggestion that they drive to King's House, not so much to inform Dr. No and Mai—which they could have done by phone—as to bask in their encouragement and seek their prayers.

When they arrived they found Jack and Dona Scibelli in the office, distraught and teary-eyed, drinking in the consolation offered by Dr. No and his wife. Mai had called the Scibellis earlier in the day to extend her sympathy. During the conversation, Dona had expressed a desire to be closer to downtown in case any news about Beth broke. Mai had opened the door to King's House for the evening, and Beth's parents had eagerly accepted.

Curtis Spooner was there too. Cole had called him after leaving County General. Spooner detected the despair in his friend's voice and hurried to the House in his rented Cadillac to be supportive.

Dinnertime had come and gone. Dr. No offered to have the kitchen crew bring food to the office, but no one wanted to eat. They sat on chairs, corners of the desks, and on the carpet rehearsing their concerns. Cole vented his frustration at not knowing what he could do to find Beth. Dona admitted her fear for Beth's life. Jack tried to be strong and positive, but he needed more Kleenex than his wife. Shelby, Theresa, Spooner, and even Jayne Watanabe attempted to alleviate the suffering with positive scenarios of Beth's soon return. Dr. No spoke less than anyone, but his affirming presence was like a strong cord holding the circle together.

Mai reminded everyone that one of the prayers prayed at King's House the previous night had been answered. The VoiceLink caller had been found and his bombs neutralized. It had been providential that Sergeant Cole and Mrs. Hornecker had gone to Pershing Square and that the bike patrolmen had mentioned Wingate's name. God was at work, Mai insisted. He was surely going to keep Beth safe and bring her home. No one responded with much enthusiasm.

"Situations like these, where we pray and hope but don't see anything, are like mountains we must tunnel through," Dr. No began, after one long, oppressive silence. "We scratch away in the dark tunnel with our picks and shovels, seemingly with little progress. The deeper into the tunnel we dig, the darker it gets. We pray, then wonder why God doesn't come into the tunnel with His power equipment and blast through to the other side.

"But often, just at our darkest, most frustrating moment, a needle of light shines into the tunnel from the impossible wall in front of us. We stand back to watch as the pinhole enlarges to the size of a fist, then a basketball. Soon it's big enough to crawl through. And suddenly, there's God. While we were scraping along feebly in the darkness doing our part by praying, He was tunneling through from the other side in response to our prayers.

"The worst thing we can do in the darkness is to give up hoping for the light. We must keep digging and watching for God's breakthrough. We must keep praying."

Conflicting thoughts were ricocheting through Cole's head like a wildly bounding racquetball off the four walls of the court. *Was it really divine providence that led me to the bike cops in the Square and the tipoff about the man with the blue and white picnic chest? Or was it just blind luck? And whichever it was, why didn't it work for finding Beth? Are the King's House financial success stories really answers to prayer? Or is the humble Dr. No just giving credit to the Supreme Being for his own shrewd management and marketing?*

What about the beautiful Shelby Hornecker? Has she tossed her entire life into the dumpster by parading this Jesus and faith stuff all over the map? Or is there really something to it? And is Curtis Spooner jumping onto the religious bandwagon just because his wheels don't get him up and down the court like they used to and he needs to cultivate a hobby for retirement? Or has he found something more reliable than an NBA paycheck?

Cole didn't have long to ponder the confusing questions. Dr. No's talk apparently inspired Spooner. He said, "Well, folks, it's still pretty dark in this tunnel of ours, so we'd better get back to praying for a breakthrough for Beth." Cole watched in amazement as his big, black friend, who had been sitting on the carpet leaning against a credenza, swung his stiltlike legs under him and rose up on his knees, resting an elbow on the back of Jayne's chair. Even in a kneeling posture he was a head taller than Jayne, who was still seated.

Shelby and Theresa immediately took the cue and assumed a kneeling position beside their chairs, as did Jack and Dona Scibelli. Dr. No and Mai found a place to kneel beside his desk.

Jayne Watanabe looked at Cole questioningly, as if asking her ranking officer, *Is kneeling for prayer to a God I'm not sure I believe in really part of my job description as a police escort?* He shrugged at her, saying, *You're on your own, partner, but I'm staying where I am until I figure out if prayer works or not.*

Then Spooner caught his eye. Cole had seen the look on his face before on the basketball court. It was Spooner's game face. It communicated, *I'm playing to win, and if you're not, get off my court. Reagan, get on your knees and pray, or leave.*

For the second time in two nights Cole found himself on his knees. He hoped that someone around him had the right words or feelings to unlock the mystery to Beth's disappearance and bring her back to him.

With the duct tape blindfold sealing her in perpetual midnight, time was still an immeasurable entity for Beth. Yet her body insisted that Hodge had been gone hours, not minutes as he had promised. She was hungry and thirsty again. Her back, hips, and legs ached from inactivity on the cot. The adhesive from the duct tape irritated her bare skin, especially across her eyes and mouth.

The room around her had felt warm when Hodge left, suggesting that its walls were exposed to midday sun. But it was cooling rapidly now, and Beth feared that night had descended. The darkness was always with her, but she dreaded spending another night in her unseen prison.

Hodge's stern warning had prevented Beth from attempting to ease her discomfort or find a way of escape. Her bonds had held secure against a mild flexing of her left arm. But she had not worked at it for fear that Hodge would burst in and find her partially free but unable to defend herself.

Using tongue and saliva she had neutralized the adhesive directly covering her mouth. Biting a small slit in the tape had served to aid her breathing. She could have torn a much larger hole had she worked at it. But to tempt her unstable and unpredictable captor so, she reasoned, could prove as disastrous as striking a match while checking for a gas leak.

So she had spent the uncounted hours in stillness scouring her surroundings with the senses that were not bound. Listening acutely for minutes at a time, she could hear nothing bleeding through the walls from the outside. Within the room she had identified the occasional drip of the faucet next to the toilet and the whir of a small electrical motor, an old refrigerator, she guessed, in the far corner of the room.

For a time Beth inspected her confines with her sense of smell. The room had a generally musty odor. It was an old building, she determined, with old, thrift shop furniture. Turning her head to one side and then the other, she smelled the years of dirt and perspiration ground into the thin mattress under her. Occasionally she caught a whiff of stale food. She imagined discarded food cans and crusts of moldy bread littering the kitchen area in the room.

Beth's feelings of fear for herself and terror for Hodge's proposed victims on Millennium's Eve blunted her attempts to calculate an advantage over the man or plot an escape. Her ploy of appearing to receive revelation from Hodge's master regarding the bombing of the Hornecker charter in Tel Aviv had been only mildly successful. But she was fresh out of "esoteric information" about Hodge. What could she pull out of her hat for an encore?

As the hours seeped slowly by her mind reached one dead end after another. She kept returning to the Our Father as a last resort. *Deliver me from evil, deliver Dad and Mom from evil, deliver Reagan Cole and the televangelists from evil . . . please,* she recited repeatedly in her mind.

Trying to twist her leg into a more comfortable position, Beth inadvertently prompted a muscle cramp in her calf. The tape across her mouth muffled a cry of pain. She jerked at the restraints trying to free her hands to massage away the excruciating cramp. The pain and helplessness brought tears to her blindfolded eyes. She could only form the words in her mind, *Help me, somebody, please!*

As the knotted muscle began to relax, a new fear slithered out of a shadowy corner of Beth's mind. *What if Hodge never comes back? The police may trace him to Pershing Square or Figueroa Street as I did. They may capture him or wound him or kill him. My prison may never be discovered. I could die of thirst, starvation, or suffocation on this smelly bed and no one would know. O God, please don't let me rot here alone,* she pleaded silently.

She was in the middle of a fervent repeat of the Our Father when she heard a key slip into the dead-bolt lock and turn. Another key clicked into the door lock. Beth was consoled even at the thought of Hodge returning. At least she was no longer alone. *Perhaps I can convince him to let me free to use the toilet and eat,* she thought hopefully, turning her head toward the sound.

The door opened slowly, as if the intruder was inspecting for danger before stepping inside. Beth felt a sudden brush of cool air through the open door. *It must be evening,* she deduced. She could hear a distant siren and the whir of a low-flying shuttle copter through the open door. *At least I'm still in the city instead of a remote cabin in Death Valley,* she thought with relief.

The hesitation at the door caused Beth to fear that the person with the keys might not be Hodge at all. The frightening possibilities darted through her mind. *Perhaps other street people have access to this room. Perhaps Hodge has sent a friend to entertain himself at my expense, someone like Wingate . . . or worse. Perhaps a burglar picking the locks has walked in on more than he bargained for.*

Beth guardedly considered another possibility, the ultimate possibility: that in seconds her bonds would be cut and her blindfold removed, allowing her to look into the face of Reagan Cole.

The door closed, and a familiar voice instantly shattered her optimism. "Good evening, my journalist friend." Hodge sounded less maniacal, more human, almost happy. Beth hoped the attitude she was perceiving bode well for her future. But how could she trust anything about a killer?

Hodge slipped out of a wrap of some kind, a nylon jacket by the sound of it. He began to talk as if someone else were in the room, but Beth could neither hear nor smell anyone else. He paced the room as he spoke.

"You should have seen the Beetle's face when I pulled out the money. He was sure he was going to sleep in a grand hotel tonight instead of under a bridge. 'Three hundred dollars, Beetle,' I said. I even waved it under his nose so he could smell it. 'All you have to do is wear my clothes and my baseball cap and carry my lunch box around Exposition Park until they find you—two men wearing gold jewelry and derbies. Keep the box in plain sight, because that's how they'll recognize you on the street.'

"I said, 'When they come up to you and say, "Are you Mr. Hodge?" give them the box. They already paid for what's inside. The $300 is your cut. Enjoy it.' Then I said, 'But if you skip out on me, Beetle, be very sure I will find you and cut your heart out.' The stupid fool couldn't trade clothes with me fast enough."

Hodge laughed for the first time in Beth's hearing. It was not a joy-filled laugh but devious, as a rattlesnake might laugh at his inept and defenseless prey.

"I watched the Beetle for a couple of hours from across the street. He walked up and down Figueroa, patting the money in his pocket, swinging that picnic chest trying to attract two men who don't even exist. Every half hour or so he ducked into a doorway and snorted a fingerful from the stash—just like I knew he would. He had so much powder in his little brain when he saw those cops on Exposition Boulevard, they must have looked as menacing as death and hell." Hodge laughed again.

Beth shivered. She was beginning to see where the strange story was headed.

"But I'll have to give the Beetle credit," Hodge continued, still shuffling in circles around the table in the center of the room. "He gave the cops a run for their money until he met up with that BMW on Jefferson. I didn't see the car hit him, but I heard it from a block away— *crunk!* I couldn't have dreamed of a better end to my trick.

"It didn't take the police long to find the diagram in poor Beetle's jacket. The bomb squad arrived at the Coliseum in less than two hours—I saw them. When they came out, they were carrying the bombs in two steel canisters, just like I knew they would. And if they found the diagram, I know they found the messages to the four horsemen in his other pocket.

"Don't you see, Mary Elizabeth? It couldn't be more perfect. The police think they have found the telephone prophet, a no-account named Hodge unfortunate enough to get himself run over in the chase. With a little bit of luck he will never regain consciousness to dispute their theory. And now they have found the decoy bombs and disarmed them. 'The danger is past,' the four infidels will say. 'The gathering in the Coliseum may go on as scheduled.' "

Hodge's voice began to rumble with emotion. "They will spend the evening shearing their sheep and leading them further astray, content that their kingdoms are secure. Then at midnight, the ten horns of the beast will execute the master's judgment on the four horsemen. 'May thy flesh be torn and thy bones be scattered and thy blood quench the parched earth.' *Boom-boom-boom-boom-boom-boom-boom-boom-boom-boom!*" Hodge accompanied each verbal explosion with a sharp clap.

Beth recoiled at the loud noise and the horrifying scene Hodge's impassioned description painted in her imagination.

"Then *he* will appear in his glory. The master's servant, risen from the grave to gather all the sheep into the master's fold, risen from the grave to commence his millennial reign, risen from the grave no more to die. Thank you, master, for choosing me as your servant. May I ever be worthy."

Hodge began to weep loudly as he paced the room. Beth was afraid the man was going to snap and, in a sudden act of cleansing judgment, plunge his knife into her. She tried to calm her fearful breathing and lie still, as if already dead. *Deliver me from evil, deliver me from evil, deliver me from evil,* she chanted inside.

Within a few minutes Hodge had calmed down. Beth heard him approach the cot. Unable to defend herself, she tensed for a blow.

Instead, with one quick pull, he ripped the duct tape from her mouth. The freedom to open her mouth and breathe normally more than compensated for the sting of the tape being removed.

Hodge said in a subdued, tired voice, "My dear journalist, it appears that the master has smiled upon us both. Indeed, your ill-advised invasion of my privacy, as inconvenient as it seemed to me, has brought me uncanny good fortune and success. The master's plan is succeeding beyond my highest hopes. You are my talisman, my totem, my good luck charm. And here you are, right where I left you. Obedience to the master's servant will not go unrewarded. Perhaps the master has a place for you in his new kingdom."

Beth couldn't believe that Hodge was attributing his success at almost killing a man, and his progress toward blowing up hundreds more, to her. But at the moment it was the only lever she had. So she quickly decided to use it.

She said, "Sir, perhaps the master's servant could use an obedient scribe, someone to record his victories and proclaim his truth to future generations of his followers. I could be that scribe."

Hodge was silent. Fearing to say more, Beth waited.

"The master says he is intrigued with your suggestion," Hodge said at last. "We must talk about this as we eat."

His knife slit the bonds and Beth's limbs were free. Unseen tears flooded her eyes as she breathed a prayer of thanks to God. She sat up cautiously, removed the scraps of tape stuck to her clothes, and tried to rub life back into her limbs. "Thank you very much, sir," she said respectfully.

Beth waited for Hodge to remove her blindfold, but he did not. Her desire to open her eyes was almost unbearable. But she decided not to press her luck by reaching for the blindfold herself.

NOVEMBER 1999						
S	M	T	W	T	F	S
	1	2	3	4	5	6
7	8	9	10	11	12	13
14	15	16	17	18	19	20
21	22	23	24	25	26	27
28	29	30				

1999 DECEMBER 1999

S	M	T	W	T	F	S
			1	2	3	4
5	6	7	8	9	10	11
12	13	14	15	16	17	18
19	20	21	22	23	24	25
26	27	28	29	30	31	

JANUARY 2000						
S	M	T	W	T	F	S
						1
2	3	4	5	6	7	8
9	10	11	12	13	14	15
16	17	18	19	20	21	22
23	24	25	26	27	28	29
30	31					

MILLENNIUM'S EVE!!

Sixty-five

Sheer exhaustion had subdued Cole's anxiety and kept him dead out for six hours. When he awoke at 7:15 A.M., he sighed with relief that the nightmare of Beth's disappearance had dissolved with the darkness of the night. With his eyes still closed, he reveled in the knowledge that she was lying beside him. He could hear her breathing. He could feel her warmth. But his fantasy lasted only seconds before he was dismally aware that Beth's warming presence in his bed was an illusion and his nightmare was indeed reality.

He forced his eyes open, grabbed the bedside phone, and dialed the number scribbled on the scrap of paper on the nightstand. This same call, for the same reason, was the last thing he had done before falling asleep six hours earlier.

It took nearly a minute for the sleepy receptionist to correctly route his call to the police officer stationed outside ICU at County General Hospital. "Officer Thorpe. May I help you?" the voice responded.

"Thorpe, this is Sergeant Cole from Southwest."

"Good morning, sarge. I was told to expect a call from you."

Cole skipped over the pleasantries. "How's Hodge doing?"

"There's been no change since the surgery."

"Has he said anything at all?"

"He's not talking, he's not moving, and he's barely breathing. If it weren't for medical technology, this guy would be in a drawer in the morgue by now."

Cole hummed noncommittally to cover his disappointment. Then he asked, "Have there been any . . . detectives . . . around to see him this morning?"

"Not since I've been here. They're not letting anyone in ICU anyway."

Cole phrased his next words to sound like an official order. "If Hodge makes any noises like he's waking up, call me right away. It's very important." Then he gave Thorpe his number.

"Sure, sergeant. But I wouldn't cancel any appointments today if I were you. The doc says he could be out for days."

Cole showered and shaved perfunctorily. Standing on the lanai in his robe and slippers staring at the ocean, he noted that the last day of the twentieth century had dawned with clear skies and balmy breezes. He could only wonder if Beth was able to appreciate the beautiful morning too.

While Cole was reading the *Times'* account of Hodge's capture, Jack Scibelli phoned to ask if the injured VoiceLink caller had offered any clues to Beth's fate. His voice was weak and tired, but Cole noted a valiant attempt at hopefulness.

Mai Ngo called to check in on Cole and remind him that people at King's House were praying. Even Shelby Hornecker called for an update and to express her concern. The encouragement that Cole felt from his new acquaintances was tempered by his frustration that all the kind words in the world didn't bring him one step closer to finding Beth.

Cole's mother also called. He exchanged as much small talk with her as he could endure before signing off without mentioning anything about Beth.

Spooner appeared from his bedroom in a T-shirt and shorts, rubbing the sleep from his eyes with his huge hands. "Are you opening a branch office for AT&T in this place?" he asked, grinning sleepily.

"Sorry about all the noise," Cole said, sipping coffee at the bar. "A lot of people apparently think I know more than I do about what's going on."

Spooner poured himself a cup and lounged on the couch opposite the bar. "So what's the plan today, Reag? Anything I can do to help you?"

Cole exhaled heavily. "I don't know what to do, Spoon. As far as the department is concerned, Beth is just one more missing person they don't have time to look for. And I don't know where to look for her. I suppose I could spend the day shaking down winos along Figueroa, but I doubt that it would do any good."

Spooner hummed his consolation.

"This is killing me, Spoon," Cole continued. "I've always been able to make things happen, to do what I set out to do. I made up my mind to play ball at UCLA even without a scholarship, and I made the team. I set a goal to be in the top 10 percent of my class at the academy, and I hit the top 5 percent. I wanted to make sergeant before my tenth year, and it happened in my seventh year.

"Ever since I was old enough to shave I've been able to attract most of the women I wanted, including Beth. Now she's gone, and there's nothing I can do to make it better. God knows I'd go after her if I knew where to go. But I . . . I just don't know what to do."

Spooner sat quietly for a moment, staring out at the tall palms swaying in the ocean breeze. Then he sang a line from a song, his rich and melodic baritone voice still a little froggy from sleep, "When I don't know what to do, Lord, I put my eyes on You. . . ."

Cole looked at his friend questioningly. He had heard Spooner sing in college, but his lyrics were seldom this decent.

Spooner explained, "It's from one of T.D. Dunne's songs. I have it on a CD at home. Great tune. It's about a king whose nation was surrounded by an enemy army. They were just minutes from being horse meat when the king stood up and prayed, 'God, we don't know what to do, but we put our eyes on You.' Then all the king's people began singing to God, and the bad guys killed each other off. The people didn't have to lift a spear."

Cole shot back quickly, "Do you really believe that stuff, man—I mean, God tunneling through your mountains, God solving all your problems?" His question came out as a cynical challenge, but it was genuine at the root.

Spooner saw through to the root. "Reag, I'm no preacher, and I don't know much about God and the Bible. What I do know is this: Life is one big mountain after another. Everybody's got problems. I thought being in the NBA and having all the money and toys and women I wanted would put me on top of everything. Well, it didn't. Living for all that stuff just dropped me deeper into the hole.

"I was kind of like that king—surrounded and ready to go under. Somebody turned me on to GoTown. I started listening to Dunne's music, then started paying attention to his talks. Somewhere along the line I told God, 'My life's a mess, and I can't do anything about it. If You want to make something happen here, take Your best shot.'

"Well, He's doing something, Reag. I'm not sure what yet. But some good stuff is happening for Natty and me. I think Dr. No is right: If we just keep our eyes on God, He'll do for Beth what none of us can do."

Cole sat silently watching his coffee get cold and mulling Spooner's words. Spooner respected his friend's thoughtfulness by refilling his own coffee cup and retiring to the bathroom to shower.

The two men spoke little as they ate the zucchini, bacon, and onion omelet Spooner prepared. Cole's guest explained that he would be attending a Millennium's Eve morning rally led by Simon Holloway, Shelby Hornecker, and T.D. Dunne at the Convention Center. Cole declined his invitation to go along, citing that he wasn't in the mood to be with a lot of people. They agreed to keep in touch by phone until they met up at the Coliseum that evening.

After Spooner left, Cole returned to the lanai to gaze at the surf and process his thoughts. He was consumed by the reality that Beth hadn't vaporized into the air; living or dead, she was somewhere, possibly still in Southern California. If he could, he would tell her how much he cared about her and how terrible he felt about not knowing how to find her or help her. He would assure her that people were concerned about her and were praying for her. He might even pass along Spooner's suggestion that she keep her eyes on God—even though he doubted that it was more than an emotional placebo.

He flashed back to their first game of one-on-one in the driveway. He remembered how she kept battling him, even though she was over-matched. He thought of her fiery spirit, her aggressiveness. He smiled as he pictured her game-winning shot from the street sailing over his outstretched arm.

She's a competitor, not a quitter, he thought. *That's what I'd tell her now if I could. "Don't let this thing beat you, Beth. Get tough. Use your head. Find a way to win."* If I could only challenge her competitive juices . . .

The sudden idea launched Cole to his feet. *I* can *communicate with Beth,* he thought excitedly, *at least with her phone, which was not discovered among Hodge's personal effects. She may not be able to answer it, but she may be near enough to hear it.*

He moved quickly to the breakfast bar and picked up his phone. He paused to remember Sergeant Cisneros' warning: A confrontational call to her captor may put Beth in greater danger. Even though Hodge was already in custody, Cole judged the warning still to be valid. She may be in the hands of an accomplice who is waiting for Hodge's return. Cole had to frame his message in such a way that it communicated his care and awareness of her predicament without raising suspicion.

Cole thought for several moments, then tapped the phone to life and entered Beth's number. He waited through the five tones and the generic message, encouraged because the instrument was still working.

When the last tone invited him to speak, he said in a positive, intentionally naive-sounding voice, "Beth, this is Reagan. I just wanted to tell you how great it was being with you this week. I also want to remind you that you owe me a dinner. Don't try to weasel out of it—I won the game fair and square. But I will give you a rematch if you think you're tough enough to take me on. Call me as soon as you have a free minute. I'm looking forward to seeing you real soon. By the way, you'll be happy to know that the big problem of Millennium's Eve has been solved. Bye."

Cole tapped his phone off. He taunted himself that his put-on voice and phony message was an exercise in futility. Dr. No's illustration seemed very appropriate at the moment. He felt like he was trying to dig through a mountain with a pick and shovel. *I sure hope somebody is tunneling through from the other side,* he thought, shaking his head.

"So there's a gentleman in your life," Hodge said after Cole's voice clicked off the phone. Beth was concentrating on plotting her phone's location on the map of the room she had sketched in her mind. The sound seemed to come from Hodge's desk. Realizing that her phone was inside the room gave her new hope for escape.

"Just an acquaintance," Beth answered, maintaining a grip on her spiking emotions. Instant elation at the sound of Cole's voice had turned to apprehension that he might say something to jeopardize her attempt to win Hodge's confidence.

Beth felt she had made definite progress with Hodge. When she proposed to serve as his "scribe" last night, he sounded intrigued. During a meal of saltines and lukewarm soup—which Beth had devoured ravenously even without being able to see—she regaled him with her past writing accomplishments. She talked at length and in detail, both to buy additional minutes of freedom from her duct tape restraints and to convince him of her expertise and availability to "the master."

Hodge hadn't said yes, but he hadn't said no—or slit her throat for proposing such an idea. Rather, he had allowed her to spend the night on her side instead of her back, hands and feet securely strapped to opposite corners of the cot. And he hadn't sedated her, though she rather wished he had for the fitful night she endured, while Hodge slept soundly on the floor. Through it all the blindfold remained securely and uncomfortably in place.

"Your 'acquaintance' has been rather persistent," Hodge said, cutting her bonds to let her up for a few minutes. "He left several messages during your first night here. He sounded quite upset when you failed to meet him at a place called King's House."

"He'll get over it; it's no big deal," Beth said, hoping to distract Hodge from Reagan and his message. But at the table, as she slowly ate two slices of dried bread and an orange while Hodge busied himself at the desk, she savored Reagan's words.

The syrupy sweet message was obviously an act designed to toss Beth a lifeline of hope without blatantly saying, "Hang on, Beth, I'm looking for you." The line about her being "tough enough" wasn't about basketball. *He knows something is wrong,* she thought. *He's challenging me, daring me to make it through the ordeal—even though he can't know for sure that I'm even alive.*

Beth also appreciated Cole's veiled reference to getting "free" and his interest in seeing her soon. The thought warmed her with hope. But she knew her first priority was living long enough to see Reagan again. Then she could think about the happily-ever-after part of the story.

All the hope communicated in the first part of Cole's message was soured by the last line. *Hodge's story about someone called the Beetle must be true,* she assessed soberly. *Apparently the Los Angeles police are convinced that the VoiceLink caller and his destructive plan have been stopped. Unity 2000 will go on as planned tonight. Simon Holloway, Shelby Hornecker, T.D. Dunne, and Morgan McClure will be sitting ducks.*

God, bless Reagan for trying to find me, she prayed. *But please let him know how important it is that he find me today in time to stop this maniac.*

It occurred to Beth as she ate that her conservative strategy for escape might need to be aborted soon in favor of a more aggressive approach. *It is well into the morning by now,* she estimated. *The gates to the Coliseum will be open in a few hours. The "ten horns of the beast" will be unleashed at midnight. Time is running out. But what more can I do? What drastic measures should I attempt?*

The first idea made her shudder. She could give her body to Hodge—an "offering" to the master's servant—in order to lure him into a posture vulnerable to a few well-placed fists, knees, and fingernails. Was she willing to make such a sacrifice? She wasn't sure.

The next idea chilled her with fear. She could wait for a moment when her hands were free and there was some floor space between her and her captor. She could rip off the blindfold and quickly grab something—a utensil from the kitchen corner, a wooden chair, anything!—with which to defend herself against Hodge and his knife.

She would have to take the fight to him to escape, and she would be seriously disadvantaged by a very sore right arm and eyes unaccustomed to the light. Such a drastic plan would require some subtle reconnaissance, a perfect opportunity, and more courage than Beth could summon at the moment.

In either scenario, Beth reminded herself gravely, she might be severely cut and perhaps killed. A man who had already blown up one planeload of people and who was cold-bloodedly prepared to kill hundreds and perhaps thousands more would think nothing of plunging a knife into her.

Beth reluctantly itemized her options.

One, I could ingratiate myself to Hodge and save my own skin while doing nothing to save anyone else. Appealing, but would I be able to live with myself if I survive?

Two, I could throw my body at him and mount a wild attack, only to lose and possibly die. Why should I give up my life if I can't save others anyway?

Three, I could take my best shot and, by some miracle, overpower him and get free in time to sound a warning.

Beth's odds for success seemed so staggering that the flicker of optimism was quickly doused. She suspended her exploration of a last-ditch, death-defying approach in hopes of finding a way to talk Hodge out of his scheme. She decided to employ her investigative skills to gain information and look for a weakness.

"When did the master reveal his plan for Millennium's Eve?" Beth asked in between slices of orange.

She heard the chair creak and imagined that Hodge had turned to face her across the table in the center of the room. He did not answer, and Beth wondered if he understood her. She was about to repeat the question when Hodge recited in cold, measured words, "Five years ago the master bid me to follow him and learn of him. Two years ago he appointed me to be his servant, lifted me to his right hand, and entrusted to me his judgment on the faithless. All is now in readiness. Tonight the infidels will be vanquished and the master's servant will be glorified."

"Has the master prepared other servants to execute judgment?"

"The master is all-powerful. He needs no other. He has chosen this servant, and I alone bear his sword. If the master desires a scribe to record his judgments, his servant will know it."

So far it's a one-man operation, Beth thought wryly, *and the possibility of expansion is still under question.*

Beth searched her thoughts for questions. *He is remarkably respon-sive. I have to keep him talking.*

"The master's judgment on Adrian Hornecker—why was it set apart from the others?" she asked.

Hodge was silent. Beth heard no writing or rustling of pages. She imagined he must still be staring at her. Had she so quickly stumped the master's servant? Had the master failed to explain to him why Shelby Hornecker instead of Adrian had been designated one of the doomed horsemen?

Finally Hodge spoke, but the edge was off his voice. "To whom greater guilt has accrued, greater judgment is due."

Beth noted the subtle lack of conviction in Hodge's response. *He's not sure of the answer, and he's trying to snow me,* she deduced with mild surprise.

Before she could respond, she heard Hodge rise and approach her. "The master tires of such talk," he said, sounding annoyed and slightly rattled. He grabbed her arm firmly and pulled her to her feet and toward the cot.

An impulse to attack suddenly seized her. Hodge was within striking distance, and one of his hands was occupied guiding her to the cot. A flurry of fists and nails might find his face. A violent, blind kick to the shins or groin might disable him long enough for her to rip off the blindfold and find a more effective weapon. She had only seconds to decide. *This may be your best chance, your only chance, your last chance!* she challenged herself.

A sharp prick to Beth's side quickly cooled her mounting fury. *The ever-present knife,* she hissed to herself, cursing. Then a shock of terror sizzled down her spine and the back of her legs. One swing, one kick would have been her last. The knife had been poised in Hodge's other hand all the time. Thinking herself to be seconds away from freedom, she had in reality been seconds away from death.

Using one hand on Beth's arm and his knife at her side, Hodge guided her to the cot and pushed her down. She assumed a position on her side, but Hodge forced her onto her stomach, heavily taping her wrists and ankles again to the sides of the cot frame. Even when Hodge was using both hands to subdue her and bind her, Beth knew the knife was within easy reach. She did not resist.

"The master is not inclined to tell his story before a scribe is appoint-ed," Hodge said, regaining a semblance of authority in his voice. "Fur-ther questions will result in a sealing of the lips." He shuffled to his desk. The chair creaked as it received him.

Beth reasoned that her chances of arguing Hodge out of his plan were now nil, and her chances of convincing him to appoint her his scribe were not helped by her questions. Time and options were drain-ing away quickly. The next time she was freed to use the toilet she would have to take her chances with the knife and try to fight her way to freedom. The thought gave her chills. *Deliver me from evil,* she prayed again. Then she began grasping for a plan of attack.

Sixty-six

The service began precisely at 11 A.M. with a timpani roll from the orchestra section and the dramatic announcement from the offstage television announcer, "Ladies and gentlemen, live from the great assembly hall of the Convention Center in Los Angeles, California, it's the Jubilee Fellowship Millennium's Eve rally!"

The maestro struck the downbeat, unleashing the orchestra's spirited introduction. The announcer continued his opening with the enthusiasm of a horse-race caller: "Your host is television evangelist Simon Holloway of Orlando, Florida. Today Rev. Holloway welcomes his very special guests, Rev. Shelby Hornecker, president and pastor of Victory Life Ministries of Dallas, Texas, and Grammy-award-winning songwriter and recording star of the GoTown Television Network, Mr. T.D. Dunne."

Shelby forced a beauty pageant smile as cameras zoomed in on the three televangelists standing together on the platform. She looked confident and attractive in the cream-colored suit, lavender silk blouse, and silver accessories Theresa had picked out for her. But after the disastrous and humbling week she had experienced, Shelby felt out of place as a center attraction in another high-powered television production. As torrents of applause echoed throughout the hall, she found herself suddenly looking forward to the anonymity and simplicity of being a King's House volunteer.

The orchestra crescendoed and the robed choir behind the platform exploded into a rousing anthem. Shelby, Simon, and T.D. broke formation on cue and took their seats on the platform among a regiment of dignitaries to listen to the choir's presentation.

Shelby assumed a well-practiced expression which suggested that she was enthralled by the music. Adrian had schooled her early in their career, "Never enjoy the preliminaries in the service too much, but always look like you are. While the music plays, rehearse your sermon opening, review your main points, anticipate your conclusion. Let the sheep enjoy the music; as the shepherd, pay attention to your responsibilities."

But Shelby was not responsible for the sermon today. Simon Holloway would likely deliver an impassioned call for unity among believers while drumming support for his Warriors and Crusaders. He had promised Shelby fifteen minutes to summarize her thoughts on Unity 2000 — a commercial for the big event, she had termed it.

Her comments, though not memorized, were well-prepared. So as the anthem rang throughout the great hall, Shelby's attention gravitated toward the 8,000 faces staring back at her from the congregation, especially the handful of people in the front row who had been part of a week she would never forget.

Jeremy Cannon sat between the Welbourns and Darin Chaumont. Looking at Jeremy, Shelby again felt the throbbing inner ache of embarrassment and remorse. But, to her encouragement, she was able to look at him and not turn away. Like a deep bruise, Shelby's failure was still painful, but it was also slowly healing. Jeremy would remain her friend. They had both come through the fiery trial humbled but stronger for the experience.

Theresa Bordeaux sat to the right of Darin Chaumont, next to Grace Ellen Holloway and her guest for the service, Valerie Dunne. Shelby considered briefly the chilling reality of the fate that had awaited herself, these women and their husbands, and perhaps hundreds of innocent bystanders, had the assassination plot not been uncovered and foiled. She thought of the ironic and divinely ordered circumstances by which her police escort, Sergeant Cole, had discovered the culprit's identity and participated in his apprehension — and she had watched the exciting events unfold with her own eyes!

Shelby scanned the front rows, casually looking for the tall police officer without really expecting him to be present in the service. Her heart went out to him. He had tracked down the mad bomber, sparing countless lives — including her own — but had been unable to rescue Beth Scibelli, who meant more to him than any of the Unity 2000 personalities he had saved. Shelby breathed a prayer for the girl's safety and for Sergeant Cole to find God's help in coping with her disappearance.

Also grappling with the loss were Beth's parents, who, at Grace Ellen's request, were sitting in the front row next to Valerie Dunne. Curtis Spooner, the basketball player and friend of Sergeant Cole, was sitting beside them. And Mark and Tim Holloway, reveling in the presence of an NBA veteran, sat next to Spooner.

Shelby was touched by the grief lining Mr. and Mrs. Scibelli's faces. How could this joy-filled service or Unity 2000 or the dawn of the twenty-first century hold any allure for them until they recovered their daughter?

Also missing from the service, Shelby noted, were Dr. No and his wife Mai. They had been specifically invited by Simon Holloway and promised preferred seating. Dr. No had graciously declined due to pressing duties at King's House. Shelby could not deny her growing attraction to a style of ministry and caregiving where the need of those being served, not the coffers and campaigns of those serving, was the center of focus.

The choir anthem was followed by an invocation, delivered by one of Holloway's staff, and two congregational hymns. Simon Holloway introduced T.D. Dunne, who performed his first song at the acoustical grand piano on the platform: an upbeat, contemporary number encouraging believers to "grab a hand, take a stand, and come together." Dunne received a roaring ovation for the number.

Simon Holloway spent the next ten minutes reciting in dramatic detail the threats against the Unity 2000 leaders, the arrest of the perpetrator, and the discovery of the lethal explosives in the Coliseum on Thursday. Several in the audience who had not seen the morning *Times* or who had been skipped over by the wildfire of gossip engulfing the auditorium before the service gasped in surprise. Spontaneous applause erupted when Simon lauded the efficiency of the Los Angeles Police Department and the mercy of God in ending the threat.

When Holloway introduced Shelby, the ovation was not as raucous as it was for T.D. Dunne's song, but it was full, warm, and respectful. She felt unworthy of the response. *If you only knew what I've been through this week*, she thought as she surveyed the applauding crowd from the pulpit, *you would not be so generous with your appreciation.*

As the applause died away, Shelby glanced again at her old friends and new acquaintances on the front row. The impact of the scene before her suddenly washed her prepared remarks from her mind. Here were twelve people, most of whom had never met each other prior to the Wednesday night gathering at King's House. *Look at them now*, she thought in awe, *sitting together as a group, differences set aside, worshiping together, supporting Beth's hurting parents.*

Shelby recognized a bond uniting the divergent dozen before her. She thought she would rather be sitting among them on the front row than standing in front of them to speak.

What pulled us together? she wondered. *Adrian Hornecker's grand plan for Unity 2000 brought us to the same city. But had it not been for the humbling failure in my life this week, the serendipitous meeting at King's House, the adversity of the murderous threat to Unity 2000, and the tragedy of Beth Scibelli's mysterious disappearance, we might have missed each other.*

Sorry, Adrian, Shelby sighed to herself, *but one glorious night together in the Coliseum doesn't produce unity. It's the grace of God and the humble hearts of people stirred generously into life's everyday triumphs and trials that bring people together in love.*

As the congregation waited, Shelby stood at the pulpit for several seconds without speaking. Her opening lines had returned to her mind, but she couldn't speak them. The hoopla of the Unity 2000 extravaganza seemed so petty in contrast to the emerging compassion and crying need she knew in the front row.

When Shelby finally spoke, her amplified voice filled the great hall.

"Ladies and gentlemen, before I share my remarks, we need to address an issue more significant than our great convocation in the Coliseum tonight. I would like us to pray for two people who are laboring under a heavy burden this morning. There is a couple in our midst whose adult daughter has been missing for two days, and I'm sure you know how these parents feel." An audible groan of compassion echoed through the crowd. Jack and Dona dropped their heads and wept.

"For them, there is no joy on the eve of the new millennium, because they don't know if their daughter is alive or dead. We need to come together in unity this morning to lift this father and mother and their missing daughter to the Lord."

There was a rustle throughout the hall as people bowed in prayer. Curtis Spooner stretched his long arm around the Scibellis' backs, touching them both. Valerie Dunne and Grace Ellen Holloway placed caring hands on them too. Stan and Eleanor Welbourn left their chairs to kneel in front of Jack and Dona and take their hands. And Shelby Hornecker lifted a heartfelt prayer to heaven.

Cole had intended to go to the station well before roll call. He wanted to lean on Sergeant Epstein and any other detectives who happened to be in the office to get busy and find Beth. But as he neared his Western Avenue exit, he reluctantly admitted to himself that his efforts would be fruitless. It was the busiest day of the century for the Los Angeles Police Department, especially the Southwest Division, whose jurisdiction included Exposition Park, the site of Unity 2000. Virtually every regular patrol officer and detective, plus as many reserves as could be corralled, were on duty. As the minutes ticked down to midnight on Millennium's Eve, the congestion, the revelry, the traffic accidents, and the crime would escalate to record proportions.

No one had time to look for a careless, unfortunate young woman who had been spirited away into the darkness, perhaps never to be seen again, Cole realized. Feeling disgusted and alone, he gunned his Kawasaki past Western Avenue and continued toward downtown. Dr. No and his wife didn't know where to look for Beth, Cole acknowledged, but at least they cared about her.

He pulled into the King's House parking lot at 1:10 P.M. and removed his flight suit. Jayne had insisted that he wear something more dressy to work today, since they would be escorting Shelby Hornecker to Unity 2000. So on the way into town he had visited a discount clothing store and quickly selected black slacks, a gray jacket, a light gray shirt and a maroon print tie, which he purchased and wore out of the store.

The young security man at the front door recognized Cole from his previous visits to King's House and admitted him with a smile. Cole nodded to several residents and volunteers as he passed them in the halls. He looked for Dr. No and Mai in the dining room, but didn't find them among several residents lingering over a late lunch.

Cole stuck his head inside the kitchen. "Are Dr. and Mrs. No in the building?" he asked a cluster of KPs at the sink scouring pots.

"I think the family is having lunch in their apartment," an Asian man called back to him above the sound of running water. "Do you want me to call them for you?" He motioned to a wall phone.

"No, no," Cole declined, "don't bother them. I'll just . . . look around for awhile."

Continuing down the main corridor, he came to the small chapel. One of the double doors stood open, so Cole looked inside. It appeared vacant. Facing away from the doors were six rows of old pews of darkly stained wood on each side of a center aisle. The aisle led to a metal lectern standing in the front. A simple wooden cross was mounted on the wall behind the lectern between two windows. Other walls bore several hand-sewn banners picturing Christian symbols and celebrating caregiving.

Cole turned to continue his wandering among the corridors. But the serenity of the chapel drew him inside. He slipped quietly into a pew near the back and released as much pent-up anxiety and frustration as he could with one long, silent sigh.

Sitting perfectly still, Cole was soon aware that he was not alone in the room. Small whispers drifted to his ears from near the front. *Prayers*, he thought. *There is someone praying up front.* He watched for confirming evidence. Presently he saw a tuft of hair wave briefly above the front pew on the left. Then the top of another head bobbed over the front pew on the right.

The prayer vigil, people praying around the clock for Beth, Cole realized. *There are at least two people on their knees up there praying for Beth's safety and return.*

Cole felt immediately out of place. Here he was, a skeptic in a place of prayer. He had come into the room to sort his thoughts in solitude. What if the whispering pray-ers saw him? What if they asked him to pray?

I have as much concern for Beth as you do—probably more, he rehearsed silently. *I'm glad you're praying. You live or work in this facility, so you're more experienced at prayer. But it's not really not my thing. I don't know the right . . . words. And I'm not exactly on speaking terms with the Lord anyway. I see too much of the dark side of life. It's hard for a cop to be very religious.*

Cole's self-conscious argument was interrupted by movement in the front of the chapel. One of the pray-ers stood up. It was a child—a black girl no more than twelve years old, Cole guessed, wearing faded jeans and a pink sweater. She picked up a small Bible and walked down the center aisle toward the rear doors. Cole dropped his head as if in prayer until he heard her footsteps fade in the hallway.

Less than a minute later another girl, younger than the first—about eight years old—and a man, apparently her father, stood in the front.

Both had Middle Eastern coloring. They collected their things and left the chapel with barely a look at Cole, provoking a sigh of relief.

The room was completely silent. *Who's praying now?* Cole thought abruptly. *This is a round-the-clock prayer vigil. Someone is supposed to be praying all the time.*

Cole listened closely again. No prayerful whispers. No movement. He stood and quietly walked to the front of the chapel. There was no one kneeling at the front pew. He was alone in the room.

Hands on hips, Cole paced across the front of the chapel. *Somebody screwed up here,* he said to himself. *Either someone left early or someone is late for his shift.* Cole felt cheated. He thought about nights as a rookie when an officer on day watch failed to get to work on time, causing him, the low man on the totem pole, to work overtime.

Perhaps this is your shift. The words came so clearly and authoritatively to Cole's mind that he jerked his head toward the back doors to see who had just walked in and spoken them. No one had.

That's ridiculous, Cole resisted. *I'm not part of this organization, and I'm not taking part in their prayer vigil. Somebody will be here any minute. Besides, I . . . I . . . I don't know how to pray.*

Standing near the end of the front pew, Cole saw in his mind's eye the two little girls kneeling and praying. He suddenly felt foolish for insisting that he couldn't do—and wouldn't even try—something children could do. He sheepishly realized that he would take on half a dozen Latin Barons if he thought it would bring Beth back, but he wouldn't attempt a childlike prayer.

Perhaps this is your shift. Dr. No wasn't in the room asking him to kneel. Nor was Curtis Spooner glaring at him. Yet Cole could not deny the strong urge he felt to go to his knees and talk to God alone about Beth Scibelli. For all the discomfort Cole felt about the idea, it seemed very right.

Cole glanced at his watch. He had to leave for work in five minutes. *I would rather spend five hours questioning drunks in Exposition Park than five minutes praying,* he objected to the urge. But it didn't go away. He checked the back door to make sure no one was entering. Then he knelt down by the corner of the pew.

Sixty-seven

Beth had been strapped to the cot on her stomach for several hours. The relief she had earlier welcomed from the new position had long since turned to agony. Her neck and back ached from being arched on the sagging cot. Her arms, twisted and taped by her side at an odd angle, throbbed. And she was weak from hunger.

Far beyond her physical anguish, Beth's heart pounded with fearful anticipation. By her calculations, it was well into the afternoon, perhaps as late as 3 or 4. The time for a last-ditch, drastic measure to overpower the demented killer—or die trying—was nearly upon her.

Hodge had completely shut down two-way communication. Prying for vital information under the guise of being thirsty for enlightenment, Beth had posed numerous questions about Millennium's Eve. How will the ten horns of the beast be unleashed? How will the master's servant accomplish such a feat? How will he make his appearance in the midst of such devastation and confusion? Hodge answered no questions and offered no information.

Plying his sympathies, Beth had complained to Hodge about her need to change positions and use the toilet. At first Hodge made no response. He continued to scribble silently and mumble. Then, wearied by Beth's attempts to engage him in conversation, he slapped a fresh piece of duct tape across her mouth and returned to his work. Beth could only wait and wish for Hodge to release her just once more and pray that she could take advantage of it.

But Hodge didn't release her. Instead, a change in his activities signaled to Beth that he was making preparations to leave. It began with the sound of sheaves of papers being collected and several books slapping shut. Then Hodge rose and moved to the sink. He slipped out of what sounded to Beth to be denim clothing, then spent several minutes at the sink with the water running. She recognized the scrape of a razor blade across facial stubble. The scent of soap and shampoo wafted near the cot. *A shave and a sponge bath*, she assessed.

Once the water was turned off, Hodge stood at the sink for a long time. Beth heard jars opening and the clatter of plastic on porcelain. Had Hodge been a woman, Beth would guess confidently that she was applying makeup. Then Beth picked up the light fragrance of cosmetics. *He* is *applying makeup*, she thought. *Apparently the master's servant is not planning to appear to his multitudes and begin his millennial reign with the grotesque face of a common street bum. He's giving himself a make-over.*

Beth listened carefully as Hodge dressed. It was not the sound of denim but a softer material. *Of course! He's dressing up for his grand appearance, perhaps in a suit or even a tuxedo.* Beth could not picture a change of clothes or a facial make-over improving her captor's homely appearance.

Hodge returned to the mirror for several minutes. Beth imagined him touching up his makeup, preening, admiring himself. Then a strong fragrance accosted her. She recognized it immediately from her days in high school theater: gum arabic in ether—spirit gum. Hodge was going beyond a make-over; he was applying a disguise—perhaps a mustache or the flowing beard of a prophet. *He must be planning to leave soon, Beth thought.*

Terrified at the thought of facing Hodge's knife in a blind fight but desperate to try an escape before he left, Beth began making noise. With the tape securely in place over her mouth, she could do little more than hum the syllables insistently, "Please let me free to use the toilet! Please give me something to eat!" She tossed her head from side to side and squirmed uncomfortably on the cot to underscore her plea.

Hodge ignored her. Instead, he began pacing the room, almost strutting, from the sound of it. While circling the table, as if Beth were not even in the room, he began announcing in his dramatic VoiceLink caller voice, "Thou shalt enter the gates of the temple in innocence as a sheep. Thou shalt descend into the bowels of the temple into the holy of holies. There thou shalt await the hour appointed by thy master."

Beth guessed Hodge's flowery recitation to be an obscure passage of judgment from the Bible, something he might have used in Pershing Square. She sensed that he was gearing up for his task, soon to leave the room for the Coliseum. She continued to squirm and make noise, but Hodge's voice overpowered her muffled cries.

"When the hour has come, thou shalt come forth and stand between the pillars of the temple. At midnight thou shalt lift up thy hands and sound the number of the beast: 666. In that moment, the ten horns of the beast shalt come forth with fury and the unfaithful shalt surely die. May thy flesh be torn and thy bones be scattered and thy blood quench the parched earth."

Hodge's voice thundered as he paced, drowning out Beth's feeble complaints.

"Then shalt thou appear in thy glory between the pillars of the temple. Every eye shalt see thy face. Every ear shalt hear thy voice. Every knee shalt bow before thee. And thou shalt rule in thy master's kingdom for a thousand years."

Hodge continued tramping around the table repeating his prophecy passionately. By the fourth time through, he was near a frenzy. Beth listened in terror, fearing that Hodge would come unhinged and turn violent. She might never have a chance to attack him or even defend herself.

Hodge's emotional tirade began to subside. Hoping that the immediate danger had passed, Beth concentrated on the message. Perhaps she could learn something about his plan from the quotation.

Suddenly it made sense. *The entire message* is *the plan!* she realized. *Hodge isn't quoting the Bible. He's reviewing his orders from the master. It all fits. The "temple" must be the Coliseum. The master has told him to enter the Coliseum "as a sheep"—in other words, in his disguise—and descend into the bowels" to "the holy of holies"—whatever that means.*

He must have a hiding place underneath the stadium, perhaps off the main tunnel.

Beth continued translating the images. *As the Unity 2000 celebration nears midnight, Hodge is to make his way to a place where there are pillars. The peristyle end of the Coliseum, high above the platform,* Beth guessed, *where seven arches stretched on each side of the main entrance form a row of pillars. He plans to touch off the ten bombs using the numbers 666—some kind of frequency or code for a remote detonator perhaps.*

And somehow in his twisted mind he is convinced that when the smoke clears and he makes his dramatic entrance down the steps, people are going to welcome him as if he is the Messiah. He's sick. He's crazy. He's possessed. God, deliver me from evil!

As Hodge's "rehearsal" subsided, Beth again begged for his attention with all the demanding noise and activity she could muster. Time was short. She made up her mind that, when he cut her free to use the toilet, she would take the first opportunity to lash out at him with all her strength. God helping her, she would succeed in time to find her phone and prevent a catastrophe in the Coliseum. If she failed, she hoped to meet her parents in heaven someday and tell them she tried.

Presently Beth heard Hodge approach the cot. "This has been a trying ordeal for you," he said with no sympathy in his voice. "But such is life in the master's kingdom. Tomorrow at this time the master will choose a scribe. Perhaps he will reward you for your endurance. But until then, I must fulfill the master's plan, and you must rest."

The reality of what Hodge intended to do gripped Beth's consciousness a half second before the hypodermic full of Halothane 3 plunged into her right shoulder. She screamed into her duct tape gag and lurched violently away from the needle. It came out, and lukewarm liquid trickled down her arm inside her sleeve.

Hodge leaned his knee hard into her upper back and jammed the needle into her again. He kept it in for two or three seconds until Beth jerked hard and snapped the needle in two at the skin line. Another stream of liquid dribbled down her arm. The imbedded needle tip seared her shoulder with pain.

Hodge stood up cursing and threw the useless hypodermic across the room.

"Go ahead, try it again!" Beth screamed bitterly, though the tape sealed her words inside her lips. "I'll break every needle you've got!" Then she blasted Hodge with unintelligible vile epithets and bounced her body on the cot in tantrum fashion as much as her bonds would allow. She challenged herself, *Whether he decides to inject me again or cut me open and let me die, I will not be a sitting target.*

There were no more needles. But the limited amount of sedative from the one which had pierced Beth twice was beginning to take effect. The skin on her face flushed hot, and her head seemed to swell like a balloon. She dropped limp on the cot. As valiantly as she struggled against it, she was going under. *God, I can't do it,* she wept, *I can't save them. Please save them.*

Seconds later a black tide of unconsciousness dragged her out to sea.

Assured that his prisoner was dead out, the assassin returned to the sink to admire once again his temporary new image. His naturally blond hair, which had not been exposed outside the bungalow for many months, was fashionably long and full. His smooth, youthful face was disguised with a close-cropped, dark blond false beard. It had been applied with such skill that most theater makeup artists would be fooled.

The man's narrow nose had been broadened slightly with a latex appliance and blended into his facial coloring with theatrical makeup. He wore contacts which shaded his blue eyes to brown, and gold-framed glasses with nonprescription tinted lenses direct from the prop room. He knew that only one in a thousand people at the Coliseum might recognize him without the disguise, and perhaps in the twilight and darkness no one would. But his mission was too important for even that slight a risk.

His conservative, medium-blue suit, blue print shirt, and solid tie, purchased at a thrift shop, had been cleaned and pressed. He added a final touch by pinning to the lapel of his jacket a blue and white Unity 2000 pin. He took one step back from the mirror for a fuller view and smiled with satisfaction. *Perfect, Mr. Farmer,* he thought. *You look respectable and trustworthy—just like a church deacon.*

A small old suitcase sat atop the bureau by the sink. The man opened it, pawed thoughtfully through its contents for a moment, then he pulled out one item and held it up for scrutiny. It was a custom-sculpted, full-head mask and wig. The thoroughly lifelike face was dark and blotchy with a large, pitted, bulbous nose. The hair was a long, straggly mat of dirty blonde and gray. The man thought of the many hours he had spent at the mirror donning the mask in the morning and removing it at night. How skillful he had become at merging the false face with his own eyes, mouth, and ears using rubber, latex, and make-up. Add the dirty yellow artificial teeth and smelly street-person costume and how perfectly natural—and utterly homely—he had looked for the part.

"Well done, R. Hodge, and thank you," the man said aloud to the mask. "Your long-running performance, though known only to myself and the master, was worthy of an Academy Award nomination."

The man dropped the mask into the suitcase and closed the lid. He allowed himself one more fond look at his new, albeit temporary, image in the mirror. Then he stepped to the desk, slipped Beth's phone into his pocket, picked up a well-used Bible, and left the bungalow, locking the door behind him.

It was sunset on the last day of the second millennium. The assassin strolled confidently down Figueroa Street toward Exposition Park, swinging his Bible in one hand. The brilliant stadium lights of the Coliseum loomed ahead in the golden twilight, stirring within him an excitement he could not yet afford to display.

Traffic along Figueroa was clogged and raucous as the city geared up for the biggest celebration of the century. Motorists blared horns, tossed firecrackers into the street, and hung out their windows whooping and cheering. Even the panhandlers crowding the sidewalk were more interested in the goings-on than in begging quarters from passersby.

The assassin crossed Exposition Boulevard with a crowd of early arriving delegates streaming toward the Coliseum. Then he walked west to the rose garden before entering the Park. He recalled with pleasure how the Beetle, R. Hodge's unwitting double, bolted from the police at this spot and ran amok, only to be conveniently struck down in the street and rendered harmless to the mission.

Exposition Park swarmed with the activity of local residents who would not be attending Unity 2000. Large family gatherings and outdoor dinner parties occupied the lawns and picnic tables in all directions. Bonfires and fireworks crackled and flashed in the shadowy semidarkness. The air was heavy with the odor of burned sulfur, cooked meat, alcohol, and marijuana.

The assassin stayed to the sidewalks, striding purposefully toward the ivy-draped walls of the giant concrete bowl. Closer to the Coliseum, large clumps of Unity 2000 delegates chatted excitedly, sang, and drifted toward the gates, which would not be open to the general public for nearly an hour yet.

Some delegates were dressed as if for a concert, others for a football game. They carried cushions and blankets and Bibles and field glasses. *Sheep without a shepherd, but only for a few hours more*, the assassin said to himself as he walked and watched.

He arrived at Gate 14 where a large, professionally painted sign announced: USHERS ONLY, A-H, I-Q, R-Z. He lined up behind a group of men and women being admitted single file through the security scan under the A-H sign.

"Norman Farmer, Silverlake Community Chapel," the man stated to the attendant, after showing his pocket phone and clearing the scan. He pulled out the usher's identification card Hodge had secured for him several weeks prior to the event. NORMAN FARMER was printed in large letters across the card. Luckily, no photograph or holograph had been required.

"Welcome, Mr. Farmer," the attendant said, glancing at the card. Then he located the name on a printout and checked it off. "Pick up a name-tag holder from the table. Usher orientation will begin on the field next to section 14 in about five minutes. Have a glorious eve-ning."

The assassin posing as Norman Farmer stepped inside the gate and took a plastic holder with a long blue and white ribbon stapled to it. He slid his card inside the holder and clipped it to his breast pocket.

Standing in a knot near the gate were four acquaintances from his days as Hodge: Sergeant Witt, Officer Coyle, Paddy Duckett, and old man Bailey, the crusty security guard. The police officers and guard looked unenthused about spending Millennium's Eve with 100,000 religious fanatics. But Paddy was in his glory. A crowd in the Coliseum meant something meaningful to do, even if most of what he was allowed to do was mere busywork.

The former R. Hodge couldn't resist addressing the four as he passed by. "Good evening," he said, showing a plastic smile. They nodded to him disinterestedly.

Norman Farmer slipped into the stream of ushers funneling through tunnel 14. When he emerged from the dark tunnel into the bright lights of the stadium, he stepped out of line to take in the scene. Ninety-five thousand empty seats waited around the bowl and on the field. At the far end of the stadium was the trademark peristyle entrance with its familiar arches, massive video displays, and towering Olympic torch. And on the field below the arches stood the Unity 2000 platform encircled with blue and white bunting.

The assassin's pulse quickened. *The master promised*, he recalled at the sight, *that when the unfaithful are judged, all eyes will look to his servant standing between the pillars. They will bow to him as to one risen from the dead. All will yield to the master. All will harken to his servant.*

"Quite a sight, ain't it?" The interrupting voice belonged to a roly-poly usher with a bad toupee and a gravy-stained tie. Emerging from the tunnel, he wrongly assessed that the short, bearded man admiring the soon-to-be packed stadium would appreciate an informative commentary.

"Gonna pack 100,000 in here tonight. Big crowd, *big* crowd. Won't be the biggest, though. Not at all. You know the record for the Coliseum? Exactly 134,254 souls. Yep, 134,254. Set back in '63. Billy Graham crusade. Wasn't here myself; I was just a kid. But my daddy was here. Sat right down there on the field."

Norman Farmer nodded without smiling and hoped to escape the man by rejoining the stream of ushers cascading down the stairs to the field. The roly-poly usher followed him.

"It'll never happen again, 134,254. Nope. The Coliseum's been re-modeled a couple of times since then. Took out a lot of seats. Made it more comfortable for us portly types, if you know what I mean." The round, jovial usher laughed for himself and everyone around him.

When they stepped off the concrete stairway and onto the grassy floor of the bowl, Norman Farmer turned right without a word as Mr. Roly-poly and the stream of ushers flowed into the back section of folding chairs for orientation. He walked confidently beside the rail separating the field from the first row of stadium seats. Then he ascended the ramp into the huge mouth of the Coliseum, the dimly lit main tunnel that curves under the west end of the stadium, past the dressing rooms, and up to the tunnel gate on Menlo Street.

He entered the lower of two doors to a long hallway parallel to the tunnel which accesses the dressing rooms and showers. The upper entrance, at the far end of the hallway, was next to the towel room where Hodge had spent many hours plying Paddy Duckett with spirits.

In the hallway, the assassin found himself among several curious ushers who had left the main stream to sneak a look into the dressing rooms where so many famous Los Angeles sports teams had prepared for battle.

Next to the towel room was the spacious Trojan team room and showers, with dressing stalls painted cardinal and gold in honor of the Coliseum's neighbors and longtime tenants, the University of Southern California. Next came the visiting team dressing room and an interview room, a small cubicle set aside for star players to meet with members of the media.

At the opposite end of the hallway from the towel room, to the left of the door where Norman Farmer entered, was a small, private dressing room for officials. With the Trojans' and Raiders' football season completed, the officials' dressing room had been converted to a storage room. Benches, chairs, and training tables had been moved there to clear the Trojan team room for a VIP lounge for the Unity 2000 leaders and their parties.

Doors to the team rooms and interview room were open. The towel room and the officials' room were locked. The entire dressing room complex would be sealed off to all visitors before the gates opened to the public at 6. The leaders were scheduled to arrive between 6:15 and 6:30.

Norman Farmer mingled with a handful of inquisitive ushers nosing into the team rooms. The Unity 2000 committee had equipped the Trojan room with comfortable chairs, a snack table spread with platters of fruits, vegetables, breads, and cold meats, and a nonalcoholic bar offering fruit juices, soda, mineral water, coffee, and tea. A security guard, a young, skinny black kid in an ill-fitting uniform, had been retained to keep uninvited guests away from the food. He sat in a metal chair beside the food table, reading a sports magazine.

The voice of an impatient usher captain boomed over the speakers in the dressing rooms, "All ushers please report to the field for orientation immediately. Come on, folks. We need to take care of business and get to our stations before the gates open."

One by one, the ushers left the dressing room to hurry through the tunnel to the field. Norman Farmer lingered behind, pretending to inspect the locker facilities in the visiting team dressing room. When all was quiet, he stepped out into the main hall. Peaking through the door to the Trojan room, he saw that the security guard was engrossed in his magazine.

The assassin quickly and silently moved to the towel room door and opened it with a key Hodge had secretly copied from Paddy Duckett's original. Inside he retrieved a plastic bag of supplies he had smuggled into the Coliseum and hidden in the towel room early in December. Checking the hallway again, he exited the towel room and walked quickly to the opposite end of the hallway. Another key admitted him to the officials' room. He closed the door and locked it behind him.

A whisper of light streamed into the room through the smoked glass window in the door. Norman Farmer climbed up on a table to twist two fluorescent tubes out of their sockets, assuring that the room would remain dark. Then he found his way through a maze of stored furniture to a back corner. He lifted a chair off a stack and set it behind a locker where he could not be seen from the door, if by remote chance someone came into the room.

He placed the plastic bag on the chair and pulled out a neatly folded garment. Reaching into the folds, he extracted a long-bladed knife, identical to the one he had left buried in the wall cavity behind the mirror in his bungalow. If he was confronted in the officials' room by an unsuspecting intruder, the knife was his insurance that his mission would not be thwarted. He placed the knife on the top shelf in the locker.

The garment was a flowing white satin robe, originally a cleric's vestment, that Hodge had picked up in a thrift store. The assassin had reasoned that the bright garment billowing in the wind would make him immediately visible when he appeared in the central arch after the moment of judgment. As the cameras noticed him there and zoomed in, the close-up of his familiar face on the giant monitor above the field would drive the survivors of the blast to their knees in contrite submission.

He slipped a hanger into the robe and hung it in the locker.

The last item in the bag was a small cosmetic bag. He removed his jacket and took the cosmetic bag to a sink in the officials' shower room. In the near darkness, he peeled off the false nose and beard and dropped them into the trash can. Then he slathered his face with cleansing cream and rubbed away the last of the makeup and spirit gum with a towel.

The assassin stood at the mirror, seeing only his shadowy outline but appreciating his clean face with his hands. Never again would he disguise his face or his voice. Never again would he appear as the downtrodden Hodge, or the insipid usher, Norman Farmer. He was now, and ever would be, only the master's servant. In a few hours, his face would be known to the world.

He returned to the locker and stowed the cosmetic bag. Putting on his jacket, he sat down in the chair and removed Beth's pocket phone from the inside pocket. His thumb moved over the keypad in the darkness touching seven familiar numbers. Immediately he began to perspire with anticipation.

The call signal sounded twice, then switched to a digital answering device in the receiving unit just as he had programmed it. The receiver was awaiting a code. He poised his thumb above the number 6. *Three touches and the platform will blow to the sky,* he thought, panting. *The master's judgment cometh swiftly, like lightning from the east.*

The rush of power and pride caused his hand to tremble. He relished the presence for a moment, then tapped the phone off, canceling the call. A dial tone again sounded in the speaker. He returned the instrument to his pocket and sat back to wait.

Sixty-eight

With the VoiceLink caller in custody, Chief DeShea Robinson had reduced the escort staff for each of the Unity 2000 personalities from two to one, beginning with day watch. Officer Jayne Watanabe, anticipating cushy duty in the Coliseum on Millennium's Eve instead of cruising the streets with the party lunatics, had arrived at roll call dressed for a theater opening. After her co-workers had complimented her appearance with the customary whistling and hooting, Lieutenant Arias broke the news that she had to change into uniform for a night on the town in a black-and-white. She sulked away to the women's locker room looking like Cinderella after her wicked stepmother announced that she couldn't attend the ball.

Jayne's absence from the Bolt also freed up the front seat for another passenger. So when Cole arrived at the Biltmore garage at 5:30 P.M. to pick up Shelby Hornecker and Theresa Bordeaux, Jeremy Cannon joined their party for the ride to the Coliseum. They pulled out of the garage behind the flashing lights of a black-and-white driven by Jayne Watanabe, who was to clear the way to the Coliseum before resuming street patrol. Stan and Eleanor Welbourn fell in behind the Bolt in their rented car.

After seeing how well his passengers were dressed, Cole wished he had spent a little more money on his Millennium's Eve work ensemble. Jeremy's custom-tailored dark suit made the policeman's $99 sport coat look like a Goodwill reject. And Cole calculated that all the jewelry he had owned in his thirty-one years didn't add up to half what the actor's pinky ring cost.

Shelby Hornecker wore a shimmering black sheath with matching long coat and several strands of pearls. Dressed more to work at the Coliseum than to celebrate, Theresa had selected a striking Prussian blue suit conservatively accented with gold jewelry.

"I'm very sorry about Ms. Scibelli, sergeant," Jeremy said, as the Bolt snaked through traffic behind its black-and-white escort. It was the first time the two men had exchanged words since their brief meeting at LAX.

Cole was pleasantly surprised, both at the actor's thoughtfulness and that he knew Beth's name and pronounced it correctly. "Thank you, sir," he said. "I'm trying not to think about it."

Trying, yes; succeeding, no, Cole admitted to himself.

"Is the suspect still unconscious?"

"Yes, sir. I checked again on my way to the Biltmore tonight."

"But at least the police know who he is, correct?"

"Not exactly, sir. The detectives were given permission to fingerprint him this afternoon. His ID didn't come back the way we expected."

Shelby, who had been listening to Cole out of the corner of her ear while talking with Theresa, leaned forward and said, "Are you saying that you have the wrong man, sergeant?"

"We still think he's the right man; all the evidence points to him. But apparently his real name isn't Hodge. However, it's not unusual for street types like him to use a variety of aliases."

Jeremy said, "That's something that puzzles me. How could a bum off the street be clever enough to build a couple of bombs, plant them in the Coliseum, and come up with those elaborate messages to the *Times?*"

"One of the first things we learned at the academy was never to underestimate any individual's capacity for crime," Cole answered. He jerked a thumb toward a clump of vagrants hunkering beside a building as they motored down Grand Avenue. "Those men weren't born on the street. Most of them had homes and jobs and relatively normal lives at one time. Some were very successful. I've run street people into

County Jail and detox who turned out to be former engineers, corporate executives, ministers, even NASA scientists.

"That guy Hodge—or whatever his real name is—may have landed on the street because of booze or drugs or religion or the devil himself. But he may also turn out to be a demolitions expert with the CIA who snapped and got himself mustered out. I don't doubt for a minute that he's clever enough to build and plant a bomb. Thank God he wasn't clever enough to keep from getting caught."

"Yes, thank God," Shelby sighed from the back seat.

After a minute of silence, Jeremy said, "What is being done to locate Ms. Scibelli?"

"Beth," Cole corrected, hoping the use of her first name would make conversation about her more palatable.

"Beth," Jeremy echoed respectfully.

"Unfortunately, not much can be done, sir. Dozens of people drop out of sight in L.A. every day, some by their own design, some by the will of other people, including the city's crime lords. We just don't have the resources to track them all down, especially those who disappear without a trace. Some of them eventually turn up in a hospital or in the morgue. At least *their* families experience some closure to their grief. Many are never found at all."

"But Beth did not disappear without a trace, sergeant," Shelby said, intending to inspire hope. "That man in the hospital must know where she is. As soon as he comes around—"

"*If* he comes around," Cole interjected.

"Twenty-first century medical technology can accomplish marvelous feats, sergeant," Shelby reminded. "Besides, I've been praying for Beth's safe return. We all have. It may look impossible, but God—"

"Yeah, I know," Cole interrupted, peeved at the pontificating which had as yet proved fruitless. "God is supposed to be digging a tunnel. Well, that sounds wonderful. But I happen to know that there are a lot of people for whom God's tunnel arrived too late. The missing persons they prayed for were found dismembered in a shallow grave in the Angeles National Forest or dumped in a back alley."

Shelby reached forward and touched his shoulder to convey her empathy. "Sergeant, if I understood why God does what He does, I would be happy to explain it to you," she said, her mind suddenly flooded with fresh memories of dire hopelessness and inexplicable mercy. "Wherever Beth is, she's in God's capable hands. Don't give up on Him yet."

Cole nodded vaguely. *What choice do I have?* he muttered to himself.

Humanity surged into the huge Coliseum through its thirty-three gates like rivers flowing into a vast lake. Opportunistic vendors, wading into the tributaries like fishermen, baited the crowd with international foods, trinkets, Unity 2000 souvenirs, and spiritual paraphernalia of every description. Beggars and religious charlatans worked the outer banks of the crowd for cash donations.

For several blocks in all directions, streets were clogged with carloads of delegates searching for nonexistent street parking. Had it not been for a black-and-white escort and a strictly controlled police lane around Exposition Park, the Bolt and its occupants could have spent Millennium's Eve hopelessly gridlocked on Figueroa Street.

Cole followed Jayne Watanabe's patrol car down the open lane on Menlo Street and through the tunnel gate, which was monitored by four uniformed LAPD officers. Shelby, Theresa, and Jeremy stepped out at the head of the two-lane concrete ramp which curved from street level past the dressing rooms and out to the field. Members of the Unity 2000 committee, wearing blue blazers with white logos embroidered on the breast pockets, were present to greet the arriving dignitaries and drive them down the ramp in glorified electric golf carts.

Cole parked the Bolt in the VIP lot nearby and walked down the ramp unescorted. The din from the crowd inside the Coliseum cascaded over the rim like a mighty waterfall. Cole couldn't resist walking past the dressing rooms to the threshold of the field for a look. Powerful stadium lights had turned night to midday inside the bowl. Circling helicopters rained brilliant, cylindrical beams down on the platform as if from heaven. The place appeared to be full, yet people continued to gush in through the tunnels. Thousands more who didn't make it into the Coliseum would fill the adjacent Sports Arena and watch the event on huge TV screens. Cole marveled at the sheer number of enthusiastic people who had chosen to spend the last night of the millennium in such a place.

When Cole entered the Trojan team room, he judged that the budding homogeneity between Simon Holloway, Shelby Hornecker, and T.D. Dunne had taken a step backward. In one corner of the room Simon and Grace Ellen Holloway clustered with Tim, Mark, Dr. Motabwa, and Dr. McGowan sipping juice from clear plastic cups. T.D. Dunne huddled at one end of the food table with Valerie, five band members, and Curtis Spooner. Shelby Hornecker's arriving entourage had joined Darin Chaumont, Dr. No, and Mai in a circle near the door, while Shelby made her rounds greeting people. And Dr. Morgan McClure, meeting everyone for the first time, sat in a far corner with Tony, his Navajo bodyguard, and Tanner, his aide, neither eating, drinking, nor enjoying himself.

Cole flashed a hello to Spooner across the room. The basketball player cocked his head as if to ask, "Anything new?" Cole shook his head, and Spooner resumed his conversation with Dunne's lead guitarist. Cole joined three other police escorts passing time in a corner by the door.

Shelby Hornecker took a position in the center of the room and called everyone to attention. "It's 6:30, people. In fifteen minutes the band will leave to begin the prelude. And at 6:55 sharp the electric carts will be in the tunnel ready to transport us to the platform. At 7, our master of ceremonies, my associate Rev. Stan Welbourn, will deliver the welcome and invocation. Then Mr. Dunne will begin the program with congregational singing and his presentation. T.D., we trust that your music will set the tone for a glorious evening of worship and fellowship with one another."

Dunne nodded and smiled.

Shelby quickly reviewed the time schedule and urged all participants to conclude their presentations on time so that the Communion service could start promptly at 11:30.

"Just before we pray and go to the platform, I would like to make a confession." Shelby's tone was abruptly personal, prompting everyone in the room to full attention. Even the four police escorts turned to listen.

"After my husband was killed nine months ago, I was tempted to cancel Unity 2000. Frankly, even before he died I saw little use for our four very independent and divergent ministries to come together. I confess that I have viewed each of you not as fellow-laborers but as rivals, and I suppose you have held a similar view toward me. I couldn't imagine that one evening in the Coliseum could produce the unity we have steadfastly avoided all these years."

Shelby's manner was so winsome and transparent that her pointed indictment of her colleagues for disunity offended no one in the room.

"However, something happened this week to launch us in the right direction, in spite of ourselves. I want to publicly thank Mr. and Mrs. Thanh Hai Ngo—whom we have come to know as Dr. No and Mai— for the hospitality they extended to us last Wednesday night at King's House. More importantly, I want to thank them for their quiet humility and sterling example of Christian love, which has been an inspiration to those of us who attended."

The Dunnes and the Holloways hummed their agreement and voiced soft thank-yous toward the Vietnamese couple. Aware that Dr. McClure had not been present, Shelby expressed her hope that he would visit King's House before he returned to Phoenix. McClure seemed to appreciate being included, but he said nothing. Though no one noticed it, the brief exchange had moved the four groups in the room a step closer together.

Shelby continued, "I also want to announce that, as a result of my visit to King's House this week, I have decided to increase my personal involvement in ministry to the disadvantaged. This afternoon I contacted Dr. No and offered my services as a volunteer at King's House for the first three months of my sabbatical leave beginning in January."

Grace Ellen Holloway, who had kept Shelby's secret, smiled broadly. Tim and Mark Holloway's mouths dropped open in surprise. Other members of the Holloway, Dunne, and McClure groups murmured their astonishment.

"Furthermore, I am directing Darin Chaumont, my very capable administrator, to investigate how we can develop a similar ministry in the Dallas area. I will recommend to our Board of Directors that we liquidate Victory Life Films and use the capital to launch this new ministry venture."

Whispers of amazement again rippled around the room.

"Mrs. Hornecker, I have also felt the impact of the King's House ministry this week." Simon Holloway's voice lacked its customary strength and self-assurance but was full of compassion. "Our two sons here, Tim and Mark, have also felt called to serve at King's House for a season. Perhaps God will use them to help us more effectively reach out to the poor in Orlando. After this week, I'm sure the vital ministry of caring for the hungry, the poor, the homeless, and the hurting will be more important to Grace Ellen and myself and our entire organization. Thank you, Dr. No."

Young Mark Holloway quickly jumped in, "Does this mean that we have your permission to volunteer at King's House, Dad?"

All eyes in the room locked onto Simon Holloway. He reached out for Grace Ellen's hand and received it. "Yes, lads, you have our permission and our blessing, that is, if Dr. No will have you."

"It would be my pleasure," Dr. No responded, smiling broadly.

Shelby initiated a round of polite applause, and many joined in.

T.D. Dunne spoke next. "Since we're such fierce rivals," he said, clearly tongue-in-cheek, "I guess I should put my two-cents worth in. I don't know if Val and I were more blessed or convicted by what we saw at King's House on Wednesday night. And I'm not sure what our response should be. Like most everything else that affects me, this experience will probably shape my music for the next several months. In fact, it has already shaped my music. You'll hear it tonight in the Unity 2000 theme song, which I wrote before we arrived in Los Angeles.

"I know we need to pray and get out there, but I have one more thing to say. I agree that our unity to this point has been at best superficial, contrived. Each of us has been more interested in our own goals than anything we might accomplish together. But maybe this week we have found something we can work on together. I'm talking about something like an interministry commission designed to reach out to the poor in a way that none of us could do alone. I for one would like to pray and brainstorm with you people on what God might want to accomplish through us."

Vigorous nods around the room revealed assent to be in the majority. Morgan McClure was again noncommittal. His thoughts were clearly elsewhere.

"Speaking of prayer," Shelby quickly interjected, "it's time to pray and make our entrance. Perhaps we could link hands in a circle to signify our desire for unity. Dr. No, will you please lead us in prayer?"

The circle was beginning to form when Dr. No added, "Most of you know that we are still praying for the safe release of Ms. Beth Scibelli. I assume we have no further word on her at this time." He looked toward Cole standing near the door who simply shook his head.

Dr. No continued, "Then, Sergeant Cole, perhaps you and your co-workers would like to join our circle as we pray." The small man extended a hand toward the four officers. They joined in with Cole appearing the least reluctant.

"Before we bow our heads," Dr. No said to the large group joined hand to hand, "take a look at what God can do."

All eyes scanned the circle. Except for Morgan McClure, who was insulated from the others with his bodyguard on one side and his aide on the other, the group was thoroughly integrated. Simon Holloway stood between Stan Welbourn and Curtis Spooner. Shelby held Grace Ellen's hand on one side and Dr. Francine McGowan's hand on the other side. T.D. Dunne was linked to Jeremy Cannon and Mai Ngo.

Dr. No said, "Let's pray that God will join our lives as we have joined our hands, and that He will spare Beth Scibelli, wherever she may be."

Then he prayed.

Beth Scibelli awoke angry. The persistent sting in her shoulder had rankled her awake like an electronic alarm, dredging her up from slumber against her will. But in only a few seconds she realized that the drilling pain had been her unwitting ally. *Stay awake*, she commanded herself. *It can't be midnight yet; there still may be time to stop him.*

Beth had to assume that Hodge was already gone. She squirmed and made angry, insistent noises, then listened for him. Nothing. She had no time for cat and mouse. She had to make something happen. If God wasn't going to deliver her from evil, she had to find a way to deliver herself. If Hodge returned and stopped her, so be it. This was the hour of truth.

She decided to marshal her anger to the cause. She remembered college basketball games in which hard-checking opponents baited her to lose her temper, hoping to ruin her concentration and distract her from her game. But Beth had never lost her cool on the court. Jack

Scibelli had coached her from their earliest days together playing driveway hoops, "You can get mad and blow up like a keg of dynamite, getting a foul or an ejection. Or you can turn that dynamite into jet fuel, release it slowly, and let it power you to a higher level of play." She must put his wise counsel to work again now, to fight the pain in her body and to get herself free.

First she tried to roll the duct tape blindfold away from her eyes by rubbing it vigorously on the cot's mattress. But the mattress offered little resistance. So the blindfold remained tightly in place.

However, in a matter of minutes Beth was able to chew away and spit out enough tape around her mouth to open a large hole to scream for help, which she did for several minutes until she decided it was useless. Hodge was probably right: the room was soundproofed.

The critical issue, Beth realized, was getting a hand free. Between the soreness in her strained right arm and the piercing pain of the needle fragment in her right shoulder, she knew that it would have to be her left hand. She was right-handed, but basketball had equipped her with better-than-average left-handed skills. How often she had fooled an opponent by driving the lane to the basket, faking right, then spinning away and laying the ball in left-handed. It was another skill her father had taught her.

Beth tested the strength of the tape on her left wrist by focusing all her strength to pull against it. Lying on her stomach, she could exert little leverage. The tape wouldn't budge. The effort made her light-headed, reminding her of her fragile consciousness, the result of Hodge's injection. She paused to focus, to breathe slowly, and to think—and command herself to stay awake.

The words came to her so clearly that she could imagine her father standing next to her as he had so often when helping her with a project in his workshop. "Sweetheart, you can't pull duct tape apart. But if you nick the edge with something sharp, you can tear it just like cloth."

Something sharp. Her left hand swept its limited range of motion. The wall—Sheetrock, unfinished, not sharp. The cold metal of the cot frame—smooth, no edges. She stretched her fingers around the frame, pulling against the tape with all her strength, searching. She scraped the tip of her longest finger against something rough. It didn't hurt; it felt wonderful; it was sharp.

She shifted her weight toward the wall and stretched out her fingers to find it again but could not. Puzzled she leaned back to her original position and reached. Again her finger grazed the tip of a pointed metal object. When she realized that the weight of her body on the cot was affecting her ability to reach the object, she knew what it was: the end of one of the small coil springs attaching the frame to the metal spring underneath the mattress.

Because of the tape, Beth couldn't get her wrist anywhere near the coil's sharp edge. Her only hope of using it to nick the tape was to detach it, which seemed impossible because of her weight on the cot.

Her outrage at the predicament flared hotly. She cursed aloud through the hole in the tape. *Steady, Beth, steady,* she cautioned herself. *Don't explode. Channel your anger. Make it work for you. Study the defense. Find a weakness.* Her head throbbed with a sedative hangover which begged her to go back to sleep.

Beth worked past the flare-up and commandeered her thoughts. *It's a game of one-on-one. The cot is my opponent, fiercely blocking my path to the goal. I must turn my adversary's strength against him and use it to my advantage.*

In seconds, the path to the goal was clear and Beth went for it.

She shifted on the cot as close to the wall as she could, then gritted her teeth, and threw her weight hard toward the open side. The wall-side legs of the cot hopped about an inch off the floor.

Beth's right arm and shoulder objected with pain. She ignored it, strained even more to the left, and threw herself harder. The legs flew upward. Fighting off her natural inclination to maintain equilibrium, she leaned hard into the fall.

The momentum toppled the cot to its side, driving Beth's shoulder into the floor. She screamed in blinding pain as the needle fragment dug deeper into her flesh. Before she could order herself not to, she blacked out.

Sixty-nine

Paddy Duckett hadn't seen such a grand spectacle in his beloved Coliseum in years. Sitting in his golf cart, parked where the main tunnel opens into the huge arena, he gazed across the rows of humanity carpeting the grassy floor to the blue and white draped platform at the peristyle end. The black singer and his guests were putting on a terrific show. The bowl reverberated with loud, upbeat music. Spotlights from the sky drenched the platform with radiance. Much of the crowd was on its feet clapping, cheering, and singing along.

Paddy had sneaked away to the towel room for a snort of booze only once since the gates opened. There had been too much going on. Easily identified as a Coliseum hand from his khaki work clothes, Paddy had been asked by the visiting dignitaries to fetch this and that and to drive here or there around the stadium in his golf cart.

He had hoped to chauffeur one of the many guests to the platform during their grand entrance and feel the thunderous roar of the crowd rain down on him. But he had been denied the privilege. So now, with the program in full swing, he was stationed conspicuously in the main tunnel, hoping to be of further service to the people running the religious show.

It was a mystery to Paddy why his good friend Hodge hadn't been around. Hodge had assured him that he would be working in the Coliseum instead of the Sports Arena on Millennium's Eve. But Paddy had been all over the grounds in the cart without seeing his friend.

Just as well, actually, Paddy thought, absorbing the noisy, exciting scene before him. *I'm too busy to visit with him anyway. There will be plenty of time to lift the glass in the towel room and swap stories about Millennium's Eve in the weeks ahead.*

The roar of the crowd rose to the level of a Concorde taking off as the band pounded out the final notes of a rousing number. Paddy found himself applauding too, along with the plainclothes police escorts standing nearby and watching with him from the tunnel's mouth. Only one policeman, the tall, sandy-haired one in the dark sports jacket, seemed not to be entertained. He restlessly paced the tunnel as if waiting for someone who was late for an appointment.

The raucous applause had only begun to abate when the entertainers on the platform burst into another driving tune. It occurred to Paddy that since the program still had four hours to run, the policemen might want to sit down and watch. He remembered that there were folding metal chairs in the dressing room area. *Not too comfortable, but better than standing for four hours*, Paddy reasoned. He decided to show himself useful by bringing chairs out for the officers.

Paddy backed the golf cart seventy-five feet into the tunnel to the lower door to the dressing room. Entering the main hallway, which was deserted, he paused to think where the nearest unused chairs might be. Looking to the left he saw the door bearing the words OFFICIALS' ROOM. He remembered helping a crew move several folding chairs and benches into the smaller room in order to clear the larger dressing rooms for Unity 2000 visitors.

Paddy pulled a bulging ring of keys off his belt and searched for the one that would admit him to the officials' room. He found it and slipped it into the door lock. He could hardly hear the jingle of the keys above the music erupting from the speakers in the hallway. Nor could he detect the movements of a figure inside the room preparing to defend himself at the sound of the key in the lock.

Opening the door, Paddy stepped into the dark room stacked with furniture. He flipped the light switch, but the room remained dark. He flipped it again and again. No light. He judged that the breaker was off or that both overhead tubes had blown out at the same time. *Odd, but not improbable*, he thought.

Normally he would have taken five minutes to go to the towel room to check the breakers or secure new tubes and install them. But it was Millennium's Eve. He had more important things to do at the moment. The room was not in use, so it wouldn't hurt to leave the tubes for another day. Besides, he could surely locate four folding chairs in the dark.

Paddy felt his way along a bank of metal lockers to the back of the room where he remembered leaning several metal chairs against a wall. Eyes unaccustomed to the dark, he walked shin first into a locker door which had been left open. The door swung backward on impact, clattered against the adjoining locker, and whipped around to bang his shin again. He grabbed his smarting leg and cursed the person who had left the locker standing open. Then he punctuated his profanity by slamming the door closed.

Paddy paused to think that if he had broken his leg or split his head open and called for help, no one would have heard him over the din of the crowd and the music. And with the room being used only for storage, had he knocked himself unconscious and bled to death, he would have been entombed here for days—perhaps weeks—before anyone found his body.

Feeling uneasy at the prospect, Paddy picked up two folded metal chairs from a stack leaning against the wall and retreated cautiously through the canyon of lockers and furniture to the door. Leaning the first two chairs against a wall in the hall, he returned for two more. The eery darkness of the officials' room, which had punished him with a sore shin for intruding, disquieted him. He quickly found two more chairs, left the room, and locked the door behind him.

The assassin released a long sigh and relaxed his grip on the knife. The unwary meddler had wandered within a few feet of his hiding place, nearly within range of the upraised blade. How easy it would have been to step from behind the locker and permanently rid himself of the intruder—and he had been poised to do so. But it had been unnecessary.

He opened the locker door Paddy Duckett had slammed shut, returned the knife to the shelf, and again sat down in the corner to wait.

When Paddy brought the first two chairs into the tunnel, the tall policeman was pacing near the golf cart while talking on his pocket phone. Crowd noise and music echoed through the tunnel like the roar of a hurricane, so the cop plugged one ear and spoke loudly.

"What's the status on the prisoner? . . . Say again, please, I can't hear you. . . . More surgery? . . . When? . . . Any hope that he will regain consciousness after surgery? . . . Right. I understand."

Paddy loaded the two chairs onto the cart and stepped back into the hall to retrieve the others. When he came back out, the officer had pocketed his phone and was returning to the mouth of the tunnel to join the other cops. He looked dejected.

Paddy drove to the end of the tunnel, hopped out, and said to the four escorts, "Any of you officers like a chair?"

Three of the four accepted the offer and thanked him. The tall, sandy-haired cop declined and kept pacing.

Beth came to again moaning at the pain boring into her right shoulder. She was lying on her side on the floor, still taped to the cot, right where she had fallen. She couldn't imagine that she had been out very long with the pain so intense. Not knowing what time it was or if she could still escape and get a message to the Coliseum was maddening. All she could do was continue to try.

Beth's new position presented new problems. Her entire right arm was on fire with pain and virtually useless, prohibiting her from searching for a coil spring on the right side of the cot. And she was no longer able to reach the coil she had discovered with her left hand before toppling the cot. She could think of only one solution.

She steeled herself for the next maneuver by reciting aloud, "Deliver me from evil, deliver me from evil." Then she again threw her weight to the left, rolling across her inflamed shoulder with a short scream of pain and pulling the metal cot on top of her. The frame slammed into the table leg on its descent and nudged it aside until Beth was flat on her back. She positioned her feet and her forehead to support most of the weight of the cot while the limp, foul-smelling mattress draped over her head.

Beth calculated that the lack of weight on the cot spring would now make the coil accessible. She twisted her left hand around the metal frame and reached for the coil. It was surprisingly easy to grasp. She jiggled the coil and discovered it to have plenty of play. All she had to do was unhook one end of the coil and she would have a sharp edge to work with. How she would get that sharp edge positioned to tear the duct tape was a mental hurdle she had yet to attempt.

Beth judged that it would be easier to unhook the coil from the cot's frame than from the mattress spring, because the frame was closer to her hand. But she also realized that the coil would offer less resistance dangling from the spring than from the solid frame, making it more difficult to use in tearing the tape. So she gritted her teeth and stretched her left hand across the coil to the place where it was hooked to the mattress spring.

The coil came free on her fourth try, and its sharp hooked end dangled beside her heavily taped left wrist.

Your next trick, Beth coached herself, *is to anchor that hook in the tape and make a tear without knocking the coil out of the frame and losing it on the floor.* It wasn't easy. She could maneuver her wrist next to the coil, but the hook on the end refused to dig into the tape.

After several minutes of futile trying, Beth's frustration was near the tantrum stage. *Don't blow up, channel your anger,* her rational self drummed at her. But after several more attempts at corralling the defiant coil, Beth lost control. She bounced the cot up and down violently with her feet and hands, slapping the loose coil with her hand as if beating it for insubordination. She slammed the frame against the table and threw her head from side to side, trying to get free of the oppressive mattress draped over her face.

Her strength soon evaporated and her angry screams turned to groans of despair. She relaxed her taut muscles and let the weight of the frame and the mattress drop on her. "God, Mary, Jesus, somebody in heaven please help me," she sobbed.

A prick of pain on her left wrist suddenly distracted her. She explored with her fingertips and discovered that her violent outburst had somehow flipped the hook of the coil into the small space between her wrist and the cot frame. The sharp edge jabbed her wrist, but as she twisted her arm carefully to escape the discomfort, she could feel the hook taking hold at the edge of the tape. What she had tried unsuccessfully to accomplish with finesse and discipline for the last ten minutes had happened almost automatically during her brief tantrum.

Suddenly hopeful, Beth held her breath and twisted her wrist to further set the hook in the tape. *If it digs into the tape too far from the edge,* she thought, *the coil will give and the tape won't tear. But the only way to know is to start twisting and let the hook do its job.*

She breathed another prayer and began turning her wrist. She could feel the tension between the coil and the tape increasing. Then she heard it: the sound of tearing fabric. The hook broke free and dangled again. The tape seemed not as tight on her wrist. She envisioned a small tear at the edge of the layers of tape, perhaps no more than a quarter-inch. She hoped it would be enough.

Beth leaned the cot frame against the wall and began working her forearm against the weak spot in the tape by pulling toward the wall. The motion was similar to the curls she used to do in weight training while playing women's basketball at USC: holding her elbows at her sides and curling weights from her waist to her chest. Beth wasn't up to her college strength, but she hoped she could do enough curls to tear the duct tape through.

One, two, three, four, five, she counted silently with each pull of her arm against the tiny tear. *Bear down, more power,* she urged herself. *Six, seven.* The tape ripped again, and Beth's hope soared. She pulled hard against the tape once more and held it, teeth clenched, left arm quivering with strength. A few more fibers gave way, then the tape split apart and Beth's arm was free.

Beth began to cry for joy, but her free left hand never stopped moving. She immediately pushed the mattress aside, pulled the tape from her mouth, and welcomed a gulp of fresh air. Digging frantically at the duct tape blindfold with her nails proved fruitless. She relocated the dangling coil spring, unhooked it from the frame, and used its sharp end to dig under the tape at her temple to start a tear.

Removing the blindfold from her eyes proved painful. Yet she worked quickly, wincing as the tape pulled away eyelashes and hairs from her eyebrows.

Opening her eyes for the first time in forty-eight hours, Beth feared she might be blind. But she quickly discerned that the room in which she was imprisoned was without light. With her eyes well accustomed to the dark, she could make out the shape of the cot still poised above her and a table leg to her left. She wiped tears and crusty matter from her eyes and thanked God for her sight.

It took three more minutes for Beth, using her trusty coil spring to cut into the tape, to finally free her throbbing right arm and ankles from the cot and push it off of her. Feeling weak and lightheaded, she rose cautiously to her feet and steadied herself by leaning on the table.

Her first impulse was to bolt for the door, get outside, and run as far from the room as she could. But she had no idea where she was or how much time was left before the deadly hour of midnight. And she was suspicious that Hodge might have stationed someone outside the door to keep her from escaping. No, first she had to turn on a light and see if there was a phone in the room to warn Reagan Cole.

Beth remembered what had sounded like the clicking of a light switch near Hodge's desk. She felt her way in the darkness toward the corner where she had pictured Hodge sitting with his papers and books. Finding the desk, she fumbled over it until she touched a lamp, located the switch, and turned it on.

The instant brilliance caused Beth to shut her sensitive eyes and turn away. Only after several seconds was she able to open them to a squint and orient herself to the room which, until now, had been no more than a crude map in her mind. An initial visual sweep of the room proved that it was even more primitive and unkempt than she had imagined. Worse yet, Beth saw no signs of a clock or telephone. She was determined to tear the place apart to find her phone and call Reagan Cole.

She started with the old desk, sweeping papers and books off the desktop and dumping the contents of the drawers onto the floor. No clock, no phone. She scoured the bookcase, the tabletop in the center of the room, and the foul-smelling kitchen area, finding nothing.

She moved around to the corner of the room which served as the bathroom. There was nothing on the toilet or sink except for a few toiletries. And the drawers in the bureau next to the sink contained only a pair of dirty socks and a threadbare T-shirt. Beth was beginning to believe that Hodge had departed with her watch, all his timepieces, and the phone to further torture her. She would have to take a chance on escaping the building to find someplace to call Reagan.

She nearly overlooked the small, old suitcase lying flat on top of the bureau. Flipping the latches open, she lifted the lid and looked inside. At first, the rubbery object lying on top looked like an expensive, full-faced Halloween monster mask. But when she pulled it out for a better look, she squealed in horror and dropped the mask into the sink as if it were alive.

The resemblance was uncanny. The deeply lined, discolored skin, the oversized, pitted alcoholic's nose, the straggly blonde-gray hair. *It's Hodge's face*, Beth acknowledged—a professionally crafted false face.

With a wary eye on the mask, Beth pawed through the remaining contents of the suitcase with morbid curiosity. It was full of makeup, sheets of latex, modeling tools, and brushes. She gasped as reality dawned on her. *No wonder he kept me blindfolded*, she thought. *Hodge is not Hodge at all. Hodge is only a character played by a pathological killer with a fascination for Hollywood makeup.*

Beth remembered the fragrance of makeup in the room before her captor drugged her and left the room. *If he's not Hodge*, she wondered, *who is he and what does he look like tonight? How can I ever find him at the Coliseum in time to stop him?* She had to find a cop or a phone right away.

Searching near the foot of the overturned cot, Beth found her shoes and sweater and slipped into them. Unwilling to open the door without something to defend herself, she searched the kitchen shelves for a knife, a cleaver, something big and menacing. But Hodge had obviously cleared the room of anything sharp Beth might use against him as a weapon. She had to settle for an old aluminum skillet.

After turning out the light, Beth unlocked the door and opened it as quietly as possible, gripping the skillet in her left hand. She peeked cautiously outside. The sight of dark sky chilled her with urgency. Seeing no one, she slipped through the doorway to find herself on the doorstep of a bungalow behind a run-down shanty of a house. Beyond the house was a dark street.

The night was alive with the sounds of celebration. Firecrackers and bottle rockets whistled, fizzed, and popped sporadically in the distance. Horns blared from a nearby thoroughfare. Beth raced out to the street to look for someone—anyone. To the left a half-dozen children were igniting fireworks in the middle of the street. She hurried toward them. In the flicker and glow of sparklers, she saw that they were Latinos. None looked over the age of eight.

"What time is it, please?" she asked urgently.

The startled youngsters turned toward her, eyeing the skillet in her hand. They didn't respond.

"Does anyone know what time it is?" she repeated, tapping her left wrist with her finger as if she were wearing a watch.

Two of the children exchanged phrases in Spanish. Beth quickly adjusted. "Que hora es, por favor?"

An older child relayed the question to a dark figure sitting in the overgrown yard of a nearby house. Beth could see the faint glow of his cigarette in the darkness.

"It's 11:10, lady," a male voice with a thick Latino accent replied.

Beth sighed with relief. Almost an hour to find a phone and call Reagan. She was ready next to ask the unseen Latino man for a phone, but thought better of it. She judged it more important to get out of a potentially dangerous neighborhood and find a public phone.

"Thank you, sir," she replied toward the glowing cigarette. "And can you tell me where the Coliseum is from here?"

The man in the darkness waved the cigarette toward the end of the dark street, saying nothing.

"Thank you," Beth said again. Then she took off at a trot on unsteady legs in that direction, keeping a tight grip on the skillet in her left hand.

Beth didn't recognize the corner when she arrived, and the street signs had long since been torn down and carried away. But, looking left, she saw the lights and stop-and-go traffic of a main street three blocks away. As she began trotting toward the well-lit street, an LAPD black-and-white came into view, easing along the stream of traffic.

"Hey, wait!" Beth cried out. "Police! Wait!" Then she tossed the skillet into the bushes and took off at a dead run toward the police car.

Seventy

Cole had watched little of the Unity 2000 program from his vantage point in the tunnel. Beth was constantly on his mind, and he couldn't stand still. He had made several calls to County General and to Southwest Area headquarters seeking new information about his missing girlfriend, but without success. In between calls he paced the length of the tunnel repeatedly.

Cole had stopped briefly to listen to his friend Curtis Spooner address the huge throng during T.D. Dunne's segment. Spooner described how God, through Dunne's music, had changed his life and saved his marriage. Serving God, not playing basketball, was his priority now, he said. Cole was impressed with Spooner's sincerity. He had to agree—something good had happened to Spooner. He wanted to talk to him about it more sometime.

Spooner had concluded his talk with a pitch Cole hadn't expected. "We're here tonight to show the world that we are one in Christ," he said, his deep baritone voice booming across the stadium. "Well, all we're really showing tonight is that we can sit together in the same arena without getting into a fight. Big deal. Even the Lakers and the Blazers can do that."

Warm laughter fluttered through the Coliseum audience.

"The real test begins when we leave here in a few hours. Christian unity will happen when we start caring about others more than we care about ourselves. There are a lot of hungry, hurting people in our world, and they don't really care that we have filled the Coliseum and the Sports Arena tonight. But if we begin to work together tomorrow the way we have come together tonight, we can meet their needs and heal their hurts. What better way is there to tell the world that God is love and that we are one?"

Dr. No has made a big impact on Curtis Spooner, Cole thought, as he watched his friend bow in response to the generous applause of the crowd.

Cole hadn't listened to much of the next guy, Dr. Morgan McClure. Nor did many others in the audience, judging from the way people traipsed to and from the snack bars during the 8:30—9:30 time slot. McClure's message was more of a big pat on his own back than a talk about unity among church people. Cole guessed that McClure was probably guilty of whatever he was about to be indicted for.

Simon Holloway and his two guest speakers had fired up the crowd again by asserting that the agenda of biotechnology is to promote a super race just as Adolph Hitler did. Cole walked away from the tunnel disgustedly just as a minor shouting match between pro- and anti-genetic engineering factions erupted on the Coliseum floor. *Great tribute to unity*, Cole thought cynically.

But the next time Cole had tuned into Holloway's segment, Simon had changed his tack. Like Curtis Spooner, the Orlando evangelist spoke of a unity of selfless service to the less fortunate in the new millennium. He described how his two sons would be returning to Los Angeles in January to give several months to a local ministry to the poor.

Holloway had challenged many in the audience to join him in his fight against godless technology as Warriors or Crusaders. Then he closed by calling *all* Christians to unite in giving their energies and substance to alleviate the suffering and heartache rampant in the nation's communities. Cole noted that the previously argumentative delegations applauded Holloway together.

By the time Holloway sat down at 10:25, the crowd was fidgety.

Aware that the year 2000 was less than two hours away, people were restless to celebrate. Fireworks could be heard and seen beyond the rim of the Coliseum, as parts of the city launched into the celebration early. A few random firecrackers popped in the tunnels around the big bowl.

T.D. Dunne had refocused the audience by leading them in singing the Unity 2000 theme during the collection of the offering. The crowd sang lustily as many people joined hands and swayed to the beat.

It's an infectious tune, Cole admitted to himself, as he listened and watched the lyrics scroll down the giant video monitor atop the peristyle end. *And it seems to fit perfectly with the unity talks given by Curtis and by Simon Holloway. Great planning on someone's part.*

At 10:30, Stan Welbourn kicked off the Victory Life segment by introducing Jeremy Cannon for his dramatization of Christ addressing His disciples. The crowd quieted to a whisper as the popular actor, in his flashy dark suit instead of a Galilean's robe, delivered his lines with authority and compassion.

As he watched, Cole admitted to himself that he probably had been wrong about Jeremy Cannon and Shelby Hornecker. From all he could see, they were sincere in their faith and circumspect in their behavior. Cole still didn't understand how they could live in such opulence when so many of their parishioners subsisted at or below poverty level. But his admiration and respect for Shelby Hornecker and her staff had risen considerably in the days he had been with them.

Following a booming ovation for Jeremy Cannon, Shelby Hornecker was introduced as the chairperson of Unity 2000. She also spoke about Christians coming together around the ministry Christ gave to all: ministry to the poor. Her warmth and transparency seemed to hold the crowd together against the distractions occurring outside the Coliseum as the giant digital clock on the scoreboard ticked into the last sixty minutes of the dying millennium.

At 11:15, Shelby introduced Dr. No for the last fifteen minutes of her segment. Despite Shelby's warm introduction, the crowd's applause of welcome for the unknown speaker was polite but tentative.

Dr. No was reading the Parable of the Sheep and the Goats when Cole's pocket phone sounded. Cole turned away from the mouth of the tunnel to pace as he answered, "Reagan Cole."

"Sergeant, this is Officer Nuñez."

"What's up, Emilio?" Cole pressed, puzzled that one of his on-duty officers would contact him by phone instead of the radio.

"Sorry to bother you, sarge, but Borges and I have a situation here, and we need your help to clear it up."

"Shoot."

"A young white female stopped us on the street at Figueroa and Twenty-third about ten minutes ago—kind of a scruffy-looking chick,

449

no ID on her. Says she's a good friend of yours. Even knew your number from memory. She insisted that we call you. She's all worked up about the bomb in the Coliseum. We told her that the bomb squad has already—"

Cole stopped in the middle of the tunnel. "Beth! Her name is Beth Scibelli!" he shouted into the phone, his voice echoing against the concrete walls.

"Well, yes, that's the name she gave us," Nuñez replied with surprise.

"Where is she?" Cole demanded.

"Right here, sarge, in the car with us."

"Give her the phone, Nuñez!" Cole ordered.

There was a brief pause, then a soft, broken voice said, "Reagan?"

"Beth! Thank God it's you! Are you all right?"

"Yes, I'm okay now," she answered, weeping. "I was foolish, Reagan, and the VoiceLink caller got to me. I'm sorry, but I'm okay."

"I'm just glad you're safe. I can't believe it! Tell Nuñez to get you—"

"Reagan, you have to listen to me," Beth demanded through her tears. "The VoiceLink caller is at the Coliseum. He has bombs—ten of them—hidden in the platform set to go off at—"

"We got him, Beth!" Cole interrupted excitedly. "His name is Hodge, and we got him. We also found the bombs."

"Reagan, listen, please!" Beth insisted forcefully. "You didn't get the VoiceLink caller. The man who was hit by the car was an impostor, somebody Hodge tricked into acting like him. The bombs you found in the Coliseum were decoys. The VoiceLink caller isn't a street bum at all. Hodge was just an act. The real killer is some kind of demon-possessed lunatic, Reagan. He's the one who blew up Adrian Hornecker's plane in Israel, and he's at the Coliseum right now. He's planning to set off the bombs at midnight and then sweep in like some kind of messiah, thinking everyone will follow him."

"Geez, you're serious," Cole gasped, gazing through the tunnel and across the field to the platform where the televangelists and his friend Curtis Spooner sat.

"I don't have time to explain everything to you now," Beth added. "But he's there somewhere. He said he would be waiting in a place he called the holy of holies. He's going to set off the bombs using the numbers 666—but I don't know what he meant. You've got to stop him, Reagan, my parents . . ." her voice was overcome with emotion.

Cole thought of Jack and Dona Scibelli, sitting somewhere near the front of the stadium, still grieving over the disappearance of their daughter. *What bitter irony,* he thought, *if the Scibellis were killed in the blast without knowing that their daughter had returned from the dead.*

"I've never heard of the holy of holies in the Coliseum," Cole said. "Where is it?"

"I've never heard of it either. He said it was in the bowels of the Coliseum. It must be a secret, out-of-the-way place."

Cole hummed and shook his head at his lack of understanding.

"What does this guy look like?" Cole asked.

"I don't know, Reagan. I was drugged and blindfolded the entire time. I think he's given up his street-person disguise. He could be anyone."

Cole glanced at his watch. It was thirty-nine minutes until midnight. A strategy began to form in his mind. "Beth, I want you to stay with Nuñez and Borges until we find this guy."

"But I want to be there with you."

"Not smart. He may see you and panic and push the button ahead of schedule. Wait in the car outside the Coliseum. I'll call you when it's safe." Beth reluctantly agreed.

Cole tapped his phone off. He shook his head in disbelief. *The crisis of my life has just been resolved, and I don't have a minute to enjoy it.*

The first thing he had to do was talk to Spooner. He hurried down the tunnel toward its mouth as he dialed his friend's number, careful to distance himself from the other escorts.

Spooner was seated behind T.D. Dunne on the platform as Dr. No continued to address the audience. Cole watched Spooner pull the small phone from his coat pocket and heard him answer, "Yes."

Cole spoke tersely and rapid-fire, not allowing his friend a chance to respond. "This is Reagan, and I'm watching you from the tunnel. Listen to me carefully, and stay cool. I hate to tell you this, but we have a big problem." In three quick sentences he explained what Beth had told him about the assassin and his bombs.

Spooner stared at him from across the stadium, remaining unruffled. "What do you want me to do?" he almost whispered.

"I need you to figure out a way to clear the platform as quickly and casually as possible. It can't look like an evacuation. The bomber may be watching. And if the crowd catches wind of a bomb threat, we'll have a stampede on our hands."

"But if this platform blows, the shrapnel will take the first twenty rows with it on all sides, Reag," Spooner warned. "We've got to warn those people."

"This guy wants the main characters on the platform, not the people in the chairs. I don't think he'll push the button if the platform is empty."

"I hope you're right, Reag."

"Me too."

"Are you calling in backup?" Spooner quizzed.

"Not until you clear the platform. A swarm of uniforms might set the bomber off."

"Okay, I'll do my best."

Cole hung up and watched Spooner subtly lean forward and whisper in T.D. Dunne's ear. Dunne responded calmly as the two men huddled together. Dr. No spoke on.

Cole approached the short man dressed in khakis who was sitting idly in the golf cart near the tunnel's opening. The name stitched above his pocket was PADDY. Cole needed information and he needed it now, but he couldn't risk arousing Paddy's suspicion.

"I'll bet you know the Coliseum pretty well, don't you, Paddy," Cole said.

"Oh, yes, officer," Paddy answered, lighting up at the attention. "Been working here forty-two years. I know the Coliseum better than my own house."

"If somebody asked to see the holy of holies in the Coliseum, where would you take them?"

"The holy of holies?" Paddy's face screwed up in puzzlement.

"You know, someplace quiet, out of the way; a place to think without being disturbed."

Paddy nodded with enlightenment. "For me, that's the towel room, west end of the hall by the dressing rooms." He aimed his finger toward the entrance door halfway up the tunnel.

"The towel room?"

"Yes, officer, a little storage room where we keep bundles of towels. It's a nice place for a fellow to . . . relax."

"Is there anyone in the towel room right now?"

"Oh, no sir. I was inside a couple of minutes ago. Nobody's there. Besides, you need a key to get into the towel room."

Cole nodded. "Anyplace else down here someone may go for peace and quiet?"

The stinging pain in Paddy's shin brought another place to mind. "We also have the officials' room at the east end of the hall. But it's stacked high with furniture from the other dressing rooms. It's locked up tight. Nobody's in there either—at least I didn't see anybody." Then he added, more to himself, "Strange that both those lights would be out at the same time. Maybe I'd better check that breaker."

"Lights?"

"Yes, when I got the chairs out of there for you officers, the lights wouldn't come on. Banged my shin a good one in the dark. Either the breaker is off or both the tubes have burned out."

"Where is that breaker panel, Paddy?"

"In the towel room, officer. Is anything wrong?"

Cole reached into his imagination for a quick, convincing fib. "No, I'm just looking for one of my men. He said he was going to sit down for awhile in the holy of holies before midnight. I don't want him to miss the fireworks."

Paddy nodded, assuring Cole that he had accepted his answer.

Cole said, "May I borrow the keys to those two rooms? My man has a way with locks. He may have let himself in and fallen asleep."

"Of course, officer," Paddy said, lifting the key ring from his belt. "Take them all. If you can't trust a police officer with your keys, who can you trust?"

Paddy fingered the two keys for Cole and handed over his ring.

Cole glanced at the platform. Everyone was still in place. It was almost 11:30, and Dr. No's talk was drawing to a close. *Come on, Spoon,* Cole urged silently, *get those people off the platform.*

Cole was backing away from Paddy's cart toward the entrance to the dressing room when his phone sounded. He saw that Spooner was holding a phone to his mouth.

"What's going on, Spoon?" Cole answered out of Paddy's earshot.

"In a couple of minutes we start the Communion service. Dunne convinced Shelby to let everyone up there help the ushers serve. We've passed the word about the bomb and about leaving the platform. Dunne will be the only one left up here."

"Dunne's got to go too," Cole argued.

"He insists on staying to lead the singing and hold the service together during Communion. Says it will look too suspicious if everyone abandons ship."

"Does he realize the danger he's in?"

"He knows. He wants to help."

Cole bit his lip at the thought of Dunne's potential sacrifice. "Okay, but tell him not to mention over the mike that the platform is being cleared. Our man may be down here somewhere listening with an itchy trigger finger."

"You really have a way of making a guy feel secure," Spooner said wryly. "I'll tell him."

Dr. No was treated to a standing ovation at the close of his speech. Cole had heard none of it and barely noticed the crowd's reaction. He stared at the platform, wishing that the event were over and the Coliseum empty. The responsibility he had so quickly assumed for the lives of hundreds of people on and around the platform had obliterated his momentary exhilaration at hearing Beth's voice again. *Why didn't I simply call Arias and wash my hands of the responsibility? Why didn't I just tell Spooner and everyone around the platform to run for their lives in hopes that the stampede killed fewer people than the bomb would?*

You're doing the right thing, he assured himself. *You're a trained professional, and right now you're the officer in charge. Respond to your instincts and training. You are the man.*

Shelby Hornecker introduced the Communion service and invited the ushers around the Coliseum to begin distributing the bread and the juice. Cole could hear a measure of anxiety challenging the self-assurance in her voice.

Then Shelby turned the service over to T.D. Dunne at the keyboard. As Dunne began to play, Shelby, Simon Holloway, Morgan McClure, and their guests descended from the platform by the steps on either side and fanned out into the crowd, ostensibly to pass platters of broken bread.

Cole sighed deeply. *It's time to go to work and catch a mad bomber.*

Seventy-one

Cole quietly briefed the three plainclothes escorts on the situation. He selected Otis Phipps, a black sergeant who had been assigned to McClure, to help him clear the dressing rooms of all civilians and then determine if indeed the bomber was holed up in the officials' room — and do so without arousing his suspicion.

He instructed Sergeant Kim Huntley, Simon Holloway's escort, to stand guard in the tunnel outside the upper door to the dressing room complex, the door nearer Menlo Street, and not let anyone inside. Cole stationed Dunne's escort, a sergeant named Krueger, outside the door nearer the field.

"Phone Lieutenant Arias and tell him we need backup and the bomb squad," Cole told Huntley. "But tell him to keep everyone in the bushes until we determine exactly where our man is hiding."

"You know that Arias will tell Captain Thomasson, and Thomasson will want to evacuate the Coliseum," Huntley returned.

Cole winced. "An evacuation announcement at this point would create pandemonium out there," he said. "An explosion might kill a couple hundred, but a stampede will kill a couple thousand. And if the bomber sees that we're evacuating, he may pull the trigger anyway."

"The brass has to make that call, Cole," Huntley pressed.

"Ten minutes," Cole insisted. "Ask Arias to give me ten minutes to find the guy. If he's not in here somewhere, he and the captain will still have fifteen minutes to try an evacuation."

"I'll give it a shot," Huntley said, pulling out her phone as she started up the ramp.

Phipps said, "Great plan, Cole, but how are we going to find out if the bad guy is hiding in there?" The two cops huddled together checking their pistols.

"I don't know yet," Cole confessed with mild chagrin, "but I'll think of something." Then the two officers slipped inside the upper door and eased quietly down the short flight of stairs leading to the hallway floor.

T.D. Dunne's music flowing through the speakers provided sufficient background noise to mute the two officers' movements. Phipps took up a position at the base of the stairs next to the towel room door with weapon drawn. At the other end of the hall, 100 feet away, stood the door to the officials' room.

Cole began a sweep through the dressing rooms with his DAB gun at his ear, pointed upward. There was only one person in the Trojan team room, the young security guard, who had been filching off the VIP food table and napping all evening. Cole ushered the wide-eyed kid quickly out to the tunnel.

The visiting team dressing room and showers were empty, as was the small interview cubicle ten feet from the door to the officials' room. Cole backed carefully away from the interview room toward Phipps. "All clear," he whispered, holstering his gun. "Keep watching while I look at the breaker panel."

Cole tested the door to the towel room. It was locked. Using Paddy's keys, he let himself in. The room smelled of bleached towels, mildew, and cheap wine. Cole switched on the light and opened the metal door to the breaker panel. All the breakers were switched on.

"The blackout in the officials' room isn't a breaker problem," he informed Phipps. "He put the lights out himself. He's in there waiting, I know it." Cole's heart began to beat rapidly. He welcomed the adrenaline rush that always accompanied pursuit and danger.

Cole ducked back into the towel room to check with Huntley on the radio. "Backup units, SWAT, and bomb squad are rolling," Huntley reported through Cole's tiny earpiece. "Arias will be on site in two minutes. Thomasson wants to evacuate, but Arias convinced him to give you ten minutes—and four of them are gone. Arias doesn't want you to rush the suspect until he arrives."

"I won't rush him," Cole answered. "I just want to make sure he's where I think he is. The lieutenant can take it from there."

Cole rejoined Phipps, who kept a wary eye on the other end of the hallway. Cole thought aloud, "How can we be sure he's in there without walking right in and spooking him to push the plunger?"

"Well, even bad guys have phones," Phipps answered sarcastically. "If we knew his number we could just call him up and ask him where he is."

Cole blinked at a startling realization. "I *do* know his number," he said. Phipps questioned his seriousness with raised eyebrows.

"Thanks, Phipps, I knew I'd think of something," Cole said. "Cover me."

Phipps began, "But what—" only to be silenced by Cole's upraised hand.

Cole started cautiously down the hallway toward the officials' room. Instead of drawing his weapon he pulled the phone from his jacket pocket. Ten feet from the wooden door with the smoked glass window, he slipped to his knees and then to his belly. He slithered along the wall, phone in hand, to within inches of the door. Placing his right ear near the point where the door frame meets the floor, he dialed the number for Beth Scibelli's pocket phone.

Seven rapid tones sent the signal on its way. Cole held the receiver to his left ear to listen. *The last time her phone was used,* he thought, *it was in the possession of the VoiceLink caller. If he still has her phone, and if he's in this room—*

The first ring sounded in Cole's receiver, as did a simultaneous tone, distant but clearly distinguishable from under the door. Silence. Then a second set of tones sounded, one from the phone in his hand and one from inside the officials' room. *Beth's phone is in there!* He *must be in there too!*

Questions flew into Cole's mind like fiery sparks from an exploding skyrocket. *Will he answer the phone or play dead? If he answers, shall I say something or hang up? If I speak, what should I say? Time is running out. Should I wait for Arias or deal with this threat myself? If there is no response at all, should I try the door or consent to an attempted evacuation?*

Just like every other call Cole had placed to Beth's number in the last forty-eight hours, the five rings were followed by a synthetic voice inviting the caller to leave name, phone number, date and time of call, and a message after the tone. When that tone sounded, Cole suddenly realized that the speaker inside the room was on. He had an open line to whoever was beside the phone.

Cole checked the time and breathed a silent sigh. No time to wait for Arias. He inched back from the door, drew his weapon with his right hand, and spoke into the phone, not altogether sure what was going to come out.

"This is Sergeant Cole with the Los Angeles Police Department. I am in the hallway outside your door with other police officers. The party is over, sir. We know who you are and we know about the bombs. The Coliseum platform has been evacuated. The entire dressing room area is surrounded. You have no route of escape. Come to the door, open it slowly, and slide your weapons and your detonator out to us in the hallway. Then step out with your hands above your head."

Cole held his breath, hoping that Dunne's music coming through the speakers would not be abruptly interrupted by the sound of an explosion from the platform. He glanced at his watch again. *Two minutes until an evacuation message from Thomasson. Come on, you maniac, answer me!*

After several seconds of silence, the stern, Slavic voice of the VoiceLink caller came through the speaker. "I know who you are, sergeant. You have been trying to reach Mary Elizabeth at this number for two days."

Cole perceived that the assassin was privy to several messages he had left on Beth's phone since she disappeared. He determined not to let the suspect's knowledge work to his advantage. "Yes sir, but I am not speaking to you as Ms. Scibelli's friend. As a police officer I order you to slide your weapons out to us and surrender peaceably."

Cole pressed the phone's mouthpiece to his leg and spoke into the tiny radio mike attached to the lapel of his jacket. "Huntley, I have him on the phone. Hold off the evacuation."

"We're listening and standing by," Huntley answered through his earpiece.

The assassin said, "Are you not aware, sergeant, that your foolish attempt to tamper with the master's mission may precipitate an act of ultimate judgment upon your lady friend?"

"Foiled again, sir," Cole answered, stifling the urge to scorn him with laughter. "Ms. Scibelli is free. She's the one who told me about your holy of holies hideout. She's sitting in a police car outside the Coliseum right now.

"Your master's mission has failed, Hodge—or whatever your name is. There will be no assassinations tonight. Now come to the door and send out your weapons and detonator—"

"The master's mission has not failed," the agitated voice insisted. "Now you listen to me, sergeant. In ten seconds I will hang up on you and dial the tiny receiver and answering device I have secreted in the platform. Don't bother sending your bomb squad to look for it. They already searched the platform and failed to find it."

A telephone detonator—station-to-station terrorism, Cole thought. *I should have known.*

The voice continued, "Once connected to the device, I need only to touch my master's number, 666, and the ten horns of the beast will erupt in fury beneath Mr. Dunne. I'm not stupid, sergeant; I know Dunne is still on the platform. And I know your superior officers don't want anything to happen to him or to the misguided sheep sitting near the platform.

"So when I appear at the door in a few minutes, the only policeman I want to see in the hallway is you—with your weapon on the floor. And standing beside you I want to see Dr. McClure, Rev. Hornecker, and Rev. Holloway."

"But sir, it's impossible to get the leaders here before—" Cole was interrupted by a call-terminating click followed by a dial tone. He quickly pushed redial to intercept the assassin's call to the detonating device in the platform. But he was too late. A busy signal told him that the assassin's call had been placed. The detonator was on-line. The lives of T.D. Dunne and hundreds seated near him were only a thumb's touch away from oblivion.

Cole berated himself for contacting the killer prematurely. *I should have waited for Arias,* he thought soberly. *But I didn't wait, so now what do I do?* The drumbeat of fear pounded loudly in Cole's ears, demanding a response.

Suddenly, he had it. It was as if someone had issued an order directly into his mind. *Thank God,* he reacted flippantly. Then, weighing his words more carefully, he thought again, *Thank God!*

Pocketing his phone, Cole stood and backed away from the officials' room. He withdrew his pistol from the holster inside his jacket and placed it on the floor about twenty feet from the door. Then he backed up another twenty feet, stopping in the center of the hall parallel to the lower door leading to the tunnel. He waved a command to Phipps who, having heard the assassin's demands through his radio, reluctantly moved up the stairs and out the upper door into the tunnel. Cole was alone in the hallway.

He spoke two terse commands into the radio. The first, directed to Phipps, was the answer to the assassin's threat. *It will work,* Cole insisted to himself, *if I can buy enough time.* The second command, to Huntley, would hopefully buy the time he needed for his idea to work. Cole silently begged Thomasson and Arias to hold off the evacuation attempt in the meantime.

The door to the officials' room opened a few inches, and Cole sucked a deep breath. He could see nothing but darkness inside. He slowly spread his hands away from his body to assure his unseen opponent that he was unarmed.

From the music pouring out of the hallway speakers, Cole recognized that the Communion service was in full swing. Dunne was leading the congregation in the theme song again. *Dear God, please don't let that brave man die on account of me,* Cole breathed.

The door opened wider and a man's left hand gripping a pocket phone slipped out of the shadows and into the light. The thumb of the hand was poised over the number six on the keypad.

"Where are the others?" the man called gruffly from the darkness.

"They're out on the field, sir," Cole answered, standing motionless with his hands spread. "I've sent for them."

"The master is displeased," the man in the shadows growled, fidgeting with the phone in his hand. "He wants them here now. He instructs me to push the first button." The thumb on the visible hand touched the 6 on the keypad. "Now get those people in here."

The answering device in the bomb is coded to three successive sixes, Cole thought soberly. *One down, two to go.*

Cole searched the darkness behind the outstretched hand for a glimpse of the man's face. It was still sheathed in shadows. But beneath the hand he saw the faint glow of white fabric, as if the man were draped in a sheet. And then he caught the quick flash of reflected light. A knife. *So that's his alternate plan,* Cole thought: *Hold Dunne and the crowd hostage while he draws the other three into the officials' room and does a Wingate number on them.*

"Sir, I assure you that I have sent for them," Cole said, in what he hoped was a calming, believable tone. "I am being told on the radio that our other officers are escorting them in from the field right now. It will just be a couple of minutes."

What Huntley was really telling him over the radio was that Morgan McClure and Simon Holloway were already at the mouth of the tunnel being briefed about playing along and buying time for Phipps to complete his assignment. But McClure was refusing to help. Cole could hear him arguing with Lieutenant Arias in the background. Shelby Hornecker, who had been farthest from the tunnel, was still being escorted in from the field.

Cole sensed that it was time to fabricate a shred of good faith. He spoke into his radio mike loud enough for the man in the shadows to hear, "You say that Rev. Holloway is there? Send him in, please."

Cole could hear Lieutenant Arias prompting Holloway to stay behind the officer in the hall and assuring him that the crisis would be over in a few minutes. Cole hoped he was right.

The door six feet to Cole's left opened slowly, and Simon Holloway stepped inside. His face was white and sweat-beaded. He walked cautiously to a point two feet behind Cole's right shoulder. "Thank you for coming, Reverend," Cole said for the assassin's benefit. "Just keep your hands clearly in sight, and you'll be fine."

Holloway swallowed hard and spread his hands outward, following Cole's example. The blade again flickered in the darkness, and Cole hoped Holloway hadn't seen it.

"Where are the others?" the man with the phone demanded.

Cole cocked his head as if listening intently to his earpiece. "I've been informed that Dr. McClure and Mrs. Hornecker are nearing the tunnel now," he answered. In reality, Huntley had said that Shelby was ready, but McClure had tried to leave the Coliseum. He and his Navajo bodyguard were being physically detained by police at the top of the tunnel ramp.

Cole wanted to delay Shelby's entry as long as possible. Standing between the suspect and one potential victim was bad enough. Having two of them in the hallway might prove too tempting to the man who seemed programmed to kill by the devil himself.

More fireworks could be heard bleeding through the music in the hallway. Midnight was approaching, but Cole couldn't make himself risk a glance at his watch while the assassin was watching. *Come on, Phipps,* Cole urged silently, *do your job. We're running out of time!*

From the darkness of the officials' room, the man with the phone began reciting in a low, spiteful tone,

King from the East, champion of might;
thy Crusaders and Warriors fight for the right.
Hear words of wisdom, hear truth from the sage;
Thou wagest a battle thy Lord doth not wage.
Thy kingdom is dust, thy crown is tin;
Thou lookest without instead of within.
Thine end is near, thy crown will fall;
The beast from heaven is all in all.

Cole said, "Sir, you must know that if you carry through with your threats you will leave this hallway only in chains or a body bag. You will not reign as messiah over anyone. I'm asking you to put down your phone and—"

"Send Holloway over here," the assassin snarled.

The man's intentions were clear, and Cole knew he could stall no longer. "I believe Mrs. Hornecker is at the door, sir," he said, motioning Holloway to stay put. "She's coming in now."

"The master is losing patience," the man hissed. "He commands me to prepare for judgment." Again, his thumb pressed the 6 on the phone's keypad.

One more tap of the 6 and Dunne and possibly Beth's parents are history, Cole acknowledged. *Phipps, where are you? What are you doing?*

"All right, Mrs. Hornecker, come in please," he said into his mike.

Shelby stepped into the hallway on cue and took a position at Cole's left shoulder. Her face mirrored grave concern and fear, but she managed a brave smile at the two men.

The man in the shadows turned his venom toward her.

Queen from the South, prophet from hell;
Entice thy people to be rich and well;
Tempt them with fatness and lust to be whole;
But fat in the flesh bringeth death to the soul.

In his exuberant recitation, the man jarred the door open another two inches. The faintest outline of his face was now visible.

Cole despised the man for his arrogance in threatening Shelby. But every second he continued to speak, they were a second closer to the life-saving message Cole awaited from Phipps over the radio.

Thy kingdom is dust, thy crown is tin;
thou lookest without instead of within.

The man in the shadows was spitting the words hatefully at Shelby. In his peripheral vision, Cole saw Shelby's head drop, and he heard her sniffing back tears.

Thine end is near, thy crown shall fall;
the beast from heaven is all in all.

Again the assassin knocked against the door with his arm, opening it several more inches. The space was now as wide as the man's shoulders, and his face, though still in shadows, was clearly in view. The man was a stranger to Cole.

Cole heard a groan to his right, then, "Oh, my dear Lord, no!" He turned to see Holloway stagger slightly backward, staring at the figure in the doorway and trembling.

Shelby jerked up her head at the sound and looked at the white-robed man holding a pocket phone in one hand and a six-inch knife in the other. The cry Shelby emitted made Cole shudder. It was guttural, primal, more of pain than of fear, as if the assassin's knife had already plunged into her.

Lieutenant Arias immediately called over the radio, "What's going down, Cole? We're coming in!"

Confused at what was happening but fearing that a charge would send the assassin over the edge, Cole cut him off with, "Hold your position! No one is hurt! Hold your position!"

Simon Holloway stood frozen with mouth agape. Shelby fell to her knees from shock. Only her hands caught her from falling prostrate. Transfixed on the man's face, she cried out again, as if her very soul was retching out its contents. Only this time her cry formed one clearly intelligible word, "Adrian!"

Seventy-two

Cole's blood ran to ice. With Shelby in near hysterics, he glanced at Simon Holloway for an explanation.

"That's him," Holloway croaked in a parched voice. "That's Adrian Hornecker standing in the doorway. But he was . . . killed. Dear God, what's happening?"

The assassin took one slow step across the threshold into the hallway's fluorescent lights. He gripped the phone and the knife menacingly. His expression was other-worldly. "Not Adrian Hornecker of the old millennium, my dear Shelby. He perished in the Mediterranean Sea. Only his shell, shrouded until now in costume and makeup, survived. Standing before you is the Adrian Hornecker of the new millennium, the master's servant. Having died and been buried in the spirit, he is now raised by the master's good pleasure to serve him in judgment and purity where you and your colleagues have failed."

"It's not really you, Adrian!" Shelby wailed. "It's not your voice! Get behind me, Satan!"

Holloway was aghast, but he quickly gathered his wits in an attempt to piece the puzzle together. He spoke to the man in the doorway, "It was all a ruse, wasn't it, Hornecker? Your death was a hoax, a demonically inspired hoax. You must have planted a telephone bomb on that plane yourself, then slipped off and dialed in the code as it was climbing out of Tel Aviv. You've been in hiding all these months. You've been plotting to kill us. Is that why you planned Unity 2000—to bring us here for this drama conceived in the pit of hell?"

"Unity under four earthly infidels was the hoax," Adrian Hornecker spat derisively, eyes flashing with hatred. "Months ago the master revealed to me that unity in the third millennium will be achieved only through the one who serves unquestioningly as his instrument of judgment. In the secret place of my heart, he told me that I was the chosen one. He promised me success. The hour is near for the unfaithful to be judged. The master's servant will be glorified and his sheep will become one flock at last."

Cole's eyes were riveted to the phone and the assassin's quaking thumb. He felt powerless, like an unwilling participant in someone else's nightmare—specifically Simon Holloway and Shelby Hornecker's nightmare. Was this wild-eyed, knife-wielding nut in the white robe really Adrian Hornecker? Was he an impostor, a ghost, or the devil himself? Cole didn't know, nor could he afford to wonder until the creature in the doorway was separated from his instruments of destruction.

"Steady out there," he reminded his colleagues in the tunnel quietly, while the assassin was momentarily distracted from him. "Phipps, I need to hear from you."

"Dear Lord, man, how did the devil get such a hold on you?" Holloway wondered aloud, still stunned.

Shelby seemed on the verge of total collapse, but she doggedly refused to let the horror of her discovery carry her away. "It was the films, wasn't it, Adrian?" she sobbed. "I saw it coming. I warned you. I begged you. But no, you had to make those films. The Last Days, the Great Tribulation, the vials, the judgments, the new millennium—they consumed you. And as if one mistress wasn't enough, you also allowed Hollywood and the film industry to seduce you, to drag you to the pit. The devil offered you a kingdom, Adrian, and you sold your soul scene by scene, film by film, to obtain it. You have become the very beast you sought to warn others about."

"Yes, it was the films, Shelby," Adrian Hornecker announced triumphantly. "But you're wrong. My calling didn't consume me; it enlightened me, it liberated me, it lifted me to the pinnacle of spiritual power.

The world must know of the coming kingdom, and the master appointed me to proclaim his gospel."

"It's not the Gospel, Adrian!" Shelby bawled. "It's darkness, it's a lie. You rejected the voice you should have heeded, and you heeded to the voice you should have rejected. You've been deceived. You wouldn't listen to me. You . . ." Shelby's words were swallowed up in hysterical sobbing.

Adrian Hornecker began waving his knife at her in a beckoning manner. "Come to me, my dear Shelby," he called with a fiendish glare, "and you will be the first to know how wrong you have been. Then Rev. Holloway will be enlightened, then Dr. McClure, and then Mr. Dunne."

Shelby remained crumpled and weeping at Cole's feet. He reached out a slow hand to her shoulder to comfort her and keep her in place.

"If you do not come," Adrian warned, "Mr. Dunne will be first, and you will hear the screams of hundreds who will be judged with him because of your stubbornness. I will count to five." He raised the phone higher. "One, two—"

"It's done, Cole." The voice in the earpiece, heard only by Cole, belonged to Sergeant Phipps. "Global has confirmed it."

"I'm sending in SWAT," Arias added.

"Three, four—"

Both doors to the hallway burst open, and a half-dozen black-clad officers with automatic weapons instantly occupied the space behind Holloway, Shelby, and Cole.

The sudden activity caught Adrian by surprise. He stood frozen. Then he bared his teeth in defiance and extended his left arm toward the sky. "You have brought this wrath on yourselves!" he howled.

"Adrian, no!" Shelby shrieked.

Then he pushed the button. Religious music had never sounded so beautiful to Reagan Cole. T.D. Dunne, backed by a choir of 95,000 worshipful voices, sang on through the speakers. Shelby and Holloway exhaled their relief and wonderment as praise to God.

"I'm sorry, Mr. Hornecker or Mr. Hodge or whatever your name is," Cole said, taking a step forward, "but your call cannot be completed as dialed. It seems that you forgot to pay your phone bill, and your service has been disconnected, effective immediately."

Adrian's expression instantly dissolved from triumph to disbelief. He jammed the 6 button repeatedly with no results. Phipps' call to Global Communications had terminated Beth Scibelli's service. The instrument in the assassin's hand was as useless as a child's toy phone. The ten bombs under the platform were for the time being as harmless as tubes of modeling clay.

Enraged, Adrian Hornecker threw Beth's phone to the floor. Pieces of metal and plastic skittered across the linoleum.

"Drop the knife and kick it toward me," Cole said, inching toward his pistol lying on the floor between them.

The disbelief on Adrian's face washed away with his color, replaced by an expression of fear and betrayal. The SWAT team slowly moved in behind Cole, while two of its members assisted Holloway and Shelby toward the door to the tunnel.

"There's still time, Adrian," Shelby sobbed over her shoulder "There's still time to turn away."

Adrian didn't hear her. Instead, with one quick step he leaped back inside the officials' room and slammed the door behind him.

The SWAT team immediately swarmed to positions on both sides of the door. "We'll take it from here, Cole," the team leader informed. "Get the civilians into the tunnel, please."

Cole complied with reluctance, retrieving his pistol and ushering Shelby and Holloway through the door and into the arms of Theresa Bordeaux, Jeremy Cannon, Grace Ellen Holloway, and a phalanx of uniformed officers crowding the tunnel. Arias moved the entire contingent of civilians to the mouth of the tunnel for safety.

Seeing that his charges were cared for, Cole turned his attention back to the scene in the hallway. The SWAT officers had pulled gas masks over their faces. The sergeant held a small canister of tear gas in his hand. "You have one minute to put down your weapon and open the door, sir," he called out with authority at the door. Thirty seconds later he repeated the warning, then pulled down his own mask.

He waited at least another minute, then nodded to the officer nearest the door. The butt of his automatic weapon smashed a large hole in the smoked glass. The sergeant tossed in a canister, received another, and tossed it in also. Cole knew it was time to step into the tunnel and close his door. He would rather have been in the first wave of officers rushing the foiled assassin.

Even with the door closed, Cole could hear the muffled pop of the canisters and the soft hiss of escaping gas from inside. A minute later, more glass shattered, and Cole recognized the shuffle of combat boots as the SWAT team stormed the officials' room. Adrian Hornecker's knife would not last long against the firepower of SWAT.

Wisps of tear gas began to escape from the door where Cole stood, so he slowly backed up the tunnel toward the street, waiting for an officer to emerge with a report. There were no gunshots. Cole was surprised that Hornecker hadn't resisted to the death.

From behind him, Cole heard a man's voice yell, "Hey, lady, you can't go down there!" He turned to see the silhouette of a tall, slender young woman, backlit by Menlo Street trotting down the ramp toward him. A pudgy old security guard was chasing her. A few uniformed cops in the tunnel also turned with alarm. The woman's long, pulled-back hair bounced behind her. Cole took two eager strides up the ramp and Beth was in his arms.

Seeing the embrace, the embarrassed guard about-faced and waddled up the ramp as quickly as he had come down it. The cops in the tunnel watched a little longer.

Beth buried her head in Cole's chest and wept. And Cole, thinking about what he had almost lost and reveling in what he had found, wept too.

After a moment, Cole pushed Beth back to look at her in the dim light of the tunnel. Her eye sockets were dark with smeared mascara. Patches of gray adhesive still dotted her forehead and cheeks and clung to her matted hair. Her lips were white and cracked. Her blouse and slacks were rumpled.

Wiping away her tears and then his own with a handkerchief, Cole said with an unquenchable grin, "I know you were upset about losing the bet and buying me dinner tonight, but the least you could do was dress up a little." They laughed together, then embraced and cried again.

A SWAT officer exited the dressing room to remove his gas mask and bark orders into his radio for an on-site ambulance to be sent to the tunnel. Recognizing Cole, the cop walked up the ramp. "We found him in the shower room, blood everywhere," he said, shaking his head. "Slashed his own throat with that big knife. Sliced open his windpipe and the carotid on one side. I don't know how a guy can do that to himself."

Beth gasped and bit her lip. Cole gripped her reassuringly in his arms.

The officer continued, "When we got to him he was coughing and sputtering something about the master calling him home. Then he passed out. He lost a bucket full of blood before we found him in the smoke. If we don't get him to County General in a hurry, he's not going to make it."

Four more of the SWAT cops hurried through the door carrying a limp Adrian Hornecker on a stretcher made from his blood-soaked white robe. The fifth officer was holding a towel, also colored deep red, to the man's throat as a compress. The stretcher-bearers, with gas masks still in place, swept by Cole and Beth toward the ambulance, which had just pulled up at the top of the ramp.

Cole glanced at the passing victim. The parts of his face not splattered with blood were pasty white. Beth turned away.

The mounting crescendo of skyrockets and firecrackers around the Coliseum announced that midnight was drawing near. "I have to find my parents, Reagan. They're inside, somewhere near the front, I think."

"Yes, of course," he said. "I'll help you."

They started down the ramp toward the mouth of the tunnel. Beth cringed and cried out when Cole squeezed her shoulder. She explained that her first task of the new millennium was to visit an emergency room and have the needle fragment removed from her upper arm.

The Communion service was nearly finished. T.D. Dunne had been leading the congregation in singing from his keyboard on the platform for nearly half an hour. Over 95,000 people had been lifted to heaven in worship by a man who knew that his life might end at any second. A signal from Spooner in the tunnel assured him that all was well.

Most of the evacuees from the platform had gathered at the mouth of the tunnel to hear about the events in the hallway and to console Shelby Hornecker. Absent from the group was Dr. Morgan McClure who, with his bodyguard and aide, had left for the airport by taxi, swearing off all allegiance to Unity 2000 and its participants.

Mai Ngo was the first to see Beth and Cole approaching through the tunnel. Her squeals of joy could scarcely be heard above the singing and the fireworks. She leaped into Beth's arms and the two were swarmed over by the Holloways, Valerie Dunne, Curtis Spooner, Dr. No, and finally by Theresa Bordeaux, Jeremy Cannon, and a dazed but courageous Shelby Hornecker. Tears flowed from the group like spring rain, both in joy for Beth Scibelli and in sorrow and shock over the bizarre appearance of Adrian Hornecker.

The singing having concluded, the jubilant throng focused all attention on the numeric display flashing from the giant Coliseum monitor: 4:01, 4:00, 3:59, 3:58, 3:57, 3:56. Pockets of the crowd were counting off the last four minutes of the second millennium aloud.

Stan Welbourn was already on the platform ready to close the service. He had invited any of the evening's special guests who wished to to join him, but he did not insist because of the explosives, disarmed though they were, still hidden in the platform's structure.

Yet the group had agreed to mount the platform together once more to ring out the old millennium and ring in the new. Having absorbed Cole and Beth as their own, the group moved en masse across the grassy field toward the peristyle end, arms locked together. A loose circle of uniformed officers surrounded the group as they marched.

The Coliseum congregation momentarily turned its attention from the clock to the convoy of Christian leaders approaching the platform. Row by row, people rose to their feet and showered the group with cheers and applause of acclaim.

"Do you know exactly where my parents are?" Beth shouted to Mai above the noise.

"I think I saw them in the second row on this side," Mai answered.

Taking advantage of their height, Beth and Cole scanned the crowd as the knot of dignitaries neared the front of the field section. But with everyone standing, they could not see beyond the first two or three files from the side aisle.

When the group approached the platform steps, Beth and Cole broke away to walk in front of the congregation and scour the first two rows for Jack and Dona Scibelli. Beth's shabby appearance raised eyebrows, but she didn't notice. She gripped Cole's hand tightly and kept looking.

The applause swelled as Shelby Hornecker, resting heavily on the arm of Jeremy Cannon, and the others mounted the platform. The jubilant occupants of the bowl picked up the chant: 2:10, 2:09, 2:08, 2:07.

Unable to watch the seconds tick away on the saddest New Year's Eve of his life, Jack Scibelli looked straight ahead instead of at the Coliseum clock. He saw Beth approaching before Beth saw him, and he cried out, "Mary Elizabeth!" He scaled the row of interlocking folding chairs in front of him with the agility of a mountain goat, plowed through the people who had been sitting in them, and engulfed his daughter in his arms. Dona made the chair climb with Cole's help and joined in the embrace. Then the tall officer watched the emotional family reunion until he was invited to join it.

Stan Welbourn commanded the crowd's attention with the clock sweeping past the one-minute mark. He led the congregation in a simple, tearful prayer of thankfulness for God's mercy and protection. The majority of the crowd would not understand the significance of his prayer until they read the full story of Adrian Hornecker and his diabolical plot the following morning in the Los Angeles Times.

At Stan's amen, the crowd immediately picked up the monitor's countdown with one boisterous voice: 27, 26, 25, 24, 23.

On the platform, hands spontaneously joined to form an unbroken chain: 18, 17, 16 15, 14.

Around the bowl and across the Coliseum floor, 95,000 pairs of hands also eagerly clasped, joining many into one. Beth, Jack and Dona Scibelli, and Reagan Cole were included in the chain across the front row. Uniformed police officers around the bowl were also absorbed into the human chain: 9, 8, 7, 6.

In the middle of the platform, Shelby Hornecker lifted her hands and tearstained face toward heaven. The links of the chain joined to her followed suit. Clasped, upraised hands rolled across the stadium like a tidal wave: 4, 3, 2, 1, 0.

For the next ten minutes, rockets exploded overhead, filling the sky with daylight, thunder, and smoke. Graphics on the monitors flashed: HAPPY NEW MILLENNIUM, JANUARY 1, 2000. People across the Coliseum cheered, whistled, tooted horns, applauded, tossed confetti, embraced, wept, and danced. Only on the platform and in a small cluster near the front row, the embraces were sweeter and the tears flowed deeper.

As the celebration began to wane, somewhere on the north side of the bowl a spontaneous, reverent a capella reprise of T.D. Dunne's song began. By the end of the third line it had engulfed the entire crowd:

Let's begin again, brothers, Let's begin again, sisters,
Let's begin again today to love the Lord our God.
Let's renew our first love, Let's walk in God's new way,
Let's begin again today to love the Lord our God.

As the Father has loved us, So we must love each other,
Lay our lives down for our brothers, As a service unto Him;
And whatever we may do, In His name for one another,
For the least of these, His brothers, We do it unto Him.

Let's begin again, brothers, Let's begin again, sisters,
Let's begin again today to love the Lord our God.

Seventy-three

Unity 2000 delegates would have lingered in the Coliseum longer to celebrate and beg autographs from the platform stars had it not been for the intervention of the LAPD. A battalion of uniformed officers gently but firmly herded the crowd out of the stadium, ostensibly to allow the cleanup crew to do its job. In reality, the cleanup crew wasn't due for another eight hours. The LAPD bomb squad was waiting in the tunnel to dismantle the platform and dispose of the explosives, and they didn't need curious onlookers.

At the invitation of Dr. No and Mai, most of the platform guests, along with Cole, Beth, and her parents, migrated to the Ngo apartment at King's House for a simple, impromptu dinner. While Mai and her daughter prepared the chicken and rice, an exhausted Beth met Dr. Alan Triplett on the fifth floor where he removed the needle fragment from her arm and examined her strains and bruises, finding nothing seriously wrong. Dr. Triplett also provided alcohol to remove the adhesive from her face and found a brush for her hair.

The mood in the crowded apartment when Beth returned was warm but far from festive, in deference to Shelby Hornecker. Though still reeling from the emotional bludgeoning she had sustained in the hallway beneath the Coliseum, Shelby had held herself together well. Instead of retreating to the Biltmore and solitude, she chose to stay with the group, remaining quiet but cordial. Grace Ellen Holloway had stayed by her side since leaving the Coliseum.

Shortly before the meal was served, Cole was notified that Adrian Hornecker was dead, this time for real. The congestion on the streets around the Coliseum had not only prevented the Life Flight helicopter from landing, but had seriously impeded ambulance transport to the hospital. Ironically, the huge crowd Adrian had hoped to win as his flock had fatally delayed the emergency medical care he needed. He died en route to County General.

Shelby wept again at the news. Then she expressed her hope that Adrian had somehow reached out to God in the last minutes of his life.

Mai and her helpers distributed plates of steaming food, and the group congregated in the living room, on the furniture and on the floor. As they all ate, Mai asked Beth to tell everyone the story of her abduction and escape. She complied, beginning with Pershing Square and the taqueria and ending with her mad dash to flag down a black-and-white on Figueroa after finding her way out of Hodge's neighborhood. Her narrative was interrupted periodically by silent pauses of remembered terror and tearful gratitude.

She thanked everyone for their prayers—Jack and Dona interjected their thanks also—and mentioned that she had done some serious praying herself. She insisted that she might not have escaped had it not been for the knowledge her father had imparted about tearing duct tape, and the coil spring she had discovered on the cot.

Beth concluded by publicly apologizing to Cole, Mai, and her parents for her poor judgment in trying to deal with Hodge alone, and for the grief it had caused everyone. T.D. Dunne theorized that God might have allowed Beth's abduction and narrow escape because, had someone not gotten close to him and discovered his demonically inspired plot, Adrian Hornecker might have succeeded. Others in the room, including Shelby, nodded their agreement.

Someone asked Cole how Adrian was able to nearly succeed in his mass assassination attempt while working virtually alone in a city full of police officers.

"I'm no criminology expert," Cole answered, "but I believe he was successful because of his planning, his patience, and his acting ability. The scheme must have formed in his head long before he announced Unity 2000. In fact, as Rev. Holloway suggested, it looks like Adrian devised Unity 2000 solely for his secret purposes: to get all of you together, do away with you, and take over your congregations."

Several in the room clucked their tongues and shook their heads in sad disbelief.

Cole went on, "Adrian carefully plotted and acted out his own 'death,' then slipped quietly into L.A. with a new identity. He took a menial job at the Sports Arena and wormed his way into the good graces of that old caretaker Paddy, who allowed him access to the Coliseum when it was time to plant the bombs."

"How could a famous personality like Adrian go unnoticed for so long?" Valerie Dunne wondered aloud.

Jeremy Cannon reflected, "Adrian loved to act, and he especially enjoyed performing in costume and makeup. He insisted on playing walk-through parts in all of our films—an Arab terrorist, a waiter, a bullet-riddled corpse, whatever. In fact, he sometimes came on the set in a disguise that fooled everybody. He was very good with makeup and facial appliances."

"As I recall," Darin Chaumont said, "Adrian's keys to the studio in Hollywood were never recovered. There are cases of theatrical supplies stored there. Maybe that's where 'Hodge' got his disguise."

"And those voice changes," Beth said. "As Hodge, he sounded like an uneducated Irish immigrant. And on our VoiceLink line, he had the voice of Count Dracula."

"Yes, he was excellent at disguising his voice," Darin said. "He used to jokingly complain about being an Oscar-contending actor trapped in the body of a television minister—at least we *thought* he was joking."

After a moment of reflective silence, Tim Holloway asked, "How did Mr. Hornecker learn to build and hide bombs? I thought only professional terrorists could pull that off."

"We used a lot of explosives in our filming," Jeremy Cannon answered, "and Adrian was fascinated at how easy it was to rig and detonate bombs. He worked with the demolitions experts on all the scenes where we blew up a car or a building. We used to kid Adrian about his preoccupation with plastic explosives. I had no idea his interest was so morbid."

"The technology for a telephone bomb is surprisingly simple, Tim," Cole added. "And you can hide it virtually anywhere. The unit in your phone that records and plays back messages is no bigger than the end of your little finger. And a chunk of plastic the size of your thumb can blow a car inside out.

"From what Adrian said in the hallway tonight, he programmed the playback unit wired to the explosives to the numbers 666. When he dialed the bomb in the platform from Beth's phone, the answering device was simply waiting for that programmed code. But instead of activating the message playback, three taps on the 6 button would have sent a charge to the detonator, and one exploding bomb would have set off the other nine."

"But where would he get plastic explosives in L.A.?" Tim pressed.

"Unfortunately, it's not very difficult if you know where to look," Cole said.

Jeremy interjected, "Adrian used to keep explosives in the basement at the studio. When I found out, I couldn't believe he would endanger the studio staff like that. Someone on the crew ratted to the fire department, and the fire marshal made him remove the stuff. Maybe he hid some of it for future use."

Mai said, "We ran a story last week about a fatal stabbing outside the studio. Perhaps Adrian went there that night for supplies or explosives.

The security guard may have caught him in the act and. . . ." Mai decided not to finish the statement in consideration of Shelby's feelings. Another wave of quiet sadness swept over the occupants of the room.

Shelby finally broke the silence. Everyone had hoped she would share her feelings about what had happened, but no one would have thought her too private for remaining quiet.

"There's more to Adrian's behavior than his fascination with playacting," she began slowly and pensively. "I began to notice it about five years ago when he preached a long series on the Revelation. The Dallas congregation loved it, and the mail-in offerings from our television audience shot up dramatically. Adrian was thrilled with the response— ecstatic, in fact. So he kept it up, preaching series after series on end-times themes: Armageddon, the Antichrist, the Rapture, the Judgment."

The Welbourns and Darin Chaumont nodded, remembering the emphasis.

"Stan and I suggested that he move on to other biblical themes in his study and preaching, but he wouldn't hear of it. He became increasingly defensive and secretive about his end-times research. He wouldn't talk to me about what he was doing; he wouldn't talk to anyone. 'You'll hear all you need to know in my messages,' he would say.

"Then he started talking about films. Adrian saw films as an excellent means to further dramatize the exciting events he thought were just over the horizon. So he bought the studio and began writing scripts, leaving most of the Dallas ministry to me.

"Sometimes when he was out of town, I would go into his office just to look at what he was working on. I found old books about the Antichrist and Satan, many of them apocryphal or mythological, few of them scriptural. He had collected charts and graphs and time lines of the Revelation and sketches of the beast and the four horsemen. I found reams of notes with verses out of context and flaky theories about the end times.

"I was suspicious then—and I see clearly now—that he was editing the truth at the whim of his imagination, while distancing himself from anyone who might challenge him about it. He was seeking guidance in his secret sanctuary all right, and he was getting it, but not from the right source. I tried to get through to him, but he wouldn't listen to me."

Shelby paused for a deep breath. The lines on her brow reflected her difficulty at verbalizing what was so freshly hurtful. But she continued on.

"When Adrian began filming the Doomsday Chronicles, he surrounded himself with Hollywood people who thought little of the Bible but adored his interpretations of apocalyptic events. Adrian became so entranced with the medium that his concern for the message was obliterated. I could see that the line between reality and fantasy in his mind was rapidly disappearing, probably because the line between truth and error had already vanished."

The crowd in the living room sat statue-still and silent, hurting with Shelby as she recounted her pain. Those few in the room who were privy to the trauma which began her week were especially prayerful that she would be able to withstand this recent and even more crushing emotional blow.

"I tried to encourage Adrian to steer his energies back to the ministry in Dallas, but I completely failed. He justified his work to me by citing the hundreds of thousands of dollars pouring into the ministry from the film division. He bought me expensive gifts trying to compensate for his absence. I kept praying for him, but I resigned myself to a position of dissatisfied but quiet tolerance.

"At times I wondered if the explosion over the Mediterranean nine months ago was God's judgment on Adrian for his growing apostasy. At other times I feared that God took Adrian in order to judge me for not being more submissive and supportive. And now, after tonight, I don't know what to believe."

Shelby seemed beyond tears. She sat gazing at the floor, clinging to Grace Ellen's hand on one side and Theresa's on the other.

Cole cleared his throat nervously. He was perched on the arm of the love seat across the room from Shelby. Beth sat on the floor beside him. He said, "I think you just need to keep digging, Mrs. Hornecker."

Shelby broke her gaze to look up at him. Her eyes begged him to explain.

Cole responded, "Last night, while Beth was still . . . missing, Dr. No said something that didn't make much sense to me. But tonight it makes a lot of sense. He said that hard times are like tunneling through a huge mountain with nothing more than a pick and shovel. We get discouraged because it's dark and we hurt and we don't seem to be getting anywhere. But he said we need to keep praying and keep working because God is digging through from the other side—we just can't see it yet. Do you remember that, Mrs. Hornecker?"

Shelby's nod was slight but sure.

Turning to the rest of the crowd, Cole said, "I know you were all praying for Beth, and, thanks to some encouragement from my friends"—he glanced at Curtis Spooner—"I even prayed myself. I can't say that I had much faith . . . but tonight, here she is." Cole reached down to Beth, being careful to pat her on the left shoulder.

Cole looked back toward Shelby. "And look at what else has happened. You all came through Millennium's Eve alive. In the process, the people in the Coliseum got a real taste of unity from your example and your leadership. That's going to continue on—I know it is. And look at this." He swept his arm across the entire group. "You all arrived in Los Angeles this week as strangers, but now you're sitting here together as friends."

Warm smiles of agreement creased many of the faces in the room. "I'd say quite a few mountains have been tunneled through this week, Mrs. Hornecker. I think if you keep praying and keep digging, you're going to come through yours just fine."

All eyes eagerly shifted to view Shelby's response. Her gaze returned to the floor, and her face was void of expression. She remained that way for thirty seconds. No one spoke.

When she looked up her eyes went straight to the tall, sandy-haired officer. "I know you're right, sergeant," she said just above a whisper. "Thank you. I *will* keep digging." The statues around the room relaxed and breathed again.

Mai welcomed the break in the seriousness to ask, "Coffee anyone?"

Several said, "Yes, thank you." Others said that they should be leaving soon. But no one moved. Mugs of instant brew were passed around.

Encouraged by Shelby's humility and transparency, Simon Holloway confessed to and apologized for a prideful, independent spirit. He expressed his desire to foster the oneness Unity 2000 had begun. Jack and Dona Scibelli offered to serve on a lay committee formed between the three ministries for that purpose. The three leaders agreed that their shares of any Unity 2000 offering surplus would be earmarked to support ongoing unity, especially as it applied to collective efforts to serve the poor.

T.D. Dunne expressed concern for Dr. Morgan McClure, and many hummed their sympathies for the man. The group quickly agreed to reach out to him and offer at least their emotional support if and when he went to trial, regardless of his guilt or innocence. "Adrian included him in Unity 2000 for his evil purposes," Dunne summarized. "We must include him for good."

"By the way," Grace Ellen said, "I think it would be good to send a letter of thanks to Mr. Malachi for arranging our first meeting here Wednesday night. Perhaps none of this would have happened without his intervention." Affirmation for the idea was unanimous.

Shelby looked at Darin. "How can we locate Mr. Malachi?"

"I don't know," he answered, shrugging. "I asked the chairman of the local committee about him last night. He didn't recognize the name or the description I gave him, and when he checked his computer, he found no William Malachi on the local committee."

Several theories were advanced: that Malachi was the victim of a computer glitch; that he was listed under another name, perhaps his African tribal name; that he had joined the committee too late to be listed; that he was from out of town and not listed.

"Yeah, maybe he was from *way* out of town," young Mark Holloway joked, pointing heavenward. Everyone laughed and secretly wondered.

Coffee mugs were drained, and guests rose in twos and threes to retrieve their wraps. Dr. No and Mai were deluged with words of appreciation. Promises to stay in touch were exchanged around the room, as were warm embraces and fond farewells.

By the time Cole and Beth stepped outside, most of the other vehicles had departed. The new millennium was nearly three hours old, and the citywide celebration was waning. An occasional firecracker could still be heard in the neighborhood around King's House.

Cole supported Beth physically as they walked toward the parking lot. Only her joy at being safely with Reagan kept her from collapsing in total exhaustion. As they approached Jack and Dona's car, Cole asked the question that had been on his mind since midnight. "When are you returning to Seattle?"

"Originally, I was scheduled to fly out Sunday. But, as you know, I have a few problems." She lifted her fingers one by one to enumerate them. "My rental car is trashed, my computer is in the shop, my phone has been destroyed, and my rented computer, my purse, wallet, watch, and all my credit cards are gone and presumed stolen. I have to stay around and sort all that out."

Cole gave her a squeeze around the waist. "Good thinking," he said in mock seriousness. "You certainly can't do that from Seattle."

Beth flashed a mischievous grin, then continued. "Also, since everything I worked on this week disappeared with the computer, I have to call my publisher and get an extension for my book. I need to stay in L.A. to redo my research. Besides, in view of everything that happened this week, I may need to start over completely. There's much more to tell than I originally thought. That could take a month."

"Or even longer," Cole added with another squeeze.

"Seriously, Reagan, I need to go home in a week or so just to touch base. But I do have three very good reasons for returning to Los Angeles soon."

"And they are. . . ?" Cole said, playing dumb.

Beth looked at Cole fondly. "Well, I have found a wonderful new friend here, and I want to . . . cultivate this relationship."

"I think new friendships are great. I'm working on one myself."

Then Beth turned her affectionate gaze toward Jack and Dona who were waiting in the car ahead. "There are two other special people in Los Angeles whom I have sadly neglected. I need to spend more time rekindling that friendship."

"I understand," Cole said. "I admire you for that."

"What about you, Sergeant Reagan Cole? Where do you go from here?"

Cole had to think a moment. "Well, I have three days off, and I don't plan to spend a minute of them in the city. Spooner flies out at 6:30 tonight, so I want to spend some time with him."

"Why don't you bring him to the house to watch the Rose Bowl game with us this afternoon? Free food, good company. . . ."

"And another opportunity to cultivate new friendships," Cole added.

"Exactly."

"I think Spoon would enjoy that, and so would I," Cole said, smiling.

"And after tomorrow?" Beth pressed.

Cole spoke more seriously. "After tomorrow, well, I have some thinking to do. I've learned a lot this week about things I never thought would interest me. Being around Shelby Hornecker and Dr. No was like taking a crash course in religion. I thought I'd hate it, but I kind of liked it. I might want to spend some time hanging around King's House learning more about digging tunnels."